C(

STEPHEN BREWEI
and *Connoisseur*
magazine editoria
editorial consulta

STEVEN K. AMSTERDAM has been a resident of New York City for over 20 years and has written extensively about Central Park. Formerly editor of Chicago's *Grey City Journal,* he is currently a free-lance writer in New York City.

ELEANOR BERMAN is a widely published travel writer. Her *Away for the Weekend: New York* guide has been a regional best seller since 1982. She has contributed to all the major metropolitan daily newspapers as well as to such national magazines as *Harper's Bazaar, Savvy, Modern Bride,* and *Diversion.*

DAVID BERREBY is a member of the Outer Critics Circle. His work has appeared in the *Village Voice, The New York Times, Ms., Diversion,* and *New York Newsday.* He reviews theater for *The New York Law Journal.*

ANDY BIRSH is a contributing editor at *Gourmet,* for which he writes a monthly column on New York dining. For a decade he edited and published *The Restaurant Reporter.*

STEPHEN R. ETTLINGER is a free-lance picture editor and photography consultant, and an independent book producer. He was formerly associate picture editor at *GEO* magazine and is currently an editor of *Photo Opportunity.* His most recent book project is *Vietnam: The Land We Never Knew, Recent Images by Geoffrey Clifford.*

SUSAN FAREWELL, a former travel editor at Condé Nast publications, writes for *Travel and Leisure, Metropolitan Home, Crain's New York Business, Child,* and other magazines. She is also the editor of the *Mobil Road Atlas and Trip Planning Guide* (1990 and 1991 editions).

DAVID FRANKEL, who was formerly an editor of *New York* magazine, has written on music for *New York* and *Rolling Stone*. He is an editor of *Artforum*.

DWIGHT V. GAST has written about the city for numerous publications. He has studied New York as an undergraduate and graduate student at the city's New School for Social Research and has been observing it as a Manhattan flâneur for over two decades. He lives in downtown Manhattan.

MATTHEW GUREWITSCH is a senior editor at *Connoisseur* magazine, where he concentrates on the performing arts. He has written about music and dance for *Opus, The New York Times, Vogue, Opera News, The Wall Street Journal,* and other publications.

ELEANOR HEARTNEY is a writer and critic specializing in contemporary art. She is a regular contributor to *Artnews, Art in America, Contemporania,* and *The New Art Examiner.*

AMY HUGHES, a free-lance editor and writer, has edited several guides in the Penguin series. She lives in the Bronx.

HEIDI KRIZ, a resident of the Upper West Side, is a graduate of Columbia University—as well as its famous bartending course. She has written about the people, places, and bars of New York City for such publications as the *Village Voice* and *7 Days.*

BARRY LEWIS, an architectural historian, has created tour programs and produced lecture series for New York's 92nd Street Y. He has also written articles on the city's architectural history for various publications and was a contributor to the Municipal Art Society's *Juror's Guide to Lower Manhattan.*

INGRID NELSON, formerly an editor of *GEO* magazine, is currently a free-lance writer living on Manhattan's Upper West Side.

JOANNA NEY is a free-lance writer specializing in dance. She was formerly dance critic for *East Side Express* and *Other Stages.* She has contributed to *The New York Times,*

Cosmopolitan, Cue, and *V.* Currently she reviews dance for WBAI radio.

DEAN J. SEAL was formerly associate editor of the *U.S. Food Journal,* a trend monitor of the American food industry. He is now a frequent contributor to food-related magazines.

RANDALL SHORT is the Theater Features writer for *Vogue.* He reports regularly on literature and the arts for *The New York Times, New York Newsday,* and *Spy* magazine.

LYNN YAEGER is the author of a biweekly column in the *Village Voice* on antiques and collectibles and was also a contributor to *The Village Voice Guide to Manhattan's Shopping Neighborhoods.* A resident of New York for over 15 years, she has written on fashion for *Cosmopolitan, Australian Woman,* and other publications.

THE PENGUIN TRAVEL GUIDES

THE PENGUIN GUIDE TO NEW YORK CITY 1990

ALAN TUCKER
General Editor

PENGUIN BOOKS

PENGUIN BOOKS

Published by the Penguin Group
Viking Penguin, a division of Penguin
Books USA Inc., 40 West 23rd Street,
New York, New York 10010, U.S.A.
Penguin Books Ltd, 27 Wrights Lane,
London W8 5TZ, England
Penguin Books Australia Ltd, Ringwood,
Victoria, Australia
Penguin Books Canada Ltd, 2801 John Street,
Markham, Ontario, Canada L3R 1B4
Penguin Books (N.Z.) Ltd, 182–190 Wairau Road,
Auckland 10, New Zealand

Penguin Books Ltd, Registered Offices:
Harmondsworth, Middlesex, England

First published in Penguin Books 1989
This revised edition published 1990

1 3 5 7 9 10 8 6 4 2

Copyright © Viking Penguin,
a division of Penguin Books USA Inc., 1989, 1990
All rights reserved

ISBN 0 14 019.919 5
ISSN 0898-8072

Printed in the United States of America

Set in ITC Garamond Light
Designed by Beth Tondreau Design
Maps by Mark Stein Studios
Illustrations by Bill Russell
Editorial Services: Stephen Brewer and Amy Hughes

THIS GUIDEBOOK

The Penguin Travel Guides are designed for people who are experienced travellers in search of *exceptional* information to help them sharpen and deepen their enjoyment of the trips they take.

The Penguin Guide to New York City 1990 highlights the more rewarding parts of the city so that you can quickly and efficiently home in on the right hotel and the best way for you to get the most out of the city.

Of course, the guide does far more than just help you choose a hotel and plan your visit. *The Penguin Guide to New York City 1990* is designed for use *in* the city. Our Penguin New York City writers (each of whom is an experienced travel writer who lives in New York and specializes in the subject he or she covers for us) tell you what you really need to know, what you can't find out so easily on your own. They identify and describe the truly out-of-the-ordinary restaurants, shops, night spots, activities, and sights, and guide you toward the best way to "do" the city.

Our writers are highly selective. They avoid the common clutter of choices in order to enhance the items of special appeal in New York City. For exhaustive detailed coverage of the city's various museums and historical sites street by street we suggest that you also use a supplementary reference-type guidebook, such as the Michelin Green Guide, along with the Penguin Guide.

The Penguin Guide to New York City 1990 is full of reliable and timely information, revised each year. We would like to know if you think we've left out some very special place.

ALAN TUCKER
General Editor
Penguin Travel Guides

40 West 23rd Street
New York, New York 10010
or
27 Wrights Lane
London   W8 5TZ

CONTENTS

MAPS

THE PENGUIN GUIDE TO NEW YORK CITY 1990

New York City's Five Boroughs

miles 0 — 2.5
kilometers 0 — 4

I-80

4

Teaneck

3

Montclair

Nutley

NEW JERSEY

3

I-95

I-95

I-95 NEW JERSEY TPK.

Lincoln Center

I-495

Lincoln Tunnel

Javits Center

Hoboken

WEST ST.

Holland Tunnel

GARDEN STATE PKWY.

Newark

World Trade Center

Manhattan Bridge

Brooklyn Bridge

I-78

22

Jersey City

NEW JERSEY TPK. EXTENSION

Brooklyn–Battery Tunnel

Newark International Airport

Liberty Island

Upper New York Bay

Elizabeth

Newark Bay

Silver Lake Park

Clove Lakes Park

BELT PKWY.

I-278

STATEN ISLAND

Verrazano–Narrows Bridge

Lower New York Bay

CONEY ISLAND

I-95 NEW JERSEY TPK.

La Tourette Park

BLVD.

Gateway National Recreation Area

WEST SHORE EXPWY.

Great Kills Park

RICHMOND PKWY.

HYLAN

N

Englewood

Wave Hill

RIVERDALE

WESTCHESTER COUNTY

Van Cortlandt Park

BRONX

SAW MILL PKWY.

THRU-WAY

PKWY.

NEW ENGLAND THRUWAY

Long Island Sound

I-95

Pelham Bay Park

PALISADES

George Washington Bridge

Fort Lee

Hudson River

HENRY HUDSON PKWY.

MAJOR DEEGAN EXPWY.

GRAND CONCOURSE

New York Botanical Garden

Bronx Zoo

BRONX RIVER PKWY.

City Island

CROSS

BRONX

I-95

BRUCKNER EXPWY.

HUTCHINSON RIVER PKWY.

Yankee Stadium

MANHATTAN

East River

FDR DRIVE

Central Park

Triborough Bridge

La Guardia Airport

Whitestone Bridge

Throgs Neck Bridge

NASSAU COUNTY

CROSS ISLAND PKWY.

CLEARVIEW EXPWY.

Rockefeller Center

Queens–Midtown Tunnel

GRAND CENTRAL PKWY.

QUEENS

BLVD.

Flushing Meadows Corona Park

Shea Stadium

I-495

Alley Park

Kissena Park

East River

Williamsburg Bridge

I-495 LONG ISLAND EXPWY.

LONG ISLAND EXPWY.

UNION TPK.

GRAND CENTRAL PKWY.

BROOKLYN-QUEENS EXPWY.

Forest Park

INTER-BOROUGH PKWY.

QUEENS

ATLANTIC AVE.

ATLANTIC AVE.

VAN WYCK EXPWY.

Brooklyn Museum and Botanic Garden

Prospect Park

BROOKLYN

SOUTHERN STATE PKWY.

BELT PKWY.

John F. Kennedy International Airport

NASSAU COUNTY

OCEAN PKWY.

FLATBUSH AVE.

(SHORE PKWY.)

ROCKAWAY

New York Aquarium

Breezy Point

Jacob Riis Park

Gateway National Recreation Area

ATLANTIC OCEAN

OVERVIEW

By Alan Tucker

Alan Tucker came to Manhattan under cover of darkness in 1964 and has lived on the Upper West Side for all but two of his years here. He is general editor of the Penguin Travel Guides and a member of the Society of American Travel Writers and the New York Travel Writers Association.

Yes, yes, we know: New York City is the cultural and creative cynosure of the entire world and still the foremost national and international financial center—the place where the big deals are made in the film industry, the broadcasting industry, in the art and theatrical businesses, in publishing and advertising, in banking and fashion and export-import.

Trends may start elsewhere, but they're not official until they're acknowledged here.

The people who live and work here create the strikingly high level of ambient human energy that fuels all this activity and is also drawn forth by it (the chicken and the egg). Talented folks from all over the country (and the world) choose to live here not just because they want to survive, but because they have something they want to *do*—and they figure this is the place to do it.

As for you, the visitor, you might want to come to see the totalitarian architecture of the World Trade Center, the robber barons' booty in the Metropolitan Museum of Art, the latest Broadway musical extravaganza, and the like. These "major attractions" are interesting, or at the very least, diverting. But Niagara Falls is interesting, too, and yet it's not quite parallel to the real lure of New York City.

We think you will probably get the most out of visiting

the city if you also look for the less obvious benefits that New Yorkers enjoy—while of course at the same time sidestepping the well-known day-to-day nuisances that living here brings (such as the privilege of paying half your salary in rent, not having your own back yard for growing tomatoes, and leaving the office at 8:30 every night).

What benefits? For example, the restaurants; the neighborhoods; the variety of people (What an understatement! More on that later) and their conversation; the easy, casual access to jazz, classical music, and other performing arts even outside the Sacred Palaces of Culture; the mania for graphic art and arresting design (everywhere); the shops and artisans and galleries (you name it, and it's on sale here—probably cheaper than it is in Hong Kong, too).

These are the things we want to tell you about in our guidebook. We have to mention Lincoln Center, the Museum of Modern Art, Macy's, and such (it may be a state law), but our hearts really lie in talking about downtown performance lofts, where to have brunch while you read your Sunday *New York Times,* where to buy private-label opera recordings, and how to take an afternoon's stroll in New York City from China to Italy to Bohemia.

To get to the goodies that you want to hear about we have had to cover the city in two dimensions.

One is in terms of *neighborhoods.* The other is by way of the city's *specialties,* such as antiques, dance, food, the literary world, fashion shopping, and so on.

The Neighborhoods

Even Midtown, the business center where most visitors huddle and where the great department stores are concentrated, is really a collection of neighborhoods (gamy Clinton, residential Murray Hill and Gramercy Park, the area around the United Nations, the Garment District around Seventh Avenue in the 30s, etc.). But there's more variety—and more of those special New York experiences we've been talking about—in some of the city's other neighborhoods.

- The **Wall Street area** is full of the history of early New York and it also has the South Street Seaport historical/shopping/dining district and the

Manhattan Neighborhoods

| 0 | miles | 1.5 |
| 0 | kilometers | 2.5 |

PALISADES INTERSTATE PARKWAY

Palisades Park

To New York State Thruway

Ft. Tryon Park

INWOOD

FORDHAM RD.

University Heights

FORT GEORGE

CROSS BRONX EXPWY

SHERIDAN EXPWY

To New England Thruway

George Washington Bridge

I-95
Ft. Lee

BROADWAY

HENRY HUDSON PKWY.

MAJOR DEEGAN EXPWY.

GRAND CONCOURSE

B R O N X

BRUCKNER EXPWY.

WASHINGTON HEIGHTS

Hudson River

155 ST.

145 ST.

HARLEM RIVER DRIVE

N

Cliffside Park

W. 125 ST.

HARLEM

E. 125 ST.

Randalls Island

Triborough Bridge

MORNINGSIDE HEIGHTS

EAST HARLEM

NEW JERSEY

BROADWAY

CENTRAL PARK WEST

W. 110 ST.

E. 110 ST.

Central Park

E. 96 ST.

GRAND CENTRAL PKWY.

Wards Island

East River

FDR DRIVE

W. 96 ST.

YORKVILLE

UPPER WEST SIDE

W. 86 ST.

E. 86 ST.

UPPER EAST SIDE

Q U E E N S

West New York

W. 72 ST.

WEST END AVE.

10th AVE.

PARK AVE.

5th AVE.

3rd AVE.

1st AVE.

Roosevelt Island

Long Island City

NORTHERN BLVD.

W. 57 ST.

E. 60 ST.

Queensboro Bridge

QUEENS BLVD.

HELL'S KITCHEN

THEATER DISTRICT

8th AVE.

6th AVE.

E. 57 ST.

Queens-Midtown Tunnel

MIDTOWN

E. 42 ST.

LONG ISLAND EXPWY. I-495

I-495

Lincoln Tunnel

W. 42 ST.

W. 34 ST.

E. 34 ST.

Union City

CLINTON

GARMENT DISTRICT

MURRAY HILL

Greenpoint

BROADWAY

AVENUE OF THE AMERICAS

W. 23 ST.

GRAMERCY PARK

E. 23 ST.

CHELSEA

STUYVESANT

W. 14 ST.

E. 14 ST.

WEST VILLAGE

EAST VILLAGE

LOWER EAST SIDE

E. 4 ST.

Hoboken

W. HOUSTON

E. HOUSTON

Williamsburg Bridge

Holland Tunnel

WEST ST.

BROADWAY

DELANCEY ST.

LITTLE ITALY

CANAL ST.

SOHO

CHINATOWN

TRIBECA

Manhattan Bridge

Jersey City

Brooklyn Bridge

BROOKLYN-QUEENS EXPWY.

WALL ST.

WALL STREET

Brooklyn Heights

WHITEHALL

NEW JERSEY TPK. EXTENSION

Battery Tunnel

B R O O K L Y N

ferry rides to the Statue of Liberty and Staten Island (the ferry ride itself is the wonderful experience here; Staten Island has a few interesting historical sites but is best left to Staten Islanders). And you'll want to see the New York Stock Exchange and the World Trade Center (have a civilized drink and get the view at the top of the north tower, number 1).

- **Chinatown** is one of the largest such enclaves in the world—and it's no living museum, either.
- **TriBeCa** is an area of artists' and arty lawyers' lofts and unusual bars, restaurants, cafés, and clubs.
- **Little Italy** is for eating.
- **SoHo** was once an inexpensive place for artists seeking large work space and is now an expensive but interesting area of galleries, boutiques, restaurants, and bars.
- **Lower Broadway** has trendy shops, punk barbershops, Tower Records, roomy if undistinguished restaurants, the Public Theater, and Cooper Union arts and sciences school—all between Canal and 8th streets. It is a sort of Luxembourg, with Little Italy, Chinatown, and the Lower East Side (or "East Village") on one side and SoHo and Greenwich Village on the other.
- The **Lower East Side** and the **East Village** are perhaps the last remaining bastions of youthful avant-garde artistic and literary activity on Manhattan Island, with attendant clubs and cafés—and lots of street crime and drug sales amid the remnants of an earlier Eastern European immigrant culture.
- **Greenwich Village** has New York University at its heart and is populated by comfortable mid- to upper-level professionals as well as (along Christopher Street in the so-called West Village) a concentrated gay community. There are lots of good bars, restaurants, and shops in the Village, but its bohemian days have given over to a sort of *New York Review of Books* gentility—ironically, the Village proper no longer even has a really good bookstore.
- **Chelsea**, its main street being along Eighth Avenue above 14th Street, has lots of rough edges, but it does have some of the bohemian ele-

ments that the Village has lost. Chelsea also has more than its share of nifty restaurants and clubs and a few leading-edge modern-dance venues, as well as punk rockers, the last especially along West 23rd Street (its northern border) near the famous Chelsea Hotel.

- The **Lower Fifth Avenue** area, also known variously as the Flatiron District, "SoFi" (*S*outh of the *Flati*ron Building), the Ladies' Mile, and the Madison Square area, has trendy restaurants and photographers' lofts on the side streets in the high teens and the 20s up to 23rd Street.

- The **Upper West Side**, north of Midtown and west of **Central Park**, is anchored at the south by Lincoln Center and at the north by Columbia University. Its now-faltering Columbus Avenue shop and restaurant strip is for those so-called bridge-and-tunnel people (Manhattan's neighbors on all sides must use one or the other to get onto the island) with more money than they should have. Amsterdam Avenue and Broadway are for the Upper West Side's own residents— who are much tighter with their money (they generally have less) and much more inclined toward the shabby genteel than their East Side compatriots. Look here for casual jazz clubs and pretty good Chinese restaurants—and some good bookstores. Many West Siders (the authentic ones, not the parvenu yuppies) look as if they've only recently stopped planning the overthrow of something or other. The ones who aren't carrying musical instruments or coming from dance or play rehearsals, that is. Finally, way up at the northern tip of Manhattan is The Cloisters, the Metropolitan Museum's bastion of Medieval art.

- The **Upper East Side** (east of the park), on the other hand, is the embodiment of everything that might *be* overthrown: Bankers, brokers, doctors, and lawyers live in apartments along Fifth and Park avenues that cost as much as the Latin American nations owe Chase Manhattan Bank; private schools occupy just about every side street; every other shop on Madison Avenue sells museum-quality art or antiques; and on Third, Second, and First avenues young corporate fodder prowl bars and restaurants with names like Tooties and J. J. Monkerton. In **Yorkville** along East 86th Street and a little down Second Avenue there are also vestiges of the earlier German and Middle European working-class presence. The Metropolitan and other museums lie along Fifth Avenue from the 70s to the 90s and even higher, and the Whitney Museum of American Art is over on Madison Avenue.

- **Brooklyn** is a sort of residential alternative to Manhattan for increasing numbers of professionals, but it is the residence of choice for genuine Brooklynites, those of "youse" and "whaddaya dune" and "geddadayear" renown from places such as Bensonhoist (as pronounced) and Bay Ridge (both heavily Italian-American), Canarsie, and Red Hook. Visitors go to Brooklyn for the adventurous Brooklyn Academy of Music (BAM) and the Brooklyn Museum (Egypt!), as well as for great Middle Eastern food on Atlantic Avenue.

- Largely residential **Queens** has its ethnic areas as well: Greeks in Astoria, Koreans and Chinese in Flushing, and more. But most Manhattanites only go to Queens to get a flight at LaGuardia or JFK airports; more's the pity.

- And then there are interesting day-trip destinations from New York City: **The Hamptons** at the eastern end of Long Island, an area that was once an artists' colony (Winslow Homer, then Jackson Pollock and Willem de Kooning) and is now a toney summer resort for rich or highly leveraged Manhattanites; Franklin Delano Roosevelt's home at **Hyde Park** up on the Hudson; the United States Military Academy at historic **West Point** not far from there; early American farms, homes, and estates in the still-beautiful **Hudson River valley**; and **Princeton** and **Yale** universities, the former being more attractive in a movie-set sort of way.

In all these places, particularly in Manhattan neighborhoods, however, what you are primarily looking for, as a visitor in search of the New York Experience, are the *people* and their colorful turns of phrase, as in the "She can't do relationships" or "He gives good phone" or "What am I, chopped liver?" genre of fast talk and one-liners. Although occasionally you'll hear talk of Poincaré or William Blake, most conversations will be on a higher plane: job complaints, money, and the price of cooperative apartments (currently about $250,000 for a one-bedroom even on the not-most-desirable Upper West Side). We've taken considerable care to place you in restaurants, bars, and other venues where you'll hear more of the citizens' patter than you may in the end want to. And places where *you* can try *your* hand at it, too; forget the nonsense about New Yorkers being inaccessible.

We've also conspired to get you into as many different neighborhoods as possible. And different each is, with its own distinct subspecies. What subspecies they are, too! Practitioners of thuggee, with orange spiked hair and chrome studs on their tongues (next year, anyway). Wild-eyed messengers looking like a cross between Don Johnson and Donald Pleasance. Female models with no ankles or muscles. Female models with 18-inch biceps. Overweight cabdrivers from Baffin Island who speak no known language. A couple wearing jellabas and dancing on stilts. A goon with no neck reading Trollope in the subway. You can stand on any street corner here—at any time of day or night—and see "types" that even the most coke-addled Hollywood director hasn't had the imagination to hallucinate for his stylish made-for-TV melodrama of discontinuity, crime, and urban decay.

These same subspecies, from our civic leaders on down (or up), will amaze and mystify you with their adaptability as well. After all, earlier New Yorkers didn't exactly earn a place in the annals of indomitable patriotic resistance when the British were comfortably ensconced here during the American Revolution. New Yorkers can figure out a way around anything. Now, we do indeed have clear principles; we're just prepared to change them as circumstances dictate.

The City's Specialties

Besides by neighborhood, the other way to come to terms with how to "do" the city is by what special interests you yourself have. Here again we've been selective, opting for the most brilliant aspects as against the more mundane. Surely no one will contest that the city's best efforts show in the areas of:

- Art
- Marketing antiques and antiquities
- Architecture
- Fashion and shopping for clothes and accessories
- Photography and filmmaking
- Classical music
- Popular music
- Dance
- Theater
- The literary world and bookstores
- Shopping (especially for unusual things)
- Food
- Museums

Another kind of specialty—and one on which we lavish quite a bit of space—is what we call "After Hours," meaning after the day's nine-to-five activities are accomplished:

- Dining
- Bars and cafés
- Nightlife and entertainment

We've tried to weed out the humdrum in order to put you *in position* to have a satisfying visit to New York City. We consider our guidebook to be a sort of starter kit. It's up to you to take it from here and begin developing your own New York for yourself. It may take a number of visits, and it will be a different town every time.

USEFUL FACTS

When to Go
A popular postcard depicts the four seasons in New York, showing the same shot of a gray, treeless street four times. However, New York actually has four distinct seasons: a hot, humid summer; crisp autumn; cold, sloppy winter; and gentle spring. Unless you enjoy extremes, April, May, September, and October are the best months for a visit, and the weeks between Thanksgiving and New Year's can be almost embarrassingly cheerful. You can expect thunderstorms in the summer, snow and rain in the winter, and showers at other times.

What to Wear
New Yorkers dress well. You will feel out of place wearing shorts at the theater and concerts, in many restaurants,

and even on the streets of Midtown during business hours. On the other hand, you will rarely feel over-dressed in this city where it is not unusual to find yourself seated next to someone in full evening dress. Women should pack skirts, dresses, or fashionable slacks; men, slacks, sports coats and/or suits, and ties (you may be able to get by with just a jacket in many places). Do not wear expensive-looking jewelry on the street and public transportation; otherwise, you may be a target for thieves.

To equip yourself for the weather, bring: *in winter,* wool clothing, gloves, scarf, raincoat with liner or over-coat, boots or galoshes, umbrella; *in summer,* lightweight cotton clothing; *other seasons,* a sweater and raincoat; *all seasons,* good, sensible walking shoes.

Getting In

The United States requires passports and visitor's or long-term visas of all visitors other than Canadians who are not United States citizens. Check with the United States Embassy or consulate nearest you before you depart. Lines for customs clearance at Kennedy and Newark airports tend to be long; non–United States citizens can expect to wait an hour and often longer at peak arrival times (between 4:00 and 6:00 P.M. for those coming from Europe).

Arrival by Air

New York is served by three major airports: La Guardia, in Queens, for shorter domestic flights (does not handle 747s); Kennedy ("JFK"), also in Queens, for domestic and international flights; and Newark, outside Newark, New Jersey, for domestic and some international flights.

Excellent public transportation links the three airports to Manhattan.

By taxi: The half-hour cab ride from La Guardia to Midtown costs about $30; the 45-minute ride from Kennedy about $40; the 45-minute trip from Newark about $50. At all airports cabs leave from well-marked stands, manned by dispatchers, outside flight arrival areas. It is illegal for cabs to pick up passengers ouside of these areas. Do not be intimidated by the long lines; they move quickly. To partake of the New York custom of "cutting on line" is a sure way of starting a row.

By bus from La Guardia: Carey buses (Tel: 718-632-0500) run every 20 minutes between 6:00 A.M. and mid-night; they leave from posted areas at curbside outside air terminal arrival areas and go to Grand Central Station at

42nd Street and Park Avenue in Midtown with connections to Port Authority and several Midtown hotels; $7.50; allow 30 to 40 minutes.

By bus from Kennedy: Carey buses run every 20 minutes between 6:00 A.M. and midnight from posted areas at curbside outside terminal arrival areas to Grand Central Station in Midtown; $8; allow 45 minutes to one hour.

By bus from Newark: Olympia Trails (Tel: 212-964-6233) buses run every 15 minutes between 6:00 A.M. and midnight from posted areas outside terminals to the World Trade Center (West Street next to the Vista Hotel in the Wall Street area downtown); $7; allow at least 25 minutes. Olympia Trails buses also run every 15 minutes between 6:00 A.M. and midnight from Newark to Grand Central Station at 42nd Street and Park Avenue in Midtown; $7; allow 35 to 45 minutes. New Jersey Transit (Tel: 201-460-8444) buses run every 15 to 20 minutes between 6:00 A.M. and midnight, with infrequent service in the small hours, from Newark to Port Authority Bus Terminal at 42nd Street and Eighth Avenue near Times Square; $7; allow at least half an hour.

By boat from La Guardia: Passengers arriving at the Marine Air Terminal on Pan Am shuttle flights from Washington and Boston may take the Water Shuttle (Tel: 212-687-2600) to Pier 11 on the East River at the foot of Wall Street; $20 one way, $38 round trip; allow half an hour. Sailings at 7:45 A.M., 8:45 A.M., 9:45 A.M., 3:45 P.M., and 4:45 P.M. Vans meet the boats and take passengers to points in the Wall Street area, free of charge. (Boats make the return trip from the foot of East 34th Street at 7:45 A.M., 8:45 A.M., 9:45 A.M., 10:45 A.M., 3:45 P.M., 4:45 P.M., 5:45 P.M., and 6:45 P.M.)

By subway from Kennedy: A bus-and-subway service, the JFK Express, a.k.a. the Train-to-the-Plane (Tel: 718-330-1234), connects Kennedy with subway stops in Brooklyn and Manhattan, including several along Sixth Avenue in Midtown; $6.75; buses stop at posted areas outside Kennedy arrival areas; allow at least an hour. (There is constant talk about derailing this service, so be sure to check in advance to make sure it is still running.)

By helicopter from Kennedy: New York Helicopter (Tel: 800-645-3494) flies from major JFK terminals to the East Side Heliport, 34th Street at the East River in Midtown, every half hour between 1:30 P.M. and 7:30 P.M.; $65.88; the trip takes just ten minutes.

Arrival by Train

Most Amtrak trains, including those travelling the busy Washington–New York–Boston corridor, arrive at Pennsylvania ("Penn") Station, at 34th Street and Seventh Avenue. Some trains, including many from Canada, arrive at Grand Central Station at 42nd Street and Park Avenue. Amtrak service to Grand Central is being phased out and as of spring 1991 all Amtrak trains will service only Penn Station. For Amtrak information, Tel: (800) 872-7245. Both stations are well served by buses and subways. As both stations are also terminals for commuter railroads, taxis are difficult to procure at rush hours; be patient and steadfast in your efforts. A tip: At Grand Central, a dispatcher speeds things along at the Vanderbilt Avenue exit.

Arrival by Sea

The only transatlantic liner that still regularly serves New York is the Cunard Line's *Queen Elizabeth II*. She and the many cruise ships that dock in New York tie up at the Hudson River piers off 12th Avenue in the West 50s. A fleet of taxis meets all ships.

Arrival by Car

If you do insist on bringing a car into already overcrowded Manhattan, you'll soon discover it really is an island, connected to the rest of the United States by a dozen or so bridges and four tunnels. It usually takes longer to traverse any of these crossings than it does to fly from New York to Paris on the Concorde. Most tolls are $3, and at most bridges and tunnels are imposed only on cars entering Manhattan. Once here, park in a garage (costly and hard to find) and walk or take public transportation. If you do park on the street, remember that New York enforces an alternate-side-of-the-street-parking law—you may not leave your car in a space for more than one night. (And *never* leave anything in your car unguarded, unless you want to lose it and one window.)

Sightseeing

Some of the many tours that will help you see New York at its best are:

Backstage on Broadway. 228 West 47th Street, Suite 346; Tel: (212) 575-8065. Actors and directors show you their behind-the-scenes domain.

Circle Line Cruise. Leaves from West 42nd Street and Hudson River, Pier 83; Tel: (212) 563-3200. A three-hour boat cruise around the Manhattan shoreline, all 31 miles of it.

Gray Line of New York. 900 Eighth Avenue; Tel: (212) 397-2600. Well-narrated bus tours give you a choice of lower Manhattan, upper Manhattan, or both.

Island Helicopter. East River at 34th Street; Tel: (212) 683-4575. Unforgettable aerial tours, from $35 to $144.

NBC Studio Tours. 30 Rockefeller Plaza; Tel: (212) 664-4444. A look at New York as television and radio capital.

New York Stock Exchange. 20 Broad Street; Tel: (212) 656-5168. A bird's-eye view of the trading floor.

Petrel. A boat tour that leaves from Battery Park at the southern tip of Manhattan; Tel: (212) 825-1976. Sails across New York Harbor on a 70-foot yawl; April through October only.

Staten Island Ferry. Leaves from Battery Park ferry terminal. Still the world's best short ocean voyage—across New York Harbor, past the Statue of Liberty—and only 25¢ for a round-trip passage.

United Nations. First Avenue and 46th Street; Tel: (212) 963-7713. Tours include the General Assembly and Secretariat.

Local Time
New York observes Eastern Standard Time from November through April and Eastern Daylight Time from May through October. The city is three hours ahead of the West Coast, five hours behind London, six hours behind Paris, and 15 hours behind Sydney.

Electric Current
Despite its dissimilarity to the rest of America, New York uses standard North American current: 110 volts, 60 cycles. Many of the better hotels have installed special wiring to accommodate European appliances.

Currency
Major foreign money exchanges in New York include: American Express, Tel: (212) 640-2000; Citicorp Foreign Currency Exchange, Tel: (718) 632-2500; and Deak International, Tel: (212) 757-6915. All have outlets throughout the city; call for locations nearest you.

Foreigners using this guidebook will probably find a branch of their major national bank in Manhattan. To name but a few: Barclays, at 300 Park Avenue and other locations, Tel: (212) 418-4600; Bank of Ireland, 640 Fifth Avenue, Tel: (212) 397-1700; Canadian Imperial Bank, 425 Lexington Avenue, Tel: (212) 856-4000; Australia and New Zealand Bank, 120 Wall Street, Tel: (212) 820-9800. Check the Manhattan telephone directory for others.

Most larger shops and restaurants accept credit cards, especially VISA, MasterCard, and American Express. Traveller's checks are also widely accepted, although a surprising number of establishments are reluctant to do so. To report lost or stolen traveller's checks, contact: American Express, Tel: (800) 221-7282; BankAmerica, Tel: (800) 227-3460; or VISA, Tel: (800) 227-6811. Bankcard holders who subscribe to the Cirrus Network (instant cash) will find outlets throughout Manhattan; Tel: (212) 424-7787.

Telephoning

New York is divided into two area codes: 212 for Manhattan and the Bronx, 718 for Brooklyn, Queens, and Staten Island. This is a distinction born of volume: Subterranean New York is crisscrossed by 20 million miles of telephone wire, and there are almost 6 million telephones in the city. (The most used set is a public phone at Penn Station on the Long Island Railroad concourse; it is used 230 times a day.) There are other public telephones on almost every corner in Manhattan, although when you try to use one you will observe a peculiarly New York phenomenon: They are almost always in use.

When calling long distance in the United States, you must dial "1" before dialing the area code.

Tipping

As a rule of thumb, tip 15 percent in restaurants (a handy way to determine the tip is to double the 8¼ percent sales tax amount shown on the bill); tip cabdrivers 20 percent of the fare; give $1 to doormen who help you carry packages or procure a cab for you; tip delivery people $1 or $2, more for heavy bundles; leave $1 or $2 a day for helpful chambermaids; give a helpful maître d' $5 or so. Don't tip anyone who is rude or decidedly unhelpful.

Business Hours and Holidays

Many shops in New York do not open until 10:00 or 10:30 A.M. and close at 6:00 or 6:30 P.M. There are a great number of exceptions. In neighborhoods outside of Midtown, many businesses open at noon and don't close until 8:00 or 9:00 P.M., so they can cater to residents on their way home from work. (Numerous New Yorkers don't report to their jobs until 9:30 or 10:00 A.M., often even later, and work until 6:00 or 7:00 P.M., often even later; a nine-to-fiver is the exception here.) Most major department stores are open, in addition to regular daytime hours, on Monday, Thursday, and Friday evenings and on Sunday afternoons. Many Jewish businesses close on Saturday for the Sabbath and open on Sunday.

Most museums are open Sunday but closed Monday; a notable exception is the Museum of Modern Art, which is open Monday but closed Wednesday.

Restaurants tend to serve lunch from noon to 2:30 or 3:00 P.M. (1:00 is the most popular time for a lunch date) and dinner from 6:30 or 7:00 to 10:30 and later (Manhattanites eat late, often at 9:00 or later). In the theater district, many restaurants offer special before- and after-theater menus.

Most bars and clubs stay open until 2:00 A.M. and many as late as 4:00, the latest they are allowed to serve liquor. A New York Sunday brunch, a popular meal in the city, rarely begins before noon, as establishments are not allowed to serve liquor until then.

Many New York businesses are always open, even on such traditional holidays as Christmas and New Year's Day. However, holidays that are commonly observed in New York include: New Year's Day; Martin Luther King's Birthday, January 15, observed the third Monday of the month; Lincoln's Birthday, February 12; Washington's Birthday, February 22, observed on the closest Monday; St. Patrick's Day, March 17, noted by the presence of a million-some inebriated suburban teenagers who descend upon the city to watch the parade on Fifth Avenue and vomit on city sidewalks; Easter Sunday; the first day of Passover; Memorial Day, May 30, observed on the closest Monday; Fourth of July; Labor Day, September 2, observed on the first Monday of September; the first day of Rosh Hashanah; Yom Kippur; Columbus Day; Veterans Day, November 11; Thanksgiving Day, the fourth Thursday of November; the first day of Hanukkah; Christmas Day.

Street Fairs and Festivals

New York graces its concrete canyons with an inordinate number of parades and street fairs, where you can expect to find booths selling exotic foods and goods. Some of the major ones are: Chinese New Year, Chinatown, January or February (an explosive event); St. Patrick's Day Parade, Fifth Avenue, March 17; Greek Independence Day Parade, Park Avenue, late March; Easter Parade (not an official parade; rather, New Yorkers parade up and down Fifth Avenue in finery and costumes), Easter Sunday, Fifth Avenue.

Ninth Avenue International Festival (meaning *food*), mid-May, Ninth Avenue from 35th to 57th streets; Amsterdam Avenue Festival, late May, Amsterdam from 77th to 90th streets; Memorial Day Parade, Memorial Day, very late May, 72nd and Broadway to Soldiers and Sailors Monument at 89th Street and Riverside Drive; Feast of St. Anthony, ten days in early June, Sullivan Street, Greenwich Village (a most nonholy mix of games of chance and carnival attractions); Second Avenue Festival, early June, 68th to 96th streets; 52nd Street Fair, mid-June, Park Avenue to Sixth Avenue; Lexington Avenue Festival, late June, Lexington from 23rd to 34th streets.

Fourth of July, Macy's Fireworks, East River; Third Avenue Summerfest, mid-August, Third from 42nd to 57th streets; Third Avenue Fair, mid-September, Third from 14th to 34th streets; Columbus Avenue Festival, mid-September, Columbus from 66th to 86th streets; Feast of San Gennaro, Mulberry Street in Little Italy, ten days in mid-September (like the feast of St. Anthony, but bigger).

Columbus Day Parade, on or around October 12, Fifth Avenue; Halloween Parade, October 31, Greenwich Village (very strange costumes); Veterans Day Parade, November 11, Fifth Avenue; Macy's Thanksgiving Day Parade, Thanksgiving Day, fourth Thursday in November, Central Park West from 77th to Columbus Circle, Broadway from Columbus Circle to Herald Square.

Getting Around

A few basic rules to keep in mind when moving around Manhattan:

Avenues run north–south and streets run east–west. Avenues increase in number from east to west—First Avenue is on the East Side and Tenth Avenue is on the West Side. Streets increase in number from south to north, with 4th Street being downtown and 74th being uptown.

Fifth Avenue is the dividing line between East and West; 1 East 50th Street would be just east of Fifth, 1 West 50th just west of Fifth.

Most streets are one way, with traffic on even-numbered

Manhattan Address Locator

To find an avenue address, cancel the last figure in the address number, divide by 2, and add (+) or subtract (−) the key number below. The result is the nearest numbered cross street. Cross-street addresses increase east or west from Fifth Avenue, which runs north to south (see examples on 57th Street below). The cross streets west of Central Park (see West 72nd Street), which increase from Central Park West, are the exception.

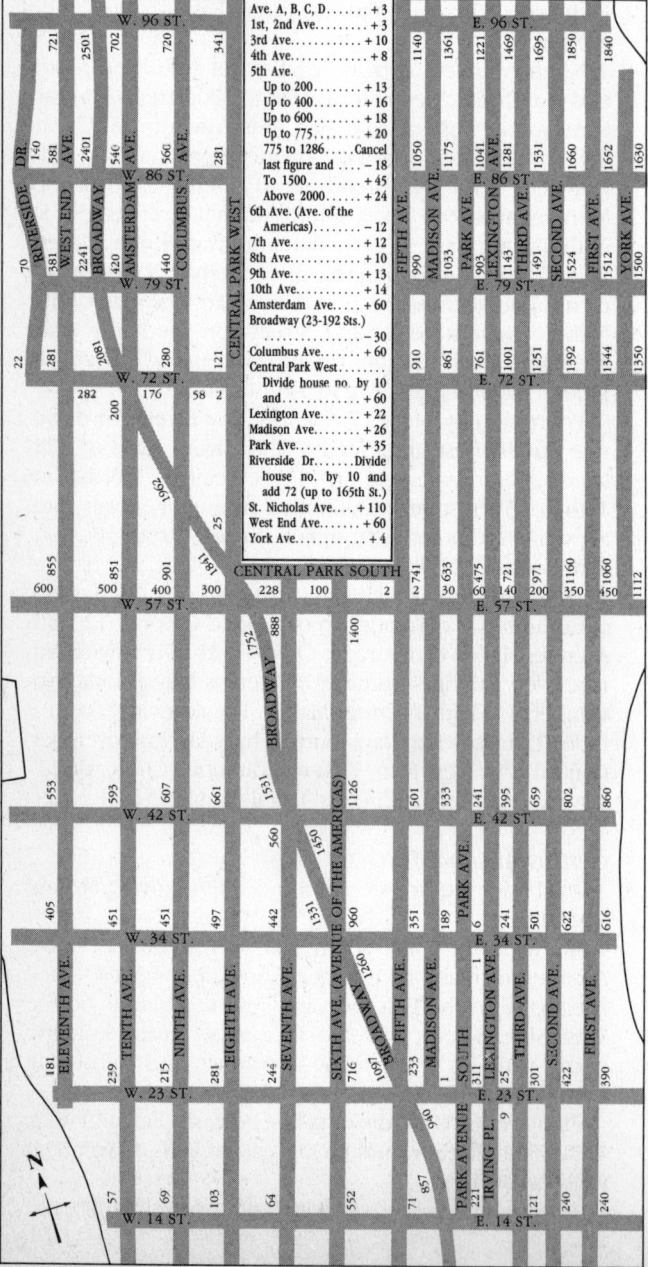

Ave. A, B, C, D	+ 3
1st, 2nd Ave.	+ 3
3rd Ave.	+ 10
4th Ave.	+ 8
5th Ave.	
Up to 200	+ 13
Up to 400	+ 16
Up to 600	+ 18
Up to 775	+ 20
775 to 1286	Cancel last figure and − 18
To 1500	+ 45
Above 2000	+ 24
6th Ave. (Ave. of the Americas)	− 12
7th Ave.	+ 12
8th Ave.	+ 10
9th Ave.	+ 13
10th Ave.	+ 14
Amsterdam Ave.	+ 60
Broadway (23–192 Sts.)	− 30
Columbus Ave.	+ 60
Central Park West	Divide house no. by 10 and + 60
Lexington Ave.	+ 22
Madison Ave.	+ 26
Park Ave.	+ 35
Riverside Dr.	Divide house no. by 10 and add 72 (up to 165th St.)
St. Nicholas Ave.	+ 110
West End Ave.	+ 60
York Ave.	+ 4

W. 96 ST. — E. 96 ST.
W. 86 ST. — E. 86 ST.
W. 79 ST. — E. 79 ST.
W. 72 ST. — E. 72 ST.
CENTRAL PARK SOUTH
W. 57 ST. — E. 57 ST.
W. 42 ST. — E. 42 ST.
W. 34 ST. — E. 34 ST.
W. 23 ST. — E. 23 ST.
W. 14 ST. — E. 14 ST.

Streets and avenues: RIVERSIDE DR, WEST END AVE, BROADWAY, AMSTERDAM AVE, COLUMBUS AVE, CENTRAL PARK WEST, FIFTH AVE, MADISON AVE, PARK AVE, LEXINGTON AVE, THIRD AVE, SECOND AVE, FIRST AVE, YORK AVE, ELEVENTH AVE, TENTH AVE, NINTH AVE, EIGHTH AVE, SEVENTH AVE, SIXTH AVE (AVENUE OF THE AMERICAS), PARK AVENUE SOUTH, IRVING PL, N streets travelling east, traffic on odd-numbered streets travelling west. Traffic flows both ways on major crosstown streets, including Canal, Houston, 14th, 23rd, 34th, 42nd, 57th, 72nd, 79th, 86th, and 96th (the last three are routes across Central Park).

Addresses on north–south streets are not consistently numbered, so 500 Fifth Avenue is actually many blocks north of 500 Second Avenue. Always get a cross street when you ask for an address.

By subway and bus: The $1.15 subway and bus fare is payable with tokens (available at subway stations) or, on buses only, with exact change, no bills. Subway lines frequently used by visitors include the IRT 1 and 9, which make frequent stops on the West Side (many along Broadway), and the IRT 6, which makes frequent stops on the East Side (mostly along Lexington Avenue). Buses run uptown on Tenth, Eighth, Sixth, Madison, Third, and First avenues and downtown on Ninth, Seventh, Fifth, and Second avenues. Some of the major east–west bus routes are 14th, 23rd, 34th, 42nd, 57th, 65th/66th, 79th, 86th, and 96th streets (the last four are the only crosstown streets that traverse Central Park).

Bus and subway maps are available at subway stations and at the office of the New York Convention and Visitors Bureau on Columbus Circle and in Times Square.

By taxi: Cabs licensed by the New York City Taxi and Limousine Commission are equipped with lighted signs on their roofs. When the sign is lit, the cab is available to pick up passengers. When the sign is not lit, the cab is occupied. When the sign reads "Off Duty" the driver is supposedly not picking up passengers. Cabs charge $1.15 for the first one-eighth of a mile and $.15 for each one-eighth of a mile thereafter. Most impose a $.50 surcharge after 8:00 P.M. A 20 percent tip is customary.

By car: A word of advice: Don't. Parking runs $20 a day. Streets are full of potholes. New York drivers are criminally insane or are in some stage of becoming so. What's the point of driving to, say, Macy's, when there's no place to park once you get there? (See also "Arrival by Car," above.)

Renting a Car

Most major rental car agencies have outlets in Manhattan. Like many other goods and services, rental cars cost more in Manhattan than they do elsewhere, and you are likely to get a better rate if you pick a car up at one of the airports. Check with your airline for fly-drive packages. Also remember that many New Yorkers do not own cars, so rental cars are often booked weeks in advance, especially on summer weekends.

Other Sources of Information

The New York Convention and Visitors Bureau distributes a wealth of information about New York from its offices at Columbus Circle and on 42nd Street in Times Square; Tel: (212) 397-8222.

For up-to-date information on shows, exhibitions, and other events, consult weekly editions of *The New Yorker, New York* magazine, the *Village Voice,* or *7 Days* as well as daily newspapers, especially the entertainment section of the Friday *New York Times.* A good radio station to tune into while you're in New York is WNYC (AM 83; FM 94), providing a lively mix of classical music, jazz, and chatter about goings on around town.

Getting Outside the City

New York is surrounded by beautiful countryside (see our Day Trips section) and you don't have to rent a car to see it. The city is served by an extensive network of public transportation. Some numbers of note: Amtrak, Tel: (212) 736-4545; Metro-North's Hudson, Harlem, New Haven, and other rail lines to Connecticut and other points north of the city, Tel: (212) 532-4900; New Jersey Transit (buses and trains), Tel: (201) 460-8444; Long Island Railroad, Tel: (718) 454-5477; Hampton Jitney (buses to eastern Long Island), Tel: (212) 936-0440; Greyhound (bus), Tel: (212) 971-6363.

—Stephen Brewer

BIBLIOGRAPHY

The best single source for books on New York is the New York Bound Bookshop, in the lobby of 50 Rockefeller Center.

History and Biography

Biographies are listed alphabetically by subject; other works are arranged alphabetically by author.

PATRICIA BOSWORTH. *Diane Arbus* (1984). An insightful look at the life and times of this native New Yorker best known for her stark photographs of freaks.

STEPHEN BIRMINGHAM. *Life at the Dakota, New York's Most Unusual Address* (1979). A highly readable blend of a hundred years' worth of architecture, social history, and gossip.

JEAN STEIN. *Edie, An American Biography* (1982). Blue-blooded actress-model Warhol groupie Edie Sedgwick caught up in the social whirl of 1960s New York.

STEPHEN GARMEY. *Gramercy Park* (1984). An illustrated history of a New York neighborhood, from Peter Stuyvesant to the present.

JOHN STEELE GORDON. *The Scarlet Woman of Wall Street* (1988). Good storytelling about mid-19th-century New York and the Erie Railway wars.

HELEN HAYES AND ANITA LOOS. *Twice Over Lightly* (1972). A thoroughly charming and sprightly account of how the "first lady of the American stage" and the author of *Gentlemen Prefer Blondes* spent a summer exploring unlikely aspects of New York City.

IRVING HOWE. *World of Our Fathers: The Journey of the East European Jews to America and the Life They Found and Made* (1976). Fascinating chronicle of arrival and assimilation; lavishly illustrated.

ELIA KAZAN. *A Life* (1988). An encyclopedic account of a long career, much of it spent on the New York stage.

ALFRED KAZIN. *New York Jew* (1978). Coming of age in the political and literary circles of mid-century New York.

JEFF KISSELOF. *You Must Remember This* (1989). New York from 1890 through World War II, as recounted by New Yorkers of the time.

JOHN A. KOUWENHOVEN. *The Columbia Historical Portrait of New York* (1972). A social and physical history of New York; richly illustrated and fact filled.

MABEL DODGE LUHAN. *Movers and Shakers* (1936). An eyewitness account of Greenwich Village before World War I.

DAVID McCULLOUGH. *The Great Bridge* (1972). A thorough and lively account of the construction of the Brooklyn Bridge.

ARTHUR MILLER. *Timebends* (1988). An autobiographical journey from Harlem to Brooklyn to the New York stage.

JAN MORRIS. *The Great Port: A Passage through New York* (1969). A chronicle of New York as a hub of transportation.

ROBERT A. CARO. *The Power Broker: Robert Moses and the Fall of New York* (1975). The highly acclaimed biography of the man who built much of the city we see today.

JERRY E. PATTERSON. *The City of New York: A History Illustrated from the Collections of The Museum of the City of New York* (1978). History at its most entertaining and attractive.

A. SCOTT BERG. *Max Perkins, Editor of Genius* (1978) and *Editor to Author: The Letters of Maxwell E. Perkins* (1987). A superb biography and selected letters document the career of New York's most famous editor, the man who published Hemingway, Fitzgerald, Wolfe, and most of the other great American writers of the 20th century.

ANDREW PORTER. *A Musical Season; Music of Three Seasons: 1974–1977; Music of Three More Seasons: 1977–1980; Musical Events, A Chronicle: 1980–1983.* These collected reviews and essays by the music critic of *The New Yorker* give a magnificent overview of the city's recent musical history.

JACOB RIIS. *How the Other Half Lives: Studies among the Tenements of New York* (1971). These sociological studies of poverty in turn-of-the-century New York instigated massive reforms in housing and social programs.

NED ROREM. *The Paris & New York Diaries* (1983). A composer's journal of his New York experiences during the 1950s and 1960s.

RON ROSENBAUM. *Manhattan Passions: True Tales of Power, Wealth, and Excess* (1987). Fascinating portraits of the rich and famous: Malcolm Forbes, Governor Mario Cuomo, gossip columnist Liz Smith, et al.

JOSEPH C. GOULDEN. *Fit to Print: A. M. Rosenthal and His Times* (1988). How the executive director of *The New York Times* rose to power; based on 317 interviews.

STEVEN RUTTENBAUM. *Mansions in the Clouds* (1986). The life of architect Emery Roth (1871–1948) and the evolution of the New York skyscraper apartment house.

PETER SALWEN. *Upper West Side Story: A History and Guide* (1989). Thorough and lively evocation of a New York neighborhood.

JAMES ATLAS. *Delmore Schwartz: The Life of an American Poet* (1977). A superb portrait of one of the century's finest poets and the New York world in which he lived.

ARNOLD SHAW. *Fifty-Second Street: The Street of Jazz* (1977). Fifty-second Street during its mid-century heyday as a jazz center.

KATE SIMON. *Fifth Avenue: A Very Special History* (1979). A very readable history of the city's poshest avenue. *Bronx Primitive* (1983) chronicles the writer's beginnings in a less glamorous part of town.

EILEEN SIMPSON. *Poets in Their Youth* (1982). Sympathetic portraits of John Berryman, Robert Lowell, Delmore Schwartz, and their like, poets who lived and worked in New York in the 1940s.

GAY TALESE. *The Kingdom and the Power* (1986). A foray into the workings of *The New York Times.*

JAMES THURBER. *The Years with Ross* (1959). A memoir of Harold Ross, founding editor of *The New Yorker,* to which Thurber contributed volumes-worth of his sardonic essays and short stories.

JAMES TRAGER. *West of Fifth: The Rise and Fall of Manhattan's West Side* (1984). Social and architectural history of a New York neighborhood.

JEROME TUCCILLE. *Trump* (1985). All you ever wanted to know about New York's biggest ego.

FLORENCE TURNER. *At the Chelsea* (1987). An affectionate history of the shabby but famous 23rd Street hotel, a favorite among New York's literati.

ELLIOT WILLENSKY. *When Brooklyn Was the World: 1920–1957* (1986). Text and photographs evoke Brooklyn in its golden days.

Literature

WOODY ALLEN. *Without Feathers* (1976), *Getting Even* (1977), *Side Effects* (1980). Humor that exposes New York as the hotbed of neurosis and anxiety it really is.

JAMES BALDWIN. *Go Tell It on the Mountain* (1953) and *Just Above My Head* (1979). Both novels are set in the author's native Harlem.

TRUMAN CAPOTE. *Breakfast at Tiffany's* (1958). The Manhattan adventures of stylish, free-spirited Holly Golightly. *Answered Prayers* (unfinished at the author's death in 1984, published posthumously in 1987) is populated by thinly disguised versions of real-life, upper-crust New Yorkers (who aren't at all happy with their portrayals).

BARBARA COHEN, SEYMOUR CHWAST, AND STEVEN HELLER. *New York Observed: Artists and Writers Look at the City* (1987). Selections from 96 writers and 51 artists.

STEPHEN CRANE. *Maggie: A Girl of the Streets* (1893). Realist fiction about life in the slums of lower Manhattan at the end of the last century.

E. L. DOCTOROW. *Ragtime* (1975). New York in the first half of this century, as experienced by a Jewish immigrant, a suburbanite WASP, and a black. *World's Fair* (1986) revolves around a middle-class New York City Jewish family in the 1930s.

JOHN DOS PASSOS. *Manhattan Transfer* (1925). Hundreds of sketches of characters and events in New York between the two world wars.

JACK FINNEY. *Time and Again* (1970). A man shuttles back and forth between the New York of today and of the 1880s, providing an exceptionally detailed and vivid account of the city in the late 19th century.

F. SCOTT FITZGERALD. *The Great Gatsby* (1925). New York before the Great Depression.

WASHINGTON IRVING. *History of New York from the Beginning of the World to the End of the Dutch Dynasty* (1809). Satirical, fact-filled account of Dutch New York, as presented by the fictional Diedrich Knickerbocker.

HENRY JAMES. *Washington Square* (1881). Greenwich Village in the middle of the last century.

TAMA JANOWITZ. *Slaves of New York* (1986). These slick tales of offbeat New Yorkers do provide a glimpse into contemporary New York—but prove just how vapid contemporary writing about New York can be.

BEL KAUFMAN. *Up the Down Staircase* (1965). Trials and triumphs of a Manhattan schoolteacher.

FRAN LIEBOWITZ. *Metropolitan Life* (1978). Humorous essays on life in the country's largest metropolis.

FEDERICO GARCIA LORCA. *Poet in New York* (1955). Early alienation poetry from the Spanish surrealist poet and dramatist.

MARY MCCARTHY. *The Group* (1963). Vassar graduates descend on New York in the 1950s.

JAY MCINERNEY. *Bright Lights, Big City* (1984). Glib, empty novel about glib, empty young New Yorkers, yet it does picture a certain New York. More of the same surfaces in *The Story of My Life* (1988).

BERNARD MALAMUD. *The Tenants* (1971). Anguish of a lonely immigrant in an abandoned New York tenement.

MIKE MARQUESEE AND BILL HARRIS. *New York, An Anthology* (1985). In poetry and prose, how writers feel about New York.

HOWARD MOSS, EDITOR. *New York Poems* (1980). Poets inspired by a common subject.

CLIFFORD ODETS. *Awake and Sing* (1935). One of the first plays by the master playwright who shaped the New York stage chronicles the life of a Jewish family in the Bronx.

CONRAD OSBORNE. *O Paradiso* (1988). An outrageous novel of New York's opera crazies.

GRACE PALEY. *Enormous Changes at the Last Minute* (1975). Short stories, many of them set in Greenwich Village.

DOROTHY PARKER. *The Portable Dorothy Parker* (1944). Poems, stories, and reviews by this renowned denizen of the Algonquin Round Table.

JOHN RECHY. *City of Night* (1952). Fictionalized account of New York's homosexual underworld.

HENRY ROTH. *Call It Sleep* (1964). A novel centered on the family life of Jewish immigrants.

DAMON RUNYON. *The Bloodhounds of Broadway and Other Stories* (1981). The author of *Guys and Dolls* explores the Broadway underworld.

J. D. SALINGER. *Catcher in the Rye* (1945). A modern classic in which Holden Caulfield, upper-middle-class son of New York, comes of age.

HUBERT SELBY, JR. *Last Exit to Brooklyn* (1964). A seething portrait of low life in a Brooklyn neighborhood.

BETTY SMITH. *A Tree Grows in Brooklyn* (1943). A sentimental novel about an Irish girl growing up in Brooklyn.

WILLIAM STYRON. *Sophie's Choice* (1976). An evocative tale of a Holocaust survivor in Brooklyn after the war.

CHUCK WACHTEL. *Joe the Engineer* (1983). A novel of working-class life in Queens.

EDWARD LEWIS WALLANT. *The Pawnbroker* (1961). Tribulations of a concentration-camp survivor in Harlem.

NATHANAEL WEST. *Miss Lonelyhearts* (1933). Economic and emotional depression as it affects an advice-to-the-lovelorn columnist in 1930s New York.

EDITH WHARTON. *The Age of Innocence* (1920). Pulitzer Prize–winning novel of upper-class life in late 19th-century New York.

E. B. WHITE. *Essays of E. B. White* (1977). A superb collection of works by this contributor to *The New Yorker,* including "Here Is New York" (1949), perhaps the best lines ever written about the city.

THOMAS WOLFE. *Of Time and the River: A Legend of Man's Hunger in His Youth* (1935). Despairing novel of New York during the Great Depression; sequel to *Look Homeward, Angel.*

TOM WOLFE. *Bonfire of the Vanities* (1987). This highly stylized novel draws on the tumultuous social realities of New York in the 1980s.

HERMAN WOUK. *Marjorie Morningstar* (1955). Social aspirations of a middle-class Jewish family on the Upper West Side.

Architecture and Photography

BERENICE ABBOTT. *New York in the Thirties* (1939). Photographs by this master who made it her business to chronicle the entire city.

MARY BLACK. *Old New York in Early Photographs: 196 Prints, 1853–1901, from the Collection of The New-York Historical Society* (1973). The best from the society's collection.

CHRISTIAN BLANCHET AND BERTRAND DARD. *Statue of Liberty: The First Hundred Years* (1985). A rich text (translated from the French) and a treasure trove of historic illustrations, many from European collections; the best book ever on the much-publicized Lady of the Harbor.

BENJAMIN BLOM. *New York: Photographs, 1850–1950* (1982). A fine collection on New York people and buildings.

JOSEPH BYRON. *Photographs of New York Interiors at the Turn of the Century* (1976) and *New York Life at the Turn of the Century in Photographs* (1985). Exquisite photographs from the Byron Collection of the Museum of the City of New York.

BARBARALEE DIAMONSTEIN. *The Landmarks of New York* (1988). Thorough documentation of historic New York, by one of the city's most visible socialites.

LORRAINE B. DIEHL. *The Late, Great Pennsylvania Station* (1985). The construction, decay, and tragic demolition in 1963 of New York's greatest landmark, one of the "few buildings vast enough to hold the sound of time" (Thomas Wolfe).

CARIN DRECHSLER-MARX AND RICHARD F. SHEPARD. *Broadway* (1988). The 293 blocks from the Battery to the Bronx along this famous street are discussed in terms of people, culture, and history.

ANDREAS FEININGER. *New York in the Forties* (1983). One of the greatest photographers of his age takes on a willing subject.

MARGOT GAYLE AND EDMUND V. GILLON. *Cast Iron Architecture in New York* (1974). A photographic record of the style that flourished in New York at the end of the last century.

PAUL GOLDBERGER. *The City Observed* (1979). The architecture critic of *The New York Times* comments on the major buildings of Manhattan.

ADA LOUISE HUXTABLE. *Classic New York: Georgian Gentility to Greek Elegance* (1964). Remarkable observations from the former architecture critic of *The New York Times.*

CHARLES LOCKWOOD. *Bricks and Brownstones* (1972). A thorough history of the New York row house.

DONALD MARTIN REYNOLDS. *The Architecture of New York City* (1984). History and commentary on 80 major buildings and monuments.

REBECCA REED SHANOR. *The City That Never Was: Two Hundred Years of Fantastic and Fascinating Plans That Might Have Changed the Face of New York City* (1988). A landing strip in Central Park and other schemes that never made it off the drawing board; well written and illustrated.

NATHAN SILVER. *Lost New York* (1967). A heavily illustrated account of New York's lost architectural landscape.

ROBERT A. M. STERN, GREGORY GILMARTIN, AND THOMAS MELLINS. *New York 1900* (1984). Monumental overview of the city's Beaux Arts architecture. Followed by *New York 1930* (1987), focusing on architecture between the wars.

J.-C. SUARES. *Manhattan* (1981). This expensive and arty photo collection is the best of our time.

JOHN TAURANAC. *Essential New York* (1979). Short, incisive write-ups on Manhattan's major buildings, parks, and bridges.

JOHN TAURANAC AND CHRISTOPHER LITTLE. *Elegant New York: The Builders and the Buildings, 1895–1915* (1985). Ninety great residential and corporate palaces.

EDWARD B. WATSON AND EDMUND V. GILLON, JR. *New York Then and Now* (1976). Old and new photographs of the same sites show how the city has and hasn't changed.

NORVAL WHITE AND ELLIOT WILLENSKY. *AIA Guide to New York City* (1988). An authoritative, building-by-building guide to New York, sanctioned by the American Institute of Architects; recently and thoroughly revised.

NORVAL WHITE AND ELLIOT WILLENSKY. *New York: A Physical History* (1988). A unique cultural, economic, and technical account of man-made New York.

Unusual Guidebooks

RICHARD ALLEMAN. *The Movie Lover's Guide to New York: The Ultimate Guide to Movie New York* (1988). Movie stars' homes, film locations, and the like; exhaustive.

JEROME CHARYN. *Metropolis: New York as Myth, Marketplace, and Magical Land* (1986). A tour of Manhattan people, places, and legends.

JUDI CULBERTSON AND TOM RANDALL. *Permanent New Yorkers: A Biographical Guide to the Cemeteries of New York* (1987). New York cemeteries as museums.

SUSAN EDMISTON AND LINDA D. CIRINO. *Literary New York: A History and Guide* (1976). This geographic tour tells who wrote what where.

MARGOT GAYLE AND MICHELE COHEN. *The Art Commission and the Municipal Art Society Guide to Manhattan's Outdoor Sculpture* (1988). Expert commentary.

JOYCE GOLD. *From Windmills to the World Trade Center: A Walking Guide to Lower Manhattan History* (1988). Personal and anecdotal guide to lower Manhattan.

HARMON GOLDSTONE AND MARTHA DALRYMPLE. *History Preserved: A Guide to New York City Landmarks and Historic Districts* (1974). Well-guided tours for history buffs.

JOSEPH LEDERER AND ARLEY BONDARIN. *All Around the Town: A Walking Guide to Outdoor Sculpture in New York City* (1975). Comprehensive and fun.

JAMES D. MCCABE, JR. *New York by Gaslight* (1882). A southern journalist's guide to the city; now in a reprint.

HENRY MOSCOW. *The Book of New York Firsts: Unusual, Arcane, and Fascinating Facts in the Life of New York City* (1982). The first balloon ascent over Manhattan and other interesting New York facts. Moscow's *The Street Book: An Encyclopedia of Manhattan's Street Names and Their Origins* (1978) provides more fun New York history.

New York City Guide (Reprint, 1982). The original, 1939 WPA guide to New York. Insightful though dated.

The New York Times World of New York: An Uncommon Guide to the City of Fantasies (1985). Essays by Vincent Canby, Nora Ephron, David Frost, and their famous like; often so clever they miss the point but good reading all the same.

LYNN SCHNURNBERGER. *Kids Love New York!: The A–Z Resource Book* (1984). Some 800 suggestions on how to keep the little ones happy in the Big Apple.

KATE SIMON. *New York: Places and Pleasures* (1971). The eloquent travel writer directs her innate charm to her home city.

Movies

New York has been a favorite film location since the movie camera was invented. *The Movie Lover's Guide to New York* by Richard Alleman (see "Unusual Guidebooks," above) is your best guide to the Big Apple as movieland. The following films are only a few of the best in which New York steals the show.

Breakfast at Tiffany's (1961). A sophisticated movie version of Truman Capote's classic, with Audrey Hepburn as Holly Golightly.

East Side, West Side (1949). Typical New Yorkers—chic, savvy, neurotic, selfish—portrayed by Barbara Stanwyck, James Mason, Ava Gardner, Nancy Davis (Reagan), others.

Easter Parade (1948). Fred Astaire and Judy Garland show how to partake of this annual Fifth Avenue tradition in high style.

Forty-Second Street (1933). Backstage drama with onstage extravaganzas by Busby Berkeley; you can also see it live on Broadway.

Guys and Dolls (1955). A snappy film version of the Broadway musical, inhabited by those amusing Damon Runyon characters.

Hester Street (1975). A nice Jewish girl from the Old Country (Carol Kane) doesn't like turn-of-the-century New York one bit.

King Kong (1933). The big hairy ape goes to the top of the Empire State Building and he doesn't even use the elevator. (He does a repeat performance at the World Trade Center in a campy 1976 remake.)

Miracle on 34th Street (1947). A highly convincing and charming argument for the validity of the Santa Claus myth.

My Sister Eileen (1955 musical version, based on the 1938 novel by Ruth McKenney). Two Ohio girls come to Greenwich Village with songs in their hearts. (The real-life Eileen married novelist Nathanael West; the couple was killed in an automobile accident in 1940.)

Next Stop, Greenwich Village (1976). Brooklyn boy explores 1950s bohemia.

On the Town (1949). Gene Kelly and Frank Sinatra dance their way up and down Manhattan.

On the Waterfront (1954). Marlon Brando sweats, scowls, and scrapes on the Jersey docks.

Prisoner of Second Avenue (1975). The city begins to get to Anne Bancroft and Jack Lemmon.

An Unmarried Woman (1978). Upper East Side housewife loses her husband, takes up with a SoHo artist, and moves into an Upper West Side brownstone: What could be more typically New York?

Where's Poppa? (1970). Ruth Gordon at her best as a batty Upper West Side Jewish mamma.

The World of Henry Orient (1964). New York as experienced by two wacky adolescents.

Finally, the films of Woody Allen, most of which are really just manifestations of the director's love affair with his native city. Of special note for their indulgence of New York: *Annie Hall* (1977), *Manhattan* (1979), *Broadway Danny Rose* (1984), *Hannah and Her Sisters* (1986), and *Radio Days* (1987).

—*Stephen Brewer*

ACCOMMODATIONS

New York's hotel roster is enlarging by the day, as a recent surge in building and renovation adds new luxury and variety for visitors. Exorbitant city real-estate values, however, mean high prices. Moderate rates are $150 to $200 a night; luxury hotels start at $210 and go way up. So many Midtown hotels have crossed the $200 boundary that it pays now to compare rates, as it is often possible to stay in a small exclusive property for almost the same tab as the large commercial hotels. Budget choices are limited, but there are some encouraging newcomers. Rates in the lower range run from $100 to $125; ambience varies from pleasant to dreary.

The selection here is divided into geographic areas and is listed *from most to least expensive in each group*. The Upper East Side north of 59th Street, with its art galleries, boutiques, and museums, is home to many of the city's most prestigious hotels. The West Side from 42nd to 61st streets gives access to Lincoln Center, Broadway theaters, and Carnegie Hall—an important advantage because cabs are hard to find just before and after performances. Midtown East is convenient for shoppers and business travellers, while the Murray Hill neighborhood, a quieter residential district in the east 30s, offers some of the most appealing accommodations in the moderate range. A final potpourri offers a rundown on the city's growing number of all-suite properties, a listing of the big convention hotels, and a selection of hotels and bed-and-breakfast options for travellers on a genuine budget.

All hotels have better rates on weekends; ask for the weekend package, then the regular rates. An 8¼ percent sales tax is added to all hotel bills.

The telephone area code for Manhattan is 212.

Upper East Side

The Pierre, a longtime favorite of the rich and powerful, has the air of a luxurious and exclusive private club and provides crackerjack service and welcome privacy for business barons and diplomats from around the world. Half the rooms are leased on a permanent basis. Chippendale and Chinoiserie are the styles, and the lobby gleams with Old World elegance. High tea in front of the grand staircase in **The Rotunda** is a daily ritual, and many a business deal has been consummated here over breakfast croissants.

2 East 61st Street (at Fifth Avenue), New York, NY 10021. Tel: 838-8000.

The Stanhope has been transformed by a recent $30-million renovation into an ornate showplace filled with Louis XVI furnishings and Baccarat chandeliers. Rooms are decorated to the last tiny corner with reproduction 18th-century armoires, displays of antique porcelain, and a mini-library of antique books. The choicest of the 50 rooms and 100 suites overlook the Metropolitan Museum across the street and Central Park beyond. Staff outnumbers guests here two to one, and the hotel provides convenient limousine transportation to Midtown. The sidewalk café outside is one of New York's most popular oases.

995 Fifth Avenue (at 81st Street), New York, NY 10028. Tel: 288-5800.

The Carlyle's understated elegance and impeccable service have kept it at the top of the New York list for decades, the choice of CEOs, society, and two United States presidents. There's a hushed quality to the dimmed lobby with its antiques and tapestries. The spacious rooms are done in fresh florals accented with antiques and greenery—nothing ostentatious, just pleasantness and quiet good taste. Rooms provide all the amenities of one of the world's best hotels, including serving pantries. Things are surprisingly lively in the evening, when top pianists play under the colorful murals at **Bemelmans Bar**—and Bobby Short holds court at the **Café Carlyle**.

35 East 76th Street (at Madison Avenue), New York, NY 10021. Tel: 744-1600.

The **Plaza Athénée** does not try to match the grandeur of its Parisian sister, but is instead a pampering, intimate sanctuary. In the small, formal lobby, softened by a blue-green pastoral tapestry and pale rugs, guests are seated at an 18th-century desk for check-in, then personally escorted by a manager to their well-appointed rooms. Duplicates of the trademark gilt clocks of the original hotel await in every room, along with traditional furnishings, fresh flowers, and such niceties as trouser pressers, tie racks, shoe trees, safes, pantries, Porthault bathrobes—even humidifiers to combat dry room heat in winter. **La Regence** serves top-caliber French food amid hand-painted panels, cloud ceilings, and chandeliers.

37 East 64th Street (between Madison and Park avenues), New York, NY 10021. Tel: 734-9100.

The **Mayfair Regent** reflects the personal warmth of manager Dario Mariotti. Once of the Grand Hotel and the Gritti Palace in Venice, he sets a cosmopolitan tone for this small and charming hotel, which attracts a loyal clientele from royalty to Italian fashion designers to Greek shipping magnates. The spacious quarters are a pretty and tasteful world of soft colors and thoughtful comforts, such as the umbrella hanging in the closet, just in case. Coffered ceilings, wing chairs, and a fireplace make the lobby a place for lingering, and the columned and mirrored lounge has become a favorite setting in the city for business breakfasts and afternoon teas. Guests also have charging privileges at the little restaurant off the lobby— the four-star **Le Cirque**.

610 Park Avenue (at 65th Street), New York, NY 10021. Tel: 288-0800.

The lobby is understated at the **Westbury** and the rooms are agreeably fussy, with stripes, flowery chintz, oriental rugs, and ruffles and plants all around, a combination that seems to appeal to the many well-dressed European travellers who keep the hotel well booked. The **Polo Lounge**, with its dark mahogany bar and paisley seats, is popular with the toney neighborhood crowd as well as with guests.

15 East 69th Street (between Fifth and Madison avenues), New York, NY 10021. Tel: 535-2000.

There's a bit of show-biz glitz to the **Regency**, the grand hotel in the Loews chain where such personages as Prince Rainier and Hollywood studio execs like to stay. The decor, recently redone to the tune of plenty of millions, is elaborate Regency style with lots of marble, brocade, and mirrors. Guests are welcome to use the fitness center in the lower lobby.

540 Park Avenue (between 60th and 61st streets), New York, NY 10021. Tel: 759-4100.

The Mark, until recently known as the Madison Avenue, is being turned into a first-class entry with an Art Deco look and rooms featuring contemporary colors and lacquer accent pieces. Eighty-five of the 185 rooms are suites.

25 East 77th Street (off Madison), New York, NY 10021. Tel: 744-4300.

The Barbizon, once a residence hotel where well-bred young ladies like Grace Kelly and Lauren Bacall were properly chaperoned when they arrived in New York, has been stylishly renovated, and the pastel contemporary rooms, while small, are a good value in the neighborhood. The tower suites with terraces and city views appeal to many celebrities; ABC puts up its top "Good Morning America" guests here. Ian Schrager and the late Steve Rubell, who did such a smashing job on the Royalton and Morgans (see below), took over the Barbizon a while back, and a renovation is underway.

140 East 63rd Street (at Lexington Avenue), New York, NY 10021. Tel: 838-5700.

Midtown West

The New York **Peninsula** was once the 1905 Beaux Arts
landmark Gotham Hotel. It reopened in 1988 as Maxim's,
with an opulent Art Nouveau theme, but in short order the
hotel was acquired by the noted Peninsula group. The Parisian touch prevails. A sweeping double staircase leads to
marble arches, antiques, and huge floral bouquets. Guest
rooms have custom cherry furnishings, three telephones,
a writing desk with leather blotters, and Art Nouveau accessories. Some baths have six-foot whirlpool tubs and bidets.
Fifth Avenue views from higher floors are striking, but the
best are from the tri-level fitness center and rooftop pool
soon to open overlooking Manhattan.

700 Fifth Avenue (at 55th Street), New York, NY 10019.
Tel: 247-2200.

The first true luxury hotel to be established near the
theater district, the sophisticated **Grand Bay** is a hit just off
Broadway. The two-story lobby, with pink marble, sculpted
pedestals, paintings of the four seasons, and a giant chandelier, is wonderfully removed from the bustle of the neighborhood. No look-alike rooms here: With decor from
French Provincial to Art Deco to black-and-white Modern,
there should be something to please everyone. There's dining on the balcony over the lobby; tea and cocktails in the
lobby café; and one of the city's more popular restaurants,
Harry Cipriani's **Bellini**, adjoins just outside. Among the
many amenities are beepers available at the front desk so
VIPs needn't miss important calls during the theater.

152 West 51st Street (at Seventh Avenue), New York, NY
10019. Tel: 765-1900.

The **Ritz Carlton** is a clubby enclave with the spirit of
an English country house. Rooms were done by noted
decorator Sister Parish at a reported $100,000 each, with
mahogany furniture from Henredon and fine print fabrics
from Brunschwig & Fils. The rooms aren't large compared to others in this price category, but the understated
English look has its appeal—judging from a reported
guest list that includes Nancy Reagan, Sophia Loren, Elizabeth Taylor, and Donald Sutherland. Things may be even
more posh when new owners begin a multi-million-
dollar refurbishing. Most in demand are the front rooms
with breathtaking Central Park views; settle for a quiet
back room and the rates go down considerably. The
Jockey Club restaurant, a meld of antique pine and
leather, has a library to keep you occupied while you wait
for your cronies in the bar.

112 Central Park South, New York, NY 10019. Tel: 757-1900.

The Plaza, New York's true grande dame, has the best location in town, at the foot of Central Park on the most European of the city's plazas. Since Donald Trump acquired this national historic landmark in 1989 and installed his wife, Ivana, at the helm, major restoration is returning the Plaza to its original turn-of-the-century glitter. In the public rooms and corridors, this means miles of burgundy carpeting, acres of gold leaf, frescoed ceilings, custom-made tapestries, and Belgian crystal chandeliers. Guest rooms have been redone in high Victorian style. Fortunately, the Trumps have elected to refurbish rather than remodel such longtime favorite meeting places as the Palm Court, the Oyster Bar, and the Oak Bar. The major change at the Edwardian Room is the addition of a new master chef and a French pastry chef.

786 Fifth Avenue (at 59th Street), New York, NY 10019. Tel: 759-3000.

The look of the **Royalton** is somewhere between a 21st-century luxury liner and the *Orient Express.* The playful new hotel incorporates the favorite travel experiences of the men who created it, Ian Schrager and the late Steve Rubell, formerly of the famous—or infamous—disco, Studio 54. Designer Philippe Starck's tapered columns, curved lines, and sweeps of mahogany and granite make for a stunning modern lobby with trendy features such as a 24-hour, high-tech lunch counter, a skylit billiard table, and a tiny round bar that seats exactly 15 people. Walking the narrow dark-blue corridors is like making your way toward a slick train compartment. Rooms are efficient affairs, with built-in seating and storage and a big bed tucked in like a captain's bunk. Love it or hate it, there's nothing else like it.

44 West 44th Street (between Fifth and Sixth avenues), New York, NY 10036. Tel: 869-4400.

For **Le Parker Meridien,** the French chain has chosen showy elegance rather than Gallic charm, with a pink-columned, two-story entry arcade setting the tone. Light-toned woods, French prints, and marble baths make for attractive if not distinctive guest rooms. A memorable bonus, however, is the glass-enclosed 42nd-floor pool and the outside sun deck and running track with soaring city views. For indoor exercise, the basement health club has a weight room, squash and racquetball courts, whirlpool, sauna, and aerobics classes. Fitness buffs and business travellers particularly enjoy the facilities, which allow them to work off the calories acquired at **Maurice**, the hotel's esteemed French restaurant.

119 West 56th Street (between Sixth and Seventh avenues), New York, NY 10019. Tel: 245-5000.

The Dorset gives off a dignified, quiet, Old English air in its gracious paneled lobby and muraled dining room. Rooms are large and attractive with modern furnishings, Picasso prints on the walls, and convenient serving pantries. Prices fall between the moderate and luxury categories because the bathrooms have not been modernized, making the hotel a relatively good buy.

30 West 54th Street (between Fifth and Sixth avenues), New York, NY 10019. Tel: 247-7300.

The **Mayflower**, a genteel dowager on Central Park, an aria away from Lincoln Center, has an Old World look in the lobby corridor lined with paintings. Rooms, however, while comfortable, are beginning to show their age. Of course, with a park view you may never notice, and there's often interesting artistic company in the **Conservatory Café**.

15 Central Park West (at 61st Street), New York, NY 10023. Tel: 265-0060.

The **Warwick** is a safe if uninspired choice with a fine location and good-sized rooms that should be more appealing after the renovation that is underway. The lobby has been spruced up, and 75 percent of the rooms will be ready in early 1990. There are a restaurant and bar on the premises.

65 West 54th Street (at Sixth Avenue), New York, NY 10019. Tel: 247-2700.

Dorothy Parker, Alexander Woollcott, and their fabled Round Table of the 1920s are gone from the **Algonquin**, but conversation still hums in the **Rose Room** and the paneled lobby sitting room–cum–cocktail lounge. The latter is a haven where authors, publishers, actors, producers, and people watchers gather, summoning the waiter with a traditional brass bell. The Algonquin is where *The New Yorker* magazine was born (and is still found in every room), where Lerner and Loewe wrote *My Fair Lady,* where Angela Lansbury lived when she starred in *Mame,* and where guests still include names like Mordecai Richler, Eudora Welty, and Maya Angelou. What the moderately priced, determinedly old-fashioned rooms lack in modern amenities they make up for in coziness, warmth, and the palpable feeling of tradition. New owners have begun modernization, and if they know what their clientele likes, will keep the old spirit intact.

59 West 44th Street (between Fifth and Sixth avenues), New York, NY 10036. Tel: 840-6800.

The spacious, pretty, old-fashioned rooms at the **Wyndham** are among New York's best buys, personally decorated by resident owners of taste who put their money into paintings and charm rather than room service or fancy new plumbing. (Everything works—it just isn't state of the art.) The deep red lobby–sitting room is as cozy as a home parlor, and you ring the bell for admittance as in a home. The hotel is a favorite of visiting performers; Jessica Tandy and Hume Cronyn keep a permanent apartment here. Reserve well in advance to join them.

42 West 58th Street (between Fifth and Sixth avenues), New York, NY 10019. Tel: 753-3500.

Midtown East

Despite her problems with the I.R.S., at press time Leona Helmsley was still proclaiming herself the queen of the **Helmsley Palace**, a hotel whose distinction lies in incorporating the opulent public rooms of the restored 1881 Villard Houses. Afternoon tea in the Gold Room is a perfect way to see the treasures, including the sweeping staircase, grand ballroom, exquisite carving, and Stanford White interiors inspired by the Palazzo della Cancelleria in Rome. The pale, oversized rooms of the 55-story hotel beyond presumably reflect Mrs. Helmsley's own Baroque tastes, which seem to appeal to many monied guests—but seldom to the truly sophisticated traveller.

455 Madison Avenue (at 50th Street), New York, NY 10022. Tel: 888-7000.

Architect Kevin Roche won a prize for the superb, soaring, contemporary **United Nations Plaza Hotel**, where luxurious guest rooms begin on the 28th floor and big windows provide the best East River views in town, particularly from the 27th-floor pool and health club (there's also a tennis court on the 39th floor). Marble, chrome, and mirrors reflecting Japanese floral arrangements mark the lobby, where a harpist offers soothing music in the afternoon. When the UN is in session, ambassadors, diplomats, and people like the secretary of state may be in residence. The hotel provides a quick Continental breakfast for busy guests in the Wickery, a bower off the lobby, and limousine service to Wall Street. The **Ambassador Grill** has a pleasant ambience, and its prices are moderate.

One United Nations Plaza (44th Street and First Avenue), New York, NY 10017. Tel: 355-3400.

The **Inter-Continental New York** is the old Barclay, revived by the distinguished international chain. The brass birdcage and Tiffany ceiling in the lobby and the air of genteel refinement remain intact. The spacious rooms have been tastefully redecorated with traditional furnishings.

111 East 48th Street (between Lexington and Park avenues), New York, NY 10017. Tel: 755-5900.

The Waldorf-Astoria, the first bastion of New York elegance, is now a busy Hilton property, but there is still cachet to the handsome Art Deco lobby. The giant clock executed for the Chicago World's Fair of 1893 is a carry-over from the original hotel (which gave way to the Empire State Building). Rooms are big and very nicely done in French Provincial style. Tucked away from the crowd with its own entrance, the **Waldorf Towers** is tonier than ever after a refurbishing that restored many of the original architectural details. The flower-adorned piano played nightly in the **Peacock Alley** cocktail lounge belonged to Cole Porter when he was a Towers resident. For those who like the variety of restaurants and services of a large hotel, this one remains special.

301 Park Avenue (between 49th and 50th streets), New York, NY 10022. Tel: 355-3000.

A contemporary hideaway in the heart of Midtown, the **Manhattan Viscount**, part of the British Trusthouse Forte hotel group, has just one hundred rooms, three or four on each of 36 floors, all done in tailored modern with plaid carpeting, lacquer furniture, and bold colors. Amenities include dressing rooms, trouser pressers, shoe racks, and bidets in many baths. Some rooms also have terraces. The lobby is divided by tall arches into a sitting area and the glass-paneled Zodiac Bar, where a complimentary Continental breakfast is served in the morning. The spiffy pinstripe-clad young ladies at the desk seem eager to please, and the Viscount itself should please those who want a slick, small, reasonable hotel.

127 East 55th Street (between Lexington and Park avenues), New York, NY 10022. Tel: 826-1100.

"Quirky" best describes the **Elysée**, a small moderately priced Midtown hotel with personality. Rooms have names rather than numbers—the Taupe Room, Le Cordon Bleu, the Italian Room, the Lanai Room—and each has a totally different look, from iron and brass headboards to chintz to shoji screens. Some are charming, some are tacky, none is boring. Off the intimate lobby, Pisces Restaurant invites with a colorful room-size mural of the Côte d'Azur; L'Atelier Simbari, an art gallery, shows work by an Italian artist; and the **Monkey Bar** serves up singers and piano entertainment amid whimsical murals.

60 East 54th Street (between Madison and Park avenues), New York, NY 10022. Tel: 753-1066.

The family-owned **Beverly** is among the best values in the lineup of commercial hotels across from the Waldorf on Lexington Avenue. There are quiet, comfortable, good-sized rooms here, as well as suites with kitchens that are good buys for families. The lobby is warm and unpretentious, and there are a restaurant, cocktail lounge, and coffee shop on the premises.

125 East 50th Street (at Lexington Avenue), New York, NY 10022. Tel: 753-2700.

If it weren't for the tour groups that clog the lobby, the **Doral Inn** would be the top choice for a reasonably priced Midtown hotel with modern, well-decorated rooms. For those willing to put up with possible waits at the desk, however, there are rewards, such as a fitness center on the fourth floor with saunas and three squash courts, a 24-hour coffee shop as well as a bar and restaurant and a convenient, money-saving, do-it-yourself laundry room.

541 Lexington Avenue (at 50th Street), New York, NY 10022. Tel: 755-1200.

The **Roosevelt** offers no glamour but it fills the bill for those who want a clean, well-located Midtown business hotel with decent rooms, all the standard services, and moderate rates. **Crawdaddy Restaurant** serves up New Orleans–style fare; commuters headed for nearby Grand Central Station favor the Crowing Cock Bar.

45 East 45th Street (at Madison Avenue), New York, NY 10017. Tel: 661-9600.

Murray Hill

An old brick façade and flower boxes filled with geraniums and trailing vines make it clear that the **Sheraton Park Avenue** is not the usual chain hotel. The paneled lobby with needlepoint upholstery and a library of leather-bound books is English country. The rooms upstairs have Chippendale-style furniture, with soft florals, long drapes, and old New York prints on the walls. Many have fireplaces (nonworking). Bookshelves and banquettes make the bar a cozy place for a fast lunch or to hear jazz at night. Guests are also welcome at the monthly lunch meeting of the Park Avenue Literary Club.

45 Park Avenue (at 37th Street), New York, NY 10016. Tel: 685-7676.

Even the tieless doorman looks like a rock star at **Morgans**, another hot property created by Ian Schrager and the late Steve Rubell (see also the Royalton). Among the celebrity guests are Giorgio Armani, Bianca Jagger, Cher, Margaux Hemingway, Brooke Shields, and Boy George. No hotel clichés here—not even a sign out front. French designer Andree Putnam's black-and-white minimalist world is clean, uncluttered Modern, from the optical-illusion cube carpeting in the lobby to the gray-and-white pinstripes on the beds and the stainless steel sinks in the bath. Furniture in the smallish rooms is functional—padded window seats lift to make room for suitcases and clutter, coffee tables have casters to roll where they are wanted—and all rooms come with both a refrigerator and a stereo. Prices are not as high as you might expect for a celebrity spot.

237 Madison Avenue (at 38th Street), New York, NY 10016. Tel: 686-0300.

The chic **Doral Park Avenue**, a small hotel with big-time ways, is treasured by those who discover it. The round entryway sets the mood, with chandeliers, marble, and brass. The newly decorated rooms are light, modern, and appealing; many have sweeping views of Park Avenue. Willing room-service people here will provide anything from breakfast in bed to a VCR to an exercise bicycle. Energetic guests are welcome at the health club at the more expensive Doral Tuscany around the corner. The Park Avenue Grill, with leather paneling and equestrian prints, has a cozy feel, and the sidewalk café out front is a Continental touch.

70 Park Avenue (at 38th Street), New York, NY 10016. Tel: 687-7050.

Doral Court, one of three sister properties in leafy Murray Hill, has just emerged from remodeling as the best value of the lot. The good-sized rooms are fresh and pretty, with entry foyers, king-size beds, and 25-inch television. Each bath has a dressing alcove with a vanity and a refrigerator. Four choice digs on the 15th floor have terraces with views of the Chrysler Building and the New

York skyline. And the **Courtyard Café** downstairs provides a greenhouse setting and a hidden garden with a gurgling waterfall.

130 East 39th Street (at Lexington Avenue), New York, NY 10016. Tel: 685-1100.

The most interesting feature of the Japanese-owned **Kitano** is its two tatami suites with bamboo rugs, floor seating, and shoji screens at the window. Otherwise, rooms are motelish modern, and some could use redecorating. But rates are moderate and the hotel does offer a different mood, with a Japanese tearoom and a serene restaurant with an indoor Oriental garden.

66 Park Avenue (at 38th Street), New York, NY 10016. Tel: 685-0022.

All-Suite Hotels

With double the space of a hotel room plus cooking facilities, each of these is a good value in its price category.

The Lowell, one of the city's smallest and most unusual lodgings, offers just 61 luxurious suites with fireplaces, libraries, full kitchens, marble baths, and a sophisticated mix of French, Art Deco, and Oriental decor. Breakfast, lunch, and tea are served in the lacy Pembroke Room, which seats just 35 and might have been lifted from a fine European hotel. The staff here outnumbers the guests, who range from California movie moguls to knowing Europeans who want both luxury and seclusion.

28 East 63rd Street (between Madison and Park avenues), New York, NY 10021. Tel: 838-1400.

The Kimberly was built as a condominium, but when the apartments didn't sell management turned it into an all-suite hotel with all the comforts of home, including a terrace with most one-bedroom apartments. The furnishings have an impersonal feel, but there's plenty of space, even in the studio suites, and 24-hour concierge service in the very tasteful lobby.

145 East 50th Street (between Lexington and Third avenues), New York, NY 10022. Tel: 755-0400.

There's no sign outside to tell you that the **Lombardy** is not just another posh New York apartment building. In fact, the studios and apartments are privately owned and are rented out hotel-style by absent owners. This means that furnishings vary according to owners' tastes, but all units are spacious, and the rates are good for the neighborhood. Guests can also enjoy full hotel service—

including room service from the excellent **Laurent** restaurant off the lobby.

111 East 56th Street (between Lexington and Park avenues), New York, NY 10022. Tel: 753-8600.

The **Beekman Tower** belongs to the Manhattan East Suite Hotels group, which has nine properties in the city, most offering roomy accommodations for less than the price of a luxury hotel room. This one has a convenient location, top views, and a lovely Old World lobby with a handsome Persian rug and brass chandelier. The furnishings are traditional and the service is caring. **La Petite Marmite** restaurant offers fine French fare, and the **Top of the Tower** cocktail lounge on the 26th floor is dazzling at night, with superb views of the East River and the Midtown Manhattan office towers.

Three Mitchell Place (off First Avenue at 49th Street), New York, NY 10017. Tel: 355-7300.

The Shelburne—Murray Hill is perhaps the most attractive of the Manhattan East Suite Hotels, with Persian rugs, chandeliers, and antiques in the lobby, and room furnishings a shade above some of the other properties. Once again, the space and facilities are exceptional for the price. Lunch and dinner are served downstairs in a restaurant that doubles as a piano bar.

303 Lexington Avenue (at East 37th Street), New York, NY 10016. Tel: 689-5200.

Other Manhattan East properties include:

▶ **The Surrey** (the priciest of the group), 20 East 76th Street, New York, NY 10021. Tel: 288-3700.

▶ **Dumont Plaza**, 150 East 34th Street, New York, NY 10016. Tel: 481-7600.

▶ **Eastgate Tower**, 222 East 39th Street, New York, NY 10016. Tel: 687-8000.

▶ **Lyden Gardens**, 215 East 64th Street, New York, NY 10021. Tel: 355-1230.

▶ **Lyden House**, 20 East 53rd Street, New York, NY 10011. Tel: 888-6070.

▶ **Plaza Fifty**, 155 East 50th Street, New York, NY 10022. Tel: 751-5710.

▶ **Southgate Tower**, 371 Seventh Avenue (at 31st Street), New York, NY 10001. Tel: 563-1800.

Convention Hotels

New York's largest properties (800 to 1,800 rooms) are first-class hotels and, while busy, can provide any needed amenity. The Vista's location near Wall Street may appeal to some travellers. Most rates are in the luxury category.

▶ **Grand Hyatt**, Park Avenue at Grand Central Terminal (42nd Street), New York, NY 10017. Tel: 883-1234.

▶ **Marriott Marquis**, 1535 Broadway (at 45th Street), New York, NY 10036. Tel: 398-1900.

▶ **New York Hilton**, 1335 Sixth Avenue (at 53rd Street), New York, NY 10019. Tel: 586-7000.

▶ **Penta**, 401 Seventh Avenue (at 33rd Street), New York, NY 10001. Tel: 736-5000.

▶ **Sheraton Centre**, 811 Seventh Avenue (at 53rd Street), New York, NY 10019. Tel: 581-1000.

▶ **Vista International**, 3 World Trade Center, New York, NY 10048. Tel: 938-9100.

Budget-priced Hotels

The **Empire**, right across the street from Lincoln Center, is one of the better budget choices in the city, offering no frills but big, freshly redecorated, attractively furnished rooms that are a sound value. **O'Neal's Baloon** on the corner facing Lincoln Center is a favorite New York sidewalk café before and after the concert.

44 West 63rd Street (at Broadway), New York, NY 10023. Tel: 265-7400.

The **Salisbury**, located near Carnegie Hall, offers a good central location, a quiet and pleasant lobby, spacious if undistinguished rooms, and the convenient, affordable Terrace Café. Most rooms also include serving pantries, making this a good bet for families.

123 West 57th Street (between Sixth and Seventh avenues), New York, NY 10019. Tel: 246-1300.

The **Gorham**, a small, quiet hotel opposite the City Center performance hall, is another good value and will be an even better one when a planned renovation— giving the hotel a modern Italian look—is complete. All rooms and suites offer kitchenettes and ample room for families. People hear about the Gorham mostly through word of mouth, and at the moment the grapevine is bringing a number of South American guests.

136 West 55th Street (between Sixth and Seventh avenues), New York, NY 10019. Tel: 245-1800.

The façade of the **Chelsea**, a historic landmark and literary shrine, bears plaques in memory of the likes of Dylan Thomas, Thomas Wolfe, O. Henry, Arthur Miller, Brendan Behan, Mark Twain, and other assorted geniuses who lived and worked here. More recently the residents have included Virgil Thomson, Sid Vicious, and artists who hope someone will know their names someday, which may tell something about the condition of the place. Rooms are big, cheap, and reasonably clean; many have kitchens, but they are *desperately* in need of refurbishing. The lobby is filled with art both Op and odd, and an equally diverse assortment of arty people. The neighborhood is similarly funky—but similarly interesting.

222 West 23rd Street (between Seventh and Eighth avenues), New York, NY 10011. Tel: 243-3700.

A recent arrival on the budget-hotel scene is Indian restaurateur Sant Chatwal, owner of New York's Bombay Palace. He seems determined to remedy the shortage of reasonably priced hotel rooms single-handedly. So far he has gathered seven hotels, all older properties now in various stages of renovation, under the **Chatwal Inns** umbrella. Many are buildings of architectural interest. While some rooms are small and furnishings simple, everything is fresh, bathrooms are new, and the values are excellent, particularly the junior suites, which are ideal for families. The smaller Chatwal Inns on 47th and 45th streets provide serve-yourself Continental breakfast. For reservations at all the Chatwal hotels, Tel: (800) 826-4667. Recommended addresses include:

▶ **The Woodward Chatwal Inn**, 210 West 55th Street at Broadway, New York, NY 10019. Tel: 247-2000.

▶ **The Chatwal Hotel**, 234 West 48th Street, New York, NY 10036. Tel: 246-8800.

▶ **Chatwal Inn on 47th Street**. 157 West 47th Street, New York, NY 10036. Tel: 768-3700.

▶ **Chatwal Inn on 45th Street**. 132 West 45th Street, New York, NY 10036. Tel: 921-7600.

More good news for budget-watchers is the reincarnation of the old Seville Hotel in Murray Hill as the **Carlton**. Behind the Beaux Arts façade everything has been spruced up, including lobby, room decor, and bathroom fixtures. While not lavish, the hotel is cheerful and attractive, and with such amenities as a concierge, room service, and valet service, it is a good buy in its category.

22 East 29th Street at Madison Avenue, New York, NY 10016. Tel: 532-4100.

The **Comfort Inn Murray Hill** offers a pleasant modern lobby, comfortable motel-style rooms, and complimentary coffee and Danish pastries in the morning. The address is actually too far west to really be part of posh

Murray Hill but it does offer some bonuses. Macy's and other Herald Square stores are steps away, and the Jacob K. Javits Convention Center is within walking distance.

42 West 35th Street (between Fifth and Sixth avenues), New York, NY 10001. Tel: 947-0200.

The turn-of-the-century **Wales Hotel** is the closest thing to a small European hotel in New York. The old marble staircase, fine woodwork, and the fireplaces have survived a $5-million renovation, but bathrooms and furnishings are new. The residential Carnegie Hill neighborhood, though inconvenient for Midtown, is quiet. Excellent shopping and Fifth Avenue museums are within walking distance. The hotel intends to add its own bistro café, but meanwhile, **Sarabeth's Kitchen**, a neighborhood favorite, is right next door.

1295 Madison Avenue at 92nd Street, New York, NY 10128. Tel: 876-6000.

New York Bed and Breakfast

The most encouraging development for travellers within limited budgets is the blooming of bed-and-breakfast lodgings in city apartments, many in some of New York's best neighborhoods, where resident hosts have decided to make use of extra space to help with the heady rent bills. Some of these rooms are short on privacy, but all are strong on friendliness. Rates are $50 to $90 nightly for a double, including breakfast, and are frequently less for longer stays. The following registries have a number of listings around the city:

▶ **Aaah! Bed & Breakfast #1, Ltd.** P.O. Box 200, New York, NY 10108. Tel: 246-4000; (800) 776-4001.

▶ **Bed & Breakfast (& Books).** (Specializes in hosts in the arts.) 35 West 92nd Street (Attn: Judith Goldberg), Apt. 2C, New York, NY 10025. Tel: 865-8740.

▶ **City Lights Bed & Breakfast Ltd.** P.O. Box 20355, Cherokee Station, New York, NY 10028. Tel: 737-7049.

▶ **Hosts & Guests, Inc.** P.O. Box 6798, FDR Station, New York, NY 10150. Tel: 874-4308.

▶ **New World Bed and Breakfast Ltd.** 150 Fifth Avenue, Suite 711, New York, NY 10011. Tel: 675-5600.

▶ **Urban Ventures, Inc.** P.O. Box 426, Planetarium Station, New York, NY 10024. Tel: 594-5650.

—Eleanor Berman

NEIGHBOR-HOODS

LOWER MANHATTAN AND THE HARBOR

By Dwight V. Gast

Dwight V. Gast has written about the city for numerous publications. He has studied New York as an undergraduate and graduate student at the city's New School for Social Research and has been observing it as a Manhattan flaneur for over two decades. He lives in lower Manhattan.

LOWER MANHATTAN

The southern end of Manhattan is where the city began, expanded, and its economic power is still concentrated. It is one of the few places in New York where you can get a feeling for the city as a port: The expansive Upper New York Bay and the bustling South Street Seaport, with their modern and historical oceangoing vessels, are both located there. So is the outgrowth of their commercial activity: the economic center of the capitalist world, known as the Financial District and exemplified by the surprisingly narrow thoroughfare called Wall Street. To keep it all running smoothly—or merely running—the city has also placed its administrative buildings near at hand: Civic Center stretches from City Hall to Chinatown.

People ebb and flow in Lower Manhattan along with its waterfront tides. If you like crowds, you'll find good company all day long. On weekends, most of the activity

takes place at the South Street Seaport and Battery Park, adding a sense of discovery to a walk in the Financial District and Civic Center; at night the entire area is always fairly deserted except for the seaport.

MAJOR INTEREST

The Statue of Liberty
Harbor views from Battery Park
The Staten Island Ferry
The Financial District
200-mile panorama from the top of the World
    Trade Center
The World Financial Center
South Street Seaport
Civic Center
City Hall
The Brooklyn Bridge

The Battery

"The Bronx is up and the Battery's down," is how New York's geography was succinctly described in the Comden-Green-Bernstein musical, *On the Town*. At the tip of downtown Manhattan, the Battery is as far down as you can go. It takes its name from the battery of cannon that protected Manhattan at what was once the island's tip, coinciding with the current Battery Place. They were aimed directly at the area now occupied by Battery Park, which has been built up over the centuries with landfill. A tide of white-collar workers from the nearby Financial District now brings their lunch to the park on weekdays, and hordes of tourists from more distant parts traipse through it on their way to the Statue of Liberty during the warmer months. In lieu of cannon, the best defense against the crowds in Battery Park is to arrive outside the lunch hour on a weekday. New York and foreign accents are then replaced by the cries of seagulls, the sounds of ships' horns at sea and ships' bells in the clock tower at the park's Pier A, and the lapping of waves at the ramparts. The smell of salt air stirred by bracing sea breezes and the panorama of Upper New York Bay can make Battery Park especially refreshing—and appetite-stimulating, but be forewarned that there are few amenable eating and drinking establishments in the area.

New York Harbor

```
0        miles        1
0      kilometers    1.6
```

Jersey City

N E W   J E R S E Y

NEW JERSEY TPK. EXTENSION

Newark Bay

Bayonne

Kill Van Kull

Staten

RICHMOND TERR.

Silver Lake
Park

Clove Lakes
Park

VICTORY BLVD.

STATEN ISLAND

STATEN ISLAND EXPWY.

BAY ST.

Ft. Wadsworth

Holland Tunnel

Hoboken

Hudson River

WEST ST.

BROADWAY

CANAL ST.

BOWERY

DELANCEY ST.

F D R DRIVE

East River

MANHATTAN

Williamsburg Bridge

PARK ROW

World Trade Center

South Street Seaport

PEARL ST.

SOUTH ST.

Liberty State Park

Ellis Island

Battery Park

Ferry

Manhattan Bridge

Brooklyn Bridge

Brooklyn Heights

BROOKLYN–QUEENS EXPWY.

Liberty Island

Ferry

Brooklyn–Battery Tunnel

Statue of Liberty

Governors Island

Ferry

FLATBUSH AVE.

Island

Upper New York Bay

RED HOOK

Gowanus Canal

Prospect Park

PROSPECT EXPWY.

BROOKLYN–QUEENS EXPWY.

FT. HAMILTON PKWY.

OCEAN PKWY.

BAY RIDGE

BROOKLYN

SHORE PKWY.

The Narrows

N

Dyker Beach Park

Verrazano–Narrows Bridge

Ft. Hamilton

Lower New York Bay

At the park's entrance on Battery Place, the Netherlands Memorial Monument briefly recounts the history of the settlement of Manhattan, in English and Dutch. A long mall then leads to **Castle Clinton National Monument**. Besides being further evidence of the defense of Manhattan (it was begun in 1807 as West Battery to provide protection against the British), the circular sandstone fort is best seen as a monument to New York entrepreneurship. In 1824 it reopened as Castle Garden, where in 1850 P. T. Barnum made a fortune staging a concert by Jenny Lind, a singer who he promoted as "the Swedish Nightingale." He drummed up even more publicity (and ticket sales) by planting anonymous letters in the papers claiming she was vastly overrated, selling out the house of 6,000 at the then-exorbitant fee of three dollars for the cheapest seat. The facilities were subsequently used as the Immigrant Landing Depot (1855–1890) and remodeled by the architectural firm of McKim, Mead & White as the New York Aquarium (1896–1941). Restored to its original incarnation as a fort, Castle Clinton hasn't forgotten its penchant for box office: It now sells tickets to the Statue of Liberty out on Liberty Island.

The Statue of Liberty

Just beyond Castle Clinton, facing the Statue of Liberty, is a plaque commemorating Emma Lazarus, author of the poem "The New Colossus" that is engraved on the base of the statue across the water. "Give me your tired, your poor . . ." it reads, "I lift my lamp beside the golden door!" The lamp itself is now newly golden, owing to an elaborate restoration of the statue and its support structure undertaken to celebrate its centennial in 1986.

Since its inception, *Liberty Enlightening the World* (as French sculptor Frédéric Auguste Bartholdi entitled his statue) has been considered more a symbol than a sculpture. The French, who paid for the statue, supported it partially as an implicit criticism of the French government. (Literally, it is supported by an iron skeleton designed by Alexandre Gustave Eiffel.) The Americans, who paid for its pedestal (designed by architect Richard Morris Hunt), have used it over the past century to invoke concepts of liberty ranging from idealistic to mawkish. Writers, artists, and filmmakers have even made use of its powerful symbolism in various ways: Franz Kafka (who had never been in the United States) describes the classic immigrant's first view of it in the opening paragraph of *Amerika*, Alfred Hitchcock uses it for the climactic scene in *Saboteur*—it also provides the dramatic close to the film *Planet of the Apes*—and sculptor Claes Oldenburg once proposed replacing it with a monumental electric fan.

The Statue of Liberty's force as a symbol is matched by the sheer magnitude of its physical presence. The Lady in the Harbor stands 151 feet tall and has a 3-foot mouth and a 35-foot waist; her pedestal lifts her up another 89 feet. The statistics take on real meaning as the ferry leaves the Battery for Liberty Island, Manhattan receding magnificently in the distance and the massive statue looming larger. Once on the island, you can visit its **American Museum of Immigration** to learn more about the huddled masses, many of whom seem to be in line for the elevator that takes visitors to an observation deck on the base of the statue after an often considerable wait in summer and on weekends. For the fit, the additional 162 steps that lead to the crown are worth the effort for views of Manhattan and the harbor.

Ellis Island, the primary point of entry for immigrants to the United States from 1892 to 1925, has long been closed to the public, but its main building is being converted to the **Ellis Island Immigration Museum**, scheduled to open in mid-1990. The new museum promises to tell the true story of the American immigrant, in the place where it all happened.

Back in Manhattan

East of the Statue of Liberty ferry landing in Battery Park, **Admiral George Dewey Promenade** offers a spectacular view of the city and the harbor. Facing out toward the bay you can see Brooklyn Heights to the left, Governors Island (the former Nut Island, the first island inhabited by the Dutch, and now occupied by the United States Coast Guard, which opens its surprising small-town-America community to the public each May during Armed Forces Weekend), the working-class borough of Staten Island, Liberty Island, and Ellis Island. Inside Battery Park are two noteworthy monuments. Just inside from the Statue of Liberty ferry landing is the monument to Giovanni da Verrazano by Ettore Ximenes. Farther south is the East Coast War Memorial, in which a giant bronze American eagle by Albino Manca is surrounded by eight granite slabs rising sharply like the lower Manhattan skyline behind them.

The **Staten Island Ferry** leaves from a terminal near the end of the Battery. Primarily used by commuters from Staten Island, at 25¢ for a round-trip fare the ferry also provides a one-and-a-half-hour pauper's boat tour of Upper New York Bay, passing near Governors Island and Liberty Island and offering spectacular views of lower Manhattan and its bridges. An especially giddy tourist was Edna St. Vincent Millay, who wrote about one such trip in her poem "Recuerdo":

> We were very tired, we were very merry,
> We had gone back and forth all night on the ferry.
> We hailed "Good morrow, mother!" to a shawl-
>   covered head,
> And bought a morning paper, which neither of us
>   read;
> And she wept, "God bless you!" for the apples and
>   pears,
> And we gave her all our money but our subway
>   fares.

Outside of Battery Park are two religious memorials. In minuscule Peter Minuit Plaza is a flagpole commemorating the first group of Jews to arrive in this country, a Spanish and Portuguese contingent that came from Brazil in 1654 and founded Shearith Israel Congregation, the oldest in the United States. Farther uptown, at 7 State Street, is the **Shrine of Saint Mother Elizabeth Ann Seton** (1774–1821), the first American-born saint, who converted from Episcopalianism to Catholicism and founded the first order of nuns and Catholic parochial schools in the United States. The shrine occupies the former James Watson House, the last of many such Federal mansions that once lined State Street. A third religious structure, the beloved Seamen's Church Institute, once stood on a site just to the north (the site was also the birthplace of Herman Melville) and was demolished in 1986 to make way for the glass-and-aluminum skyscraper at 17 State Street. The loss of Seamen's Church caught many by surprise, since preservationists had been especially watchful in New York after the demolition of Pennsylvania Station in 1963, an act of brutality that brought about the formation of the New York City Landmarks Preservation Commission. But as Henry James wrote in *The American Scene:* "If it had been the final function of the Bay to make one feel one's age, so, assuredly, the mouth of Wall Street so proclaimed it, for one's private ear, distinctly enough; the breath of existence being taken, wherever one turned, as that of youth on the run and with the prize of the race in sight, and the new landmarks crushing the old quite as violent children stamp on snails and caterpillars."

Farther north on State Street is the former **United States Custom House**, built in 1907 to the designs of Cass Gilbert. (Customs operations have since been moved to the World Trade Center.) The customhouse is one of the city's finest examples of the ornate Beaux Arts style American architects learned from the Académie des Beaux-Arts in Paris. The entrance sculptures, *The Four Continents* by Daniel Chester French, represent telling turn-of-the-century American attitudes. *Asia* and *Africa* sit at the most removed extremes (*Africa* is actually asleep), *Europe* is surrounded by icons of education, and *America* looks progressively forward with her own torch of liberty and enlightenment, accompanied by Labor turning the wheel of progress. On the cornice are 12 statues representing commercial powers from history, past and present (*Germany* was renamed *Belgium* during World War I). A more recent vision of commerce is provided by the Reginald Marsh murals of nautical themes in the oval rotunda indoors on the second floor.

Across from the customhouse is **Bowling Green**, the city's first park. Originally part of the Dutch cattle market, it became a green for the sport of bowling and later contained a statue of King George III, which was melted down for bullets after the Declaration of Independence was read publicly on July 9, 1776. The exuberant patriots also tore off the crowns that once topped the iron fence erected around the park in 1771, but the rest remains and was recently restored to its pre-Revolutionary glory. While there, have a look at the Bowling Green subway station. Clean, spacious, and bright with glazed orange tile, it is the most pleasant station you'll see in New York's heavily criticized system.

Two nearby buildings recall the area's former importance as the center of the city's shipping industry. The immense Renaissance-style structure at 25 Broadway was designed by Benjamin Wistar Morris and built in 1921 for the Cunard line. Its lavish lobby is now occupied by the United States Postal Service, which has preserved the ornate interior with its intricate (if badly illuminated) ceilings and frescoes. (Number 26 Broadway across the street, the former headquarters of the Standard Oil Company, has another fine lobby.) At 1 Broadway is the United States Lines–Panama Pacific Lines Building. It recalls more than shipping because it occupies a site that was once the tip of Manhattan, where the original Dutch Fort Amsterdam, the headquarters of George Washington and, later, Richard Howe, once stood.

THE FINANCIAL DISTRICT

Some of the most expensive land in the world lies in this area of lower Manhattan, and only a privileged few can afford to occupy it. In fact, except for the residents of Battery Park City (and their permanent counterparts in Trinity Church cemetery), the Financial District, like London's City, is hardly residential at all. The vast majority of its population consists of dayworkers for large corporations. In his 1853 short story, "Bartleby, the Scrivener," Herman Melville described a Wall Street "which of weekdays hums with industry and life, at nightfall echoes with sheer vacancy, and all through Sunday is forlorn." That aspect of the area has not changed.

What *has* changed are the buildings owned by the banking and other institutions that give the Financial District its name. Many corporations have built their headquarters in the area—the World Financial Center being the latest example—and the corporate emphasis on edifying edifices makes architecture one of the great pleasures of a visit to the area. But don't worry about neck strain: Down-to-earth attractions such as some of the finest outdoor public sculpture this side of Chicago and the salt air of the South Street Seaport will keep you pleasantly level-headed.

The World Trade Center

Dominating the Financial District (and most of the New York metropolitan area, for that matter) are Minoru Yamasaki's twin towers of the World Trade Center, two 110-story buildings rising like the prongs of a colossally unaligned tuning fork from the depths of Manhattan. The scale and monotony of the buildings are, in fact, completely out of tune with the romantic skyscrapers that surround it. If record-breaking height was the goal, the buildings lose on that scale as well, since their altitude was soon surpassed by the Sears Tower in Chicago.

Though there are attempts to humanize the seven-building complex (sprawling westward from the base of Church Street) with such works of art as a tapestry by Joan Miró and sculpture by Fritz Koenig, Masayuki Nagare, James Rosati, Louise Nevelson, and Alexander Calder, the scale of the buildings is too overpowering to allow the works to stand on their own. What humanization has occurred at the World Trade Center has taken place outside of the architects' plans, such as the outdoor greenmarket held Tuesdays from June to December and Thursdays year-round. Some of the more spectacular human activities that have occurred there have been appearances by tightrope artist Phillip Petit, who gave new meaning to the term "high wire" when he walked on one stretched between the towers, and mountain climber George Willig, who scaled the towers. There was even a spectacular animal feat at the Trade Center when King Kong, in the 1976 film, also climbed to the top.

The more conventional means of ascent are the high-speed elevators, which whisk visitors to the observation decks on the 107th and 110th floors of the south tower (number 2) and the bars and restaurants of the north tower (number 1). **Windows on the World** is a popular brunch spot among New Yorkers hosting out-of-town guests (with a waiting list as long as the building is high, so reserve well in advance; Tel: 212-938-1111), but the **City Lights Bar** will give you much of the same 100-mile view, in this case over Brooklyn and Long Island.

If you are interested in the theater, note the **TKTS booth** on the mezzanine level of 2 World Trade Center (south tower) before leaving. It sells half-price tickets for shows on the day of performance, and there is usually a shorter line than at its counterpart in Times Square.

A recent aesthetic and commercial challenge to the World Trade Center has been the **World Financial Center** in the heart of Battery Park City, a modern residential complex. It lies just east of the World Trade Center but is miles ahead of it in its humanness, including public sculpture worth a visit even for nonresidents. One good example is Ned Smyth's *The Upper Room,* a playful outdoor environment made of concrete embedded with glass, stone, and mosaic.

The World Financial Center was designed by Cesar Pelli and Associates and consists of four 34- to 51-story

MURRAY ST.

GREENWICH ST.

WEST BROADWAY

PARK PL.

BROADWAY

WEST ST.

Woolworth Bldg.

BARCLAY ST.

VESEY ST.

6 W.T.C.

St. Paul's Chapel

to Tribeca

5 W.T.C.

CHURCH ST.

FULTON ST.

North Tower
1 W.T.C.

DEY ST.

WEST ST.

World Trade Center

World Financial Center

CORTLANDT ST.

3 W.T.C.

South Tower
2 W.T.C.

4 W.T.C.

LIBERTY ST.

LIBERTY

CEDAR ST.

CEDAR ST.

THAMES

ST.

PINE ST.

BATTERY

ALBANY ST.

WASHINGTON ST.

TRINITY PL.

Trinity Church

PARK

CARLISLE ST.

GREENWICH ST.

WEST ST.

SOUTH END AVE.

CITY

RECTOR ST.

New York Stock Exchange

WEST THAMES ST.

EXCHANGE PL.

BROADWAY

NEW ST.

BATTERY PL.

BROOKLYN–BATTERY TUNNEL

WEST ST.

MORRIS ST.

BEAVER ST.

WHITEHALL

Bowling Green

STONE ST.

Hudson River

BATTERY PL.

BATTERY PL.

U.S. Custom House

STATE ST.

BRIDGE ST.

PEARL ST.

N

Castle Clinton

Battery Park

PROMENADE

Ferry to Ellis Island

Ferry to Statue of Liberty

City Hall

PARK ROW

AVE. OF THE FINEST

ST. JAMES PL.

ROBERT WAGNER SR. PL.

BROOKLYN BRIDGE

SPRUCE ST.

BEEKMAN ST.

DOVER ST.

ANN ST.

PEARL ST.

PECK

NASSAU ST.

BEEKMAN ST.

WATER ST.

SLIP

GOLD ST.

FULTON ST.

FRONT ST.

SOUTH ST.

JOHN ST.

CLIFF ST.

South Street Seaport

MAIDEN LA.

PLATT ST.

WATER ST.

Fulton Fish Market

ST.

WILLIAM ST.

CEDAR ST.

PEARL ST.

JOHN ST.

Pier 17

FLETCHER ST.

Federal Hall National Monument

MAIDEN LA.

WALL STREET

PINE ST.

FDR DRIVE

WILLIAM ST.

FRONT ST.

GOUVERNEUR PL.

SOUTH ST.

PEARL ST.

OLD SLIP

(ELEVATED HIGHWAY)

BROAD ST.

Fraunces Tavern

East River

WATER ST.

Downtown Heliport

PETER MINUIT PLAZA

Staten Island Ferry

Wall Street Area

0   yards   200

0   meters   200

towers clad in granite and reflective glass and topped with geometrically shaped copper roofs, visible along the entire length of Sixth Avenue. It comprises some of the most exciting new public spaces to open in New York in years. Outdoors is the city's first plaza on the Hudson River, and indoors is the Courtyard—a glass-covered European-style plaza—as well as the Winter Garden, a 120-foot-high vaulted glass- and-steel structure graced by palm trees, where free concerts are often held during the lunch hour and after work; Tel: (212) 945-0505 for information. Dozens of shops, restaurants, and cafés cater to those who work at the center, world headquarters for such firms as American Express, Merrill Lynch, and Dow Jones. As modern as the facilities are, a stroll through this *dernier cri* in New York's public spaces somehow recalls the promenades depicted in Currier & Ives prints of old New York, in a much more genuine way than in the city's more obvious tourist attractions.

Lower Broadway

Vesey Street leads east out of the World Financial Center's northern edge. After one block you'll encounter 140 West Street, the entrance to the New York Telephone Building, a 1926 skyscraper by Voorhees, Gmelin & Walker, complete with Art Deco detailing on the façade and in the lobby. Its Vesey Street side has a sheltered arcade. At 20 Vesey Street is the former New York Post Building, a soaring Art Nouveau structure topped with statues by John Gutzon Borglum, the sculptor of Mount Rushmore. Take Church Street to Cortlandt Street, which crosses Broadway to become Maiden Lane, named for the young girls who did the family washing in a brook that once flowed along the site. On the northeast corner of Broadway and Maiden Lane you can check the hour at an unusual glass-covered clock set in the sidewalk. At 33 Maiden Lane is the entrance to Federal Plaza, where on the lower level is the newly reopened downtown branch of the **Whitney Museum of American Art**. It houses space for temporary exhibitions put together by the museum's younger curators, so the shows vary from just-on-the-edge avant-garde to just-out-of-the-classroom academic.

Maiden Lane leads to William Street, where in a small park called **Louise Nevelson Plaza** there are seven black constructions by the sculptor, who until her death in 1988 had a home and studio in downtown Manhattan and was an active figure in the city's cultural life. Around the corner, at 33 Liberty Street, is the **Federal Reserve Bank of New York**, a rusticated stone building inspired by various Florentine Renaissance palazzi. The building stores one-quarter of the official monetary gold of 80 countries—more than Fort Knox. These billions of dollars of gold bars are available for public viewing during free one-hour tours (Tel: 212-720-6130 at least one week in advance; tickets will be mailed to you). Nearby is another fanciful edifice, the Beaux Arts New York Chamber of Commerce Building at 65 Liberty Street.

Returning to Broadway, you'll pass through Chase Manhattan Plaza, the first in a series of open spaces that eventually leads to the World Trade Center. Decorated with a sunken garden by Isamu Noguchi and the *Group of Four Trees* sculpture by Jean Dubuffet, the plaza is dominated by the glass-and-aluminum Chase Manhattan Bank building by the architectural firm of Skidmore, Owings & Merrill. The same team was responsible for the Marine Midland Bank, just ahead of it at 140 Broadway, which has a dark matte-black-steel-and-glass façade that plays nicely off the ornamentation of the nearby buildings reflected in it. The spacious plaza in front of the building, with its huge sculpture *The Red Cube* by Isamu Noguchi, is the most welcoming of the series of spaces. It is certainly more inviting than 1 Liberty Plaza across Broadway, another Skidmore, Owings & Merrill creation, this one a cynical concession to the newest zoning law, which requires public open space in exchange for more floor space. Even J. Seward Johnson, Jr.'s sculpture *Double Check,* a banker immortalized in bronze in the plaza, seems oblivious to his surroundings.

The Equitable Building at 120 Broadway was what brought such zoning laws into existence. Its massive bulk caused such a commotion when it was built in 1915 that the following year the nation's first law was passed requiring that buildings be stepped back at certain levels in order to admit light to the street, thus forming the "zoning envelope," or legal limit to building proportions, that has since shaped so many of the city's skyscrapers. Farther downtown, at 100 Broadway, is the Bank of Tokyo, an 1895 Beaux Arts building restored and adapted for use as a modern bank in 1975. The contrast of old and new extends to the building's art: outdoors are Greek-inspired statues above Ionic columns, indoors an aluminum sculpture by Noguchi.

Farther down Broadway, at the head of Wall Street, is the 1846 **Trinity Church**, the third such Episcopal church on the site. Its Gothic Revival complex with its well-maintained cemetery is an architectural oasis in this part of Manhattan. It has also long been a spiritual oasis. "And in this yard stenogs, bundle boys, scrubwomen, sit on the tombstones, and walk on the grass of graves," wrote Carl Sandburg in his poem "Trinity Peace," "speaking of war and weather, of babies, wages and love." People still go to the churchyard there to visit the graves of Alexander Hamilton and Robert Fulton, as well as to hear the concerts held during the lunch hour. The cast-iron lamppost in front of the church adds another old-fashioned touch to the scene. Dating from 1896, it is one of some 30 such "bishop's crooks" that remain on the city streets.

Wall Street gets its name from the wall Dutch Governor Peter Stuyvesant built on the site in 1653 to protect New Amsterdam from the Indians. Today it is better known as the location of the **New York Stock Exchange**, that bastion of capitalism founded in 1792 when 24 brokers met beneath a buttonwood tree at the corner of Wall and William streets. The entrance to the building is around the corner of Wall, at 8 Broad Street; above its Corinthian columns is a pediment depicting *Integrity Protecting the Works of Man*. For a look at the trading floor, go to the visitors' center through the 20 Broad Street entrance weekdays between 9:20 A.M. and 4:00 P.M.; displays and recorded narration explain the chaotic activity.

Across from the stock exchange on Wall Street is another Greek-inspired building, **Federal Hall National Memorial**, a Doric temple built of Westchester marble. It stands on the site of the first English City Hall, later Federal Hall, where George Washington took his oath of office in 1789 (a bronze statue by John Quincy Adams Ward commemorates the event). The present building dates from 1842 and houses exhibits related to George Washington and other aspects of American history.

Farther down, Broadway leads to two other noteworthy buildings. The Morgan Guaranty Trust Company at 23 Wall was built by financier J. Pierpont Morgan in 1913 as an understated symbol of his wealth. The symbolism was not lost on anarchists, who in 1920 exploded a bomb in front of the bank, killing 33 people and leaving marks in the building that are still visible. At 55 Wall Street is Citibank, a blend of Ionic and Corinthian elements housing an impressively classical interior space.

At its intersection with Pearl Street (the original East River shoreline) you get the definitive view of Wall Street as the canyon of Manhattan, with the steeple of Trinity Church, once the tallest structure in the city, rising at the end. Pearl leads south to Hanover Square, where the Italian palazzo–style India House stands at number 1. Originally built as the Hanover Bank in 1851, it is made of the same brownstone so associated with the later town houses on Manhattan's Upper West Side, and though the square is commercial, the mellow stone and the innocuous monumental statue in the middle of the square make it easy to imagine the area's former days as a residential district. The building also houses **Harry's at Hanover Square**, a meat-and-potatoes restaurant that gets such a serious drinking crowd from Wall Street that it might as well be called "Harry's at Hangover Square."

At 54 Pearl Street is **Fraunces Tavern,** a 1927 reconstruction of a tavern where George Washington bade farewell to his troops. Inside are displays of memorabilia from the Revolution and a restaurant serving food that some claim dates from the same period—but having a drink here is a harmless way of paying homage to history. More recent American history is commemorated nearby at the New York Veterans' Memorial in Vietnam Veterans Plaza (55 Water Street), a translucent wall of glass block engraved with letters from Vietnam soldiers and other writings. It is especially effective at dusk, when interior lights give the memorial an eerie glow. At the 55 Water Street building to the north there is another plaza, accessible by escalator, with fine views across the East River.

South Street Seaport

Water Street passes many interesting sights on its way uptown. At the corner of Old Slip is the Postmodern Engine Company No. 10, and just down Old Slip is the Renaissance palazzo–style First Precinct Police Station. There are more plazas at 77 Water Street and at the I. M. Pei–designed building at 88 Pine Street, where a sculpture by Yu Yu Yang reflects passersby in a mirrored disk. The delightful public space at 127 John Street is full of brightly colored metal tubes and canvas canopies, and in case you miss the point, a lobby plaque announces with characteristic Gotham candor, "This building was designed to create an atmosphere of pleasure, humor and excitement for people." At the corner of Water and

Fulton streets is a small lighthouse that marks the entrance to South Street Seaport.

New York's busiest port district during the 19th century, the area fell into disuse over the intervening years, except for the ever-thriving Fulton Fish Market and a few pleasantly seedy seafood restaurants. Over the past couple of decades the area has been undergoing renovation as a pedestrian mall by the Rouse Company, which was responsible for similar projects at Faneuil Hall in Boston and Harbor Place in Baltimore. The old salt of the area has been substituted with a somewhat salt-free version of New York history, attracting everyone from tourists to beer-guzzling traders from the Financial District, with such attractions as a multimedia show called "The Seaport Experience" and a plethora of bars and restaurants with contrived names. For a more singular seaport experience, avoid the area on Friday evenings and weekends.

Despite the theme-park atmosphere, there is much history to be found amid the histrionics here. The old **Fulton Fish Market** itself, most of which is now located in a new brick building also housing suburban-style shops, supplies the most authentic energy at South Street Seaport—and is a perfect place for insomniacs, since the boisterous transactions are in full swing by 4 A.M. (Tours given later, at 6 A.M., may be reserved by calling 212-669-9400.) **Schermerhorn Row**, which runs from 2 to 18 Fulton Street, is an original group of warehouses dating from 1811 built by Peter Schermerhorn on landfill some 600 feet from the original shoreline; it gives an idea of what much of the area was like until just a few decades ago. Water Street houses the "museum block," where at number 211 there is an operating 18th-century print shop and at 215 the **Seaport Gallery** with nautical exhibits. Historic ships are moored in the East River at Piers 15 and 16, from which harbor cruises on the *Andrew Fletcher* and the *Pioneer* also depart during the warmer months. Pier 17 is topped by a pavilion with magnificent views over the East River. Many of the above sights may be seen on the guided tours leaving from the visitors' center at 207 Water Street.

Present-day attractions at the South Street Seaport include various concert series held throughout the year, its own greenmarket (on Front Street) Wednesdays and Saturdays from June to December, and the well-known comedy club **Caroline's**. For an amusing preview of the Brooklyn Bridge, walk north on Fulton to 41 Peck Slip, where the real thing looms over a painted version of it in a mural by trompe l'oeil artist Richard Haas.

CIVIC CENTER

Fulton Street leads from South Street Seaport a few blocks west to Nassau Street, another pedestrian mall, this time catering to the food and clothing needs of white-collar workers from the Financial District. Fortunately, not all the shops and streets in the area are so lacking in character.

At the north end of Nassau is Park Row, known as Newspaper Row at the turn of the century because of the newspaper offices that once lined the street, a fact commemorated by a statue of printer Benjamin Franklin at the intersection. (Park Row is now lined with discount electronics stores.) The street veers toward the left to **St. Paul's Chapel** of Trinity Parish on the other side of Broadway. Modeled on St. Martin's-in-the-Fields in London, it was designed by Thomas McBean in 1766. George Washington worshiped in the elegant Georgian interior, which contains a starburst (over the high altar) designed by Pierre L'Enfant, who laid out Washington, D.C. St. Paul's is the oldest surviving building in Manhattan—a fact to contemplate while gazing at its steeple rising before the towers of the World Trade Center in the background.

On the northwest corner of Broadway and Barclay Street is everyone's favorite skyscraper, the **Woolworth Building**. Designed with heavy Gothic detailing (it was nicknamed "The Cathedral of Commerce" when it opened) by Cass Gilbert, the building was completed in 1913 and remained the world's tallest until the Chrysler Building went up in 1930. Frank Woolworth of the discount store chain paid for his building entirely in cash, an act depicted along with other amusing scenes in bas-reliefs in the ornate three-story lobby.

Across from the Woolworth Building is **City Hall Park**, the southern end of the few blocks where the city's civic buildings are scattered. Decorated with statues of patriot Nathan Hale and newspaper mogul Horace Greeley, the park's real centerpiece is palatial **City Hall**, a surprisingly small and genteel building for such a large and noisy metropolis. When it was built between 1802 and 1811 it was faced in marble on the south side and cheaper brownstone on the north side, the side then facing away from the city. Though the city is pinching pennies as tightly as ever, in 1959 it loosened up enough to replace the entire façade with limestone and later converted the second-floor Governor's Room into a museum and portrait gallery.

The Brooklyn Bridge

Opposite the east side of City Hall Park is the Manhattan pedestrian entrance to the Brooklyn Bridge. Immortalized in poetry by Walt Whitman and Hart Crane, captured on canvas by Joseph Stella, and gloriously illuminated by the Grucci family's fireworks during its centennial celebration in 1983, the bridge's practical significance was perhaps best described by architecture historian James Marston Fitch: "The nineteenth century saw three great developments in structural theory: the enclosure of great areas in the Crystal Palace, the spanning of great voids in the Brooklyn Bridge, and the reaching of great heights in the Eiffel Tower."

A series of tragedies befell its designers John A. and Washington Roebling. Father John died of gangrene following a crushed foot he incurred while taking measurements for the bridge, and his son Washington developed the bends from taking pressurized caissons underwater to work on the foundations. After the loss of many men, the bridge was completed in 1883. It is composed of two Gothic-style granite towers, from which the world's first steel span is suspended from four huge cables and a vast network of wires. One of the best ways of seeing it is to accept poet Elizabeth Bishop's "Invitation to Miss Marianne Moore":

> From Brooklyn, over the Brooklyn Bridge, on this
>   fine morning,
> please come flying.
> In a cloud of fiery pale chemicals,
> please come flying,
> to the rapid rolling of thousands of small blue
>   drums
> descending out of the mackerel sky
> over the glittering grandstand of harbor-water,
> please come flying.

You can go walking to Brooklyn on the boardwalk that runs down the middle of the bridge, elevated above the traffic. A fine evening at sunset is another nice time to do so.

NORTH OF CITY HALL

On the Chambers Street (that is, north) side of City Hall Park is the old **New York City Courthouse**, a Victorian building now familiarly called Tweed Courthouse after William Marcy "Boss" Tweed, the corrupt New York City official who made off with $10 million of the $14 million budgeted for the construction of the building. You can see present-day politicos in action at lunchtime in two of their favorite restaurants nearby, **Ellen's Café** at 270 Broadway and **Roeblings** at 11 Fulton Street.

Across the street, on the northeast corner of Broadway and Chambers, is the last remnant of the area's past as a center for newspaper publishing—the outdoor clock that marks the building that once housed the offices of the *New York Sun.* (The Italian palazzo–style building, originally built for the A. T. Stewart Department Store, began a trend for Italianate commercial buildings in the city.) There are also two lobbies worth looking into on Chambers Street: Number 51 is the Emigrant Savings Bank Building, with its stately banking facilities on the first floor; number 31 is the Surrogate's Court or Hall of Records, an ornately façaded Beaux Arts building (the sculpture, by Philip Martiny, represents *New York in Its Infancy* and *New York in Revolutionary Times*) with a theatrical foyer to match.

Rising across Centre Street, which runs north of Chambers, is the **Municipal Building**, another Beaux Arts skyscraper, designed by McKim, Mead & White. Built in 1914 to house city offices, it, too, has become too small for the job, but many of the city's functions remain there—including the Marriage License Bureau. Many a couple can be seen ceremoniously leaving the building beneath its central arch, through which Chambers Street once flowed. In typical Beaux Arts fashion, the building is adorned with statuary. Adolph Alexander Weinman's *Civic Fame,* the tallest statue in the city (25 feet), graces the top of the building.

Through the arch, a pedestrian mall leads to three-acre Police Plaza, Manhattan's largest public space, dominated by an aptly arresting Cor-Ten steel sculpture by Bernard Rosenthal, *Five in One*. The Police Headquarters building is the large red brick structure toward the river. Like many of the nearby modern buildings, it was designed by Gruzen & Partners in the 1970s as part of a redevelopment program for this part of the city. The Neo-Georgian church in the plaza is St. Andrew's, which adds a comforting touch to its large-scale surroundings, as do the food vendors' booths set up during the warmer months.

Cross Foley Square, a low-lying area that was once the site of the Collect Pond, the city's reservoir during its early years. At 60 Lafayette is the Family Court Building, a black granite mass that seems somewhat alien to its function. A steel sculpture by Ray Gussow, *Three Forms,* stands in front of the building. Farther up the street is the side entrance to the Civil and Municipal Court Building, a plain façade enlivened by Joseph Kiselewski's bas-relief, *Justice.* (William Zorach's *Law* bas-relief is at the main entrance at 111 Centre Street.) Across White Street at 87 Lafayette is a fanciful building housing a community center for nearby Chinatown. Though it looks like a French château, it was originally a fire station.

Returning downtown on Centre Street: At number 100 is the notorious, towering Art Deco prison known as **The Tombs**. The name was originally given to an Egyptian-style prison that once stood across Centre Street, though the menacing appearance of the present structure has equally deadly connotations. Architecture critic Paul Goldberger has described its front door as "one of the most brilliantly contrived, if evil, stage sets in the City of New York." Officially called the New York Criminal Courts Building, it hosts courtroom procedures in a system so overloaded that some take place at its special night court, a fascinating and free spectacle—especially if it's not compulsory.

The site of the intersection of Baxter, Park, and Worth streets a block south of The Tombs was the most dangerous slum in the city in the mid-19th century. Known as Five Points, it was the center for such street gangs as the Dead Rabbits, the Shirt Tails, and the Plug Uglies. People in the area lived in the kind of squalor recounted by Jacob Riis in *How the Other Half Lives:* "The family's condition was most deplorable. The man, his wife, and three small children shivering in one room through the roof of which the pitiless winds of winter whistled. The room was almost barren of furniture; the parents slept on the floor, the elder children in boxes, and the baby swung in an old shawl attached to the rafters by cords by way of a hammock. The father, a seaman, had been obliged to give up that calling because he was in consumption, and was unable to provide either bread or fire for his little ones."

Riis's documentation changed public attitudes toward social injustice, and the construction of the Foley Square courthouse complex beginning in the 1920s transformed the slum dwellers' former domain into a display of the justice system. Its strongest architectural statements are the templelike New York County Courthouse designed by Guy Lowell and the United States Courthouse by Cass Gilbert and his son, Cass, Jr. Both court buildings are replete with allegorical sculpture to the point that you begin to feel overwhelmed by the spirit of Justice. Lest you get carried away, venture into the New York County Courthouse and take a look at the fantastic zodiac depicted in its rotunda pavement.

Right behind The Tombs lies the southwest corner of Chinatown. But before venturing into Manhattan's corner of the Orient, we go west into TriBeCa.

CHINATOWN TO THE VILLAGES

By Dwight V. Gast

The generous section of Manhattan extending south of 14th Street roughly to City Hall is generally referred to as downtown. Its residents are fiercely proud of the entire area, often claiming to suffer nosebleeds if they venture above 14th Street. To be able to say "I live downtown" implies, at least to them, a character and creativity they find lacking in other parts of the city.

They have much to be proud of. Downtown Manhattan has the history, ethnic variety, and free spirit that for many is the essence of life in New York City. Those qualities, combined for the most part with a human-scale architecture missing elsewhere in Manhattan, make the extensive area a particularly pleasant place for the outsider as well. From its shops and art galleries by day to its restaurants and clubs by night, downtown Manhattan is perhaps the most exciting part of New York City.

ELEVENTH AVE.

Madison
Square
Garden

Penn
Station

MADISON AVE.

PARK AVE.

Madison
Square
Park

W. 23 ST.

TENTH AVE.

NINTH AVE.

EIGHTH AVE.

SEVENTH AVE.

SIXTH AVE. (AVENUE OF THE AMERICAS)

FIFTH AVE.

BROADWAY

CHELSEA

Union
Sq.

W. 14 ST.

GREENWICH AVE.

GREENWICH ST.

HUDSON ST.

W. 4 ST.

GREENWICH ST.

W. 8 ST.

UNIVERSITY PL.

WEST ST.

WEST VILLAGE

Washington
Square
Park

WAVERLY PL.

Hudson River

CHRISTOPHER

SEVENTH AVE.

BLEECKER

New York
University

W. 4 ST.

BLEECKER ST.

WASHINGTON ST.

W. HOUSTON ST.

WEST BROADWAY

PRINCE ST.

SPRING ST.

SOHO

BROOME ST.

VARICK ST.

CANAL ST.

HOLLAND TUNNEL

GREENWICH ST.

HUDSON ST.

TRIBECA

BROADWAY

N

WEST BROADWAY

Tweed
Courthouse

WEST ST.

CHAMBERS ST.

City Hall

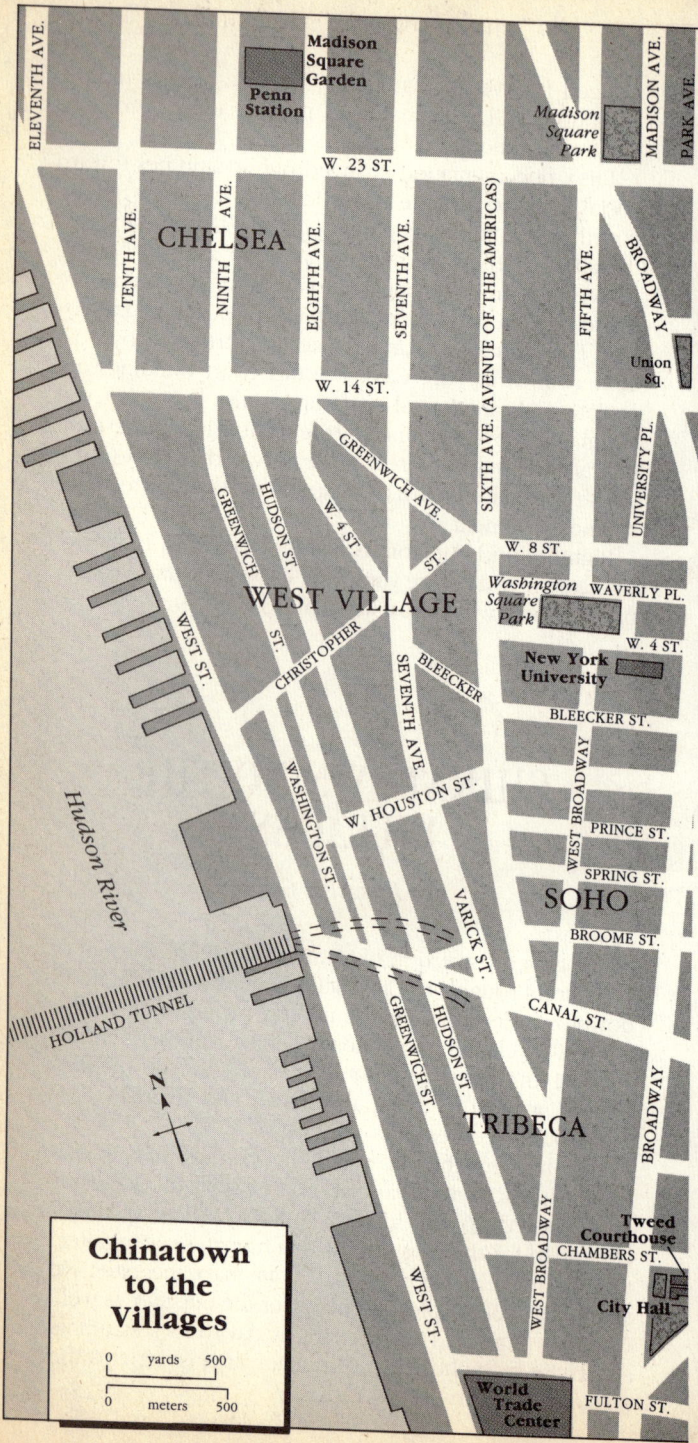

**Chinatown
to the
Villages**

World
Trade
Center

FULTON ST.

0   yards   500

0   meters   500

MAJOR INTEREST

Avant-garde art in TriBeCa
Chinatown
Remnants of immigrant life on the Lower East Side
Little Italy
Contemporary art and cast-iron architecture in
  SoHo
Greenwich Village
Counterculture in the East Village

TRIBECA

Farthest downtown in the downtown area is TriBeCa, one of many portmanteau names so popular with real-estate developers in this part of town. It stands for *Tri*angle *Be*low *Ca*nal, referring to the West Side area roughly defined by three streets: Canal Street, Broadway, and West Street, with Hudson and West Broadway its main thoroughfares. The area's stalwart cast-iron and masonry buildings, many of them dating from the 19th century, were originally used for industrial and commercial purposes, and indeed many still are (therefore they usually have ample loft space). Following the gentrification of the SoHo area to the north, however, artists began to find cheaper space in TriBeCa, which became a sort of appendage to SoHo. Though development has inevitably occurred (the area provides convenient accommodations for Wall Street lawyers and others who consider living in a loft "a lifestyle option" rather than a practical necessity), TriBeCa is still somewhat of a vestigial organ. Its art galleries have never quite reached the blue-chip status attained above Canal, nor have trendy boutiques yet opened in the area—though there are some good bars and restaurants. It is that rough, experimental edge that characterizes the area today; mixed in with honest and often anonymous architecture, it makes TriBeCa one of the most visually rewarding places in Manhattan for the adventurous boulevardier.

One of the oldest of TriBeCa's cultural institutions is at 346 Broadway, the former New York Life Insurance Company. Its clock tower was added at the turn of the century by the architectural firm of McKim, Mead & White, and now houses **The Clocktower**, a gallery of the Institute for Art and Urban Resources, whose art exhibitions are always worth a look (see the Art section). So is the view from its terrace, where giant eagle sculptures stand watch over TriBeCa as its unofficial culture vultures. Looking north, you can also get a glimpse of the stretch of lower Broadway (amusingly dubbed LoBro), which extends as far as the bend at the spire of Grace Church at East 10th Street and is lined with discount clothing and home-furnishings stores.

A block south, at Broadway and Worth Street, is the monolith called the AT & T Long Lines Building, actually a giant piece of electronic equipment clad in pink granite. At 8 Thomas, the next street, there is a Victorian building mixing brick, sandstone, granite, and cast iron as well as a number of architectural styles. Its ground floor houses the **Thomas Street Inn**, one of the area's most established restaurants. If you're interested in more contemporary art, walk two blocks farther south at this point, where at 22 Reade Street is an outdoor mural, *Sens Dessus Dessous,* by French artist François Morellet. Follow Reade across Church Street, another main thoroughfare for serious dis-count shopping, though the mural there by Jerry Johnson, *Oceana by the Sea,* adds a touch of whimsy. Between Reade and Chambers streets on the west side of Church is the **Cary Building**, which dates from 1856, making it one of the oldest cast-iron buildings in existence. The next block west is West Broadway (which continues north across Canal Street to become SoHo's main drag); a block north on West Broadway, Hudson Street leads to Duane Park (the once-trendy TriBeCa restaurant, **The Odeon**, is at 145 West Broadway). The park is a pleasant urban oasis, formerly lined with Federal houses and until recently the center of the Washington Market, New York City's food market, be-fore the area was slated for redevelopment. There are still a few butter and egg wholesalers in the vicinity, and if you're there on a Wednesday or a Saturday during the warmer months you can pay homage to the past by doing some marketing at nearby Independence Plaza, which on those days hosts a greenmarket that adds a spot of life to a somewhat sparse and empty-feeling area. Otherwise there are a number of alternatives for sustenance near Duane Park: Tommy Tang's, a Thai restaurant around the corner at 323 Greenwich Street; Puffy's Tavern at 81 Hudson; and the Sporting Club, at 99 Hudson, where jocks served by wait-resses dressed as cheerleaders watch sports TV on a giant screen.

If you'd rather feast your eyes, there are other architec-

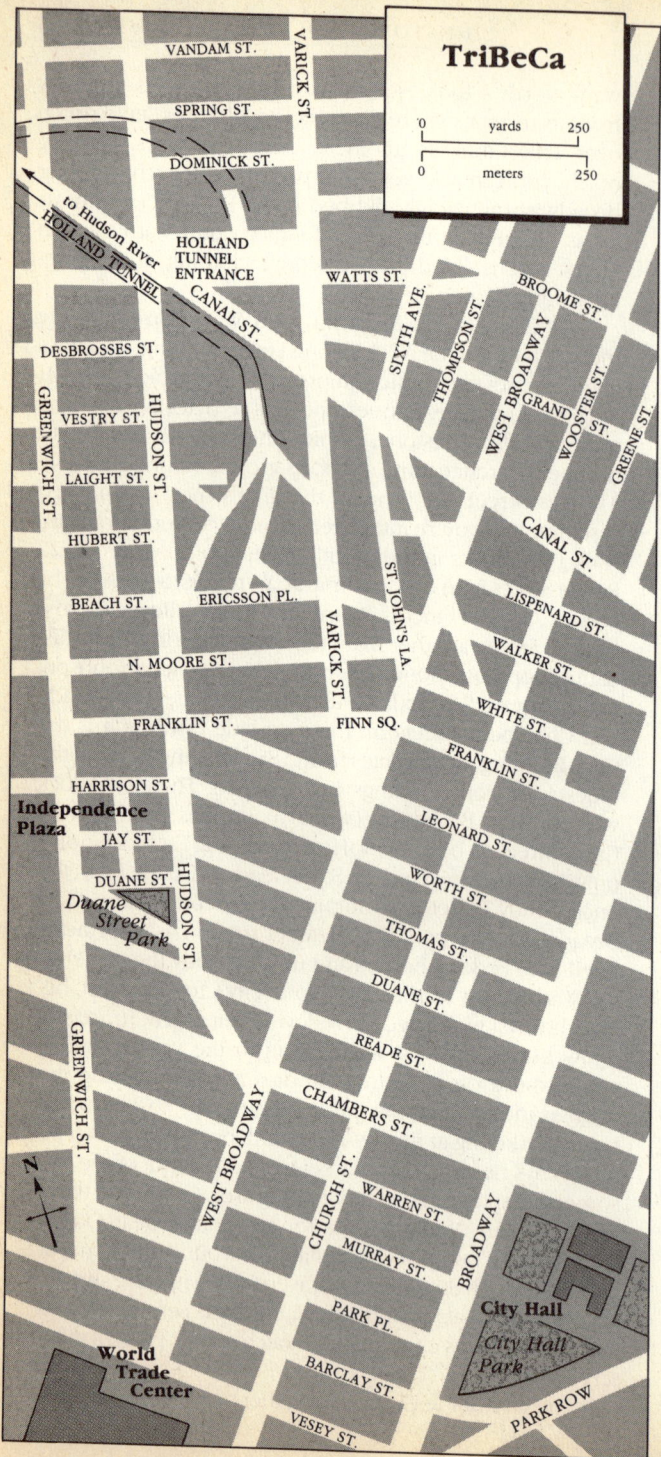

TriBeCa

yards 0 — 250

meters 0 — 250

VANDAM ST.

VARICK ST.

SPRING ST.

DOMINICK ST.

to Hudson River

HOLLAND TUNNEL

HOLLAND TUNNEL ENTRANCE

CANAL ST.

WATTS ST.

SIXTH AVE.

THOMPSON ST.

WEST BROADWAY

BROOME ST.

GRAND ST.

WOOSTER ST.

GREENE ST.

DESBROSSES ST.

GREENWICH ST.

HUDSON ST.

VESTRY ST.

LAIGHT ST.

CANAL ST.

HUBERT ST.

LISPENARD ST.

BEACH ST.

ERICSSON PL.

WALKER ST.

N. MOORE ST.

VARICK ST.

ST. JOHN'S LA.

WHITE ST.

FRANKLIN ST.

FINN SQ.

FRANKLIN ST.

HARRISON ST.

LEONARD ST.

Independence Plaza

JAY ST.

WORTH ST.

DUANE ST.

HUDSON ST.

Duane Street Park

THOMAS ST.

DUANE ST.

READE ST.

GREENWICH ST.

CHAMBERS ST.

WEST BROADWAY

CHURCH ST.

WARREN ST.

BROADWAY

MURRAY ST.

PARK PL.

City Hall

City Hall Park

World Trade Center

BARCLAY ST.

VESEY ST.

PARK ROW

N

tural sights around Duane Park. The Art Deco Western Union Building at 60 Hudson is clad in some 19 different shades of brick; the Mercantile Exchange at 6 Harrison Street is an admirable pile of stone and brick; farther down Harrison are six examples of Federal town houses transplanted from the Washington Market.

Head up West Broadway for further cultural pursuits. **Artists Space** at number 223 sponsors exhibitions by emerging artists; half a block east at 112 Franklin Street is the equally innovative **Franklin Furnace** art exhibition center; a block north at 17 White is the **Alternative Museum**, where contemporary art exhibits also take place. Finally, to read about the art and artists you've been seeing (and more), browse through the **Printed Matter Bookshop** at 7 Lispenard. You can digest your reading matter at **Barocco**, a trendy and inexpensive restaurant at 301 Church; at **Exterminator Chili**, a comfortable and cheap chili parlor at 305 Church; and at the roomy bar and restaurant **Smoke Stacks Lightning** at 380 Canal, on the southeast corner of West Broadway.

North across Canal is SoHo, but we will move east instead now, into Chinatown.

CHINATOWN

Go east on the "Ca" of TriBeCa—**Canal Street**, named for the 40-foot-wide canal dug on the site in 1805 to drain the waters of the Collect Pond (then New York's reservoir) into the Hudson River—to Chinatown. Here, in New York's most ethnically distinctive neighborhood, the signs are predominantly Chinese and many structures (including phone booths) are topped with pagodas. The area becomes especially animated during the Chinese New Year festival held in January or February (depending on the lunar calendar), when a giant dragon puppet snakes through the streets, banqueters fill the restaurants, and firecrackers explode nonstop. Gone are the opium dens that during the Jazz Age made the expression "going to Chinatown to kick the gong around" synonymous with getting high, but Chinese street gangs such as the Ghost Shadows still make drug trafficking of other types one of Chinatown's problems, which also include dense overcrowding from an influx of immigrants from a soon-to-become-Communist Hong Kong. Add to it the enormous hordes of tourists who flock to its famous restaurants each weekend and you have the fascinating bazaar that is Chinatown.

Canal Street East provides a good introduction to the raw ingredients of Chinese food. Fish, meat, exotic vegetables, and fruits are sold in shops and stalls along its south side between Centre and Mulberry streets, and **Kam Man** at 200 Canal between Mott and Mulberry offers the area's widest selection of Chinese food, cooking utensils, and unusual pharmaceuticals.

Mott Street is Chinatown's main drag, where the dragon and other revelers parade during New Year's. This is the place to wander freely, to stop in at practically any of its restaurants for an inexpensive and excellent meal (tradition dictates ordering several dishes per table and sharing); coffee shops for such snacks as pork buns and custard tarts with tea or coffee routinely served with real cream; Chinese bookstores (**Hong Kong Bookstore** at number 72 and **Chinatown Books** at 70A have good selections); a Buddhist Temple (number 64); curio shops (try Tai Heng Lee at number 60); and the bizarre **Chinatown Fair Amusement Arcade and Chinese Museum** (number 8), a sideshow-type emporium where amusements include a live chicken that answers questions, wax displays of Chinese food, and the dragon that winds through the streets during the New Year's festivities. Don't neglect the side streets for further diversions: Especially rich is the arcade between Elizabeth and Bowery, which contains, among other things, the ever-popular **Phoenix Garden Restaurant**.

At the end of Mott Street is Chatham Square, surrounded by architecturally distinguished modern apartment buildings such as Chatham Towers (170 Park Row) and Chatham Green (85 Park Row) as well as the towering red-brick curve of Confucius Plaza, with its bronze statue of the sage by Tiu Shih. The Chatham Square area's architectural distinction is over a hundred years old, however. The Chatham Square Branch of the New York Public Library at 33 East Broadway was designed by McKim, Mead & White in 1903; the Mariners' Temple and Baptist Meeting House at 12 Oliver Street was built in 1842; St. James Roman Catholic Church at 32 St. James Place in 1837; the Chinatown Mission at 48 Henry in 1830; the William Clark House at 51 Market Street in 1824; the Sea and Land Church at 61 Henry Street in 1817; 6 Bowery (the site of the former Olliffe's Apothecary, the oldest drug store in America) in 1803; and a Federal-style house at 18 Bowery in 1785. On

Chinatown and Little Italy

| 0 | yards | 250 |
| 0 | meters | 250 |

E. HOUSTON ST.

JERSEY ST.

PRINCE ST.

MULBERRY ST.

SPRING ST.

BOWERY

DELANCEY ST.

CLEVELAND PL.

LAFAYETTE ST.

KENMARE ST.

CHRYSTIE ST.

FORSYTH ST.

ELDRIDGE ST.

ALLEN ST.

CROSBY ST.

BROOME ST.

CENTRE ST.

GRAND ST.

BAXTER ST.

LITTLE ITALY

HOWARD ST.

HESTER ST.

MOTT ST.

ELIZABETH ST.

CANAL ST. to East River

WALKER ST.

CANAL ST.

MULBERRY ST.

CHINATOWN

ST.

BOWERY

MANHATTAN BRIDGE

WHITE ST.

Civil Municipal Courthouse

"The Tombs"

BAYARD ST.

BAXTER ST.

PELL ST.

DOYERS ST.

MOTT ST.

DIVISION ST.

CHATHAM SQ.

BROADWAY

CATHERINE ST.

FRANKLIN ST.

HOGAN PL.

Columbus Park

PARK ST.

E. HENRY ST.

OLIVER ST.

LEONARD ST.

WORTH ST.

Federal Plaza

LAFAYETTE ST.

CENTRE ST.

New York County Courthouse

PARK ROW

JAMES ST.

MADISON ST.

PEARL ST.

DUANE ST.

ELK ST.

FOLEY SQ.

U.S. Courthouse

Police Plaza

PEARL ST.

ST. JAMES PL.

Alfred E. Smith Houses

READE ST.

Municipal Building

Police Headquarters

AVE. OF THE FINEST

CHAMBERS ST.

Tweed Courthouse

City Hall

PARK ROW

R. F. WAGNER SR. PL.

BROOKLYN BRIDGE

N

the south side of the square is the area's—in fact, Manhattan's—earliest extant artifact. It is the First Shearith Cemetery, the original burying ground for the city's Spanish and Portuguese Jewish community, dating from 1683. Return to Mott Street and follow it uptown to Canal Street, the unofficial border between Chinatown and Little Italy.

LITTLE ITALY

Though the Chinese now own the majority of the real estate in Little Italy, and the area's Italian residents have been systematically moving to Brooklyn and suburban areas, Little Italy retains much of its Italian character. It is most pronounced—almost theatrically so—along **Mulberry Street** north of Canal, where Italian community leaders have quietly asked the Chinese to post their signs in Roman letters only, a request they haven't refused. The street is lined with Italian restaurants, shops selling Italian food and other goods, and black limousines parked in front of brick-faced "social clubs" solemnly guarded by elegantly coiffed young men in tight clothing. Occasionally, *Godfather*-style gun wars break out, as occurred in 1972 when a member of the Colombo crime family allegedly shot rival Joey Gallo at Umberto's Clam House (there are bullet holes in the window to prove it), but the everyday street scene the tourist is likely to encounter is lower key, more akin to the infighting among street toughs in Martin Scorsese's film, *Mean Streets*.

The **Feast of San Gennaro** is the best or worst time to visit Little Italy, depending on your point of view. The street fair is named after the patron saint of Naples, reflecting the neighborhood's original residents' southern Italian origins. During the ten days around September 19 on which it takes place, amid the Baroque swirls of arches made of light bulbs and the batteries of Port-a-Potties set up especially for the occasion, thousands of people descend upon Mulberry Street determined to have a good time. Young Italian-Americans from outside the neighborhood prowl the streets along with busloads of tourists. The saint, whom old-time residents recall used to be celebrated by dancing in the street to the strains of a small orchestra, is currently commemorated by drinking beer, eating greasy versions of Italian (and, increasingly, Latin American and Asian) food on sale in stands along Mulberry, and playing games of skill or chance in other booths. Some come for what they sincerely believe is a taste of Italy; others are drawn to its decidedly grotesque carnival atmosphere. San Gennaro himself smiles on it all, his image decorated with dollar bills and paraded around the streets on September 19, then displayed through the end of the feast in a special grandstand constructed for the purpose.

The rest of the year, Little Italy is a quiet and peaceful place. Mulberry Street, as it leads north from Canal, is lined with restaurants and cafés ranging from the old-fashioned style of **Paolucci's Restaurant** (at number 149) in the former Stephen Van Rensselaer Federal-style house dating from 1816, to the high-tech elegance of **Caffè Biondo** at number 141. (Conversely, Richard Haas has given the area a retro touch by painting one of his trompe l'oeil murals of old storefronts on a wall space along the east side of Mulberry Street between Hester and Grand.) Most of Little Italy's restaurants serve a heavy cuisine mutated from southern Italian immigrant cooking and virtually nonexistent in the mother country.

The intersection of Mulberry and Grand streets is the heart of Little Italy, where you'll find a variety of restaurants, cafés, and excellent neighborhood food stores (Italian Food Center at 186 Grand, Alleva Dairy at 188 Grand, and Piemonte at 190 Grand). If they were located in any other part of town, the food stores would be called gourmet shops, but here they are part of the remaining Italian residents' daily marketing routine. **Ferrara Café** (195 Grand) gets a particularly large crowd for dessert after dinner in Little Italy and Chinatown; **Caffè Roma** (385 Broome), a little farther north on Mulberry, is more intimate. While in the area, don't miss one of the most delightful examples of the Chinese influx: **Pearl River** department store at 200 Grand, which carries a huge selection of Chinese merchandise of all sorts.

The copper dome you see looming to the west above Little Italy is the top of the former New York City Police Headquarters (the entrance is at 240 Centre Street), a Renaissance-style palazzo topped with a Baroque-type cupola. After years of debate about what to do with it after its abandonment, the building has now been converted to luxury condominiums.

A block east of Mulberry, Mott Street (with its marvelous views of the Empire State Building neatly framed by the street's tenements) is becoming increasingly Chinese, but still has some of the most typically Italian institutions in the area. At 116 Mott is Fretta Bros. butcher shop, which sells a variety of domestic and foreign Italian sausages, as does DiPalo's at 206 Grand Street (on the corner of Mott), along with homemade and imported Italian cheeses. Farther uptown, Caruso's Fruit Market at 152 Mott Street is a remnant of the pushcart days (and one of the few places to get fresh basil in the neighborhood), and **Parisi Bakery** at 198 Mott sells loaves of fresh bread or makes them into sandwiches for you.

Finally, the pride of Little Italy is **Old St. Patrick's Cathedral** at 260–264 Mott Street. The site of the original 1815 Roman Catholic cathedral of New York, the present church was gutted by a fire and restored in 1868, only to have the archdiocese move to the uptown St. Patrick's in 1879. The church and its adjacent walled cemetery are well maintained and add a dignified air to the neighborhood.

THE LOWER EAST SIDE

A large segment of New York's Jewish history is alive and well in the area to the northeast of Chinatown, called the Lower East Side. Though the city has had a Spanish and Portuguese Jewish community from its very beginning, in the 19th century Jewish refugees came from Eastern Europe as well. Most of them settled on the Lower East Side with the other immigrant populations and remained there well into this century. Two films by Joan Micklin Silver, *Hester Street* and *Crossing Delancey,* offer historical and contemporary glimpses, respectively, into the area's Jewish community.

The Jewish population that occupied the area during much of the 19th and 20th centuries has since dispersed throughout the city, giving the New York metropolitan area a larger Jewish population than all of Israel. The Lower East Side is still about 25 percent Jewish (the rest is largely Hispanic and Chinese, with an increasing minority of artists attracted by cheap rents—an early sign of gentrification in an area that still has a long way to go to become another SoHo). Remnants of Jewish culture— most of them admittedly run-down—include synagogues, delicatessens, restaurants, and discount clothing stores, all of which attract Jewish and Gentile visitors alike. One note before going: Because the Jewish Sabbath runs from sundown Friday to sundown Saturday, most of the area's nonreligious sights are closed on Saturday.

Of the area's numerous synagogues, the first built for use as such (and still the most impressive) is **Congregation K'Hal Adath Jeshurun** at 14 Eldridge Street between Canal and Forsyth streets. An eclectic blend of Moorish, Gothic, and Romanesque architectural elements, it contrasts greatly with the surrounding tenements. Though it, too, is in a sad state of repair, it is slowly being restored to its former glory. (In better shape is the Bialystoker Synagogue at 7 Willett Street, between Grand and Broome, originally a Methodist Episcopal church built in 1826.)

Jewish history continues toward the east, where at 175 East Broadway is the building where the *Forward,* the Jewish newspaper, was originally published. Down the street, at 197 East Broadway, is the Educational Alliance, an organization founded by wealthy uptown Jews in 1883 to assist recent Jewish immigrants. Across the street, at 192 East Broadway, is the Seward Park Branch of the New York Public Library, where Leon Trotsky studied when he was in town. A block south and two blocks east is the Henry Street Settlement, a still-functioning community service organization that served as the prototype for such programs around the country.

Outside, the drama of contemporary life on **Orchard Street** continues with the passionate pursuit of shopping for discount clothing by famous designers from around the world (see Fashion), while the Essex Street area is the principal thoroughfare for more specifically Lower East Side institutions. One of its most distinguished contributions to American gastronomy—pickles—may be purchased fresh at Guss's Pickle Stand (42 Hester Street), Pickleman (27 Essex Street), or Hollander Kosher Pickle Stop (35 Essex Street), which pickles many other vegetables as well. Baked goods of all kinds can be sampled at Gertel's Kosher Bakery at 53 Hester Street. If you're still hungry you can try the **Grand Dairy Restaurant** (341 Grand Street) or **Ratner's** (138 Delancey Street), both of which are as famous for their meatless cuisine (Jewish law proscribes the eating of dairy products with meat products) as they are for their rude waiters. Crossing Delancey Street (that's the Williamsburg Bridge at its east end), Essex leads to the two-block-long **Essex Street Market,** an indoor food market catering to the area's Chinese, Hispanic, and Jewish clientele. Between Rivington and Stanton streets are even more exotic delights for the palate: Schapiro's House of Kosher and Sacramental Wines, the only winery in the city (tours and samples of

The Lower East Side

0 yards 250 250
0 meters 250 250

N

East River

East River Park

FDR DRIVE

WILLIAMSBURG BRIDGE

FDR DRIVE

CHERRY ST.

JACKSON ST.

LEWIS ST.

KAZAN ST.

MADISON ST.

GOUVERNEUR ST.

MONTGOMERY ST.

COLUMBIA ST.

WILLETT ST.

HENRY ST.

CLINTON ST.

LOWER EAST SIDE

PITT ST.

RIDGE ST.

ATTORNEY ST.

DELANCEY ST.

BROOME ST.

GRAND ST.

EAST BROADWAY

JEFFERSON ST.

CLINTON ST.

SUFFOLK ST.

RUTGERS ST.

NORFOLK ST.

AVE. B

ESSEX ST.

LUDLOW ST.

ORCHARD ST.

ALLEN ST.

HESTER ST.

CANAL ST.

AVE. A

STANTON ST.

RIVINGTON ST.

ELDRIDGE ST.

MANHATTAN BRIDGE

FIRST AVE.

E. HOUSTON ST.

FORSYTH ST.

CHRYSTIE ST.

SECOND AVE.

BOWERY

ELIZABETH ST.

MOTT ST.

MULBERRY ST.

KENMARE ST.

BOWERY

LITTLE ITALY

HESTER ST.

CHINATOWN

CLEVELAND PL.

CENTRE ST.

HESTER ST.

CANAL ST.

BOND ST.

LAFAYETTE ST.

CROSBY ST.

BROADWAY

LAGUARDIA PL.

BLEECKER ST.

PRINCE ST.

SPRING ST.

MERCER ST.

GREENE ST.

WOOSTER ST.

BROOME ST.

GRAND ST.

CANAL ST.

LISPENARD ST.

WALKER ST.

SOHO

the syrupy stuff are given on Sundays), is at number 126 Rivington Street; Economy Candy (131 Essex Street) sells marzipan and halvah; and **Bernstein-on-Essex Street** (135 Essex Street) is a combination Jewish deli and kosher Chinese restaurant.

The area's largest deli restaurant is **Katz's** at 205 East Houston Street. The same street also has a number of other food shops (Ben's Cheese Shop and Moishe's Bakery at number 181, Russ and Daughters delicatessen at 179, and Yonah Schimmel's Knishes Bakery at 137), but for the grandest bouffe of all, have a meal (it may be your last) at the not-so-cheap **Sammy's Famous Rumanian Restaurant** at 157 Chrystie Street (just north of Delancey). Each table comes equipped with, in addition to the usual salt and pepper, a jar of rendered chicken fat (*schmaltz*) as a cholesterol-laden condiment; there is also a bottle of seltzer water (the owners call it "Jewish Perrier 1936"), and a container of milk and a bottle of chocolate syrup for making your own egg cream, the quintessential Lower East Side comestible. You'll note that it contains no egg and no cream.

THE BOWERY

Once the road that led to Peter Stuyvesant's farm, or *bouwerie,* the Bowery today is famous for the derelicts who live on its streets and in its flophouses. Even its squalor is historical, however, having been where songwriter Stephen Foster died destitute in 1864 and the setting for *Maggie: A Girl of the Streets,* the 1893 novel by Stephen Crane, who called the Bowery "the only interesting street in New York." He sketched the scene there: "Long streamers of garments fluttered from fire escapes. In all unhandy places there were buckets, brooms, rags and bottles. In the street infants played or fought with other infants or sat stupidly in the way of vehicles. Formidable women, with uncombed hair and disordered dress, gossiped while leaning on railings, or screamed in frantic quarrels. Withered persons, in curious postures of submission to something, sat smoking pipes in obscure corners. A thousand odors of cooking food came forth to the street. The building quivered and creaked from the weight of humanity stamping about in its bowels."

The Bowery was New York's theater and music-hall district in the mid-19th century and achieved renewed vitality after Crane's day when the Third Avenue elevated train brought people to its popular entertainments: John Sloan and other early-20th-century artists depicted the era in numerous prints and drawings. The theaters are gone, but the area retains a certain amount of architectural fantasy in the palatial Bowery Savings Bank (130 Bowery) by McKim, Mead & White, dating from 1894, and the 1909 Beaux Arts approach to the Manhattan Bridge (at the intersection of Canal Street at the edge of Chinatown), with its monumental sculpture representing *The Spirit of Commerce, The Spirit of Industry,* and, of all things, *Buffalo Hunt.* Today most people only see the Bowery through their windshields (often aided by an unexpected cleaning from one of the area's squeegee-brandishing derelicts) on their way to and from the Manhattan Bridge or Chinatown, or to shop in the restaurant-supply and lighting-equipment stores that line the wide street.

SOHO

From Little Italy west of the Bowery, you can reach SoHo—*So*uth of *Ho*uston Street (pronounced House-ton)—by taking Prince west across Lafayette Street. First take a detour past the huge store selling pricey castoffs of office buildings and their furnishings, **Urban Archaeology** at 285 Lafayette, to look at the **Puck Building** at 295 Lafayette, on the corner of Houston Street. It is the former headquarters of the satirical magazine *Puck*— hence the two statues of the Shakespearean imp above the entrance and at the building's northeast corner—and continues the tradition by housing the offices of *Spy,* a contemporary satirical magazine. Then follow Prince west to LoBro, or Lower Broadway, where SoHo begins.

There is nothing lowbrow about SoHo, though. Such is its enduring trendiness that hip directors such as Woody Allen (*Hannah and Her Sisters*), Paul Mazursky (*An Unmarried Woman*), and Martin Scorsese (*After Hours*) have all set films there in recent years. Before that, however—in the 1960s—the area was "discovered" by two distinct groups: preservationists and artists. Preservationists liked the outsides of the buildings in the area, the largest and most important concentration in the world of structures made of cast iron, a cheap and malleable material widely used in the construction of warehouses in the mid-19th century. Artists liked the buildings' insides, former industrial space that gave them large studio space at low rent. "Oh, to be young and come to New York and move into your first loft," wrote Thomas Wolfe in *In Our Time,* "and look at the world with eyes that light up even the rotting fire-escape railings, even the buckling pressed-tin squares on the ceiling, even the sheet-metal shower stall with its belly dents and rusting seams. . . ."

Our times have changed. In just a few years, the area's lofts have become luxuriously appointed, and most artists can no longer afford either to live in SoHo or show in its galleries. SoHo has become the most important center in the world for contemporary art, and its boundaries have spread every which way from West Broadway, still its main drag. Art-world figures engage in a regular ritual of looking at the new shows on Saturdays (the serious SoHo galleries are closed on Sundays and Mondays) during the art season, which extends roughly from Labor Day through Memorial Day. Gallery hopping has become a social event as well, so Saturday is also a good time to see the latest fashions being worn in the galleries, on the streets, or in such wateringholes as the **Cupping Room** (359 West Broadway near Broome) for coffee or tea, the **SoHo Wine Bar** (461 West Broadway between Houston and Prince) for a wide selection of vintages, and the **Manhattan Brewing Company** (40 Thompson Street) for beer.

Galleries and Shops

Saturdays are when SoHo is most crowded and active, but if for some reason you'd prefer to avoid the scene, the galleries are open Tuesdays through Fridays as well, and the cast-iron architecture is always there. Most galleries and other shops, don't open until noon.

In the past few years, Broadway has given serious competition to West Broadway (note that the latter is a separate street four blocks west of Broadway) for the area's largest concentration of institutions—only appropriate since this area was New York's main shopping thoroughfare in the mid-19th century. The gourmet shop **Dean & DeLuca** recently opened a huge new store at 560 Broadway (at Prince Street), which quickly filled with croissant- and cappuccino-consuming regulars. The building is also occupied by such prestigious galleries as Salvatore Ala and Max Protetch. This stretch of Broadway also has some of the area's most important buildings. Across

W. 14 ST.

W. 13 ST.

LITTLE W. 12 ST.

GANSEVOORT ST.

HORATIO ST.

JANE ST.

W. 12 ST.

BETHUNE ST.

BANK ST.

W. 11 ST.

PERRY ST.

CHARLES LA.

CHARLES ST.

W. 10 ST.

CHRISTOPHER ST.

EIGHTH AVE.

GREENWICH AVE.

St. Vincent's Hospital

WAVERLY PL.

SEVENTH AVE. SOUTH

Abingdon Square

W. 4 ST.

BLEECKER ST.

GREENWICH VILLAGE

Sheridan Sq.

GROVE ST.

BEDFORD ST.

HUDSON ST.

GREENWICH ST.

BARROW ST.

MORTON ST.

ST. LUKES PL.

LEROY ST.

WASHINGTON ST.

CLARKSON ST.

WEST SIDE HWY.

WEST ST.

N

Hudson River

Holland Tunnel

WATTS ST.

DESBROSSES ST.

VESTRY ST.

SoHo and Greenwich Village

0   yards   250

0   meters   250

Union Sq.

W. 14 ST.   E. 14 ST.

W. 13 ST.

W. 12 ST.   E. 12 ST.

BROADWAY

FOURTH AVE.

Grace Church

W. 11 ST.   E. 11 ST.

SIXTH AVE. (AVENUE OF THE AMERICAS)

FIFTH AVE.

W. 10 ST.   E. 10 ST.

MILLIGAN PL.

PATCHIN PL.

W. 9 ST.   E. 9 ST.

WANAMAKER PL.

GAY ST.

W. 8 ST.   E. 8 ST.

WASHINGTON MEWS

ASTOR PL.

Cooper Union

MACDOUGAL ALLEY

Washington Arch

WAVERLY PL.   WAVERLY PL.

UNIVERSITY PL.

Cooper Sq.

JONES ST.

CORNELIA ST.

Washington Square Park

WASHINGTON PL.

W. 4 ST.   E. 4 ST.

New York University

W. 3 ST.   E. 3 ST.   GREAT JONES ST.

MINETTA LA.

BOND ST.

CARMINE ST.

DOWNING ST.

BLEECKER ST.

LA GUARDIA PL.

____ ST.

W. HOUSTON ST.   E. HOUSTON ST.

KING ST.

MACDOUGAL ST.

SULLIVAN ST.

THOMPSON ST.

WOOSTER ST.

GREENE ST.

MERCER ST.

CROSBY ST.

CHARLTON ST.

VARICK ST.

VANDAM ST.

PRINCE ST.

S O H O

SPRING ST.

SPRING ST.

DOMINICK ST.

SIXTH AVE. (AVENUE OF THE AMERICAS)

WEST BROADWAY

BROADWAY

LAFAYETTE ST.

BROOME ST.   BROOME ST.

GRAND ST.

HOWARD ST.

LAIGHT ST.

YORK ST.

CANAL ST.

LISPENARD ST.

the street, at 561 Broadway, is one façade of the L-shaped Singer Building (the other façade is on Prince) by Ernest Flagg. Toward the south is the Haughwout Building at 488 Broadway—a pleasant Palladian pastiche best known for its Otis elevator, which was the first in the world when it was installed in 1857. At 478 Broadway is another important cast-iron building, the Roosevelt Building, designed by Richard Morris Hunt in 1874.

SoHo's largest proliferation of galleries is currently at 568 Broadway, where you may want to stop into the John Gibson and Curt Marcus galleries to see what the art world is looking at. For a complete and current listing of the city's gallery shows, pick up a copy of *Art Now Gallery Guide* or *Art in America New York Galleries and Museums,* both available free of charge at most dealers' front desks.

At 583 Broadway is the **New Museum of Contemporary Art,** a noncommercial institution that mounts exhibitions from around the world. And more than the art world extends to this stretch of Broadway, the heart of LoBro. At 611 Broadway is the 1894 McKim, Mead & White–designed Cable Building, technically not in SoHo because it is north of Houston Street. On the ground floor of its Mercer Street entrance is the recently opened Angelika Film Center, one of the few movie houses south of Greenwich Village. Opposite it, on the north side of 599 Broadway, is a wall sculpture by Forrest Myers. While in this part of "NoHo" (or LoBro), cross Broadway to 65 Bleecker Street for a look at the 1898 Bayard/Condict Building, the lone example of Louis Sullivan's architecture in New York. Trendy Cajun chef Paul Prudhomme just opened the restaurant **K-Paul's-New York** at 622 Broadway. Altogether, the Broadway sidewalks between Canal Jean north of Broome Street and Astor Place Hair Designers at the corner of Astor Place, crammed with street vendors and youth-oriented stores such as **Tower Records** at number 692 and **Unique Clothing** at number 726, are a teenage mall rebel's dream—not to mention other pedestrians' nightmare.

If you haven't gotten lost in the crowd, head west off Broadway on Prince Street. At the corner of Prince and Mercer streets is **Fanelli,** which has existed since SoHo was known only as the Eighth Ward in the 19th century, serving truck drivers from the nearby warehouses. It is still the only serious bar in SoHo, though its ownership has changed and the stains on its clientele's clothing are less likely to be from motor oil than from Italian extra-virgin olive oil. Take a side trip to 163 Mercer to look into the Tony Shafrazi gallery.

Continuing on Prince: **Jerry's Restaurant** at number 101 has become the most popular hangout in SoHo, reflecting another sort of dead seriousness in the contemporary art world. ("New York is not the cultural center of America," Chicagoan Saul Bellow once remarked, "but the business and administrative center of American culture.") Next door, at 103 Prince, stop into the Edward Thorp Gallery above the post office. It has one of the nicest spaces of any SoHo gallery, with a lovely skylight illuminating the art.

On the southwest corner of Prince and Greene streets is another mural by Richard Haas, this one a painting of the building's cast-iron façade on the brick wall of its east side and incorporating real windows. Important Greene Street galleries include Metro Pictures (number 150), Sperone Westwater and John Weber, at 142, and Barbara Gladstone at 99. While there, you might want a sample from the extensive wine list of the **SoHo Kitchen** (at number 103), perhaps accompanied by an inexpensive hamburger at the bar. Among Greene Street's cast-iron masterpieces are the buildings at 72–76 and 28–30, both dating from 1872.

Another nearby option for food is **150 Wooster**, SoHo's and maybe New York's hottest meal ticket of the moment, serving an eclectic Continental and Brazilian menu. Wooster Street is also the location of the Paula Cooper gallery at 155, which was the first to move to SoHo in the 1960s and still shows many of the same minimalist artists from that era. Across the street is 130 Prince Street, a former bakery that has been renovated and is now SoHo's newest gallery building. Its colorful Postmodern façade is entirely appropriate to one of its best-known tenants, the **Louver Gallery, New York**, the East Coast branch of the well-known Los Angeles gallery.

Prince next runs into West Broadway, considered the main street of SoHo. Toward the north are two Italian oases: **Rizzoli Bookstore** (454 West Broadway), with its Postmodern façade and staff to match, specializes in international art books and international periodicals and is a great place for browsing while listening to music on its excellent sound system; **I Tre Merli** (463 West Broadway) is a cavernous, high-tech Italian restaurant serving palatable food or sparkling *prosecco* wine for a quick pick-me-up. Toward the south, at 417 West Broadway, is the Mary

Boone gallery, whose high prices and patronizing gallery assistants have made it the Gucci of the contemporary art world, though it often functions as a chic toll both from an artist's studio to a major collection. The building at 420 West Broadway has housed so many well-known galleries—currently Leo Castelli, Charles Cowles, 49th Parallel, Germans Van Eck, Marilyn Pearl, and Sonnabend—that its entrance has become a rendezvous for friends and tours meeting in SoHo. Down the street at number 396 is the recently opened **Barolo**, which serves the cuisine of Italy's Piedmont region.

Spring and Broome streets are better known for sights other than art galleries. Among them, **Spring Street Books** at 169 and **Jaap Rietman**'s art bookstore at 134 Spring draw a lively crowd, as does the **Spring Street Bar and Restaurant** (number 162). The outstanding piece of architecture on the street is the 1870 cast-iron building at number 101, which has a façade pierced with ample expanses of glass. On Broome Street, the **Broome Street Bar** (363 West Broadway) is a good place for an inexpensive hamburger in preparation for an architectural field day: number 484 is an 1890 Romanesque-style brick building; numbers 478 (1885), 475 (1873), 461 (1871), and 455 (1873) are all cast-iron buildings.

Before leaving the area you may want to locate some socio-cultural phenomena in SoHo that might bring you back to pursue special interests. On its southern fringes are the **Performing Garage**, a long-established experimental theater at 33 Wooster, and the **Museum of Holography** at 11 Mercer, where there are crowd-pleasing displays of three-dimensional laser photography. Toward the west are the **Film Forum**, at 57 Watts, which shows noncommercial films (the Thalia SoHo, at 15 Vandam Street, is a revival house); the **New York City Fire Museum** at 278 Spring, which has the most comprehensive collection of fire-fighting equipment in the country; **White Columns**, a sculpture gallery at 325 Spring; and the **Ear Inn**, a funky café-restaurant at 326 Spring. The latter contrasts greatly with the studied 1930s decor of the **Canal Bar** at 511 Greenwich Street around the corner—still one of New York's hottest celebrity hangouts.

The South Village

Perhaps the most relaxing part of what is now called SoHo is the long-standing residential area at its west end, once

CHINATOWN TO THE VILLAGES

known as the South Village, incorporating Thompson, Sullivan, and MacDougal streets south of Houston. Formerly predominantly Italian, the area retains that flavor in such quaint shops as the Vesuvio Bakery at 160 Prince, **Café Borgia II** at 161 Prince, Lanciani Pastry at 177 Prince, and the Melampo food store at 105 Sullivan. Over the past few years, however, its Portuguese population has quietly increased. Its parish church, dedicated to Saint Anthony of Padua (who, coincidentally, was born in Lisbon), holds an Italian street fair on Sullivan in June, but celebrates mass in Portuguese. The M & O Market at 124 Thompson is one of the few places in town where you can purchase Portuguese fish, cheese, sausages, olives, olive oil, and mineral water.

There is a pleasant Federal–Greek Revival house at 203 Prince and Federal houses on the residential streets of Charlton, King, and Vandam—now given landmark status—beyond Sixth Avenue. However, a simple stroll in the area with no preconceived notions about compulsive sight-seeing adds a nice down-to-earth, real-people touch after spending a day among lofty trend setters. You can fortify yourself with provisions from the aforementioned Italian or Portuguese food shops, or perhaps some *charcuterie* from **Raoul's Butcher Shop** at 179 Prince (no pretense here either—they really are French); if you'd prefer sitting down, dinner at either **Raoul's** at 180 Prince (the steak and *pommes frites* at the bar is a less-expensive option here) or **Provence** at 38 MacDougal will end the day's ramblings on a mellow, Continental note.

GREENWICH VILLAGE

If you ask people in SoHo how to get to Greenwich Village, their answer might require some translating. "The Village?" they'll say, meaning Greenwich Village, "Take Sixth Avenue" (what all New Yorkers call Avenue of the Americas) "across House-ton uptown" (north). Indeed, at that point Avenue of the Americas really does live up to its good-neighborly name. Thanks to a 1976 restoration, it almost resembles a boulevard from some South American capital in its broadness and the use of pattern in its pavement and provides a great entrance (and contrast) to the narrow, winding streets of the Village.

And wind they do, even though they lie within the area of the grid plan imposed on Manhattan beginning in

1811. (West 4th Street intersects with West 10th, 11th, and 12th streets in the Village, to the consternation of tourists and residents alike.) The reason is that the area had long been established, first as an Algonquin Indian settlement, then as a Dutch tobacco plantation, and finally as a small British town called Greenwich, which enjoyed such a pleasant climate it was used by residents of New York in the early 19th century as a refuge from smallpox and yellow-fever epidemics. Its reputation as a haven for artists and writers dates from the late 19th century, when John La Farge, Winslow Homer, Mark Twain, Henry James, and others lived there. In this century John Sloan, Edward Hopper, Eugene O'Neill, Edna St. Vincent Millay, Edmund Wilson, and many others continued the tradition, which died out after the inevitable rising rents drove the Beat poets and beatniks away. Paul Mazursky's film *Next Stop, Greenwich Village* represents the swan song of that era.

Somehow, Greenwich Village maintains its mystique. As recently as 1971 John Lennon said, "I should have been born in the Village, that's where I belong." And today a bohemian feeling can still be sensed in its cafés, restaurants, and clubs, which are, admittedly, visited mostly by outsiders. Even among its residents, however—students and professors, gays and straights, ethnics and middle class—a tolerant and pleasant community spirit prevails. It can be experienced on a person-to-person basis during the area's numerous "block parties," fund-raising and social events held throughout the year by community groups; the ragtag Annual Village Halloween Parade also attracts a good-natured group of revelers and outrageously costumed marchers from inside and outside the area.

The West Village

The area west of Sixth Avenue between Houston and 14th streets has the largest amount of the atmosphere and architecture associated with the Village, and you can get a preview of it by looking east up narrow Minetta Street near the intersection of Sixth Avenue and Bleecker. For a strong taste of Greenwich Village's Italian community, follow **Bleecker Street** north: The parish church of Our Lady of Pompeii (which holds a street festival each July) is at the intersection of Carmine Street; there are baked goods at Rocco's (number 243), Dellarovere and Musa (245), and Zito's (259); various foods are sold at Faicco's

Pork Store (260), Zampognaro (262), Mario Bosco (263), and Ottomanelli & Sons (281).

Take Leroy Street (which has a nice array of residential architecture) across Bedford and Seventh Avenue South to St. Luke's Place, a stunning row of brownstone houses dating from the 1850s. Mayor Jimmy Walker lived at number 6, which accounts for the lanterns at the entrance, an old New York custom for indicating the mayor's residence. St. Luke's leads to Hudson Street, where just south of number 487 is the church of St. Luke-in-the-Fields, which stood on the river's edge when it was built in 1821, before the landfill that extended the island. Number 487, the first in a series of Federal houses, was once the residence of Bret Harte, whose tales of life in California mining camps earned him a literary reputation in the United States and Great Britain in the late 19th century.

A block north is **Christopher Street**, the center of New York's gay community. Gone are the days of the pre-AIDS 1970s so sensationalistically depicted in William Friedkin's film *Cruising,* but the street scene still gets quite active on Gay Pride Day each June, when participants in the parade down Fifth Avenue—including Rollerina, a drag queen who has achieved celebrity status by roller-skating in the streets in a flurry of chiffon waving her magic wand—congregate in and around Christopher Street afterward. There are a number of establishments in the area that cater to a homosexual clientele: On Christopher itself are two men's bars—Ty's at number 114 and Boots & Saddle at 76—as well as the **Oscar Wilde Memorial Bookshop** at number 15. The Grove Club (70 Grove Street) and The Cubbyhole (438 Hudson) are lesbian bars; **Marie's Crisis Café** (59 Grove Street) is where men gather to sing show tunes in Thomas Paine's former home (the name of the establishment is a reference to one of the patriot's publications); and The Monster (80 Grove) offers drag cabaret and video. Rougher bars are found, appropriately enough, closer to the waterfront at the west end of Christopher. The community is also tolerant of outsiders, who come for off-Broadway theater at the **Lucille Lortel** (121 Christopher), shopping at such specialty shops as Li-Lac Chocolates at 120 Christopher, McNulty's Tea & Coffee provisioners at 109 Christopher, and the Pleasure Chest at 156 Seventh Avenue South, which sells sexual equipment for all persuasions.

From Christopher, head south down Bedford Street for a leisurely stroll around the West Village's most characteristic residential streets, where many of the houses date from the early 1800s. The ramshackle structure at 102 Bedford has a characteristically Greenwich Village history: Originally a town house built in 1830, in 1926 it reopened in its elaborate present state as "Twin Peaks," a haven for artists, writers, and actors. Number 86 Bedford is the secret entrance to **Chumley's,** a quiet bar that was formerly a speakeasy with a back door leading to Barrow Street for hasty retreats; 75½ Bedford is the narrowest residence in the city (9½ feet wide), but once housed one of the Village's most expansive residents, the poet Edna St. Vincent Millay (given her middle name from another Village institution, St. Vincent's Hospital). If you are interested in historical residences, turn right on Commerce Street where Washington Irving lived at number 11 and Aaron Burr at number 17.

Nearby, 17 Barrow houses **One If By Land,** a restaurant serving excellent Continental cuisine, but there are a number of options nearby for traditional American cuisine well suited to the neighborhood's architecture: **Ye Waverly Inn** up at 16 Bank Street is famous for its chicken potpie; **The Coach House** at 110 Waverly Place east of Sixth Avenue serves southern food in a town-house setting; and the **Pink Teacup** at 42 Grove Street specializes in soul food. Traditional Village drinking establishments include the **White Horse Tavern** at 567 Hudson Street (where Dylan Thomas had his booze-laden last supper before being taken to St. Vincent's Hospital) and the bar at the **Lion's Head** at 59 Christopher east of Seventh, which still gets a literary crowd from the days when the *Village Voice* offices were nearby.

Jefferson Market Area

Across Seventh Avenue South, Waverly Place leads to—characteristically—Waverly Place. The street intersects itself at the triangle-shaped Northern Dispensary, which once dispensed medicine to Edgar Allan Poe and is known as the building with one side on two streets (the junction of Grove and Christopher) and two sides on one street (Waverly Place). Follow Waverly Place east to Gay Street, which, though it intersects Christopher, was so called as far back as 1827, long before the word got its present-day homosexual connotation. The street's original connotation of frivolity is best recalled at number 14, where Ruth McKenney wrote *My Sister Eileen,* the definitive play (later made into a musical and two films) about the time-honored tradition of Midwesterners moving to New York City.

At the other end of Gay, follow Christopher east to Greenwich Avenue (Note: Greenwich *Street,* way to the west, is a different entity); turn left on Greenwich and right on West 10th Street to see two more narrow Village streets: **Patchin Place** to the left before Sixth Avenue (John Masefield, Theodore Dreiser, and E. E. Cummings all lived there), and Milligan Place to the left on Sixth.

Take Sixth Avenue a block north to 11th Street, where on the northwest corner is one of many pizzerias in town that claims the prestigious title, The Original Ray's Pizza: The permanent line of loyal patrons is testimony that this is one of the best, if not the oldest. Across Sixth Avenue, at 76 West 11th Street, is the Second Shearith Israel Cemetery, a peaceful triangular plot (it was twice its present size until 11th Street was expanded in 1830), used by the congregation of the city's Spanish and Portuguese synagogue from 1805 to 1829. Across the street is an entrance to the main buildings of the **New School for Social Research**, founded in 1919 as an educational institution for adults, and referred to by Thomas Wolfe as the "School for Utility Cultures." Its graduate school at 65 Fifth Avenue enjoys a reputation for excellence in the academic world, particularly in the social sciences (Hannah Arendt and other exiled European intellectuals taught there), but its adult education division is better known among New Yorkers, who take courses for edification in an unusual variety of subjects ranging from basket weaving to Byzantine history (often merely as a pretext for meeting other adults, married and single) in its evening division. Walk through the school's pleasant sculpture garden in the main building to the 12th Street exit for a look at its 66 West 12th Street building. Room 712 in the building houses the recently restored 600-square-foot mural *The Coming Together of the Races,* painted by Mexican artist Jose Clemente Orozco in 1931.

Heading back down Sixth Avenue, take a look at the towering Victorian Gothic building at number 425. It was originally a courthouse, designed by Frederick Clarke Withers and Calvert Vaux (the architect of Central Park) in 1876. It is now the last remnant of a complex that included a women's jail, firehouse, and market on the adjacent property, now a bright spot of landscaping. Thanks to a 1967 conversion by Giorgio Cavaglieri, the building houses the **Jefferson Market** branch of the New York Public Library, though the neighborhood's most gentrified marketing takes place across the avenue at Balducci's, number 424. At 414 is **C. O. Bigelow Chemists**. Begun in 1838, it is New York's oldest continuously operating pharmacy. The famous counter that Truman Capote, Mel Brooks, and others once lunched at is gone; in its place, however, are more of the fine domestic and imported pharmaceuticals and grooming products for which the establishment is famous.

Head east on West 10th Street, which, like West 9th, 11th, and 12th streets between Sixth Avenue and University Place, is a neatly combed version of the twisting streets found in the West Village, complete with trees, 18th-century architecture, and literary associations (Mark Twain lived briefly at number 14, as its plaque commemorates). On the northwest corner of Fifth Avenue and West 10th Street is the 1840 Church of the Ascension, which contains stained-glass windows and an altar mural by John La Farge and a marble altar relief by Augustus Saint-Gaudens. At 47 Fifth Avenue, between 11th and 12th streets, is the Salmagundi Club, the oldest artists' club in America. The club was founded in 1870 at its present site, an 1853 mansion (the avenue was once lined with such residences). Among its members were John La Farge, Louis Comfort Tiffany, and Stanford White, and it still sponsors exhibitions, worth attending more for a look at the building's Victorian interior than its members' art—the best places for that nearby are the **Forbes Magazine Galleries** at 60 Fifth Avenue, famous for their Fabergé eggs, and the **Grey Art Gallery** at 33 Washington Place, which mounts temporary exhibitions to suit all shades of fancy.

Washington Square

Head south toward the arch of Washington Square—traditionally considered the heart of the Village—on this stretch of Fifth Avenue, one of the most pleasant few blocks for strolling in the city. At 1 Fifth Avenue is a towering apartment building with a popular bar-restaurant, **One Fifth,** on the ground floor; the building's south side flanks **Washington Mews**, originally stables behind the town houses along Washington Square North and now housing New York University faculty. (Its continuation, **MacDougal Alley,** lies behind the huge building at 2 Fifth Avenue and is entered from MacDougal Street.) The houses themselves are considered the finest examples of the Greek Revival style in America and provided the setting for Henry James's novel *Washington Square,* though the actual house, number 18, where his grandmother lived was torn down in 1950 for the cumbersome 2 Fifth Avenue apartment building. Over the years, John Dos Passos, Edward Hopper, and others were all fortunate enough to have lived in the houses, known as The Row.

The **Washington Arch**, which marks the beginning of Fifth Avenue, was designed by McKim, Mead & White in 1892 to replace a wooden arch erected on the spot in 1889 for the centenary of George Washington's presidential inauguration. The statue of *Washington as President* on the west pier of the arch is by Alexander Stirling Calder; Herman MacNeil is responsible for the east-pier statue, *Washington as Commander-in-Chief.*

As if in homage to the staid Washington Square residents portrayed by Henry James, both statues have their backs turned on the lively scene in the square. A walk through it can often be an urban obstacle course—dodging joggers, frantic frisbee players, and skateboarders, and drug dealers offering what sounds like "Sex! Sex!" but is actually street parlance for a type of marijuana called sensimillia. The more Jamesian residents of the area may wish that the square return to its former function as a hanging gallows (executions took place from the giant elm tree—said to be the oldest in the city—in the northwest section of the park) and potter's field, but the scene is generally quite harmless, dominated by the youth of **New York University**, the institution that owns most of the real estate around Washington Square.

On the square's south side is the Judson Memorial Baptist Church, an 1892 Romanesque church by McKim, Mead & White that contains more stained glass by John La Farge and a relief by Herbert Adams done to the designs of Augustus Saint-Gaudens. In the 1960s and 1970s it housed the Judson Dance Theater, where such seminal figures in the dance world as Trisha Brown, Simone Forte, Yvonne Rainer, and Twyla Tharp gave performances early in their careers. At 70 Washington Square South is a prominent New York University building that the *AIA Guide to New York City* amusingly dubs one of The Redskins: the hulking red-granite Elmer Holmes Bobst Library designed by Philip Johnson. (The other two, from the same quarry, are the André and Bella Meyer Physics Hall at 707 Broadway and Tisch Hall at 40 West 4th

Street.) Equally hulking buildings in the area are the I. M. Pei apartment blocks at 100–110 Bleecker Street and 505 La Guardia Place (a northern extension of SoHo's West Broadway), though the scale is somewhat softened by the Picasso sculpture, *Portrait of Sylvette,* in the building's central plaza. A plaque on the northwest corner of Washington Place and Greene Street commemorates the Triangle Shirtwaist Fire of 1911, in which 146 people perished in a blaze in a garment factory in the building because the fire exits had been locked by supervisors.

Before leaving the area, head south on **MacDougal Street** to one of the area's Italian cafés. Most evocative of Greenwich Village bohemia is **Caffè Reggio** at 119 MacDougal near 3rd Street, with its walls covered with paintings and discolored from decades of smoke and steam from its espresso machine. Farther down the street, at the corner of Bleecker, **Café Borgia** and **Le Figaro Café** sit opposite each other like funky Village versions of Café Flore and Les Deux Magots, while at 81 MacDougal is **Caffè Dante**, decorated with scenes of Florence. Any one of them makes a pleasant place for an afternoon of people watching, or to cap off a night at one of the nearby theaters such as the historic **Provincetown Playhouse** (133 MacDougal), where Village resident Eugene O'Neill had a number of plays produced, and the Sullivan Street Playhouse (181 Sullivan), where the charming production *The Fantasticks* has been running since 1960.

THE EAST VILLAGE

In the 19th century, parts of the East Village were pleasant residential areas. Believe it or not, Tompkins Square once had the appearance, almost, of an English park; the Astor, Vanderbilt, and Delano families all had town houses on what was at the time the most fashionable address in New York—Lafayette Street, then Lafayette Place.

The area has now gone from high culture to counterculture. Funky street-artist mosaics decorate sidewalks and lampposts. Its principal street, **St. Mark's Place** (the equivalent of 8th Street), is the main drag of the city's residual punk population, with the attendant fashion and music scenes, as typified by Susan Seidelman's film *Desperately Seeking Susan*. The seeds of the 1960s grass-roots movement have sprouted somewhat scraggly results in the East

Village, with the proliferation of social-realist murals and public gardens along its eastern perimeter.

Though the eastern portion of the East Village (the area including Avenues A, B, C, and D—called Alphabet City) is a center of New York's heavy drug trade, there is much to see elsewhere in the vicinity. The best time to go is on a warm Sunday morning, when most of the usual crowd is sleeping off the previous night's excesses, for a punk-watching brunch at, say, **Kiev** (117 Second Avenue at 7th Street), which serves Eastern European specialties. Preceded by a visit to the **Astor Place** area, an afternoon in the East Village can still be a pleasant experience. There's not much to the architecture of the eastern part of the East Village beyond what longtime resident Allen Ginsberg described in his poem "Waking in New York" as "tenement streets' brick sagging cornices" and the spontaneous temporary shelters put up by the homeless residents of Tompkins Square Park, which occupies the area between 7th and 10th streets and Avenues A and B.

Bernard Tony Rosenthal's huge, rotating, black steel cube called *Alamo,* at Astor Place, is one of the principal rendezvous of the East Village. Its shape unconsciously echoes many of the hairdos created just down the street at Astor Place Hair Designers (2 Astor Place), where the line of punks and New York University students waiting to be cheaply shorn and shaped often extends around the block. Walk south down Lafayette Street to Colonnade Row at 428–434, a group of four of the original nine town houses called La Grange Terrace that once stood on the spot (number 430 houses **Indochine**, a popular and trendy Vietnamese restaurant). The houses date from 1833, but the Corinthian columns could almost be original, they are in such bad shape. Number 376 Lafayette is an 1888 warehouse building designed by Henry J. Hardenbergh, architect of the Plaza Hotel and the Dakota Apartments. Cross Lafayette Street and continue back uptown to the northeast corner of East 4th Street, where at 399 Lafayette there is another noteworthy warehouse, the De Vinne Press Building, designed by Babb, Cook & Willard in 1885. Down East 4th Street, at number 29, is another remnant of the area's fashionable days, the Old Merchant's House, a Greek Revival residence dating from 1832. Back up Lafayette, number 425 is the **Public Theater**. Originally the Astor Library, it was converted to theater spaces in 1966 by Giorgio Cavaglieri.

At the corner of Lafayette and Astor Place, step through

The East Village

yards 250
meters 250

East River

East River Park

FDR DRIVE

AVENUE D
AVENUE C
AVENUE B
AVENUE A

E. 8 ST.
E. 7 ST.
E. 6 ST.
E. 5 ST.

E. HOUSTON ST.

Stuyvesant Town

Tompkins Square Park

E A S T

V I L L A G E

E. 16 ST.
E. 15 ST.
E. 14 ST.
E. 13 ST.
E. 12 ST.
E. 11 ST.
E. 10 ST.
E. 9 ST.
ST. MARK'S PL.
E. 4 ST.
E. 3 ST.

FIRST AVE.
SECOND AVE.
THIRD AVE.
BOWERY

IRVING PL.
PARK AVE. SOUTH
Union Sq.
FOURTH AVE.
UNIVERSITY PL.

LAFAYETTE ST.
ASTOR PL.
BROADWAY
WAVERLY PL.
WASHINGTON PL.
E. 8 ST.
GREAT JONES ST.
BOND ST.
E. 3 ST.
BLEECKER ST.
LAGUARDIA PL.

Washington Square Park

the morass of vendors selling what seem to be articles lifted from poor people's refuse bins, and walk past the Cooper Union Foundation Building, the centerpiece of **Cooper Union for the Advancement of Science and Art**, an important art, architecture, and engineering school. Its 1859 brownstone exterior masks a total reconstruction, which gave the building a high-tech interior in 1975. On the south side of the building is an 1894 bronze statue of the school's industrialist founder, Peter Cooper, by Augustus Saint-Gaudens, with a base by Stanford White.

Continue back to St. Mark's Place for a strong dose of street theater. (Real avant-garde theater can be still found at another area cultural landmark, the **La MaMa Experimental Theater** on 74 East 4th Street.) To get a taste of the variety of the neighborhood's activities, take a look at the bulletin board of the recently enlarged **St. Mark's Bookshop** at 12 St. Mark's Place. Boisterous punks, shops, and restaurants characterize St. Mark's, which has the appearance of unusual width because most of its buildings were built farther back from the sidewalk than on other streets in the city. Pause at **Gem Spa**, on the southwest corner of St. Mark's Place and Second Avenue, for an egg cream. The traditional Lower East Side refresher is now made here by East Indians, but they prepare the concoction well (though not as well, perhaps, as the Indian food served in the profusion of Indian restaurants on and around East 6th Street—**Gaylord's** at 87 First Avenue is one of the best).

Head up Second Avenue, where at number 140 is the Ukrainian National Home, the center for the area's sizable Ukrainian community: There is an excellent and inexpensive restaurant inside, and a museum of Ukrainian folk art at number 203. On the northwest corner of Second Avenue and 10th Street is the area's most historic building, the **Church of St. Mark's-in-the-Bowery**. Built on the site of Dutch Governor Peter Stuyvesant's original mansion (he is buried in the cemetery next to the church), it dates from 1799. Its Episcopalian congregation is far from stodgy, however, sponsoring an innovative program of poetry and performing arts.

To the west is Stuyvesant Street, a remaining tract of the former carriage lane that once extended from the Bowery to the governor's mansion (the Stuyvesant Fish House at number 21 dates from 1803). Refreshment may be taken locally at **The Cloister**, a relaxing indoor-outdoor café-restaurant at 238 East 9th Street, or **McSorley's Old Ale**

House (15 East 7th Street). A pleasant, dingy dive taken over by Cooper Union and New York University students during the academic year, McSorley's dates from 1854 and claims to be the oldest bar in the city.

MIDTOWN

By Dwight V. Gast

Midtown, the huge chunk of Manhattan between 14th Street and Central Park, is where most of the city's business is conducted. Midtown's boisterous street scene reflects its high-pressured essence. Besides the handfuls of Rolaids gulped down behind closed doors, there is much evidence of the relentless level of stress in this part of town. Construction workers hammer away with pneumatic drills as sidewalk superintendents voice their criticism of the new buildings shooting up throughout the area. Office clerks, coffee cups and food from a sidewalk vendor in hand, flock to feed in any space with a vaguely horizontal surface. Pedestrians crowd the sidewalks during the rush and lunch hours. Messengers whiz by on bicycles, often the fastest-moving vehicles in an impatient procession of honking trucks, taxis, buses, and cars on the rigid grid pattern of the streets.

But whether or not their business takes them there, New Yorkers and out-of-towners occasionally go to Midtown to have fun in spite of themselves. In addition to the charms of the older neighborhoods of its southern portion, Midtown is where you'll find major department stores and minor specialty shops, a strong concentration of bars and restaurants, Broadway and off-Broadway theaters, some of the most famous and glamorous buildings of the New York skyline, and—chances are—your hotel.

MAJOR INTEREST

Union Square area
Gramercy Park area
Madison Square and the Ladies' Mile
The Empire State Building

Times Square
The New York Public Library
Grand Central Station
The United Nations
Rockefeller Center
The Museum of Modern Art
Major department stores
Broadway Theater District

UNION SQUARE

Just north of the East Village, above 14th Street between Broadway and Third Avenue, is the Union Square–Gramercy Park area. Originally named Union Place after its role in uniting Bloomingdale Road (now Broadway) and Bowery Road (Fourth Avenue), Union Square was a residential square with its own private park in the mid-19th century, much as Gramercy Park is today. (One vestige of that genteel era is **Grace Church**, four blocks south at Broadway and East 10th Street. Built in 1845 by James Renwick, Jr., it served the area's Episcopal congregation.) After a brief stint as New York's theater district in the 1850s, Union Square became the city's rallying point for radical political groups, a fact somewhat abstractly alluded to in the statue of Gandhi in its southeast pedestrian section. Until fairly recently the area flourished as a center for budget department stores. Klein's "On the Square" was recently replaced with considerable disunion by a towering apartment complex immodestly named after its developer and topped with pyramids. It blocks the classic view of the Consolidated Edison power company clock tower, which was somewhat of a symbol of the square—though, tellingly, it often gave the wrong time.

After a period of decline, most of the area's famous book dealers moved on (**The Strand** at Broadway and 12th Street is the last of them), and the square was primarily used by drug dealers. Union Square, however, has made a complete turnaround. On Wednesdays, Fridays, and Saturdays, New York's largest greenmarket takes place there: New Yorkers, often pushing infants in strollers, come to finger the radicchio, sample the goat cheese, and generally exchange pleasantries instead of the usual business cards. Trendy American restaurants such as the **Union Square Café** (21 East 16th Street) and **America** (9 East 18th Street) have given the area the finishing touches

W. 60 ST.

W. 59 ST.

COLUMBUS
CIRCLE

*Central
Park*

CENTRAL PARK SOUTH

Roosevelt
Hospital

W. 58 ST.

W. 57 ST.

**Carnegie
Hall**

W. 56 ST.

**City
Center**

W. 55 ST.

TENTH AVE.

NINTH AVE.

EIGHTH AVE.

BROADWAY

SEVENTH AVE.

W. 54 ST.

W. 53 ST.

W. 52 ST.

W. 51 ST.

**Radio City
Music Hall**

W. 50 ST.

W. 49 ST.

T H E A T E R

W. 48 ST.

D I S T R I C T

W. 47 ST.

SIXTH AVE. (AVENUE OF THE AMERICAS)

W. 46 ST.

N

W. 45 ST.

W. 44 ST.

Times
Sq.

**New York
Convention and
Visitors Bureau** →

W. 43 ST.

W. 42 ST.

*Bryant
Park*

W. 41 ST.

**Port Authority
Bus Terminal**

W. 40 ST.

W. 39 ST.

TENTH AVE.

DYER AVE.

NINTH AVE.

EIGHTH AVE.

SEVENTH AVE.

BROADWAY

W. 38 ST.

W. 37 ST.

← To Javits Convention Center

W. 36 ST.

W. 35 ST.

Herald
Sq.

Macy's

W. 34 ST.

G A R M E N T

W. 33 ST.

D I S T R I C T

W. 32 ST.

**Felt
Forum**

**Madison
Square
Garden**

Penn Station

Midtown

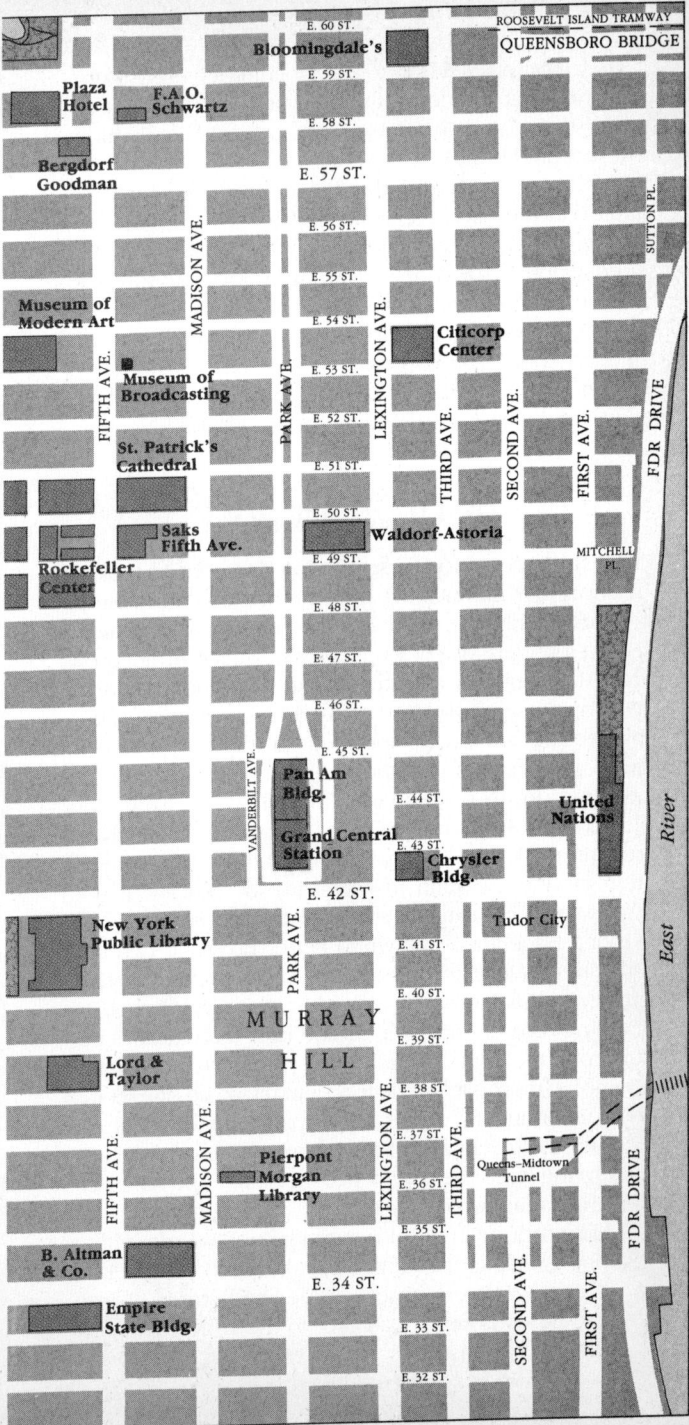

of gentrification, leading to the opening of even more meteoric establishments throughout the general area (see also the Madison Square and Ladies' Mile/Fashion Row sections below).

In addition to Gandhi, there is an unusual amount of statuary in the park. Henry Kirke Brown's 1855 *George Washington* is the city's first monumental bronze; the same sculptor's *Lincoln* is also there; Frédéric Auguste Bartholdi, who created the Statue of Liberty, was given another chance to honor his native France with his *Lafayette*. Karl Adolf Donndorf designed the square's elaborate drinking fountain, and Anthony de Francisci did bas-reliefs for the base of the Independence Flagstaff.

GRAMERCY PARK

Take 14th Street a block east to Irving Place. Have a look at the enormous mural above the entrance to the **Palladium** at 126 East 14th Street. The club was New York's trendiest disco a few seasons back but has since been invaded by what Manhattanites call "the bridge-and-tunnel crowd," meaning those whose entry to the island is via one of the engineering structures specified in the expression—therefore, outsiders. (Another disparaging term for almost the same group of people is "BBQ," which stands for "Bronx, Brooklyn, and Queens.") The mural, by Hank Pressing and Jeff Green, contains an image of Pallas Athena pulling aside a curtain to reveal a rock concert. If not exactly social realism, it is at least one sort of social reality.

Irving Place leads uptown to **Pete's Tavern** at 129 East 18th Street. Like McSorley's Old Ale House in the East Village, it claims to be the oldest bar in the city, though its founding date of 1864 is a decade later than McSorley's. But from the look of the lively young crowd usually assembled there for simple food and drink, no one seems to be counting on more than a good time, let alone accuracy: Both Pete's and **Sal Anthony's**, a restaurant back at 55 Irving Place (near 17th Street), claim to be the place where O. Henry wrote *The Gift of the Magi*.

Head north on Irving Place to Gramercy Park, with a sidelong glance at East 19th Street between Irving Place and Third Avenue, a peaceful tree-lined street. To see how the peace is kept, head over to the **Police Academy Museum** at 235 East 20th Street, which has the world's largest collection of police memorabilia.

Gramercy Park and Chelsea

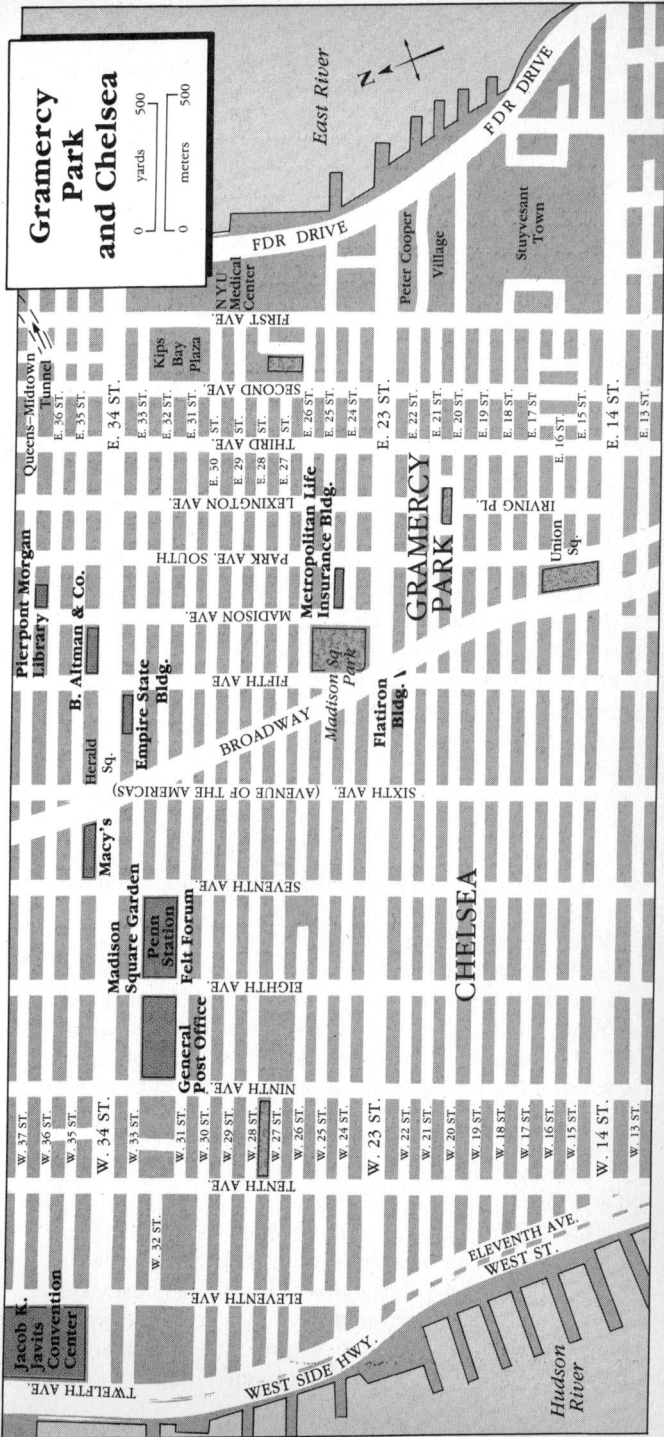

Jacob K. Javits Convention Center

Macy's
Madison Square Garden
Penn Station
Felt Forum
General Post Office

Herald Sq.
Empire State Bldg.

B. Altman & Co.
Pierpont Morgan Library

Madison Sq. Park
Flatiron Bldg.
Metropolitan Life Insurance Bldg.

Kips Bay Plaza

NYU Medical Center

GRAMERCY PARK

Union Sq.

IRVING PL.

CHELSEA

Peter Cooper Village
Stuyvesant Town

East River

Hudson River

FDR DRIVE
Queens–Midtown Tunnel

WEST SIDE HWY.
WEST ST.
ELEVENTH AVE.
TWELFTH AVE.
ELEVENTH AVE.
TENTH AVE.
NINTH AVE.
EIGHTH AVE.
SEVENTH AVE.
SIXTH AVE. (AVENUE OF THE AMERICAS)
BROADWAY
FIFTH AVE.
MADISON AVE.
PARK AVE. SOUTH
LEXINGTON AVE.
THIRD AVE.
SECOND AVE.
FIRST AVE.

0   yards   500
0   meters   500

N

W. 37 ST.
W. 36 ST.
W. 35 ST.
W. 34 ST.
W. 33 ST.
W. 32 ST.
W. 31 ST.
W. 30 ST.
W. 29 ST.
W. 28 ST.
W. 27 ST.
W. 26 ST.
W. 25 ST.
W. 24 ST.
W. 23 ST.
W. 22 ST.
W. 21 ST.
W. 20 ST.
W. 19 ST.
W. 18 ST.
W. 17 ST.
W. 16 ST.
W. 15 ST.
W. 14 ST.
W. 13 ST.

E. 36 ST.
E. 35 ST.
E. 34 ST.
E. 33 ST.
E. 32 ST.
E. 31 ST.
E. 30
E. 29 ST.
E. 28
E. 27
E. 26 ST.
E. 25 ST.
E. 24 ST.
E. 23 ST.
E. 22 ST.
E. 21 ST.
E. 20 ST.
E. 19 ST.
E. 18 ST.
E. 17 ST.
E. 16 ST.
E. 15 ST.
E. 14 ST.
E. 13 ST.

Gramercy Park begins at East 20th Street, there called Gramercy Park South. The park was built in 1831 and bears a striking similarity to squares in London, a fact that status-conscious New Yorkers often point to with pride. The park is private (area residents have their own keys to the stately iron gates), but if you peer through the iron fence you can catch some interesting statuary. Children especially enjoy a bronze in the southeast corner, Gregg Wyatt's *Fantasy Fountain,* with the water spouting from dancing giraffes. In the corner of the park is Edmond T. Quinn's statue of *Edwin Booth as Hamlet.* It faces the actor's former residence at 16 Gramercy Park South, which now houses The Players, a club founded by Booth, who commissioned Stanford White to remodel it. Besides Booth and White, Thomas Nast and Winston Churchill have counted themselves among the club's members. (Churchill's mother, Jennie Jerome, was born nearby, in a mansion that once stood on the site of the southeast corner of Madison Avenue and 26th Street.) The mansion at number 15 Gramercy Park South, remodeled by Calvert Vaux, is another club, the National Arts Club.

A stroll around Gramercy Park is enough to get a general sense of the square's charms: Specific points of interest include numbers 3 and 4 Gramercy Park West, with their fine cast-iron porches.

Walk west on 21st Street to Park Avenue South, where you'll see Gothic-style Calvary Church, designed in 1846 by James Renwick, Jr., who was also responsible for Grace Church and St. Patrick's Cathedral. Eleanor Roosevelt was baptized there in 1884.

If the Roosevelt family intrigues you, walk down to 28 East 20th Street, the birthplace and boyhood **home of Theodore Roosevelt**, now owned by the National Park Service. The home is actually a reconstruction, an architect and decorator's understated interpretation of "Speak softly and carry a big stick." From there, the most convenient place to end your visit to Gramercy Park would be **Positano** (250 Park Avenue South near 20th), a professional's wateringhole where the speaking is far from soft. If you prefer more meditative surroundings, it's a short walk to 108 Lexington Avenue, between East 27th and East 28th streets, in an area increasingly becoming known as **Little India** because of its influx of East Indian businesses. There you'll find **Annapurna**, an Indian restaurant with a mural of a sunset over the swaying palms of an Indian beach. If you like what you eat, you can purchase some of the ingredients (along with other Indian products) at the Annapurna Indian store around the corner at 126 East 28th Street.

THE MADISON SQUARE AREA

Located at the intersection of Broadway and Fifth Avenue, between East 23rd and East 26th streets, Madison Square is another version of Union Square, although rather than greengrocers filling its expanses, you're likely to find residents from the nearby hotels: Once the most glamorous in the city, the accommodations are now inhabited by welfare recipients. Madison Square has also been newly refurbished, has its own nearby clock tower (the Metropolitan Life Insurance Company headquarters), and boasts an abundance of statuary. One of its earliest monuments was the long arm of the Statue of Liberty, placed there as an early (and unsuccessful) ploy to raise funds for the statue's erection after it had been exhibited in the Philadelphia Centennial Exposition in 1876. The long arm of Chester Alan Arthur is also commemorated in Madison Square: Bronzes of the president and his associates William H. Seward, David Glasgow Farragut, and Roscoe Conkling adorn the park. Of these, the Admiral Farragut Monument on the north end of the park is the most interesting. Created by Augustus Saint-Gaudens in 1880, it is especially noteworthy for the relief sculptures of Loyalty and Courage adorning its base, which was designed by Stanford White.

White was responsible for the square's most famous architectural monument—the original Madison Square Garden, which stood on the northeast corner of East 26th Street and Madison Avenue. Demolished in 1925, the Garden was also the scene of White's demise: He was shot dead in 1906 in its Roof Garden Theater by Harry K. Thaw, the jealous husband of one of White's former mistresses, Evelyn Nesbit. Almost as dramatic architecturally is the 1900 Appellate Division of the New York State Supreme Court, a block south of the site, at the northeast corner of 25th Street and Madison Avenue. A small Palladian palace, it is a decorator's extravaganza, covered with idealized statuary depicting historical personages and lofty themes, and outfitted with an ornate interior. Among its noteworthy decorations is Daniel Chester French's *Justice,* the fourth statue from the left as you face the façade.

Today the most famous piece of architecture near Madison Square is the 1902 **Flatiron Building**, across 23rd Street from the square at the intersection of Broadway and Fifth Avenue. Immortalized in the photographs of Edward Steichen, the building is one of Chicago architect Daniel H. Burnham's masterpieces. When completed, it was the tallest building in the world and had an observation platform on top. Its triangular shape gave the building its name (it was originally called the Fuller Building), but to some it also suggests the prow of a ship and indeed does create a sense of movement. The shape also creates an unusual flurry of air currents, and in the building's first years men used to gather to watch the billowing skirts of 23rd Street's female shoppers blown about, giving rise to the expression "23 skiddoo!" which constables used in order to shoo gapers from the area. Real-estate developers are now trying to attract them, and the name of the area they've dubbed "SoFi" (*So*uth of the *Fi*atiron) has caught on at least with one local establishment, an elegant restaurant called **Sofi** at 102 Fifth Avenue, between 15th and 16th streets.

Though the new development has attracted publishing companies and advertising agencies to the area, the photographers whose flashes brightened local lofts in recent years are now being driven farther west to less expensive studio space in Chelsea as many of the buildings are being converted to apartments.

North of Madison Square are two churches of note. At 272 Fifth Avenue, on the northwest corner of West 28th Street, is the Marble Collegiate Reformed Church, an 1854 Gothic-style church by S. A. Warner. Dr. Norman Vincent Peale, author of *The Power of Positive Thinking,* was pastor here. Around the corner, at 1 East 29th Street, is the Gothic-style Church of the Transfiguration. Built from 1849 to 1856, in 1870 it was the site of the burial rites for an actor named George Holland, after a nearby church refused to perform them and referred the funeral party to a "little church around the corner." Since then it has been known as the Little Church around the Corner, and is a favorite spot for actors. It contains a stained glass window by John La Farge depicting Edwin Booth as Hamlet, and sponsors a small acting company. Around the corner from the Transfiguration, up at 120 Madison Avenue, is McKim, Mead & White's 1905 Colony Club, now home of the American Academy of Dramatic Arts.

CHELSEA

Just west of the Flatiron District is Chelsea, which lies roughly between 14th and 30th streets from Sixth Avenue to the Hudson River. It was named for the estate of Captain Thomas Clarke, which covered most of the area when it was laid out in 1750. His scholarly grandson Clement Clarke Moore, the author of the *Compendious Lexicon of the Hebrew Language* but better remembered for the Christmas poem *A Visit from St. Nicholas* ("'Twas the night before Christmas," etc.), grew up in the family mansion on the site of Eighth Avenue and West 23rd Street. Though Clement Clarke Moore donated a block of his land for the General Theological Seminary in the 1830s, much of Chelsea's later history is undistinguished. The Hudson River Railroad brought warehouses and tenements along 11th Avenue in the 1850s, and New York's first elevated railroad brought crowds to a flourishing theater district in the 1870s. Artists and writers moved in when the theaters moved to Times Square (the old theaters and warehouses were briefly recycled as movie studios), and creative residents—including rock musicians—still add a touch of character to the area. Its predominant impression, however, comes from the large-scale apartment buildings scattered throughout the area and the palatial cast-iron buildings that once housed department stores along Sixth Avenue. The combination of settled dust and its current version raised by widespread construction gives the neighborhood a rather gritty feel.

You'll most likely go to Chelsea for a specific purpose. The area's single largest concentration of retail clothing is at **Barney's** (Seventh Avenue and West 17th Street). Dance concerts are held at the **Joyce Theater** (175 Eighth Avenue, at 19th Street) and the **Bessie Schönberg Theater** (219 West 19th Street west of Seventh Avenue); theater is performed at the **Hudson Guild Theatre** (441 West 26th Street between Ninth and Tenth avenues) and the **WPA Theatre** (519 West 23rd, at 10th Avenue). Several interesting bars and restaurants—such as **Chelsea Trattoria** and **Rogers and Barbero**—cluster around the Joyce Theater on Eighth Avenue. However, there are a few other sights that make Chelsea a pleasant enough stroll in its own right.

Start at the **Chelsea Hotel** at 222 West 23rd Street. One of the city's first cooperative apartment buildings when it was built in 1884, it is even more famous for the roster of celebrity artists who have lived there, from Mark Twain and O. Henry to Virgil Thomson, Janis Joplin, and Sid Vicious. The lives and deaths of these last two figures (Vicious was the subject of the Alex Cox film, *Sid and Nancy,* part of which was shot in the Chelsea) were eerily prefigured in a poem called "The Hotel Chelsea," written by another of the hotel's noted residents, Edgar Lee Masters:

> Today will pass as currents of the air that veer and
> die.
> Tell me how souls can be
> Such flames of suffering and ecstasy.
> Then fare as winds fare?

The pleasant eclecticism of the hotel's architectural style still extends to its guest roster; after inspecting its façade, take a look at the lobby to see its grand staircase and perhaps some of the regulars.

Walk down Eighth Avenue to West 20th Street, the heart of the Chelsea Historic District, a quiet area filled with late 18th-century residences ranging from town houses to large apartment buildings. On the north side of West 20th Street between Ninth and Tenth avenues is the General Theological Seminary, a conglomeration of 19th-century buildings, the oldest of which is the 1836 West Building at 5–6 Chelsea Square. Note the row houses on the south side of West 20th Street: 406–418, known as Cushman Row, dates from 1840; the Italianate houses at 446–450 from 1855.

Head up Tenth Avenue to West 23rd Street, where the entire north side of the block is taken up by a vast apartment complex called London Terrace, built in 1930. A more appetizing homage to the era is the **Empire Diner** at 210 Tenth Avenue at the corner of West 22nd Street, a 24-hour Art Deco–style eating establishment, which gets a glassy-eyed crowd (largely of the *Saturday Night Fever* variety) from the nearby discos during the wee hours. Just up Tenth Avenue at the corner of 24th Street is **Chelsea Commons**, a local hangout with good burgers, a fireplace, and an outdoor terrace.

LADIES' MILE/FASHION ROW

Aficionados of cast-iron buildings should head back east at this point, where on Sixth Avenue between West 23rd and West 18th streets they'll pass the cast-iron skeletons of the department stores that flourished in the area in the late 19th century. This part of town was so devoted to shopping that Broadway was known as the Ladies' Mile, and Sixth Avenue was called Fashion Row. The northern part of the area is now given over to wholesale florists, on Sixth Avenue around West 28th Street, and garment manufacturing—one of New York's largest industries—centered slightly to the north on Seventh Avenue in the 30s: the **Garment District**. Seventh Avenue, in fact, is called Fashion Avenue between 26th and 28th streets, where the **Fashion Institute of Technology**, a school for those interested in the clothing industry as a profession, is located.

Begin back down at 32–36 West 23rd Street, the site of the 1878 Stern's Dry Goods Store. At 695–709 Sixth Avenue is what was originally the 1889 Erlich Brothers Dry Goods Store; 675–691 was the 1900 Adams Dry Goods Store (the third and final cemetery of the Spanish and Portuguese Synagogue, used between 1829 and 1851, is just around the corner from it at 98–110 West 21st Street); the former 1875 Hugh O'Neill Dry Goods Store is at 655–671 Sixth Avenue (across the street at 47 West 20th Street is the 1846 Church of the Holy Communion by Richard Upjohn, preserved for better or worse as the **Limelight discotheque**); 621 Sixth Avenue was the site of B. Altman from the building's beginning in 1876 until 1906; and the 1895 616–632 Sixth Avenue building housed the Siegel-Cooper Dry Goods Store.

To best get an authentic taste of the era, head back east over to the **Old Town Bar** near Union Square, at 45 East 18th Street, between Broadway and Park Avenue South. It serves inexpensive sandwiches and drinks in an original, unpretentious 1892 setting. Once fortified, you might want to take a look at some more stores of the Ladies' Mile. Numbers 881–887 Broadway (at 19th Street), by Griffith Thomas, housed the Arnold Constable Dry Goods Store in 1869 (extensions were made in 1873 and 1877); a block north, 900 Broadway is an 1887 loft building by McKim, Mead & White; 901 Broadway was the Lord & Taylor Dry Goods Store in 1869; and finally, a block west at 153–157

Fifth Avenue, is the first headquarters of Charles Scribner's Sons publishing company, built in 1894 by Ernest Flagg.

THE EMPIRE STATE BUILDING

With the demise of Pennsylvania Station, there is little of architectural interest in the 30s. The old station has been replaced with the present-day **Penn Station** (currently undergoing renovation) and **Madison Square Garden**, which architecture critic Paul Goldberger calls "graceless, sloppy, cheap." You may be drawn to the neighborhood for any number of practicalities, however. You could be taking part in a gathering at the immense **Jacob K. Javits Convention Center** (at 655 West 34th Street, near the Hudson River). You may have business at McKim, Mead & White's classically inspired 1913 General Post Office at Eighth Avenue and 33rd Street (open 24 hours), or at **Macy's** (Herald Square, at the intersection of Broadway and Sixth Avenue at West 34th Street). There are variety stores along Fifth Avenue between 34th and 57th streets whose "going out of business" signs are such permanent fixtures they seem to announce the name of a local chain store. Or you may want to attend an exhibition from the extensive permanent collection of drawings and manuscripts at the **Pierpont Morgan Library**, a genteel 1906 McKim, Mead & White mansion built for banker and financier John Pierpont Morgan, Sr. (33 East 36th Street at Madison), followed by a stroll past the fine town houses on East 36th Street between Third and Lexington avenues. The 30s, in short, are a spotty area for sightseers.

One sight towers above it all, however: The Empire State Building. Though it opened in 1931 after a brisk two years of construction, by 1949 the Empire State Building had already accumulated enough history to be thus lauded by E. B. White in *Here is New York:*

> It even managed to reach the highest point in the sky at the lowest point of the depression. The Empire State Building shot twelve hundred and fifty feet into the air when it was madness to put out as much as six inches of new growth. (The building has a mooring mast no dirigible has ever been tied to; it employs a man to flush toilets in slack times; it has been hit by an airplane in a fog, struck countless times by lightning, and been jumped off by so many unhappy

people that pedestrians instinctively quicken step when passing Fifth Avenue and 34th Street.)

In spite of the higher elevations of the Sears Tower in Chicago and the World Trade Center in their own city, to New Yorkers the Empire State will always be the tallest building in the world—they are inhabitants of the Empire State, after all. Its observation deck is as popular for its views of the city as it was when the building opened, its power to amuse and excite as alive now with the bright lights—color-coordinated for the holidays—that illuminate its crown as it was when used for the final scene in the original 1933 *King Kong*.

So just enjoy it. Enjoy its superlatives, beginning with the **Guinness World Records Exhibit Hall** in its lobby. Enjoy the high-speed elevator ride up to the 80th floor, the shorter ride to the observation decks (open from 9:30 A.M. to midnight) on the 86th floor and the 102nd floor. And, above all, enjoy the views, which extend imperially 50 miles in every direction.

42ND STREET

True to the lyric in the title song of its namesake 1933 Busby Berkeley musical, 42nd Street truly is "where the underworld can meet the elite." Its western end, particularly the area around Times Square, is still occupied by the underworld (though legions of pimps, prostitutes, and pornographers have replaced the Irish street gangs that gave the area the name Hell's Kitchen), while the apartment complex of Tudor City at its eastern end remains one of New York's better addresses.

Times Square

Be prudent if you begin your visit in darkness before an evening at one of the area's Broadway theaters, because Times Square is every bit as "naughty, bawdy, gawdy," and "sporty" as it was when Ruby Keeler used those adjectives to describe it in the 1933 musical. That was a far cry from the carriage-trade days of the late 19th century, when it was called Long Acre after the London district. Times Square was at its gaudiest earlier in this century. Dozens of legitimate theaters—later replaced by movie palaces— flourished, and the signs were made up of neon lights with such added attractions as real waterfalls and gargantuan smoke rings. Even some of the current plans for redevelopment are playful Postmodern adaptations of this tradition, calling for sparkling sidewalks, colorful reflective façades, and more neon.

Darkness is the optimal time to witness the dazzling effect of Times Square's lights, best described in 1923 by British writer G. K. Chesterton in *What I Saw in America:*

> When I had looked at the lights of Broadway by night, I made to my American friends an innocent remark that seemed for some reason to amuse them. I had looked, not without joy, at that long kaleidoscope of coloured lights arranged in large letters and sprawling trade-marks, advertising everything, from pork to pianos, through the agency of the two most vivid and most mystical of the gifts of God; colour and fire. I said to them, in my simplicity, "What a glorious garden of wonder this would be, to any one who was lucky enough to be unable to read."

There is plenty to read, of varying usefulness, on the signs as well as by way of the literature dispensed at the New York Convention and Visitors Bureau at 158 West 42nd Street. Take a look at the building at its southern edge, 1 Times Square, which used to be Times Tower, the headquarters of *The New York Times.* The sphere that marks the beginning of the New Year still descends to a celebratory crowd each New Year's Eve, but if you're there at other times of the year you can still get into a celebratory mood at the bar-restaurant called **The View** (1535 Broadway, between 45th and 46th), the only revolving restaurant in New York, and true to its name, atop the Marriott Marquis hotel. More traditional amenities in the area range from hot dogs with the hoi polloi at one of Nathan's two locations in the vicinity (1482 and 1515 Broadway) to hobnobbing with show folk, either expensively at **Sardi's** (234 West 44th Street, between Seventh and Eighth avenues) or more moderately at **Joe Allen** (326 West 46th Street). This last place is on a block called Restaurant Row, a group of restaurants between Eighth and Ninth avenues in front of which you're likely to see a patrol of young men sporting red berets and tee-shirts. Called the Guardian Angels, they are part of a self-appointed peacekeeping force that keeps watch in the subways and other potentially dangerous parts of the city and were recently hired by the street's restaurateurs to keep drug dealers off the block.

If you go under cover of daylight, you may want to look at specific pieces of architecture: The 1931 McGraw-Hill Building at 330 West 42nd Street (unfortunately located next to the squalor in and around the Port Authority Bus Terminal) is a Modernist masterpiece, complete with jazzy Art Deco lobby and a blue-green terra-cotta skin. Returning to Times Square, you'll notice a long lineup of movie houses between Eighth and Seventh avenues. They were originally legitimate theaters when they were built in the 1890s, and if you venture into one of the action-adventure movies that predominate along with pornography, you can still watch a strangely theatrical phenomenon: The lively and largely harmless spectators scream and shout back at the screen as if the movie were an audience-participation theatrical performance.

Of the Broadway theaters still used for their original purpose in the **Theater District**, the oldest and most interesting is the 1903 **Lyceum** at 149 West 45th Street. Before leaving the area, note the **TKTS** booth at the north end of Times Square near the statue of George M. "Give My Regards to Broadway" Cohan. It sells half-price tickets to Broadway shows on the day of the event (after 10:00 A.M. for matinees, 3:00 P.M. for evening performances).

New York Public Library Area

Walk east on 42nd Street to Sixth Avenue, where construction and drug dealers currently obscure Bryant Park and you'll find another discount-ticket booth, specializing in music and dance. The park is named for William Cullen Bryant, who is commemorated there by a 1911 bronze.

Continue east along 42nd Street toward Fifth Avenue. The ski-slope building at 41 West 42nd Street is the W. R. Grace Building, Skidmore, Owings & Merrill's answer to the setback requirements of the zoning regulations. Its shape has been heavily criticized, but it does provide plenty of the requisite space for public amenities at its base (there is a passageway through it to West 43rd Street), and along with the plaza of the Graduate Center of the City University of New York next to it, at number 33, it is a popular spot for office workers to sun themselves during warm weather.

Office workers, scholars, and monumental lion sculptures alike sun themselves in front of the Central Research Division of the **New York Public Library**, between 40th and 42nd streets on Fifth Avenue. The wonders of the 1911 Beaux Arts masterpiece by Carrère & Hastings, which with Bryant Park occupies the site of the former city reservoir, can be pointed out to you by the volunteers who conduct free tours of the building (Monday through Saturday, 11:00 A.M. and 2:00 P.M.). You may also inspect its lavish interior yourself and test the strength of its research collection of over six million volumes by calling up a title on the computer system recently installed in its main reading room, number 315. Exhibits of works from its collection are often held throughout the building.

East 42nd Street

Continue across East 42nd Street to another Beaux Arts landmark, the 1903–1913 **Grand Central Terminal** by Reed & Stem and Warren & Wetmore, at 42nd and Park Avenue. The Municipal Arts Society gives enthusiastic tours of the building free of charge on Wednesdays at 12:30, but at other times feel free to wander its expanses on your own. It only becomes "as busy as Grand Central Station" during rush hour; at most other times it is almost a refuge, as the homeless people inhabiting its bowels will attest. Its most intimate cranny is near the entrance to the Oyster Bar restaurant on the lower level. Stand in one corner of the brick vault and whisper sweet nothings: Through an acoustic oddity, they can be heard clearly in the opposite corner. The **Oyster Bar** is also an excellent place for a meal, the expense of which may be mitigated by ordering a simple bowl of clam chowder at the lunch counter. Upstairs, note the constellations twinkling on the ceiling before you venture outdoors onto 42nd Street to admire the sculpture group by Jules-Felix Coutan entitled *Transportation* above a stately clock. Mercury's flight seems somewhat grounded by the Pan Am Building, a 1963 monolith by Pietro Belluschi and Walter Gropius rising behind it over Park Avenue and dwarfing everything in sight.

There is more art across the street at the branch of the **Whitney Museum of American Art** in the Philip Morris Building (entrance on the southwest corner of West 42nd Street and Pershing Square). Another Midtown refuge, it mounts exhibits of contemporary art on a temporary basis, but permanent fixtures are the creditable cappuccino and espresso served at its counter.

Continue east on East 42nd Street for more architectural marvels, each of which sports a highly decorative lobby. At 110 East 42nd Street is the 1923 Romanesque Bowery Savings Bank. At 122 East 42nd is the 1929 paisley-skinned Chanin Building, and across from it another familiar shape on the New York City skyline, the **Chrysler Building**. Designed by William Van Alen and built in 1930, it was the tallest building in the world until the Empire State surpassed it, but it is detail, not height, that makes it New York's quintessential skyscraper. Admire the African marble and chrome steel of its lobby, and the detailing of gargoyles and automobiles on its upper floors. On its ground floor is Con Edison's Conservation Center, a didactic display of common energy-saving concerns popular with energetic children and their energy-conscious parents. At 200 East 42nd Street is New York's last authentic Horn & Hardart Automat; this branch was built in Art Deco style in 1958, long after the first one opened in Philadelphia in 1912. The cafeteria-style restaurant dispenses food out of glass-covered pigeonholes, opened with coins or special tokens available at the cashier.

At 220 East 42nd Street is Howells & Hood's 1930 Daily News Building, with a globe in its lobby right out of Superman's *Daily Planet* (it was, in fact, used in the *Superman* films). Between First and Second avenues on the north side of the street is the 42nd Street entrance to the Ford Foundation, a 1967 building by Kevin Roche, John Dinkeloo & Associates with an elaborate atrium garden that inspired many others throughout the city. Across the street from it is Tudor City, the exclusive 1925–1928 apartment building.

At First Avenue and East 42nd Street begins United Nations Plaza, the main attraction in an otherwise quiet and elegant residential neighborhood known as Turtle Bay. The visitors' entrance to the **United Nations** is three blocks north, at East 46th Street, which is where you begin the one-hour guided tours conducted seven days a week from 9:15 A.M. to 4:45 P.M. They are the best way of seeing the 18-acre site, designed by an international team of architects between 1947 and 1953. The Secretariat Building is the tall box of a building that rises above the scoop of the General Assembly Hall to the north; the library sits to the south, and the conference building stretches east beyond the Secretariat. Artworks from all member nations decorate the complex. Besides the architectural and artistic highlights that will be shown to you by the tour guides, note the UN Craft Shop and post office, both in the basement of the General Assembly building. After the tour you can rub elbows and forks with diplomats in the **United Nations Delegates Dining Room** (for reservations, Tel: 212-754-7625) on the fourth floor. A less official place in the vicinity, popular with the diplomats and trysting couples (sometimes one and the same), is the cocktail lounge on the top floor of the **Beekman Tower Hotel**, at 3 Mitchell Place on the northeast corner of First Avenue and East 49th Street.

PARK AVENUE

Head back west across East 45th Street. Across Lexington Avenue, on the south side of the street in front of the entrance to the Pan Am Building, you'll find another international lineup, this time of sidewalk food vendors. The Pan Am lobby was recently remodeled at great expense if not taste, removing the Josef Albers mural and sculptures that once graced the space. Go in anyway, for a laugh. The hideous sculptures resembling enormous earrings that replaced the artwork will prepare you for the oddball art you will be seeing on Park Avenue. From the Pan Am building go north through the arch marked "Helmsley Walk East," named after the owner of this and much other New York real estate, Harry Helmsley. You may recall his name from the recent tax-evasion case in which his wife, Leona, provided press fodder for a time. The entertainment is of a more permanent nature, however, in the passageway where cloud paintings on the ceilings are accompanied not by a Baroque concerto as you might expect but by elevator music. You emerge in neither heaven nor a disco but on the broad boulevard of Park Avenue, a stretch of which has some interesting architecture and rather unusual art. In the plaza before 245 Park Avenue is *Performance Machine, Big O's,* a 1986 kinetic sculpture by Lowell Jones, which is solar-powered and twists around like a giant chromosome. On the southeast corner of Park Avenue and East 48th Street is *Taxi!* Though it is actually a lifelike 1983 bronze by J. Seward Johnson, Jr., depicting an executive in the act of hailing a cab, frustrated New Yorkers have interpreted it as the petrified result of waiting for one. The **Waldorf-Astoria**, still one of the city's most prestigious hotels, is at 301 Park Avenue, between East 49th and East 50th streets. A block north, between East 50th and East 51st streets, is St. Bartholomew's Church, the parish church of the city's most affluent Episcopalian congregation. The church's Romanesque entrances, by McKim, Mead & White, were relocated from its earlier incarnation and attached to the Byzantine building designed by Bertram G. Goodhue. A block north, in front of 345 Park Avenue, is *Dinoceras,* a 1971 abstract sculpture by Robert Cook that looks like a ball of wax and in fact was an enormous lump of beeswax stretched on a bamboo frame before it was cast in bronze.

In the next uptown block is the **Seagram Building**, the 1958 modernist masterpiece designed on the outside by Ludwig Mies van der Rohe and on the inside by Philip Johnson. It houses Johnson's **Four Seasons** restaurant (entrance at 99 East 52nd Street), a sleek and expensive eatery that best exemplifies the New York phenomenon of combining dining with business deals known as the "power lunch." At 100 East 53rd Street, between Park and Lexington, is the **Brasserie**, a more modestly priced establishment to which patrons seeking only caloric power come at all hours, since it is one of the few places in town open around the clock. Two other imaginative examples of Johnson's architecture, done in collaboration with John Burgee, are nearby: the building at 885 Third Avenue (East 53rd Street), called the Lipstick Building because of its slick cylindrical shape; and the 1984 AT & T Building at 550 Madison Avenue (East 56th Street), which has been referred to as the Chippendale Building because of the similarity of its broken pediment to the furniture style.

Across the street from the Seagram Building, at 370 Park Avenue, is McKim, Mead & White's 1918 Racquet and Tennis Club, one of many private clubs in the area. At 390 is Skidmore, Owings & Merrill's 1952 **Lever House**, a glass box that spawned many less successful spinoffs. Next, take a look at the Chase Manhattan Bank branch at 410 Park Avenue (East 55th Street), which has a mobile by Alexander Calder on the second floor, visible from the street when the curtains are not drawn. The final piece of Park Avenue architecture worthy of inspection is the Mercedes-Benz Showroom at 430 Park Avenue (East 56th Street). It was Frank Lloyd Wright's first work in New York, designed in 1955. From here, look back toward the Pan Am Building for the full effect of its dwarfing the New

York Central Building (now called the Helmsley Building), a 1929 Warren & Wetmore skyscraper that once grandly marked the end of the avenue.

FIFTH AVENUE AND ENVIRONS

For an appropriately commercial crescendo to your Midtown promenade, return to the busy intersection of Fifth Avenue and 42nd Street and head uptown. Interesting sights fill practically all of the side streets to the west toward Sixth Avenue. On West 43rd and West 44th streets are some of Midtown's private clubs. The Palladian-style Century Club is at 7 West 43rd Street; the boxy Princeton Club is at 15 West 43rd Street. On West 44th Street is the sedate Georgian Harvard Club (by McKim, Mead & White) at number 27; the fanciful Beaux Arts New York Yacht Club is at number 37; and the **Algonquin Hotel** is at number 59. Though not a private club per se, its **Oak Room** was the setting for the Round Table—Robert Benchley, Heywood Broun, Edna Ferber, George S. Kaufman, and Dorothy Parker were among its most famous "members"—a group of self-styled wits (or, as Anita Loos called them, "a boring set of exhibitionists") who gathered there regularly to engage in banter and boozing. A drink or tea in the lobby lounge is a must.

At 551 Fifth Avenue, on the northeast corner of East 45th Street, is the 1927 French Building, designed by Fred F. French. Note the multicolored faience on the building's upper floors and the jazzy lobby.

West 45th and 46th streets have been virtually taken over by Brazilian shops and restaurants. Among the best restaurants is **Via Brazil** (34 West 46th Street), the only place in town that serves the all-you-can-eat meat extravaganza called churrasco. It is traditionally accompanied by a strong herbal tea called *erva mate,* which may be bought along with many other Brazilian products at **Coisa Nossa** down the street at 57 West 46th Street. Incidentally, if you look east on 46th Street, you'll get an idea of how imposing the New York Central Building must have once looked on Park Avenue, because it, rather than the Pan Am building, dominates the view from that angle.

West 47th Street is the heart of New York's **Diamond District,** where predominantly Jewish merchants trade their precious wares in noisy negotiations reminiscent of the Lower East Side. Scattered among them is the equally energetic **47th Street Photo** (67 West 47th Street), where great savings, if not service, may be had on electronic equipment when you know what you're looking for. It is but the most prominent of many such stores in the area. More relaxing is the **Gotham Book Mart** (41 West 47th Street), perhaps the city's most revered literary emporium, with hardly a current best seller dirtying its dusty shelves.

For best sellers (and at a discount) you'll have to go to **Barnes & Noble**, around the corner at 600 Fifth Avenue, between West 48th and West 49th streets. The former Scribner bookstore, an ornate iron-and-glass building across the street at 597 Fifth Avenue, was designed by Ernest Flagg in 1913 for the specific purpose of housing a bookstore (his brother-in-law's). The space was remodeled recently to accommodate a new tenant, Brentano's bookstore, but the exterior of the building—which has landmark status—remains unchanged.

Up the avenue, between East 50th and East 51st streets, is **St. Patrick's Cathedral**, the seat of the Roman Catholic archdiocese in New York. Though built in 1879 to the designs of James Renwick, Jr., its Gothic-style spires work well with the modern towers of Rockefeller Center across the street and are nicely reflected in the brown glass of Skidmore, Owings & Merrill's 1976 Olympic Tower a block north. The block of brownstone buildings on the east side of Madison Avenue facing the cathedral once housed the offices of the archdiocese, though they were built in 1884 by McKim, Mead & White as a mansion for Henry Villard. Developer Harry Helmsley later purchased them with the intention of demolishing them but was convinced to preserve them as the entrance to the **Helmsley Palace Hotel**. Number 457 Madison Avenue, the northernmost of the group, houses the city's best architectural bookstore, **Urban Center Books**.

Rockefeller Center

On the west side of Fifth Avenue, from West 47th to West 51st streets between Fifth and Sixth avenues, is Rockefeller Center, the sculpture-studded Art Deco business and entertainment complex that inevitably draws crowds of visitors and office workers alike. Built between 1931 and 1940, it was given landmark status in 1988 by the National Trust for Historic Preservation. It is most effectively approached on the promenade called **Channel Gardens** (because it separates the British Building from the Maison Française), between 49th and 50th streets. Channel Gardens, with its bronze fountainhead figures by René Paul Chambellan, is either elaborately planted or decked out with Valerie Clarebout's heraldic angels, depending on the season. It leads to a sunken area occupied by café tables in warm weather or an ice-skating rink in the winter, when it and its golden statue of *Prometheus,* by Paul Manship, is towered over by a gigantic Christmas tree. Behind it looms the 70-story RCA Building (the landmark's new owners call it the G.E. Building, but to the New Yorker on the street it will always be RCA; note Lee Lawrie's 1933 panels depicting Wisdom, Light, and Sound at the entrance). One-hour tours may be taken of the NBC television studios. Television enthusiasts should note that tickets to tapings are often handed out free on the Fifth Avenue side of Rockefeller Center and that the **Museum of Broadcasting** is located nearby at 1 East 53rd Street—but will be moving to 23 West 52nd Street in September. The RCA Building also houses the **Rainbow Room** (65th floor), a newly renovated Art Deco restaurant ideal for romantic dining, dancing, or drinks.

The most traditional spot for entertainment at Rockefeller Center, however, is **Radio City Music Hall**, at 1260 Sixth Avenue at the northeast corner of West 50th Street. There, a seasonal stage show featuring the leggy Rockettes takes place in the huge auditorium. The building was also recently restored to its Art Deco splendor, and may be fully appreciated by taking one of the music hall's special hour-long tours; Tel: (212) 246-4600.

At the new McGraw-Hill Building (1221 Sixth Avenue), the multimedia extravaganza **The New York Experience**, which for many years has been the best condensation of the touristic aspects of this part of town, has been temporarily closed but plans to reopen in 1990. To see its equivalent in contemporary art, take 51st Street west (where art furniture by Scott Burton sits squatly on the north side of the sidewalk) to see one of the temporary exhibits usually held nearby at the **Whitney Museum at Equitable Center**, 787 Seventh Avenue, between West 51st and West 52nd streets. Its permanent sculpture collection includes *Hare on Bell* (1983) and *Young Elephant* (1984) by Barry Flanagan. Back to the east, on the northeast corner of Sixth Avenue and West 52nd Street (51 West 52nd Street), is the CBS Building. Built to the plans of Eero Saarinen in 1965, it is the only skyscraper the Finnish-born architect ever designed.

Farther ahead on West 53rd Street are two more museums, the **American Craft Museum** at 40 West 53rd Street, and the **Museum of Modern Art** at 11 West 53rd Street, both between Fifth and Sixth avenues. MoMA (as the latter is called in the acronym-obsessed art world) was the world's pioneer institution for the exhibition of modern painting and sculpture, and initiated the first museum departments in photography, film, architecture, and design as well. Its own buildings are noteworthy pieces of architecture: Museum Tower, at 15 West 53rd Street, is a condominium erected in 1983 to the designs of Cesar Pelli as a fund-raising adjunct to the museum. The original building dates from 1939 and was designed by Philip L. Goodwin and Edward Durell Stone; Philip Johnson added extensions in 1951 and 1964, and Cesar Pelli doubled the gallery space with extensive renovations in 1984.

Brochures explaining the highlights of the collection, which range from French Impressionist paintings to a hovering 1,380-pound helicopter, are available at the front desk: Among its most popular attractions are Pablo Picasso's *Les Demoiselles d'Avignon,* Claude Monet's *Water Lilies,* and Andrew Wyeth's *Christina's World.* The museum also has some of the most interesting shops in town: an extensive art bookstore and a shop specializing in modern design objects. MoMA is open every day except Wednesday, unlike most of the rest of the city's museums, which close on Monday. After you exit the museum, look east across 53rd Street. The opalescent skyscraper that seems to hover at the end of the street is actually in Queens. Occupied by the Citicorp bank, at 48 stories it is the tallest building between Boston and Philadelphia outside Manhattan.

If you haven't ended your tour of MoMA with a visit to its sculpture garden, cross Fifth Avenue and walk to **Paley Park** at 3 East 53rd Street. The tiny enclave of seats, trees, and a waterfall is swarmed by office workers during the lunch hour, but provides welcome respite the rest of the day.

Before you continue up Fifth Avenue, if you're well dressed and well heeled (and have a reservation) you might want to backtrack to pause for some refreshment at the **"21" Club,** at 21 West 52nd Street. The last remnant of the many speakeasies that once lined 52nd Street during Prohibition, when the street was also known for its jazz and swing clubs, the veritable institution was recently refurbished and given a trendy gallicized menu. But many New Yorkers continue to swing with the punches, and pay $21 for its venerable hamburger. On the way there you'll pass 666 Fifth Avenue on the west side between West 52nd and West 53rd streets. Go into its lobby arcade, where the late sculptor Isamu Noguchi installed a waterfall and a white louvered ceiling. At the other end of the building, on the 39th floor, is **Top of the Sixes**, a bar-restaurant with mediocre food but marvelous views to the north.

Head back toward Fifth Avenue, where at 1 West 53rd is St. Thomas Church and parish house, designed by Bertram Goodhue in 1914. The reredos over the altar is just one noteworthy element of its lavish Gothic-style interior. At the northwest corner of Fifth and 54th Street (1 West 54th Street is the address) is the grandest private club of them all, the University Club, designed by McKim, Mead & White in 1899 along the lines of a Florentine palazzo. A private club of a different sort across the street, the Elizabeth Arden beauty salon at 691 Fifth Avenue, inspired the following lines from poet-humorist Ogden Nash:

> In New York beautiful girls can become more beautiful
> by going to Elizabeth Arden,
> And getting stuff put on their faces and waiting for it to
> harden. . . .

The stepped-back building at the northeast corner of Fifth Avenue and East 56th Street is the 1983 Trump Tower, a garish newcomer. The imposing effect is somewhat softened by the trees placed in its recesses high above the street. Its pink-marbled, gilded lobby propels you immediately (if unintentionally) into the connecting lobby of the *next* building, Edward Larrabee Barnes's 1983 IBM Building (590 Madison Avenue), where free concerts may be heard on Wednesday afternoons at 12:30 in the bamboo-and-flower-filled atrium (Tel: 212-745-5214 for information) and the **IBM Gallery of Science and Art** usually has an interesting exhibition taking place.

Back at 727 Fifth Avenue is **Tiffany's**, which has lovely displays of gems in its tiny windows on the avenue and around the corner on 57th Street. Cross 57th Street and walk two blocks north on Fifth toward the southeast corner of Central Park. On the west side of the street is **Grand Army Plaza**, an open square modeled on Paris's Place de la Concorde. In its center is Karl Bitter's 1913–

1916 Pulitzer Fountain, in which Scott and Zelda Fitzgerald once romped. Behind it looms Henry J. Hardenbergh's 1907 **Plaza Hotel**, one of the most romantic in the city. Its **Oak Bar** is a popular Midtown wateringhole, and its **Palm Court** is a cozy place for tea, a special favorite of shoppers from the elegant shops and department stores nearby.

WEST 57TH STREET

One such department store is **Bergdorf Goodman**, on Fifth Avenue between West 57th and West 58th streets. Take a look at its windows, and if you can resist the temptation to go in, turn west on 57th Street. In addition to its shops, the area is known for its art galleries. (The art and antiques area extends for a couple of blocks east on 57th from Fifth as well and way up Madison from 57th. If you'd like to see some shows, ask for a copy of *Art Now Gallery Guide* at one of the dealers in the closest gallery building, 20 West 57th Street, for an up-to-date listing.) The galleries—along with such other commercial attractions as another slope-façaded building (number 9), the **Henri Bendel** up-market department store (number 10), **Hacker Art Books** (number 45), the plush and fashionable **Russian Tea Room** restaurant (number 150), and the boisterous **Hard Rock Café** (number 221, with the line in front and the rear end of a Cadillac above)—will keep you busy on West 57th Street as you make your way to **Carnegie Hall**, at the southeast corner of West 57th Street and Seventh Avenue. The 1891 building was recently refurbished, some say to the detriment of its famous acoustics, but it's as popular a concert hall as ever, and New Yorkers still dare not ask how to get there, for fear of the wisecracking answer, "Practice, practice, practice!"

You'll likely hear that Borscht Belt chestnut and others if you end your visit to Midtown with a corned beef or pastrami sandwich at the **Carnegie Delicatessen and Restaurant** around the corner at 854 Seventh Avenue, used extensively as the scene for such banter in Woody Allen's *Broadway Danny Rose,* though with the death of owner Leo Steiner the place is rumored to have relaxed its standards. If you'd rather finish with a flourish of higher culture, walk across West 57th Street past the ornate Osborne Apartments at number 205 to the Art Students League, an 1892 French Renaissance structure by Henry J.

Hardenbergh at number 215, and thence to **Coliseum Books** at Broadway and 57th Street—at the gateway to the Lincoln Center/Upper West Side area.

THE UPPER WEST SIDE

By Stephen Brewer

Stephen Brewer, who was formerly an editor at GEO *magazine and is the editorial consultant for this guidebook, has lived on the Upper West Side for many years.*

You have probably read and heard of the Upper West Side many, many times. Theodore Dreiser's Sister Carrie lived here, in a fifth-floor flat on Amsterdam Avenue. J. D. Salinger's fictional Glass family occupied a roomy apartment on Central Park West, not far from the Morningstars, that parvenu clan of Herman Wouk's *Marjorie Morningstar,* or, for that matter, from Oscar and Felix of "The Odd Couple." The tough denizens of *West Side Story* walked the same streets that you will if you choose to travel just north of Midtown to see this neighborhood, and you certainly should.

One reason to go to the Upper West Side is, of course, to see its major attractions, the Lincoln Center for the Performing Arts and the American Museum of Natural History foremost among them. The neighborhood's location is in itself an attraction. These 200-some blocks occupy a narrow strip of land between the Hudson River on the west and Central Park on the east, running from Columbus Circle north to Columbia University at 114th Street. This means that an Upper West Sider who steps out for a bit of air can stroll along the shores of the river that the writer Thomas Wolfe found so comforting ("like long pipes and old tobacco"), walk across the neighborhood to sit for awhile on a bench in Central Park, the most successful of all urban greenswards, and be back in the apartment in less than an hour.

You may also want to go to the Upper West Side to see for yourself traces of the reputation it has won over the years for harboring New Yorkers of artistic tempera-

The Upper West Side

| 0 | yards | 500 |
| 0 | meters | 500 |

To Columbia University

W. 105 ST.
W. 104 ST.
W. 103 ST.
W. 102 ST.
W. 101 ST.
W. 100 ST.
W. 99 ST.
W. 98 ST.
W. 97 ST.

Central Park

MANHATTAN AVE.

Symphony Space

POMANDER WALK

W. 96 ST.
W. 95 ST.
W. 94 ST.
W. 93 ST.
W. 92 ST.
W. 91 ST.
W. 90 ST.
W. 89 ST.
W. 88 ST.
W. 87 ST.

HENRY HUDSON PKWY.

Hudson River

Riverside Park

RIVERSIDE DR.

WEST END AVE.

BROADWAY

AMSTERDAM AVE.

COLUMBUS AVE.

CENTRAL PARK WEST

W. 86 ST.
W. 85 ST.
W. 84 ST.
W. 83 ST.
W. 82 ST.
W. 81 ST.
W. 80 ST.

Children's Museum of Manhattan

Zabar's

Hayden Planetarium

79th St. Boat Basin

W. 79 ST.
W. 78 ST.
W. 77 ST.
W. 76 ST.
W. 75 ST.
W. 74 ST.
W. 73 ST.

American Museum of Natural History

New-York Historical Society

Central Park

W. 72 ST.

The Dakota

W. 71 ST.
W. 70 ST.
W. 69 ST.
W. 68 ST.
W. 67 ST.
W. 66 ST.
W. 65 ST.
W. 64 ST.
W. 63 ST.
W. 62 ST.
W. 61 ST.

Museum of American Folk Art

BROADWAY

AMSTERDAM AVE.

FREEDOM PL.

WEST END AVE.

COLUMBUS AVE.

CENTRAL PARK WEST

Juilliard School

Lincoln Center

Damrosch Park

Fordham University

W. 60 ST.
W. 59 ST.

COLUMBUS CIRCLE

NY Convention & Visitors Bureau

W. 58 ST.
W. 57 ST.

HENRY HUDSON PKWY.

Hudson River

N

ments. Edgar Allan Poe wrote much of *The Raven* on West 84th Street, a Herculean task given that he had on his hands a tubercular wife and a brood of starving children. Two houses on the block bear plaques marking the site where the poor man allegedly lived, and no one really knows which is accurate.

The neighborhood still attracts many writers, musicians, and actors, and an Upper West Sider who returns home from a night at the theater on the M 104 bus may have the pleasure of sitting next to one of the performers he has just seen on stage. (The M 104 begins at the United Nations on the East Side, crosses 42nd Street to Times Square, then proceeds north along Eighth Avenue and Broadway; if you are staying in Midtown, it is an excellent way to reach any of the sights on the Upper West Side.)

The mainstays of the neighborhood, though, have always been the bourgeoisie. As soon as the neighborhood began to develop, which was not until the late 19th century, the prosperous middle classes fled from the cramped downtown neighborhoods to take up residence on the West Side in what are still some of the city's best apartment houses and in brownstones. Edith Wharton, as much an elitist as the inhabitants of her novels about New York life at the turn of the century, thought these high, narrow houses were simply hideous.

The real reason to go to the Upper West Side, though, is not to partake of literary traditions or take in famous sights. Rather, even a brief walk here will give you the chance to see a quintessential New York neighborhood, a place where New Yorkers eat and sleep and go about their daily business, however eccentric that may be compared to quotidian activities elsewhere.

MAJOR INTEREST

Lincoln Center for the Performing Arts
The Dakota and other grand apartment houses
Central Park West
American Museum of Natural History
Columbus Avenue shopping and street life
Zabar's and other food shops on Broadway
Riverside Drive and Park and the Hudson River
Columbia University and neighborhood
Cathedral Church of St. John the Divine
The Cloisters and other north Manhattan museums

COLUMBUS CIRCLE AND LINCOLN CENTER

If you walk north from Midtown, you will approach the Upper West Side from its southern boundary, Columbus Circle. This vast, open space could have the monumental presence of, say, the Place de la Concorde—that is, were it not almost always full of a rush of traffic roaring around a tiny statue of the explorer, perched atop an 80-foot pedestal. Pedestrians scurry around the circle's periphery, first past the white marble pseudo-Islamic mosque at the southern tip of the intersection that has inspired jokes about Persian brothels since A & P heir Huntington Hartford put it up as a gallery of modern art in 1965. The building's saving grace is its current tenant, the **New York Convention and Visitors Bureau,** which distributes pamphlets and maps of the city from its ground-floor office.

As you make your way around the circle in a counter-clockwise direction, you will pass the extravagant, white marble *Maine* Memorial, which commemorates the incident that sparked the Spanish-American War in 1898 and marks one of the main entrances to Central Park. You will then come to the foot of an utterly banal office tower once known by the name of the corporation that built it in 1970, Gulf & Western. The edifice is now the property of Paramount Communications, but its only mark of distinction is still a pronounced tilt to the east, suggesting that it might one day have the good grace to topple out of sight.

From here begin the walk north on Broadway. As you leave the circle, you will see on your left the old New York Coliseum, an ugly, functional structure that became dysfunctional when the five million some conventioneers that New York hosts every year moved their shows to the new Jacob K. Javits Convention Center in Midtown near the Hudson. No sooner had the city announced plans to demolish the hall than New Yorkers, who had never paid any attention to it before, began to protest, fearful that the two snazzy skyscrapers that are to go up in its place will cast mile-long shadows over the circle and, worse, the southwestern corner of Central Park. Some variation of these buildings will undoubtedly go up, but the protest gives you a good idea of just how protective New Yorkers are of their land and the air above it, even when the space in question is as unremarkable as Columbus Circle.

Follow Broadway north for just seven blocks to the **Lincoln Center for the Performing Arts**. New Yorkers have been taking pot shots at the pedestrian appearance of this 12-acre complex since it opened in 1962. (You can see the neighborhood that once stood in its place in the film *West Side Story;* it was shot in the deserted streets and buildings of the slum that the center replaced just before the wreckers moved in.) To fuss about the appearance of Lincoln Center is to miss the point. The world's most accomplished performing artists grace its theaters, which surround a large marble plaza that is irresistibly charming despite its cold formality. The best time to take a seat on the rim of the fountain is 10:30 P.M. or so, when the performances end and the audiences spill out onto the plaza, looking much happier than New Yorkers usually do en masse.

Perched atop one of the buildings across Broadway is one of New York's favorite unheralded landmarks, a miniature Statue of Liberty. When the designs for Lincoln Center were being laid, there was a movement afoot to tear down this and other surrounding buildings to extend the plaza all the way to Central Park—a dream that soon faded in the face of the realities of Manhattan real estate.

Anyone who comes to New York for even a short stay should try to buy a ticket and step off the plaza into one of the surrounding halls. **Avery Fisher Hall**, on the north side of the plaza, was originally called Philharmonic Hall. But when the esteemed New York Philharmonic moved into its new quarters and sounded its first notes, the acoustics were so bad that the audience made a beeline for the doors. The symphony made a plea to electronics czar Avery Fisher, and the hall was lined with oak paneling. As a result, Mr. Fisher is immortalized in one of the world's favorite venues for classical music, and the rest of us are treated to the best acoustics to be found anywhere.

The **Metropolitan Opera House** occupies center stage at the far western end of the plaza. This hall, home to the Metropolitan Opera Company and the American Ballet Theater, wins the prize for showmanship even before the curtain goes up. From the six-story height of its glass-fronted lobby hang two murals by Marc Chagall—they are visible even from a bus passing by on Broadway, except in the morning when they are shrouded to protect them from the sun. Inside, the theatrics begin when the huge

crystal chandeliers float into the ceiling just before curtain time so they won't interfere with the sight lines,
which are unobstructed from all but a dozen or so seats.
The **New York State Theater,** where the New York City
Opera and the New York City Ballet perform, occupies
the south side of the plaza. The theater is the property of
the state, and when the governor comes to the city he
often throws official parties in the foyer and on the
second-floor loggia.

The rest of Lincoln Center stretches to the north behind
the Metropolitan Opera House. The **Vivian Beaumont
Theater,** which stages plays and musicals, shares a building
with a branch of the New York Public Library, the **Library
and Museum of Performing Arts.** The real treasures
amongst this amazing collection of books on the performing arts and sheet music are some 12,000 recordings that
musically inclined New Yorkers can borrow. The reflecting
pool outside with a Henry Moore sculpture rising from its
midst is a wonderful place to sit. Just beyond is the esteemed **Juilliard School,** whose well-trained graduates often return to perform on Lincoln Center's stages. Excellent
tours, taking in the center's stages and labyrinthine costume storage rooms, leave frequently from the Metropolitan Opera House; Tel: (212) 582-3512. Across Broadway
from Lincoln Center, Columbus Avenue begins its northward run (more on the avenue's shops later in this chapter). The **Museum of American Folk Art** has just moved its
noted collection of paintings, textiles, furniture, and decorative arts into bright new quarters at the foot of Columbus, at 65th Street. A glossy gift shop adjoins.

The Hotel des Artistes is just up the avenue and around
the corner at number 1 West 67th Street. This fine building has been popular with creative New Yorkers since the
earliest days of this century. Its double-height apartments
were built to accommodate painters, but it has been years
since any normal boheme has been able to afford them.
Isadora Duncan, Norman Rockwell, Rudolph Valentino,
and Noel Coward have called the des Artistes home, but it
was the debauched Harry Crosby who gave the place its
racy élan. One evening in 1929, this nephew of J. P.
Morgan and founder of the Paris-based avant-garde Black
Sun Press locked the door to an apartment here, made
love to and then shot his lovely mistress, and put the gun
to his own handsome young head. You, too, can enter
these bohemian portals and partake of a fine meal at the
extremely attractive **Café des Artistes** on the ground

floor. One of the café's famous neighbors is the equally popular **Tavern on the Green**, set just inside Central Park at 67th Street. Festooned with Christmas lights and decorated in an eclectic style, the place makes even regulars feel like tourists out for a night on the big town; it's a good place to stop in for a drink, though, especially in the summer when the garden is open. Many of the buildings here in the West 60s house television studios. ABC has just moved into its sleek new semicircular headquarters between 66th and 67th streets—just across Columbus from the studio where "All My Children" is shot, attracting to its stoop every day a faithful group of fans.

THE 72ND STREET AREA

If you continue north from Lincoln Center on Broadway you will soon come to its busy intersection with 72nd Street, where just 100 years ago stood the ramshackle homestead of Jacob Harsen. His farm was then one of many on the Upper West Side. Less than 200 years ago Washington Irving described vast tracts of this area as "a sweet rural valley . . . enlivened here and there by a delectable little Dutch cottage." At the very center of the intersection you will see a brick kiosk, the entrance to the subway that, when it opened in 1904, finally brought civilization to the Upper West Side.

New Yorkers had already begun to take up residence in huge new apartment houses on Broadway in the decade or so before the arrival of the subway. One of these, The Dorilton, at 71st Street, opened to an onslaught of sour reviews, the most dire of them claiming "the sight of it makes strong men swear and weak women shrink afrightened"; New Yorkers have survived a full century of the building's ornate, Beaux Arts presence and have become quite comfortable with its hideous appearance. When **The Ansonia** opened at 73rd and Broadway in 1901, it sported two swimming pools, a lobby fountain populated by seals, and a roof garden where a bear roamed freely. These trappings, as well as its apartments of as many as 18 rooms, have wooed some of New York's most flamboyant citizens over the years, including Theodore Dreiser, Florenz Ziegfeld, and Babe Ruth. The building's most shameless tenant, though, was a recent one: a tawdry club called Plato's Retreat to which couples retired for the peculiar purpose of copulating in public, next to bubbling whirlpools. The place finally closed a few years ago, but will long be remembered—if only as proof that the West Side is bohemian at heart.

You should leave Broadway now and walk east on 72nd Street, toward Central Park. If you want a snack, you can do no better than **Gray's Papaya**, a gaudy stand-up counter on the southeast corner of the 72nd Street and Broadway intersection. Two dollars here will get you two of New York's best frankfurters ("better than filet mignon," their motto claims) and a fruit drink, and will also bring you closer than you may want to be to some very seedy clients. Many of them are habitués of Verdi Square across the street. This tiny patch of greenery has long been known as Needle Park, in part because of its triangular shape but more so because of the lively drug trade that goes on beneath a statue of composer Giuseppe Verdi, put up by New York's Italian citizenry in 1906.

Could you have stood here a hundred years ago on a Sunday, you would have witnessed an extraordinary sight. By the thousands, New Yorkers of the day used to drive their carriages and ride their bicycles—only just invented—north from the Grand Circle (now Columbus Circle) up the Boulevard (now Broadway), across 72nd Street to Riverside Drive, and follow it north to roadhouses along the Hudson River. "After dark Riverside Drive seemed alive with fireflies, so numerous were the varicolored lamps flashing under the trees," wrote one observer of the day trippers returning home.

Seventy-second Street's few remaining kosher restaurants and butchers have long served the neighborhood's large Jewish population. The most notable of these is the **Eclair**, between Broadway and Columbus Avenue, a pleasant restaurant and pastry shop that is still a gathering spot for European Jews who came to New York half a century ago.

The Dakota, New York's first great apartment house, is at the corner of 72nd and Central Park West. When Edward Clark, heir to the Singer Sewing Machine fortune, put up this yellow-brick building in 1881, it was so far from the rest of Manhattan that his detractors said it may as well have been in the Dakota Territory, giving the house its now very famous name. The well-to-do were then still wary of apartments, considering it vulgar to share halls and elevators, invented only a few years before, with strangers. Accordingly, Clark fashioned the Dakota in the style of a château, even surrounding it with a moat. So convincing was the effect that the Russian composer Tchaikovsky, visiting music publisher Gustav Schirmer here, thought that his host owned the entire house and that Central Park was his alone. The Dakota has also been home to such other musically inclined tenants as Theodore Steinway, the piano manufacturer, and, more recently, Leonard Berstein and Roberta Flack, the latter of whom fell out of favor with the neighborhood when she stripped her apartment of its mahogany woodwork and replaced it with stainless steel.

The building's most famous tenant, of course, was John Lennon, who was shot to death outside its gates in 1980. You can pay tribute to the musician across the street in **Strawberry Fields**, an acre of Central Park that Yoko Ono had landscaped in her husband's memory. This is a very nice place to enjoy the park, sitting beneath the arbor that leads off 72nd Street or wandering down to one of the gazebos alongside the rowing lake. If you come here at night you will notice a curious phenomenon: New Yorkers do not enter the park after dark (except in large groups of half a million or so to attend concerts on the Great Lawn), even in the hottest days of summer. They are heeding the advice of Ogden Nash, who warns anyone who finds himself in the park after dark to "hurry, hurry to the zoo, and creep into the tiger's lair, frankly you'll be safer there."

From the Dakota walk north on Central Park West, a handsome avenue whose big apartment houses facing the park are some of the neighborhood's best addresses. Aside from the Dakota, the most impressive buildings are the San Remo, at 74th Street, and other twin-towered apartments that went up in the 1930s to house, among others, well-to-do Jewish families who had arrived on the Lower East Side from Europe only a generation before.

The West Side Museums

At 77th Street you will come to the **New-York Historical Society**, a quiet, stodgy institution-cum-museum that gave into temptation recently and arranged to sell its side garden to a developer of high-rises. The neighborhood set up a roar that rattled the society's rich collection of Tiffany glass and portraits, and made its point—this part of Central Park West, at least, will not soon be overshadowed by an apartment tower.

Just across 77th Street is the **American Museum of**

Natural History, a wonderful if rather musty collection totaling 37 million items—the world's largest—of bones, gems, and just about any other object relating to natural history. Anyone who grew up in New York counts among his or her happiest school days those field trips here, parading past dioramas of African scenes and dark rooms lined with mummies to the top floor galleries, where the dinosaurs are exhibited. The museum has expanded haphazardly and somewhat confusedly since it opened in 1877, so you may want to stop at the information desk at the main entrance and join one of the excellent tours. The Hayden Planetarium is adjacent, just to the north.

COLUMBUS AVENUE

If you leave the museum by the 77th Street exit, you will be just a few steps away from Columbus Avenue. On the evening before and early morning hours of every Thanksgiving, Macy's uses this stretch of 77th Street as a staging ground for its parade, blowing up the huge balloon figures that will float down Central Park West and then Broadway to the department store in Herald Square. Many Upper West Siders stand here through the night, watching the familiar figures take shape.

Columbus Avenue from Lincoln Center to 86th Street is almost always crowded with the well-dressed patrons of its fancy shops and restaurants. Until recently, though, Columbus was decidedly middle class. The elevated subway, the "El," rushed above it, and the stores below did a lively business supplying the apartment houses of Central Park West. Of all these long-gone shops, the best remembered is Hellman's delicatessen, whose homemade mayonnaise has achieved fame far beyond the Upper West Side. The avenue now belongs to suburbanites in for a day's or evening's jaunt, and to the well-reared, well-dressed, well-educated young New Yorkers who pay as much as $2,000 a month rent for a few rooms in a brownstone that their grandparents could have rented in its entirety for $100. Seeing so many well-heeled young people crowd into the neighborhood's bars and restaurants on weekend evenings, it is hard not to be cynical. These pampered youth bring to mind what Dorothy Parker, who grew up in this neighborhood, said when half a century ago she was asked to comment on the attendees of a Yale prom: "If all those sweet young things were laid end to end ... I would not be at all surprised." Keep in mind, though, that young professionals like those who now inhabit so much of the Upper West Side have always formed a sizable portion of Manhattan's population. Keep in mind too, that the difference between the haves and have nots is shockingly distinct in New York. Within blocks of this affluent strip are sordid tenements housing welfare families, and it is impossible to walk these streets without seeing, and often being approached by, at least a few of the city's 75,000 homeless citizens.

SHOPPING AND DINING ON THE UPPER WEST SIDE

Of the many good shops and restaurants that line Columbus, some of the best are those that have been here for a decade or more. On 71st Street, just east of the avenue, is **Café La Fortuna**, a pleasant little coffee house where you will be encouraged to linger over your cappuccino and Italian pastry. **Victor's**, a Cuban restaurant, 240 Columbus at 71st Street, is a holdout from the 1960s, when as many as 100,000 Cubans and Puerto Ricans settled in the neighborhood. Many have resettled in other boroughs, but Victor's continues to serve the best Latin food in the city. With its cookbooks and mail-order gourmet food business, the **Silver Palate** has cornered a nationwide reputation—from its tiny headquarters on the west side of Columbus at 73rd Street. Freshmade breads and the shop's own specialty mustards and vinegars are packed high to the ceiling. Nathan Cohen, a former network cameraman, sells his favorite toys, both antiques and reproductions, at **The Last Wound-Up**, on the west side of the street near 74th. **Mythology**, on the same side of the avenue at number 370, north of 77th Street, also sells toys, as well as a tastefully eccentric collection of books, posters, and other bric-a-brac. **Maxilla and Mandible**, across the avenue just north of 81st Street, takes advantage of its proximity to the natural history museum to stock a gruesomely fascinating collection of bones and taxidermic specimens.

The natty building across the avenue is the Endicott, an expensive cooperative apartment house that typifies the renovation that has reshaped so much of the Upper West Side in recent years. Before its conversion, the Endicott was a hotel of dubious distinction, losing on the average a guest a month to homicide. In an irony typical of this neighborhood, **Endicott Bookseller,** one of the smart new shops on the ground floor, is a gathering spot of local literati. There is still a hotel nearby, a very good one, the **Excelsior,** overlooking the museum on 81st Street between Columbus and Central Park West. A large double room here still costs less than $100, and slightly more will put you in a suite with a kitchenette; Tel: (212) 362-9200.

You will probably notice that a number of the shops on Columbus stand empty. Their former tenants learned a lesson: However high the aspirations of Upper West Siders may be, they are unwilling to pay $200 for a shirt—and you have to sell a good many shirts at that price to meet rents that average as much as $10,000 a month for even a small space.

To shop the way Upper West Siders do, walk west two blocks to Broadway. Like residents in European cities, New Yorkers tend to shun supermarkets—some in Manhattan maintain shoddy standards of cleanliness and service that would send Betty Crocker into a swoon—in favor of specialty shops. **Fairway,** 2127 Broadway at 74th Street, is a pleasure; even if New York's largest selection of greens and fruits isn't high on your New York shopping list, the cheeses, breads, coffees, and other specialty foods sold here may well be. The store serves some 30,000 customers a week, many of whom stop in every day on their shopping rounds. Just up Broadway, at 75th Street, is **Citarella's,** a fishmonger that is as noted for its piscine window displays as it is for its exquisite selection of fresh fish. Even if you can't accommodate a red snapper rotting in a corner of your hotel room, you can partake of local shellfish at Citarella's stand-up clam bar.

La Caridad, at 78th and Broadway, is the best of a breed of Cuban-Chinese restaurants unique to New York. These places are run by Chinese who immigrated to Cuba, then fled to New York after Castro's takeover; La Caridad was once the favorite hangout of taxi drivers but is now packed with affluent young newcomers to the neighborhood. The large, white apartment house across 78th Street is the Apthorp, one of New York's best addresses, occupying an entire block and built around a dark though luxuriously quiet courtyard.

The Upper West Side's, and New York's, most famous food store is **Zabar's,** north on Broadway at 80th Street. The store's 160 employees sell 10,000 pounds of coffee, 10 tons of cheese, and 1,000 pounds of salmon a week—

as well as CuisinArts, microwave ovens, pots and pans, even tea towels, for total sales of $25 million a year. Most notable, Zabar's charges the lowest prices in New York for every item it stocks, be it a vacuum cleaner or a loaf of bread.

There is still much else to see on the Upper West Side, and you would do well to fortify yourself with coffee and pastry in Zabar's busy little coffee room. After that you might continue to pursue the neighborhood's two passions, food and books. For yet another sample of the former, walk across 80th Street to **H & H Bagels**, the city's largest manufacturer—70,000 a day—of this New York staple. **Shakespeare and Company** bookstore, north of Zabar's on Broadway at the corner of 81st Street, has only slightly less character than its Paris namesake and is very well stocked. **Gryphon**, just across Broadway, has a very fine, rather dusty collection of secondhand books (and an annex around the corner). The **Children's Museum of Manhattan** has just opened on 83rd Street, between Broadway and Amsterdam. Its young visitors study the human mind in the Brainatarium and execute computer-generated self-portraits.

For New York's best smoked fish, you need walk only a few blocks north up Amsterdam to **Barney Greengrass the Sturgeon King**, a deli and restaurant at number 541, just north of 86th Street. The Greengrass family counts among its past and present clientele the likes of Franklin D. Roosevelt, Groucho Marx, and Woody Allen. Some of the neighborhood's nicest restaurants are on this shabby avenue, and they are eclectic indeed: Peruvian, Caribbean, Indian, Mexican, Japanese, kosher. If you are hungry, just follow Amsterdam north from 79th to 88th streets. The best meals to be had are at **Baci**, an expensive and popular Italian trattoria at 80th Street, and **Good Enough to Eat**, at 84th Street, where very good American-style classics (ham, catfish, and the like) come out of the kitchen. By all means avoid the much-frequented bars that are beginning to open on Amsterdam—they are easily recognizable by names like the Raccoon Lodge and Mugamba Bay—unless you enjoy the company of sloppily inebriated college students.

RIVERSIDE DRIVE
AND THE PARK

It would be a shame to come to the West Side without having at least a glimpse of the Hudson River, and there is no better vantage point than Riverside Drive. Walking west from Broadway anywhere above 72nd Street, you will first cross West End Avenue, a street of tall, handsome apartment buildings that seems more typical of a residential quarter of Paris or old Berlin than of New York. What makes West End Avenue unique is the absence of shops and the uniformity of its architecture. (Oddly enough, when the West Side was being laid out in the late 19th century, Broadway was to have been the residential street, serviced by businesses on West End.) Most of these solidly middle-class buildings went up in the 1930s. In New York, leases are often passed from generation to generation, and many of these apartments are still occupied by the original tenants or their children and grandchildren. In recent years many of the buildings here and elsewhere on the Upper West Side have become cooperatives, and a comfortable two-bedroom apartment selling for less than $350,000 is a bargain. The same size apartment rents for $2,500 a month or more.

If you follow West End as far north as 94th Street, you will find one of the West Side's hidden treasures: **Pomander Walk**, a row of little town houses that look for all the world like cottages in a British village. Indeed, the walk, built in the 1920s, was modeled on stage sets from a then popular British play of the same name. Suitably, these tiny rooms have been home to Humphrey Bogart, the Gish sisters, and many other actors.

Riverside Drive, one block to the west of West End, curves gently above the banks of the Hudson, which flows a hearty stone's-throw away on the far side of narrow Riverside Park. New Yorkers once built mansions along this still lovely, exclusively residential, noncommercial avenue. None was more exquisite than the 65-room French château, complete with private chapel, that steel tycoon Charles Schwab built at Riverside Drive and 74th Street in 1904. Alas, in an uncharacteristic show of modesty, the city fathers decided not to buy the palace and make it the official mayor's residence, and the house came down to make way for an apartment building in the 1940s.

There are still a few survivors from the old days, though, including a dilapidated mansion at the corner of 89th Street and a whole block of fine French town houses between 105th and 106th. For the most part, the apartment buildings that have replaced the private homes are very pleasant places to live. As for **Riverside Park** itself, laid out, like Central Park, by Olmsted and Vaux in the 1870s, you will find it decidedly shabby or utterly romantic. It is both, and, given its isolation next to the river, you should confine your daylight exploration to well-trodden footpaths and at night venture no farther north than the Soldiers and Sailors Monument, perched above the park on the drive at 89th Street.

A good place to see both park and river is the **79th Street Boat Basin** (just follow 79th Street all the way west). It may be hard to believe, but this shabby little marina often harbors the fleets of Donald Trump, Malcolm Forbes, and other rich and famous yachtsmen. It is also home to the few New Yorkers who live on houseboats, and the grassy slope stretching up from the broad, noble river is as peaceful a place as any in New York for a picnic.

COLUMBIA UNIVERSITY AND ITS NEIGHBORHOOD

Many residents of the Upper West Side went to school here, at Columbia University. You can walk to the campus, a straight shot up Broadway to 114th Street, or you can board the M 104 bus anywhere along Broadway.

Columbia bows to its Ivy League status with a large green quadrangle, but this is a decidedly urban, overbuilt campus. The university's major real-estate holding is not here but in Midtown—Columbia owns the land upon which Rockefeller Center was built. Like most universities, Columbia is surrounded by some good bookstores and inexpensive restaurants. Of the former, the best is **Barnard Book Forum**, just across Broadway from the main entrance to the campus and especially strong in history, philosophy, and literature, as well as books published by the Columbia University Press.

The students' favorite eateries are next to one another

on Amsterdam Avenue between 110th and 111th streets. The **V & T Pizzeria** serves a pie that alone justifies a trip this far north. The **Hungarian Pastry Shop** allows its patrons to sit and read, downing strong coffee and rich poppy-seed rolls, as long as they wish, and the **Green Tree**, next door, serves hearty Hungarian fare in a homey atmosphere. For a Columbia student, or for that matter any Upper West Sider, a Saturday night often begins at one of the Chinese restaurants on Broadway around 96th Street and the blocks just to the north. These places change names and hands so frequently that it is almost impossible to keep up with them—but it is hard to go wrong at any of them.

At 112th Street and Amsterdam is the **Cathedral Church of St. John the Divine**, which will be the world's largest cathedral if it is ever completed. The monstrous Episcopal edifice has been so long in the making, since 1892, that no one would recognize the site if it weren't buzzing with stone carvers. (Replicas of the gargoyles they make are for sale in the cathedral shop.) The neighborhood's other two monuments are west, on Riverside Drive. New York cab drivers are wont to ask out-of-towners if they know who is buried in **Grant's Tomb**. The answer lies at Riverside and 122nd Street, where the former president, who retired to New York four years before he died in 1885, lies next to his wife in a pompous marble mausoleum. The even colder, more imposing structure next door is **Riverside Church**, built by John D. Rockefeller in the 1920s.

THE MUSEUMS OF NORTH MANHATTAN

Some of New York's finest smaller museums are north of Columbia in Harlem and elsewhere in upper Manhattan, and you needn't let the area's deservedly bad reputation keep you from seeing them. On Madison Avenue you can board an M 1 bus, which will deposit you at the **Schomburg Center for Research in Black Culture**, at 135th Street and Lenox Avenue. This amazing collection of materials relating to blacks, the world's most extensive, counts among its holdings some 50,000 prints and photographs, a small portion of which are on display at any one time.

Audubon Terrace, to the west at 155th Street and Broadway—take a cab from the Schomburg or, if travelling from areas farther south, the number 1 Seventh Avenue subway or M 4 or M 5 Madison Avenue buses—is a pleasant cluster of Neoclassical buildings that houses a delightfully eclectic mix of exhibitions: the **Museum of the American Indian**, the nation's largest collection of Native American artifacts; the **Hispanic Society of America**, which owns a collection of paintings by Goya, Velázquez, and El Greco that is the envy of many a larger museum; the **American Numismatic Society**, the world's largest collection of coins; the **American Geographical Society**, the Western Hemisphere's largest collection of maps; and the **American Academy of Arts and Letters**, which has changing exhibits of American art.

If you travel still farther north, to the tip of Manhattan, your reward will be **The Cloisters**. You can reach the museum on the M 4 Madison Avenue bus, which will afford you a good look at Harlem and Washington Heights, a middle-class Jewish and Hispanic neighborhood whose lower rents have in recent years attracted the young, creatively inclined New Yorkers who once settled in Greenwich Village and on the Upper West Side. A faster route is the A line of the Eighth Avenue subway.

The Cloisters is a collection of five Medieval European cloisters, a 12th-century chapter house, and other substantial treasures collected piecemeal in the early years of this century by George Bernard, a sculptor and architecture enthusiast. Mr. Bernard often had to pry discarded pillars and stones away from European homeowners who were using them as garden ornaments. He managed to reassemble the lot upon his return to New York and sold it to John D. Rockefeller. He in turn presented the artifacts and a building to house them to the Metropolitan Museum of Art.

The Cloisters are now handsomely planted with herb gardens and flowers, making it very easy for you to imagine you are in Europe and not in Manhattan—which will, nonetheless, lure you back after a pleasant afternoon here.

CENTRAL PARK

By Steven K. Amsterdam

Steven K. Amsterdam has been a resident of New York City for over 20 years and has written extensively about Central Park. Formerly editor of Chicago's Grey City Journal, *Amsterdam is currently a free-lance writer in New York City.*

Where else might you expect to hear the sounds of the New York Philharmonic filling the night sky, to catch a glimpse of Madonna jogging, or to witness such seasonal spectacles as a 12-foot-high brontosaurus carved out of ice? Where else can you find, on a fine summer's day, several hundred thousand New Yorkers enjoying the great outdoors? And, for that matter, where else but in Central Park is the Manhattan topography dominated by 840 acres of woodland and meadows?

The origins of this magnificent greensward date to the 1850s, when the New York legislature wanted to create some pleasant grounds for walking, something along the lines of London's manicured and formal Kensington Gardens. William Marcy "Boss" Tweed, then city alderman, argued for a large, central park on some of the island's swampiest, rockiest land, which the city purchased from Tweed's friends at the absurdly inflated price of $7,500 an acre. A contest was held to find the best original plan for the park, and the award went to Frederick Law Olmsted (landscaper) and Calvert Vaux (architect). In an area between what is now 59th Street to the south and 110th Street to the north, Fifth Avenue to the east and Central Park West to the west, hills and valleys were created so that the footpaths would meander instead of march across the landscapes. Transverse roads were constructed to pass underneath the footpaths so visitors would not have to see the horse carriages. The style—the revolutionary idea of creating a wilderness—became a model for parks around the world.

More than a century later, Central Park is a romantic place where New Yorkers retreat to engage in such pastimes as Polish folk dancing, ice-skating, bike racing, gondola rides, theatergoing at free performances of Shakespeare, tree climbing, and simply the chance to sit and smell the roses. In fact, recent commissioners of the Parks Department have restored much of what Olmsted and Vaux intended, and the park is looking more rustic now than it has in 50 years.

You should give Central Park at least an afternoon. Start at the new **Central Park Zoo** at 65th Street on the East Side. Its small but high-tech habitats allow secular Manhattanites to gawk at natural wonders: penguins (whose squawks are amplified over the speaker system), seal feedings, and an indoor rain forest complete with monkeys, snakes, free-flying birds, and bats.

Other sites in the southern portion of Central Park have given it a reputation as "The Children's District." Originally a distribution spot for fresh milk, the **Dairy** is now the visitors' center. At **Wollman Rink**, renovated a few years ago with funds from Donald Trump, there is ice-skating or roller-skating under the trees, depending on the season (rentals are available), and miniature golf on a course studded with models of the landmarks and skyscrapers that loom just beyond the trees. The nearby **Carousel**, built in 1908 (making it one of the oldest in North America), has been completely overhauled.

A walk along the elm-lined **Mall** to the north is likely to bring you to a magician, accordion player, clown, or a company volleyball game and a flamboyant circle of disco skaters. The Naumberg Band Shell's stage is given over to experimental musicians, actors, and artists as long as the weather permits. Organized events, such as jazz, blues, and reggae shows, go on each weekend of the summer.

The **Sheep Meadow**, just east of the Mall, hasn't had sheep on it since the Great Depression, when Mayor La Guardia decided the city couldn't afford their upkeep at a time when Hoovervilles were being built on the same grass. In the 1960s and 1970s, too many lively peace rallies and well-attended New York Philharmonic concerts threatened to destroy the terrain. The Meadow, replanted, is currently fenced and occasionally off limits to visitors, in order to let the grass grow greener. When open, it is a good place to stretch out and enjoy a thick, well-tended lawn and a panoramic view of the city.

At 68th Street on the West Side, you can buy a picnic lunch at the Tavern on the Green bus, a concession stand for picnickers outside the pricey but picturesque restaurant of the same name (the building was formerly a sheep hold).

Central Park

| 0 | yards | 250 |
| 0 | meters | 250 |

To Lasker Rink and Conservatory Garden ↑

To Museum of the City of New York and Museo del Barrio

Reservoir

International Center of Photography

Jewish Museum

E. 92 ST.

Cooper-Hewitt Museum

National Academy of Design

E. 89 ST.

Guggenheim Museum

Jogging Path

N

W. 86 ST.

W. 85 ST.

CENTRAL PARK WEST

E. 86 ST.

E. 85 ST.

E. 84 ST.

E. 83 ST.

FIFTH AVE.

Great Lawn

Metropolitan Museum of Art

W. 81 ST.

Delacorte Theatre

Hayden Planetarium
American Museum of Natural History

Turtle Pond

Belvedere (Castle)

E. 79 ST.

W. 77 ST.

To Whitney Museum →

E. 76 ST.

New-York Historical Society

Ramble

Lake

Loeb Boathouse

Alice in Wonderland Statue

Model Boat Basin

Bow Bridge

Bethesda Fountain

Bethesda Terrace

W. 72 ST.

E. 72 ST.

Strawberry Fields

E. 71 ST.

Frick Collection

Naumburg Band Shell

W. 69 ST.

E. 69 ST.

The Mall

W. 67 ST.

Sheep Meadow

E. 67 ST.

W. 66 ST.

Tavern on the Green

FIFTH AVE.

E. 66 ST.

W. 65 ST.

Children's Zoo

E. 65 ST.

To Lincoln Center ←

Carousel

Dairy

Central Park Zoo

E. 64 ST.

W. 62 ST.

Wollman Rink

E. 61 ST.

BROADWAY

Pond

E. 60 ST.

E. 59 ST.

COLUMBUS CIRCLE

CENTRAL PARK SOUTH

SEVENTH AVE.   SIXTH AVE.

Plaza Hotel

From there make the pilgrimage to the John Lennon memorial, **Strawberry Fields**, across from the Dakota at the park's West 72nd Street entrance. New Yorkers are not too jaded to appreciate the *Imagine* mosaic at the center of the newly landscaped hill, and choose this pleasant acreage, a gift from Lennon's widow, Yoko Ono, as a meeting ground. There are no strawberries here, by the way, but there are plants donated by more than 20 countries, including a cluster of white birch trees from the USSR.

The **Bethesda Fountain**, in the center of the park at 72nd Street on the edge of the Lake, is the park's busy, central piazza. If you cross the Lake from here on Bow Bridge, you will come to the **Loeb Boathouse**, where you can rent a rowboat or board a gondola. There are two eating establishments here, one providing *nouvelle cuisine* and the other sandwiches. Behind the boathouse is the extensive and uncharted **Ramble**, a maze of small overgrown paths and streams and a haven for the adventurous who enjoy solitude.

Except in the dead of winter, toy sailboats, motorboats, and subs sail every weekend on the **Model Boat Basin**. A statue with magnetic charm is situated at the northern end of the pond: **Alice in Wonderland**, sitting on a mushroom, usually crawling with children.

If you are not ready to brave the Ramble, you can walk north along the Drive, through the back end of the Ramble, and up to **Belvedere Castle**. From here you can see the busy Midtown skyline as well as the more majestic and less congested views of Central Park West and Fifth Avenue. Just to the north are the Turtle Pond and the Great Lawn.

The open-air **Delacorte Theatre**, just under the cliffs of Belvedere Castle, offers free performances of Shakespeare's plays all summer long (Tel: 212-861-PAPP). Last year's program included Jeff Goldblum, Gregory Hines, and Michelle Pfeiffer in *Twelfth Night*. Do not pass up an opportunity to see the plays, with the backdrop of Belvedere Castle, the pond, and the stars; Broadway cannot offer an experience as evocative or as inexpensive. When the reviews are good, however, getting a seat involves sitting out on the Great Lawn for the afternoon until the tickets are distributed at 6:00. However, with a few trips to Zabar's delicatessen at Broadway and 80th Street for sustenance, this is not an altogether painful experience.

Currently, the **Great Lawn** is what the Sheep Meadow

was in the 1970s—a playing field and gathering spot, a place for baseball games, kite flying, ice-sculpture competitions, and all sorts of performances (from *La Bohème* to Elton John).

The **Conservatory Garden** at 105th Street and Fifth Avenue is a northern point well worth the exploration, as it is a reminder of what the deliberately rusticated park is not. When Olmsted began importing trees and bushes to the agriculturally barren region—before the project was launched there were only 42 species on the site—a nursery had to be established. Over time, 1,300 varieties of trees and shrubs were planted here in orderly rows, resembling a formal garden. The Conservatory Garden now has a perfectly timed procession of flowers in bloom throughout the spring, summer, and fall. The symmetrical paths of the garden circle around two delicate fountains.

For skating, the **Lasker Rink** (just in from the 110th Street entrance to the park) is less expensive and less crowded than the Wollman, though the clientele is a bit more rowdy. On the park's northernmost edge, the Harlem Meer looks like a city dump and beyond it is a burned-out building. But the Parks Department is not far behind. By 1991 they expect to have the water completely dredged, the area relandscaped, and the building refurbished as an activities center for children.

All of Central Park can be done on foot, but you will be exhausted. Possibilities to explore are: bike rentals, (212) 861-4137; boating, (212) 517-2233; group walking, (914) 439-5155; group running, (212) 860-4455; horseback riding, (212) 724-5100; horsedrawn carriage riding, (212) 246-0520; Wollman Rink, (212) 517-4800; Lasker Rink, (212) 397-3142; public tours, (212) 397-3080; other information, (212) 397-3156.

THE UPPER EAST SIDE

By Susan Farewell

Susan Farewell, a former travel editor at Condé Nast Publications, writes for Travel and Leisure, Metropolitan Home, Crain's New York Business, Child, *and other publications. She is also the editor of the* Mobil Road Atlas and Trip Planning Guide *(1990 and 1991 editions).*

On the Upper East Side, scrubbed streets (roughly those between 59th and 96th, east of Central Park) are lined with ivy-covered town houses, opulent mansions, and solid apartment buildings guarded by white-gloved doormen. In front of them, limousines often await the residents within. The Upper East Side is home not only to New York's most wealthy citizens, but also to the Metropolitan, the Guggenheim, and the city's other great museums and to the world's largest concentration of antiques shops and art galleries. Its endlessly fascinating architecture is as varied as the palazzo-like Metropolitan Club and the tenement houses of Yorkville. Like the rest of New York City, the Upper East Side is best seen à pied.

MAJOR INTEREST

Frick Collection
Temple Emanu-El
Antiques shops and boutiques
Art galleries
Whitney Museum of American Art
Asia Society
Bloomingdale's
Restaurants and bars

Yorkville
Carl Schurz Park
Gracie Mansion
Henderson Place Historic District
Church of the Holy Trinity
Sotheby's auction house
The night scene

Carnegie Hill
Millionaires' Row mansions and town houses

The Upper East Side

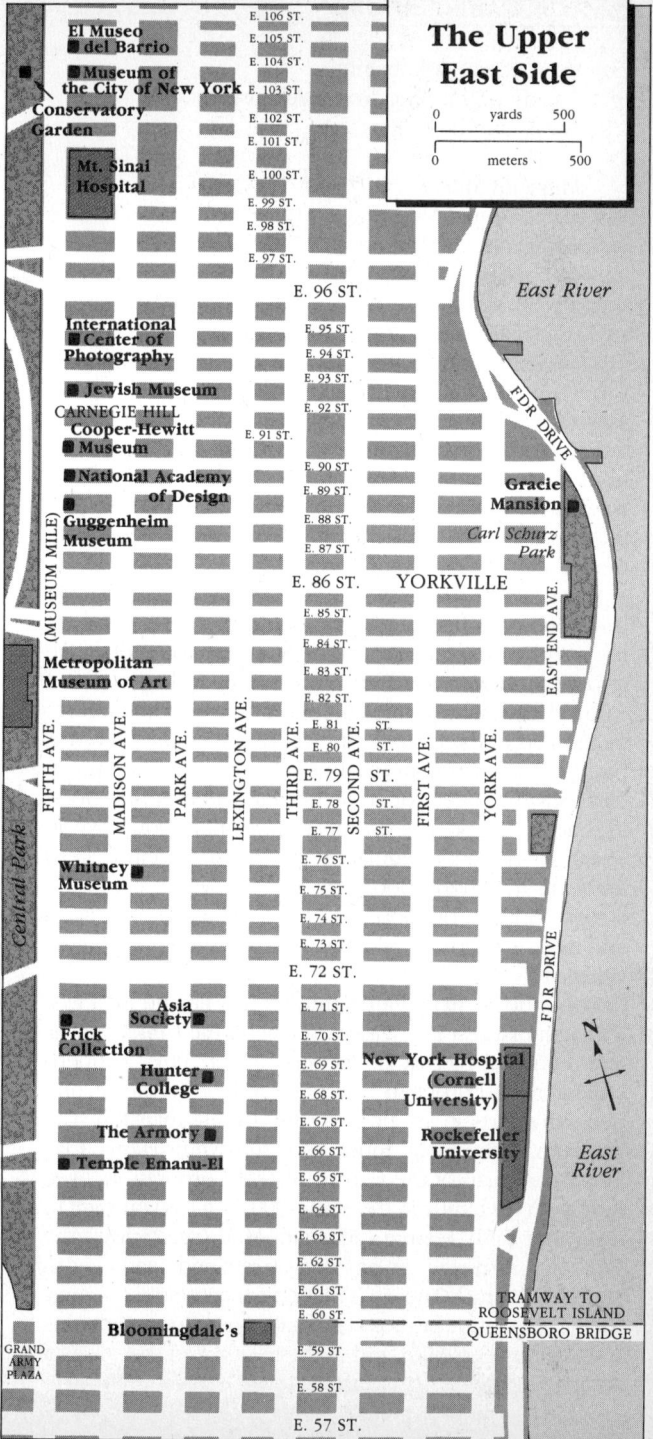

| 0 | yards | 500 |
| 0 | meters | 500 |

El Museo del Barrio
Museum of the City of New York
Conservatory Garden
Mt. Sinai Hospital

International Center of Photography
Jewish Museum
CARNEGIE HILL
Cooper-Hewitt Museum
National Academy of Design
Guggenheim Museum

Metropolitan Museum of Art

Whitney Museum

Asia Society
Frick Collection
Hunter College
The Armory
Temple Emanu-El

Bloomingdale's

East River

FDR DRIVE

Gracie Mansion
Carl Schurz Park

YORKVILLE

New York Hospital (Cornell University)

Rockefeller University

East River

TRAMWAY TO ROOSEVELT ISLAND
QUEENSBORO BRIDGE

Central Park

GRAND ARMY PLAZA

(MUSEUM MILE)

FIFTH AVE.
MADISON AVE.
PARK AVE.
LEXINGTON AVE.
THIRD AVE.
SECOND AVE.
FIRST AVE.
YORK AVE.
EAST END AVE.

E. 106 ST.
E. 105 ST.
E. 104 ST.
E. 103 ST.
E. 102 ST.
E. 101 ST.
E. 100 ST.
E. 99 ST.
E. 98 ST.
E. 97 ST.
E. 96 ST.
E. 95 ST.
E. 94 ST.
E. 93 ST.
E. 92 ST.
E. 91 ST.
E. 90 ST.
E. 89 ST.
E. 88 ST.
E. 87 ST.
E. 86 ST.
E. 85 ST.
E. 84 ST.
E. 83 ST.
E. 82 ST.
E. 81 ST.
E. 80 ST.
E. 79 ST.
E. 78 ST.
E. 77 ST.
E. 76 ST.
E. 75 ST.
E. 74 ST.
E. 73 ST.
E. 72 ST.
E. 71 ST.
E. 70 ST.
E. 69 ST.
E. 68 ST.
E. 67 ST.
E. 66 ST.
E. 65 ST.
E. 64 ST.
E. 63 ST.
E. 62 ST.
E. 61 ST.
E. 60 ST.
E. 59 ST.
E. 58 ST.
E. 57 ST.

N

View down Park Avenue
Façade of the Squadron A Armory
Shops and boutiques

Museum Mile
Metropolitan Museum of Art
Guggenheim Museum
Cooper-Hewitt Museum
Jewish Museum
International Center of Photography
Museum of the City of New York

As you move north of Midtown on the East Side, you'll notice that the streets are less crowded and the energy level isn't as frighteningly high—especially on summer weekends, when the entire population of the Upper East Side seems to flee to the Jersey Shore, upstate New York, Connecticut, or the Hamptons.

Where to start is always a good question. Basically, you can hopscotch back and forth between avenues and hit the most worthwhile attractions. Start with a cup of coffee at **Caffè Strada,** a state-of-the-art pushcart parked at Grand Army Plaza (Fifth Avenue and Central Park South, in front of the Plaza Hotel). In a city where the coffee served is often as transparent as tea, this is a real find. The proprietors saw the need for some decent coffee in New York, especially for people on the run. So here you have it, $1.00 for decaf or regular, $2.25 for cappuccino. Steps away are the **Strand Book Store kiosks,** where you could spend an hour or more looking through books, tapes, and maps spread out on tables and in large kiosks on the sidewalk.

Continue north up Fifth to the **Temple Emanu-El** (1 East 65th), the largest Reform synagogue in the United States, and then to the **Frick Collection** (1 East 70th), a superb collection of European paintings, antique furniture, and decorative arts in an elegant Fifth Avenue mansion. The museum today looks much as it did when Henry Clay Frick, chairman of the Carnegie Steel Corporation, lived here with his family in the early 1900s. Unless you want to do upper Fifth Avenue's Museum Mile (see below) the same day, turn right on any cross street and head over to **Madison Avenue.** The city's biggest concentration of toney boutiques, antiques shops, and galleries is located on this stretch between 59th and 79th streets. And, because of zoning, most are in attractive town houses or brownstones and often have residences on higher floors. Among the shops, you'll find Villeroy & Boch, Ralph Lauren Polo, Saint Laurent Rive Gauche, and Kenzo-Paris, all lined up like contestants in a beauty contest. (See the Fashion section for more on Madison Avenue shopping.)

You'll also find on the East Side the fine-arts auctioneer **Christie's** (502 Park Avenue, at 59th Street) and its branch, **Christie's East** (219 East 67th Street, between Second and Third; Tel: 212-546-1000 for information).

At 75th Street and Madison stands the **Whitney Museum of American Art**, which you might want to save for a Tuesday night when admission is free and it becomes a buzzing hive of mingling singles who show more interest in one another than in the works by Georgia O'Keeffe and other contemporary artists. Veer off to Park at 70th Street if you're interested in seeing the **Asia Society** (725 Park), founded under the guidance of John D. Rockefeller III, who wanted to increase American awareness of Asian culture. The society achieves this goal with its fine collection of Asian ceramics and sculpture and an ambitious film and lecture program. Back on Madison, you'll pass the **Carlyle Hotel** (35 East 76th Street), which is worth returning to for dinner: The **Carlyle Restaurant** serves classical French cuisine in one of New York's most elegant and sophisticated rooms, and after-dinner, pianist Bobby Short is on hand. Farther down Madison you'll come to **Le Relais** (712 Madison between 63rd and 64th), a fashionable bistro packed with Europeans. It's a great lunch spot, especially if you sit outside on a beautiful day.

At some point in the 60s, start inching your way east, so you can sample a bit of Lexington Avenue. It's chockablock with a variety of boutiques and shops (not all as prohibitively expensive as those on Madison) and Greek-owned coffee shops where you can still get a meal for less that ten dollars (today in New York City that's close to a miracle).

Next stop: **Bloomingdale's** (Lexington Avenue at 59th Street). Absolutely every visitor to New York includes this department store on his or her sightseeing list. It's right up there with the Empire State Building and the Statue of Liberty. You might want to go there with your defenses up: Mannequinlike men and women stand with index fingers ready to tap the sprayers of different fragrances as they call out the names of their products. Bloomingdale's is *always* busy, so don't go when you're feeling pressed for time, and don't go on Sunday, when it is usually closed.

Some of the East Side's best restaurants are in the Bloomingdale's area, including **Arizona 206** (206 East 60th, near Third Avenue; Southwestern cuisine); **Malvasia** (108 East 60th Street; creatively prepared fish, chicken, and duck dishes); **Felidia Ristorante** (243 East 58th Street; boar with rosemary, pheasant, and a satiating selection of Northern Italian dishes); **Arcadia** (21 East 62nd, between Madison and Fifth; down-home American food); and **The Sign of the Dove** (1110 Third Avenue at 65th Street; a costly brunch spot). And of course there's **Le Cirque** (58 East 65th, between Madison and Park), the ultimate French restaurant in New York City—it's very expensive and reservations are very difficult to get.

YORKVILLE

You have to have a really great imagination to picture what this shore of Manhattan Island looked like in the late 18th century. At that time it was considered "upstate New York," where only the fabulously wealthy could afford to have country homes. With the advent of the railroad linking New York City with Harlem in 1834, Yorkville was "suburbanized" and attracted Eastern European and German immigrants. Though many of the Germans, Czechs, and Hungarians have since migrated to the suburbs, there are still traces of their heritage—especially in small restaurants and businesses from the low to mid-70s and up to 96th Street, between Park Avenue and the East River. Today's Yorkville residents are predominantly young working couples and singles.

Although 86th Street and Second Avenue are the main streets of Yorkville, a good starting place for a walking tour is **Carl Schurz Park**, which is built directly over Franklin D. Roosevelt Drive, smack-dab on the East River, stretching from 90th Street to Gracie Square at 84th Street.

The centerpiece of the park is the official mayor's residence, **Gracie Mansion**. The original part of the house was built as a country home for merchant seaman Archibald Gracie; it later passed through a series of wealthy owners, each of whom eventually lost his fortune. In 1924 it was taken over by the Museum of the City of New York and later—during Mayor La Guardia's term—turned into the official mayor's residence. Mayor Koch is to thank for opening it up to the public. Tours are conducted on

Wednesdays (Tel: 212-570-4751 for an appointment). The house as it stands today is actually a historic re-creation, not a restoration, of the Federal style. Many of the interior pieces are on loan from museums and private collections or are reproductions. There are a perennial exhibit called "Merchants to Mayors" and a gift shop in the basement.

The park's waterfront esplanade—the John Finley Walk—is a fine place to perch yourself for a rest. Grab a bench that looks out at the churning East River and you'll have a hard time leaving. This is one of those places that keeps New Yorkers in love with their city.

Just outside the park (86th Street) there's a stunning block of Queen Anne–style row houses, the **Henderson Place Historic District**, with slate roofs, charming windows of all shapes and sizes, turrets, and double stoops. Continue on west through Yorkville and you'll pass hundreds of row houses (each one is usually just 20 to 25 feet wide), stately town houses (fancy row houses for people who could afford to have pieds-à-terre), and innumerable nondescript high-rise apartment fortresses. Sadly, these towers are eating up the old neighborhoods.

On sight of the **Church of the Holy Trinity**, between First and Second avenues on 88th Street, you'll think you're in the Loire Valley. The church is French Gothic style with gargoyles, flying buttresses, arches, and ornate copper work. The inside is just as impressive, with Medieval-style stained-glass windows and an incredible rank of organ pipes. Check the newspapers for information on Holy Trinity's winter organ recitals and classical-music concerts.

Also in Yorkville, you'll find Sotheby Parke Bernet, known as **Sotheby's** (1334 York Avenue at 72nd Street; Tel: 212-606-7000), the American branch of the world's oldest firm of arts auctioneers. This is the auction house that sold most of Andy Warhol's estate and van Gogh's *Irises* for $53.9 million.

For dining in Yorkville, consider **Bistro Bamboche** (1582 York Avenue, between 83rd and 84th streets), where French specialties are prepared with flair. **Le Refuge** (166 East 82nd, between Third and Lexington) is a quiet, refined bistro with country French decor. Its clientele is made up largely of Upper East Siders who show up dressed in anything from casual weekend clothes to Brooks Brothers suits. If you want to do a little celebrity watching, try **Lusardi's** (1494 Second Avenue, between 77th and 78th), where the Italian cuisine is unfailingly good. Though everyone will tell you that **Elaine's** (1703 Second Avenue, between 88th and 89th) is where to go stargazing, don't bother. Not only is the food lamentable, but ordinary people are made to feel like real nobodies. However, it used to be a bastion of New York literati, including Woody Allen, who used it as a location in *Manhattan*. One of the last remaining Eastern European restaurants in Yorkville is **Vasata** (339 East 75th, between First and Second avenues), which serves New York City's best Czechoslovakian food in an old Bohemian setting.

The Upper East Side is famous for its profusion of bars, mostly on First Avenue in the 60s and on Second and Third from 72nd to 94th streets (see also the After Hours chapter). If you want to sample the bar scene here, drop in at **Jim McMullen** (1341 Third, between 75th and 76th). In a city where bars open and close like flowers, this one has managed to stay hot for years. The clientele is made up of many regulars, most of whom are fashion models and professional athletes. Tops on the list of trendy spots is **The Outback** (between 93rd and 94th on Third), a scuzzy-looking bar with cigarette butts on the floor and music that is much too loud. Pour down an Aussie beer, pull out all the Down Under phrases you know, and you'll fit right in. On weekend nights it's so popular that the spillover crowds bide their time across the street at **The Launch Café** until they can get in. The Upper East Side is also home to two very good comedy clubs: **The Comic Strip** (1568 Second, near 81st Street) and **Catch a Rising Star** (1487 First, near 77th).

CARNEGIE HILL

Carnegie Hill is more a state of mind than an actual neighborhood. It stretches from about 86th to 96th streets, from Fifth to Park, but sometimes reaches over as far as Lexington and Third, as indicated by some shop and building names. You won't find it marked on most maps and will come across few—if any—New Yorkers who can tell you exactly where it begins and ends.

The area became known as Carnegie Hill in 1901 when Andrew Carnegie built a mansion (now the Cooper-Hewitt Museum) on 91st and Fifth. Up until that point, the socially acceptable place to live was south of 59th Street. His bold step set off a trend, and before long several mansions sprang up along a section of Fifth facing the park. The Astors, the Vanderbilts, and other wealthy families began migrating to upper Fifth Avenue, which soon became known as **Millionaires' Row**. The growth of Madison Avenue and the side streets between Madison and Fifth followed. Today, Carnegie Hill continues to be one of the most exclusive neighborhoods in the world (Richard Nixon couldn't get in after his presidency).

To get a feel for the area, just wander aimlessly. Most of the mansions and lavish town houses line Fifth (many now house small museums or consulates) or are tucked away on side streets, especially in the lower 90s between Fifth and Madison. Make a point of getting over to see 120 and 122 East 92nd Street, two wooden town houses that were built in the late 1800s, complete with shutters and columned front porches. Over on Park at 92nd, there's a Louise Nevelson sculpture called *Night Presence,* a 22-foot-high steel work donated to the city by the artist in 1972. A block north is the headquarters building of the Synod of Bishops of the Russian Orthodox Church Outside of Russia, which was owned in the late 1920s by banker George F. Baker, who had a private railroad car that would stop directly beneath the building (the railway tracks for Grand Central Station run under Park here). It's not open to the public, but you can peek in at a garden courtyard that leads to a ballroom that Baker added to the original 1918 structure.

The view south down Park Avenue from Carnegie Hill is spectacular. The avenue dips down like a rolled-out carpet, with the cornices of its grand apartment houses aligned, drawing your eye to what used to be the New York Central Building (now the Helmsley Building) between 45th and 46th streets, with the Pan Am Building looming over it. And though the color gray predominates, there's a central divider planted with a colorful profusion of flowers, trees, and bushes in fair-weather months. During the winter season, delicate white lights strung in the trees give the avenue a delightful carnival spirit at night. Most Park Avenue buildings are compatible in size (from 15 to 18 floors) and materials (all are brick, many have limestone trim), with the exception of the occasional town house or church. With the "Gold Coast" (as Fifth Avenue facing Central Park is called), Park Avenue is one of New York's most coveted addresses. An average apartment (often just a pied-à-terre) might sprawl over a dozen rooms.

In contrast to the present-day vista, before 1900 Park

Avenue was not a coveted address. The railroads ran above ground and were lined with rather humble dwellings and unattractive factories. Beginning in 1872 the tracks were moved below street level as far north as 56th Street. It was not until after the completion of Grand Central Terminal in 1913, however, that the tracks were depressed as far north as 96th Street. By the 1920s, the avenue had become very desirable real estate, with one luxury residential building going up after another. Today it continues to be one of New York's most fashionable areas—up to 96th Street, where Spanish Harlem abruptly begins.

If you follow 93rd Street back west toward Madison, you'll pass a classical mansion with Palladian and bull's-eye windows and a discreet sign identifying it as the Smithers Alcoholism Treatment Center. It was originally a house built for William Goadby Loew, a stockbroker, and later was owned by Billy Rose, a producer and art collector and a husband of Elizabeth Taylor. The façade of the former **Squadron A Armory** between 94th and 95th on Madison is hard not to notice. It's a massive fortresslike building with arched doorways, towers, and battlements. Walk through the entrance and you'll find yourself in the middle of a playground that serves next-door Hunter High School.

Carnegie Hill architecture can keep you mesmerized for hours, but so can the shops along Madison Avenue—especially if you're in the market for antiques. If money is no object, you can have a glorious time. Many of the small boutiques and shops sell European imports. You never have to walk more than a few blocks to find a gourmet shop in the neighborhood, where chances are good that you will find that rare mustard you thought you could only get in Lyons.

Consider brunching at **Sarabeth's Kitchen** (1295 Madison, between 92nd and 93rd). The setting is delightful, with high ceilings, light floral wallpaper, small round tables covered with crisp white tablecloths, and vases spilling over with daisies. The food is wholesome and good: typical breakfasts here are whole-wheat pancakes topped with fruit and wheatberries, pumpkin waffles, and cheddar and apple-butter omelets. It's connected to the **Hotel Wales**, a longtime favorite among loyal guests, with some of the most reasonable rates in town (see Accommodations section). The **Bistro du Nord**, Madison at 93rd, is very European and comfortable, and across the street is the fashionable restaurant **Island**. Just down Madison between 91st and 92nd streets, **Equense Mangeria**, a new family-owned Italian-American restaurant, serves warm spinach salads, marinated funghi, and delicious *saltimbocca*.

MUSEUM MILE

Museum Mile is a consortium of nine cultural institutions on Fifth Avenue between 82nd and 104th streets. The grande dame is the **Metropolitan Museum of Art** (The Met), a gargantuan building on the edge of Central Park between 80th and 84th streets. Especially impressive is its Egyptian Wing. The American Wing is rich with more than 3,000 paintings and decorative arts from the Colonial period to the 20th century. Other outstanding collections, each worth at least half a day, are the European Painting rooms, the Meyer Galleries of 19th-century European paintings, the new modern-art wing, and the Rockefeller primitive-art collection. The museum shops are spectacular, too. You'll need a break afterward, so stop for drinks at the Stanhope Hotel's **Terrace**, a pleasant sidewalk café directly opposite. The Stanhope's **Le Salon** serves a wonderful tea, with scones and Devonshire cream, salmon and watercress sandwiches, and, to top it all off, fruit tartlets.

The eight other museums are spread out along Fifth on the east side of the street. Walking north, you'll pass them all. First, you'll come to the **Yivo Institute for Jewish Research** (1048 Fifth at 86th Street), housed in one of Fifth Avenue's most exquisite mansions, with Ionic pilasters, balustrades, rosettes, and bull's-eye windows. The museum is devoted to the history of Eastern European Jews. Frank Lloyd Wright's **Solomon R. Guggenheim Museum** (1071 Fifth, between 88th and 89th streets) is one of the city's most distinctive buildings. It contains painting and sculpture from the Impressionist period to the present; most of the exhibit space is devoted to temporary exhibitions.

A block north, between 89th and 90th streets, is the **National Academy of Design** (1083 Fifth), which holds a rich collection of 19th- and 20th-century American art. At 90th stands the Protestant Episcopal **Church of the Heavenly Rest**, a Gothic church with a tiny side chapel. Directly across the street is the main meeting place for joggers warming up to do "the loop"—a run around

Central Park's Reservoir. The entrance of the **Cooper-Hewitt Museum**, the Smithsonian Institution's museum of design, is at 2 East 91st Street. This was millionaire Andrew Carnegie's home, a 64-room mansion now housing exhibits that change regularly but always focus on some aspect of design. Directly across the street is the Convent of the Sacred Heart (1 East 91st), a neo-Italian palazzo, now a girls' school. (This area contains many of the city's private schools, most on the side streets.) Continue up Fifth and you'll come to the **Jewish Museum** (1109 Fifth) in a French Renaissance–style mansion. In addition to its permanent collection of Judaica it runs temporary exhibits.

The International Center of Photography (1130 Fifth) has changing exhibits by 19th- and 20th-century photographers and photojournalists. Several blocks up (at 103rd Street) is the **Museum of the City of New York**, where the city's history is re-created. Call for information (Tel: 212-534-1672) about their Sunday walking tours. At 104th Street, **El Museo del Barrio** (1230 Fifth) completes the Museum Mile. It's the only museum in America devoted to the cultures of Puerto Rico and Latin America.

BROOKLYN

By Randall Short

Randall Short is the Theater Features writer for Vogue. *He reports regularly on literature and the arts for* The New York Times, New York Newsday, *and* Spy *magazine.*

"When the sun is shining and the wind is right," says a character in Richard Condon's *Prizzi's Honor,* "there ain't no place like Brooklyn!" If Manhattan is flash and glitter, Brooklyn (perhaps recalling its origins as Dutch-colonized farmland in the 1600s) is the gentler side of urban living in New York. Although Manhattanites used to regard Brooklyn simply as a bedroom community across the river, that attitude has given way in recent years to a vigorous, renewed sense of local pride perceptible even to the casual visitor. The borough owes much of its character to close-knit neighborhoods, a diverse ethnic mix—West Indies blacks, Hasidic Jews, Norwegians, Russians, and Middle Easterners barely begin to exhaust the list—and a superbly preserved heritage of 19th-century architecture.

Older Brooklynites still joke about a time when "fine dining" meant one thing: chow mein and egg rolls in one of the borough's numerous Chinese restaurants. In the 1930s and 1940s these were a Canarsie kid's usual introduction to foods more exotic than bagels or corned beef. At that time the borough was home to working-class Irish, Italian, and Jewish families, whose distinctive accents and don't-try-to-bullshit-me attitudes still characterize the Brooklynite. Now, however, Brooklyn offers variety in dining comparable to that in Manhattan—often at significantly lower prices—and its row houses are being snatched up by Manhattanites for a relative song, compared to prices across the East River.

Brooklyn lies to the east and south of Manhattan, connected to it by three bridges and a network of subways. Prior to its annexation into New York City in 1898 ("the Big Mistake," one Brooklyn-born writer calls it), the borough's 77 square miles formed a separate city composed of six principal towns and numerous small independent villages. Much of the area still has a strong regional feel; inhabitants consider themselves Bay Ridgers or Williamsburgers or Park Slopers first, Brooklynites second, and the neighborhoods bear strong witness to several successive waves of immigrant history.

MAJOR INTEREST

Brooklyn Bridge
Promenade view of Manhattan skyline
Brooklyn Heights' Brownstone Belt
Atlantic Avenue's Middle Eastern community
Brooklyn Academy of Music
Prospect Park
Brooklyn Botanic Garden
Brooklyn Museum
Brighton Beach's Little Odessa
Coney Island
Greenpoint

Subways and cabs will take you from Manhattan into Brooklyn with no trouble, but it may be more difficult to hail a cab going the opposite direction—drivers tend to prefer the crowded Midtown district for pickup business. However, there are numerous car services to ferry you around. Or—an alternative solution—rent a bike and make the trek from Manhattan over the pedestrian walkway atop Brooklyn Bridge, from which there's no finer view anywhere.

Take the IRT number 2 or 3 train to the Brooklyn Heights stop (20 minutes from Midtown Manhattan), walk two blocks to the small park square at the end of nearby Montague Street, and you're at a natural point of entry to the borough, the Esplanade, commonly called the **Promenade**, a pleasant bench- and tree-lined walkway built by legendary city commissioner Robert Moses. (You may remember Judy Holliday waltzing on its edge with Dean Martin to "Just in Time" in *Bells Are Ringing*.) Fronting the East River and lower Manhattan, it offers an unparalleled view of the harbor, the Financial District, and the borough's best-known symbol, **Brooklyn Bridge**, the 1883 dedication of which opened Brooklyn to large-scale industrial and residential development. Built by the immigrant German father-and-son team of John and Washington Roebling, pioneers in the engineering and construction of modern suspension bridges, it was at the time the largest such structure in the world. If you find yourself interested in a closer look at the bridge, a walk to the end of the Promenade and down a sharply sloping hill will bring you to its foundations—and to the **River Café** (1 Water Street; reservations, Tel: 718-722-5200), which offers pleasantly elegant (and expensive) waterside dining from a French-style menu featuring American classics.

BROOKLYN HEIGHTS

Some 70 years before the bridge's completion, when steam-ferry service between Brooklyn and Manhattan was begun, the riverbank neighborhood **Brooklyn Heights** became America's first suburb, conceived as an oasis of genteel *rus in urbe* living for harried Wall Street businessmen. Today it's the center of the gentrified "Brownstone Belt," a swath of magnificent urban architecture rediscovered in the late 1950s by young professionals resisting the call of Levittown-style housing developments farther out.

A walk down any of the surrounding streets will reveal dozens of meticulously preserved Greek Revival and Federal-period brownstones crowned with gargoyles, oriel windows, and finely detailed ornament. A convenient route might be to start out south down Hicks near the northern end of the Promenade and make side excursions, as the whim takes you, on Middagh, Pierrepont, Montague, Henry, Strawberry, Joralemon, and Warren streets.

If, on the other hand, you should find your interest in Brooklyn taking a more methodical turn, tour the **Brooklyn Historical Society** (128 Pierrepont Street). The society spent several years refurbishing its handsome, mansionlike premises and adding a new museum gallery and has just reopened its doors to the public. Besides acting as custodian for a large collection of papers and artifacts relating to the borough's history, it offers a wide variety of tours, educational programs, and lectures. Many of these are held in a lecture hall where Mark Twain and Rudyard Kipling, among others, entertained 19th-century audiences with tales of their travels abroad.

In the 1800s Brooklyn acquired the nickname "Borough of Churches" for the number and distinction (both architectural and clerical) of its ecclesiastical institutions; several of the most prominent still stand in central Brooklyn Heights, just around the corner from the historical society. **St. Ann's and the Holy Trinity**, an Episcopal parish at Clinton and Montague streets, possesses the first stained-glass windows made in the United States and hosts a popular arts series. From the pulpit of nearby **Plymouth Church** at Orange and Hicks streets— formerly known as "the Grand Central Terminal of the Underground Railroad"—the clergyman and abolitionist Henry Ward Beecher preached against "the peculiar institution" and harbored large numbers of fugitive slaves on their way to sanctuary in the North.

Montague Street, the Heights' main shopping thoroughfare, is filled with bookstores, clothing boutiques, art galleries, and lots of convivial, moderately priced places for a bite and a swallow. The bars at **Peter Hilary's Bar and Grill** (174 Montague Street), **Slade's** (107 Montague Street), and **Montague Street Saloon** (122 Montague Street) draw a young professional crowd from the nearby downtown City Hall and court districts; try **Foffe's** (155 Montague Street) down the block for lovingly prepared traditional Italian specialties. If you're in the mood for game, **Henry's End** (44 Henry Street) regularly features dishes like pheasant, quail, bear, buffalo, and reindeer; a 52-selection beer list is available to help wash them

NEW JERSEY

PULASKI SKYWAY

Holland
Tunnel

MANHATTAN

Hudson River

East River

NEW JERSEY TPK. EXTENSION

WEST ST.

BROADWAY

LAFAYETTE ST.

CANAL ST.

DELANCEY ST.

FDR DRIVE

WILLIAMSBUR

Williamsburg
Bridge

BEDFORD

Ellis Island

Liberty Island

Governor's
Island

WALL
STREET

Brooklyn
Bridge

Brooklyn-
Battery
Tunnel

Manhattan
Bridge

BROOKLYN
HEIGHTS
Promenade

COURT ST.

Borough Hall

FULTON ST.

FLATBUSH

BROOKLYN

BEDFORD AVE.

BEDFORD-
STUYVESANT

ATLANTIC AVE.

RED HOOK

Brooklyn
Academy
of Music

Brooklyn
Botanic
Garden

Upper
New York
Bay

Gowanus
Bay

BROOKLYN-QUEENS EXPWY.

Brooklyn Museum

FOURTH AVE.

Grand
Army
Plaza

PROSPECT EXPWY.

PARK SLOPE

Prospect Park

BEDFORD AVE.

39 ST.

CATON AVE.

N

BAY RIDGE
AVE.

FORT HAMILTON PKWY.

BOROUGH
PARK

CONEY

Brooklyn College

BAY
RIDGE

FOURTH AVE.

65 ST.

OCEAN

ISLAND

AVE.

MIDWOOD

The
Narrows

Fort
Hamilton

Dyker Beach Park

BENSONHURST

86 ST.

BAY PKWY.

AVENUE P

PKWY.

KINGS HWY.

AVENUE U

Verrazano-
Narrows
Bridge

STATEN
ISLAND

Gateway National
Recreation Area

Hoffman Island

BELT PKWY. (SHORE PKWY.)

Gravesend
Bay

STILLWELL AVE.

CONEY
ISLAND
AVE.

NEPTUNE AVE.

BRIGHTON
BEACH

Atlantic Ocean

Swinburne Island

CONEY ISLAND

SURF

AVE.

New York
Aquarium

Brooklyn

0　　miles　　1

0　　kilometers　　1.6

LONG ISLAND EXPWY. I-495

QUEENS EXPWY.

GREENPOINT

GRAND AVE.

GRAND ST.

QUEENS

BROADWAY

MYRTLE AVE.

BUSHWICK AVE.

Forest Park

INTERBOROUGH PKWY.

ATLANTIC AVE.

ATLANTIC AVE.

CROSS BAY BLVD.

CONDUIT BLVD.

EASTERN PKWY.

CROWN HEIGHTS

EAST NEW YORK

LINDEN BLVD.

LINDEN BLVD.

PENNSYLVANIA AVE.

KINGS HWY.

FLATBUSH

FLATLANDS AVE.

CANARSIE

BELT PKWY. (SHORE PKWY.)

Jamaica Bay

FLATBUSH AVE.

KINGS HWY.

FLATLANDS

BEDFORD AVE.

Marine Park

GERRITSEN AVE.

KNAPP ST.

SHEEPSHEAD BAY

Floyd Bennett Field

Gateway National Recreation Area

SHORE PKWY.

Sheepshead Bay

ORIENTAL BLVD.

MANHATTAN BEACH

Rockaway Inlet

Marine Pkwy. Bridge

BEACH CHANNEL DRIVE

ROCKAWAY (QUEENS)

Jacob Riis Park

down. And, after a few anxious months spent in the shadow of the wrecker's ball, the classic wood- and mirror-paneled 1870s salon of **Gage & Tollner** (372 Fulton Street, in the nearby downtown shopping district; Tel: 718-875-5181) has been rescued by restaurateur Peter Aschkenasy and restored to its full gastronomic glory. "Brooklyn's Landmark Restaurant," as it bills itself, now offers both its hallowed seafood specialties (try the clam bellies) and Virginia-style dishes (Smithfield ham, homemade breads and preserves) by the renowned Southern chef Edna Lewis.

ATLANTIC AVENUE

A walk of two or three blocks will bring you to the center of New York's—and America's—largest Arab community. Atlantic Avenue is lined with shops and restaurants, many of them operated by and catering to the recent wave of Middle Easterners that have relocated in Brooklyn. An antiques district with dozens of small independent stores has sprung up here to service the growing crowd of new home buyers. It offers prices substantially lower than those in Manhattan. After you've loaded up on porcelain and sconces, try the kebabs, curries, and couscous at **Tripoli** (156 Atlantic Avenue), one of the area's more elegantly appointed Arab restaurants. Slightly more modest, but just as good, are **Adnan** (129 Atlantic Avenue) and **Near East** (136 Court Street), whose motto hangs on a sign over the door: It Pays To Eat Well.

Brooklyn Academy of Music

Avant-garde performance is alive and flourishing just off the intersection of Atlantic and Flatbush avenues at the **Brooklyn Academy of Music** (20 minutes from Midtown Manhattan on the D train to the Atlantic Avenue station; box office, Tel: 718-636-4100), America's oldest continuously operating performing arts center. BAM, as it's commonly known, operates out of a superb 1908 opera house and offers New York's largest ongoing concentration of experimental dance, music, and theater. The fall Next Wave festival regularly premieres new work by the likes of Pina Bausch, Philip Glass, and Robert Wilson. Around the corner, BAM's newly opened **Majestic Theater**, a turn-of-the-century variety stage, has been renovated in the Postmodern manner by director Peter Brook, who makes his American creative home here.

PARK SLOPE

From BAM, Flatbush Avenue runs through a renovated commercial district, into Park Slope, a magnificent enclave of late Victorian homes developed in the 1880s for Brooklyn's prosperous English and German upper middle classes. The houses' satisfying combination of sober practicality and fancifulness (elaborately carved stone detailing, delicate cast-iron filigree, decorative castings) today seems more modern—certainly more popular—than ever.

The neighborhood's focal point is the center of old Brooklyn, **Grand Army Plaza** (40 minutes from Midtown Manhattan on the number 2 or 3 West Side IRT train to the Grand Army Plaza station; 20 minutes on the D train to the Seventh Avenue station), a European-style traffic circle with a memorial arch built in 1892 to honor Brooklyn's Union Army war dead. The group of statues at its summit, featuring Columbia (the pre–Uncle Sam symbol of America) at the center of a victory quadriga, are by the prominent 19th-century American sculptor Frederick Mac-Monnies; relief panels over the inner entrance doorways by Thomas Eakins are the only public Eakins sculptures in New York City.

Walk from the plaza down the wide, pleasant spaces of Eighth Avenue and its side streets (Carroll, Garfield, Montgomery Place) for a look at the comfortable gentility of the 19th-century good life; then skip over for drinks on Seventh Avenue, the main shopping drag, at **McFeely's** (847 Union Street), a Victorian-style saloon from which waitresses (such as Kelly McGillis) routinely go on to become movie stars, or **Rex** (222 Seventh Avenue), an old Irish bar with a new Caribbean flair. **Cousin John's Café**, with two Seventh Avenue locations, makes its own pastry and fresh ice cream on the premises. And, a little farther down, the kitchen of **Aunt Suzie's** (247 Fifth Avenue between Carroll and Garfield) turns out inexpensive trattoria fare in a homey atmosphere. Slightly pricier, and well worth it, are two French-style restaurants that have opened on the south edge of the Slope within the past year: the "new American" haute-cuisine **Adele** (501 11th Street), whose chef left Manhattan's renowned Montrachet for greener pastures in Brooklyn (reservations a must; Tel: 718-788-4980); and the airy, pleasant, country bistro **Tartine** (426A Seventh Avenue).

From the plaza, three of the borough's proudest attractions are within a few minutes' stroll of one another. **Prospect Park**, a pastoral, 526-acre expanse of trees, grass, and water (its Long Meadow offers the largest green vista unbroken by buildings in New York City), is the masterpiece of urban designers Frederick Law Olmsted and Calvert Vaux, who also created Manhattan's Central Park. Begun in 1866, it was built on land from the estate of city father Edwin Litchfield, whose palatial Italianate villa is the park's headquarters. Contemporary Brooklynites of every stripe now come from all over to picnic, ice-skate, play ball, and enjoy concerts in the band shell, site of the popular Celebrate Brooklyn summer festival. Across from the band shell is **Raintree's** (142 Prospect Park West), a restaurant in a converted drugstore with tile floors and stained-glass windows that open onto the park. A couple of blocks down, **Aunt Sonia's** (1123 Eighth Avenue), named for the neighboring Ansonia Clock Factory, serves classic American dishes with a piquant twist in an intimate, friendly atmosphere.

Dismayed by the intrusion of not entirely appropriate buildings (like the Metropolitan Museum) into their design for Central Park, Olmsted and Vaux didn't make the same mistake twice: They insisted that the Prospect Park commissioners set aside a tract of land separate from the park proper to accommodate subsequent developments. So cross the street and you're in the **Brooklyn Botanic Garden** (1000 Washington Avenue; Tel: 718-622-4433). With a design reminiscent of an English estate and grounds, this assemblage includes a Japanese scholar's garden, a cherry esplanade that bears great clouds of soft pink blossoms in the spring, the Cranford Rose Garden (third largest in the United States), and the new Steinhardt Conservatory of tropical and desert plants. The number 2 and 3 subway lines stop at its (Eastern Parkway Station) door and at that of the **Brooklyn Museum** (200 Eastern Parkway). The museum's stately Beaux Arts building is undergoing expansion these days. Its collection of Egyptian art is the most comprehensive outside of Cairo and London; the Chinese and African galleries are also strong. After you've taken them in, **Michele's** (350 Flatbush Avenue) and **New Prospect Café** (393 Flatbush Avenue), comfortable, wood-and-mirror-paneled bistros just a few minutes away, are convenient for a light lunch or supper.

BRIGHTON BEACH

If you're in the mood for a longer trip, 40 minutes on the D train from Midtown Manhattan will land you in Brighton Beach, just up the boardwalk from Coney Island and until the last decade best known as a fertile breeding ground for Jewish-American comedians and humorists (Moss Hart, Neil Simon, Woody Allen). It's now familiarly known as Little Odessa for the massive numbers of Russian nationals who relocated to this seaside neighborhood when Soviet emigration restrictions eased in the early 1970s. On **Brighton Beach Avenue**, the area's commercial center, bookstores (a recent big seller: Gorbachev's *Perestroika*), restaurants (caviar, *shashlik*), and omnipresent balalaika music attest to its status as America's largest Russian community. Check out the Saturday crowds shopping for smoked fish and garlicky sausage at **M & I International Foods** (number 249); then cross the street for a lunch accompanied by vigorous Slavic renditions of American pop tunes at **Primorski** (number 282). (You've never heard Elvis till you've heard him in Ukrainian.) Fifteen dollars here will bring more food than one human being can reasonably consume; Russians, explains the owner, "like good value for their money." **Café Europa** (number 306) and **Café Zodiac** (number 309) offer slightly lighter fare in the same vein, but dinner visitors to **National Restaurant** (number 273) should be prepared to do things in a big way: For $25, you get dinner, drinks, dancing, a nightclub show, and the chance to participate in the most passionate audience singalongs this side of Kiev. You might want to plan a walk in the salty air of the boardwalk along the beach first in order to whet your appetite.

CONEY ISLAND

A ten-minute stroll from the Brighton area along the same beachfront will put you in the center of an authentic American landmark. Lawrence Ferlinghetti named one of the first volumes of Beat poetry for it; Maksim Gorki, who visited it in the early days of the Soviet Union, came away with a phantasmagorical vision of American urban intensity; it's the birthplace of the hot dog. It's Coney Island, of course, and since the 1840s—first by railroad, later, and more democratically, by subway—this first and best-known of American seaside parks has enabled stressed-out New Yorkers to leave behind the hot summer city for a few hours of sun, sand, and surf. Frankness compels an admission that the resort is not in the best state of repair these days. The carousels, roller coasters, and fantasy rides that made its Luna and Steeplechase parks famous at the turn of the century (Steeplechase's Ferris wheel, visible 38 miles out to sea, was often the first piece of America sighted by European immigrants) were allowed to decay in the 1960s, when amusement parks everywhere suffered a decline in popularity. The good news, however, is that a private developer has recently signed an agreement with the city to restore the concessions to their full former glory; completion is projected for 1992. In the meantime, you can take in the **New York Aquarium** (Boardwalk and West 8th Street), rent a fishing pole and catch dinner from one of the city-operated piers, or simply enjoy the waves. As might be expected, there are quite a number of good, inexpensive seafood restaurants in the neighborhood, but no serious eater would consider visiting Coney Island without paying his respects to **Nathan's Famous**, the mecca of tube-steak—all right, all right, hot dog—lovers. Many older New Yorkers can still recall heading for a day at "Coney" in the 1920s with four nickels in their pockets: two for the subway ride there and back, two for a pair of Nathan's mustard-and-sauerkraut *specialités de la maison*. Nathan's continues to feed thousands of visitors a day at Surf and Stillwell avenues—garish, yellow-green, and eternal.

GREENPOINT

In 1862, the ironclad *Monitor* emerged from the Continental Ironworks in Greenpoint to fight for the Union against the Confederate *Merrimac*. At the northernmost point of the borough, this area was responsible for the the international reputation as an industrial center that Brooklyn wielded by the 1890s. Its numerous factories and plants specialized in cast-iron manufacture, pottery, printing, and petroleum. Although all of those enterprises have long since departed, the neighborhood is still populated by the descendants of the Polish, Italian, and Irish immigrants who came over to work in them. The Polish community has recently expanded to include a large number of Solidarity activists who left the homeland when martial law was imposed in 1981. Many of the community's activities are centered about St. Stanislaus Kostka Church (607 Humboldt Street), where a brass plaque commemorates the 1969 visit of Polish Cardinal Karol Wojtyla before he became Pope John Paul II.

If you go to Greenpoint (a ten-minute trip from lower Manhattan on the M or J subway to the Marcy or Lorimer stations), try the Polish pastries at the **White Eagle Bakery** (600 Humboldt Street) or **Little Europe** (888 Manhattan Avenue). **Bamonte's** (32 Withers Street) and **Crisci** (593 Lorimer Street) are landmark Italian restaurants, each boasting several generations of family ownership.

There's no real debate about this area's most exceptional dining experience, however: **Peter Luger** (178 Broadway; Tel: 718-387-7400), under the shadow of the elevated train in neighboring Williamsburg, is by itself worth the trip—from anywhere. This Teutonic *keller,* with worn wooden floors and an atmosphere redolent of more than a century's worth of beer, tobacco, and red meat, serves the finest steaks in New York City, aged to perfection in the restaurant's own warehouse and served in classic German-American style by waiters in high, white, starched aprons. The way there via subway (D or N lines from Midtown) is slightly inconvenient, so take a cab; there's not a driver in greater New York who doesn't make the trip regularly.

QUEENS

By Barry Lewis

Barry Lewis, an architectural historian, has created tour programs and produced lecture series for New York City's 92nd Street Y. He has also written articles on the city's architectural history for many publications and was a contributing writer to the Municipal Art Society's Juror's Guide to Lower Manhattan. *He lives in the borough of Queens.*

Queens: To residents of Manhattan it's New York's Midwest, the Archie Bunkerville where dwell the cab drivers, the firemen, the secretaries, and the plumbers of New York City. Built up half before World War II and half after, Queens was considered, in the 1950s and 1960s, the "suburbia" to Manhattan's "city." But things change—New York always does—and this borough of nearly two million has changed with it.

Queens is New York's London. It doesn't look like London, but it acts like it. Its dozens of small towns and small cities are, like London's boroughs, instinctively independent and terribly insular. If nuclear testing were planned for Flushing, the people in Jackson Heights—two "towns" away—would wonder what it had to do with them. Each neighborhood is different in class, in ethnic texture, and even in architectural scale. From the Brooklyn-style row houses of Ridgewood to the upstate, small-town atmosphere of College Point, from the modernistic factories of increasingly artsy Long Island City to the bustling Hong Kong–like downtown of Flushing, Queens is a mosaic of how New York is really lived in, away from the media-soaked atmosphere of Manhattan.

For those who can spare only an afternoon to cross the East River and visit Queens, a walk around Astoria's Greek enclave at Ditmars Boulevard and 31st Street or a visit to the Noguchi Museum and Socrates Sculpture Park and nearby Broadway might give you a taste of this other-side-of-the-world quality. Similarly, Jackson Heights' South American district along 82nd Street and Roosevelt Avenue or downtown Flushing's "Little Asia" along Main and Union streets can give you a quick take of this other New York perspective.

MAJOR INTEREST

Garden-city planning
The Seven Sister neighborhoods
Queens melting pot
Greek Astoria
Latin American and Indian quarters in Jackson
    Heights
Flushing's Little Asia
Forest Hills' Russian enclave
Corona Avenue's Italian enclave
Long Island City's Socrates Sculpture Park
Isamu Noguchi Museum
American Museum of the Moving Image
Queens Museum

Queens, first settled just after the Civil War, was annexed
to New York in 1898 and achieved full throttle with the
opening of the Queensboro (59th Street) Bridge and the
Long Island Railroad (LIRR)/Penn Station complex around
1910. In the next 30 years Queens boomed. The city had
arrived, but it was a verdant city, where architects and
developers often tried to thread gardens and greenbelts
around their apartment buildings and private homes.
Some neighborhoods were built up in the repetitive
patterns of Archie Bunker–type developments. Others,
however, like Astoria in the northwest or the older sections of Rego Park in the center of the borough, were
built with the kind of garden-style apartments and row
houses that give much of prewar Queens a leafiness
absent in over-bricked Manhattan.

A word about the Queens street system: There appears
to be a "system," but there really isn't. After the 1898
consolidation, city hall imposed a Manhattan-style grid on
the new borough. Old names were replaced by numbers
with, theoretically, 1st Street at the East River end and
250th Street at the Nassau County eastern end, and First
Avenue along the northern Long Island Sound shoreline
and 150th Avenue at the southern end near what is now
Kennedy Airport. But the old patchwork of separate street
systems resisted easy codification. The result is a crazy
quilt of numbers pretending to be organized. An address
like 83-10 125th Street means, theoretically, the building
is on 125th Street near 83rd Avenue, but usually that's
only the beginning of your quest. The best advice is to
call ahead to the restaurant or museum and get explicit

directions. When you get there, you can then set out to explore the surrounding neighborhood.

The western half of the borough is mostly prewar, except for the huge 1960s apartment complexes in Rego Park and Forest Hills. The northeast quadrant of the borough was built up after the war and resembles any postwar suburb; but don't overlook the older communities like **Bayside** (take the LIRR from Penn Station, Port Washington line), an early 20th-century town strung out along Bell Boulevard near the station, or **Douglaston** (LIRR, Port Washington line, walk north of the station), a planned early 1900s community nestling on the marshy shores of Little Neck Bay.

In the southeast there is another series of verdant 1920s neighborhoods, most of these black or integrated communities like Laurelton (LIRR, the Far Rockaway line). The one serious problem here is the poverty belt of South Jamaica that runs south of downtown Jamaica along Sutphin and Guy Brewer boulevards. But South Jamaica's plight too often blinds us to the handsome solidity of the black middle-class communities nearby. The row-house-lined streets of Cambria Heights and the eclectic mansions of St. Albans were early suburban areas opened to upscale blacks coming out of Manhattan's Harlem or Brooklyn's Bedford-Stuyvesant area. St. Albans in particular had, in the 1950s, a stellar residents' list that included Roy Campanella, James Brown, and Count Basie.

Downtown Jamaica (along Jamaica Avenue from Parsons Boulevard to 169th Street), the borough's historic county seat, is now, like many other old downtowns, struggling to revive itself. If you find yourself there try to see the Tabernacle of Prayer (90-07 Merrick Boulevard at Jamaica Avenue), the former Loew's Valencia, a grand 1929 atmospheric movie palace in the Spanish Baroque style, now remade with a new color scheme into an evangelical church, where everyone is welcome for Sunday services. Or visit, a few blocks west, the **Jamaica Arts Center** (161-04 Jamaica Avenue, at Union Hall Street), a cultural center and art gallery housed in the small but flamboyant City Register Building built soon after the 1898 annexation.

THE SEVEN SISTERS

Amid the patchwork of towns and developments that covered Queens there was a group of planned neighborhoods of real quality. Today known as "The Seven Sisters," these seven independently developed neighborhoods brought 19th-century garden-city ideals to the often crass New York real-estate scene. Sports facilities, parkland, and community clubhouses were built for homeowners and apartment dwellers, giving residents "rest and recuperation" from the frenzy, noise, and dehumanizing congestion of modern industrial life.

The Seven Sisters began with **Richmond Hill**, an 1880s speculative development, whose Shingle-style "Meet-Me-in-St. Louis" Victorians fan out from a village center and town common clustered around the intersections of Hillside, Jamaica, and Myrtle avenues and Lefferts Boulevard (take the E or F subway line to Union Turnpike, Kew Gardens, and the Q-10 bus to Hillside Avenue). Some of the best houses stand north of Myrtle Avenue between 112th and 115th streets; a few blocks farther on Myrtle is the 500-acre, densely wooded Forest Park. The 1890s town center is nostalgic (if slightly run-down), and the tiny common became, in 1905, the campus for one of the libraries that industrialist Andrew Carnegie built throughout the East toward the end of the last century (at Lefferts Boulevard and Hillside Avenue). Inside, in one wing of the library, is a 1937 WPA mural by Philip Evergood depicting in exuberant 1930s optimism, *The Story of Richmond Hill.* For a meal, there is the **Triangle Hofbrau**, at 117-13 Jamaica Avenue at Myrtle, a long-standing German restaurant— Mae West frequented it when she lived nearby—whose premises were originally an 1860s way station on the Jamaica Turnpike (now Jamaica Avenue). For just a hamburger, across the street at 117-33 Myrtle Avenue is the **Junction Diner**—streamlined inside, 1980s remodeling outside—a *real* diner, not one of the cleverly packaged mock-ups so popular in Manhattan.

To the north, developed in the 1910s, is **Kew Gardens** (LIRR Main line to Kew Gardens, or the E and F subway lines to Union Turnpike, Kew Gardens), with its Neo-Tudor "village" centered around the railroad station at Lefferts Boulevard and Austin Street. Its eclectic mixture of apartments and row houses, and especially its variety of private homes that range from modest to mansion, are carefully sited to fit respectfully into the rolling, hilly landscape. The Neo-Tudor and Neo-Colonial buildings lie in the shade of 80-year-old pin oaks that line the streets.

Adjacent and to the west of Kew Gardens is the most famous of the Sisters, **Forest Hills Gardens** (take the LIRR

Queens

| 0 | miles | 2 |
| 0 | kilometers | 3 |

Throgs Neck Bridge

GREAT NECK

WHITESTONE

Little Neck Bay

LITTLE NECK

FLUSHING

FRANCIS LEWIS BLVD.

CLEARVIEW EXPWY.

BELL BLVD.

CROSS ISLAND PKWY.

BAYSIDE

DOUGLASTON

I-495

NORTHERN BLVD.

NORTHERN STATE PKWY.

PARSONS BLVD.

Alley Park

Kissena Park

UNION TPK.

HILLSIDE AVE.

LONG ISLAND EXPWY.

Cunningham Park

164 ST.

FRESH MEADOWS

QUEENS VILLAGE

JERICHO TPK.

UNION TPK.

GRAND CENTRAL PKWY.

HOLLIS

NASSAU COUNTY

JAMAICA

HILLSIDE AVE.

JAMAICA AVE.

ST. ALBANS

FRANCIS LEWIS BLVD.

CAMBRIA HEIGHTS

CROSS ISLAND PKWY.

VAN WYCK EXPWY.

SUTPHIN BLVD.

GUY BREWER BLVD.

LINDEN BLVD.

SPRINGFIELD BLVD.

PARK

SOUTH JAMAICA

SPRINGFIELD GARDENS

SOUTHERN STATE PKWY.

LEFFERTS BLVD.

LAURELTON

SOUTHERN STATE PKWY.

SUNRISE HWY.

ROSEDALE

ROCKAWAY BLVD.

John F. Kennedy International Airport

PENINSULA BLVD.

ROCKAWAY TPK.

BURNSIDE AVE.

FAR ROCKAWAY

Cross Bay Bridge

BEACH CHANNEL DRIVE

ROCKAWAY

Rockaway Beach

Atlantic Ocean

Atlantic Beach

to Forest Hills, or the E and F lines to Continental Avenue, Forest Hills, and walk south), the "fairy tale suburb" of Sinclair Lewis's *Main Street,* a superb example of garden-city planning. Lushly landscaped by Frederick Law Olmsted, Jr. (his father designed Central Park), the "Gardens" includes housing of all types, from apartment towers to mansions to experimental poured-concrete row houses made friendlier with Neo-Tudor detailing. Station Square, the 1912 "town center" by architect Grosvenor Atterbury that clusters around the LIRR station, is a fine example of urban design, as much Expressionistic as it is Medieval Revival, evincing character and a sense of place without ever being cloying or cute. While visiting the Gardens, you might want to try the well-prepared nouvelle cuisine at closet-sized **My Kitchen** (72-24 Austin Street, between Continental and Ascan avenues) or the varied and freshly made Mexican dishes at **Sgt. Garcia's** (70-09 Austin Street, upstairs). Both are located in the bustling shopping district near the railroad station.

Closer to "the city" (always meaning Manhattan) is **Jackson Heights** (number 7 IRT subway line from Times Square or Grand Central to 82nd Street; walk north), built in the 1910s and 1920s with apartment-house blocks of imaginative historic revival designs, threaded with greenbelts running through the blocks and with superior apartment layouts boasting three and four exposures, floor-through plans, and separate service and bedroom wings. (Restaurants in Jackson Heights will be mentioned below in the ethnic section.)

Farther west, with Midtown's skyline rising in the background, is **Sunnyside Gardens** (number 7 IRT subway line from Times Square or Grand Central to 48th Street, and walk north; for information contact the Sunnyside Foundation, Tel: 718-392-9139), a utopian experiment of the late 1920s designed by the gifted team of Clarence Stein and Henry Wright. Home for many years to urban critic and *New Yorker* columnist Lewis Mumford, and once known as the "Nursery of Greenwich Village" for the number of ex-Village artists who moved there to raise their families, Sunnyside was built as a model housing complex, including verdant commons within the blocks and a still extant Community Park that is New York's only private park besides Manhattan's Gramercy Park. The two remaining Sisters are Douglaston, already mentioned, and **Fresh Meadows**, two miles east of Forest Hills Gardens, a moderate- and middle-income garden-city complex built in 1949 by the New York Life Insurance Company as a low-rise, more spaciously laid-out sibling of Manhattan's Stuyvesant Town. These seven communities are now being rediscovered and have come to be considered classics of American urban and suburban design.

THE QUEENS MOVIE INDUSTRY

Queens was America's first Hollywood. During the days of the silents and the early talkies, before producers discovered Los Angeles, Astoria Movie Studios was one of the principal centers of the movie industry. Today that studio, renamed **Kaufman/Astoria Movie Studios**, is thriving again, and its new addition, **The American Museum of the Moving Image** (at 34-31 35th Avenue at 36th Street) has itself become a box-office smash, giving visitors a multimedia understanding of TV, video, and film production. The museum, which also hosts screenings in both its main and experimental theaters, is four blocks from the R train's Steinway Street station—that's three stops from Bloomingdale's in Manhattan.

Queens was also the first Beverly Hills; the stars of stage and screen (and jazz as well)—including Charlie Chaplin, Al Jolson, Will Rogers, Billie Holiday, Bix Beiderbecke, and the immortal Louis Armstrong—settled in from Corona to Forest Hills to Bayside, some to lead quiet lives away from Manhattan's din and others to lead the North Shore Long Island lifestyle that would soon move to "West Egg" and be immortalized in *The Great Gatsby*.

ETHNIC QUEENS

Queens is today's melting pot, serving New York as the Lower East Side once did. Only here, the number of people is far larger, their origins more exotic, and their lifestyles more prosperous than those of their 19th-century predecessors along Manhattan's Rivington, MacDougal, and Mott streets. Queens is one of the most densely mixed ethnic melting pots in the world. Los Angeles has a mix, but they're all in cars and only fenders brush, not people. In Hong Kong it's largely Asian, while in Queens there are Greeks, Latins, Middle Easterners,

West Indians, and Russian Jews besides denizens from the entire arc of eastern and southern Asia.

Queens is the place where almost any kind of ethnic foodstuff, cooking gadgetry, or ethnic restaurant can be found. But this is not Manhattan, where retail stores and eateries are often slickly packaged and merchandised. Restaurants and food stores in Queens are not written up; you simply have to know about them. Restaurants here are not glitterized with Postmodern decor; they just have plain cloths on the tables and simple pictures on the walls. The food, however, is excellent, cheap, and abundant. The atmosphere is home-style—home, that is, to a Greek, an Indian, or an Argentine. Queens is where you can see an Indian woman in a sari eating Italian pizza made by an Argentine in what is basically an Oriental district, where churches announce services in Korean, and an Indian temple rises among Victorian homes.

Here is Greek **Astoria**, clustered around the stations of the elevated N line (from Bloomingdale's) that rumbles above 31st Street. Once German, then Italian, now one of the largest concentrations of Greeks outside of the home country, Astoria's major activity is at the N line's terminus, Ditmars Boulevard, where Greek coffee and pastry shops (and Italian pastry shops as well), Greek-language newsstands, and a Greek-language movie house serve the local population. **Nea Hellas Restaurant** (31-15 Ditmars Boulevard, east of 31st Street), **Tony's Ristorante** (33-12 Ditmars Boulevard, two blocks east of 31st Street), **Lefkos Pirgos Bakery** (at 31st Street and 23rd Avenue, one block south of Ditmars), and **Europa Delicacies** (22-42 31st Street, under the "El"—or elevated train—just south of Ditmars) are just the appetizers to a culinary feast. Broadway, near the El station, is another frenzy of food shops, with **Roumely Taverna** (33-04 Broadway, east of the El) and **Karyatis Restaurant** (35-03 Broadway, two blocks east of Roumely's) being two excellent restaurants in that stretch.

Latin American **Jackson Heights** is centered at 82nd Street and intersects 37th Avenue, which is one block north of the IRT number 7 El train route, Roosevelt Avenue. Exit at the 82nd Street station and bring your Spanish phrase book with you. Two wonderful Colombian restaurants nearby are **Tierras Colombianas** (82-18 Roosevelt Avenue, east of 82nd Street) and **La Pequeña Columbia** (83-27 Roosevelt Avenue, one block farther east). On Baxter Avenue, south of Roosevelt Avenue and

84th Street, is **La Fusta,** 80-32 Baxter Avenue, an Argentine restaurant specializing in *parrillada,* Latin American–style barbecue. And under the El on Roosevelt are several Latin nightclubs and elegant eateries, including **Uncle Peter's** (76-18 Roosevelt Avenue at 76th Street), an excellent, upscale restaurant with adjoining bar and music room. Farther east on the number 7 line, at the Junction Boulevard station, is an expatriate Cuban restaurant, **Rincon Criollo,** at 40-09 Junction Boulevard, just south of the El. On the western side of Jackson Heights is one of New York's Little Indias (number 7 IRT line to the 74th Street station, or the E and F lines to the 74th Street/Roosevelt station): 74th Street, north of Roosevelt, is a veritable "Saree Alley," and it and the surrounding area are filled with Indian saree shops, restaurants, and grocery stores.

Then there is downtown **Flushing**'s Little Asia (Main Street from Sanford Avenue to Northern Boulevard, and side streets, including Union Street, parallel to and east of Main Street), where the intense small-scale retailing, billboards in foot-high Oriental letters, and mixture of Koreans, Chinese, Indians, and Japanese will make you feel that you have just flown across the China Sea.

The entry to Flushing is via the IRT number 7 line, nicknamed "The Orient Express," from Times Square and Grand Central to its terminal at Main Street (the LIRR's Port Washington line also stops there). When you exit from the subway at Main Street and Roosevelt Avenue you will be right in the heart of the business district. **Cho Sun Ok** (136-73 Roosevelt Avenue, upstairs, one block east of the subway terminal) is a Korean restaurant specializing in hibachi-based barbecue. **Flushing Yuet Tung** (136-11 38th Avenue, two blocks north of the subway and east of Main Street) serves *Haka*-style Chinese dishes, such as salt-baked chicken (Haka is the soul food of China). **Crystal Garden** (136-40 39th Avenue, three blocks north of the subway and east of Main Street) prepares excellent *dim sum.* **Hwa Yuan** (41-97 Main Street, two blocks south of the subway) specializes in such Szechwan dishes as cold noodles in sesame sauce.

Asian supermarkets and food stores also dot Flushing's streets. Nippan Daido is a Japanese supermarket (with an attached Dosanko fast-food restaurant) at 137-80 Northern Boulevard at Union Street; several excellent Chinese and Korean supermarkets line Main Street near Sanford and Maple avenues (about three blocks south of the subway), and Indian grocers and delis cluster on Main Street another block farther south. Nearby, to the east of Main Street, a Hindu temple built by Indian craftsmen flown over from the subcontinent sits beside the surrounding Victorian houses. Home to the Hindu Society of North America (45-57 Bowne Street at Holly Avenue; Tel: 718-961-1199), the temple has a richly decorated interior of shrines and Hindu gods and goddesses and always has a welcome mat out for strangers (call for hours and directions).

In **Forest Hills** on 108th Street north of 65th Avenue (it's about 20 blocks north of Forest Hills Gardens; the nearest subway is the 63rd Drive, Rego Park station of the R and G lines; walk east from the station) Russian Jews have established a small colony far from the better-known settlement in Brighton Beach, Brooklyn. Two Russian delis, **Misha & Monya's** and **Loxtown**, face each other across 108th Street at 65th Avenue, duelists in the game of freshly made sour cream, dried fish, pickles, and pirogi. A block north, at 64th Road, **Carmel Middle Eastern Grocery** (64-27 108th Street), serving the local population of Sephardic Jews, specializes in freshly made hummus, *babaganouj,* olives, pickles, and Middle Eastern grains and spices.

CULTURAL INSTITUTIONS

The list of neighborhoods and their specialty stores could go on and on. Yet Queens is also beginning to attract the kinds of cultural institutions that people—even Manhattanites—will go out of their way to visit. Housed in a fortresslike 19th-century school, **P.S. 1** (46-01 21st Street at Jackson Avenue; Tel: 718-784-2084) is a combination of art gallery, artists' working lofts, and sometime performance space that pioneered Long Island City's role as a new center for the "downtown" art scene. The number 7 line's Court House Square/45th Road station (three stops from Grand Central) and the E and F's 21st Street/Ely Avenue station (one stop from Citicorp Center) are only a few blocks away.

Farther north, along Long Island City's industrial riverfront, is the **Socrates Sculpture Park** (31-29 Vernon Boulevard at Broadway and the East River), where large-scale modern sculpture can be seen against the spectacular backdrop of the Manhattan skyline. From the N line's

Broadway station it's an eight-block walk west to the riverfront and Socrates. The park is open daily during the summer but only on weekends in the winter and is near the food shops and restaurants of Astoria's Broadway. Just two blocks south of the Socrates, at 33rd Road, is the **Isamu Noguchi Museum** (32-37 Vernon Boulevard, which is the riverfront road; Tel: 718-204-7088), in the late sculptor's former studio. Open only Wednesdays and Saturdays, the museum displays the artist's works in a redesigned industrial loft of almost monastic simplicity and an austerely beautiful garden. Nearby, on the other side of Astoria, is the aforementioned **American Museum of the Moving Image**. From Noguchi or Socrates you would have to walk back east on Broadway, five blocks past the El to 36th Street and turn right, or south, two blocks to 35th Avenue to reach the Moving Image. It's a "schlepp," as New Yorkers say, but the sights and aromas of Astoria's Broadway might make the walk less taxing than you think.

In Flushing Meadows Corona Park, once the dusty "ash heaps" of F. Scott Fitzgerald's *The Great Gatsby* and subsequently the site of two world's fairs, stands **Shea Stadium**, home of the Mets, and, just to its south, the **National Tennis Center**, site of tennis's U.S. Open championships. Both are near the number 7 line's Shea Stadium station and both are only a few minutes away from the gustatory delights of both downtown Flushing and Jackson Heights. Just south of the tennis center is the **Queens Museum**, with excellent art and photography shows; within the museum (housed in the New York City pavilion of the 1939 World's Fair) is the **New York Panorama**, a Lilliputian-scaled model of the entire New York City, including every building and street within the five boroughs.

On Flushing Meadows' western edge, in Corona Park, is the **New York Hall of Science** (in the park, 47-01 111th Street at 48th Avenue, Corona; Tel: 718-699-0005), a tremendously popular hands-on experience of applied science and high technology housed in a reinforced concrete "amoeba" originally built for the 1964 World's Fair. If you're visiting just the Hall of Science, it's best to take the number 7 line to the 111th Street station and walk south eight blocks to 48th Avenue.

Getting hungry? From the Hall of Science walk south on 111th Street (that's a left on exiting the hall) three blocks to 51st Avenue and turn right one block to 108th Street (only in Queens is 108th one block from 111th). There, where Corona Avenue intersects 108th and 51st, is Joseph Lisa

Square, the heart of an Italian neighborhood. On the square the **Lemon Ice King of Corona** (52-02 108th Street) still makes New York's best Italian ices in an endless variety of flavors. The **Parkside Restaurant** (107-01 Corona Avenue, on the 51st Avenue side of the square) serves Italian cuisine in a posh style that attracts people from all over the city; for more modest but still excellent dining, nearby is **Army's Italian Cuisine** (51-01 108th Street at 51st Avenue). Take-out sandwiches and heros with fresh Italian cheeses and deli meats can be had at the **Corona Park Salumeria** (14-46 122nd Street), and for cappuccino and pastry there is **Baldi's Italian Pastry Shop** (108-15 Corona Avenue at 53rd Avenue). Don't be fooled by Corona's small-town atmosphere. It was the longtime home of jazz great Louis Armstrong, whose house is now a national historic site and archives (34-56 107th Street; Tel: 718-478-8274). Nearby, though long closed and picked clean of debris, was Louis Comfort Tiffany's studio (96-18 43rd Avenue), where many a Tiffany lamp and Favrile glass vase was fabricated.

All this gives you a few good reasons to cross the East River and chart "the unknown borough." Don't listen to what your Manhattan friends tell you; being Manhattan people, they really don't know New York. Queens is worth the trip.

DAY TRIPS
FROM MANHATTAN

By Eleanor Berman

Eleanor Berman is a widely published travel writer. Her guide Away for the Weekend: New York *has been a regional bestseller since 1982. She has contributed to all the major metropolitan daily newspapers, as well as to such national magazines as* Harper's Bazaar, Savvy, Modern Bride, *and* Diversion.

For visitors caught up in the Manhattan maelstrom who wonder, How does anybody live here? here's the secret: New Yorkers get away—often—to incredibly appealing places only a day trip away. Why not join them? Greenery, scenery, history, prime beaches, ivy-clad campuses, and even early American charm are nearby. Here are some of the escapes the natives favor.

MAJOR INTEREST

The Bronx
Bronx Zoo
New York Botanical Garden
Wave Hill mansion and grounds

Hudson Valley
Philipsburg Manor's early Dutch farm grounds
Washington Irving's retreat, Sunnyside
Van Cortlandt Manor colonial house
Union Church of Pocantico Hills
Franklin D. Roosevelt National Historic Site at
    Hyde Park
United States Military Academy at West Point

Yale University
Litchfield, Connecticut, historic New England town
The Hamptons, beaches and resort towns
Princeton University
Donald M. Kendall Sculpture Gardens in Purchase,
    New York
Storm King Art Center and Sculpture Park
Spring Lake on the New Jersey Shore
Doylestown in Bucks County, Pennsylvania

BRONX OASES

In the city's northernmost borough, generally better known for Yankee Stadium than for its beauty spots, there are three magnificent, leafy retreats less than an hour from Manhattan. Contact each for directions by subway, public bus, or Metro-North train. Liberty Lines express buses go within walking distance of all three (Tel: 212-652-8400 for routes and schedules).

The Bronx Zoo, the nation's largest urban zoo, founded in 1899, still has its famous central court of stately exhibit buildings, but the rest of the 265 wooded acres is undergoing a renaissance. Spectacular natural habitats are replacing the cages for the 4,000-plus animal residents, to make it

Metropolitan Region

```
0        miles        10
0        kilometers        16
```

Rhinebeck

THRUWAY I-87

9

Hyde Park
FDR House

New Paltz

Poughkeepsie

NEW YORK STATE

N E W   Y O R K

I-84

17

I-84

Newburgh   **Beacon**

Fahnestock State Park

Middletown

9W

Mountainville   **West Point**
Highland Falls

Brewster

9

TACONIC STATE PKWY.

17

Bear Mountain State Park   **Peekskill**

Palisades Interstate Park

Croton-on-Hudson
Van Cortlandt Manor

I-684

NEW YORK
NEW JERSEY

Harriman State Park

PALISADES INTERSTATE PKWY.

Hudson River

Suffern

NEW YORK STATE

Pocantico Hills
Tarrytown

THRUWAY I-87

Purchase
I-287

Greenwich

HUTCHINSON PKWY.

I-95

N

I-80

Paterson

GARDEN STATE PKWY.

I-80

Clifton   I-95

Bronx Zoo
BRONX

East River

25A

N E W   J E R S E Y

Newark   **MANHATTAN**

I-278

New York City   **QUEENS**

BROOKLYN

I-278

STATEN ISLAND

Coney Island

Rockaway Beach

Atlantic Beach *Long Beach*

to Doylestown (PA)

U.S. 1

NEW JERSEY TPK.

GARDEN STATE PKWY.

Gateway National Recreation Area

to Spring Lake

Atlantic Ocean

Princeton

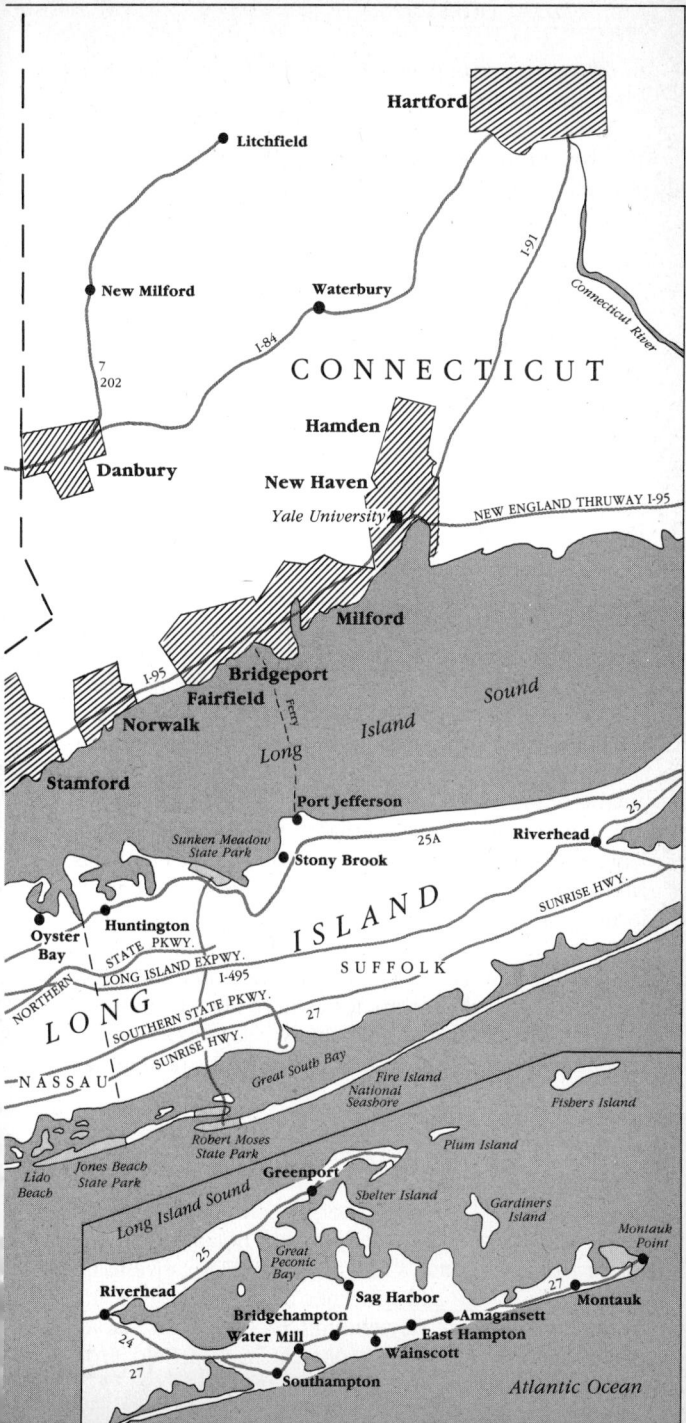

all the more exciting and realistic for the human beings who come to call.

Siberian tigers, Asian elephants, and Indian rhinoceroses roam the plains of Wild Asia, while red pandas and rare and beautiful snow leopards are in residence in the Himalayan Highlands, a habitat that re-creates the high passes and remote mountains of their homeland. Lions, gazelles, giraffes, zebras, and cheetahs roam the African Plains, where predator and prey are safely separated by moats. The environments are authentic down to the fencing and signs based on native art. In good weather the monorails and trams bring you right into some of the habitats.

The most lavish of the new environments is the indoor Jungle World, a 55-foot-high, glass-enclosed complex that comes complete with clouds, rain, lakes, and waterfalls. The wooden walkway leads through an Indonesian scrub forest, a mangrove swamp, and a Southeast Asian rain forest where it is almost impossible to distinguish the 100 species of actual tropical plants from the man-made rocks, trees, and vines among them. Some 800 animals, including black leopards, white-cheeked gibbons, sleepy crocodiles, and brightly hued Bali myna birds, live here, separated from people and one another only by ravines, streams, or cliffs.

One of the park's latest additions is the Keith W. Johnson Zoo Center, which replaces the former Elephant House with enlarged, naturalistic habitats for elephants, rhinoceroses, and Malay tapirs. It also serves as a centrally located information center.

Other innovative indoor exhibits are the World of Birds, a three-story space where multicolored fliers soar free, and the World of Darkness, where night is simulated so that such nocturnal animals as bats, foxes, and supergliders can be seen in action during our regular daytime hours.

In the whimsical Children's Zoo, kids can crawl into a giant snail shell, explore a giant spider web, sit in a child-size nest, or compare their jumping ability to that of a frog.

To reach the zoo (and the New York Botanical Garden) by car from Manhattan's East Side, take FDR Drive to the Triborough Bridge and Bruckner Expressway east to the Bronx River Parkway northbound. From the exit marked Bronx Zoo, turn left to the Bronxdale parking field. From the West Side, take the West Side Highway/Henry Hudson

Parkway north to the Cross Bronx Expressway east to the Bronx River Parkway; at the Bronx Zoo exit turn into the Bronxdale parking lot. The botanical garden is directly opposite, across Fordham Road.

The New York Zoological Society, Fordham Road and Bronx River Parkway, Bronx, NY 10460. Tel: (212) 367-1010.

The New York Botanical Garden, across Fordham Road from the Bronx Zoo (enter on Southern Boulevard; see above for directions by car), is part of the same vast urban park that was once the private domain of the Lorillard family. Since 1891 it has devoted itself to showing off nature at her exuberant best. The 250-acre site is part unspoiled woodland with nature paths along a winding river, part formal gardens.

The undisputed star of the botanical garden is the Enid A. Haupt Conservatory, 11 shimmering pavilions of glass around a courtyard and reflecting pools. The glass dome over the central pavilion, inspired by London's Crystal Palace, soars 90 feet over a leafy palm court below. The conservatory also houses desert and tropical plant collections, a fern forest, and showy seasonal floral displays.

Outdoors there are formal gardens planted with more than 200 varieties of roses, a perennial garden, herb and rock gardens, a conifer garden, and a garden of native New York plants. In spring, flamboyant bulb displays and clouds of pink and white flowering trees greet the season.

The Peggy Rockefeller Rose Garden is a lush two acres planted with 2,700 rose bushes. The stone museum building on the grounds houses a garden shop that sells horticultural items, an orchid terrarium, and the extensive Harriet Barnes Pratt Library, an excellent collection of literature on horticulture.

New York Botanical Garden, Southern Boulevard and 200th Street, Bronx, NY 10458. Tel: (212) 220-8777.

Wave Hill is a small, perfect jewel, a 28-acre enclave of velvet lawns, gardens, greenhouses, two manor houses, and an incomparable view of the Hudson River and the geological wonder beyond: the stony cliffs of the New Jersey Palisades. The astonishing beauty of this setting in the Riverdale section of the Bronx has drawn a roster of rental tenants that includes Theodore Roosevelt, Mark Twain, and Arturo Toscanini.

The main house at Wave Hill was built in 1843 by jurist William Lewis Morris as a summer home away from the heat and noise of a growing city. In 1866 it was acquired by publishing mogul William Henry Appleton, who transformed it into a Victorian estate, building a greenhouse and stable and bringing in exotic plants. William Thackeray and Thomas Henry Huxley were likely to stop in for tea here.

Wave Hill and the neighboring manor house of Oliver Harriman, called Glyndor, were bought by George F. Perkins in 1903. Perkins brought in Albert Millard, a royal landscape gardener from Vienna, to help him further develop the gardens. The estate remained in the Perkins family until 1960, when the property and the two houses were donated to New York City as a public park. Nature trails connect it to Riverdale Park, a 97-acre sanctuary along the Hudson with three miles of hiking trails. A good time to visit is on Sunday afternoons, when chamber-music concerts are offered in the Wave Hill house several times a month from September to May and guided walks are given in summer. Outdoor dance programs are performed on Thursday nights in summer.

Wave Hill is a short drive from Manhattan by car. From the East Side take the Major Deegan Expressway northbound. Exit at Henry Hudson Parkway and take the first right to H. Hudson Parkway, *southbound*. Take the 254th Street exit, turn left at the stop sign, left again at the light, right at 249th Street to Wave Hill. From the West Side take the West Side Highway/Henry Hudson Parkway northbound. Get off the parkway at the 246th–250th Street exit; continue north to 252nd, go left at the overpass, left again, and right at 249th Street.

Wave Hill, 249th Street and Independence Avenue, Bronx, NY 10471. Tel: (212) 549-3200.

HISTORIC HUDSON VALLEY

Farther north, much of the early history of New York was forged in the great manor houses along the river. Historic Hudson Valley, a nonprofit corporation, was formed more than 35 years ago, with financial aid from John D. Rockefeller, Jr., to preserve some of the most important properties.

Philipsburg Manor in North Tarrytown is a farm that was the domain of a Dutchman who came to the New World in the early 1650s as Peter Stuyvesant's carpenter and amassed his own fortune through the clipper trade and a good marriage. The Upper Mills site, built in 1682, was a trading and shipping center where tenant farmers brought grain to be ground, bagged, and shipped. It has been restored to approximate its appearance during its most prosperous period, 1720 to 1750. The mill still grinds, the garden grows the kinds of plants that were cultivated in the 18th century, and the cows, sheep, and chickens roaming the farm have been "back bred" to reproduce the breeds of an earlier day. The simple stone farmhouse with its whitewashed walls contains samples of rustic early New York furniture and Dutch Delft ceramics.

Sunnyside, in nearby Tarrytown, is the quaint Victorian cottage and gardens of author Washington Irving. The estate, which he appropriately called his "snuggery," contains Irving's furniture, possessions, and library.

Antiques lovers should definitely plan a visit to handsome **Van Cortlandt Manor,** north of Sunnyside, in Croton-on-Hudson. This was also the domain of a Dutchman, Oloff Stevense Van Cortlandt, who arrived in New Amsterdam in 1638 and sired a prominent family that boasted a mayor of New York City and a lieutenant governor of the state. The house has been restored to the elegant period between 1790 and 1814. Most of its fine furnishings were made in New York and belonged to the Van Cortlandts, who remained in residence here until 1945.

Outdoors there are fruit orchards, flower gardens along the brick "long walk," and display gardens filled with herbs, flowers, and vegetables typically grown in this country prior to 1814. The ferry house looks as it did when it served as a rest stop for travellers on the Albany Post Road to New York City; it was at this spot that stages were ferried over the Croton River. The smoke house, necessary house, ice house, and other estate buildings also have been restored.

The **Union Church of Pocantico Hills** in North Tarrytown, the final select Westchester County property, still has an active congregation and is the worshiping place of the Rockefeller family, whose estate is nearby. It boasts the only cycle of church windows created in this country by Chagall, including eight luminous side windows in blues, greens, and golds and an enormous rear window dedicated to John D. Rockefeller, Jr.; its vivid colors fill the small sanctuary with light even on the darkest days. The small circular rose window by Matisse, his final work, shimmers over the altar with cutouts in green, yellow, pale blue, and white. It is a memorial to Abby Aldrich Rockefeller, John D., Jr.'s wife, who was a patron of the arts and an active member of the church. Visiting hours are limited, so phone Historic Hudson Valley for information (see below) before you plan a trip.

Tappan Hill, Highland and Benedict avenues, Tarrytown (Tel: 914-631-3030), is the place for dining with a hilltop Hudson view after you've seen the sights.

All of the Westchester properties are off Route 9 on the east side of the Hudson and can be reached by taking the New York State Thruway (Route 87) to exit 9, Tarrytown; follow Route 9 south 1 mile to Sunnyside, north 2 miles to Philipsburg, north another 9 miles to Van Cortlandt Manor. To reach the Union Church, go east on Route 448 from Route 9 in North Tarrytown. Signs mark the turnoffs clearly. To see all the sites, a car is necessary.

Historic Hudson Valley, 150 White Plains Road, Tarrytown, NY 10591. Tel: (914) 631-8200.

FRANKLIN D. ROOSEVELT NATIONAL HISTORIC SITE

The lavish mansions of a later era were built in the mid-Hudson highlands farther up the east side of the river. The best known of these is Franklin Roosevelt's home, officially called Springwood but usually referred to as **Hyde Park**.

Few memorials offer such personal glimpses of public figures. The main house (overlooking the Hudson River), the Roosevelt Museum and Library, and Eleanor Roosevelt's own modest home, Val-Kill, provide visitors with a new awareness of the public and private lives of one of our most remarkable presidents—and his equally remarkable wife.

The museum of the Franklin D. Roosevelt Library contains a series of photos and displays about the life of the only man elected for four presidential terms, who guided the nation out of its worst depression and through its most perilous war. Franklin's bout with polio, his campaigns and presidency, and the worldwide mourning at his death in 1945 are all recorded.

The library contains Roosevelt's study (where he gave some of his famous radio fireside chats) and his presidential desk, preserved just as it was on his last day in office, covered with "toys"—miniature Democratic donkeys and

replicas of his pet scottie, Fala. An uncanny lived-in quality is reinforced by the presence of Eleanor's knitting,
Franklin's collection of ship models and many gifts he
received in office, and his elegant Ford Phaeton convert-
ible with hand controls.

Both Franklin and Eleanor are buried in the rose garden beside the house. Eleanor, however, never felt at
home at Hyde Park, where Sara Roosevelt, Franklin's
mother, reigned. With Franklin's blessing, she built a
small retreat on the estate two miles away from the big
house in 1926. It was often her weekend escape, and it
was in this unpretentious pine-paneled house, Val-Kill,
that she lived from 1945 until her death in 1962—the
years when she became known as First Lady of the World.

Hyde Park is a two-hour drive from New York City. Follow the New York Thruway (Route 87) to exit 18 (New
Paltz); go east on Route 299 for 5 miles and then right on
Route 9W south to the Mid-Hudson Bridge. Cross the
bridge and follow signs for Route 9 north to Hyde Park.
While in Hyde Park, enjoy a meal prepared by the soon-to-
be-greats at the **Culinary Institute of America** on Route 9,
the nation's top training ground for chefs. For the formal
lunch or dinner, reservations are needed far in advance
(Tel: 914-471-6608), but no reservations are required for a
light lunch weekdays in their St. Andrew's Café.

Franklin D. Roosevelt National Historic Site, Route 9,
Hyde Park, NY. Tel: (914) 229-9115.

The Hudson Valley merits an overnight stay—to see the
foliage, pick apples, hike in the mountains, or explore the
great estates along the river: Montgomery Place, Clermont, Mills Mansion, and Olana north of Hyde Park, and
the Vanderbilt Mansion and Boscobel to the south. An
excellent guide to the area is *The Hudson River Valley: A
History and Guide* by Tim Mulligan. The most pleasant
overnight accommodations are at the **Beekman Arms,** a
stagecoach inn dating back to 1700, 10 miles north of
Hyde Park on Route 9 in Rhinebeck (Tel: 914-876-7077).

THE UNITED STATES
MILITARY ACADEMY

Standing on a crest on the west bank of the Hudson River,
the gray stone buildings of the United States Military

Academy at West Point are intended to impress, as they indeed do. There's a strong sense of rich history here, and the pride of the young cadets who are carrying on the "long gray line" of patriots who marched before them is tangible.

West Point is also one of the Hudson Valley's great beauty spots. The site from which colonial troops kept watch for British ships up and down the river still provides an unsurpassed Hudson overlook.

The visitors' center outside Thayer Gate in Highland Falls supplies all the information needed for a rewarding visit, including a self-guiding tour map and a movie about cadet life. Guided tours are available for a fee. The new Olmsted Museum houses one of the largest collections of military history in the Western Hemisphere.

From Trophy Point you can see the links of the Great Chain, which was stretched across the river during the Revolution as a barrier to enemy ships. In days when America's rivers were its highways, the Hudson was a vital artery. In fact, if Benedict Arnold had succeeded in turning strategic West Point over to the British, they might have won the war.

The Cadet Chapel, noted for its Gothic architecture, contains the largest church organ in the world (18,000 pipes) as well as outstanding stained-glass windows donated by past graduating classes. Beyond the chapel are the gracious 19th-century homes of the superintendent and the commandant, facing the parade ground known as The Plain. On the roster of cadets who have marched here are Ulysses S. Grant, Robert E. Lee, Thomas J. "Stonewall" Jackson, Douglas MacArthur, Dwight Eisenhower, and astronauts Buzz Aldrin, Frank Borman, and Michael Collins.

Dress parades, with cadets in full regalia, are held on The Plain on football weekends in autumn and at various times throughout the year (phone for current schedules).

There are many other buildings and monuments to be seen at West Point, including Fort Putnam, the original 1778 garrison constructed under the supervision of General George Washington. A one-and-a-half-hour Hudson Highlands river cruise runs in summer months (Tel: 914-446-7171 for reservations). While you are at West Point the **Thayer Hotel** on campus is the best place for meals.

West Point is 50 miles from New York City. By car, take the George Washington Bridge to the Palisades Interstate Parkway northbound, to Bear Mountain Circle, then

Route 9W north, following signs to Highland Falls and West Point.

United States Military Academy, West Point, NY 10996. Tel: (914) 938-2638.

YALE UNIVERSITY

Founded by ten clergymen in 1701 and named for an Englishman who saved the fledgling school from bankruptcy, Yale University has grown from its puritan beginnings into one of the nation's great centers of learning. The Gothic-spired campus, an attraction in itself, boasts cultural treasures that are a more than ample incentive for a visit. Among them is America's top collection of British art.

Guided tours of the campus leave twice daily on weekdays, once on Saturdays and Sundays, from the information office at Phelps Gate on College Street, off the New Haven Green. If you prefer, you can wander on your own, armed with the center's walking-tour map. Touring begins on the green, one of nine squares laid out in 1638 in America's first planned city. Among its three notable churches, the 1812 Center Church is considered a Georgian masterpiece.

Though it is now a sprawling university of 11,000 students, the historic heart of the school remains the old campus bounded by Chapel, High, Elm, and College streets. Nathan Hale, Noah Webster, Eli Whitney, and William Howard Taft all lived in Connecticut Hall, a 1753 Georgian structure that is the oldest on campus. It is now the Department of Philosophy, and the rest of the old campus buildings serve as freshman dormitories.

From sophomore year, Yale undergraduate life centers around a college plan similar to that of English universities, dividing the students into 12 colleges, each a separate entity under the guidance of a master. The first seven of these distinctive colleges, each arranged around a quadrangle, came into being in 1933; eight of the first ten were designed by one architect, James Gamble Rogers. The newest buildings, Ezra Stiles and Morse, completed in 1962, were designed by Eero Saarinen.

The misty sea- and landscapes of Constable and Turner, the bawdy London of Hogarth, and the portraits of Gainsborough and Reynolds hang in the **Yale Center for British Art**, the 1977 gift of philanthropist Paul Mellon. Mellon, who had amassed the largest collection of British art outside England, endowed a modernistic building designed by Louis Kahn to show off his paintings with natural radiance from skylights.

Yale also boasts the nation's oldest college art museum, the **Yale University Art Gallery**, whose eclectic exhibits span the continents and the centuries. The Yale collection of musical instruments is world renowned, numbering some 850 antique and historical instruments from the 16th to 19th centuries. The **Beinecke Library** has its own displays of rarities, including a Gutenberg bible, original Audubon bird prints, and Medieval manuscripts.

Theater lover's might catch one of the excellent productions at the **Yale Repertory Company** or New Haven's **Long Wharf Theater**, an outstanding regional company where many Broadway hits have been born.

Robert Henry, 1032 Chapel Street, is the acknowledged gourmet headquarters in town. Wooster Street is famous for its Italian restaurants; the pizza at **Sally's** and **Pepe's** is legendary in Connecticut—come early or late to avoid the lines.

New Haven is a 1-hour-and-45-minute train ride from New York via Amtrak or Metro-North; take a cab or buses A, J, or U from the station to the campus. By car, follow Route 95 north to exit 47.

New Haven Convention and Visitors Bureau, 900 Chapel Street, Suite 344, New Haven, CT 06510. Tel: (203) 787-8367.

LITCHFIELD, CONNECTICUT

You may recognize the steepled Congregational Church on the green· in Litchfield. It has been the subject of countless photographs of the typical New England town. And indeed, it would be hard to find a more idyllic setting than this community, which is considered by many to be the finest authentic 18th-century town in America.

Once a prosperous stage stop between Boston and New York, Litchfield attracted political and intellectual leaders from the time of its founding in 1720. The nation's first law school and first women's academy were founded here, and the Reverend Lyman Beecher first preached against the evils of intemperance in the Litchfield village meetinghouse. His son, abolitionist Henry

Ward Beecher, and his daughter, Harriet Beecher Stowe, were born in the 1787 parsonage next to the church.

The three dozen or so choicest homes, those forming the central historic district around the village green, can easily be seen on foot because they are concentrated on two long blocks, North and South streets, radiating from the green. Little restoration has been necessary; many of Litchfield's homes have been continuously occupied— some by their original families—since they were built.

Most are still privately owned, but you can visit the 1773 home where Tapping Reeve opened the nation's first law school, with his brother-in-law Aaron Burr as his first pupil. Eventually, the pupils outgrew the house and a one-room school was erected next door in 1784. Among its alumni were three Supreme Court justices, 26 senators, some 90 congressmen, two vice presidents, and 14 governors. When he was a student here, John C. Calhoun lodged in the rectory next door and planted some of the elms that remain along the street.

Farther down the street is the 1736 home where Ethan Allen, Revolutionary War leader of the fabled Green Mountain Boys, is believed to have been born. Also on South Street is a white clapboard house, circa 1775, that was the home of Oliver Wolcott, Sr., a signer of the Declaration of Independence who became governor of Connecticut. And there is the obligatory structure boasting "George Washington Slept Here"—in this case the former Elisha Sheldon Tavern.

The Litchfield Historical Society Museum is expected to open soon with renovated exhibits that will cover 250 years of local history. Displays of locally made furniture include the tall case clocks for which Litchfield was famous.

Toll Gate Hill Inn on Route 202, a 1700s Colonial, is the appropriately historic spot for a meal or lodging (Tel: 203-567-4545). And while it is strictly 20th century, gardeners won't want to miss a stop at Litchfield's White Flower Farm, on Route 63 south, nationally known for its 1,200 varieties of unusual perennials.

Litchfield is 85 miles from New York. Take the New York Thruway (Route 87) north to Route 287 east to Route 684 north, then Route 84 east into Connecticut. At Danbury pick up Route 7 north and at New Milford follow Route 202 into Litchfield.

Litchfield Hills Travel Council, P.O. Box 1776, Marble Dale, CT 06777. Tel: (203) 868-2214.

THE HAMPTONS

If you think you spy your favorite actor or your favorite author sitting across the room in a restaurant in the Hamptons, you are probably right.

This chain of half a dozen towns on the east end of Long Island (South Fork) is summer home to countless celebrities. Socialites live in shingled mansions behind the tall hedges in Southampton; artists, writers, and publishing executives tend to settle in East Hampton; and prominent faces from the arts and entertainment world are legion in either town or nearby villages such as Bridgehampton, Water Mill, Amagansett, and Sag Harbor. Many of them show up in July for fellow resident George Plimpton's annual fireworks show, a benefit for Guild Hall, the arts center in East Hampton.

But celebrity watching is only a small part of the lure of the Hamptons for visitors. The main attraction is what brought everyone here in the first place—miles of magnificent, unspoiled, dune-backed white-sand beaches that are among the finest in the East. The ocean beaches are wide and beautiful all the way from Southampton to Montauk; each town also has bay beaches with calmer waters. Most popular are **Main Beach** in East Hampton and **Atlantic Avenue Beach** in Amagansett, both favored by the many young, single New Yorkers who share summer homes in the area. All beaches are free, but beach-parking permits are an absolute necessity if you go by car. Permits are expensive for short visits—about $10 a day in most places. Each village imposes its own rules and regulations. In Southampton, you may purchase a daily permit from the Parks and Recreation Department, Hampton Road; Tel: (516) 283-6000. East Hampton Village oversees five local ocean beaches (at Main Beach, pay at the beach office. For information: Village Hall, Main Street; Tel: 516-324-4150). The rest of the beaches are under the umbrella of the Town of East Hampton (apply at Town Hall, Pantigo Road, East Hampton; Tel: 516-324-4142). Many lodgings make parking permits available to their guests; it pays to ask before you reserve.

In addition to the beauty of the beaches, these are historic towns still graced by the windmills, village greens, and clapboard homes of their 300-year-old colonial heritage. Southampton dates back to 1640, and its Old Halsey House is the oldest frame house in the state. Along East

Hampton's picturesque green are half a dozen notable homes including the Studio, the home of watercolorist Thomas Moran, and, two doors down at 217 Main Street, the Summer White House of President John Tyler. The town's wind-powered Hook Mill—rising above the ancient stones in the nearby Hook Mill Burying Ground—is still grinding.

The Hamptons are also known for the many stylish boutiques, antiques shops, art galleries, and excellent restaurants that have sprung up to serve such a distinguished clientele.

Gordon's, Main Street, Amagansett, just east of East Hampton, is a longtime favorite Hamptons dining spot, as is the **1770 House**, 143 Main Street, East Hampton. There are two branches of Manhattan's pricey **Palm** steak house in East Hampton, at the **Huntting Inn**, 94 Main Street, and **The Hedges**, 74 James Lane. Trendy favorites opened recently by New York restaurateurs are **Sapore di Mare**, Route 27 and Wainscott Road, Wainscott, and **Karen Lee's**, Main Street, Bridgehampton. For the best lobster, drive to the very end of the island and join the waiting line at **Gosman's Dock** at Montauk harbor.

If you choose to stay and enjoy the beach, East Hampton's 1770 House (Tel: 516-324-1770) and The Hedges (Tel: 516-788-7269) are among the most appealing lodgings, along with the **Mill Garth** (Tel: 516-267-3757), cottages in a garden, on Windmill Lane in Amagansett.

Southampton is 96 miles from Manhattan—but it feels like 296 in Friday-night traffic in summer. Drive *only* at nonpeak hours. Take the Long Island Expressway to exit 70, go right for 3 miles to Sunrise Highway (Route 27), then follow 27 east. Long Island Railroad has frequent service from Manhattan (Tel: 718-454-5477), as does the Hampton Jitney bus (Tel: 212-936-0440).

Southampton Chamber of Commerce, 76 Main Street, Southampton, NY 11968. Tel: (516) 283-0402. East Hampton Chamber of Commerce, 4 Main Street, East Hampton, NY 11937. Tel: (516) 324-0362.

PRINCETON UNIVERSITY

Princeton would merit a visit even if it were not home to one of America's great universities. The shaded lanes of this historic town are lined with outstanding Colonial and Federal architecture. Add the beautiful, ivy-clad campus that dominates the center of town, and its extraordinary outdoor art collection, and the trip becomes a double pleasure.

First stop is Maclean House, just inside the main campus gate, to sign up for a free, one-hour Orange Key guided tour or to pick up a do-it-yourself tour guide. Either way, the place to begin is where Princeton began—at **Nassau Hall**. The building, one of the largest in Colonial America, housed the entire college for nearly 50 years beginning in 1756. It also played an important part in the nation's history, serving as home to the Continental Congress for six months in 1783.

Move on to Firestone Library, where three million volumes fill the shelves. Whig and Clio halls, twin buildings, just west of the library, that resemble Greek temples, once housed the rival societies where two 18th-century students, James Madison and Aaron Burr, honed their debating skills (the two groups merged in 1929).

Princeton's University Chapel boasts glorious stained-glass windows, oak pews, and a 16th-century pulpit from France. It took 100 men a year to carve the choir and clergy stalls, which are made of wood from England's Sherwood Forest.

The striking Woodrow Wilson School of Public and International Affairs and the **Princeton University Art Museum** show the progression of campus architecture. Chinese paintings, and prints and drawings are among the special strengths in the museum's fine collections, which range from African ritual masks to paintings by Cézanne and van Gogh. The Picasso sculpture just outside is part of the outstanding outdoor collection that covers the campus and includes dozens of works by such masters as Louise Nevelson, Henry Moore, Alexander Calder, and Jacques Lipchitz.

For information on other historic sites in and around town, stop for a guide at Bainbridge House, the headquarters of the Princeton Historical Society on Nassau Street. Among sights worth seeing are Rockingham, George Washington's onetime headquarters; Morven, the former official residence of the governor of New Jersey; the Stony Brook (Quaker) Meeting House; and the homes of Woodrow Wilson, Albert Einstein, and Aaron Burr. There are dozens of fine historic homes to be viewed on Nassau Street and its side streets Alexander, Mercer, and Stockton. Nearby are the attractive Neo-Gothic Graduate School and the world-famous **Institute for Advanced Studies**.

Princeton's fine dining choices include **Le Plumet Royal** in the Peacock Inn, 20 Bayard Lane, and **Lahiere's**, 5 Witherspoon Street. The **Omni Nassau Inn** in Palmer Square is newer than you might expect but is pleasant and convenient for lunch (accommodations reservations 1-800-922-3432 or 609-921-7500).

New Jersey Transit (Tel: 201-460-8444) runs frequent trains to Princeton from Penn Station, with a change at Princeton Junction. The trip takes an hour and the center of the university is a three-minute stroll from the station. Bus service is available via Suburban Transit (Tel: 212-868-7367) from the Port Authority Bus Terminal to the center of town. To reach Princeton by car, take the New Jersey Turnpike south to exit 9, then Route 18 north to Route 1 (Trenton exit). Drive approximately 15 miles on Route 1 south to the Princeton–Hightstown Road exit, and go right on Route 571. At the third traffic light make a left on to Nassau; this puts you right in the middle of Princeton.

Princeton Chamber of Commerce, P.O. Box 431 (entrance 2–4 Chamber Street, Suite 127), Princeton, NJ 08542. Tel: (609) 921-7676.

OTHER DAY TRIPS

In brief, some other places that are well worth a trip:

Donald M. Kendall Sculpture Gardens, Pepsi corporate headquarters in Purchase, New York: Some 112 acres of formally landscaped grounds are an outdoor gallery for 40 works by a virtual Who's Who of important 20th-century artists—Calder, Dubuffet, Rodin, Miró, Moore among them. The grounds are open to the public daily, year round, free of charge. On the campus of the State University of New York at Purchase, across the street, the Neuberger Museum exhibits American and primitive art. To reach the sculpture gardens, take Route 87 (the Deegan Expressway) north to exit 4, then the Cross County Parkway eastbound. Exit onto the Hutchinson River Parkway northbound, continue to exit 28, go north on Lincoln Avenue, turn right at the end of Lincoln onto Anderson Hill Road. Depending on traffic, allow 45 minutes to an hour for the 35-mile trip from Manhattan.

PepsiCo, Inc., Anderson Hill Road, Purchase, NY 10577. Tel: (914) 253-2000.

The Storm King Art Center and Sculpture Park, Mountainville, New York: Mountain peaks are a dramatic backdrop for 130 post-1945 sculptures, many of them massive in size, set on 400 acres of woodland and open terraced lawns. Take the George Washington Bridge to the Palisades Parkway to the New York Thruway (Route 87). At exit 16 (Harriman) turn north on Route 32 for 10 miles and follow signs to the center, about 55 miles from Manhattan. Storm King is open from April to November only.

Storm King Art Center, Old Pleasant Hill Road, Mountainville, NY 10953. Tel: (914) 534-3190.

Spring Lake, New Jersey: A turn-of-the-century boardwalk and shady avenues lined with gingerbread-trimmed hotels and gracious Victorian homes with canopied porches are the stage sets for an old-fashioned day by the sea. The spring-fed lake that gave Spring Lake its name is in a sylvan park in the heart of this pretty village, once known as the "Irish Riviera" because so many wealthy Irish families summered here.

Normandy Inn (Tel: 201-449-7172) and Ashling Cottage (Tel: 201-449-3553) are small, charming Victorian homes turned bed-and-breakfast inns. Take your meals at The Breakers (Tel: 201-449-7700) and other big hotels.

Follow the New Jersey Turnpike south to the Garden State Parkway. Take exit 98, then Route 34 south to the traffic circle, and Route 524 east into town. Spring Lake is about 65 miles from Manhattan.

Greater Spring Lake Chamber of Commerce, P.O. Box 694, Spring Lake, NJ 07762. Tel: (201) 449-0577.

Doylestown, Pennsylvania (the county seat of scenic Bucks County): Archaeologist Henry Chapman Mercer was so intrigued with the work of the old Pennsylvania German tile makers that in the 1890s he apprenticed himself to a master. He became so proficient that Mercer tiles can be seen today in the casino at Monte Carlo and the Gardner Museum in Boston. Mercer's **Moravian Pottery and Tile Works** factory is now a museum but still turns out tiles according to his patterns. His collection of 25,000 early American tools is on view nearby at the **Mercer Museum**, with an interior spiral design that is said to have inspired Frank Lloyd Wright's design for New York's Guggenheim Museum. Most intriguing of all is Mercer's home, **Fonthill**, a concrete fantasy of columns, balconies, beams, towers, and winding staircases, with tiles everywhere. The three attractions are known collectively as the "Mercer Mile." Doylestown's James Michener Art Center salutes the work of the many artists who over the years have called Bucks County's stone farmhouses home.

Good bed-and-breakfast inns in Doylestown are Highland Farms, the former Oscar Hammerstein estate (Tel: 215-340-1354), and the Inn at Fordhook Farm, once the estate of seed king David Burpee (Tel: 215-345-1766). The Pear and Partridge Inn serves a nice dinner (Tel: 215-345-7800).

To get to Doylestown, take the New Jersey Turnpike south to exit 10, then go north on Route 287 15 miles and stay left for another exit 10, Route 22. Drive west for about 3½ miles and turn right at the sign marked Flemington-Princeton. This is Route 202, which leads across the Delaware River to Doylestown, about 85 miles from Manhattan.

The Mercer Mile, Doylestown, PA 18901. Fonthill, East Court Street. Tel: (215) 348-9461. Mercer Museum, Pine Street. Tel: (215) 345-0210. Moravian Pottery and Tile Works, 130 Swamp Road. Tel: (215) 345-6722.

THE CITY'S SPECIALTIES

MUSEUMS

By Amy K. Hughes

When Amy Hughes is not busy editing and writing, she is often in a museum. She specializes in art, travel, and natural history.

One of the first things you will notice when you are exploring the city's museums is that they are full of New Yorkers, and it's because of this sophisticated, hard-nosed clientele that New York's museums are among the best in the world. From the largest, stuffiest, wealthiest institution to the smallest and quirkiest, each has its own appeal, and when you put them all together, there truly does seem to be a museum for everyone.

Most museums in New York are open on weekends and closed on Mondays (exceptions are noted). Some close on Sundays or Tuesdays as well, to make a "weekend" of it. Many are open late one or two evenings a week, as noted. Like everything else in New York, the hours of museums are subject to change, as are the addresses and phone numbers; we recommend you telephone a museum before setting aside time or going out of your way to visit it.

All museums are in Manhattan (telephone area code 212) unless otherwise indicated.

A late eighteenth-century carriage house quarters the **Abigail Adams Smith Museum**, with music room, dining room, kitchen, bedrooms, and sitting rooms decorated in period furnishings. 421 East 61st Street at Second Avenue. Tel: 838-6878. Open Mondays, closed Saturdays.

The **Alternative Museum** shows contemporary political and sociopolitical art that you won't find in the uptown museums. They also put on solo, mid-career shows for artists out of the traditional mainstream. 17 White Street near lower Sixth Avenue. Tel: 966-4444. Closed summers.

If you equate crafts with summer camp, the ceramics, glass, textiles, woodwork, metalwork, and basketry by craftspeople of today and yesterday on display at the **American Craft Museum** will change your outlook forever. 40 West 53rd Street between Fifth and Sixth avenues. Tel: 956-6047. Open late Tuesdays.

The **American Museum of Immigration**, located beneath the Statue of Liberty, celebrates the age of immigration; special exhibitions highlight the stories of different immigrant groups in America. Liberty Island. Tel: 363-3200 for ferry information; 363-8834 for the museum. Open every day.

The **American Museum of the Moving Image** is dedicated to demonstrating, displaying, portraying, explaining, analyzing, and celebrating television, video, and film—in an exciting, exhilarating arena. 35th Avenue at 36th Street, Astoria, Queens. Tel: (718) 784-0077.

Most native New Yorkers share Holden Caulfield's memory of tramping through the **American Museum of Natural History** on a school field trip. The kids are still here, marveling at the massive dinosaur skeletons and the giant whale hanging from the ceiling. The exhibits include dioramas with life-size models of peoples and animals from around the world and through time, a spectacular mineral and gem collection, a giant-screen movie theater, and the Hayden Planetarium, which brings you the universe. Central Park West at 79th Street. Tel: 769-5100. Open every day; open late Wednesdays, Fridays, and Saturdays.

The **Asia Society**'s special exhibitions, programs, films, and lectures focus on the art, culture, and history of the East. The society's permanent holdings include the John D. Rockefeller collection of Oriental arts. 725 Park Avenue at 70th Street. Tel: 288-6400.

Thousands of dolls, teddy bears, and toys fill **Aunt Len's Doll and Toy Museum**, operated by a former New York City school teacher. 6 Hamilton Terrace at West 141st Street. Tel: 281-4143 for an appointment.

Intriguing displays of local artists, local themes, and

local history can be found at the **Bronx Museum of the Arts**. 1040 Grand Concourse at 165th Street, Bronx. Tel: 681-6000. Closed Fridays.

Everyone with kids should spend a day among the bright, colorful hands-on exhibits at the **Brooklyn Children's Museum**. Natural history, science, and technology are brought to life in an environment that inspires and ignites young imaginations. 145 Brooklyn Avenue. Tel: (718) 735-4400. Open Mondays closed Tuesdays.

You'll find all the wonders of Brooklyn—Coney Island, the Dodgers, Brooklyn Bridge, even "The Honeymooners"—documented and exhibited in the newly refurbished **Brooklyn Historical Society**. 128 Pierrepont Street, Brooklyn Heights. Tel: (718) 624-0890.

A world-famous collection of Egyptian art, Colonial American furnishings, Oriental prints, and European paintings (and everything and anything in between) can be found at the superb **Brooklyn Museum**. Be sure to check out one of the best, most affordable museum shops in New York. 200 Eastern Parkway near Washington Avenue. Tel: (718) 638-5000. Open Mondays, closed Tuesdays. (Easily reached from Manhattan via number 2 and 3 subway lines, Eastern Parkway station.)

The **Center for African Art** brings the traditional arts of Africa's myriad cultures to New York, with changing exhibitions, films, and lectures. 54 East 68th Street between Madison and Park. Tel: 861-1200. Open late Tuesdays.

Members of the advisory committee of the new **Children's Museum of Manhattan** range in age from 5 to 14. They have been opining on the installation of such exhibits as a walk-in model of the human brain, hands-on electrical exhibits, and a simulated countryside with cows, a mooing machine, and scratch-and-sniff smells of the great outdoors. 212 West 83rd Street between Broadway and Amsterdam avenues. Tel: 721-1234.

The Medieval and Gothic **Cloisters** invite you back into the Middle Ages. The treasures and artworks are augmented by the monastic setting, the herb garden, and the view of the Hudson and the Palisades. West 190th Street and Fort Washington Avenue in Fort Tryon Park. Tel: 923-3700. (From Midtown, take either the A subway line or M 4 Madison Avenue bus.)

In Andrew Carnegie's 64-room mansion, the **Cooper-Hewitt Museum**, an affiliate of the Smithsonian Institution, displays superb collections of wallpapers, drawings, prints, glass, porcelain, textiles, embroidery, lace, woodwork, metalwork, and anything else that falls into the categories of design and decorative arts, both the old and the new. 2 East 91st Street at Fifth Avenue. Tel: 860-6868. Open late Tuesdays.

The restored registry building that houses the **Ellis Island Immigration Museum** was the site of the foreign emigrant's first, and often frightening, encounter with American bureaucracy. This new museum, with its authentic setting, oral histories, and it-happened-here realism, promises to tell the true story of the American immigrant. Scheduled to open in spring 1990. For information, contact the Statue of Liberty, Tel: 363-3200, or the National Park Service, Tel: 264-8711.

The stone on which George Washington stood during his presidential inauguration is one of the displays at **Federal Hall National Memorial**, a museum devoted to New York's and America's early days. 26 Wall Street at Nassau Street. Tel: 264-8711. Closed weekends.

The Fabergé eggs are the stars of the **Forbes Magazine Galleries**, which also house 500 toy boats, 12,000 toy soldiers, and a fine collection of master paintings. 62 Fifth Avenue at 12th Street. Tel: 206-5548. Free.

The exhibits on the second floor of **Fraunces Tavern**— in the room where George Washington took leave of his fellow officers after the Revolution—document the culture and history of New York City in its colonial days. 54 Pearl Street at Broad Street, at the southern tip of Manhattan. Tel: 425-1778. Closed weekends in summer, Saturdays in winter.

The **Frick Collection** of old-master paintings, sculptures, furnishings, and decorative arts could not be shown to better advantage—in what was once Henry Clay Frick's home. 1 East 70th Street at Fifth Avenue. Tel: 288-0700.

The **Solomon R. Guggenheim Museum** is as famous for its spiraling Frank Lloyd Wright building as it is for its extensive modern-art collections. 1071 Fifth Avenue at 88th Street. Tel: 360-3500. Open late Tuesdays.

Spanish and Portuguese paintings (by Goya, Velázquez, and El Greco), sculptures, artifacts, and mosaics from Roman times to the 20th century are in the fine collection at the **Hispanic Society of America**. Audubon Terrace, Broadway at 155th Street. Tel: 926-2234.

Besides the science and computer exhibits you might expect, the **IBM Gallery of Science and Art** has changing displays of paintings, sculptures, photographs, and architecture—sometimes from the company's own excellent collection. Madison Avenue at 56th Street. Tel: 745-6100. Free.

Past and present photographers and photojournalists are represented in one-person and theme shows at the **International Center of Photography**. 1130 Fifth Avenue at 94th Street. Tel: 860-1777. Open late on Tuesdays. There is also a branch at 1133 Sixth Avenue at 43rd Street. Tel: 768-4682. Open late Thursdays.

Aboard the **Intrepid Sea-Air-Space Museum** (housed on a decommissioned aircraft carrier), military history is conveyed through exhibits, films, authentic aircraft, and the carrier itself. Hudson River, Pier 86, West 46th Street. Tel: 245-2533.

A reconstruction of a Tibetan temple, gardens and a lotus pool, and a remarkable collection of Tibetan and Buddhist art are some of the attractions of the **Jacques Marchais Center of Tibetan Art** (also called, simply, the Tibetan Museum). Besides students and lovers of Orientalia, its visitors include Buddhist monks from a New Jersey monastery. 338 Lighthouse Avenue, Staten Island. Tel: (718) 987-3478. Closed December through March.

The permanent collections of art, artifacts, and treasures at the **Jewish Museum** are augmented by changing exhibitions that highlight different aspects of Jewish life and culture. 1109 Fifth Avenue at 92nd Street. Tel: 860-1888. Open Mondays, open late Tuesdays, closed Fridays and Saturdays.

As soon as you enter the Great Hall at the **Metropolitan Museum of Art** you know you are in New York's biggest and best. Wander through such sections as the Egyptian Temple of Dendur, the American Wing, and the Chinese Blumenthal Patio and you'll feel as if you've been around the world and through time. Paintings by masters old and new, sculptures from ancient Greece and Rome to modern times, the Costume Institute, the primitive-art collection, and famous collections of the arts of Egypt and the Orient are just a few of the wonders that await. Fifth Avenue at 82nd Street. Tel: 535-7710. Open late Fridays and Saturdays.

El Museo del Barrio displays paintings, sculpture, photographs, and films by contemporary artists of Puerto Rican, Central, and South American heritage, as well as historical and cultural artifacts. 1230 Fifth Avenue at 104th Street. Tel: 831-7273.

Quilts, weathervanes, tin toys, decoys, and furniture are some of the things you might find at the **Museum of**

American Folk Art, most with a quirky twist that characterizes this type of art. 2 Lincoln Square, Columbus Avenue at 65th Street. Tel: 977-7298. Open 9:00 to 9:00 every day. Free.

The displays of clothing, artifacts, sculpture, jewelry, and masks at the **Museum of the American Indian** are designed to further the understanding of the cultures of the native peoples of the Americas. Audubon Terrace, Broadway at 155th Street. Tel: 283-2497.

Radio and television buffs shouldn't miss the **Museum of Broadcasting**, where they can listen to old broadcasts, watch old TV shows or commercials, and look up favorite scripts. 1 East 53rd Street near Fifth Avenue. Tel: 752-7684. Open late Tuesdays. The museum plans to move into much larger quarters and expand their hours in September 1990. The new address will be 23 West 52nd Street between Fifth and Sixth avenues.

You can find out anything you want to know about New York City at the **Museum of the City of New York**. Their Sunday walking tours of different neighborhoods are among the best in town. 1220 Fifth Avenue at 103rd Street. Tel: 534-1672.

Changing exhibitions of drawings, paintings, and sculptures are on display at the **Museum of Contemporary Hispanic Art** (MoCHA). 584 Broadway, seventh floor. Tel: 966-6699. Open late Thursdays.

Since its opening in 1929, the **Museum of Modern Art** (MoMA) has been a major force in promoting the arts of this century and the end of the last, when modern art was born. All the important movements of modern art and design are represented here, be they photos, paintings, sculptures, furniture, or household appliances. 11 West 53rd Street between Fifth and Sixth avenues. Tel: 708-9480. Open Mondays, closed Wednesdays, open late Thursdays.

Samuel F. B. Morse and Rembrandt Peale were among the founders of the **National Academy of Design**, which houses an impressive collection of paintings, drawings, and sculptures, many of them from Renaissance times. 1083 Fifth Avenue at 89th Street. Tel: 369-4880. Open late Tuesdays.

For a glimpse at art that is perhaps too avant-garde for the more button-down galleries and museums, stop in at the **New Museum of Contemporary Art**. 583 Broadway between Prince and Houston at the eastern edge of SoHo. Tel: 219-1355. Open late Fridays and Saturdays.

What better place to learn about the history of fire-fighting than in the old firehouse that quarters the **New York City Fire Museum**, featuring old engines and equipment and exhibits on the city's great fires. 278 Spring Street, between Hudson and Varick. Tel: 691-1303.

The **New York Hall of Science**, on the site of the world's fairs of 1939 and 1964, houses a fascinating assemblage of hands-on space, technological, and science exhibits. Flushing Meadows Corona Park, 47-01 111th Street at 48th Avenue, Queens. Tel: (718) 699-0005. (From Manhattan, take the number 7 subway line to 111th Street in Queens.)

Learn what's made New York tick for 350 years at the **New-York Historical Society**, a repository of furnishings, prints, fine art, artifacts, and documents pertaining to New York and early America. 170 Central Park West at 77th Street. Tel: 873-3400.

For a glimpse into the 1830s, don't miss the **Old Merchant's House**, which contains the original furnishings, mementos, and clothing of the family that lived there. 29 East 4th Street. Tel: 777-1089. Open Sundays only for walk-in tours; call to try to join a group tour during the rest of the week. Hours may expand in early 1990.

The **Pierpont Morgan Library** is a stunning backdrop for its superb exhibitions, including old-master drawings, Medieval and Renaissance artworks, valuable manuscripts, and inspired temporary shows. 29 East 36th Street at Madison Avenue. Tel: 685-0610. Usually closed last two weeks of August.

A giant scale model of the five boroughs of New York featuring every building is one of the displays at the **Queens Museum**, housed in the New York City pavilion from the 1939 World's Fair. Flushing Meadows Corona Park. Tel: (718) 592-5555. (From Manhattan, take the number 7 subway line to the Shea Stadium stop.)

The Staten Island Historical Society's **Richmondtown Restoration** is a series of historical buildings—school, grocer, general store—that have been restored and furnished to particular periods in the area's history. 441 Clarke Avenue and Arthur Kill Road. Tel: (718) 351-1611. Open every day.

Docks, nine ships, and five square blocks of historic buildings are all part of the bustling **South Street Seaport Museum**, which endeavors to keep the spirit of its early 18th-century heyday alive. South Street at Fulton Street. Tel: 669-9424. Open every day.

The **Studio Museum in Harlem** is a showcase for contemporary black artists (of Africa, the Caribbean, and the Americas); its permanent collections and special exhibitions are among the finest, and most thought-provoking, in the city. 144 West 125th Street. Tel: 864-4500.

The **Theodore Roosevelt Birthplace** is a re-creation of the childhood home of the New York City police commissioner who became president. 28 East 20th Street. Tel: 260-1616.

The history and the traditional arts and crafts of the Ukraine are on display at the **Ukrainian Museum**, devoted to keeping that culture alive in the American melting pot. 203 Second Avenue at 12th Street. Tel: 228-0110.

For an impressive overview of the most influential American artists of this century—from Edward Hopper to Georgia O'Keeffe to Andy Warhol—visit the **Whitney Museum of American Art**. 945 Madison Avenue at 75th Street. Tel: 570-3676. Open late Tuesdays. The Whitney has three branches, which feature special exhibitions: The Whitney Museum Downtown, 33 Maiden Lane at Nassau Street; Tel: 943-5655; closed weekends. The Whitney Museum at Equitable Center, 787 Seventh Avenue; Tel: 554-1113; closed Sundays, open Mondays. The Whitney Museum in the Philip Morris Building, 42nd Street and Park Avenue; Tel: 878-2453.

ART

By Eleanor Heartney

Eleanor Heartney is a writer and critic specializing in contemporary art. She is a regular contributor to Artnews, Art in America, Contemporania, *and* The New Art Examiner.

New York City is haunted by the ghosts of art worlds past. You can stroll around Union Square and nod to the spirits of Isabel Bishop and Reginald Marsh as they toss off rapid sketches of the inhabitants of a quieter America between the wars. Then, heading south along University Place, you pass near the sites of such legendary watering-holes as the Cedar Tavern and the 10th Street Bar, where Jackson Pollock, Willem de Kooning, Philip Guston, and their cronies tipped their bottles in the raucous hours between their solitary labors. A detour along Washington Square takes you past the Judson Church, which during the 1960s served as a stage for happenings, experimental dance and theater productions, and environmental installations by such avant-gardists as Red Grooms, Allan Kaprow, Allen Ginsberg, and Yvonne Rainer. Of course, the most obvious places to partake of New York's rich artistic heritage are the city's many art museums, covered in our Neighborhoods section and Museums listings.

However, to penetrate the heart of *today's* art world, you must continue on across Houston to SoHo, that once shabby warehouse district that now boasts what is undoubtedly the richest concentration of artists, artworks, and art talk in the world. There are, by conservative estimate, roughly 500 art galleries in New York City, more than half of them in SoHo, and perhaps as many as 90,000 artists living in the city and its immediate environs. Such sheer numbers, at once the cause and effect of the burgeoning art market, have re-created the art world in ways that would have seemed unimaginable even 15 years ago. As art, money, and hype mix here in a sometimes unwholesome stew, bohemia today wears a distinctly modern face, and though black remains the sartorial color of choice, the notion of starving in garrets or repulsing the bourgeoisie is definitely passé.

You can chart the rising respectability of respectability by the changing fortunes of the late, lamented East Village art scene. Back in the already distant early 1980s, an enterprising group of young artists decided to challenge the hegemony of the art establishment by opening their own collection of motley storefront galleries on the then unfashionable Lower East Side. This guerrilla action, begun almost as a lark (one trailblazer opened her first exhibition in her bathroom), evolved into an astonishingly successful assault on the taste-making process, and for a few short years it was not uncommon to see limos parked along the garbage-strewn streets of Alphabet City (Avenues A, B, and C) while their owners hopped from tiny storefront to tiny storefront in search of the latest manifestation of the avant-garde.

Times change, and in the end the East Village art scene has been undone by its own success. The influx of dedicated and well-heeled art lovers lured new restaurants and real-estate developers to the neighborhood, rents shot up, and gallery owners found themselves edged out of the market. Meanwhile, the more successful artists and art dealers have outgrown both the cramped quarters and the aggressively raunchy style that was once the signature of the East Village art scene. Many have moved on to conquer SoHo.

THE GALLERY AS SHOWCASE

Ensconced in clean white exhibition spaces and equipped with an open-door policy, a revolving schedule of exhibitions, and a quasi-educational function, most galleries today attempt to duplicate the museum experience. Yet, unlike museums, they support themselves through the sale of work. This lends them a slightly schizophrenic character, a fact forcefully brought home recently when the New York Department of Cultural Affairs decreed that galleries, like all other retail businesses, must display an up-to-date price list of all items on display. Some galleries quietly complied, others protested vigorously that too much emphasis on commerce would detract from aesthetic contemplation—and a few evaded the regulation entirely by preselling entire shows.

The price-list furor dramatizes the complicated role galleries play in the contemporary art world. Commercial galleries today are the primary mechanism through which artists emerge into the art mainstream (due in part to the decline of the alternative space; see below). Hence a gallery exhibition is far more than a display of wares for sale; it is a crucial milestone in an artist's career, a way to enter the art dialogue, to get reviewed, to be considered for museum exhibitions. Therefore, it is important for everyone involved that the exhibition be open to the general public and be seen by a larger audience than that composed of potential buyers.

At the same time, however, the gallery is a place of sale. Typically, each gallery represents a "stable" of artists, whose works are available for viewing and sale at all times in the back room. Most galleries support themselves as much or more through the back room as through sales of exhibited work. In theory, at least, this allows them to present work that may be risky and potentially unsalable out front.

DOING THE GALLERIES

Given the number of galleries and the varieties of art currently on display, "doing" the galleries in New York can seem a somewhat daunting task. Once an activity that might fill a pleasant afternoon, gallery going now threatens to overwhelm the unselective visitor. In order to survive a day of gallery hopping, begin with a definite plan of attack. The indispensable tool is the *Art Now Gallery Guide,* a monthly listing of the exhibitions currently on view in more than 500 galleries and museums around the city. The *Gallery Guide* is available free from the listed galleries (though toward the end of the month they tend to become a very scarce commodity) and at select bookstores. The guide divides the city into areas, and each section is accompanied by a small map.

Because they benefit from spillover traffic, galleries tend to cluster together. The greatest concentrations exist in **SoHo**, of course, where you can expect to find the work of the most hotly debated new artists and styles. The galleries on **57th Street**, with several lively exceptions, focus on artists of more solidly established reputations. And those on the Upper East Side along **Madison Avenue**, in elegant converted brownstones, present art of historical and contemporary importance with a quiet decorum that contrasts strikingly with the downtown scene's noisy self-promotion.

The first-time visitor wanting to get the flavor of New York art could do worse than focus on the various multi-gallery buildings, such as those at: 420 West Broadway and 560, 568, and 578 Broadway in SoHo; and 41 East 57th Street, 50 West 57th Street, and 724 Fifth Avenue in the 57th Street area. Those with more time or specific interests will want to venture as well to the more dispersed galleries listed in the *Gallery Guide*.

Though distinctions have begun to blur somewhat, the old division between haughty uptown and hip downtown remains largely in force. What follows are a few thumbnail sketches of some notable galleries in the three major art zones. No effort is made here to be comprehensive (an impossible task anyway), and this selection should be taken as a mere starting point for gallery exploration. (You'll find exact street locations in the *Gallery Guide;* we do give addresses for galleries outside of the major concentrations in SoHo and on 57th Street.)

SoHo Galleries

Less an art purveyor than a tourist attraction in her own right, **Mary Boone** has almost single-handedly redefined the gallery business in the 1980s. Her talent for showmanship and marketing and her uncanny ability to position herself at the crest of whatever wave is breaking over the art world at the moment make her gallery must viewing for casual observers and cognoscenti alike.

By contrast, the grand old man of the New York art scene is **Leo Castelli**, who made his reputation in the early 1960s with his unwavering support of the then-brash newcomers like Andy Warhol, Roy Lichtenstein, and Jasper Johns. The work of these artists can still be seen in Castelli's newly remodeled West Broadway gallery, along with that of several younger generations.

One of the elegantly apportioned East Village transplants, **Jay Gorney Modern Art** is a showcase for the conceptual-based, opulently appointed New Object art. Both artworks and setting resonate with the aura of temperate luxury that marked the spirit of the late 1980s.

For the "old" austere Conceptual and Minimal art, the place is **John Weber Gallery**, whose stable includes such venerable names as Sol LeWitt, Alice Aycock, and Robert Smithson, as well as younger artists with a compatible outlook.

Ronald Feldman Gallery, one of the more independent and idiosyncratic galleries in town, offers artists as different as the elegantly restrained Conceptualist Arakawa, the boisterous Russian expatriates Komar and Melamid, and the self-appointed nouveau Andy Warhol, Mark Kostabi.

A cryptic, cerebral, ironic aesthetic is to be found at **Metro Pictures**. Home of the so-called Pictures Generation, whose politically attuned media explorations offered a counterpoint to Neoexpressionism in the early 1980s, Metro shows artists credited with spawning the momentarily trendy "Neo Geo" movement.

The core of the **Phyllis Kind Gallery** are the brash aesthetics of the Chicago "Hairy Who" artists who Kind discovered and promoted when she was centered there in the 1970s. In most cases, Kind's other artists are faithful to the gallery's orientation toward fantastic figurative painting.

The only gallery in New York specializing exclusively in work that celebrates the marriage of art and architecture, **Max Protetch** offers architectural drawings and models as well as quasi-functional and architecturally inspired sculpture.

For relief from too much seriousness, there is **Gracie Mansion Gallery**, one of the first East Village galleries. This last bastion of the scene's original cartoon-inspired funky energy continues to resist the subsequent sobering of the art world in its new SoHo location.

57th Street Galleries

A gallery with a venerable history (its proprietor was linked to the discovery of Pop Art in the 1960s), **Sidney Janis Gallery** is noted for the museum quality of its exhibitions of the art of such historical figures as Giacometti, Mondrian, and Albers as well as its surprising embrace of the ill-fated graffiti movement of the early 1980s.

New work by the major figures of the color-field school is frequently the fare at **André Emmerich Gallery**, whose stable boasts, among others, Jules Olitski, Lawrence Poons, Kenneth Noland, Helen Frankenthaler, and Sam Francis.

The decorative movement, which had its great moment in the mid-1970s, remains the inspiration for many of the artists represented at **Holly Solomon Gallery**, while ambitious installations, provocative theme shows, and a taste for the fashionably eccentric are the hallmarks of **Kent Fine Art Gallery**.

The focus at **Marian Goodman Gallery** is on the European avant-garde, with an emphasis on *arte povera,* Conceptualism, and large-scale sculpture projects. This is the place to see the work of artists who have achieved major reputations in Europe but are still little known here.

Uptown Galleries

M. Knoedler & Co. (10 East 70th Street), one of the oldest and most elegant galleries in New York (founded in 1846), is home to a distinguished stable of artists that includes such illustrious names as Frank Stella, Nancy Graves, and Richard Diebenkorn as well as historical figures such as Adolph Gottlieb, David Smith, and Alexander Calder.

Also offering uptown's characteristic mix of old and new, **Hirschl & Adler Modern** (851 Madison Avenue) focuses on 20th-century modernists as well as contemporary artists concerned with figuration. Meanwhile, the gallery's original branch, **Hirschl & Adler** (21 East 70th Street), concentrates on historical material from the 18th through the early 20th century; newly opened **Hirschl & Adler Folk** (851 Madison Avenue) presents 19th-century American folk art from paintings to weather vanes to quilts.

Traditional Art

While the vast majority of galleries in New York feature contemporary art or a mix of contemporary and modern (late 19th and 20th century) art, there are a number of dealers who specialize in historical work. Most of these operate privately and are open by appointment only to serious buyers. There are, however, several that balance private sales and public exhibitions, offering one or two carefully handpicked shows a year. Occasionally these are fleshed out with works on loan from museums or prestigious private collections. Some of the most interesting of these galleries follow.

Galerie St. Etienne (24 West 57th Street) specializes in an odd mix: Austrian and German Expressionist painters from the turn of the century and contemporary and 19th-century American folk art. This gallery, operating in New York for 50 years, was the first to introduce an American audience to such artists as Gustav Klimt, Paula Modersohn-Becker, and Grandma Moses.

Colnaghi USA Ltd. (21 East 67th Street) is the American branch of a London gallery that was founded in 1760. The New York gallery specializes in old master drawings, prints, and paintings and English watercolors ranging from the 14th to the early 20th century. The gallery has two large exhibition spaces and annually offers two or three exhibitions of drawings and prints from its own stock. It sometimes draws on outside loans for its two painting shows a year on scholarly themes.

Wildenstein and Co. (19 East 64th Street) also has an impressive pedigree. Founded in Paris in 1875 and established in New York in 1902, it offers a broad scope of historical work ranging from the 12th to the early 20th century and specializes in such areas as 18th-century French art, French Impressionism, and Postimpressionism. Its two or three exhibitions a year are often of museum quality and may include the works of artists of the stature of Goya, Rembrandt, Monet, and Manet.

HANGING OUT

The best experience of the art world as theater is to be obtained at gallery openings. Ostensibly, the purpose of these receptions is to inaugurate a new exhibition, but they are actually opportunities to see and to be seen, to network, to party. Once the gallery begins to fill up with artists, collectors, and well-wishers, the art becomes invisible anyway, so anyone seriously interested in viewing the exhibition is advised to return another day.

On any given night through the art season (which lasts from September to June or July) there are likely to be multiple openings, so that a determined opening aficionado can take in quite a variety of different scenes. Times and dates of openings are listed in the back of the *Gallery Guide* or can be obtained from the galleries.

One warning: Most galleries long ago abandoned the practice of serving food at openings and most offer only inferior wine. Plan instead to stop off afterward at such SoHo art hangouts as **Fanelli** (at Prince and Mercer) or the **Spring Street Bar** (at Spring and West Broadway), where post-opening crowds gather.

BUYING ART

Buying a work of art is not always a simple proposition. Some of the tonier galleries, maintaining that they have a responsibility to place their artists in only the most important, most visible collections, practically require an audition before they will part with a work of art. Other dealers, especially those specializing in non-superstars, younger, or emerging artists, or in specialty items such as prints, photographs, drawings, or old master works, are more than willing to steer potential collectors through the art labyrinth. A listing of reputable dealers, which includes information on their areas of specialization, can be obtained by writing or calling the Art Dealers Association, 575 Madison Avenue, New York, NY 10022; Tel: (212) 940-8590.

Other important sources of information for a novice art collector are the major art magazines: *Art in America, Artnews, Arts,* and *Artforum,* which publish reviews of recent exhibitions and articles on important contemporary artists and trends. The Friday edition of *The New York Times* and the weekly *Village Voice* may be even more helpful, because they contain reviews of shows currently on view.

Once you have determined what kind of work you are interested in purchasing, it may help to focus on galleries specializing in that medium or approach. A short (and once again, by no means comprehensive) list of various specialties includes:

Photography: Marcuse Pfeifer Gallery, Light Gallery, Laurence Miller Gallery, Pace/MacGill Gallery.

Prints: Castelli Graphics, Multiples, Pace Prints, Diane Villani Editions, Crown Point Press, Editions Ilene Kurtz, Pelavin Editions.

Old Master and Period Works: Richard L. Feigen & Co., Barry Friedman, Daniel B. Grossman, Hirschl & Adler, Coe Kerr, David Tunick.

Art Auctions

For those who like a little adventure with their art hunting, it is also possible to purchase art at auction. Prices are not always lower than those attainable at the galleries, but the astute collector can find some bargains. Contemporary art auctions are held twice a year, in November and May. The evening sales are for the heavy hitters, but the daytime sales focus on younger artists with shorter track records and on smaller works. Also of interest to the novice collector are the weekend previews held before the major auctions, at which the works to be auctioned off can be viewed.

The two major auction houses are **Sotheby's** (1334 York Avenue; Tel: 212-606-7000 or 606-7245) and **Christie's** (502 Park Avenue at 59th; Tel: 212-546-1000 or 371-5438). Neck and neck in competition for the best offerings, Sotheby's and Christie's are practically indistinguishable in the range and quality of their art lots. A distant third is **Phillips** (406 East 79th Street; Tel: 212-570-4830).

In order to participate in the auctions, you will want to subscribe to the catalogs for the sales you are interested in (contemporary, modern, prints, etc.). The catalogs, distributed before every sale, cost about $20 each and contain pictures of the works to be auctioned and the high and low estimates of the sale price, along with information about the work's ownership history. Generally there is also an unstated reserve price below which the seller will not go.

One interesting development of recent years is the tendency for collectors and dealers to use the auction as the testing ground for the prices of works by younger artists. When a work by someone like Julian Schnabel or David Salle goes at auction for as much or more than the gallery price, this confirms the validity of those prices. Thus, astute collectors follow the auctions closely to gauge the ups and downs of major reputations.

A final bit of advice: A lot of ink has been spilled in recent years about art as investment, but for most collectors the old advice is still the best—buy only the works you truly love. Then, whether their value rises or falls, you will still be a winner.

ALTERNATIVE SPACES AND UNORTHODOX INSTITUTIONS

During much of the 1970s, the art market seemed to be running on empty. In response, artists began to organize their own not-for-profit, cooperatively run exhibition spaces to provide commercially unviable and emerging artists with a means of exposure. Many of the most prominent artists today were first presented to the art world under the auspices of the alternative space, as these institutions came to be known. With the resurgence of the art market in the early 1980s, commercial galleries began to reassert their role as taste makers and talent scouts. The alternative movement faded—but did not die away completely. Those few alternative spaces that survived have had to carve out a new place for themselves in today's art landscape. One common strategy is to show work that is by nature unsalable—installations, performance art, and the like—or that is politically sensitive or otherwise unsuited to the commercial gallery. Other spaces have begun to function in a quasi-museum fashion, putting together theme exhibitions that explore a particular aspect of contemporary art or life. As a result, some of the most provocative shows in town are to be found in these stalwart survivors of the 1970s. Among the most interesting:

Artists Space. One of the most respected alternative spaces, both for the innovative quality of its exhibitions and for the intelligence of its choices, Artists Space (223 West Broadway between Franklin and White in TriBeCa; Tel: 212-226-3970) boasts that the artists who received their first exposure in its modest galleries include such contemporary heavyweights as Laurie Anderson, Jonathan Borofsky, Robert Longo, David Salle, and Cindy Sherman. It has long focused on such noncommercial forms as video art and installation and maintains a computerized slide registry that outside curators, dealers, and critics may peruse to locate artists who do not necessarily have a gallery affiliation.

P.S. 1 and the Clocktower. Two outposts of the same organization, the Institute for Art and Urban Resources, P.S. 1 is located in a rambling red-brick schoolhouse (at 46-01 21st Street) in Long Island City, Queens (Tel: 718-784-2084), while the Clocktower occupies the top two floors in the old courthouse building (including the rather spectacular clock tower itself) at 108 Leonard Street, between Broadway and Lafayette in lower Manhattan (Tel: 212-233-1096).

Both offer a schedule of provocative special exhibitions but their most innovative feature is the studio program. Each year a group of local, national, and international artists are awarded working space in the P.S. 1 and Clocktower buildings. Visitors may catch glimpses of artists at work, especially during the three or four openings a year, when resident artists transform their small cubicles into exhibition spaces for their work. As the artist stands by ready to discuss his or her work with curious passersby, it is possible on these occasions to view a dizzying variety of work, ranging from traditional painting and sculpture to video works, environmental installations, and multimedia performance art set side by side in jolting juxtaposition. Not to be missed as well at P.S. 1: James Turrell's *Meeting,* a permanent site installation (consisting of a sitting room whose ceiling is open to the sky) that is one of the most serene, contemplative spots in the city. (To get to P.S. 1 take the number 7 subway line from Times Square or Grand Central Station to the 45th Road/Courthouse Square exit; or the E or F line to the 23rd Street/Ely Avenue exit.)

The Dia Art Foundation. The Dia Foundation, founded in 1976, reflects the expansive ambitions of the art of that era. Dedicated to the encouragement of projects that "cannot obtain sponsorship or support from other public or private sources because of their nature or scale," Dia has exhibited a commitment to long-term installation and environmental projects in New York and elsewhere in the United States. In SoHo, Dia has maintained two works by Walter De Maria since 1977: *The New York Earth Room* (literally that, a room filled with earth), at 141 Wooster between Prince and Houston, and *The Broken Kilometer* (a magical gallery space where the floor is lined with a kilometer's-worth of metal pipe), at 393 West Broadway between Spring and Broome. In 1987 it opened a huge new exhibition space on the far West Side (548 West 22nd Street, between 10th and 11th avenues) that will present a series of year-long exhibitions of specially commissioned works by important contemporary artists. Dia is unique among New York's not-for-profit art institutions both for the high-profile nature of the participating artists (the 1987/1988 exhibitions involved Joseph Beuys, Imi Knoebel, and Blinky Palermo, while the 1988/1989 roster was composed of Robert Ryman, Francesco Clemente, and Jenny Holzer) and the generous financing it provides for its contributors' projects.

In addition to the commissioned works, Dia maintains an exhibition space in SoHo (77 Wooster Street, between Spring and Broome) that features changing shows often drawn from the foundation's extensive holdings. For all Dia locations, Tel: (212) 431-9232.

The New Museum of Contemporary Art. In a category all its own—not exactly an alternative space, but not a traditional museum either—is the New Museum. Founded in 1970 by former Whitney Museum curator Marcia Tucker, the New Museum, at 583 Broadway between Houston and Prince (Tel: 212-219-1355), was originally run in a spirit of radical egalitarianism. Eventually the idea of paying all employees the same rate and rotating jobs proved impractical, but the institution's resistance to orthodoxy remains strong. Shows tend to be conceptual, political, or for one reason or another on the fringes of the mainstream. Despite, or perhaps because of, its antiestablishment stance, the New Museum was one of the first institutions to seriously consider the art of commodity critique that eventually was dubbed "Neo Geo" and swept the art scene for a season. It is also one of the few museums in New York that makes a concerted effort to incorporate works by regional artists in its group shows.

The offerings at the New Museum tend to be a mixed bag: The museum can be excessively leery of popular themes or artists. Nevertheless, the New Museum remains a remarkable and admirable experiment.

Other not-for-profit spaces worth a visit are White Columns, 325 Spring Street (Tel: 212-924-4212), 55 Mercer (Tel: 212-226-8513), and the Storefront for Art and Architecture at 97 Kenmare Street in SoHo; the Alternative Museum, 17 White Street (Tel: 212-966-4444), in TriBeCa; and Fashion Moda, 2803 Third Avenue (Tel: 212-585-0135), in the Bronx.

ART AND CRAFT SUPPLIES

David Davis, 346 Lafayette, is revered among artists for its informed help, selection of imported materials, and overall quality.

Pearl Paint, 308 Canal Street, is generally cheaper, though not quite as comprehensive for the fine artist. Pearl also carries hardware and supplies for designers and crafts people.

Just a step below the above (which are by overwhelming consensus the best art-supply outlets in the city) is **New York Central Art Supply**, 62 Third Avenue at 11th Street, which also carries an excellent selection of papers.

Utrecht, 111 Fourth Avenue, between 11th and 12th streets, is also popular among fine artists. It carries its own line of paints, which are less expensive but not as high in quality as the name brands.

OTHER ART AND CRAFT SPECIALTIES

Arthur Brown, 2 West 46th Street, carries materials of interest to designers and art directors.

Charrette, 212 East 54th Street, offers a variety of fine-art and commercial materials, with a particularly good selection of architectural and drafting supplies.

Jam Envelope and Paper, 621 Sixth Avenue at 19th Street, is a wholesale outlet specializing in paper.

Polk's Model Crafts, 314 Fifth Avenue at 32nd Street, carries wood products.

CK & L Surplus Store, 307 Canal Street, carries metal screening, wire, and the like.

AIN Plastics, 300 Park Avenue South, between 22nd and 23rd streets, and **Industrial Plastic**, 309 Canal Street, specialize in plastics, acrylic, acetate, buterate, and so forth.

See the Bookstores section in the chapter on Literary New York for shops that specialize in **art books**.

ANTIQUES, ANTIQUITIES, AND COLLECTIBLES

By Lynn Yaeger

Lynn Yaeger is the author of a biweekly column in the Village Voice *on antiques and collectibles and was also a contributor to* The Village Voice Guide to Manhattan's Shopping Neighborhoods. *A resident of New York City for more than 15 years, she has written on fashion for* Cosmopolitan, Australian Woman, *and other publications.*

Whether the collector is visiting New York for a few months or a fortnight, whether he or she is an avid accumulator of objects from the past or maintains a purely academic, scholarly interest in such items, New York City provides a scope and variety of antiques, antiquities, and collectibles probably unrivaled in the world today. (Did somebody say London? But London is full of old English things. New York City is full of old things from *all* over.)

Anywhere you go in New York you are likely to run into antiques and collectibles shops, whether nestled in the shadows of the Washington Square Arch or buried in the small streets radiating from the major museums. Certain areas, however, have clusters of stores, and the serious shopper should head to these places first to get an idea of what is currently popular in the Manhattan antiques world and what prices the New York City market will bear.

Serious money might begin its tour with the axis of 57th Street and Madison Avenue. On **57th Street** proper, between Fifth and Lexington avenues, are a number of antiques dealers with internationally known names, displaying goods (mostly furniture and decorative accessories) of exquisite manufacture and rigorous provenance.

Turn up **Madison Avenue** and you will find a number of additional prestigious shops, and most have been at their addresses far longer than the foreign fashion stores snuggling up next to them. Their aristocratic presence is felt in varying intensity up to about 96th Street, where Madison Avenue sheds its golden glow and begins its rapid decline.

A visit to the Madison Avenue antiques shops stuns all but the wealthiest traveller into shocked, impoverished silence. Jump on the Lexington Avenue downtown local subway (number 6) and alight at the Spring Street stop in **SoHo**, which, while not inexpensive, gives the ordinary working person at least a fighting chance at shopping survival. The mood down here is rampant Art Deco and French bistro, and there is a growing enthusiasm for mission oak and the Arts and Crafts movement. The atmosphere is relaxed, and even when the price tag is astronomical the salesroom will lack the pin-drop hush of 57th Street.

From SoHo, the inexhaustible visitor might walk northwest to **Greenwich Village**, where on Hudson Street or Greenwich Avenue he or she will find lots of furniture stores with jumbled-up stock that looks inexpensive but isn't, really. Higher priced things are for sale on Bleecker between Christopher and Bank, where for some reason the shops seem equally divided between delicate, austere French and Biedermeier furniture on the one hand and folk-art galleries full of quilts, Beacon blankets, and moth-eaten dolls on the other.

Those young urban professionals who do not mind being identified as such can hop on the Seventh Avenue train (numbers 1, 2, 3, or 9) to 72nd Street and stroll with their compatriots up **Columbus Avenue** (to about 92nd) and back down **Amsterdam Avenue**, where a selection of stores sell old and antique furniture and accessories that are appropriate for the furnishing of one's new co-op or first home in Westchester.

Heartier souls not intimidated by Wholesale Only or To the Trade signs might want to check out the huge repositories of furniture, lamps, bronzes, and so on in the **wholesale antique district** located up and down Broadway and University Place and intervening streets between 8th and 14th streets. Though you are neither dealer nor decorator, a tough-talking demeanor and the willingness to pay quickly and in cash may succeed in getting you past the door.

Specific recommendations regarding individual antiques and collectibles stores have built-in limitations, because stock may vary enormously and the buyer tends to rely on the inspiration of the moment. Furthermore, the assiduous antiques shopper is ever on the lookout for that one-in-a-million baby in a five-and-ten store and may in fact turn up nothing of interest in any store described below, but rather find his or her heart's delight in some alleyway hovel unknown to us. (Note: Be sure to check the other shopping sections of this guide, where a number of additional stores specializing in collectibles are described. Vintage-clothes wearers, for instance, will find their haunts listed in the Fashion section.) Keeping all of the above in mind, we suggest the following.

Furniture

A huge and intense variety of styles, ages, countries of origin, and prices exists. (In fact, it is difficult to ascertain which preoccupation is more intense among New Yorkers: their personal appearance or the way their houses look.) The market groans with everything from 19th-century Portuguese and Spanish furniture at **Cobweb** (116 West Houston Street) and French working-class pieces at **T & K French Antiques** (120 Wooster Street) to Scandinavian country pine at **Evergreen Antiques** (120 Spring Street and 1249 Third Avenue).

Collectors of the newly fashionable vintage furnishings from the 1930s through the postwar era will be serviced by **First 1/2** (131 Thompson Street), **Fifty-50** (793 Broadway between 10th and 11th streets), **Retro-Modern Studio** (88 East 10th Street), and **Depression Modern** (150 Sullivan Street). **Alice's Antiques** (552 Columbus Avenue) specializes in 19th-century American iron beds, and the nearby **Better Times Antiques** (500 Amsterdam Avenue) can provide likely companion pieces in English pine. In SoHo, **Bertha Black Antiques** (80 Thompson Street) sells small pieces of hand-painted furniture that evince a Hudson River School influence. At **Peter-Roberts Antiques** (134 Spring Street) the hunky, chunky look of mission oak is much in evidence.

Those preferring sleek, polished examples of the Art Deco movement should dip around the corner to **Alan Moss Studios** (88 Wooster Street) or travel to the Village to **Maison Gerard** (36 East 10th Street). If you have money to burn you should proceed uptown in a taxi to where the finest of the finest English and French 17th- to 19th-century antique furniture is for sale, at such establishments as **Stair & Company** (942 Madison Avenue), **Didier Aaron, Inc.** (32 East 67th Street), and **Dalva Brothers** (44 East 57th Street). Highly desirable American furniture, pre-Revolutionary to early 19th century, is available from the eminent **Israel Sack** (15 East 57th Street). Those whose eyes gaze wider than their pocketbooks can open should not despair but rather visit **A B C Antiques** (888 Broadway between 18th and 19th streets) or the **Salvage Barn** (523 Hudson Street between 10th and Charles streets), both of which sell interesting pieces (mostly late 19th and 20th century) from various countries for reasonable prices. In SoHo, **Fleur De Lis Antiques** (489 Broome Street) is a big, friendly warehouse sort of place, open only Friday through Sunday, where bargains can be hunted and where famous faces have been known to pop out from behind dusty armoire mirrors.

Jewelry

Jewelry is one collectible category traversed even by those who otherwise shy away from antiques and collectibles. Much interesting jewelry is available from the variety of dealers at the **New York Center for Art and Antiques** (fairly affordable) and at its more glamorous sister, the **Place des Antiquaires** (less so)—see below under Antiques Centers for locations. Edith Weber, in Antiquaires, has a distinguished collection of English lovers' eyes (painted on ivory, under glass) from the turn of the 18th century. **Fred Leighton** (Trump Tower and 773 Madison Avenue) has Cartier Art Deco diamonds and other signed pieces of early 20th-century jewelry, as does **Primavera** (808 Madison Avenue) and **Macklowe Gallery & Modernism** (667 Madison Avenue). **A La Vieille Russie** (781 Fifth Avenue) carries jewels that look as if they would have fallen out of the czarina's Gladstone had she crossed the border into Finland. **James Robinson** (15 East 57th Street) has wonderful fine jewelry in its street-level store, but take the elevator up to six for relatively more affordable Edwardian and Victorian paste, cut steel, and Scottish agate. Still less expensive antique jewelry may be found down in the Village, where **The Antique Buff** (321½ Bleecker Street), **Claudia Kable Antiques** (106

MacDougal Street), and its next-door neighbor **Den of Antiquity** (number 108) all offer a range of late 19th- and early 20th-century possibilities.

Those interested in acquiring a vintage wristwatch are advised to visit **Time Will Tell** (962 Madison Avenue) or **Chiuzac Gallery** (510 Madison Avenue). Prices will be higher here than at the flea markets, but the shopkeeper will at least provide a guarantee. Shoppers in search of fashionable, less expensive vintage merchandise might like the 1930s Bakelite bracelets at **The Good, The Bad, and The Ugly** (143 East 13th Street). Fans of the rather overblown costume jewelry of Miriam Haskell will want to know that there are always many pieces available at **Norman Crider Antiques** (Trump Tower).

Folk Art

American folk art has burgeoned in popularity over the last several years, and with it has come an attendant boom in fakes and reproductions. Foreign visitors, who may never have seen a drunkard's path quilt or yellowware bowl close up, should exercise special caution when considering items such as these at outdoor markets. The following shops will of course provide annotated receipts assuring the quality and provenance of your purchases.

Susan Parrish (number 390), **Cynthia Beneduce** (388), and **Kelter-Malcé** (361) are all near one another on Bleecker Street in the Village, and among the three of them their stock approximates a veritable museum of hooked rugs, indigenous textiles, Adirondack furniture, Indian souvenir beading, and various other items in the folk-art fashion. **Laura Fisher**, in the New York Center for Art and Antiques (see Antiques Centers, below), is a nice person who sells hundreds of quilts and knows a lot about them. **Hirschl & Adler Folk** (851 Madison Avenue, second floor) is a serious gallery where browsing is expected and purchasing is a more private affair.

Clocks

A man walked into a New York City clock shop some years ago, looked around, saw something he favored, and brought it over to the shopkeeper. "I'll give you $300 for it," the man said. "Well, I'll tell you," said the proprietor, "I'm not going to sell it for that—Mr. Fanelli on Madison Avenue will give me at least $400 for it." "I am Mr.

Fanelli," said the first gentleman, "and I will give you $300." Mr. Fanelli's shop, **Fanelli Antique Timepieces, Ltd.**, is located at 1131 Madison Avenue, near 85th Street.

Silver

Tudor Rose (28 East 10th Street) has a sizable stock of English and American silver, including many small items (boudoir accessories, picture frames), and exceptionally reasonable prices. **Sutton Antiques Mews**, at number 34, has an interesting selection as well. **Alice Kwartler Antiques**, in the Place des Antiquaires at 125 East 57th Street, sells a rigorously curated collection, with a lot of things at the level of signed Tiffany dresser sets. Antique silverplate and sterling coffee and tea services, along with early flatware (sold individually or in sets), are among the specialties at the venerable **S. Wyler Inc.** (941 Lexington Avenue at 69th Street).

Antiquities

Strong as it is in most areas of collecting, the New York market collapses a bit when it comes to purveyors of ancient art and objects of antiquity. Nonetheless, take time out to visit **Royal-Athena Galleries** (153 East 57th Street), where more than 1,500 ancient sculptures, vases, and other objects (Greek, Roman, pre-Columbian, etc.) are for sale by an enthusiastic staff. In the rarefied upper reaches of Madison Avenue, **Antiquarium Fine Ancient Arts Gallery** (number 948) or the **Safani Gallery** (960) might be worth looking into as well. And **Ares Rare** (961), among its other jewelry offerings, features authentic ancient Greek and Roman bibelots.

Rugs and Textiles

Cora Ginsburg (19 East 74th Street, third floor; open by appointment only, Tel: 744-1352) is usually whispered to be the high bidder at textile auctions, and presents a scholarly collection of early examples (including rare 18th- and 19th-century day clothing, shoes, and lingerie) at her gallery. For carpets and tapestries, the toney name is **Doris Leslie Blau** (15 East 57th Street), where exceptionally high tariffs justly reflect the quality of the merchandise. Across town, shoppers with less money who are forced to be more flexible in their requirements might find an acceptable antique floor covering at the **Rug Warehouse** (2222 Broadway at 79th Street), or around the corner at **Central Carpet** (424–426 Columbus near 80th Street). Both these places usually have on hand an assortment of desirable 1920s Chinese Art Deco rugs.

China, Glass, and Porcelain

A revival of interest in Tiffany, Gallé, Daum, and other art glass has priced most examples right out of the market, but those who like to look at these things should visit **Minna Rosenblatt** (844 Madison Avenue). French and English cameo glass and highly collectible glass paperweights are specialties at **Leo Kaplan** (967 Madison Avenue). **Susan P. Meisel Objets D'Art Gallery** (141 Prince Street) in SoHo holds down a corner of the world market of the British Art Deco chinaware by the bizarre artisan Clarisse Cliff.

Flea markets and travelling antiques shows remain excellent sources for early 20th-century glass and porcelain, but a careful and prudent eye is advised. (The tiniest chip, of little interest to the casual user, can devalue the object considerably.) Shoppers desiring depression-era proto-American Fiestaware dishes are advised to visit **Mood Indigo** (181 Prince Street), where stacks in several colors and sizes are always on hand at reasonable prices.

Orientalia

Bargains on authentic examples in this area may be ferreted out by experts—we only have the ability to recommend highly reputable if costly outposts. **Ralph M. Chait** (12 East 56th Street) specializes in Chinese pottery, porcelains, and handstones dating from the Neolithic period (2500 B.C.) through the heady days of the early 18th century. **Flying Cranes Antiques** (in the New York Center for Arts and Antiquities at 1050 Second Avenue) sells cloisonné, satsuma, bronzes, and the like from both Japan and China from 1690 to 1890. Nestled in a corner of the Carlyle Hotel is **Michael B. Weisbrod** (987 Madison Avenue) and his fine Chinese works of art, including inlaid lacquer, though you may require a few stiff ones at the hotel's well-known Bemelmans Bar before you garner the confidence to sign the enormous check.

Decorative Accessories

Almost every antiques store in town sells items that may be construed as decorative accessories, so suggestions in this area will necessarily be cursory and eccentric.

Those wishing to decorate their domiciles in the manner of the American home circa 1935—be it a cottage with sagging porch and cabbage-rose wallpaper or an oilcloth-covered Sears & Roebuck–furnished Bronx apartment—will find authentic rolls of wall-covering and linoleum at **Second Hand Rose** (270 Lafayette Street). Lamps by which to curl up with the latest issue of *The Smart Set* may be located at **Louis Mattia** (980 Second Avenue at 52nd Street) or **Barry of Chelsea** (154 Ninth Avenue). If you live permanently out of a suitcase, visit **Eclectiques** (483 Broome Street), where you will find a large selection of rare vintage Louis Vuitton trunks as well as antique hatboxes, Pullman cases, and other bags covered in a variety of exotic animal skins, from ostrich to elephant.

You may find a vintage pedestal sink or tub for sale—along with old columns, mantels, staircases, and the like—at **Great American Salvage Co.** (34 Cooper Square), a place that claims it has 25,000 items in its computer memory bank. Furnishings that once graced the interiors of now-defunct barbershops, saloons, and ice-cream parlors now grace **Urban Archaeology** (285 Lafayette Street). Smaller items in a similar vein (world's fair standing ashtrays, old Coney Island peep-show machines) can be found at **Lost City Arts** (275 Lafayette Street).

Toys and Memorabilia

Aficionados of old toys, games, dolls, and assorted childhood memorabilia are among the most zealous visitors to flea markets and antiques shows, where genuine bargains may still surface and careful searching can really pay off. Those interested in visiting stores that specialize in this sort of thing should take in **Second Childhood** (283 Bleecker Street) for tin toys, soldiers, and interesting, small Celluloid dolls, and **Darrow's Fun Antiques** (309 East 61st Street). In the shadow of the 59th Street Bridge, under the intermittent gaze of the Roosevelt Island tram, Darrow's sells vintage games and rarer items like big 1930s toy zeppelins.

A jumbled-up but excellent selection of dolls is for sale at the **Antique Doll Hospital of New York** (787

Lexington Avenue), where the proprietor is a real crafts-man. ("Can I repaint a doll's eye? I can fix anything. I am an artist.") Boyish types of any age will probably like the **Soldier Shop** (1222 Madison Avenue between 88th and 89th), specializing in highly collectible, not inexpensive antique toy soldiers and military miniatures. Those evinc-ing unlimited enthusiasm and funds to match should visit **Monde Magique**, in the Place des Antiquaires, for museum-quality 19th-century automata, dolls, toys, and early games.

Markets

Of course, many people eschew conventional antiques stores entirely in favor of flea markets, antiques shows, and public auctions. For these collectors, the thrill of the chase is all, and the heart leaps as they sidle up alongside shop-keepers at markets, ready to buy what has momentarily been replaced on the shelf, or, even better, succeeding in outbidding these same merchants at auction houses all over town.

There are a number of year-round weekend markets in Manhattan, the most recommended being the one lo-cated in two adjacent parking lots on Sixth Avenue be-tween 24th and 26th streets. Although this market is open on Saturdays, the offerings then are paltry, since for 22 years this has operated as a Sunday market, and dealers are by nature creatures of habit. Half the market is cor-doned off and requires that you pay one dollar admis-sion, presumably to discourage diamond thieves who might otherwise enter and have a field day. Other markets include one in the schoolyard of Public School 183 (York Avenue and 67th Street) on Saturdays, and its superior cousin on Sundays at P.S. 87 (Columbus Avenue and 77th Street). Both of these also have small, depressing indoor sections in school cafeterias still redolent of lunches but transformed for the weekend into collectibles dens.

Shows and Street Fairs

There are any number of specialty shows (paper ephem-era, dolls, baseball, etc.) and street fairs that make their way to New York City. For current listings of these, buy the Friday and Sunday editions of *The New York Times* and check the antiques classified advertisements. Shows of a more general, eclectic nature spring up all the time as well. Highbrow ones take place in fall, winter, and spring at the Park Avenue Armory (the winter show, in January, is the fanciest), and there is a wonderful show of more than 600 dealers held on three Hudson River piers each year in November and March. Once a year (March also) a huge and highly regarded collectibles show takes place on the boardwalk in Atlantic City, easily accessible from New York City by the buses that shuttle thousands of unregenerate gamblers to and from Atlantic City on a daily basis.

Antiques Centers

Somewhere in the shadowy world between a table of junk for sale in the broiling sun and a full-fledged antiques store lies the province of the antiques center—a collection of glass-enclosed booths owner-operated by individual dealers. There are two major centers in New York City. **The New York Center for Art and Antiques** (1050 Second Avenue at 55th Street), with 104 galleries, sells everything from toys to rugs and objects of virtue, with a heavy concentration on fine jewelry. The newer, smaller, and very elegant **Place des Antiquaires** (125 East 57th Street) contains 64 expensive miniature shops showing admittedly expensive merchandise. There are also a number of small, less diverting antiques malls in town. If you find yourself stranded in that shopping desert known as the East 30s, you can seek temporary relief at the **Murray Hill Antiques Center** (201 East 31st Street). You might also choose to visit the indoor center on Canal Street off West Broadway, where, among much undistinguished merchandise, one woman sells a spectacular collection of antique powder compacts, vinaigrettes, and other early purse accessories, and another has a showcase full of excellently priced, exceptionally attractive gentlemen's vintage wristwatches.

Auction Houses

Those visitors possessed of steel nerves who disdain paying preordained prices for anything might care to try their hand at a Manhattan auction. These take place at **Christie's** and **Sotheby's** at least weekly, and there are often interesting items at **Doyle Galleries** and **Phillips** as well (see the Art chapter). Check the advertisements in *The New York Times,* paying careful attention to notices of Christie's

Collectibles or Sotheby's Arcade auctions, as these often feature lower priced, more amusing merchandise.

ARCHITECTURE

By Barry Lewis

New York is a great maw for architecture. Throughout its existence New York has built itself up as a city, played out history in that city, and then ripped it out a generation later only to replace it with yet another city. Some downtown lots have been redeveloped five times since 1800. In Europe, buildings stand for centuries; in New York, a lifetime for a building might be only 30 years.

And yet, peruse certain neighborhoods and it would seem as if time has stood still: the brownstone-lined streets of Chelsea, the Greek Revivals of Greenwich Village, the 19th-century row houses of the East 50s hard by the soaring towers of Midtown. Ghostly department stores of the Victorian Ladies' Mile still line Broadway above Union Square, and Federal row houses still stand among the industrial buildings of SoHo. So much of New York is surprisingly old; so much of it can be harshly new.

New York's buildings are eclectic beyond imagination. The city has the well-deserved reputation of trying to mimic the airs of European aristocracy, and is often unfavorably compared to Chicago and California, where a fresh American originality was encouraged. Nonetheless, New York's buildings are far more varied than historians will admit. To see this, roam the streets around Union Square, where a modern commercial style was hammered out in turn-of-the-century loft buildings; or the Upper West Side, where from the 1880s to the 1930s new forms for urban residences were developed in row houses and apartment houses. Walk the Grand Central Terminal area, where in the 1920s the image of the skyscraper was indelibly etched in the world's imagination— and you can see that New York was no slouch in forging its own original style and flair.

New York, being completely American, is the product of

private speculators, some of whom have demanded architectural quality, most of whom have demanded the cheapest product. This has resulted in a good deal of banality and some extraordinary exceptions, but the sum total is quite impressive. The city's buildings, like its people, are numerous, jammed together, and at times rise to dizzying heights making an estimable silhouette—especially from afar. That's why some of the best views of Manhattan are from "offshore" looking back: from atop the Jersey Palisades in Weehawken's Hamilton Park, along the Brooklyn Heights promenade, or from the Socrates Sculpture Park on Long Island City's East River shore. But walking the city's streets and seeing it in detail is rewarding as well. The new, the old, and the older are layered along the same block. New York may seem to be a chaotic jumble of buildings, but actually there is an order, a sequence, and a logic. Like any archaeologist, you only need to know the "key" in order to understand the hieroglyphics.

THE ROW HOUSE

Back in the 1810s New York was a town clustered hard by the Battery and extending no farther than the brand-new **City Hall** (1802–1811; Mangin & McComb). This delicate Federal gem is still one of America's most impressive city halls, but it was plagued by extended deadlines and cost overruns, proving that certain civic practices have a deep-rooted tradition. The city's merchants were fast making their town America's busiest port and most populous metropolis. Earning their money from the sailboats lining the East River docks—parts of today's **South Street Seaport** are all that remain—they lived in handsome town houses along lower Broadway and along Greenwich Street near the verdant Hudson River shoreline, where they could stroll in evening promenades and "take the air." Built in the Federal style, with fanlights in their entrances, brick and marble-trimmed fronts, and delicate interiors, these houses represented a simplified, "Yankee" version of England's richly ornamented, brilliantly colored late Georgian or Adams style. Although hundreds of these town houses were built for the newly prosperous lawyers, merchants, and bankers, all that remains intact is a relative handful, among which the most elegant is the **James Watson House** (1793–1806; John McComb, Jr.), at 7 State Street, opposite Battery Park, now part of a Roman

Catholic shrine to Elizabeth Ann Seton, the first American saint.

As the city grew, the wealthy residential district pushed northward to Canal Street and, by the 1820s, beyond. Federal row houses scattered among the circa 1900 tenements and factories of Chinatown, Little Italy, and SoHo attest to those areas' former roles as the Upper East Side of a bygone era.

The Erie Canal, opening in 1825, put New York over the top. First the canal and then the railroads funneled America's—and the world's—raw produce and goods through New York's harbor. In the 1830s the city began an explosion of growth that, until the financial troubles of the 1970s, seemed to be without end. By 1835 the city had reached and engulfed the rural town of Greenwich, and the emerging Greek Revival style would embellish the new precincts of Washington Square and lower Fifth Avenue. Especially distinctive are the houses of West 10th Street (between Fifth and Sixth avenues) and **The Row** on Washington Square North (numbers 1–13 and 21–26; 1831; Martin Thompson, architect), which, though slightly altered, evoke the stiff-backed restraint of antebellum society.

Though larger and more monumental than the Federal houses, the Greek Revivals followed the same basic elevation and plan. The configuration of the New York row house had been essentially set by 1800. The stoop had already appeared, a New York phenomenon dictated by the lack of back alleys (New York developers balked at cutting alleyways through expensive real estate). No back door meant deliveries, garbage, and honored guests all had to pass through the front. The stoop allowed for an "upstairs-downstairs" double entry, with service personnel entering the ground-floor servants' quarters and guests entering the first-floor parlor and dining room. These monumental exterior staircases were actually a poor solution to the problem of a double front entry, dictating clumsy exteriors and a cramped interior layout. But rich New Yorkers loved them as their descendants would love Cadillacs; a house with a stoop indicated that the family within had finally arrived. Designers of the day, from James Renwick (architect of St. Patrick's Cathedral) to Olmsted and Vaux (creators of Central Park), railed against the crowded interiors that a stoop dictated, but New Yorkers turned a deaf ear. They would not give up their stoops until the later, more sophisticated generation of the early 1900s would be persuaded by the likes of Stanford White and Edith Wharton to adopt the more graceful, street-level-entry town-house designs of London and Paris.

Around 1845 a war of styles broke out, as the Greek Revival was challenged by the newer Neo-Gothic and Italianate. Within five years the dust had settled and the Italianate had won. It was obvious that New Yorkers, preferring the Renaissance palazzo look, identified themselves with the Medici and Sforze rather than Medieval prelates or ancient Athenians. But the New York palazzo was of brownstone (a material native to Connecticut and New Jersey, not Tuscany), and the streets were soon lined with what Edith Wharton disparagingly called a "chocolate sauce." Thousands of these new town houses were built along the streets of Chelsea, Longacre Square (now Times Square), Turtle Bay, and Murray Hill. So many brownstone-fronted houses went up in New York, Brooklyn, and the Jersey towns atop the Palisades that to this day New Yorkers habitually call any old row house—of whatever material or style— a "brownstone."

Behind the brownstone façades a revolution in domestic technology was unfolding. Modern water systems, sewers, and gas lines meant indoor bathrooms, gas-fed globes to replace dripping candles, modern kitchens with stoves, hot and cold running water, and "refrigerators" (they were actually iceboxes), and, thanks to cheap coal from Pennsylvania, central heating systems. The "modern" house had arrived. By the 1860s the average New York bourgeois could boast of a high-tech domesticity, smugly knowing that the great palaces of Europe still remained cold and unplumbed. It's no wonder that the people of those times thought theirs was truly "The Century of Progress."

After the Civil War the French mansard style, with all its nouveau-riche flamboyance, became popular, though often all New Yorkers did was take a prewar brownstone and stick a mansard on top of it. Instead of the Italianate, the new rage was a mechanistically rendered Neoclassicism, called the Neo-Grec, reflecting the growing Victorian interest in an honest, machine-age style. These Neo-Grec, mansard-roofed brownstones lined the streets of the Upper East Side, a new district opposite newly built Central Park. Thoroughly middle class—the rich then lived on Fifth Avenue in the 50s—the neighborhoods' breadwinners commuted down to Wall Street on the equally new elevated railroads.

In the 1880s brownstone fell out of favor and Eclectic styles ranging from the Queen Anne to the Neo-Romanesque became popular. It was the age of Richardson, Sullivan, and Furness; their intuitive genius for the simple rendering of materials is reflected in the glorious palette of stone, brick, tile, and terra-cotta that New York architects used for this new generation of city houses. Streets from the West 70s to the West 130s, just then being developed, were alive with brilliant coloration and texture. The Eclectics were also interested in new interior layouts (it wasn't easy squeezing a home into a narrow row-house plot), and they introduced bay windows, interlocking balconies, terraces, and towers to make the rooms inside both more interesting and more open. There are superb examples of this era's accomplishments on West 76th Street off Riverside Drive, around the corner on West End Avenue, and on Harlem's **Striver's Row** on West 138th and 139th streets between Seventh and Eighth avenues.

Of all the thousands of row houses built since the 1830s only two remain totally intact and open to the public as house museums. One is the 1832 **Old Merchant's House** at 29 East 4th Street (between Bowery and Lafayette), a late Federal gem, and the other is the **Theodore Roosevelt Birthplace**, 28 East 20th Street (between Broadway and Park Avenue South), a rebuilt, Neo-Gothic brownstone from 1848 (rebuilt in 1923). Go first to the Old Merchant's House and notice its spare Yankee simplicity, then visit Roosevelt's boyhood home to see firsthand the growing Victorian penchant for decoration and embellishment.

By 1900 the price of Manhattan real estate had made row-house living prohibitive for the middle class. Between 1900 and 1930, the last major era of the Manhattan town house, these houses went up almost exclusively in the new wealthy precincts of the Upper East Side. The rich had been displaced by the growth of Midtown, so they moved north of 59th Street, where they built Beaux Arts–style town houses and freestanding Fifth Avenue mansions reflecting the Neoclassicism of Italy, France, England, and colonial America. Of the town-house-lined side streets, East 79th Street off Fifth is an excellent example. As for the mansions, few are left and almost all have been recycled for other uses. Among the earliest and the best are the **Villard Houses** (1883; McKim, Mead & White) at Madison Avenue and 50th Street, a group of six houses expertly arranged to give the look of a Renaissance palazzo. (How different they are from the provincial brownstones of the 1850s!) The gem of the group was Villard's own house, today the south wing of the Helmsley Palace Hotel. The clarity, simplicity, and sophistication of the interior, which is now well restored, was 20 years ahead of its time. Other grand mansions still extant are the French 18th-century-style Duke mansion (1912; Horace Trumbauer; Fifth Avenue at 78th Street), now the **New York University Institute of Fine Arts**; the Loire Valley–style Warburg mansion (1908; C. P. H. Gilbert; Fifth Avenue at 92nd Street), now the **Jewish Museum**; and two Neo-Georgian houses that are today the homes of the **Cooper-Hewitt Museum** (Andrew Carnegie's home; 1902; Babb, Cook & Willard; with its interior beautifully restored) at 91st Street; and the **International Center of Photography** (Willard Straight's house; 1914; Delano & Aldrich) at 94th.

Built to last forever, many of these houses were demolished within a few decades. In typical New York fashion they were removed by the 1930s to make way for a new city, one of elegant department stores south of 59th Street and elegant apartment houses north of it.

THE APARTMENT HOUSE

Middle-class Americans of the 19th century insisted, like the English, on living in their own private homes. Tenements were fine for the immigrant poor, but the middle class would have nothing to do with multiple dwellings.

Tenements first appeared before the Civil War in the ethnic slums like the Irish Five Points (now Chinatown) and the German Bowery district (now the Lower East Side), but middle-class New Yorkers were adamant. They would not adopt the Continental style of apartment-house living until they had to. By 1900, they had to. Real-estate prices made town houses a luxury commodity, and the New York bourgeoisie began moving into new "apartment-hotels."

The luxury apartment house first appeared en masse on the Upper West Side and in Harlem, the two New York districts most associated with the solid middle class. The famous **Dakota** (Henry J. Hardenbergh) at Central Park West and 72nd Street, opening in 1883, was a bit ahead of its time. By the 1900s the city's first subway line, the IRT, linked upper Broadway with Wall Street— and the apartment-house boom was on. **The Ansonia**

(1904; Graves & DuBoy; 2109 Broadway at 73rd), **The Apthorp** (1908; Clinton & Russell; Broadway between 78th and 79th streets), and **The Belleclaire** (1903; Emery Roth; Broadway at 77th Street, southwest corner) were typical of the new breed. The Ansonia especially, with its blowsy Neo-Baroque style, reminds us of a Parisian extravagance of the Belle Epoque. But the New York version was far taller and contained more high-tech gadgetry than any Parisian apartment house.

These new high-rise residences were state-of-the-art palaces with garages (equipped with outlets for electric cars), underground shopping centers, and health clubs. Elevators, built-in refrigerators, pneumatic mail-delivery systems, and miles of piping and wiring for gas, electricity, water, and heat made these new luxury apartment houses the equivalent of oceangoing steamships anchored to the New York streets. To assuage the "shame" of living in a ten-room flat, these early apartment houses offered hotel-like amenities including maid service, room service, elegant in-house restaurants, and rooftop gardens and pavilions for private soirees.

The super rich, as well, finally capitulated to apartment-house living, but they insisted on doing it in their own aristocratic manner. McKim, Mead & White's elegantly proportioned **998 Fifth Avenue** (1910; 81st Street, northeast corner) set the pattern. Rejecting the West Side's middle-class flamboyance, the East Siders preferred the subtleness and simplicity of a Renaissance palazzo. This restrained academicism took hold, and when New York went apartment-house wild after World War I, when Park Avenue on the East Side, Fifth Avenue opposite Central Park, and West End Avenue on the West Side were rebuilt to the new scale, it was flat-topped, porticoed Neo-classicism that prevailed.

In the 1930s the new Moderne or Art Deco style emerged. It was especially popular in the new apartment towers of Central Park West, such as **The Century** (1931; the Chanin Co.) at 62nd Street, **The Majestic** (1930; the Chanin Co.) at 72nd, **The San Remo** (1930; Emery Roth) between 74th and 75th streets, and **The Beresford** (1929; Emery Roth) at 81st—though the last two are a mixture of Moderne and Mannerist. The new skyscraper-style apartment houses emphasized wraparound corner windows (only possible in a steel cage building), spacious foyer-plan interior layouts, and soaring towers housing magnificent apartments with four exposures—literally "mansions in the sky"—making that era seem, by today's standards, the golden age of the New York apartment house.

Though undecorated brick boxes predominated after World War II, interior layouts continued their prewar spaciousness. Beginning in the 1960s, however, apartments and their rooms began to shrink, and materials seemed to "shrink" as well. Today's elaborate Postmodern decor, concierges' desks, and in-house health clubs cannot hide the fact that often the apartment itself, considering the price, is a pale shadow of its magnificent Beaux Arts and Art Deco predecessors.

DEPARTMENT STORES, THEATERS, AND COMMERCIAL BUILDINGS

Traditionally, New York's downtown (Wall Street) was where the money was made and Midtown—the city's retail, theater, and café district—was where the money was spent. Downtown remained stationary, though growing taller every generation, but Midtown followed the northward expansion of the luxury class that frequented it and moved constantly farther uptown.

In the 1840s Midtown settled at Broadway near City Hall Park, producing America's first department store, **A. T. Stewart's** (Snook & Trench), which rose at Chambers and Broadway (northeast corner) in 1845 and is still standing. (It is now called the Sun Building after a newspaper tenant of later years; being city owned, it is in terrible shape.) Stewart's was not only a new phenomenon in retailing, it also brought the Italianate style to New York, sparking a fashion in architecture that would sweep the city during the next two decades.

By the 1850s Midtown had moved to what is today called SoHo, with Tiffany's at 550 Broadway (now altered) and Lord & Taylor (now demolished) at Grand Street. Cast-iron construction, a modern modular system for erecting buildings (much like a kid's erector set) became all the rage; and so many cast-iron department stores in the guise of Venetian palazzi rose along Broadway that New Yorkers dubbed that thoroughfare "the Grand Canal." The Venetian Renaissance style was not popular for mere sentimental reasons. Its open, well-fenestrated arcading allowed architects to exploit cast iron's possibilities, creating Victorian "glass boxes" framed in Neoclassical packaging. The

1857 **Haughwout Store** (J. P. Gaynor) still stands at Broadway and Broome Street (northeast corner). Its cast-iron framing was originally a glistening white painted with faux marble veining to give the illusion of antiquity. It mattered little to New Yorkers that their "palazzi"—bigger and glassier than anything in Renaissance Venice—would have been impossible to build before the age of iron.

After the Civil War, Midtown jumped north to the Ladies' Mile: Broadway and Sixth Avenue from 14th to 23rd streets. Grand department stores in the French Second Empire style, with cast-iron framing and iron-crested mansard roofs, lined Union and Madison squares and Sixth avenue from 18th to 23rd streets. Many still stand, like so many ghosts from a vanished past. The new money of the infamous Gilded Age, an era expertly captured in Jack Finney's novel *Time and Again,* had a chance to display itself strolling fashionable 14th or 23rd streets. The department stores were generally built with skylit interior atriums, open-cage elevators, and acres of glass windows and skylights, making each store a veritable Crystal Palace. **Tiffany's** (now severely altered to house a labor union) moved to Union Square West and 15th Street in 1869; **Arnold Constable** (1869; Griffith Thomas) opened at Broadway and 19th Street (southwest corner), and serves today as the home of ABC Carpets (across the street ABC also occupies the old 1881 W & J Sloane store); and **Lord & Taylor** (1869; James Giles) settled in at Broadway and 20th Street, part of it (the altered part) now occupied by Saint Laurie Clothiers. The opening of Lord & Taylor prompted Teddy Roosevelt, Sr.—whose brood, including the future president, lived just down the block—to exclaim that the neighborhood was changing, and it was time to move. That they did in 1873, to the new address of note, West 57th Street.

By 1910 Midtown had moved again, this time to Fifth Avenue north of 34th Street. **B. Altman & Co.** (Trowbridge & Livingston) opened in 1906 at 34th Street, where the building still stands, though the venerable department store just closed its doors. Acknowledging the Beaux Arts fashions of the day, Benjamin Altman wrapped his 11-story steel-cage department store in the elegant detailing of a Renaissance palazzo (a far more sophisticated version than A. T. Stewart's back in 1845), and the other great shopping emporia followed suit. In the same year **Tiffany's** moved into McKim, Mead & White's glass palazzo at the southeast corner of 37th Street (it's now the Reverend Moon's printing plant); **Lord & Taylor** (Starrett & Van Vleck) opened at 39th Street in 1914; **Arnold Constable** moved to 40th (now the Mid-Manhattan Library); and **Saks Fifth Avenue**'s "palazzo" (Starrett & Van Vleck) capped the trend when it opened in 1924—way uptown!—at its current location at 50th Street. By this time a distinct middle-class shopping district had blossomed at Herald Square (Macy's opened there in 1902), and the theater district had followed its own path up Broadway, settling down around 42nd Street and Times Square in the 1900s.

Midtown shifted slightly again—to 57th Street—in the 1930s and 1940s. **Bergdorf Goodman** (Buchman & Kahn) moved into its streamlined headquarters on 57th Street in 1928. **Tiffany's** (Cross & Cross), moving again, built a Classical-Moderne "safe" for its jewels at 727 Fifth Avenue in 1940. This time, however, the central business district was moving northward as well, and for the first time in the city's history corporate skyscrapers joined the department stores and retailers to share Midtown's streets.

The Beaux Arts–embellished Heckscher Building (Warren & Wetmore; now the **Crown Building**, recently restored and spotlit) opened at Fifth Avenue and 57th Street, southwest corner, in 1922, and ten years later Rockefeller Center rose opposite Saks Fifth Avenue and St. Patrick's Cathedral. Midtown, continuing to shift, had always been moving up the island's spine. In 1910 people assumed that by the 1950s (way in the future), Midtown would probably reach 125th Street—but it never happened. Midtown New York, having moved northward for over 100 years, finally stopped at the southern gates to Central Park.

PUBLIC BUILDINGS

New York's unrelenting grid gives few public buildings a chance to shine—no vistas or grand boulevards here. But when New York entered its great age of civic design, the Beaux Arts era between 1890 and 1930, its architects produced a handful of buildings whose qualities of planning and design we had not seen before and may never see again. The 1898 consolidation of New York created a five-borough city of four million people that demanded new public facilities. The New York architectural establishment rose to the occasion by producing buildings of extraordinarily skillful planning and outstanding civic presence. This new generation of professional, Beaux Arts–trained American architects married the sublimity of European Neoclassicism with the pragmatism of the Yankee mind. The result was great Neoclassical palaces fine-tuned to become machines for modern life, criticized by a later, so-called Modern generation for stylistic irrelevancy. In today's Postmodern era we have put aside those prejudices to appreciate once more the masterworks of that earlier generation.

The American Museum of Natural History and the **Metropolitan Museum of Art** (both begun in the 1870s) received new Beaux Arts fronts, though in these instances the Neoclassical faces, though skillfully done, masked decades of willy-nilly additions. There were, however, four public buildings built from scratch that became instant landmarks for all times. In typical American fashion, indicative of how we build our cities, three of these four "public" buildings were in fact built by private corporations.

The former **United States Custom House** (1907; Cass Gilbert) on Bowling Green is the only true public building of the group. Reminiscent, in its palatial guise, of the deep-rooted traditions of Western architecture, behind its Beaux Arts façade it is a paradigm of skillful functionalist planning. Separation of freight and people was achieved by giving cars and trucks a street-level basement entrance in back and pedestrians a first-floor monumentalized entry in front. The statue-flanked Neo-Baroque grand entrance (Daniel Chester French did the *Four Continents*— and are they kitsch!) made New Yorkers understand instantly where the customhouse was and where they should enter. The grand stair leads, in the Neoclassical tradition of an architectural promenade, to the nerve center of the building, a skylit rotunda where the customs officials waited for the business at hand. In 1937 Reginald Marsh, under the auspices of the Work Projects Administration, embellished the ceiling of the rotunda with gritty scenes of New York Harbor showing its piers bustling with passengers and freight. In 1973 the United States Customs Service moved to the World Trade Center (where, thanks to the Modern idiom, you can't even find the customhouse and, if you do, you can't figure out how to get in), and the 1907 customhouse came close to being demolished. Saved after a preservation battle, it has recently been proposed as the future home of the Museum of the American Indian. At present it is sometimes used for temporary exhibits, and if it is open don't miss the chance to see it.

The **New York Public Library** (1902–1911; Carrère & Hastings; actually a private institution) rose on Fifth Avenue between 40th and 42nd streets in the same decade as the U.S. Custom House. Though it is usually compared unfavorably to its inspiration, the Boston Public Library (1890; McKim, Mead & White), people often forget that Boston's library, though aesthetically richer and more sophisticated, is a building that never worked. The New York Public Library, on the other hand, was designed by librarians with the help of architects (an unusual shift in architects' priorities) and is as superbly functional today as it ever was—and is undergoing a badly needed restoration program (by Davis, Brody & Associates with Giorgio Cavaglieri).

The library's practical layout, ingenious use of natural light, and its deft mixture of specialized libraries and the more modern stack system (via a 1911 pneumatic-tube system that is still state-of-the-art today) make it a working machine for everything from scholarly research to casual reading. Its varied rooms, as they come out from under the restoration wraps, are a marvelous synthesis of sensibility and function. Its newly restored (1987) Bartos Forum, originally the circulating library, skylit and metal-framed, is a gem of Beaux Arts–influenced, machine-age design. The main entrance plaza, facing Fifth Avenue, is one of the city's great public spaces, its steps and flanking terraces a constantly shifting scene of street theater and schmoozing. Its exhibitions in the reopened Gottesman Hall are usually first rate, and the daily tours by trained docents worth attending. No city can call itself civilized without a great library at its heart, and New York's, after years of sad neglect, is again becoming the vibrant core it once was and should always be.

Grand Central Terminal (1902–1913; Reed & Stem, Warren & Wetmore) shares kudos with the library. Replacing an earlier terminal on the same site, the new GCT is actually a city-within-a-city, mixing long-distance and commuter trains, subways, taxis, automobiles, and pedestrians. The steel-framed Beaux Arts building sits atop a double-deck underground railroad yard that stretches from Lexington to Madison avenues, from 42nd to 50th streets. As Park Avenue developed in the 1920s and 1930s, every building on the avenue, from the terminal to the

Waldorf-Astoria, was positioned on the roof of that yard, one of our earliest examples of "air rights" development. An iron-framed highway, planned in 1904 and one of the nation's first, carries Park Avenue traffic around the building, and underground "streets" link the terminal to over half a dozen skyscrapers and two major hotels.

The terminal itself is an ingenious interlocking of specialized spaces, lit by a system of skylights and interior windows that fully exploit its steel frame. Its monumental concourse is one of the city's great plazas, a roofed piazza San Marco, serving the dashing commuter and the casual pedestrian alike. The Municipal Art Society (Tel: 212-935-3960) conducts tours of the terminal every Wednesday at 12:30 P.M. Few complexes today combine with such skill the efficient and the humane. It is truly one of the nation's great architectural works.

The same could have been said of its sister railroad complex, Pennsylvania Station. McKim, Mead & White's 1910 architectural wonder (Seventh and Eighth avenues, 32nd to 34th streets) modeled its concourse in front on the Baths of Caracalla, and built its train platforms in back in a totally functionalist idiom of exposed iron and glass. No one could accuse these architects of using historical styles for lack of imagination. As in the three other public buildings we've mentioned, the station's designers used history where they felt its symbolism was appropriate, and utilized modernity where the building program demanded it. But Penn Station is gone, buried under the cracker-box skyscrapers and garish arena of Madison Square Garden. The station's demolition in 1960–1963 so infuriated the New York public that it led to the establishment of the New York City Landmarks Commission, given authority to prevent that kind of vandalism from ever happening again.

The great tradition of public architecture might be revived in the Postmodern era, but that remains to be seen. Fans of high-tech will be interested in the new **Jacob Javits Convention Center** (1987; I. M. Pei's James I. Freed; the Hudson River at 37th Street), whose steel-and-glass superstructure has given New York City its own Crystal Palace. But the great public buildings of the Beaux Arts period have yet to be surpassed—or even equaled—in their skillful integration of function, beauty, and humane concern for the private citizen. That kind of architectural largesse may in fact be a lost art.

THE SKYSCRAPER

The skyscraper, invented in Chicago in 1885, arrived in New York in 1890. The first New York skyscraper, at 50 Broadway, lasted less than 30 years, when, characteristically for New York, it was torn down to make way for a bigger building. In the ensuing generations Chicago and New York vied with each other for superlatives of height. The Chicago style often won the acclaim of critics for its no-nonsense, flat-topped rationality; New York came in a poor second, criticized for its costume-y historicism and "vulgar" flamboyance. But if the scholars preferred Chicago, the public preferred New York, and a new generation of critics is beginning to swing around to give New York its due.

New York's first steel-cage buildings popped up downtown in the Financial District and in the wholesale belt from Canal to 34th streets. Using a Neoclassical formula, the New York architects artificially divided their buildings' façades into a base-shaft-capital arrangement based on the parts of a classical column—even though steel-cage construction is modular and uniform from bottom to top. The critics charged "façade-ism" and "artifice," but on closer look we find that the New York architects were not such dummies.

The tripartite formula allowed for a decorative base at the sidewalk level where pedestrians can relate to it (no one ever looks above the third floor—unless you're on a walking tour); an austere midsection to keep the decorativeness in check; and a fanciful top that announced the building's presence in the city's skyline. The romantic top, later so despised by the Moderns, often served parenthetically as a "billboard" for the corporation located within. Chrysler's spire, Bankers Trust's ziggurat (at Wall and Nassau streets), and Standard Oil's oil lamp (22 Broadway, seen best from New York Harbor) were the best advertisements a company could buy.

In the Wall Street area the designs were largely Neoclassical, because prestige and "image" were so important to financial institutions. The narrow streets, soaring towers, masonry street walls, and the recurring Beaux Arts formula encouraging decoration disciplined by a rhythmical order created streetscapes not seen anywhere else in the world. Midtown, with its broad avenues and river-to-river streets opening up views in all directions, does not compare. Downtown New York is its own special place. Typical is lower Broadway, where Bowling Green, framed by the 1907 customhouse, and the Beaux Arts–era skyscrapers create one of the city's finest vistas.

Around 1900 a satellite office district emerged uptown in the Madison Square area (23rd Street and Fifth Avenue). After part of the old Ladies' Mile was ripped out, the new construction produced two of New York's more notable skyscrapers, the **Flatiron Building** (1902; Daniel Burnham; Fifth Avenue at 23rd Street) and the **Metropolitan Life Tower** (1909; Napoleon Le Brun & Sons; Madison Avenue at 24th Street). The former briefly held the record as the world's tallest building.

In the wholesale district, east and west of Broadway from Canal to 34th streets, the buildings were more anonymous but no less interesting. Perhaps feeling less restrained, the architects gave the façades of their loft buildings eclectic treatments that melded (Louis) Sullivanesque modernity with Beaux Arts formality. Brick, stone, iron, glass, and terra-cotta were used to create high-rise tapestries of incredible originality. Blocks to notice include West 12th and 13th streets between Broadway and University Place. Down in SoHo, the "little" **Singer Building** (1904; Ernest Flagg; 561 Broadway) and the **New Era Building** (1893; Alfred Zucker; 495 Broadway) both give Chicago stiff competition in the game of high-rise aesthetics.

As buildings grew to astronomical heights it became obvious that their massiveness would have to be pruned back—if only to allow light and air to penetrate the streets below. Ernest Flagg's magnificent Singer Building (1908; Broadway and Liberty Street; now demolished!) pointed toward a solution with its narrow, ornamented tower rising from a stubby base, but it was the **Woolworth Building** (1913; Cass Gilbert; Broadway at Barclay Street–Park Place) that gave the basic formula to the next generation of skyscraper designers. Its secular Neo-Gothicism made the building's unprecedented 795 feet soar into the clouds. Its multiuse base included shops, a luxury restaurant, a health club (still in operation), and a direct link with the new BMT Broadway subway line, making it more a "city" than just a building. Its two-story-high mosaic-tiled lobby served as grand entrance and interior "court" (a must-see; the Woolworth personnel are very hospitable), giving access to all the building's multiple functions. The world's tallest building until 1930, it still remains today—thanks to the Woolworth Company's vigilance—one of the finest skyscrapers of its day and a template for all times.

When in 1916 New York adopted America's first zoning code requiring setbacks and narrow towers, the Woolworth Building was its prototype. In the unparalleled building boom of the 1920s the city's skyline was reshaped largely in the Woolworth image. The great Art Deco skyscrapers of the 1920s were built mostly in Midtown on the "new Wall Street" (as the area around Grand Central was then called). Skyscrapers such as the **Chanin Building** (1929; Sloan & Robertson; Lexington Avenue at 42nd Street, southwest corner), the **Chrysler Building** (1930; William Van Alen, Lexington Avenue at 42nd Street, northeast corner), and the **Empire State Building** (1931; Shreve, Lamb & Harmon; Fifth Avenue at 34th Street, southwest corner) gave the world its definitive image of what a skyscraper should look like. No Chicago skyscraper ever captured so intensely the public's imagination as these did.

They borrowed their silhouettes from the American skyscraper Gothic, their details from the German Expressionists, and their nomenclature from the French Exposition des Arts Décoratifs of 1925. Traditional materials such as marble and stone were mixed with new materials like stainless steel and Monel Metal, so that references to both the past and the future were interwound. The Chrysler Building with its Art Deco marble lobby, elevators paneled with inlaid wood, and stainless steel tower is the epitome of its time. Its top was planned to be brilliantly lit (finally achieved in 1985), as in Fritz Lang's Expressionistic film *Metropolis*.

Downtown Art Deco skyscrapers were pinstriped and bankerish, though one of the finest, the **Irving Trust Co.** at 1 Wall Street (1932; Voorhees, Gmelin & Walker) houses a brilliant red and gold mosaic banking hall, now used as an office but accessible to the public. Uptown the Deco buildings were more colorful, both outside as well as inside, whether serving as a corporate headquarters— like the **Fred F. French Building** (1927; Fred F. French Co.; Fifth Avenue at 45th Street, northeast corner)—or as commercial loft space, such as **2 Park Avenue** (1927; at 33rd Street), Ely Jacques Kahn's confection of Vienna Secessionist color and form.

The boom went bust as we all know, but the depression era produced one of the finest skyscraper complexes the world has ever seen. Pushing the Midtown office district farther north to around 50th Street between Fifth and Sixth avenues, **Rockefeller Center** (1931–1938; the Associated Architects) put slab towers atop low-rise bases (for more light and air both in the building and on the street) and tied its buildings together with a vast underground shopping center. The center gave the public an unprecedented pedestrian promenade and sunken plaza (used for ice-skating in the winter), direct access to the new IND Sixth Avenue subway, and provided for underground truck deliveries (below the skating rink), making its streets more civilized to negotiate.

Its two music halls (one is now gone) and cinema (the Guild, at 50th Street) provided entertainment, while sculpture, art works, and museums (the latter are now all gone) provided culture. Raymond Hood, the project's chief architect, melded Le Corbusier's insistence on light, airy slabs with the German Expressionists' insistence on symbolism. The result was a then-unique type of "city" that was friendly and familiar, light-filled and open in spite of its gargantuan scale. Yet it gives us "character" as few Modern buildings ever do: The G.E. Building (newly spotlit), the center's visual focus, anchors the city as Medieval cathedrals once anchored old European cities. Many complexes have tried to emulate Rockefeller Center, but few have achieved its balance of size, scale, and civility.

After World War II the Modern "glass box" school came into vogue. Skidmore, Owing & Merrill's Gordon Bunshaft shocked New York with his Manufacturers Hanover Trust glass bank (1954) at Fifth Avenue and 43rd Street (southwest corner) and the floating glass slabs of **Lever House** (1952) at Park Avenue and 53rd Street (northwest corner). Here was an urban world of shimmering glass, light, air, and sun. Glass skins began to be wrapped around old-fashioned setback silhouettes.

Mies van der Rohe and Philip Johnson's **Seagram Building** (1958; Park Avenue at 53rd Street, southeast corner) changed the shape of the skyscraper radically and created the template for a generation. Mies's brilliant rendering of bronze, glass, and marble expressed perfectly that generation's search for a new functionalist, machine-age style. The building's pristine glass tower, set in a podium-style plaza, was reproduced superficially by the thousands in cities across the country. In New York itself the Seagram's imagery permeated everything as Midtown pushed up

Park, Third, and Sixth avenues, and as downtown expanded from Water Street to the World Trade Center.

The Seagram is perfection both as a piece of sculpture and as an aesthetic statement. But its popularity among developers did not stem from its refined proportioning. Rather, because the building is actually fatter and more complicated than it first appears to be, the Seagram gave them a sleek corporate image while allowing them to stuff a good deal of office space behind the glass façade. Its pristine lobby had no room for messy retail tenants, and the tower-in-a-plaza siting was the perfect expression of the Suburban Decade's dislike of anything remotely urban.

The Seagram is a work of art, but what turned out to be a prototype for mass production was itself, ironically, not truly capable of being mass produced. Most of the building's features—from its bronze mini I-beams, used as decorative mullions, to its bronze-tinted glass windows and special interior lighting (which gives the Seagram at night a totally different effect)—were custom designed and custom made. This classic image of a machine-made product was in fact a custom-made arts-and-crafts artifact costing twice as much as other buildings. Knocked off cheaply, it lost the genius that made its minimalism work. When repeated on a large scale the Miesian city was lifeless, boring, and scaleless, giving 1960s cityscapes an almost fatal case of visual anomie.

Everything the Seagram eschewed has come back in the Postmodern 1980s. Decoration, romantic silhouettes, flamboyant tops, intensely active plazas all are now *de rigueur*. One of the first of the Postmodern towers, the **Citicorp Center** (1977; Hugh Stubbins; Lexington Avenue at 53rd Street), is still one of the best, creating a truly urbane interior court that has consistently attracted the public. Others of note are the **AT & T Building** by Philip Johnson (1979; Madison Avenue at 55th Street, northwest corner), known for its Chippendale top (which is probably the building's best part), the **IBM Building** next door (1983; Edward Larrabee Barnes; Madison Avenue at 57th Street, southwest corner), with its own quite popular glassed-in court and the excellent **IBM Gallery** downstairs, and **Trump Tower** (1979; Swanke Hayden Connell; Fifth Avenue at 56th Street, northeast corner), whose opulent, marble-swathed, vertical shopping center is a fitting altar to New York's worship of the loud and the flashy. Three blocks east at **135 East 57th Street** (Lexington Avenue, northwest corner) the architectural firm of Kohn Pederson Fox has just completed a new concave office tower with a pergola entranceway and the adjoining Place des Antiquaires, a building whose only tenants are antiques dealers (125 East 57th). The entire complex, with its lavish use of rich marbles and High Renaissance detailing, is the quintessential expression of the firm's Postmodern Neoclassicism, carefully tuned to the scale of today's corporate Medici.

Downtown, **Battery Park City** (BPC) gives us in one fell swoop all the Postmodern standards on a single stage. Cesar Pelli's **World Financial Center** has mosaic-domed lobbies, a shop-lined walkway system, and the glass-enclosed, café-filled **Winter Garden**, which give us the commercial side, while BPC's new residential districts, with their traditional city streets and apartment buildings reminiscent of prewar designs, show us Postmodernism on the domestic front. The open-space planning and landscaping here is the most imaginative in years, and includes a new version of Gramercy Park as well as waterfront esplanades and parks designed with a refreshing sensibility.

Though it is too early to tell, the Postmodern style is probably the beginning of a new Eclectic era, when romantic silhouettes, decoration of whatever kind, intense urban activity, and design sources from both the past and the future will predominate. But Postmodern decor cannot mask the changing facts of city life. In the service economy of the postindustrial world, our buildings are being built for computers more than for people. Though Midtown office buildings might be slender and notched to give each member of their corps of corporate executives a corner office, most skyscrapers are now built on a massive scale to give the computerized back-offices and trading floors the immense amount of room they need. Large floors mean fat buildings: Though the World Financial Center's towers average 40-odd stories, each contains at least the square footage of the 102-story Empire State Building.

In addition, record-breaking real-estate costs mean gargantuan towers, whether commercial or residential. Every one of Manhattan's desirable residential sections is being glutted with apartment houses of unprecedented size.

Whither goes Manhattan? Nobody knows. Looking back over the previous 20-year period, we can with hindsight see that no one could have predicted the changes that would take place five years down the road from any particular time. Who knows when we'll see the next masterpiece—or the next abysmal flop. Whenever it is, you can be sure it won't be long in coming.

MUSEUMS AND BOOKSTORES FOR ARCHITECTURE

The Museum of Modern Art. Books, galleries, and occasional exhibitions on, of course, Modern-movement architects. Don't miss the gallery highlighting modern consumer products. 11 West 53rd Street (between Fifth and Sixth avenues). Museum bookstore.

The Metropolitan Museum of Art. Period rooms including French 18th-century salons, an American Neo-Gothic library, and a Frank Lloyd Wright living room. Fifth Avenue at 82nd Street. Museum bookstore.

Cooper-Hewitt Museum. The Smithsonian's decorative-arts branch, which often has architectural exhibitions. Its building is a major exhibit in itself: the 1901 mansion built for Andrew Carnegie. Check the bookstore's inventory. Fifth Avenue at 91st Street.

The Urban Center. Located in the north wing of the 1883 Villard Houses, with the rest of the complex now functioning as the Helmsley Palace Hotel. Often has small exhibits on architectural and city-planning topics especially relating to New York and/or historic preservation. 457 Madison Avenue at 51st Street. **Urban Center Books,** located in the Urban Center, is *the* New York bookstore for architecture, city planning, and urban design.

Rizzoli Bookstore. As handsome a bookstore as the books it sells. Its design section features lush volumes on art and architecture. 31 West 57th Street between Fifth and Sixth avenues. There are also branches at 454 West Broadway in SoHo and in the new World Financial Center in lower Manhattan.

GALLERIES

Max Protetch. Devotes one of its galleries full time to architectural exhibits and has original architectural drawings for sale. 560 Broadway at Prince Street at the edge of SoHo.

The Drawing Center. This nonprofit gallery occasionally has smashing shows on architectural drawings. 35 Wooster Street, between Broome and Grand streets, SoHo.

Storefront for Art & Architecture. Offbeat, interesting architectural shows. 97 Kenmare Street, near Lafayette Street, not far from SoHo.

For up-to-the-minute schedules of gallery and museum shows of architectural interest, see the listings in *Blueprint* magazine, a British publication that covers the New York scene, or *Metropolis* magazine, published locally, devoted to architecture, urban design, and the decorative arts. Both are available at Urban Center Books and Rizzoli Bookstore.

FASHION

By Lynn Yaeger

From its earliest days as a metropolis, nascent New York displayed an enthusiasm for the culture of beauty, the cult of fashion, and the vagaries of style quite out of proportion to the circumstances of most of its residents. "I have known young ladies supporting themselves," wrote one Anne Royall in the early years of the 19th century, "sit up til 12 o'clock at night, to complete a suit of clothes, the proceeds of which was to purchase a fine cap, or a plume of feathers, to deck herself for church. Hundreds of those females thus maintain themselves in a style of splendor; no ladies in the city dress finer. A ten dollar hat, a thirty dollar shawl, with silk and lace, is common amongst the poorer class of females."

By the middle of the 19th century, A. T. Stewart, considered the first true department store in the United States, had opened on lower Broadway, employing good-looking gentlemen to shepherd the ladies from counters of the finest European laces and linens to the revolutionary displays of ready-made cloaks and mantles. Other dry goods stores were also expanding (many dispensing with the traditional custom of selling "wet" goods—rum—on one side of the establishment and necessities for the ladies on the other), including Lord & Taylor, which had a great currency during the Civil War years at the now almost irredeemable intersection of Grand and Chrystie streets.

As the century progressed the big stores moved uptown,

and by about 1885 "Fashion Row"—as Sixth Avenue was called from 14th to 23rd streets, with some offshoots on Broadway—was filled with towering cast-iron emporiums. ("Meet you at the fountain!" shoppers said to one another in 1895, referring to the waterworks in front of Siegel-Cooper Dry Goods Store, Sixth Avenue at 18th Street, years before the Biltmore clock came into fashion.)

No sooner had Fashion Row and the Ladies' Mile (Broadway in the same area) become firmly entrenched in the shopper's imagination than the stores pulled up stakes and moved again. (Lord & Taylor, having left the Lower East Side in 1869 for Broadway and 20th Street, packed up again in 1906 and relocated to its present Fifth Avenue location.)

Of course, not everyone dressed in silks and proper bonnets, genteelly attempting to ape their betters. There were those, then as now, who stuck their stylistic tongues out at the passing show and elected a wildly bohemian style. The Bowery G'hirls of the 1840s, with their garish yellow shawls, scarlet dresses, and giant feathers and boas, scandalized society with bold manners and ankle-length skirts (floor-dragging being the only respectable length). Now their spiritual descendants, in torn black leather, nose rings, and spiked hair, tread the same streets with identical *épater les bourgeois* intentions occupying their youthful minds.

Why is it that New York remains at the crossroads of style and fashion, century after century? Is it because for 150 years Manhattan has been a center of clothing manufacture, of design, of intense wholesale and retail activity? By the 1920s the clothing business had moved from its squalid cottage-industry origins to large-scale factories in the neighborhood once known as the "Tenderloin." A noon visit to this **Garment District**—Sixth to Eighth avenues in the 30s—will dispel any doubts the reader may harbor that Manhattan has somehow passed its peak as the apex of the fashion industry. Choking racks of clothing impede all but the hardiest pedestrian, trucks with screaming drivers stall aggressively at loading docks, and the whir of 10,000 sewing machines is dimly audible in the distance.

Today as yesterday young designers rush from fashion school to Manhattan, where they apprentice themselves to established designers or set up storefront couture houses on their own. And when the time comes to show the fashion collections of the major designers, there are no "American" or "United States" collections for the press and society to flock to. The only important fashion showings this side of the Atlantic are the appropriately named, aptly situated, and justly famous "New York" collections.

SHOPPING

The Upper East Side

Eclipsing Fifth Avenue, challenged by SoHo, but still holding strong at the center of the shopping firmament, *Madison Avenue* is the street of dreams for those who dream of the best clothes, from the fanciest shops, offering the most uncompromising service. Although there are a few interesting outposts below 59th Street (**Itokin Plaza**, at 520 Madison, contains some serious contenders), the real action begins north of the new AT & T Building. The only way to canvass the area properly is to walk uptown along the avenue (or down from 96th Street), since several stores are scattered on each block. Take plenty of breaks for coffee—or sherry—and grab a taxi home or back to the hotel.

Not in geographical order, but rather grouped according to tastes, some of the interesting Madison Avenue shops are as follows: For the youthful shopper, **Susan Lemor** (number 697) has flat-heeled, peculiar, amusing shoes at (given the location) surprisingly reasonable prices. This shopper will also like the brightly colored clothing at **Kenzo** (824) as well as the judiciously edited collection of European items at **Betsey, Bunky, Nini** (746). **Joseph Tricot** (804) can provide properly unserious knitwear; visit **Stewart Ross** (754) for shelves crammed with hand-knitted bulkies—some wacky, some ditsy, most originating in the British Isles.

The marginally more mature shopper might prefer to buy her pullover at **Cashmere Cashmere** (840), where styles are casual but the materials at hand are almost insufferably elegant. At **Missoni** (836) the stock features unique jaquard wool items, from socks to coats. **Sonia Rykiel** (792) plies her snug, knitted costumes (considered quite revolutionary at their introduction 20 years ago) from a comfortable, busy store nearby. And the phenomenally well-received shoes of **Robert Clergerie** inhabit their own shop a half block off Madison at 41 East 60th Street.

Although the well-fixed but not unhip matron will probably head next for **Giorgio Armani** (815) and **Gianni**

Versace (816), both of which sell famous, luxuriously appointed Italian separates, she should also consider a visit to **Milan D'Or** (910), which offers less well known Italian designs, so she won't see herself coming and going at embassy cocktail parties. For Francophiles, **Yves St. Laurent** (855), **Pierre Balmain** (795), and **Emanuel Ungaro** (803) offer their labels in relatively close proximity to one another.

Americans experiencing a burst of civic pride (and foreign visitors weary of encountering similar designer merchandise in all the major cities on the globe) should visit **Polo/Ralph Lauren**, sequestered in the old Rhinelander mansion at the corner of 72nd Street (867), of interest to students of architecture and interior design as well as those in search of fashion. The old mansion still sports its original interior, the lower floors being full of Lauren clothing interspersed with antiques (both fine and homely), while the upper floors, where Ralph sells furniture and decorative accessories, stand ready with their old-fashioned bedsteads, travel trunks, lace panels, and even the occasional birdcage, all for the pleasure of a long-lost Rhinelander princess, as she rushes to the window to catch the sunrise over Madison Avenue.

Fifth Avenue–57th Street Area

The corner of 57th Street and Fifth Avenue, sunk deeply in myth from the time that Zelda swam in the Pulitzer Fountain and the morning Holly broke fast at Tiffany's, remains for many the cosmopolitan center of the universe, and the shops fanning out in all directions do nothing to disabuse them of this notion.

Those who wish to approach this zenith from a southerly direction should begin their walking tour at **Saks** on 50th Street, or perhaps make a brief visit to St. Patrick's Cathedral before setting off. Though this stretch of Fifth lacks the stupendous allure it once held, there are still some excellent shops, including **Mario Valentino** (645 Fifth) and **Ferragamo** (number 717), both featuring Italian clothing and leather goods. Directly off Fifth, at 15 West 55th Street, the international coterie that follows the fancy footwork of the shoemaker **Manolo Blahnik** will find a shop devoted to his designs. Readers as yet unconvinced that Mr. Mencken spoke the truth when he asserted that "no one ever lost money underestimating the taste of the American people" can dispel any lingering doubts with a visit to Trump Tower. This pink marble and waterfallencrusted edifice, attended by embarrassed-looking security guards dressed in Gilbert and Sullivan costumes, actually contains a few not uninteresting shops (Aspry, Charles Jourdan, etc.).

Now turn west briefly, where half a block away stands **Charivari 6**, at 18 West 57th, the newest and for many connoisseurs the best of the Charis, with four floors of designer merchandise plus the video screens, good-looking salespersons, and blaring music some people consider indispensable company when they spend their money. East of Fifth Avenue, 57th's reputation as a shopping street is confirmed. **Chanel**, at number 5 East 57th Street (the company waited a long time for this particular address), sells its famous collarless brass-buttoned suits, but there is also a full range of makeup and accessories available (including the quilted bag) for those wishing to commit a few hundred rather than a few thousand. The popular **Ann Taylor** (3 East 57th) has reasonably priced, stylish clothing, a glass elevator, and a highly regarded shoe department. **Laura Ashley** (21 East 57th) specializes in the maid-of-the-moors look, with its flowery prints, high-waisted dresses, puffy sleeves, and sashes. Those preferring a more androgynous appeal should turn instead to **Burberry's** (9 East 57th) or **Jaeger** (19 East 57th), both of which will accoutre the serious person, with not a sprig in sight.

On the next block (between Madison and Park) you will find, among the many other high-priced offerings, shoes by **Maud Frizon** (49 East 57th), internationally renowned for their blend of grown-up gamin (round toes, bows) and glamour girl (gold kid, high heels). At **Matsuda** (461 Park Avenue) the clothes are World War I as filtered through the artistic sensibility of modern Tokyo; while the palette is sober and conservative, the prices are not.

Upper West Side

Once, not so long ago, the Upper West Side was a shabby-genteel neighborhood, full of butcher, hardware, liquor, and shoe-repair shops. Then came the co-ops, and the traditional stores found themselves replaced by places selling antiques and tostadas. Lately the more esoteric of these shops are beginning to disappear, in favor of branches of European clothing chains and fancy ice-cream depots.

Charivari 72, on the corner of 72nd Street and Columbus Avenue, deals in high-priced men's and women's big-name European clothing from its triplex shop. (The Charivari shops were among the first fancy stores to open on the Upper West Side and have since reaped the profits of their prescience.) Among the other offerings spread out along Columbus Avenue, you might like **Caroll of Paris** (number 315), which sells working women's French sweaters; **Sacha London** (294), interesting shoes with low prices; or **French Connection** (304), hip, collegiate clothing. Those with more exotic tastes should look into **Street Life** (422), a house line of oversize cotton shirts and smocks, with a lot of items in the rare under-$100 range. **Charivari Workshop** (441 Columbus Avenue, across the street from the American Museum of Natural History) is especially strong in the area of gender-neutral clothing from Japan. Over on Amsterdam Avenue, **Nana** (number 414) sells Dr. Martens and other post-punk bohemian footwear.

Chelsea

Though it has experienced something of a renaissance lately, Chelsea still does not qualify as a serious hunting ground for the fashion-minded tourist. **Barney's** (Seventh Avenue and 17th Street) remains the only real reason to travel to Chelsea for shopping, and although its six floors of very stylish, very desirable European and American clothing, shoes, and accessories for men and women are intriguing, the consistently high tariffs have left tourists and natives alike stampeding to the elevators and into the street. Still, all the major (and a lot of the minor) labels are represented, and the physical setting is impressive.

After Barney's, you can walk east a few blocks to Fifth Avenue in the teens, an area that is experiencing definite retail revival. The neighborhood boasts two recently opened sartorial palaces: **Emporio Armani** (110 Fifth Avenue), with its house line of somewhat less expensive (but hardly inexpensive) Armani clothing from Italy, and the even newer flagship shop of **Matsuda** (156 Fifth Avenue), featuring high-priced, but undeniably interesting, avant-garde Japanese clothing. Here you will also find **Folklorica** (89 Fifth Avenue), with clothing and decorative objects from South America, Africa, and other Third World locales; **Willie Wear** (119), stylish and casual reasonably priced clothing; and the excellent **Royal Silk** (79 Fifth Avenue), three floors of silk blouses, dresses, skirts, shirts, nighties, and so forth, all dramatically underpriced.

West Village

For almost a hundred years "Greenwich Village" has conjured images of bedraggled painters starving in attics, bearded poets ranting in parks, and bohemian wine parties of astonishing debauch. Those in search of this lost world will reel in horror at the reality of streets full of squeaky clean suburban teenagers and nice respectable couples pushing baby carriages where once the middle classes feared to tread.

Still, it is possible, with a little determination, to uncover a few interesting shops in these confines. **Patricia Field** (10 East 8th Street), despite its proper-sounding name, has some of the weirdest, most uncompromising getups to be found around town, and **Capezio**'s upper floors (177 MacDougal Street) can still outfit the aspiring ballerina or black-clad modern dancer. **Modern Girls** (169 Thompson Street) has an ever-changing stock of punk-influenced items, many one-of-a-kind (well, it might be difficult to sell more than one of most of these things). At **Untitled** (26 West 8th Street) the items are upper-crust British rock star, and the designs lean heavily to the brocaded waistcoat and the odd, displaced ruffle. Both **Ibiza** (46 University Place) and **Lo: New York** (22 Greenwich Avenue) sell clothing suited for the rich hippie whose taste is rooted in yesteryear—the former specializing in printed rayon, 1930s-influenced dresses and long skirts, and the latter featuring a unique line of drippy, drooping flaxen-knitted garments that can be dyed any color desired and would have been the perfect thing to wear to the long-ago wedding of John and Michelle Phillips, had you been invited.

For reasonably priced, stylish, youthful clothes, you should not miss the huge and justly famous **Reminiscence** (74 Fifth Avenue), located at the very northernmost tip of what is considered Greenwich Village, but well worth the walk.

East Village

The undeniably shabby East Village, with its tottering tenements, luncheon counters, and crackpots of every persuasion, nonetheless pulls like a magnet at the heart of every would-be hipster from Bangkok to Bailey's Beach. The shops, as you would expect, are tiny, eccentric, ever-changing holes-in-the-wall—some cluttered, some streamlined by recent art-school graduates, all selling things either stitched up on the home sewing machine or hammered together in a garret (or perhaps special ordered from the wilds of punkdom in the United Kingdom). At **109 St. Mark's Place** (located in typical East Village fashion at 115 St. Mark's Place) a number of neighborhood designers show their work, ranging from the borderline wearable to the outrageous, such as a fringed Saran Wrap burnoose. **Enz** (5 St. Mark's Place) is home to the heavy-metal aficionado, though it may be possible to turn up something like a fuchsia mohair sweater mixed in with the spikes and chains. **Ponica** (325 East 5th Street), comfortingly located next to the local police precinct house, sells transparent, drifting dresses suitable for the Mad Hatter's tea party. Both **Lilla Lova** (117 East 7th Street) and **Shrimpton & Gilligan** (70 East 1st Street) have storefront couture items that someone might actually wear to work—assuming she toils for, say, a struggling theater troupe rather than the president of General Motors.

SoHo

Once purely a center for painting, sculpture, and performance art (and, for a century before that, a warehouse district with a lingering reputation of 19th-century licentiousness), SoHo in the last few years has come to rival Madison Avenue as a place to view, purchase, and parade around in expensive, interesting clothes. Stores open, close, and replace one another with dizzying rapidity down here, because of the spiraling rents and the shifting buying moods of the crowd.

Visitors to SoHo will probably arrive and proceed on foot, as this is preeminently strolling territory. Most people start at West Broadway, which, between Houston and Canal streets, is full of fashionable shops selling predictably fashionable, avant-garde items. Neighboring streets (Greene, Wooster, Thompson, etc.) also contain many interesting stores, some of which, due to the cheaper rents obtained by moving off the main drag, feature rather more esoteric merchandise.

On West Broadway proper, shoppers can visit **If** (474) for an outstanding selection of European clothing, with labels running the gamut from Azzadine to Zoran, with Clergerie shoes and Gaultier corselets wedged between. For even more esoteric European designers check **Bagutta** (402 West Broadway). **Victoria Falls** (451) presents a collection of the Southern France–influenced white-silk-and-straw-boater variety, while **Nicole Farhi** (435) has clothes for women from the same country of origin who work as executives in the towering glass monsters of Montparnasse. (Suitable clothing for this entrepreneur's secretary, or her lycée-attending daughter, is available at **Agnès B.**, off West Broadway at 116–118 Prince.)

One block west, Thompson Street features a number of smaller shops with growing reputations. **Peter Fox** shoes (105 Thompson Street), with their curved court heels and delicately laced napes, appeal to a faithful coterie, as do the offerings of **FDR Drive** (109 Thompson): its fine gabardine 1930s- and 1940s-influenced separates and its oversize, unisex printed rayon shirts are made from authentic vintage fabric. **Betsey Johnson** (130 Thompson) sells weird skintight clothes for shoppers young enough to be amused by such things.

Readers anxious to spend more money should now proceed west to Wooster Street, where **Comme des Garçons** (116) holds forth with its world-renowned collection of Rei Kawakubo–designed Japanese esoterica, including oddly shaped and sized coats, shirts, dresses, and accessories. **Yohji Yamamoto** (103 Grand Street) has similarly priced and draped oddments (though fans of the two will turn purple with rage at the allegation that these two giants are at all comparable). **Tootsie Plohound** (110 Prince, women; 124 Prince, men) sells clunky beribboned clodhoppers, many with the obligatory serrated rubber sole, which lots of people think looks great with droopy, flappy Japanese costumes.

Those who wish to lurk near the heart of fashion darkness might like the black belted overcoats with shoulder pads and epaulets that, along with a full line of other seasonless items, are usually available at the huge and loftlike **Parachute** (121 Wooster).

Department Stores

A visitor overwhelmed by the number of small stores in New York, or desiring a crash course in the scope, price ranges, and general diversity of merchandise in Manhattan, should plunge headlong into Manhattan department-store shopping. Those who desire hair-raising excitement can elect to visit **Macy's** at 34th Street and Sixth and Seventh avenues first—purportedly the world's largest department store and containing departments covering all of humankind's basic needs in every price range and to suit every taste. There are floors of inexpensive merchandise, but lots of less democratically priced high-fashion goods as well.

Those reeling from the mobs at Macy's might seek refuge a block away, at the brand new **A & S** store, which, hoping to break the curse that kills New York department stores, has optimistically opened in the spot once inhabited by the now deceased Gimbels. Farther up Fifth at 38th Street, **Lord & Taylor** tries valiantly to hang on to its superlative reputation, but the inelegance of the surrounding neighborhood has taken its toll, and the old girl (despite an excellent collection of American country-style clothing) is a shadow of her former self. **Saks Fifth Avenue**, luckier in its location at 50th Street and Fifth Avenue across the street from Rockefeller Center and St. Patrick's Cathedral, offers a predictable cross-section of high-quality merchandise.

Bloomingdale's at 59th and Lexington, which started life as an East Side bargain basement, has transformed itself over the past 20 years into the epitome of glamorous, new-wave fashion. The entire fourth floor is given over to individual boutiques, and the big names—Chanel, Ungaro, St. Laurent, plus more obscure avant-gardists like Romeo Gigli and Workers for Freedom—evince a merchandising sensibility not to be trifled with.

A number of the traditional, carriage-trade department stores have updated and upgraded recently as well. **Bergdorf Goodman**, for years a dependable if fading flower on the corner of 57th and Fifth, has recently blossomed with a burst of excellent European and American designer merchandise (Gaultier, Donna Karan) in its newly renovated interior. A new, smaller **Bonwit Teller** at 4 East 57th (the old one was destroyed by Donald Trump several years ago) is trying mightily to compete with interesting merchandise. **Henri Bendel**, 10 West 57th, longtime home of the moneyed anorexic set, still features lots of one-of-a-kind obscure merchandise in its innovative street-of-shops format, but the store has recently been taken over by the comparatively lowbrow Limited corporation, and change hangs ominously in the air.

Discount Shopping

Visitors who are incorrigible, incurable bargain hunters, or those temporarily overawed by the bold, unblinkingly high price tags that pass for normal in Manhattan, will be happy to know that there is a shadow world of shopping in New York, where bare metal racks and dusty linoleum floors yield delectable merchandise at genuinely encouraging prices.

In these hidden districts of the city, no one ever pays full price for anything. Tentatively acclimate yourself to lower prices by visiting the area of lower Fifth Avenue (between 16th and 23rd streets) for off-price men's wear (**Moe Ginsburg** at 162 is prototypical) or visit West 14th Street for extremely cheap, appealing children's clothes (try Bunnie Baby Wear or Jacks Bargain Store). At **Daffy's** (111 Fifth Avenue) the motto is "Clothing Bargains for Millionaires" and the three full floors may indeed yield possibilities for intrepid hunters who don't mind communal fitting rooms. Thus primed, plunge headlong into the land that time forgot, the bargain center of the universe—the creaking but thriving, ancient Lower East Side neighborhood of **Orchard Street**, where the impoverished and the savvy bargain hunter have met for the past 100 years. (The entire district is open every day but Saturday; Sunday is the day for lovers of hyperactive crowds and screeching, hen-pecked proprietors.) Lots of Orchard Street stores confine themselves to ordinary merchandise, but a few break out with high-class, high-style European designer goods. Investigate **Chez Aby** (79 Delancey Street) for likely French and Italian items, or visit the slightly more prosaic **Breakaway** (125 Orchard Street), where American designers mingle with European closeouts. Extraordinarily chic shoes, all heavily discounted if not absurdly cheap, are carried by the **Lace-Up Shoe Shop** (110 Orchard Street). Shoppers willing to stand in line (sometimes extending outside the door) may reward themselves with a name-brand off-price handbag from the famous **Fine & Klein** (119 Orchard Street).

Of course, there are those who blanch at the highly charged atmosphere of the Lower East Side. These visitors might prefer several of the other discounters scattered throughout Manhattan. Young women, or those who have preserved the physiques of their younger selves, might like the offerings at **Strawberry** (all over town) or **Joyce Leslie** (20 University Place and numerous other locations), both of which specialize in very inexpensive, up-to-the-minute imitations of designer merchandise. The more bohemian reader will prefer **Unique Clothing Warehouse** (726 Broadway, between Washington and Waverly places) or **Canal Jean Co.** (504 Broadway between Spring and Broome streets), two cavernous holes in the wall near New York University with immense collections of hip, cheap things. (Young gentlemen of the painter-writer-filmmaker persuasion can purchase suitable outfits at these places as well.)

Fashion connoisseurs with more taste than money might wish to investigate two shops lurking in the very heart of the fancy Madison Avenue shopping district: **Damages** (768 Madison at 66th Street) and **22 Steps** (746). The former specializes in off-price Italian fashions, with a strong selection of silk afternoon dresses and blouses. The latter features discounted items from illustrious designers (with label intact), including the likes of Yves St. Laurent, Sonia Rykiel, and Comme des Garçons. (Neither of these shops is breathtakingly cheap, but they do feature impressive merchandise.)

Shoppers who wish to experience a genuine Third World bazaar atmosphere while remaining on the isle of Manhattan should head for one of the **Conway** stores (225 West 34th Street and other locations), where overstuffed hausfraus and irascible teenagers compete for groaning racks of ridiculously inexpensive merchandise. The offerings spill right out of the giant plate-glass, garage-type doors, covering adjacent sidewalks, and encroaching on neighboring storefronts. The resultant bulging pink paper shopping bags can be seen draped over the arms of bus and subway riders all over town.

Accessories

If, as has been alleged, God is in the details, then surely your outfit, whether at home or abroad, would benefit from a few distinguished accessories. These popular items (scarves, hats, gloves, handbags, etc.) have an additional benefit as souvenirs, since any size will fit the recipient; they are available over the complete spectrum of prices and, most important, they are usually small and travel well.

Due to their currency as both business and fashion, *handbags and briefcases* of surprising beauty and interest are available all over town. If utility is paramount: **Coach** (710 Madison Avenue at 63rd Street) has American softly tailored leather products, or visit **Lederer** (613 Madison) for classic French styles. At the old-line **Crouch & Fitzgerald** (400 Madison), traditional styles crowd the first floor, while upstairs the complete line of Louis Vuitton items waits in chains. (Crouch was the first place in town to carry L. V., years before it assumed its current popularity.)

Higher priced fashionable bags are available from **Bot-**

tega **Veneta** (635 Madison between 59th and 60th); this place also carries especially impressive small leather goods (wallets, card cases, etc.), but beware of scorching prices. Likewise, **Loewe** (711 Madison Avenue) and **Prada** (45 East 57th Street) stock distinctive, expensive handbags, attachés, and smalls. More youthful designs are sold by the famous French house **La Bagagerie** (727 Madison at 64th Street), and the even more ambitiously stylish should seek out the Italian **Furla** (705 Madison). Downtown, **Il Bisonte** sells its signature bleached calf accessories at 72 Thompson Street in SoHo. Among an impressive array of items made up from quilted printed Provençal fabrics, **Pierre Deux** (870 Madison at 71st Street) offers commodious duffel bags suitable for weekends in Westhampton. And for those willing to cash in their airline tickets and stow away for the trip home, **La Jeunesse** (989 Lexington between 71st and 72nd streets) sells incomparable evening reticules, composed of antique frames (some inset with semi-precious stones) with new leather purses added.

Shoes. It sometimes seems that even if each resident owned a thousand pairs, they would not be able to support the number of shoe stores flourishing in Manhattan. Although quite a few booteries are scattered elsewhere throughout this guide, the true shoe enthusiast should not fail to visit West 34th Street between Fifth and Sixth avenues and West 8th Street between the same avenues. Both thoroughfares are crowded with shoe shops, and while styles there are always up-to-date, corresponding price tags are unassuming. Shoe-lovers who have come to New York expressly to find items they can't locate at home will find a number of venues that specialize in the creation and fitting of custom-made footwear. At **Vogel**, located for more than a hundred years at 19 Howard Street, the specialty of the house is made-to-measure boots. For exquisite slippers, the like of which you rarely see outside of a Marlene Dietrich movie, go to **Mathias** (20 East 69th Street). Bring thousands, not hundreds.

Lingerie. Visitors who possess a sentimental longing for underthings of the past will enjoy the neo-Victorian, neo-hippie look of lingerie at **Michelle Nicole Wesley** (126 Prince Street in SoHo). Plenty of pristine white cotton, tiny satin bows, and seed pearls are in evidence, and there is usually a corner piled high with crushed velvet items as well. Those who crave handmade pure silk camisoles and drawers will like **Montenapoleone** (789 Madison between 66th and 67th streets), popular with daughters of deposed dictators, or **La Lingerie** (792 Madison), beloved by movie stars and/or wives of movie moguls. Those lacking sufficient funds should visit **Victoria's Secret** (34 East 57th), where items in satin and faux silk materials are glamorously cut and reasonably priced.

Scarves. For that prototypical souvenir, the silk scarf, many travellers visit **Hermès** (11 East 57th) or **Gucci** (683 Fifth Avenue), where the haute bourgeois merchandise is always dependable. The slightly more original shopper might prefer to travel down to the Orchard Street area, where **Bernard Krieger & Son** (316 Grand Street) has been offering men's and women's cotton and linen handkerchiefs by the dozens (that's the only way they're sold) at ridiculously low prices since 1936. In the East Village, a few surviving nativist shops still sell brightly colored, floral printed, wool challis Ukrainian peasant scarves out of piles of cardboard boxes stacked up on ancient, creaking showcases.

Hats. Though only a decade ago it seemed as if the custom millinery business in New York was all but dead and buried, the corpse has in fact been resuscitated over the past few years, and a couple of establishments can actually be described as thriving. **Victoria Dinardo** (68 Thompson Street in SoHo) has a number of appealing designs—ranging from the winsome to the downright strange—and will listen to and attempt to incorporate your suggestions into her work.

Cosmetics. **Boyd Chemists** (655 Madison Avenue between 60th and 61st streets), despite its elegant location, is anything but subdued—the wildly enthusiastic, overly made-up sales staff will push products on you no matter how reluctant you are to buy. The selection is very impressive (it includes hard-to-find foreign brands), and there is a spectacular array of hair accessories, leaning heavily toward the fake tortoise and rhinestone variety and hailing mainly from France. For still more hair accoutrements, investigate **Halina's** (160 West 55th), an obscure hairdressing shop that sells vintage (and vintage-looking) tortoise barrettes, clips, and hard-to-locate, dramatic Spanish-style combs.

Downtown at **Kiehl's** (109 Third Avenue between 13th and 14th streets), considerations of health outweigh those of glamour. The store sells a house brand of potions and ointments, and many New Yorkers swear by their efficacy. **Caswell-Massey** (Lexington at 48th), the oldest pharmacy in the city, also has a private label and the accompanying claque of enthusiastic fans.

To renovate your complexion with a complete and rigorous workout, call for an appointment at **Georgette Klinger** (501 Madison Avenue between 52nd and 53rd streets) or **Janet Sartin** (480 Park Avenue between 58th and 59th streets); either of these ladies will slather, slap, and massage your face in accordance with her particular expensive regimen.

Furs. The fur coat, once strictly the province of the moneyed classes and once emblematic of female sophistication and implied indolence, is no longer synonymous with the life of leisure. It has been embraced by the working woman, the gentleman stroller, and even the (fur) swaddled babe in arms. Reasonably priced middlebrow coats are available all over town, but the stoical of heart are urged to take on the area of Seventh Avenue in the high 20s, where office buildings bursting with innumerable showrooms and workshops sell coats in various price ranges, depending on the skins in question and the complexity of design. The fur district has an aura of a wholesale-only operation, but many (most) of the businesses are more than happy to entertain the retail customer. **Steven Corn Furs** (141 West 28th Street, ground floor) is huge and bustling and will keep the undecided customer occupied for hours; at **Harry Kirshner** (307 Seventh Avenue between 27th and 28th streets, fourth floor), a typical factory/salesroom operation, the service is unusually cordial and solicitous. Shoppers intent on owning one of the shearling sheepskin coats that are now popular should visit **Sport and Travel** (511 Madison Avenue) for traditional women's styles or **Michael Max** in the Village (163 West 4th Street), which features *outré* shearling outerwear to suit the adventurous dresser of either sex.

Uptown, **Jindo Furs** (41 West 57th) sells a wide range (from under $1,000) of fur jackets and coats; some of the less expensive models are conspicuously stylish. To examine the dramatic, ground-breaking designs that have left fur fanatics breathless over the past several years, don't hesitate to visit the Fendi coats at **Henri Bendel** (10 West 57th Street), even when potential purchase (never under $10,000) remains remote.

Jewelry

Many of the old-line jewelry houses may claim at least partial responsibility for lending the words "Fifth Avenue" their international connotation of wealth and glamour. **Cartier**, snug in its landmark building at the corner of 52nd Street, remains hushed and intimidating to all but the most brazen and well-heeled shopper. **Tiffany's**, by contrast, exudes a bustling, almost egalitarian air. (Take the elevator to two for less expensive silver items, still packaged in the famous Tiffany blue box and brought to you from the stockroom by an antiquated system of dumbwaiters and pneumatic tubes.) Upper Fifth also features branches of **Fred Joaillier** (703), very fine, fashionable French jewelry, and **H. Stern** (645, across the street from St. Patrick's), Brazilian and a specialist in the innovative use of colored gemstones. The venerable **Harry Winston** (to whom Ms. Monroe alludes when she explains why diamonds are a girl's best friend) occupies a site at 718 Fifth.

Intersecting Fifth Avenue at 47th Street is the **Diamond District**—one solid block (to Sixth Avenue) of stores, booths, workshops, and showrooms dedicated to the design, renovation, repair, but mostly the sale of diamond, colored gemstone, and gold jewelry. Though it looks and behaves like a wholesale area, most of 47th Street talks retail enthusiastically. Bring cash and prepare to bargain. (A similar, but smaller, less boisterous wholesale-retail jewelry district exists downtown in the area of Canal Street and the Bowery; proximity to Chinatown accounts for its interesting supply of high-karat red-gold charms and chains.)

Shoppers attracted to Fifth Avenue gems but lacking corresponding funds should consider visiting **Kenneth Jay Lane** (in Trump Tower), who made his reputation with beautifully executed copies of high-priced pieces. Those who leave the real thing in the vault, or wish to appear as though they do, should stop at **Jolie Gabor** (699 Madison Avenue), where individual pieces can be copied or "fabulous fakes" bought off the shelf. Much less expensive is **Gould Jewelry** (20 East 58th Street), whose imitation baubles would be perfectly illuminated by the dim light of dusk on board an ocean-liner deck.

If it's pearls you're after, there is **Mikimoto**, the veritable inventor of the cultured variety, at 608 Fifth Avenue between 48th and 49th streets. **Buccellati** (in Trump Tower) will seat you on a comfortable chair and spread before you individual specimens of heartbreaking luster and intensity, to be strung at your behest. Stagger out of Buccellati to the nearest magazine stand, from whose wooden frames many news dealers are selling one-dollar strands of ersatz pearls—just to make sure these things truly become you.

For a wristwatch, veer nominally off Fifth Avenue to **Tourneau Corner** (500 Madison Avenue at 52nd Street) for a staggering collection of watches, ranging from reasonably expensive to rarefied Rolex. An entirely different world of watches—namely, the oversize, comical, bubble-headed variety—is accessible to those willing to travel downtown to 8th Street, where **Savage** (59 West 8th) sells a likely selection.

At **Charles' Place** (234 Mulberry Street) rhinestone-bedecked animal earrings (the gamboling pigs are nice) can be custom tailored to your specifications or bought ready-made. Gentlemen who are looking for shops that will sell them a single earring will want to know that the stretch of 8th Street between Fifth and Sixth avenues, as well as eastern Greenwich Avenue, should prove particularly fruitful. **Einstein's** (96 East 7th Street in the East Village) can provide perverse, almost threatening pieces of jewelry to those in search of same.

People who want something unusual but still have to work for a living will find amusing but wearable examples at **Ylang Ylang** (4 West 57th). Modernists who don't mind spending a bit may prefer **Artwear** (456 West Broadway). Unusual metals like titanium are experimented with here; the results often decorate the mannequins at prestigious fashion shows. If your financial sky has no limit, there are interesting one-of-a-kind items for sale at the **Neil Isman Gallery** (1100 Madison Avenue near 83rd Street), where important new jewelry artists are represented.

Lastly, shoppers in search of something completely different (as well as those who find themselves temporarily in queer street) might benefit from a visit to **Gem Pawnbrokers** (608 Eighth Avenue), a classic place (three balls outside, glass window) with a surprisingly comprehensive display of "out of pawn" offerings.

Vintage Clothing

The popularity of vintage clothing, which began its worldwide ascendance in the 1960s, has hung on with surprising tenacity in New York City. Many of the locals pride themselves on dressing funny and find that their innate taste and "ideas" about clothing, usually crippled by their lack of funds, can find full expression at the secondhand store.

There are fine antique clothes (1920s through 1940s, excellent condition and presentation) at **Panache** (525 Hudson Street between 10th and Charles streets), **O'Mistress Mine** (143 Seventh Avenue South), and the vintage racks at the always appealing **Reminiscence** (74 Fifth Avenue at 13th Street). **Harriet Love** (412 West Broadway between Prince and Spring), the grandmother of antique clothing stores in New York, now stocks a variety of new clothing along with the special old pieces (beaded jackets, cashmere sweaters, rayon dresses) for which she is so justly famous. At **Jana Starr/Jean Hoffman Antiques** (236 East 80th) there is a preponderance of Victorian white-work, and hard-to-find accompanying accessories like boudoir caps and early satin dancing shoes. (These ladies outfit a lot of weddings, graduations, and christenings, and thus provide a high level of service—with prices to match.) Madame Liza of **Liza's Place** (132 Thompson Street in SoHo), boasts that her shop sells authentic Chanels and Schiaparellis, and even when these are not in evidence you will find unparalleled beaded flapper dresses among her permanent collection.

Shoppers seeking to spend vastly less money will be happier visiting **Andy's Chee-Pees** (14 St. Mark's Place) or **Cheap Jacks** (841 Broadway betwen 13th and 14th Streets), two stores with lower priced rough-and-tumble merchandise, where condition is often dubious but you are sometimes able to uncover a diamond in the rough. At **Alice Underground** (481 Broadway downtown and 380 Columbus Avenue on the Upper West Side) the surroundings are more presentable and price tags are still extremely reasonable. The East Village contains a number of inexpensive possibilities, among them **Unlimited Debris Inc**. (148 Second Avenue), the long-lived **Love Saves The Day** (119 Second Avenue at 7th Street), and the densely packed, filthy, and infamous **Bogie's** (201 East 10th Street).

Men's Clothing

The main line of gentlemen's clothiers is in the area of Madison Avenue in the lower 40s. Here are **Brooks Brothers** (346 Madison Avenue at 44th Street), justly famous, predictably conservative, surprisingly affordable; **Paul Stuart** (Madison at 45th Street), more ambitious merchandise; and **F. R. Tripler** (336 Madison at 46th) for old-fashioned items including the hard-to-find gentleman's Edwardian nightshirt. If you are looking for the loud, off-

center style peculiar to the American country-club denizen, investigate **Chipp** (342 Madison), club ties depicting
90-plus breeds of dogs; and J. **Press** (7 East 44th Street),
indescribable madras-plaid patchwork baggy trousers. Farther uptown, at **Sulka** (430 Park Avenue at 55th Street), the
extremely refined goods are strictly for the silk-undies set.
Cashmere robes here are $700 plus, but an ascot might
prove affordable—and makes a lovely souvenir.

The new-to-New York **Louis, Boston** (Lexington at 57th)
brings with it a well-established reputation for exquisitely
tailored overcoats and dress suits. **Burberry's Ltd.** (9 East
57th Street) has the plaid-lined raincoats synonymous with
its name. The gentleman traveller should be aware that
Bergdorf Goodman contains boutiques bearing two interesting old names, Hackett and Charvet, from Britain and
France respectively, and has the largest selection of Turn-
bull and Asser shirts outside of London.

For another new shirt to wear home visit the English
outpost of **Paul Smith** (108 Fifth Avenue) for oversize
shirts with unusual details, or the **Custom Shirt Shop** (618
Fifth Avenue, between 49th and 50th streets, and other
locations), which makes chemises to order, as the name
would indicate. Profligate guys who must be the cynosure
of all eyes can fulfill that intention with a new outfit from
that wildly admired Italian, **Giorgio Armani** (815 Madison
Avenue between 68th and 69th streets).

An entirely different sort of man, who looks as if he
rolled out of a haystack dressed in the same black sweat
shirt and jeans you've seen him in for 20 years, may also
be a secret shopper—albeit of a radically different persuasion. His requisite leather jacket can be purchased at the
N.Y. Leather Co. (33 Christopher Street in the West Village), and accompanying baggy, shapeless trousers are
available from **Aca Joe** (313 Columbus Avenue and other
locations). On the rare occasion (his wedding day?) that
this guy dresses up, he might consent to wear a neo-
1940s outfit (pleated pants, gabardine shirt) from an excellent in-house collection at **FDR Drive Men** (80 Thompson Street at Spring Street in SoHo). **Enz** (5 St. Mark's
Place), which he will surely saunter past on his nocturnal
treks to the East Village, will happily accoutre the aspiring
rock star. If he suddenly wins the local lottery or has a
successful day at the races, the visitor might enjoy a
shopping trip to the elegant, austere **Comme des Garçons** (116 Wooster Street), **Yohji Yamamoto** (103 Grand
Street), or **Matsuda** (465 Park Avenue, 156 Fifth Avenue),

all of which feature expensive, extreme, avant-garde designs from Japan.

Finally, the man whose sartorial style was fixed for all time during his freshman year at the University of Wisconsin circa 1968 (or the University of London, or Sydney, or the Sorbonne) will find everything he requires down among the canteens, gas masks, and goggles at the **Army & Navy Stores** (221 East 59th Street and other branches) or at **Weiss and Mahoney** (142 Fifth Avenue at 19th Street).

Children's Fashions

The fairly recent but undeniably virulent national obsession with childbirth, babies, and their attendant requirements has spawned a serious increase in the number of stores serving small persons in Manhattan. Wee shops with teensy, adorable names are springing up all over, and autos with Baby on Board signs trudge from the East River to the Hudson and back in search of the perfect snowsuit and the most elegant bunny pajamas.

If you are travelling with a child or know one at home you'd like to buy something for, you will soon find that the New York kiddie market divides itself into two distinct branches: one approximating the taste of the (pre–Fergie and Di) British royal family—a lot of tartan plaid, velvet collars, and patent-leather Mary Janes—and its polar opposite, a sort of 1960s redux, with the prevailing themes being tie-dyed or painted tee-shirts and bib overalls.

Those shopping for the former style should visit **Liberty of London** (630 Fifth Avenue), where printed smocked dresses with round collars and sashes are available for fruity little girls. **Cerutti** (807 Madison Avenue between 67th and 68th streets) has French and Italian items as well as things from England, and will suitably accoutre the luckless little pretender to one or another royal throne. The unpronounceable **Swantje-Elke** (1031 Lexington at 74th Street) sells similar items, albeit slightly less conventional and conservative. Readers who resent spending a week's wages on an outfit consisting of a quarter-yard of fabric should stop down at **Klein's of Monticello** (105 Orchard Street), where heavily discounted, high-toned European children's clothes have been available for years.

Converts to the Woodstock school of children's fashion will find diminutive hipster clothing at **Space Kiddets** (46 East 21st Street). **Dinosaur Hill** (302 East 9th Street) is a preeminent tee-shirt source, and **Peanut Butter & Jane** (617 Hudson Street between 12th and Jane streets) will outfit a child appropriately for West Village life. Miniature Bianca Jaggers, who wear baby Maud Frizons and seek outfits to match, may like the selection at **Bebe Thompson** (98 Thompson Street in SoHo).

Finally, if the child in question lacks only a set of horns and a tail to make his true character known, if this small person is driving you to the hotel balcony where you sip what you claim is your last gasp of Champagne and make threatening promises to the pedestrians below, attempt to mollify your tormentor (at least temporarily) with the gift of a kiddie Ninja suit, available from **Bok Lei Tat Trading Co.** (213 Canal Street).

PHOTOGRAPHY AND FILMMAKING

By Stephen R. Ettlinger

Stephen R. Ettlinger is a free-lance picture editor and photography consultant in New York City, and is also an independent book producer. He was formerly associate picture editor at GEO *magazine, and is currently an editor of* Photo Opportunity. *His most recent photo book project is* Vietnam: The Land We Never Knew, *by Geoffrey Clifford.*

Visual artists of all stripes from all over the world make pilgrimages to New York City to do business, and thousands work, study, and live here. The main draw to the city for professional photographers is the concentration of major advertising agencies, magazines, and publishing companies. An editorial photographer from out of town may spend a week here, making appointments to see as many as six editors in a day at such publications as *Time, Life, Newsweek, Vogue, GQ, Connoisseur,* and the like. He or she may stop in to see any of the major photo agencies, all of which also have their headquarters here: Magnum, Gamma-Liaison, Contact, Woodfin Camp, Comstock, Im-

age Bank, Freelance Photographers Guild, Photo Research-
ers, Associated Press, Bettmann Archives, and so on. The
attendant organizations and associations are also here.
There is no reason why a professional or even a devoted
follower of photography could not stop in at any of these
places to at the very least absorb some of the atmosphere.

There is not one main street or neighborhood for
filmmakers, though groups of them are found in SoHo,
TriBeCa, and the East Village, and a concentration of
services is found near the television studios in the West
40s and 50s. However, photographers have definitely developed something akin to their own neighborhood,
called the **Photo District**, anchored by the venerable
Flatiron Building at Fifth Avenue and 23rd Street. Among
the city's first skyscrapers, it was the location of a 1905
movie featuring the wind blowing women's skirts up in
a revealing way. This windy locale gave birth to the
phrase "23 skiddoo." Warren Beatty found it a perfect
1902 setting for Diane Keaton's New York City arrival in
the film *Reds*. Although there are no official borders, the
consensus is that the Photo District extends from 23rd
Street to 14th Street and from Park Avenue South to
Sixth Avenue.

The area has been home to advertising and fashion
photographers for years because of its commercial loft
buildings and low rents. Recently, following the usual
pattern of gentrification, rents and purchase prices have
skyrocketed, forcing new photographers to look elsewhere for living or studio space, while professional-
oriented stores and labs, on the other hand, have moved
into the area. In fact, the equipment-rental business is
growing rapidly in the area, which is good news for a
visiting photographer: Everything from the studio to
the camera can be rented. Some of the upward pressure
on rents has been generated by the arrival of several
major advertising agencies and publishers, who have
taken over large loft buildings in the district after total
renovations.

Photographers themselves are not as much in evidence in the streets of the Photo District as are the
businesses that serve them. Beyond the obvious labs
(the more established ones occupy entire buildings and
have reception areas buzzing with messengers, assistants, and students—all displaying the latest in street fashion) are more traditional businesses that have adapted
to serve their photographic neighbors. Antiques stores

have signs in the windows proclaiming that their goods are available as rental props, and a plethora of gourmet stores cater photo shoots.

For some reason there are not any famous, traditional photographers' hangouts in the area, though if anything comes close it would be the **Old Town Bar** at 45 East 18th Street, a resolutely dark, dingy, and inexpensive place that has vociferously resisted any attempts at gentrification. The owner has gone so far as to post signs in his dirty window that say his place is not for sale to any well-dressed developers (earlier signs used to say, "Don't stare at the artists," etc.). It is one of the few spots that regular photographers and assistants can afford. Nearby there are some elegant restaurants that cater to visiting art directors or celebrated photographers, but this clientele is apparently quite fickle, as the hot spots rise up in glory and go out of business in a flash with astounding regularity. Only one place has tried a definite photo orientation complete with ongoing displays of photography: **Portfolio Restaurant and Gallery**, 4 West 19th Street. The real action in the district is in the labs and photo stores concentrated around West 19th and 20th streets.

It is fitting that New York City would have a major museum devoted solely to photography: the **International Center of Photography** (ICP), 1130 Fifth Avenue at 94th Street, and a Midtown branch at 1133 Sixth Avenue at 43rd Street. Between the two locations ICP hosts about 20 major shows each year, accompanied by crowded and jolly opening celebrations (be sure to ask when the next one is). Photographers tend to work alone, and the editors and agents seem to have been colleagues since whenever they started in the business, so the openings smack of reunions. ICP offers a full program of courses, workshops, and lectures, all of which are open to the passing traveller.

Two other major museums, the **Museum of Modern Art** and the **Metropolitan Museum of Art**, have excellent photo exhibitions. MoMA's permanent collection is one of the most important for any photographer to see, and the bookstore's selection supplements the experience.

In order to find out what's happening here, photographers can turn to a local monthly of some renown, *Photo District News*. (Filmmakers rely on the national paper *Variety*.) *PDN* is distributed free at various labs and photo stores, or may be had at the publication's offices, 49 East 21st Street. The classified ads would be of help to anyone planning a prolonged stay and in need of free-lance assistant work or a studio to rent.

Films and Filmmaking

Film buffs need not look far in New York to find satisfaction: There are dozens of theaters and spaces showing absolutely every kind of film made, from the most experimental avant-garde to the most cherished classics. Listings are easily found in daily and weekly magazines such as *The New York Times,* the *Village Voice* (new issues on Wednesday), *New York* magazine, and *The New Yorker.* The Sunday *New York Times,* which is available around 11:00 P.M. Saturday evening, always has thorough reviews and news of festivals.

One of the best places to see the widest range of classics, including a good number of silent films, is at the **Museum of Modern Art**, which has a regular program (Tel: 212-708-9490 for the daily features). Through MoMA's Film Study Center, the complete archive and film library is open to qualified students and scholars who write in advance for an appointment in a private screening room.

The New York Public Library shows and circulates films, mostly from the comprehensive **Donnell Library** Media Center, across from MoMA (at 20 West 53rd). The Donnell Library is one of the more relaxed and yet complete branches in the city, excellent for someone in need of a convenient Midtown office for a few hours. The **Performing Arts Library at Lincoln Center** (111 Amsterdam Avenue) does not circulate films but has an amazing collection of books on cinema, clippings, periodicals, memorabilia of all kinds, posters, and a reference service at the Billy Rose Theater Collection that is open to all but is a particular boon to film scholars. They even have a catalog of film memorabilia from which you can call up items.

Each September and October there are two film festivals of note: the **New York Film Festival**, with the subgroupings of the New Directors series, and the **Independent Feature Project Market**, which also includes workshops and is oriented toward low-budget films, including documentaries. Well-known pros often participate in workshops at New York Women in Film (Tel: 212-512-8022). The New York University filmmaking, video, and broadcasting studies department at the School of Continuing Education, 50 West 4th Street, Tel: (212) 998-7140, offers weekend workshops as well.

While most people link Hollywood with the origins of filmmaking, it all started back East. In fact, New York claims as many movie landmarks as Los Angeles. This is in part because Thomas A. Edison invented the whole idea in nearby West Orange, New Jersey; his laboratory and home is now a national park most definitely worth a pilgrimage (Tel: 201-736-5050). The first westerns were shot in New Jersey. These days movie and television productions bring New York almost $3 billion yearly in gross revenue, and a major studio, the Kaufman/Astoria Studios, has just reopened in Queens. Its clients past and present range from D. W. Griffith to Woody Allen. The city even has a one-stop department devoted to assisting filmmakers with permits and resources. The Mayor's Office of Film, Theatre and Broadcasting at 254 West 54th Street issues permits overnight and arranges for the police film unit to coordinate traffic and control bystanders during chase or fire scenes. They keep lists on hand of locales, such as a penthouse apartment overlooking rooftops that give a 1930s feeling, or the one place in Manhattan where you can walk directly into a river (under the George Washington Bridge).

Filmdom has its own brand-new museum in New York City: the **Museum of the Moving Image**, located within the studio complex at 35th Avenue and 36th Street in the Astoria section of Queens, near the 59th Street Bridge. Unique in this country, it is a wonderful blend of education and entertainment and contains a small theater, a large screening room, and special and permanent exhibits on both the art and the business of movie and TV-show making. (See the Queens Neighborhood section for directions.)

BOOKSTORES

The Drama Bookshop, 723 Seventh Avenue; the **Gotham Book Mart**, 41 West 47th Street; and the **Theatre Arts Bookshop**, 405 West 42nd Street, all go beyond film into theatrical work. **Applause Cinema Books**, 100 West 67th Street (near Lincoln Center and ABC Studios), is an excellent place to find elusive screenplays. Mainline art bookstores such as **Rizzoli** (main store at 31 West 57th Street) are good, too, but the best is probably the **New York University Bookstore**, 18 Washington Place, which supports all the courses in film theory and the like at their famous film school.

A Photographers Place, in SoHo at 133 Mercer Street,

not only has a huge selection encompassing damaged bargains and old classics, but also has a regular mail-order catalog. Some antique paraphernalia is displayed, along with occasional shows. They will also search out a rare title for you on request. The **ICP** bookstore at 94th Street and Fifth Avenue has one of the city's most complete selections of contemporary work as well as related texts and technical books. Their Midtown store, at 1133 Sixth Avenue at 43rd Street, is more limited. Both feature photographer appearances from time to time, although at any time uptown you may find the photographer of the very book you are perusing looking over your shoulder—a good place to keep your criticisms to yourself.

Both the Met and MoMA have photo books for sale, but MoMA's selection is broader. Surprise bargains as well as regular discounts are found at both **Barnes & Noble** bookstores across the avenue from each other at Fifth Avenue at 18th Street, as well as at the nearby venerable secondhand store, **Strand** (828 Broadway at 12th Street). A newer store, **Untitled II**, across from New York University at 680 Broadway, has a growing reputation among serious photo-book collectors.

PHOTOGRAPHY AND FILM SHOPPING

While there are no guides to New York City for photography buffs, there is something that is sort of a major photographers' Rollodex in book form, listing every conceivable potential supplier of goods or services to photographers: the *Professional Photo Source*. Available at a number of photography industry vendors in the Photo District for $12.95, it is also available by phone or mail order from 568 Broadway, New York, NY 10012; Tel: (212) 219-0993. There are 350 headings ranging from acrylic ice to walkie-talkies, including dealers specializing in various categories of cameras, such as "collectible" or "panoramic." The ads in *Photo District News* are also a decent guide (their articles are useful as well).

A concentration of large department-store-type camera stores developed in the early postwar period around Macy's, and some are still there. However, bargains take considerable digging to find, and little advice is given. The better stores, concentrated in the Photo District, include the ultimate bargain places as well as those that may not offer the best prices but make up for that considerably with personal advice, equipment loans, and excellent service. In those you will be rubbing shoulders with

a professional crowd. A good number of places are open
seven days a week (some close on Saturday but open on
Sunday), and weeknights until quite late, some until midnight. Most advertise in *PDN* or are listed in *Professional
Photo Source*. They attract an international clientele.

For the quintessential New York purchasing experience, two places stand out. **Gould Trading**, 41 Union
Square West, Room 225, is found at the end of a long,
dark corridor in a very dingy building. If they don't have
what you want, with a little cajoling they'll find it for you
through their network of dealer friends. (They are especially good with used Nikon equipment.) They'll also pay
cash for your own equipment. Bargaining is a way of life
here. Gould also makes excellent, inexpensive 35-mm
duplicate slides and sells film in bulk at a terrific discount. Similar in atmosphere is **Adorama**, 42 West 18th
Street, with old gadgets piled side by side with the latest
Zeiss attachments. At both places it helps to have a good
idea of what you want before entering, as neither has a
display area for wandering. It is more like a bar where
you belly up and order.

The **Lens & Repro Equipment Corporation**, 33 West
17th, is noted for its large selection of used and new
large-format cameras, including a Japanese brand made
of ebony and its own brand. Amazingly, they have a
selection of the rare handmade Deardorfs. **Ken Hansen
Photographic**, 920 Broadway at 21st Street, is more or
less the Leica king, though he has a full range of other
equipment and a huge lighting equipment display. But
Hansen prides himself more on the personal service
angle of the business, actually publishing the names of his
salesmen in his ads, and having many telephone lines so
clients can make appointments if they so desire.

Hasselblad maniacs will find therapy at **Gil Ghitelman
Cameras**, 166 Fifth Avenue, especially if they are looking
for trades. **Olden Camera**, 1265 Broadway between 31st
and 32nd, is favored by students, which keeps the place
lively in a pleasant way, and Olden carries a wide range of
lines, including used equipment.

Every photographer has his favorite laboratory, but for
quick service of all kinds the larger labs do an excellent
job. **K & L** (222 East 44th Street), **Ken Lieberman** (118
West 22nd Street), and **Duggal Color Projects** (9 West
20th Street) will do virtually anything you can think of,
any way you want it. Duggal actually has an entire building and is something like the hub of the Photo District.

The outfit is owned by a legendary Indian who has helped many of his countrymen immigrate, and they have in turn left to start their own smaller custom labs: Baboo, L & I, and Tony (acronym for "To New York," the only English this man knew when he came here). They are all very aggressive marketers, operating 24 hours a day, and anxious to please. K & L is in a building that houses services for the video and film industries as well.

Rentals

Photographics Unlimited, at 17 West 17th Street, rents not only equipment but darkrooms as well, both color and black-and-white, and has something of a Woodstock-era feel to it.

Professionals in the Photo District tend to rent equipment at **Ken Hansen** (920 Broadway at 21st Street; especially good for lighting), **Lens & Repro** (33 West 17th), **Photo Marketplace** (11 West 20th), **Foto-Care** (170 Fifth Avenue), and **Profoto** (128 West 31st Street), which is actually a branch of a Hamburg store.

Probably the most amusing place to visit is **The Set Shop**, at 37 East 18th Street. Set Shop has one of the biggest and most cluttered bulletin boards, a direct line on the doings of the district, but, more importantly, has a superb display of foam-rubber rocks, plastic ice cubes, and rubber fish that fill out its line of props. They have a complete catalog, too, which includes backgrounds, building supplies, studio equipment, and all kinds of gadgets undoubtedly useful in all the visual or theatrical arts. **The Camera Mart, Inc.**, at 456 West 55th, rents any movie- or TV-related items you may need, whether for the usual use or as a prop.

Repairs

For years, the pros have all gone to **Professional Camera Repair Service** at 37 West 47th Street.

SHOPPING FOR PHOTOGRAPHY IN GALLERIES

New York City supports a wonderful range of galleries that show photography on a more or less regular basis, and you can easily buy pictures from day one of the medium to the absolute cutting edge. Many of the leading painting galleries show the latest "in" photographers, generally one with connections in the fashion or advertising world, and these would be featured in the standard gallery listings (see Art section). (Galleries are usually open Monday to Saturday from 10:00 or 11:00 A.M. to 5:00 or 6:00 P.M.)

Collectors who are interested in experimental work of both early and contemporary 20th-century photographers from both sides of the Atlantic and Latin America should visit **Lieberman & Saul**, at 155 Spring Street at West Broadway. They are credited among dealers as having some of the most exciting work in the city in this small space, though not in a style that attracts mainstream media attention. For example, a recent show featured portraits of Jean Cocteau.

Mid-century American work in the tradition of the Farm Security Administration and the Esso Collection is found across the street at **Photofind**, 138 Spring Street. Their emphasis is on reportage—modern for them means Robert Frank.

No doubt the gallery the farthest off the beaten track belongs to dealer Alan Klotz, who holds a very personal European-style salon in his Upper West Side apartment. His **Photocollect Gallery**, at 740 West End Avenue between 96th and 97th streets, features vintage 19th- and early 20th-century quality work, ranging from $200 to $20,000 in price. Although he maintains regular gallery hours, a phone call is recommended in case he has just dashed off to make a new acquisition; Tel: (212) 222-7381. A close second to Photocollect in terms of being small and personal is **The Union Square Gallery**, 32 Union Square East, which is photographer Todd Weinstein's studio. On Fridays and Saturdays he packs all his gear into his darkroom, hangs some terrific work, and sets up a table with wine and cheese in the hallway. His neighbors are his biggest fans.

The more expensive work of living and dead greats, such as Irving Penn and Brassaï, can usually be found in the main art gallery area at the **Marlborough Gallery**, 40 West 57th Street. Current stars are often exhibited at the **Pace/MacGill Gallery**, 32 East 57th Street, as are well-known painter-photographers.

The **Witkin Gallery**, at 415 West Broadway, is probably the most prominent of the commercial galleries featuring work by the best contemporary photographers, and it also sells a good selection of photo books. Openings are well attended by noted critics, writers, and, of course, photographers. **Ledel** and **Marcuse Pfeifer** are two other galleries showing consistently good work.

Probably the most exciting place to buy photography is at one of the auction houses. Four major houses organize among themselves to present a series of auctions for one week in late October or early November, and again in early May. The Friday and Sunday editions of *The New York Times* are the best places to see what is being offered. The venerable houses of **Christie's** (502 Park Avenue at 59th Street; Tel: 212-546-1000) and **Sotheby's** (1334 York Avenue on the East Side at 72nd Street; Tel: 212-606-7000) usually have the largest number of items, but often **Phillips** and **Swann Galleries** have excellent items for sale. Sales at these places are usually confined to three-hour sessions, and their expensive catalogs are very well produced. There is much greeting and cooing among the small group of dealers who find themselves moving from one seasonal event to another.

CLASSICAL MUSIC

By Matthew Gurewitsch

Matthew Gurewitsch is a senior editor at Connoisseur *magazine, specializing in the performing arts. He has written about music and dance for* Opus, The New York Times, Vogue, Opera News, The Wall Street Journal, *and other publications.*

In the late 1980s, a wild spirit haunted New York in the person of a gaunt, scruffy pianist with unsmiling eyes who turned up (usually after dark, usually near a brick-strewn vacant lot on the east side of Broadway south of the 1960s monumental architecture of Lincoln Center) to bang out Liszt, Chopin, and Tchaikovsky above the din of the street. A tin can—he did not deign to pass it—stood at the ready for collections. As urban surrealism, nothing quite matched the sight of him dragging his instrument to work of an evening through Amsterdam Avenue's pre-theater gridlock or dragging it back home-ward after midnight. The ruin of a fabulously ornate upright, decked out with candelabra and inky gorgons and mounted on casters, it followed him on a chain like a domesticated dragon. Making a living at music in this city takes nerve, resolve, and invention. What has become of that roving pianist is anybody's guess, but his memory has not faded. He was a heraldic device come to life.

Close to curtain time every day of the week, in buses and subways, you encounter other musicians en route to their jobs: men of all ages, lacking only bow ties to complete their evening dress, negotiating luggage in the telltale shapes of cellos and horns, or, more discreetly, attaché cases; women in long dresses and sneakers wrestling harps. A glance at their datebooks would confirm that, like our street player, they have to cobble together the existence that suits them. Artistic and economic necessities require it, even of the musicians with the greatest job security.

Thus, many principal players with the New York Philharmonic, with multiple-season contracts running 12 months a year, double as faculty at the Juilliard School, across 65th Street from Avery Fisher Hall. Regular players in such busy Manhattan-based ensembles as the self-conducting chamber orchestra Orpheus or the Orchestra of St. Luke's free-lance regularly, in accord with their private interests, with groups dedicated to early or contemporary music. Some switch-hit as soloists (as in another country the flutist James Galway did before cutting loose from the Berlin Philharmonic) or establish trios or quartets. The studious-looking international crowd of children, adolescents, and young adults who disappear into Juilliard each morning are headed for careers checkered in just this fashion. The most precocious among them are already on the circuit.

The Musical Places

Though guidebooks for travellers usually don't mention it, the **Juilliard School** is well worth the musical visitor's attention. What with recitals by students and faculty, concerts by student orchestras (often with students or illustrious recent graduates as soloists), master classes, and fully staged productions of operas both familiar and rare, the school offers more than 300 performances a year. Quality, as you might expect, varies; at best, it is superb. Prices, as you might also expect, are low (often, admission is free). And the Juilliard Theater, though obscurely situated—the entrance is from a dark underpass on 65th Street—is

Manhattan's only opera house built on a human scale. (It seats 933, comfortably and with good sight lines.) For information, consult the billboards by the bus stop on the west side of Broadway between 65th and 66th streets, or call the concert office; Tel: (212) 874-7515.

Lincoln Center for the Performing Arts, of which Juilliard is a constituent, boasts the city's highest concentration of stages for music. At the center's epicenter is a fountain: a black marble circle enclosing vertical jets of water whose play, in its abstract fashion, is as ecstatic as any of the Baroque cascades of Rome. But in the summer, it, too, has been covered to double as a platform. Around the fountain spreads a rectangular plaza, bounded on three sides by grandly scaled houses for opera, dance, and concerts: **New York State Theater** (2,737 seats), with its soothing gleam, shared by the New York City Opera and the New York City Ballet; the plush, crystal-studded **Metropolitan Opera House** (3,718 seats); and **Avery Fisher Hall** (2,738 seats), articulated like the inside of a cream-colored accordion, home to the New York Philharmonic. Add to these the open-air band shell of **Damrosch Park** at the southwest corner of Lincoln Center; **Alice Tully Hall** (1,096 seats), in the same building as Juilliard and to the north of Avery Fisher, built for the Lincoln Center Chamber Music Society; and impromptu outdoor spaces devised for free summer events—and it is hard to imagine that you would ever need to look elsewhere for musical enjoyment.

And to an extent, that is now true. Time was when the New York music scene was divided neatly into "uptown" and "downtown." Uptown meant little beyond mainstream classics from the Continent, a canon closed, after several largely wasted decades, when Richard Strauss finished his "Four Last Songs" and laid down his pen. Downtown meant the esoteric John Cage, pixieish guru for the few, heard in cellars, lofts, and assorted holes-in-the-wall; then it meant the minimalists from Terry Riley through Steve Reich and Philip Glass, who after a quiet start have entranced multitudes. Since have come fast-rising children of the tape age from A (Anderson, Laurie) to Z (Zorn, John).

In the late 1960s, downtown found its temple across the river, at the Brooklyn Academy of Music, whose success has been so phenomenal as to create demand for its artists where else but uptown? And Lincoln Center has come through, scheduling special events and even whole series (like the recent summertime creation "Serious Fun!") designed not to hurt a bit.

Carnegie Hall, a short walk away from Lincoln Center at 57th Street and Seventh Avenue, cannot compete for sheer quantities of programming, but after all, how many concerts can you attend at once? And it is still the incomparable prestige address. Since its construction in 1891, it has ranked not only as the nation's premier concert hall but as the concert hall's Platonic ideal. (You've heard the story: A man stops a man with a violin case on a New York street corner. "How do I get to Carnegie Hall?" asks the first. "Practice!" comes the reply. It has been correctly observed that the punch line is really the set up. Substitute any other concert hall and there is no joke.)

In 1986 the main hall (2,784 seats) was sumptuously refurbished, and so was the smaller space upstairs then known as Carnegie Recital Hall and since rechristened the **Weill Recital Hall** (268 seats). The public heard many assurances beforehand that the fabled warm acoustics, traditionally equaled only by the Amsterdam Concertgebouw, Boston's Symphony Hall, and the Vienna Musikvereinsaal, would be preserved intact. At the reopening, it was instantly apparent that the sound had changed—and few listeners indeed thought it had changed for the better.

Most agree that the hall has become brighter, colder, more space-age, more aggressive. Some have wondered whether the impression originates in what amounts to an optical illusion: Now that all the dowdy gray drapes and tacky screens have been removed from the stage area (and now that the palette has gone to ivory, rose, and gold, and the ushers have been outfitted by Ralph Lauren), Carnegie Hall certainly *looks* brighter, in a Postmodern-retro way. Nevertheless, experiments with acoustic panels and other fine tuning have begun and are bound to continue for years. So is the bickering among the experts. Meanwhile, a time-honored flaw in the hall remains: The rumble of the subway is still plainly audible.

Since the departure of the New York Philharmonic to Lincoln Center in 1962, Carnegie Hall has had no resident orchestra. However, the symphonies of Boston, Philadelphia, and other major American cities provide continuity with their regular seasons there. In addition, the hall produces and presents dozens of series with leading international artists. On dates when the hall does not have plans of its own, it is available for rental, which will explain the presence of a decidedly second- or third-tier attraction from time to time. The monthly schedule, available at the box office, is color-coded to distinguish the rentals from Carnegie Hall's own offerings, which can give the critical concertgoer a useful signal when confronted with unfamiliar names. Book especially warily at Weill Hall, a venue much favored for once-in-a-lifetime vanity recitals. But here, too, Carnegie Hall as an institution grows more ambitious with each passing season.

So far, the talk has mostly been of the big venues. For more intimate material—solo recitals or chamber music—there are many smaller spaces, too, frequented faithfully by all but the hugest box-office stars. You would not expect to encounter Jessye Norman or Dietrich Fischer-Dieskau at the **92nd Street Y**, on upper Lexington Avenue, for instance, but Elly Ameling and Hermann Prey are regulars. The **Metropolitan Museum of Art**, for its part, has long presented, in its **Grace Rainey Rogers Auditorium**, such internationally acclaimed artists as the Guarneri String Quartet, the Beaux Arts Trio, and Les Arts Florissants.

The Frick Collection, ten blocks down Fifth Avenue from the Metropolitan Museum, retains its character of a connoisseur's private mansion and boasts—apart from a glorious assemblage of paintings—a fine music room, where late-afternoon concerts are held once or twice a month. Important performers appear here with minimal fanfare. No advance notices are published in the newspapers, but the concerts are broadcast on WNYC radio, and the audience is often extremely distinguished. Tickets are free with admission to the museum, but the procedure for obtaining them is Byzantine to the point of impossibility. For information on dates, phone (212) 288-0700. To get in, queue up a half hour or so before the concert and hope for the best. Your patience is likely to be rewarded; there are always plenty of no-shows. One more tip on high-class, free concerts: From October to June, the radio station **WNCN** broadcasts hour-long recitals each Tuesday at 8:00 P.M. A live studio audience attends. For information and reservations, call (212) 730-9629.

If you enjoy music in beautiful surroundings, you should know that the **Metropolitan Museum of Art** offers performances not only in the Grace Rainey Rogers Auditorium, which has no cachet, but also in its Medieval Sculpture Hall, the Temple of Dendur, the Velez Blanco Patio, and elsewhere—as well as at the Funtedueña Chapel at **The Cloisters**, its bastion of Medieval art, surrounded by rambling Fort Tryon Park at the northern tip of Manhattan. Often the performances at the Cloisters coincide with church holidays; they almost always have a deliberately archaic cast. (To get to the Cloisters, take the uptown-bound A train to 190th Street and Overlook Terrace, exit by elevator, and walk through the park; or hop the M 4 bus marked "Fort Tryon Park, The Cloisters." The bus comes up from lower Manhattan via Madison Avenue, but it is a waste of several hours to take it from points downtown or Midtown.)

The **Museum of Modern Art** has adapted the Cloisters' example in its own way, offering end-of-summer concerts of small-scale 20th-century works amid the Nadelmans, Maillols, Picassos, and Oldenburgs in the outdoor sculpture garden. Splendid artists appear in imaginative programs. Alas, this is Midtown, and the urban racket intrudes. Ambient noise is a problem in **Central Park**, too, where the New York Philharmonic and the Metropolitan Opera—heavily amplified—play beneath the stars and the airplanes and the mosquitos to the picnicking multitudes on various midsummer nights.

The **Brooklyn Academy of Music**, better known as BAM, has already been cited in passing for its role in legitimizing downtown music. In the process, it has turned itself into something very like the Alternative Lincoln Center, housing under a single roof the festive Opera House (2,085 seats), a well-proportioned playhouse (1,011 seats), and a black box, reconfigurable any which way, called the **Lepercq Space** (seating 350 to 550). In addition, BAM has recently refurbished the Majestic Theater (875 seats), a dilapidated former vaudeville house several blocks closer to Manhattan, enshrining its very disrepair.

All of BAM's auditoriums serve many muses, notably the muses of music and dance. The **Next Wave Festival**, held each autumn, juxtaposes ground-breaking American work with adventurous work from abroad. Thanks to the festival's enduring success, BAM is associated above all with the commercially viable avant-garde. In the future, BAM may be equally famous for its contributions in opera. Plans call for importing front-line productions from innovative companies outside New York, for mounting challenging productions of lesser-known, smaller-scale pieces, and for commissioning new works. As of 1991, the Metropolitan Opera will be BAM's partner in this venture. In the meantime, BAM has gotten off to a roaring start, and certainly, operatic New York, notorious for its conservatism, desperately needs the shot of creativity.

All the BAM theaters are easily accessible by subway. From Manhattan, take the Broadway express lines (numbers 2 or 3) or the less-circuitous Lexington Avenue express (numbers 4 or 5) to Nevins Street for the Majestic; ride one stop farther, to Atlantic Avenue, for BAM proper. The Q, R, B, and N trains will also get you to BAM (though not to the Majestic) from Manhattan; the stop to look for on those lines is Pacific Street. Another convenient option is the BAM Bus, which departs from the Summit Hotel, Lexington Avenue and 51st Street, one hour before curtain time at the Opera House or the Majestic. On the way back the bus makes several stops, the first in Greenwich Village, the last on Broadway at 72nd Street. For BAM information, call (718) 636-4100.

One last tip for opera buffs and anyone else with a taste for musical theater not weighted down with convention: **Opera at the Academy**, at 419 Lafayette Street (next door to Joseph Papp's downtown bastion, the Public Theater, and developed under his benevolent eye), mounts two or three lively productions each season. The art-school quarters are spartan, the sensibility is European, and the audience is with it. Inventive reduced orchestrations and cheeky production values are the rule in this bohemian haunt, and the performances are sharp, meticulously rehearsed, and full of cross talk to concerns of the present day. If you're lucky enough to hit town when a show is on—and if the tiny house is not already fully booked—go. For information, Tel: (212) 677-8960.

Listings and Tickets

The Arts & Leisure section of the Sunday *New York Times* is indispensable for long-range planning, but for a visitor the weekly magazines and newspapers provide more helpful calendars. The best-organized listings are in *New York* magazine (see the Cue listings section). In "Goings on about Town" each week, *The New Yorker* prefaces its calendar information with a polished, very short essay on some event of special note and proceeds to give just the facts (but often not enough of them) about a reasonable selection of smaller events and all the majors. Following the music columns, *7 Days* magazine offers a similar overview, with capsule descriptions that attempt with mixed success to be a little more judgmental.

Each day, the **Bryant Park Ticket Booth**, on 42nd Street behind the New York Public Library, sells half-price tickets for music and dance events taking place that evening. The very hottest attractions (Bernstein and the Vienna Philharmonic, Solti and the Chicago) will not be represented, but many first-rate ones often are. Call (212) 382-2323 to find out what is on offer—and what the booth's hours are; they vary from day to day.

Apart from this booth, ticketing is mostly decentralized. All the leading institutions and most marginal ones will take ticket reservations over the phone and charge them to any of the standard array of credit cards. Such sales are final. When ordering by phone, it is usually impossible to find out exact seat locations (you are generally promised "best available" within the price range). Fussy patrons are advised to go to the box office, *Stubs* in hand. *Stubs,* available at magazine stands in the Broadway Theater District, contains seating plans for all but the smallest of the city's theaters and concert halls. Though these plans are posted at theaters and concert halls, they are usually posted too far from the box office to be of any use.

SHOPPING FOR MUSIC AND MUSICAL INSTRUMENTS

Not surprisingly, the prime shopping area for musical instruments is within a few steps' radius of Carnegie Hall. The **Steinway & Sons** showroom, at 109 West 57th Street, is an institution. **Jacques Français**, 250 West 54th Street, is the place to go for rare string instruments. Amatis, Guarneris, and Strads probably pass through here as frequently as anywhere else in the world. For the keyboardist of the future, the **Yamaha** showroom, 142 West 57th Street, is a must. Apart from conventional concert-quality grands, Yamaha has acoustic pianos with brains that allow you to correct mistakes, transpose, speed up, or slow down your live performance, and then to play it back (cleaned up) with no hands. Other Yamahas produce sound electronically so that, if the occasion requires, you alone, in headphones, can hear what you are up to. The top-of-the-line synthesizers are virtual symphony orchestras in a console, awaiting their New Age Beethoven. For band instruments, stroll down to West 48th Street between Sixth and Seventh avenues and browse.

Classical musicians shopping for scores head for **Patelson**, 160 West 56th Street, across from Carnegie Hall's stage door. The shop also stocks the city's best selection of books on classical music and musicians, and an interesting array of recordings. Another exclusive feature: The latest concert reviews from *The New York Times* (the only reviews in town that really matter) are pasted into a loose-leaf album by the door.

If you are after sheet music for show tunes, go to **Colony Records Center**, 1619 Broadway (at 49th Street), where the bossy sales help can probably set you up with whatever you want—even private tapes of musicals never commercially recorded.

SHOPPING FOR RECORDS

Compact discs are significantly cheaper in the United States than anywhere else, so it is not uncommon to see visitors from abroad loading up on them by the armful. For the latest classical releases (often issued here several months later than in Europe) the most reliable source is the **J & R Classical Outlet**, 33 Park Row, near City Hall. It is the store you can count on to order sufficient stock. Nevertheless, *the* name in this game is **Tower**, at two locations: 1965 Broadway, just north of Lincoln Center, and 692 Broadway (at 4th Street), downtown, in Greenwich Village. The downtown location has a more knowledgeable sales staff and a larger selection, though to find a specific title you may have to check both stores. For music lovers still interested in vinyl, an attraction at the downtown Tower is the sales annex, at 4th and Lafayette streets, where conventional LPs, cassettes, and even CDs are available at rock-bottom prices.

The LPs at **Gryphon Records**, 251 West 72nd Street, second floor, are often pricey, with good reason: They are collector's items. The pleasantly Dickensian emporium specializes in "Proudly Archival Sound," so audio fetishists will disapprove. But for anyone with a tolerance for a recently obsolete technology and an appreciation for historic performance, Gryphon is a gold mine. So is **G & A Rare Records Ltd.**, the new shop nearby at 139 West 72nd Street (another second-story outlet), which is a little sprucer to look at and charges more outlandish prices. Still, if they have what you've always been looking for. . . . Another stop for the serious collector of out-of-print records is the **Academy Book Store**, 10 West 18th Street— dusty, cramped, and full of surprises. **Footlight Records**, 113 East 12th Street, specializes in hard-to-find Broadway albums, movie sound tracks, big band music, jazz, country, and rock 'n' roll. For rare rock, drop in at **Midnight Records**, 255 West 23rd Street.

A word of caution: Examine all merchandise critically. While it is possible to find copies of fairly commonplace material in mint condition, many rarer items are decidedly worse for the wear. If you want to hunt further, consult the Yellow Pages of the Manhattan telephone directory under the heading "Records-Phonograph-Retail." Phone before travelling out of your way. Used-record shops are forever going out of business, as anyone who wants to sell used discs quickly discovers.

DANCE

By Joanna Ney

Joanna Ney is a free-lance writer specializing in dance. She was formerly dance critic for East Side Express *and* Other Stages. *She has contributed to* The New York Times, Cosmopolitan, Cue, *and* V. *She also reviews dance for WBAI radio.*

T he sheer quantity and diversity of dance in New York guarantee that there is something for the visitor to see at any given time of the year. Whether you crave the formality of classical ballet or the improvisational quality of performance art, you are likely to find it in an opera house or a loft. Once considered an exotic art reserved for a select coterie, dance now appeals to a much wider audience in New York.

At the heart of New York's dance explosion is the **Lincoln Center** complex, which includes the New York State Theater, the official home of New York City Ballet (NYCB), and the Metropolitan Opera House, which plays host to American Ballet Theatre, as well as to a variety of other major companies from around the world.

When Lincoln Center was built 25 years ago the neighborhood was a wasteland dotted with tenements. Today it is packed with restaurants, cafés, boutiques, and much frenetic activity. Strolling up Broadway from Columbus Circle to 79th Street, you can see famous dancers and ballet students making their daily rounds. Dancers are easy to spot, walking briskly in ballet's proverbial first position. Their favorite hangout is the Plaza Fountain at Lincoln Center; it takes on a movie-set glitter when illuminated at night.

New York City Ballet, the creation of Lincoln Kirstein and George Balanchine, has undergone major changes; last November, Lincoln Kirstein retired, and artistic director Jerome Robbins resigned to pursue personal projects, leaving Peter Martins as the sole artistic director. (The troop will present a retrospective of Robbins' ballets in the spring of 1990.) The company performs November through February and May through July, with December reserved for the perennial favorite, *The Nutcracker*. Traditionally, the company has stressed choreography, specifically that of George Balanchine, over a star system. Since Balanchine's death the company has faced an identity crisis, but the dancing, especially at the principal level, remains top-notch. NYCB also has its own professional school, the School of American Ballet, which gives dance lovers an opportunity to witness dancers in the making when it presents its annual spring workshop on the stage of the Juilliard School.

Although NYCB has many faithful subscribers, some tickets are usually available the day of performance, unless it happens to be a company premiere or a dancer's debut in a particular role. Even when a performance is sold out, balletomanes know that if they wait outside the theater before curtain time someone is likely to sell them a ticket.

Across the plaza, the imposing Metropolitan Opera House, with its gigantic Chagall murals and red and gold trappings, is the home of **American Ballet Theatre** (ABT), which from 1974 to September of last year was under the artistic direction of Mikhail Baryshnikov, who quit after a dispute with the company's management board. Until a new director is appointed, the company will be run by a triumverate of Jane Hermann, the recently appointed executive director; Oliver Smith, formerly co-artistic director with the late Lucia Chase; and John Taras, Baryshnikov's associate director. Formerly a star-studded glamour company, under Baryshnikov's aegis the ABT has become "Balanchinized" and now stresses ensemble dancing rather than star "turns." The company's corps de ballet is virtually unparalleled, and many exciting principals (for example, Susan Jaffe and Amanda McKerrow) have risen from its ranks. The repertory includes 19th-century classics such as *Swan Lake* as well as contemporary works by modernists such as Twyla Tharp and Paul Taylor, but thanks to *glasnost,* one of the Bolshoi's most exciting dancers, Andris Liepa, is on loan to ABT for a second year and adds some needed dazzle to its male contingent. It is difficult to predict how the company's artistic profile will change with Baryshnikov's departure, so keep an eye on repertory and dancers in the season to come.

When ABT is touring the Met has no shortage of other illustrious guests. Internationally renowned ballet companies that appear there include the Paris Opéra Ballet, run by Rudolf Nureyev; Denmark's Royal Ballet; Germany's Stuttgart; and the Soviet Bolshoi and Kirov. It is an ironic fact that the formerly insular Russians have given new life to American ballet, beginning with Balanchine's contribution and continuing with such present-day idols as Nureyev, Baryshnikov, and Natalia Makarova.

The Moorish-style **City Center**, at 131 West 55th Street, is another major showcase for both ballet and modern dance. At various times of the year you can catch the spirited **Joffrey Ballet**, now under the leadership of Gerald Arpino, who succeeded its late founder, Robert Joffrey; the **Alvin Ailey Company**, with its unique blend of modern, jazz, and blues arising out of the black experience; the classical **Dance Theater of Harlem** (led by NYCB alumnus Arthur Mitchell), which combines Neoclassicism with a flair for drama; and the twin masters of modern dance, **Paul Taylor** and **Merce Cunningham**. City Center is one of the most congenial dance spaces in the city and a favorite with dancegoers.

A newish addition to the dance scene is a former offbeat movie house converted into the **Joyce Theater**, at Eighth Avenue and 18th Street in the gentrifying Chelsea area. The Joyce offers works by established choreographers such as **Eliot Feld**, as well as many bold newcomers, all in an agreeably intimate setting. One of the pluses of the Joyce experience is the number of restaurants, both modest and chic, virtually on its doorstep. The Joyce season runs from September to May, and single performance tickets are often available.

Nearby, at 219 West 19th Street, is the **Dance Theater Workshop** (DTW), a haven for experimental dance. Up a narrow flight of stairs is the **Bessie Schönberg Theater**, a small, informal space with bleacherlike seating. Devotees don't mind the slight discomfort: DTW is known as a leading pioneer of new dance in the country. The theater is accompanied by an attractive gallery that presents solo art and photo exhibits.

The area between Park Avenue South and Broadway is fast becoming the new center for dance schools and dance companies. Alwin Nikolais and Murray Louis started this downtown trend in the 1970s when they moved their school and company headquarters to the area. Now they have converted a huge loft dance studio on the seventh floor of 38 East 19th Street into a lovely 100-seat theater, the **Nikolais and Louis Choreo Space**, perfect for small dance companies. The seats are well raked, and there is not a bad sight line in the house. Additional cushion seating on the floor is available for 20 people. The theater's schedule includes performances by many new and exciting dance companies, and the neighborhood is a hub of night life.

For the committed dancegoer, the **Brooklyn Academy of Music**, or BAM, as it is affectionately called, is a definite must. The main building has three theaters—the Opera House, the Carey Playhouse, and the smaller Lepercq Space. Bam's Majestic Theater is across the street. The turn-of-the-century Opera House is a spacious, beautifully appointed theater on whose stage appear some of the most exciting innovators in dance, performance art, and contemporary music. This is where you'll see the theater pieces of Robert Wilson and Pina Bausch and hear the work of Philip Glass and other minimalists.

BAM can be reached via the IRT subway line on the number 2 or 3 train on the West Side and the 4 or 5 on the East Side, as well as the Q, B, R, and N on the BMT line. The BAM stop for the IRT trains is Atlantic Avenue; for the BMT, Pacific Street. The BAM Manhattan Express Bus is an option available for events taking place at the Opera House and the Majestic Theater. It leaves Manhattan one hour prior to curtain time from the Summit Hotel at 51st Street and Lexington Avenue. On return it makes stops in the West Village, Midtown on the East Side, and the Upper West Side. For reservations and BAM information, Tel: (718) 636-4100, Monday to Friday 10:00 to 5:30; Saturday and Sunday on performance days, 12:00 to 3:00.

BAM has a concession area in the lobby where you can stave off hunger pangs with a hot or cold sandwich or salad and a cup of coffee or a soft drink. There is also a full bar. For something more leisurely try **Gage & Tollner** at 372 Fulton Street (a 15-minute walk from BAM; a dangerous excursion after dark). This old New York establishment has specialized in steaks, chops, and seafood since 1879. The dark wood paneling and colored glass lighting fixtures provide an authentic traditional flavor; Tel: (718) 875-5181 (closed Sunday). For a more informal, family-style restaurant you might choose **Junior's** at 386 Flatbush Avenue (Tel: 718-852-5257), known for its roast beef and brisket of beef and justly famous countrywide for its cheesecake.

Apart from the formal dance events, you can also experience New York's dance wave in many outdoor performances that take place all over the city in the summer. For basic information on all dance events, it's a good idea to check the listings in *The New York Times,* as well as the *Village Voice, The New Yorker,* and *7 Days.*

DANCE APPAREL AND EQUIPMENT

Capezio, in Greenwich Village at 177 MacDougal Street off 8th Street, is definitely the one-stop place to get outfitted for a dance studio or gym. Its dance shoe department on the second floor carries a full line of ballet, aerobic, character, and tap shoes. The salespeople are knowledgeable and helpful. The adjoining Dance Body Shop stocks every conceivable item you will need for a dance, exercise, or aerobics class. Styles range from traditional to the latest in spandex and decorated dancewear. The shop also carries socks, stockings, and lingerie. There are other Capezio stores in Manhattan: one at Steps Dance Studio at 2121 Broadway at 74th Street, and the big main branch at 755 Seventh Avenue at 50th Street (with a more hectic pace than the others).

For superior quality soft ballet shoes and pointe shoes there is also **Freed of London** at 922 Seventh Avenue at 58th Street. The footwear is of fine and durable leather. They also carry leotards, tights, and accessories. There are no bargains here, but the service is efficient and courteous.

On Stage, at 197 Madison Avenue between 34th and 35th streets, is a small dance apparel store nestled between the tall buildings of Madison Avenue, across the street from B. Altman. This store specializes in a full line of dancewear and carries all the major brands as well as the biggest selection of lycra and cotton leotards and tights in the city. Everything a dancer needs for class—dance bags, leg warmers, headbands, socks, and sports bras—is available here. The store also carries ballet, jazz, and tap shoes. Other pluses: The personnel are knowledgeable about correct fit and know their merchandise; the dressing room is well lit and ample for try-ons; leotards are arranged on hangers by color, so you can see at a glance what is in stock. Price range is in the medium to high category, but if you happen to find something in your size in the "sale basket" you've got yourself a real bargain.

Paragon Sporting Goods, 867 Broadway (between 17th and 18th streets), also has a section devoted to dancewear. Traditional styles are limited, and the emphasis is on the aerobic and jazzy types. You'll find the top sports lines—Avia and Nike—and a full line of Baryshnikov dancewear, including spandex tights and sweatpants. Another line, Marika, offers basically the same merchandise at lower prices.

DANCE MEMORABILIA AND COLLECTIBLES

The Ballet Shop at 1887 Broadway (at 63rd Street near Lincoln Center) is a one-of-a-kind establishment owned by Norman Crider, a former champion baton twirler and collector. For the past 16 years the shop has been on this site and managed by the knowledgeable Tobias Leibovitz and his assistant, Joe Marshall, a former ice skater. There is nothing these two don't know about *la danse*. Here you'll find rare prints and lithographs from the romantic era on, as well as out-of-print books, signed photographs, statuary dating back to the pre-1840 period of ballet, class records for ballet, modern, jazz, and tap, the largest video selection from technique to documentary performances, as well as the more mundane fare, such as tee-shirts and dance-related gift items. If you've been looking for an original signed Chagall sketch, a rare original Leon Bakst ballet design, or a 19th-century bronze statuette of Fanny Elssler, The Ballet Shop is likely to have it.

The Performing Arts Shop, underground at Lincoln Center, has a more limited and popular selection of items related to dance, such as tee-shirts, ceramic mugs, and books, records, and cassettes. Opera and music items are highlighted.

THE THEATER

By David Berreby

David Berreby is a member of the Outer Critics Circle. His work has appeared in the Village Voice, Ms., Diversion, *and* New York Newsday. *He reviews theater for* The New York Law Journal.

One late summer afternoon in Midtown Manhattan, a film crew was carefully choreographing an attractive couple, a mounted policeman, a dancer in pink pants wearing headphones, a hot-dog cart with its distinctive umbrella, great clouds of smoke from a dry-ice device, and, in the center of it all, a gleaming red Ferrari. A happy crowd watched the crew shoot take after take in the glow of theater marquees and immense neon signs, ignoring the honk and roar of passing traffic. Meanwhile, across the street, a posse of young break dancers gyrated to the beat of a powerful portable radio, while, a couple of blocks up, a rival group danced to a live drummer. A block up from *them,* a duo played show tunes on a bongo and a steel drum. The whole honking, drumming, banging, yelling chaos seemed to harmonize into a single purposeful scene, over which hovered the electronic headlines of the Times Tower (where the ball drops at New Year's) and a perpetually wheeling flock of irritated pigeons.

This is Times Square, where Seventh Avenue and Broadway meet to form the Crossroads of the World, as it was known in the 1920s. In many ways, the square and the blocks of the West 40s immediately adjacent still form the heart of New York. And, not coincidentally, the neighborhood is also the heart of New York's **Theater District**.

You need only a few minutes here to see how New York's essence is bound up with the theater. It's a fact of geography (the world's greatest concentration of theaters is here, just off Broadway in the center of the center of town). It's a fact of economics (drama is a major industry and tourist attraction). But more important, it's a fact of the spirit. Like the theater, New York City is high-class yet not entirely respectable; artistic yet crass; insular yet eager for attention and approval from outsiders. Perhaps that's the reason why when the city works, it acts like a well-choreographed show.

Of course, the Broadway Theater District (especially at its southern boundary, 42nd Street, and at Eighth Avenue) has its low-down, sleazy, and menacing blocks, where drugs and sex are sold. And it's also true that the cost of putting on a Broadway show nowadays is so immense that "Broadway" to many people stands for safe dull plays and homogenized international musicals imported from London. Nonetheless, this part of town remains the repository of the city's theatrical tradition, where you can have cheesecake at **Lindy's** on Broadway near 45th (a strictly Disney version of the original haunt of show biz, bootleggers, and wise guys immortalized by Damon Runyon), get in a gawk at **Sardi's** (234 West 44th), where opening-night parties are still held, and contemplate the Brill Building farther up on Broadway, where Kern and Gershwin once toiled.

The city has embarked on a multimillion-dollar office development plan to tone up the area. The neighborhood is already pocked with construction sites, and the lights may not stay as bright as the corporate towers go up. See it while you can.

Getting Tickets

Times Square is a good place to start hunting for a show to see, even if you've decided to skip the astonishingly high costs of Broadway, where the top ticket price is now $70. Many non-Broadway theaters are in the neighborhood, and it's easy to reach others from this central location.

The best way to cut your ticket expenses is to go to one of the booths where the Theatre Development Fund sells seats for Broadway and off-Broadway shows for *half price* (plus a $1.50 fee per ticket). The catch is you have to take what's available the same day you buy your ticket. There are three in the city, each marked with a big **TKTS** sign (it's pronounced "tickets," as in "I'll meet you on the tickets line"). The largest is right in Times Square, at 47th Street. It opens at 3:00 P.M. and doesn't close until curtain time, 8:00 P.M. (It's within sprinting distance of a number of theaters, and hence is still selling at three minutes to the hour.) On Wednesdays and Saturdays, when there are matinee performances at 2:00 P.M., the booths open at noon, close at curtain time, and reopen an hour later for the evening shows. Any show that isn't a sold-out hit will turn up on the TKTS listing of available shows. Naturally, you'll have a better chance (and a much shorter wait) if you go on a Tuesday or Wednesday rather than a Friday or Saturday, and the earlier you turn up, the better. (On Mondays, most theaters are "dark"—closed—so if you go then you'll have little to select from.) Count on waiting in line 30 minutes or so if you come midweek before people escape from their offices; it'll take longer if you arrive at, say, 6:30 P.M., or if you come on a weekend.

Unless the weather's bad, the Times Square TKTS line is not an unpleasant place to wait. You've got a perfect perch for watching Times Square go by, and you'll likely be approached by hawkers trying to interest you in less-than-sellout shows. Often, they'll offer you a "twofer"—a ticketlike slip that allows you to purchase two tickets for the price of one. You can then leave the line and go directly to the theater box office. (Twofers are also widely available in stores, hotels, and at offices of the New York Convention and Visitors Bureau on Columbus Circle and in Times Square.) Naturally, the more popular a show, the less likely it is that you'll find twofers for it.

If you hate to wait, the lines are generally shorter at the other TKTS booths: One, in the financial district, is in 2 World Trade Center (the south tower); the other is in Brooklyn Heights, at the foot of Montague Street in front of the state court building.

If the show you're living to see is sold out until next Christmas, you might consider forgoing a seat. Most Broadway houses sell standing room for a fraction of the usual ticket price; inquire at the box office. You can also get on line to buy last-minute cancellations (be early, though, because the cancellation line for a hit show will start to grow at least two hours before curtain time).

If you want to be sure of seeing one exact show on one exact date, you can always reserve with a ticket agent: **Golden and LeBlang** at 1501 Broadway, Tel: (212) 944-8910, for example, or **Hickey's** at 251 West 45th, Tel: (212) 586-2980. If you're staying in the area, your hotel can put you in touch with a ticket agency, too. Their nominal fees are set by law.

What to Look for

If you've arrived in New York without a show in mind, you can find listings for all major productions in *The New Yorker* or in *New York* magazine, both sold at newsstands. Shows are listed as "Broadway," "off-Broadway," and "off-off-Broadway"; knowing these categories can give you a good idea of what to expect.

"Broadway" is not really a geographic term (most Broadway theaters aren't on Broadway). Broadway is a type of contract, covering a big house, providing big salaries, and generally portending high ticket prices and a certain sumptuousness of staging that visitors expect from one of the city's premier tourist attractions. "Off-Broadway" contracts cover the kind of smaller productions that sprang up 25 years ago in reaction to Broadway's expense and conventionality. These days, though, off-Broadway itself is part of the mainstream. (Many off-Broadway shows are offered at TKTS.) Still, it's free of the immense financial pressures of Broadway, and it's less expensive (with a top ticket price of about $40 versus Broadway's $70). Off-Broadway in turn engendered off-off-Broadway—smaller, more experimental, more daring (in theory), and cheaper still. Many small off-off-Broadway shows are actually "showcases," in which the actors aren't paid at all, but play because it's a chance to do something professional and (you never know) the show might get discovered. Such plays may run only on weekends, take place in a church basement, and charge you a mere ten dollars, but they can be excellent theater, and they give you a chance to get off the beaten path.

Directly adjacent to the Broadway area is one of the city's happier urban renewal efforts, **Theater Row**. It's a long block of off-Broadway theaters and restaurants stretching from Ninth to Tenth avenues on 42nd Street. Here you can usually find something worth seeing—and a good meal. (It's also the site of the Manhattan Plaza Garage, which offers one of the lowest parking rates in the area.)

Elsewhere in the city, a number of off- and off-off-Broadway productions are sponsored by long-standing theatrical institutions with records of offering high-quality, interesting work. Perhaps the foremost of these is **The New York Shakespeare Festival**, founded and run by the legendary Joseph Papp, who produced *A Chorus Line, Pirates of Penzance,* and *The Mystery of Edwin Drood,* among other unconventional hits. In the 1960s Papp successfully overcame objections and won permission to stage free plays every summer in Central Park. Summer visitors can still enjoy free Shakespeare at the Delacorte Theatre in the park—but be warned: If the show's a hit, you should arrive in the late morning and spend the afternoon picnicking under the trees on line, until the 6:00 P.M. ticket distribution.

These days most of Papp's lively, often controversial productions of both classics and new works are to be seen indoors, at **The Public Theater**, 425 Lafayette Street near 8th Street/Astor Place. The huge building is a converted library that houses legitimate theaters and a movie house. Appropriately enough for a combative, controversial theater, nearby Astor Place is where, in 1849, a different theatrical *contretemps*—the fight between supporters of the American tragedian Edwin Forrest and fans of English actor William Macready—led to 31 deaths in the infamous Astor Place Riot. (New York theatergoers have always been passionately opinionated.)

Not far from Papp's empire is one of the most venerable avant-garde theater groups in the world, the **La MaMa Experimental Theater Company**, 74A East 4th Street, in the East Village. Founder Ellen Stewart's ideal is to create a genuine world theatrical community, and so La MaMa's offerings have ranged from Andrei Serban's stunning reinterpretation of the Trojan War to Eskimo drama performed by Eskimos (Stewart would have had pygmy dancers come, too, but the government of Zaire refused). Another bastion of innovation is **The Brooklyn Academy of Music**, 30 Lafayette Avenue, Brooklyn, where Ingmar Bergman, Peter Brook, Robert Wilson, Peter Sellars, and Laurie Anderson, among others, have presented their work. BAM, as it's known, has been many an experimentalist's ticket into the mainstream. It's the place to go to see work the year before everyone else learns about it. (See Classical Music or Dance for directions, or call BAM; Tel: 718-636-4100.)

Several other companies are worth seeking out. The **Circle Repertory Theater**, at 99 Seventh Avenue South, on Sheridan Square in Greenwich Village, was long the home company of Lanford Wilson and has presented many fine new American plays. **The Roundabout Theatre Company**, 100 East 17th Street, sticks staidly to classics and revivals, and does them well. The **Jean Cocteau Repertory**, 330 Bowery, likes to stage neglected works in its tiny theater on the city's traditional skid row. Performance art meets theater at **The Performing Garage**, 33 Wooster Street. **Mabou Mines** is an experimental troupe with a commitment to language as well as image. Headquartered at P.S. 122, a former public school at 150 First Avenue, they often perform elsewhere, and their work is worth hunting for in the listings. And finally, when you get fed up with the wonder of it all, go see **Forbidden Broadway**, a hilarious, constantly updated spoof of the theater scene and of the latest hits. After five years in a cabaret, it's now lodged at the Theater East, 211 East 60th Street.

Theatrical Hangouts

If you haven't gotten enough of the cast at the show, you can try to rub elbows afterward. Waiting at the stage door for an autograph is a venerable Broadway tradition, and well worth it if you have the patience. Not only could you meet your favorite performer, but you'll encounter a curious cast of regulars—autograph hunters and photographers—who live in a subculture all their own.

There are also a number of Theater District restaurants where you'll likely find actors unwinding after shows. If you want to go in comfort, **Orso**, at 322 West 46th (near Eighth Avenue) is a pleasant Italian restaurant where you might find the stars of major shows and visiting celebrities. Immortal Sardi's (see above) still gets its share of the prominent and would-be prominent. And **Café Madeleine**, at 43rd and Ninth Avenue, gets after-show clientele from both Broadway and Theater Row.

On the other hand, if you'd like to see how most actors really live, try **Barrymore's**, 267 West 45th (between Seventh and Eighth avenues), a large, dark bar where you'll see a lot of people wearing the nylon jackets emblazoned with logos that Broadway shows issue to their casts and crews. Nearby is **Charlie's Restaurant**, 705 Eighth Avenue between 44th and 45th, another good bet. Neither of these will send you to gastronomic nirvana, but you won't get ptomaine either, and you'll be seeing life as it's lived by the majority of actors (or at least actors who are working—to see life as it's lived by most New York actors, you'd have to go to an unemployment line or become a waiter).

Finally, if you're not satisfied to see the show, wear the sweatshirt, buy the album, get the autograph, and eat next to one of the cast, you can always follow the actors home. The M 104 bus goes up Eighth Avenue to the Upper West Side, haunt of many actors (though fewer these days, since rents have skyrocketed). The Seventh (numbers 1, 2, and 3) and Eighth (A, B, C, and D) Avenue subways are the closest to Theater Row and Broadway. Between 11:30 P.M. and 1:00 A.M. these public conveyances bear many actors (looking incongruous without their makeup, costumes, and stage auras) back to their homes. Try not to stare.

THEATER BOOKS AND MEMORABILIA

Many a city has theaters, but New York has a theater culture. With a little effort, you can find a 1964 Broadway poster, a book on Kabuki, or the script of the new play you saw last night. The city's major bookstores have well-stocked drama sections, but the best place to start hunting (especially for a new play) is in one of the bookstores that cater to the trade. They make an effort to have available everything currently showing, as well as thousands of other plays, memoirs, works of scholarship, and such books as *Foreign Dialects* and *How to Market Your Play*.

Many new scripts are quickly published in inexpensive, pamphletlike editions by one of two major publishers: Samuel French and Dramatists Play Service. **Samuel French** maintains a bookstore of its own, at 45 West 25th Street (between Fifth and Sixth avenues), where you can purchase its own editions and other theater books. Another publisher, **Applause Theatre Book Publishers**, bills itself as "the unavoidable source" and offers everything from the essays of Eric Bentley to recently published Australian plays, as well as a wide selection of other publishers' titles at its store at 211 West 71st (between Broadway and West End Avenue). Cinema books are offered at their second store, at 100 West 67th, between Broadway and Columbus.

For rare theater books and old prints of theater productions, an excellent source is **Richard Stoddard Performing Arts Books**, 18 East 16th Street, Room 202 (between Fifth Avenue and Union Square). In the theater district itself there are three comprehensive bookstores: **The Drama Bookshop**, 723 Seventh Avenue near 48th Street; **Theatrebooks**, at 1600 Broadway, Room 1009 (near 48th Street); and the **Theatre Arts Bookshop**, 405 West 42nd Street (just west of Ninth Avenue, on the north side of the street). A good place to hunt for show scores and sheet music is **Colony Records Center**, 1619 Broadway (at 49th Street).

New York's theater culture offers a wide selection of souvenirs and memorabilia, ranging from the plastic *Phantom of the Opera* masks sold everywhere around Times Square to framed, original drawings by Hirschfeld, *The New York Times*'s indestructible caricaturist of 50 years.

The most "touristy" of places to hunt memorabilia (but worth a look, nonetheless) is **One Shubert Alley**, a tiny shop tucked into an outside wall of the theater where *A Chorus Line* has been playing for as long as anyone can remember. (Shubert Alley extends between 44th and 45th streets, in the block between Broadway and Eighth Avenue.) This is the place for tee-shirts, mugs, postcards, the latest posters, and the like. Slightly to the west on 44th Street is **The Actors Heritage**, at number 262; here they have photographs, movie stills, programs, posters, scripts, and some records and scores. The Theatre Arts Bookshop, mentioned above, also has a decent collection of posters, and offers more memorabilia around Christmastime.

The biggest seasonal break for souvenir hunters, though, is early October, when Lincoln Center's **Performing Arts Library** has its annual sale. Every conceivable kind of memento relating to theater, dance, opera, and music is offered at prices that begin at 25¢. The sale items are not merely the library's castoffs: Theater people often donate things (the proceeds help the library). The library's sale is one of the best sources in the city for one-of-a-kind theatrical souvenirs. For information, Tel: (212) 870-1670.

Finally, for the serious collector (spending serious money) there are a number of galleries that offer posters and original drawings. Two that have a strong emphasis on theater are the **Triton Gallery**, at 323 West 45th (between Eighth and Ninth avenues), featuring Broadway and foreign posters; and **Margo Feiden Galleries** (11th Street and University Place, in Greenwich Village), which has, among other things, those Hirschfeld drawings.

LITERARY NEW YORK

By Ingrid Nelson

Ingrid Nelson, formerly an editor of GEO magazine, is a free-lance writer living on Manhattan's Upper West Side.

Few writers have character strong enough to write in New York. For all the hoo-haw that surrounds it, writing is the least glamorous of professions: It is slow, laborious, and ultimately solitary work. To attempt it in a city as distracting as New York can be disastrous, and while there have been times when writing has flourished here, the names of the talented writers who have died from overindulging in Manhattan's fleshpots could also serve as a reading list for a survey course in American literature. Writers with sense head for tamer spots, like Chicago, when there's work to be done.

Nonetheless, New York is essential to American writers for two reasons: It provides inspiration and it promises fame. Nowhere else is such a variety of human beings and human pursuits packed into such a small area; the inspirational potential of this pure human concentrate is boundless. And once words have been set down on paper the city becomes the writer's marketplace.

New York is the seat of publishing, the home base of most important magazines and journals, the headquarters of the country's largest wire service (the Associated Press), the stage upon which playwrights make their reputations, and the country's chief forum for the dissecting, analysis, and judgment of literature. The novelist Thomas Wolfe, whose relationship with New York was as ambivalent as any writer's has ever been, described the city he adopted in *From Death to Morning*: "The great vision of the city is burning in your heart in all its enchanted colors just as it did when you were twelve years old and thought about it. You think that some glorious happiness of fortune, fame, and triumph will be yours at any minute, that you are about to take your place among great men and lovely women in a life more fortunate and happy than any you have ever known—that it is all here, somehow, waiting for you."

In the beginning—that is, before 1850—there wasn't much that was literary about New York. Publishers lived in Boston. Most American writers were from elsewhere. An exception was Washington Irving, who had been born in lower Manhattan in 1783. This was merely an accident of birth; after he gained his early and considerable fame from humorous essays about New York society, Irving moved to Europe, which he far preferred, and stayed there for much of his adult life. When it came time to retire, he installed himself and his extended family in an eccentric mansion called Sunnyside in Tarrytown, about

25 miles north of Manhattan. (Sunnyside is now a museum, open to visitors; see Day Trips chapter.)

Around 1850, however, publishers began to migrate south, drawn by New York's growing population (and thus, pool of book purchasers). With them came editors, illustrators, and the usual literary hangers-on. The city was ripe for them. Having made money in trade, wealthy New Yorkers were ready to invest it in less tangible assets: They were endowing museums, amassing art collections, and reading for pleasure.

At the time, New York was also the occasional home of two genuinely great writers: Herman Melville and Edgar Allan Poe. Neither prospered from his writing, nor did either find the city to be a sympathetic place. There was something about New York, even in these early days, that didn't like writers.

Herman Melville was born at 6 Pearl Street in lower Manhattan in 1819. When he was 12 his father died. A few years later, Melville ran off to sea and lived the adventures he described in two early books, *Typee* and *Omoo*. Both were wildly successful, and Melville purchased a farm near Pittsfield, Massachusetts, and settled in to write his masterpiece, *Moby-Dick*. It was a complete flop, denounced by the critics and ignored by the public. Destitute and discouraged, Melville returned to New York. He moved his family into a brick house at 104 East 26th Street, and took a job as a customs officer at a dock on the East River. The pay was about four dollars a day. He died 28 years later, in 1891, having written a series of brilliant but unrecognized novels and stories. Melville is buried at Woodlawn Cemetery in the Bronx, under a headstone engraved with a blank scroll. During his career, he earned less than $8,000 from his writing; in his obituary, *The New York Times* called him Henry.

Edgar Allan Poe was a Bostonian, but in 1844 he moved to Greenwich Village with his child bride, Virginia, and took a job at the *Evening Mirror* newspaper. Although a collection of his tales was published in this period, and he wrote several well-known poems, including "Annabelle Lee," the Poe family was impoverished, and Poe himself was regarded more as a hack critic than a real artist. Virginia suffered from consumption, and by 1846 she was so ill that Poe rented a house (now open to visitors) in Fordham in the Bronx, where the air was clean. The rent was $100 a month. This put such a strain on his precarious finances that Virginia's mother (who lived with them) had to beg the neighbors for food. Virginia died in 1847. Two years later Poe himself died during a trip to Baltimore. He was found in an alcoholic stupor outside a voting booth where presumably he had been earning a few dollars as a repeating voter.

Fortunately for literature, New York City's next great writer chose to live abroad. Edith Wharton was born here in 1862 and grew up in a brownstone at 28 West 25th Street. She married Teddy Wharton in a church across the street, and the affluent young couple embarked on a comfortable but ultimately stultifying life together. In her mid-forties Edith fled to Europe and eventually settled in Paris. Her novels, however, are wicked dissections of the city she left, set in and around her old neighborhood. In *The Age of Innocence,* the Archer family lived in a brownstone on West 28th Street, where similar buildings still stand. Of them Wharton wrote in *A Backward Glance:* "the narrow houses so lacking in external dignity, so crammed with smug and suffocating upholstery . . . the little low-studded rectangular New York cursed with its universal chocolate-colored coating of the most hideous stone ever quarried."

Whatever it was about early New York that drove these writers to Europe or to their deaths—perhaps the city's crass materialism or its stuffy provincialism—was about to change. The first wave of European immigrants arrived in Manhattan in 1860 or so. The contribution they have made to this city, and this country, is incalculable—they brought vitality to New York, and they formed a bond between America and Europe, a kind of vibrating chord linking the Old World to the New. They also created a whole new social climate, one in which teeming slums existed cheek by jowl with uptown brownstones. The city became a different place altogether, and as such it was the geographical center for a remarkable group of writers, men and women of enormous energy, sophistication, optimism, and humanity, all imbued with a strong social conscience.

An early member of this group (actually, a precursor) was Walt Whitman of Long Island. Whitman was an editor of the *Brooklyn Eagle,* among other newspapers, for many years. In his free time he roamed through lower Manhattan and composed some of the poems that would eventually make him one of the best-known and most acclaimed of all American poets; poems about the Brooklyn Bridge and "Mannahatta," written with exuberance, sensuality, and a strong sense of individualism. Unfortunately, the New York curse on writers was still partially in evidence, for Whitman never achieved in his lifetime the fame that came to him after his death.

The writers of the next few decades did, however. O. Henry (William Sydney Porter), who lived on Gramercy Park, wrote a story a week for the *New York World* newspaper, and earned $100 for each—remarkable affluence for a New York writer. The legend goes that he wrote "The Gift of the Magi" in Pete's Tavern, still just around the corner from the park on Irving Place.

Something of a writer's colony grew up around Washington Square in Greenwich Village, the New World's closest equivalent to the Latin Quarter. Theodore Dreiser and Sinclair Lewis both struggled with naturalistic novels there early in their careers. Lincoln Steffens, the New York journalist for whom the word "muckraker" was invented, lived in the Village too. Proclaiming that "the city is human nature posing nude," he travelled throughout the country recruiting like-minded writers to join him in New York. One who did was John Reed (author of *Ten Days that Shook the World*). Reed lived at 42 Washington Square (now the address of New York University's law school), and wrote a poem about his apartment:

> In the winter the water is frigid,
> In the summer the water is hot;
> And we're forming a club for controlling the tub
> For there's only one bath to the lot.
> You shave in unlathering Croton,
> If there's water at all, which is rare—
> But the life isn't bad for a talented lad
> At Forty-Two Washington Square.

Reed belonged to a small theater group called the Provincetown Players. It may have been the most talented amateur theatrical group in history—other members were Edna St. Vincent Millay, Sherwood Anderson, E. E. Cummings, and Eugene O'Neill.

Another group of writers, critics, and wits congregated uptown, at a round table in the Rose Room of the Algonquin Hotel on West 44th Street. Robert Benchley, Alexander Woollcott, George S. Kaufman, and the riveting Mrs. Dorothy Parker formed the inner circle. One afternoon, Mrs. Parker was asked to use the word "horticulture" in a sentence. "You can lead a whore to culture," she instantly replied, "but you can't make her think."

And, farther uptown, the Harlem Renaissance was just getting underway. It was, as the name suggests, a new birth of black writing. Countee Cullen was an early leader; the poet Langston Hughes was an usher at Cullen's wedding in a Harlem church, and a disciple of his work.

All these literary stirrings and rumblings in New York attracted more writers, some of whom came here to write about someplace else. Sherwood Anderson was physically present in New York City while his imagination populated small towns in the American Midwest and evoked them in several novels. The novelist Willa Cather lived on Park Avenue and wrote about Nebraska; at the Society Library on East 79th Street she once ran into Truman Capote, another writer from elsewhere (Alabama) who had come to make his reputation in New York. Capote wrote that Cather's appearance, "rather mesmerized me—her eyes especially: blue, the pale brilliant cloudless blue of prairie skies." At their first meeting, and before they exchanged names, she asked Capote what writers he liked. He named several, then added, "I really like Willa Cather. Have you read *My Mortal Enemy*?

"With no particular expression," Capote continued, "she said, 'Actually, I wrote it.'"

The subjects and styles of these uptown, downtown, and out-of-town writers differed; they were not always familiar with one another's work, or even aware that one another existed. Nevertheless, they fermented together in this city, and together they created a literary community, the first New York had known. They were drawn here by New York's growing sophistication and variety; they in turn gave to the city the two essentials of lyricism and passion.

Of course, where there are writers there are also editors, and New York's publishing industry thrived. Practically every important American publisher was based in Midtown New York, close to former speakeasies turned literary wateringholes. (The "21" Club on West 52nd Street is one, but it has since degenerated into an expensive see-and-be-seen hangout and is best avoided.)

Publishing for the most part is a fairly dull business conducted by penny-pinching businessmen, but occasionally an editor will come along who is as much an artist as the writers he works with; great editors, it has been said, are artists whose medium is the work of other artists. One was Maxwell Perkins who, during much of this period, worked for Scribners. Perkins's other artists included Ernest Hemingway, F. Scott Fitzgerald, and Thomas Wolfe.

New York's literary community would prove to be lasting, although its hospitality to writers turned out to be a fleeting thing. After World War II, rents began to rise, and many of the writers who had been dispersed by the war moved to cheaper places. But the template of a literary community remained, and it wasn't too long before a new group of New York writers emerged.

The term *beatnik* seems curiously outdated; its literary equivalent, beat, is hardly ever heard now. And Allen Ginsberg and his fringy, offbeat contemporaries—Gregory Corso, the late Jack Kerouac, and William Burroughs—are practically grand old men of mainstream American letters today. When they started out, however, they shuttled between the Upper West Side (where Ginsberg was a student at Columbia University) and the Lower East Side (where they took their various pleasures) like ragged urchins. Nobody believed that the free-form, experimental writing they were touting as poetry would last. It did, of course. However, the Beat poets did not stay for too long in New York; the whole movement shifted to the West Coast and San Francisco.

In postwar Harlem, James Baldwin, the son of a preacher and a preacher himself for a brief period, brought the original Harlem Renaissance into a more militant phase with his uncompromising and beautifully written book, *Go Tell It on the Mountain*. Baldwin too left New York, and settled in France.

The handful of writers who did try to work in New York had, often as not, sadly truncated lives. Notable among them are the poet Delmore Schwartz, who died an alcoholic in 1966, and Dylan Thomas, who perished in 1953 in St. Vincent's Hospital in the Village after a monumental drinking binge. Clearly there is still something about New York that drives certain writers to Europe or to their deaths.

It's worth mentioning that the exact opposite is true of New York's intellectual community. The city is and has long been a haven for thinkers of all persuasions. Edmund Wilson and Lionel Trilling are two American critics who found employment and success in New York. Philosopher Hannah Arendt and art critic Meyer Schapiro were both refugees from Europe; Arendt taught at the New School for Social Research in the Village, and Schapiro at Columbia University; both became essential parts of the New York intellectual landscape.

What of the current literary situation in the city? Where are the presses hottest, the writers most talented, the poetry most modern? For one thing, publishing houses have moved downtown in recent years, to the lofts and low office buildings around Union Square.

Lunching is a large part of the business. If you were to wander into the **Union Square Café** at one o'clock or so and see a pair of diners, one casually but carefully dressed, the other looking slightly disheveled, you are probably witnessing an expense-account meal between editor and author. If that evening you wish to go to a real literary wateringhole, you should know that there aren't any left in New York. There are those with historic interest—the **White Horse** in the West Village, where Dylan Thomas hung out, and the **Lion's Head** at 59 Christopher, which has long been a meeting place for journalists from the *Village Voice*. But young writers in New York today tend to frequent the posh restaurant and club scene—those establishments that are photographed for the latest issues of *New York* magazine, *Vanity Fair,* and *Details*.

Instead, one of the best ways to get a good feel for literary New York is to visit bookstores. Few cities have so many that are so good. If you frequent the idiosyncratically-stocked shops scattered throughout Manhattan, you will discover that part of New York where ideas are wealth, and talent is currency. And this may very well be the real soul of the city. Below is a highly selective list of some of New York's best bookshops.

BOOKSTORES

Downtown

The **Academy Book Store** (10 West 18th Street) is a used-books store. It is not nearly as large as the Strand (see below), and, as a consequence, the books out on the shelves (about 100,000 at any one time, with 200,000 in reserve) are carefully chosen and rotated regularly. The tone here is generally quite serious; humanistic subjects such as philosophy and history are stressed. The Academy also has a superb collection of used records, including some classic recordings that are elsewhere unavailable.

Barnes & Noble (105 Fifth Avenue at 18th Street; 128 Fifth Avenue at 18th Street; and at Columbia University) has about a dozen branches around town, but only these three are worth going to. The main store, at 105 Fifth, has a really remarkable collection of books: shelf upon shelf of the newest fiction and nonfiction in both paperback and hardcover; a large room full of the latest in medical books; and a rear annex of university texts. The sales annex across the street has terrific prices on current books and an uneven, but immense, selection of over-stocks and out-of-prints that are even cheaper. The up-town branch is actually the Columbia University book-store, but nonstudents are welcome, and the paperback fiction collection is wonderful.

The Biography Bookshop (400 Bleecker Street near 11th Street) specializes in people—books about people, that is. Biographies, autobiographies, diaries, letters, and anything else pertaining to lives both famous and obscure can be found here.

Bob Fein Books (150 Fifth Avenue, Room 623, near 20th Street) has a wonderful collection of books, new and old, about the Indians of North and South America. Mr. Fein also sells photographs, prints, and lithographs of Indian themes and has a revolving collection of small sculptures on sale.

Books of Wonder (132 Seventh Avenue at 18th Street) is a children's bookstore with a collection so good that adults will almost certainly find something to read too. There is a small case of first editions and fine bindings and a nice selection of posters and cards.

East West Books (78 Fifth Avenue at 14th Street and 568 Columbus Avenue at 87th Street) deals in philoso-phy, spiritualism, and self-help. The emphasis here is on Eastern writers and thinking; the atmosphere in the small store is appropriately serene and contemplative.

Forbidden Planet (821 Broadway at 12th Street) doesn't look like a bookstore. In fact, it looks a bit like the alien bar in the first Star Wars film. The resemblance must be inten-tional, for the specialty here is science fiction and fantasy (with a sideline in comics).

Judith's Room (681 Washington Street, between West 10th and Charles streets) sells books by or about women, along with magazines and newspapers that ad-dress women's concerns.

The Literary Bookshop (15 Christopher Street, just underneath Oscar Wilde—see below) is brand-new and stocks a good assortment of serious fiction and nonfiction. The emphasis here too is on books by women, although the list is by no means limited to such.

Oscar Wilde Memorial Bookshop (15 Christopher Street) claims it is the oldest gay and lesbian bookstore in the world. At the age of 22, it may very well be. The collection here consists of books by or about gay people; all titles costing more than $7.95 are discounted.

Russica Book and Art Shop (799 Broadway near 11th Street) is not set up for browsers. However, its collection of books in the Russian language, books published in Russia, and books about Russia is unrivaled in the West.

St. Mark's Bookshop (13 St. Mark's Place) had a near brush with bankruptcy recently, but is flourishing again. The collection of fiction and literary journals here is so good that New Yorkers from as far away as the Upper West Side trek down to shop.

St. Mark's Comics (11 St. Mark's Place) sells comics, old and new, along with baseball cards, Batman paraphernalia, posters, video tapes, and other accoutrements for the frivolously inclined.

Samuel French, Inc. (45 West 25th Street) deals in single-volume editions of plays and musicals (including scores). Just about any play or musical currently in production, or ever in production for that matter, is available here.

Science Fiction Shop (56 Eighth Avenue, near Horatio Street) is tiny and packed as neatly as a submarine with (mostly paperback) science fiction.

Spring Street Books (169 Spring Street at West Broadway) has several racks of magazines up front. In keeping with this neighborhood of galleries, the selection of art magazines is terrific. In the rear is a well-chosen collection of books.

The **Strand Book Store** (828 Broadway at 12th Street) claims to have eight miles of books—used, overstocks, out-of-prints, reviewer copies, and some of the oddest paperbacks that have ever been printed. But how anyone could measure anything in this rabbit-warren of a place is a mystery. Whatever the mileage, this is New York's biggest used-books store, and thus the biggest in the country. By mysterious means, previously owned books from as far away as China find their way here. They are arranged by subject, the staff is adept at negotiating the maze of shelves to find what you may be looking for, and you can spend hours browsing through the splendid selection. There is also a section of fine bindings and rare books.

Three Lives (154 West 10th Street, between Sixth and Seventh avenues) is one of the superb, general-interest bookstores in New York. Mostly, such bookstores mirror the special interests of their owners; here, these happen to be fiction and art.

University Press Books (65 Fifth Avenue near 14th Street) stocks only a selection of those books published by American, Canadian, and British university presses. Not all are thick, academic tomes; on the contrary, some university press books are quite current. Normally, they are hard to find, but this store makes it easy.

Midtown

The Antiquarian Booksellers' International, Inc. (125 East 57th Street, Gallery 48) is a store/showroom that was founded by a group of rare-book dealers. Browsers are welcome, though, and the books, prints, autographs, maps, and manuscripts on display will provide a brief introduction to the fascinating subject of rare books and incunabula.

Argosy (116 East 59th Street between Park and Lexington avenues) has a vast collection of used books, which range in price from less than a dollar to several hundred times more. Prints are also available here, notably many Audubons.

B. Dalton, the huge chain with outlets across the country, has its flagship store on Fifth Avenue (at 666). It's a soulless, cheerless place, but there is an up-to-date selection of current titles here, as well as a good stock of standard titles, especially in paperback.

Coliseum Books (1771 Broadway at 57th Street) has an amazing number of books, mostly paperback, on all subjects. This is a great place to browse; even if you don't find what you're looking for you will certainly find something you like.

The Complete Traveller (199 Madison Avenue at 35th Street) specializes in travel books. It stocks most of the Nagel guides—expensive but authoritative—and also has a terrific selection of maps.

Doubleday (724 Fifth Avenue) has several branches, but it's best to shop in this one, at 57th Street. The selection of new fiction is excellent—occasionally, books are on sale here before the official release date. The reference section is also particularly good, and in the store's other special sections, spread out over three floors, you'll find most standard books in stock. The store is open until midnight, six days a week.

The Gotham Book Mart (41 West 47th Street) has a sign over the awning that says, "Wise men fish here." Indeed they do, and even the unwise may learn something here. The Gotham has made no concessions to fleeting fashion or modern marketing in its 50 or so years of existence. It remains a book-lover's bookstore, with a new and used collection of poetry, fiction, books on film and the theater, and journals that reflects the taste and interests of its founder, the late Frances Steloff, who was an early reader and supporter of James Joyce, Ezra Pound, Henry Miller, and Dylan Thomas, among many others. Give yourself an afternoon, at least, for the Gotham.

Hacker Art Books (45 West 57th Street) bills itself as the largest art-book shop in the world. Size aside, its collection is probably the broadest—every period of fine and applied art is represented here.

Librairie de France and **Libreria Hispanica** (610 Fifth Avenue and 115 Fifth Avenue), actually one store with a downtown branch, sells French and Spanish books, tapes, guides, and posters, and English books in translation. The Rockefeller Center store stocks more French books, while the 19th Street store is a bit heavier in the Spanish department. Also in the downtown branch is a sub-store called the Dictionary Store, which offers an unusual assortment of dictionaries, in a dozen or so languages.

Mysterious Book Shop (129 West 56th Street) is a chummy spot stocked with mysteries of every genre and populated by mystery lovers of every description. Hardcover and paperback, new and used whodunits are available.

New York Bound Bookshop (50 Rockefeller Plaza, in the lobby) limits its merchandise to things pertaining to New York City, old and new. As this collection demonstrates, however, there is no limit to the ways that writers, artists, and photographers have described and depicted New York.

Patelson (160 West 56th Street) is just behind Carnegie Hall and, appropriately, stocks the city's largest collection of books on classical music and musicians, as well as sheet music and recordings.

Rizzoli (31 West 57th Street) is a handsome store

where the oak shelves groan under the weight of the finest art, photography, and fashion books published in the United States and Europe. On hand here, too, is one of New York's finest selections of foreign periodicals. Rizzoli's store at 454 West Broadway in SoHo has a similar though smaller selection, with an emphasis on art.

The Travellers Bookstore (22 West 52nd Street) is a good place for both real travellers and armchair travellers. The standard guides are available, as well as a good collection of travel writing, old and new, fanciful and factual.

Urban Center Books (457 Madison Avenue at 51st Street) is suitably located in the historic Villard Houses, former private residences that are now part of the Helmsley Palace Hotel. The store is run in part by the Municipal Arts Society and stocks 4,000 titles on anything that has to do with cities: architecture, historic preservation, and the like.

Uptown: East Side

Books and Co. (939 Madison Avenue at 74th Street) is a relatively new addition to New York's roster of bookstores and it has won a wide following. This is probably because it's carefully designed to appeal to a toney crowd—classical music plays softly in the background; books about art, philosophy, and literature (with a capital L) are stressed; and there's a well-bred mein to the salespeople. Despite all this niceness, the books here are really quite good, and it's a wonderful place to browse.

Kitchen Arts & Letters (1435 Lexington Avenue near 93rd Street) is the right place to go when you're hungry. It stocks cookbooks of every persuasion and the work of food writers of every kind.

Military Bookman (29 East 93rd Street just west of Madison Avenue, in a brownstone ground floor) carries books about military history, from the taking of Troy to the present, although the emphasis is on classic battles of earlier wars. Some of the books are rare and quite valuable, posters and periodicals are in stock, and the salespeople here are nice as well as knowledgeable.

Wittenborn Art Books (1018 Madison Avenue at 78th Street) is, as its name suggests, an art-book shop. The definition of art here, however, is broad enough to include books about archaeology and fashion—and not all the books on sale are necessarily in English; they just have to be good.

Uptown: West Side

Applause Theatre Books (211 West 71st Street) deals mainly in drama—British, American, and European—in anthologies, annotated versions, and single-play books. Although there is an emphasis on British drama, it is not necessarily serious; it's possible to find, for instance, a collection of Monty Python skits. Applause also has a branch that specializes in the cinema at 100 West 67th Street.

Eeyore's (2212 Broadway near 78th Street and 25 East 83rd west of Madison) is a terrific children's bookstore with a unique service: They will select and send books to kids at summer camp.

The **Gryphon Bookshop** (2246 Broadway near 80th Street, with an annex upstairs around the corner) sells used books and records. The selection is good, particularly in the children's section where all (it seems) of the Oz books are available in any edition you would care to own. Used records are also on sale; in the annex some of the books have been marked down.

Murder Ink (271 West 87th Street) sells mysteries, new and used. The books are arranged according to an impenetrable shelving system, but the salespeople can produce titles at will. Business hours are eccentric, so call in advance: 362-8905.

Papyrus Books (2915 Broadway at 114th Street) is not worth a special trip uptown, but if you are in the neighborhood, you should certainly stop by. It has a good collection of new and used fiction, particularly paperbacks, but it has a truly amazing collection of periodicals. You'll have no trouble finding *Nicaraguan Perspectives* here, for instance.

Pomander Bookshop (955 West End Avenue at 107th Street) is an airy, well-lighted room full of out-of-print and used books. It is an exceedingly pleasant place to shop.

Shakespeare and Company (2259 Broadway at 81st Street) is an Upper West Side institution, and on sunny Sunday afternoons it gets almost as crowded as next-door Zabar's. The stock of new fiction and nonfiction here reflects the neighborhood: eclectic, offbeat, and brainy.

OTHER SHOPPING

By Lynn Yaeger

It stands to reason, New York City being as it is the home base for eccentric, offbeat, oddball citizens who have emigrated here from all over the globe, that attendant unusual shops have sprung up to meet their peculiar needs. "There's a nut for every street lamp in New York," as the saying goes, and often enough there's a store shimmering under that light as well. People only visiting us will want to avail themselves of our plethora of one-of-a-kind, out-of-the-way venues in order to carry back to their peaceful homes talismans of Manhattan life.

HOUSEWARES

Those who would rather equip their homes than themselves face an almost unlimited selection of domicile-related shops and items. Postmodernists will find matte-black metal and glass home accessories at the always mobbed **D. F. Sanders** (386 West Broadway between Spring and Broome Streets and 952 Madison Avenue at 75th Street); accompanying plain boudoir furnishings—namely the rigorously streamlined bedroll known as the futon—can be purchased at the **Futon Shop** (491 Broadway, between Spring and Broome). Parties who prefer a Georgia O'Keeffeian southwestern atmosphere in their sitting rooms can pick up a bleached animal skull from **Maxilla & Mandible** (78 West 82nd). Wicker furnishings, having recently expanded their scope beyond the exclusivity of the sagging summer porch and now bedecking rooms for all seasons, are in good supply at **Deutsch** (31 East 32nd Street). For the ultimate in avant-garde discomfort, the gallery/shop **Modern Stone Age** (111 Greene Street) features slabs of rock converted into modern pieces of Fred Flinstonian furniture. Possessors of ill-shaped windows, who travel with or have memorized the dimensions of their unfortunate vitrines, can order custom-made lace-patterned French-style curtains from the always charming **Wolfman Gold & Good** (116 Greene Street near Prince).

Linens are the specialty at **E. Braun** (717 Madison near 64th Street), an old-fashioned holdover from the days when Madison Avenue was just the local shopping street for rich people. **Descamps** (723 Madison) has modern, very popular sheets, towels, and pillowcases from and for upper-crust France. At **Christofle Pavillon** (680 Madison) silver-plated flatware and other more elaborate items appeal to the conservative, good-taste crowd, while across the street, **Georg Jensen** (683 Madison) flogs the Scandinavian design items that have been staples of the ritzy (but unglitzy) home for more than 40 years. Those who subscribe to a rather more slap-dash style of home decoration may prefer the whimsical offerings at the **Mad Monk** (500 Sixth Avenue), a hand-thrown-pottery store (it also sells Zen books) at the northern end of the West Village.

Shoppers who wish to buy into the English country-home look (of late smothering rooms all over America under oceans of chintz, mottled and faded carpeting, and hairy dogs) should head uptown to **G. Elter** (740 Madison), where antique reproduction picture frames can be purchased. Other dust collectors can be found at the **Mediterranean Shop** (876 Madison), where hand-painted faux naïf pottery is the specialty, and the line includes some unusual items like slotted pencil cups and place-card holders. Your castle walls, albeit sagging beneath the groaning display of oil-painted Irish setters and dead relatives, should include some of mummy's needlepoint, which can be made up from kits purchased at **Erica Wilson Needle Works** (717 Madison, in the same building as E. Braun). If the duke and duchess and their 15 progeny are ambling over to dinner, matching silver for incomplete sets of flatwear may be located at **Jean Silversmith** (16 West 45th). After supping, recline on Fortuny-inspired Venetian pillows from **Portantina**, the narrow, velvet-encased shop at 886 Madison.

PERSONAL EMBELLISHMENT

The number of small stores in Manhattan catering to the whims and fancies of the eccentric shopper is practically uncountable. Tiny variations in personal embellishment and style assume enormous proportions in this town, and new visitors will no doubt be taken aback by the seriousness of the pursuit.

A whole shop, **Tender Buttons** (143 East 62nd), splendid as an art gallery, is devoted to these humble items—antique, vintage, and new—sometimes made up into cuff links or earrings, but most often left in their natural state to adorn your most prosaic garments. (Those eschewing this high-class enclave and yearning for wholesale ribbons, laces, and trimmings are directed to the area of Sixth Avenue in the high 30s, where cardboard boxes showcase the wares, and trading, though brisk, will tolerate the retail customer.) Persons who wish to purchase leather skins straight off the animal's back should go to **Grosz Leather** (74 Spring Street in SoHo), a shop selling ordinary to obscure hides.

To distinguish yourself with a swaggering gait, pick up a walking stick or cane, as well as all manner of umbrellas, at **Uncle Sam** (161 West 57th). Or go even further: Purchase a leather riding crop at **M. J. Knoud** (716 Madison) or **Kauffmans** (139 East 24th) or **Millers** (123 East 24th), all of which are equestrian stores selling boots, bits, feed bags, jodhpurs, and fashionable riding habits.

Shoppers in search of the lost world of bohemian Greenwich Village may be inspired, after an interval of watching the perennial chess players at the southwest corner of Washington Square Park, to purchase a chess set of their own, available in an impressive range of styles and prices from **The Chess Shop** (230 Thompson Street). The **Glori Bead Shoppe** (172 West 4th Street) will supply appropriate strands for the neck, wrist, and ears of a surviving Joan Baez look-alike. Sinister sunglasses can be selected from an array at **Shades of the Village** (167 Seventh Avenue South).

The studious traveller, desiring neither riding crop nor rawhide, may still be able to do some satisfying shopping in New York. Exquisitely marbleized Venetian papers, in the form of stationery but also made up to cover a wide range of desk accessories, are for sale at **Il Papiro** (1021 Lexington and in Herald Center across 34th Street from Macy's). The correct pen and/or pencil for the scholarly-journal underliner is at **Arthur Brown** (2 West 46th); the right cigar for late-night musing at **Nat Sherman** (711 Fifth Avenue). Horn-rimmed or tortoiseshell-framed spectacles (as well as some other examples of the most stylish eyeglasses in the city) are at **Joel Name** (65 West Houston and 353 Bleecker) and **Robert Marc** (190 Columbus Avenue and 1046 Madison) and the extremely fashion-forward **Alain Mikli** (100 Fifth Avenue).

ETHNIC SHOPPING

Despite varying tendencies among New Yorkers to alternately embrace and deny their immigrant origins, shops catering to merchandise from the old country abound. In addition, disparate nationalities continue to arrive and, once here, open specialty shops importing goods associated with the life left behind.

Although in no way comparable to their numbers 50 or even 30 years ago, there are still plenty of Irish in Manhattan whose ancestral longings can be assuaged by a visit to **Shamrock Imports** (205 East 75th), where, among a selection of emerald-green ephemera, hand-knit fisherman sweaters, wide caps, and *claddagh* rings are available. Fiercely nationalist remnants of the Ukrainian community, still hanging on in the rapidly gentrifying East Village, go to **Surma** (11 East 7th Street) for traditional painted Easter eggs and embroidered linens. Though burgeoning Chinese immigration is pushing northward beyond Canal Street and spilling into the Little Italy area, the Mulberry Street corridor continues, for the time being, to sell ornate Italian pottery, posters of Sophia Loren, and cappuccino machines. Chinatown's endurance as a tourist attraction, meanwhile, supports the type of (souvenir-laden) stores you would anticipate.

The needs of those recently arrived from India are met by a variety of stores located in the area of Park Avenue South and Lexington Avenue in the 20s. Sari fabric off the bolt and sticks of incense are always available, and there are numerous other products less immediately accessible to the North American consumer. Those other Indians—the ones Americans like to watch on TV westerns—are an almost strictly imaginary community in New York City. Their indigenous merchandise, however, is available at a number of venues, among them the Village's **Common Ground** (50 Greenwich Avenue), handling baskets, weavings, and silver and turquoise jewelry.

Antique and modern Japanese kimonos are available in the East Village at **Yuzen** (318 East 6th Street) and due west at **Shinbi** (55 Greenwich Avenue). Tibetan textiles, mirrored caps, silver charm bracelets, and other accessories from Tibet's far-flung outposts have found a peaceful home in the heart of the West Village at **Tibet West** (19 Christopher Street). Visitors whose taste remains deeply entrenched south of the equator will like **Craft Caravan** (63 Greene Street), which sells African handcrafted tin toys among other artifacts. From this hemisphere, Mexican folkloric furniture, pottery, and glass are sold at **Amigo Country** (19 Greenwich Avenue) and likewise at the charming **Buen Dia** (108 West Houston Street).

TOYS AND GADGETS

Although there remain in Manhattan a number of toy stores dedicated exclusively to a clientele composed of the under-12 set, many places that specialize in these types of things (games, kits, tricks, gadgets, miniatures) also cater to an adult audience that can't seem to get enough of this merchandise. **Mythology** (370 Columbus on the Upper West Side) is full of faddish robots, inflated dinosaurs, and the like, and is always packed with young prodigies and their proud parents. **The Last Wound-Up** (290 Columbus at 73rd Street, 889 Broadway at 19th Street, and at the South Street Seaport) got famous selling mechanical toys, and the range of sizes and prices remains exhaustive. At **B. Shackman** (85 Fifth Avenue) the specialty is reproduction Victoriana manifested in bisque-headed dolls, paper ephemera, and miniatures, including dollhouse furniture. Prices are always inviting. Those readers obsessed with the diminutive (and this includes the growing number of adults who like to play with dollhouses) should visit **Gulliver's** (50 Grove Street in the West Village) for a full line of stunted furniture and accessories.

Children who enjoy annoying others by performing tedious magic tricks (and who among us does not know at least one of these small persons) will benefit from a trip to **Hornmann Magic Co.**, located upstairs in the office building at 45 West 34th Street. Youngsters (as well as certain older persons) whose idea of a brilliant practical joke rests at the level of the whoopie cushion should head for **Jimsons** (30 East 18th Street), where kindred items crowd the chaotic shelves.

The young science and science-fiction fanatic should visit **Forbidden Planet** (821 Broadway at 12th Street), where comic books and merchandise pack two stories in an atmosphere that can only be described as scholarly. Dungeons and Dragons partisans will enjoy the **Compleat Strategist** (11 East 33rd), a place filled with stimulating boxed mind-games and patronized by a passionate group of any-age devotees. Visitors seeking to take a break from mental activity can indulge themselves at **Big City Kites** (1201 Lexington Avenue between 81st and 82nd streets), where the merchandise, once properly constructed, will (presumably) soar.

Of course, try as you may, some things remain deeply embedded in one's childish years and must inevitably be put away as one grows older. At the famous F.A.O.

Schwartz (767 Fifth Avenue at 59th Street) the merchandise is insufferably young, and, assuming you can abide the giant singing clock at the entrance ("Welcome to our world, welcome to our world of toys"), you'll find the scope and selection to be more than impressive. Tiny infants (are there any other kind?) can be mollified with a cozy, affectionate stuffed toy, the kind that grandma used to make, still handmade by anonymous grandmas at the charitable **New York Exchange for Woman's Work** (660 Madison). **The Lighthouse** (111 East 59th), which sells items handcrafted by the visually impaired, has extremely inexpensive crocheted farm and barn animals, of which the pastel kangaroo-en-famille is especially engaging.

UNCLASSIFIABLE ODDITIES

Defying every attempt to codify, classify, or otherwise order Manhattan shopping venues, certain stores stand proudly outside the law of rational organization. These places sell what would be considered unsalable outside a great metropolis and are often the chief reason people fall in love with New York City.

Prototypical of this breed of store is **Rita Ford's Music Boxes** (19 East 65th), a 19th-century sort of place featuring obviously tuneful, if not inexpensive, merchandise. At the other end of town, **It's Only Rock N Roll** (49 West 8th Street) serves a far different clientele with vintage record albums, back issues of fanzines, and assorted pop memorabilia. Old radios and phonographs (Edison wind-ups through the Art Deco years) are for sale at **Waves** (32 East 13th Street). Contemporaneous movie posters, lobby cards, and other motion-picture ephemera are available at Jerry Ohlinger's **Movie Material Store** (242 West 14th Street between Seventh and Eighth avenues). A few blocks farther south is **Mouse N' Around** (197 Bleecker between Sixth Avenue and MacDougal), a mercantile homage to Disney, featuring Mickey-embellished items in a silly, slap-happy atmosphere. Likewise, **Little Rickie** (49½ First Avenue at 3rd Street), with its 1960s ephemera, Barbie-related accessories, and one of the last extant black-and-white photo booth machines in town, appeals to the laugh-riot crowd. The inveterate collector of baseball cards can visit **Jeff's** (150 Second Avenue between 9th and 10th streets). Those preoccupied with the pursuit of mummified butterflies will not want to miss the very pleasant **Mariposa** (in the South Street Seaport).

Unusual telephones (in the shape of, say, juicy puckered

lips, Snoopy dogs, or cheeseburgers) are for sale at the **Phone Booth** (12 East 53rd). Set one next to a raw gemstone from **Astro Mineral** (155 East 34th) for stolen moments of contemplation. Utilitarian restaurant china and glass, not usually sold on a per-piece basis, can be found at **Wooden Indian** (60 West 15th). The vintage red, blue, and white ocean-liner tableware is especially desirable.

Travellers who desire high-quality gadgetry should visit **Hammacher Schlemmer** (147 East 57th), famous for upper-class items on the order of bun-warming frankfurter steamers and solar-charged garden sprayers. Less rarefied though still amusing items can be examined at **The Sharper Image** (4 West 57th), and younger visitors will undoubtedly enjoy the thought-provoking widgets (microscopes, fossils, and the like) sold by **The Nature Company** (8 Fulton Street in the South Street Seaport area).

Readers who have long since acknowledged that a gadget won't solve their problems and are still searching for answers can investigate **The Magickal Childe** (35 West 19th) or **Enchantments** (341 East 9th Street), both of which serve New York's active witch and warlock community.

Lastly, visitors desperately thrashing in the throes of wretched homesickness should pull themselves together long enough to visit **Hotalings**, the gigantic news dealer smack in the middle of Manhattan at 142 West 42nd Street. If there's anyplace in town that carries a copy of your hometown paper, this is it.

FOOD

By Dean J. Seal

Dean J. Seal was formerly associate editor of the U.S. Food Journal, *a trend monitor of the American food industry. He is now a frequent contributor to food-related magazines.*

This international city can arguably be described as the food capital of America. People from all over the country, and the world, bring their demanding tastes here, and whether they take up residence or just visit, they expect the best. And they get it—at world-famous restaurants, at Korean grocery stands, at gourmet food shops.

COMING TO MARKET

Meat comes into New York on the west side of Greenwich Village, by the Hudson River. Whole loins of choice beef can be had at a steep discount, if you know what you want, and a visit to **Florent**, a 24-hour neighborhood restaurant at 69 Gansevoort Street in the area, is alone worth the trip.

Fishing boats have unloaded at the **Fulton Fish Market** at the South Street Seaport (east end of Fulton Street next to the Financial District downtown) for more than a hundred years. Tours can be arranged, but be aware that the market opens at 3:00 A.M. The Fulton retail shop, though it may be less picturesque, keeps more reasonable hours and is geared to serving the public.

The Hunts Point Terminal Produce Market in the Bronx calls itself the world's largest single produce market, supplying the needs of both grocers and restaurants. However, many prefer one of the "greenmarkets" the city sponsors around town. Three—Union Square, West 77th Street at Columbus Avenue (Sundays only), and Federal Plaza—are year-round, and another dozen locations host seasonal markets. The produce, wine, flowers, and honey from four states get top ratings for freshness and quality.

SPECIAL EVENTS

Some neighborhoods sponsor street fairs and festivals, which usually include food specialties of the area. The **Feast of San Gennaro**, held for two weeks at the end of September in Little Italy, for example, is an orgy of sausage-and-pepper sandwiches; and the **Ninth Avenue International Festival** (south from around 42nd Street) in May draws a million eaters to sample diverse ethnic fare. More than 60 fairs take place annually in the five boroughs.

As a convention city, New York also hosts special events for the food industry. Among them is the megashow at the

Jacob K. Javits Convention Center, which combines the New York Food and Beverage, Gourmet Products, Entirely Tabletop, and Glass and China shows all at once every fall. Consult the New York Convention & Visitors Bureau at 2 Columbus Circle (58th Street and Eighth Avenue; Tel: 212-397-8222) for specifics on fairs, festivals, and conventions.

SEASONAL FOODS

Given the variety of foods imported to New York, a diner here is almost totally free of seasonal restrictions. If there is something you want to eat, you can get it here. Everything is coming in all the time. As Douglas Levy of gourmet caterers Fisher and Levy says, "When it's winter here, it's summer somewhere else. In this day and age of cargo planes, you can find anything you want for a price." But there are seasonal highlights. Fall and spring are best for deep-water halibut; summer visitors can look forward to shad roe (a mass of shad eggs, best done gently, steamed or poached) and soft-shell crab (blue crabs recently molted, that can be crunched down shell and all, cooked on a fast, high heat by broiling or sautéing in butter and capers). Abalone oysters are here in spring, summer, and fall. Fruits and vegetables to watch for include broccoli, apples, and pears in the winter and fall, as well as a variety of squash; and fiddlehead ferns in fall. Spring is the time for spring cherries and blackberries in welcome abundance. And New York is one of the few places where Long Island duck can be had fresh, not frozen. And if you really want to indulge in indigenous food from the city itself, Steve "Wildman" Brill will give you a free tour of Central Park, pointing out edible foods that can be harvested there—mushrooms, carrots, nectarines, mustard greens, various berries, and the like. You can't get any fresher. (Call Steve at 718-291-6825.)

EATING ON THE RUN

Manhattan's neighborhoods differ in age, makeup, and traditions, but they all share accessible food sellers that cater to America's toughest, most mobile clientele.

Upper West Side

The food mecca of this neighborhood is the **Silver Palate** (Columbus Avenue between 72nd and 73rd). This tiny room gave birth to a nationally distributed packaged-goods business and three best-selling cookbooks; a gastronomically historic spot. For fresh produce, Broadway offers **Fairway** (between 74th and 75th), with heaps of fruits and vegetables, a great cheese department, and some of the most outrageous signs ever (Fresh Figs, Raw Sex, Same Thing).

Nonetheless, the hot spot is **Zabar's**, 2245 Broadway (between 80th and 81st), arguably the best food (and kitchen equipment) store in the world. It's famous for top-quality smoked fish, sausages, caviar, coffee, and cheeses; a cookware selection that is complete and competitive; and a take-out deli that cannot be beat. When it's open, it's busy, and when it's busy, it's a nuthouse. It is one of the few mandatory stops on this tour.

Upper East Side

This is one of the richest neighborhoods in the world, and this wealth is apparent in the food available. Mango curried chicken salad, fresh mozzarella with tomatoes and basil, exotic ham sandwiches on freshly baked bread abound at notables like Neuman & Bogdonoff (1385 Third Avenue between 78th and 79th streets), Fraser-Morris (931 Madison at 74th), William Poll (1051 Lexington between 74th and 75th), and the multiple locations of August and Co.

Yorkville, in the northeast, is the home of an old German neighborhood, and you will get a taste of it at **Bremen House**, 218 East 86th Street near Third Avenue, where you can stock up on wurst, cheese salad, even German-made cookware. Hungarians and Czechs maintain cooking traditions at shops like **Paprikas Weiss**, 1546 Second Avenue between 80th and 81st, the best source for Middle European spices. For Western European spices try **Saint Remy**, at 818 Lexington off 62nd Street, which specializes in French herbs and spices. **Ottomanelli Brothers**, at 1549 York (82nd Street), is known for game. Two of the most modern gourmet places are on Third Avenue: **Sweet Victory**, near 67th Street (pizza, ice cream, and restaurant serving low-calorie, high-flavor foods), and **Gourmet Gazelle**, between 69th and 70th (superb local deli).

Great bakeries flourish, notably two on East 78th Street between First and Second avenues: **Orwasher's** for bread and neighboring **Rigo** for "Hungarian Viennese" pastries. And the country's leading food bookstore is here, **Kitchen Arts & Letters**, at 1435 Lexington, between 93rd and 94th. Finally, **Grace Balducci's Marketplace** (from the famed Balducci family), at 1237 Third Avenue between 71st and 72nd, is a great grocery, where the superb produce, meats and cheeses, and deli are imbued with a warm Italian flavor.

Midtown

This heart of corporate headquarters is a great place for lunch, except from noon to 1:00 P.M. Before or after this rush try **Piatti Pronti** for sandwiches (34 West 56th Street), or **Savories**, downstairs next to the skating rink/café in the 30 Rockefeller Center concourse, for take-out food of all types. Specialty stores attest to the proximity of the United Nations and the presence of international businessmen: **Caviarteria** (caviar and vodka), 29 East 60th between Madison and Park; **Petrossian** (caviar and smoked fish), 182 West 58th at Seventh Avenue; **Old Denmark** (smorgasbord and café), 133 East 65th between Lexington and Park; **Maison Glass** (European spices), 111 East 58th between Park and Lexington; **Nyborg and Nelson** (Swedish and Scandinavian foods), 153 East 53rd at Lexington; and **Katagiri** (Japanese), 224 East 59th between Second and Third avenues. For one-stop shopping, try **Macy's Cellar**. It's a selection of "boutique" outlets of small Manhattan specialists like Otto-manelli, plus Macy's own departments to fill out the line. You might find a few bargains, but mostly they offer quality and convenience with acceptable service.

Ninth Avenue

Host to the biggest street food fair in the city (late May), Ninth Avenue in the 30s and 40s offers a cornucopia of international foods year round. Greek pastries with mouth-watering phyllo are at **Poseidon Bakery**, number 629 between 44th and 45th. Bargain fish, served fresh by a smart staff, is at **Central Fish Co.**, number 527 between 39th and 40th. Next door is **International Grocery Store**, famous for spices and baby lamb and kid, at number 529. For Italian sausage and suckling pig, go down to **Esposito & Sons Pork Store**, number 500 at 38th Street. And top it off with a visit to java headquarters at **Empire Coffee and Tea**, number 486 between 37th and 38th, for 75 different kinds of coffee beans and a similar selection of herbs, teas, and spices.

Greenwich Village

The West Village is New York's single best spot for buying food. Specialists proliferate: pasta (Raffetto's, 144 West Houston between Sullivan and MacDougal); pork (Faicco's, 260 Bleecker at Sixth Avenue); spices (Aphrodisia, 282 Bleecker Street, between Sixth and Seventh avenues, for a wide selection of culinary and medicinal herbs); bread (Zito's Bakery, the best Italian baker in town, 259 Bleecker Street between Sixth and Seventh avenues); and coffee (Schapira, which roasts their own, at 117 West 10th Street between Greenwich and Sixth avenues; McNulty's Tea & Coffee, 109 Christopher Street between Bleecker and Hudson; and Longo's, also called Porto Rico Importing, at 201 Bleecker Street between Sixth Avenue and MacDougal Street).

Jefferson Market, on Sixth Avenue between 10th and 11th, is long on service and expertise for their meats and fishes, superb choices, and reasonable pricing, plus a selection of gourmet goodies. But **Balducci's**, a block south at 424 Sixth, is the real Italian treat. They have what may be the best produce selection in town, a dynamite deli, cheeses and charcuterie for the ages, and an extensive mail-order system. Balducci's is more authentic than anything in Little Italy; you will sense a real love of food here, springing from three generations of tradition. Crowds can be competitive for all this good stuff, so try to come off-peak. For a real taste of New York, this is another mandatory stop.

Little India

In this neighborhood (Lexington Avenue in the 20s) that offers incredibly cheap Indian restaurants are also a few places to dig up staples and exotic spices of that national cuisine. **Spice and Sweet Mahal**, at 135 Lexington Avenue at 29th Street, is the place for Indian sweets. **Tashjian Kalustiyan** is herb and spice headquarters for Indian and

Middle Eastern groceries and spices; find them at 123 Lexington Avenue between 28th and 29th streets. **Annapurna Indian Groceries**, at 126 East 28th Street between Park and Lexington, is a great place not only for hot spices but also is an information vortex about all things of India. **Foods of India**, at 121 Lexington Avenue between 28th and 29th streets, is the most extensive when it comes to cooking utensils, spices, and an energetic staff.

Lower East Side

After perusing the latest schmattas in the punked-out East Village, a visit to the old Jewish areas of the Lower East Side can be a soothing return to reality. Russians, Ukrainians, and Poles mingle on East Houston Street, awaiting the kosher delights of **Yonah Schimmel**'s knishes (number 137); **Ben's Cheese Shop**'s cream cheese and farmer cheese (number 181); or **Russ and Daughters** for Nova, lox, smoked fish, and caviar (number 179). (Calvin Trillin singled out Russ's and Ben's as Best in Class for the perfect cream cheese and lox combo.) Bialys can be had fresh at **Kossar's** (367 Grand Street), and Ukrainian meat specialties are available at **Kurowycky Meat Products** (124 First Avenue). **Bernstein-on-Essex** (between Stanton and Rivington) calls itself the first-ever kosher Chinese restaurant, and they also have a *glatt* (strictly) kosher deli for, among other things, kosher won tons (Chinese kreplach) or Romanian pastrami fried rice. Finally, hit the **Second Avenue Deli** (at 10th Street) for traditional Yiddish K rations: kasha, kugel, kishke, and knaidel. (The *Journal of Gastronomy* quotes an exchange that could have been heard anywhere around here. Customer: "I don't like the looks of this whitefish." Waiter: "You want looks, you shoulda ordered goldfish!") Finally, one of the great unheralded spice emporiums is **Angelica's Herb and Spice Company**, 147 First Avenue between 8th and 9th, featuring over 2,500 varieties of herbs and spices.

SoHo and TriBeCa

Aside from modern-design stores and renowned art galleries, SoHo also offers a place to find artistically prepared food. **Dean & DeLuca** (560 Broadway at Prince Street) has been a pioneer of better eating in America, deserving of the moniker "the Rolls-Royce of food shops." Food to go, great breads, cheeses, oils, coffees, and esoterica make this place second only to Zabar's, and then just barely. The store also has cookware and cookbook departments and does a strong mail-order business. This is another mandatory stop, if only to see the airy, elegant surroundings; expensive only compared to places that offer less.

TriBeCa has only recently been "discovered" and is becoming a chic residential quarter for artists and stock-brokers, but it has two established food specialists too. **Cheese of All Nations** (153 Chambers Street between Greenwich Avenue and West Broadway) is not kidding—they have everything. They allow sampling, they ship, and they put together gift packages. There is also **Commodities Natural Foods** (117 Hudson at North Moore Street), for a huge selection of organic whole foods.

Little Italy and Chinatown

Aside from the pastry that can be had almost anywhere in Little Italy, the **Italian Food Center** at 186 Grand Street and the **Alleva Dairy**, next door, are the only two spots for special Italian materials. The first is a complete source for all things Italian, the second specializes in ricotta and mozzarella.

Chinatown offers a much more vibrant street scene, especially in the fish markets. A department store of all things Chinese, including foods and cookware, is **Kam Man** (Golden Gate) at 200 Canal. But nose around the neighborhood for little stands, especially the one that sells what can only be called Chinese doughnut holes, made for a dollar a dozen right in front of you.

The Other Four Boroughs

Brooklyn has a Middle Eastern contingent on Atlantic Avenue, a big Russian community at Brighton Beach, West Indians in Flatbush, a thriving community of Poles in Greenpoint, and three distinct Jewish communities: Hasids in Williamsburg, Lubavitchers in Crown Heights, and Sephardics on Kings Highway and in the Borough Park area. Queens is home to many Greeks, in Astoria; Chinese, Japanese, Indians, and Koreans, in Flushing; and, in Jackson Heights, an old-fashioned immigrant neighbor-hood with a new-fashioned selection of immigrant food-stuffs: Argentine, Colombian, Cuban, Peruvian, Filipino, Salvadoran, Thai, Indian, and Irish populations all offer up at least a restaurant or two of home-style cooking, and most also have a store that stocks the essentials of their culinary heritage. To get to Jackson Heights, take the number 7 subway from Times Square or Grand Central to the 69th Street/Fisk stop for the Filipino area, or get off at any of the next four stops (74th, 82nd, or 90th streets or Junction Boulevard) for the Latin areas. There are Italian enclaves in all five boroughs.

The Food Lover's Guide to the Real New York is an excellent source for finding these areas, though the coverage for Manhattan is curiously spotty.

SHOPPING FOR GOURMET ITEMS

Restaurateur Alice Waters once said, "I think transportation, in general, is a bad thing." This is true for many foods, but not all. Prepared foods like smoked fish, packaged goods like caviar or wine, most chocolates, and baked items like bagels can travel well, especially if they are bought the day of your departure.

Many delis put their prepared foods in containers so durable that they could conceivably be used to bring things all the way back home. When in doubt, ask the people who are selling it to you if the item is something that travels well and if it needs to have more than the usual protective wrapping. Many places also have selections of gift baskets of their most popular, and most portable, foods. Just ask. Any of the big five—Zabar's, Dean & DeLuca, Balducci's, Grace's, or Macy's Cellar—can help you with this. Other specialty shops named here and elsewhere can do this too; again, don't be shy.

For wine, four stores stand out. **Garnet Liquors** (929 Lexington, between 68th and 69th) offers the best prices for those who know what they want. **William Sokolin,** on Madison between 33rd and 34th, offers the best learning experience for those who want to know more, with reasonable prices. **Morrell & Company,** 535 Madison (between 54th and 55th), offers the best selection, especially of exotic, rare, and expensive wines, and has an excellent staff. And **Sherry-Lehmann,** 679 Madison at 61st Street, has probably the best selection of New York State wines.

This town loves chocolate and has a selection of Belgian (Godiva, Le Chocolatier Manon), Swiss (Neuchatel, Teuscher), and Italian (Perugina). But the hometown entries—**Li-Lac** in the West Village (120 Christopher) and **Mondel,** 2913 Broadway at West 114th Street, by Columbia—have their own fans. Mondel has a great diet chocolate (How do they do it?), and Li-Lac has a wicked fudge they've been making since 1923. Li-Lac also has an endearing habit of closing when they've sold enough for the day, so go early.

SHOPPING FOR GOURMET COOKWARE

For regular home cookware, try **Conran's** first, not only because they have a number of locations (at the Citicorp building in Midtown, on Astor Place in the Village, and at Broadway and 82nd Street on the Upper West Side), but also because their quality gets very high marks, and they use their international buying clout to get great stuff worldwide for cheap. For the more adventurous, **Bridge Kitchenware** at 214 East 52nd Street, between Second and Third avenues, has the best selection and top quality, but they discourage retail customers, preferring the pros. So go only if you know what you want, because service is scarce.

Robin Importers, 510 Madison Avenue between 52nd and 53rd streets, has a decent selection of knives and tablewear, and they offer good prices too. **Zabar's** has a great selection of equipment and is relatively competitive in general cookware but is very good in discounting kitchen appliances, like CuisinArts. You can also get occasional loss leaders here. **Macy's** has a pretty good selection, but high prices to match.

There is a street of suppliers where the pros go for kitchen equipment, and if you want the very best deals, you should go there, too: the Bowery, between Houston Street and Cooper Square. The neighborhood is a bit gamey and should not be visited alone, but **King Glassware**, at 112 Bowery at Grand Street, can be worth it. From major appliances to small gadgets, everything is at hand here, and most of it for just 10 percent above wholesale. Top chefs call it the best source, period.

AFTER HOURS

DINING

By Andy Birsh

Andy Birsh is a Contributing Editor at Gourmet, *for which he writes a monthly column on New York dining. For a decade he edited and published* The Restaurant Reporter.

The standard estimate of the number of restaurants in the city of New York is 15,000. Even by limiting the word "restaurant" to mean just those places where gracious and potentially enjoyable full meals are served, the number is still in the low four figures. In other words, there are years and years of interesting lunches and dinners to be had in New York—and one of the amazing things about longtime New Yorkers is the number, and the variety, of these meals that they have consumed. New Yorkers virtually live in restaurants, and restaurants easily outstrip any other sort of public place when it comes to where New Yorkers spend their often hard-won free time.

What follows is a selective survey of places to eat in Manhattan (with some forays to other boroughs). These are restaurants that please New Yorkers and convey the flavor of the city as well as the flavors of the many culinary styles that have made a home for themselves here. Missing are establishments whose tables are mostly filled with weary tourists, and missing, too, are many fine places that could easily have been included had space permitted.

Exact prices are not quoted, but general levels of expense may be gauged from the descriptions of the restaurants. Bear in mind that eating out in New York is more expensive than eating out nearly anywhere else. An ample meal that is inexpensive in relative terms will probably cost $25 to $30 per person, once drinks, sales tax, and an expected gratuity of at least 15 percent are factored in. Dinners in the middle of the local range are liable to run $40 to $60 per person (on the bottom line), and dinners at the topflight places can easily top $100 per person without anyone's ordering caviar and Champagne.

But while New York's restaurants can reveal the city at its most extravagant they can also show it at its wisest and simplest; they preserve its oldest ways and make some daring stabs at the future; some exemplify the city's competitive, fame-seeking edge, while others offer blessed relief from it. They can also provide travellers from anywhere on earth with what may be the most delightful mealtimes they will ever know.

All restaurants listed are in Manhattan (telephone area code 212) unless stated otherwise.

ITALIAN

It would be fair to say that although the competition is fierce, the best eating in New York is to be found in Italian restaurants. This is no surprise when you consider how very much Italian restaurants have to offer: meals that can be either quick, light, and sustaining or grand feasts; ingredients that ought to be, and usually are, of the most evident freshness; plenty of genially affordable wine (except in the loftiest places); and, of course, pasta, veal, garlic, olive oil, *calamari,* crusty bread, tomatoes, exotic mushrooms, beautiful cheeses, and on and on. New York's Italian cooking has its roots in every corner of Italy, and regional digressions go a long way to keep New Yorkers interested in the subject. Travellers to the city are usually amazed by the vast difference in variety and quality between Italian food here and that in most of the rest of America.

The portion of the Lower East Side that is still called **Little Italy** (in spite of the near-total relocation of Italian-Americans to the suburbs) teems with Sicilian and Neapolitan restaurants, many of which, unfortunately, serve dreary food. There are exceptions. **Villa Pensa**, at 198 Grand Street near Mulberry, which has been discreetly in business since 1898 and has been owned by only two families, makes its own excellent ravioli and manicotti, one of which will do very nicely halfway between an antipasto and some veal or chicken. The same specials have been offered on the same days of the week for generations. Caruso and Valentino ate here. Tel: 226-8830.

Far newer is **Taormina**, a spacious, bright, immaculately maintained establishment nearby at 147 Mulberry Street that is somewhat more expensive than Villa Pensa. Big tables convey a sense that families of 12 are always welcome, and the circulating antipasto cart is a nicely dated touch. The very exacting chef-proprietor is descended from cooks in the noble houses of Naples. Tel: 219-1007.

People, well . . . mostly guys who have been waiting all week, or all their lives, to behave disgracefully in public, head unerringly for **Puglia**, at 189 Hester Street near Mulberry. The kitchen does nothing to distract them from the rowdiness at hand, and the management has the decency to charge very little for what it sends out. Tel: 226-8912.

Greenwich Village, particularly on the blocks around certain churches, is also a longtime Italian enclave; and here some restaurants have also had their doors open for decades, such as the readily affordable **Grand Ticino**, at 228 Thompson Street near West 3rd (Tel: 777-5922), or **Minetta Tavern**, at 113 MacDougal Street, on the corner of Minetta Lane (Tel: 475-3850). Others are part of a Florentine tide of eateries that has brought real trattoria fare to an area that ought to have real trattorias. **Cent'Anni**, at 50 Carmine Street (between Bleecker and Bedford just west of Sixth Avenue), has simple decor and a tiny kitchen, but is justly renowned for its cooking. Wild mushrooms, handfuls of fresh herbs, and rich fruity olive oils find their way into a remarkable range of dishes, which includes perhaps the best bowl of soup in New York. Add some rare Tuscan wines and the check will start to climb, but most of the customers are in raptures over their meals and don't care. Tel: 989-9494.

Da Silvano, an older Florentine standout, at 260 Sixth Avenue between Bleecker and Houston, is priced higher than Cent'Anni but has a more worldly, fashionable air and some sidewalk tables for the good weather. The place gets quite busy in the evening, but when the midday customers (some of whom are SoHo art dealers) carefully work on their artichokes, a sophisticated leisureliness prevails. The printed menu provides only a portion of the news on what's available. Tel: 982-2343.

Some newcomers seem to be here to remind New Yorkers that Italy stands for sleek design and that pasta is an art form and not just a chore for *mamma*. **Rosolio**, at 11 Barrow Street (off Seventh Avenue near Sheridan Square), doesn't require customers to appear in Milanese tailoring, but they do anyway. Low-slung black leather chairs allow for lingering conversations after the consumption of superb hand-cut pasta. Tel: 645-9224.

It may well be true that there is a good Italian restaurant out there for everyone. The well-heeled downtown art crowd takes its calamari and *tiramisù* at **Arqua** and **Barocco**, 281 and 301 Church Street (a few blocks below Canal Street). Both are modishly stark and very noisy and both belie their black-clad patrons' apparent disenchantment with life. Cooking as good as this can put a song in the heart of the most studied nihilist. Tel: 334-1888 for Arqua; 431-1445 for Barocco.

The Florentines have set down in Chelsea, too. **Chelsea Trattoria**, at 108 Eighth Avenue south of 16th Street, is snug and small and friendly, and serves food that is far better (and a little costlier) than its unassuming façade suggests. Tel: 924-7786. **Da Umberto**, at 107 West 17th Street west of Sixth Avenue, is more expensive and more of a show, especially the mouth-watering layout of antipasti, the floor-to-ceiling bins of Italian wine, and the dizzying array of off-the-menu special dishes. This is a wonderful place to order an unlikely Florentine favorite: a juicy grilled T-bone steak served with nothing but big wedges of lemon. Tel: 989-0303. **Onini**, at 217 Eighth Avenue (corner of 21st Street), is a husband-and-wife operation that has grown from a hole-in-the-wall into a commodious and rather tranquil neighborhood place for lunch as well as dinner, with unconventional dishes, such as salads that creatively incorporate Italian ingredients in ways not seen in Italy. Onini is also one of the rare Italian places that makes fine desserts—one of which is *prugne farcite,* surprisingly delightful stuffed prunes that must be tasted to be believed. Tel: 243-6446.

For the most part, the American public recognizes a distinction between Northern and Southern Italian cooking. Southern is synonymous with "tomatoey," and Northern means "kind of expensive." In its deep fascination with Italian cooking, New York has pushed beyond this simple formula. The cooking of Southern Italy is not only preserved (to some extent) in Little Italy, but also celebrated in stylish new places that have introduced something of a second wave of *Southern Italian* cuisine.

Siracusa, at 65 Fourth Avenue between 9th and 10th streets, has bare floors, nearly bare walls, and a short menu (in Sicilian) of antipasti, salads, and pasta. Quite a festive little repast can be made from a big communal plate of marinated vegetables, hard salami, cheese, and other nibbles, followed by pasta in the best Sicilian manner, such as with fresh sardines and buttery bread crumbs. For dessert: probably the best *gelato* in Manhattan, of which the hazelnut is the best of the best. Tel: 254-1940.

A Sicilian chef named Maria Sindoni owns a pair of very good restaurants, **Azzuro** and **Baci**, on opposite sides of town, that have more extensive menus than Siracusa but that vie just as tenaciously for the eggplant crown. Marinated, thin-sliced swordfish also reaches an apogee at these places, and Sindoni's poached pears with winy *zabaglione* may be the stuff of future legends. Baci, at 412 Amsterdam Avenue near 80th Street, is the more casual of the pair—no reservations or credit cards, and it is open midday. Tel: 496-1550. Azzuro, where nearly everything is indeed a vibrant blue, serves dinner solely and is found at 1625 Second Avenue between 84th and 85th streets. Tel: 517-7068.

Bright, airy, and multi-tiered, **Positano**, at 250 Park Avenue South at 20th Street, perches its tables at various elevations, like the hotels and houses on the Amalfi coast. As befits its namesake town, the kitchen emphasizes fish and shellfish (although not at the expense of pasta), and offers a genuine *torta di mandorle,* the mild Amalfian chocolate almond cake, for dessert. During the cold and gray months in New York, the sunniness of Positano is a tonic. Tel: 777-6211. Similar homage is offered at **Sistina**, a snug, superior outpost of home-style cooking on the Upper East Side, at 1555 Second Avenue between 80th and 81st streets. Tel: 861-7660.

Northern Italian comes in many different shapes and sizes. Apart from the Florentines, there are Venetians, Milanese, Piedmontese, and some culinary free agents who have built styles of their own. While not necessarily cooking by the old rules, these innovators would make centuries of traditional Italian cooks proud. Some of these places also have the questionable distinction of being the most expensive Italian restaurants on earth; no meal in Italy could possibly cost as much.

Primavera brings Old World comfort to an otherwise characterless corner of Yorkville, at 1578 First Avenue (82nd Street). Park Avenue's denizens have no trouble negotiating the distance east from their co-ops when the late autumn brings white truffles from Alba to Primavera and the waiters are shaving the precious fungi onto steaming bowls of fettucine. When the season ends, the gang gets by with meltingly tender *capretto* (baby goat), sweetly delectable veal, and game birds. An expensive outing, but a great one. Tel: 861-8608.

Palio, at 151 West 51st Street, not only has a major kitchen—which is run by Andrea Hellrigl, an Italian from the Alpine region who also owns the Villa Mozart in Merano, Italy—but is also a design tour de force. The downstairs bar is dominated by a four-sided depiction of *il Palio,* the reckless annual horse race run through the streets of Siena, painted by the Italian Neo-Expressionist Sandro Chia. The upstairs has an almost Japanese orderliness, and tables are set with the sort of fine wafer-thin crystal that can't possibly go into dishwashers. Risottos are to be adored here and so is venison. Pre-theater menus are offered daily, although it's a toss-up whether or not Palio is the better show. Tel: 245-4850.

Similarly tied to a great restaurant name in Italy is **San Domenico,** at 240 Central Park South (equivalent to 59th Street, between Seventh Avenue and Broadway). It is sister to a much-heralded establishment in Imola, near Bologna, whose chef may sometimes be found in the New York kitchen. It faces the park across the street, which means that plenty of light comes through the gauzy curtains, but even if it did not, the delicious food would brighten the place. Look for any version of homemade spaghetti and for dishes that utilize baby artichokes or lobster. A generous bowl of crudités is served before dessert in lieu of salad. The wine list goes on forever, an array of hundreds of Italian names that perhaps 90 people in the world can sort through with any authority. It helps prove a point about Italy's bounty and sophistication, however. Tel: 265-5959.

The imaginative, unusually beautiful restaurant **Toscana** suffers somewhat from its installation as part of the lipstick-shaped skyscraper that John Burgee and Philip Johnson's firm perpetrated a few years ago at 54th Street and Third Avenue. Toscana, run by the courtly Sergio Bitici is, in opposition to the building, an example of

Postmodernism gone right. Pear wood, marble, stucco, and glass form an environment as easy to love as the carefully concocted dishes. Service, in keeping with the high prices, is smooth and very gracious. The front door is at 200 East 54th Street. Tel: 371-8144.

Simpler pleasures (at lower cost) can be sought at **Café Trevi**, at 1570 First Avenue between 81st and 82nd streets, where the tablecloths are blue-checked and the amiable owner loves a bowl of pasta with a bottle of red wine just as much as you do. This is the sort of place that ought to be in every neighborhood in every city, but few others are so lucky. Tel: 249-0040.

As an interesting departure, the cooking of the old Jewish quarter in Rome is re-created nightly at **Lattanzi Ristorante**, 361 West 46th Street, on the Theater District's generally unstimulating Restaurant Row. The dishes offered pay tribute to the people who introduced eggplants and artichokes to the Italian diet, for which they are owed a big round of thanks. Another signature of the cuisine is a delicious plate of tomatoey pasta with tuna. The meal is not kosher, however, just an homage. Tel: 315-0980.

ITALIAN IN BROOKLYN

For those willing to travel, an expedition to Coney Island, where Brooklyn meets the Atlantic Ocean, can be an experience to treasure. Either take the B or F subways all the way to the end (about an hour), or drive along the Belt Parkway, passing under the Verrazano-Narrows Bridge, until the skeleton of the old parachute-jump tower appears on the horizon. At 2911 West 15th Street (between Surf and Mermaid) is **Gargiulo's**, a monument to generations of having a really big dinner. In case Coney Island doesn't whet your appetite for seafood (Coney Island was prettier 80 years ago), the giant plaster octopus stretched across Gargiulo's ceiling should bring seafood to mind. Share a Deep Sea Royal (plenty of seafood, plenty of pasta), lotsa wine, and pray that you pick the lucky number from 10 to 100 that means dinner is on the house. It happens at least once a night. Tel: (718) 266-0906. Then hit Surf Avenue and its clackety, terrifying landmark roller coaster, The Cyclone. Your car should be quite safe behind the high brick walls (topped with jagged glass) in Gargiulo's lot.

ITALIAN IN THE BRONX

The Bronx has a thriving Italian neighborhood centered on Arthur Avenue, not far from the New York Zoological

Society (the Bronx Zoo). From Manhattan take the Metro-North train on the Harlem Line from Grand Central Station to Fordham Road; walk four blocks east to Arthur Avenue. By car, cross the Willis Avenue Bridge to the Bruckner Expressway; take that to the Bronx River Parkway, and then take the Bronx River to Fordham Road, which meets Arthur Avenue at a gas station.

There are shops here that make traditional sausages, salamis, cheeses, and pastries, and several restaurants that whip it all up into finished dishes. One is **Dominick's**, at 2335 Arthur Avenue between 186th and 187th streets, which is so informal that customers all sit packed together at long communal tables and waiters heft platters of food over heads. They never prepare nearly enough divinely good stuffed peppers. No reservations, no credit cards; Tel: 733-2807. Across the street is **Mario's**, at 2342 Arthur Avenue, which has tablecloths, printed menus, and waiters with note pads. If the food is a little short of Dominick's gusto, at least no one's windbreaker is in your linguine. Tel: 584-1188.

FRENCH

BISTROS

Cutting more and more deeply into the devotion New Yorkers feel for their Italian restaurants are the carefully replicated French bistros. It may well be because bistros have the reputation for bringing a certain gladdening vigor to everyday eating. Whatever the cause, they're all over town, and new ones crop up constantly. Never has so much *cassoulet, choucroute garni,* and *rillettes* of pork been dished out in Manhattan.

In its own way, the West Village has the charm of a Parisian arrondissement. It seems natural, then, to find some of the city's best bistros wedged in among the shaded, crooked streets of this neighborhood. **Quatorze**, at 240 West 14th Street near Eighth Avenue, is a classic: a quaint and handsome setting with relaxed atmosphere and lusty, authentic bistro food. It is also fairly inexpensive (a big salad with *lardons* is easily enough for two as a first course) and therefore crowded. Reservations are essential; Tel: 206-7006.

A wooden girl in traditional French country dress announces the entrance to **Chez Jacqueline**, at 72 MacDougal Street. She holds the menu card for the day, which may list such delights as quail stuffed with chicken mousse or roast pork with Dijon mustard. Other house specialties are solidly Niçoise (as are the owners), so look for *pissaladière* and *brandade de morue*. The restaurant inside is handsome and comfortable, the service and wine list exemplary. Tel: 505-0727.

"Straightforward" is the word for **Café Loup**, a loyalty-inspiring bistro that recently relocated to roomy digs at 105 West 13th Street near Sixth Avenue. Warmed rounds of garlic sausage, steaks with slender *pomme frites,* and a selection of fruit tarts are always on hand, as are a museum-grade display of photographs and a changing list of intriguing wines (at merciful prices that may make them seem even more intriguing). Tel: 255-4746.

James Beard used to catch lunch at **La Gauloise**, 502 Sixth Avenue near 13th Street. Mirrored panels reflect the amber light from handsome wall sconces and the pleased faces as they dig into such traditional bistro fare as *choucroute garni* and steak au poivre. The manner is determinedly old-fashioned. Service, though, can sometimes lack warmth. Tel: 691-1363.

Florent, 69 Gansevoort Street, was once a meat-packing-district diner and is still open 24 hours a day. Downtown types now sit elbow-to-elbow with Wall Streeters here, and they all seem to enjoy the flow of wine and the rough country cooking. Tel: 989-5779.

Eze, at 254 West 23rd Street near Seventh Avenue, is a bit of the South of France. The restaurant is starkly beautiful, but the food is luscious with the strong flavors of the Mediterranean. A dish such as red snapper stuffed with saffron-perfumed couscous leaves little to be desired. Eze asks a fairly steep fixed price for dinner, but its consistent high quality justifies the cost. Tel: 691-1140.

Farther uptown is **La Colombe d'Or**, 134 East 26th Street off Lexington Avenue. Its rooms have the feeling of a country inn. Large parties can sit at a big round table in the back of the room. The Provençal cooking has recently improved in a big way, so it's worth a visit for more than the pots of *tapenade*—olive and anchovy paste—to spread on the delicious yeasty bread. Tel: 689-0666.

Chez Napoleon, 365 West 50th Street between Eighth and Ninth avenues, is a popular place to come before or after the theater. After decades of service, the decor is a little frazzled but nevertheless comfortable, and the food is always dependably good and affordable. Tel: 265-6980.

Another popular theater restaurant is **René Pujol**, at 321 West 51st Street between Eighth and Ninth avenues. There is nothing chic about this place, but the food is reliable, the service friendly, and you'll be in your theater seat on time. It is a bit more cushy than a bistro, but the food still has gusto. Tel: 246-3023.

Chez Josephine, 414 West 42nd Street between Ninth and Tenth avenues, set amid a group of playhouses called Theater Row, is named for Josephine Baker and is run by one of her adopted French children, Jean-Claude. Her semiclad likeness hangs everywhere, and her *joie de vivre* lives on in cooking that cheerfully varies between bistro and Deep South. The house's well-thumped piano is, in fact, the same instrument Ms. Baker practiced with in Harlem before her epochal trip to Paris in 1925. Tel: 594-1925.

Bistro Bamboche, at 1582 York Avenue between 83rd and 84th streets, takes up barely a storefront, but the narrowness of the room is quickly forgotten with the skillful cooking of the young chef. Old standbys are vibrant, and the desserts, especially a piping hot soufflé small enough for one person, are memorable. Only wine is served. Tel: 249-4002.

FRENCH RESTAURANTS

French restaurants, as in the phrase "fancy French restaurant," have a shorter history in New York than you might suspect. A hundred years ago, in the city's first heyday of grand public eating, the action was controlled by Germans and Italians. There were traditional French influences on the highest priced meals, and an evocation of Paris was always good for a few extra pennies on the right-hand column of the menu, but proud, authoritative French cooking was little known here until after World War II.

Even then there was not much of the real thing. Good little bistros that specialized in the cuisines of rigorous French frugality (plenty of tongue, kidneys, and mussels on the menu; beef and birds fit for stewing in the pots) dotted Manhattan, but *haute cuisine* meant some mushrooms and a little wine in the sauce for the Chateaubriand and, for a big occasion, lobster Thermidor—the cooking, in fact, not of the restaurants of France but of the first-class dining rooms on ocean liners.

The lighter, fresher, more delicate manner of cooking that emanated from the kitchen of Fernand Point of La

Pyramide in Vienne only took hold later, at the legendary Le Pavillon (which was a holdover from the French pavilion at the 1939 World's Fair). For more than 30 years Le Pavillon was considered the best restaurant in New York, and even now, nearly two decades after the place's extinction, former employees still work many of the best dining rooms and kitchens in the city. Le Pavillon was one of a kind for many years, until other equally ambitious restaurant owners began to open places that played variations on Pavillon's theme of restrained richness of decor, exacting, laborious cooking, waiters trained in Europe, daily attention to costly flower arrangements, and prices that were unapologetically stiff. For many Americans, Le Pavillon was the only place they had ever been where their dinner gave them a thrill.

The pattern set by Le Pavillon was picked up by the newcomers La Caravelle, Lutèce, Le Cygne, and La Côte Basque (the less formal offshoot of Le Pavillon, installed in the original site when Le Pavillon moved).

All of these restaurants were, and still are, anointed with praise from newspapers, magazines, and a steady flow of testimonials from the business community (whose presence gave these restaurants their air of stodginess—a trait that is not natural to restaurant people themselves). By the late 1970s French restaurants in New York found themselves no longer setting tastes but instead reacting in a haughty, grumpy manner to changes in life around them. There were the fusses over whether women would be allowed through the door in pants, and whether a woman ought ever to see the menu with the prices on it if she was out with a grown man. But the greatest flap was over the food. A new generation in France sought to make fine cooking lighter still, more spontaneous (although spontaneity was to be granted only to those who had served grueling, unspontaneous apprenticeships), and more worldly; it was no longer possible to treat Asian cooking as less than an equal of the best European.

The top French restaurants in New York reacted badly, for had not the art of cooking reached near perfection in Vienne in the 1930s? Pantsuits were pushing through the front door, and nouvelle cuisine was trying to break into the kitchen. How these places have survived is interesting.

Lutèce has simply stood above it all. This fixedly old-fashioned restaurant had its firmly committed regular clientele in place before the changes took place, and it only changed when the traffic would allow it. Today,

Lutèce is a cozy place, an out-of-the-way restaurant that is essentially a mom-and-pop operation (Mr. and Mrs. André Soltner) in which Pop, who could be overseeing legions of cooks in some huge, frightfully posh hotel, would rather just cook (or oversee the cooking) for a few people a day and keep things cheery, personal, and actually on a higher standard than you can hit in one of those hotels with so many people coming and going.

In fulfillment of all this, Lutèce is set in a relatively unassuming town house at 249 East 50th Street, near unfancy Second Avenue. Even after a recent redecoration, the rooms still feel like those in a town house and the meal like a well-catered party. The food has gotten lighter, but only in ways that are hard to detect (sauces haven't been thinned out to broths, although they are no longer so rich as to constitute a food in their own right). Should you go to Lutèce when you have only a relatively short time to spend in New York (assuming a reservation can be obtained)? Only if some very pampered time-travel is in order, or if you know you'd like an escape from hard-driving New York while you're still in the city. Tel: 752-2225.

La Caravelle nearly turned into a ghost town. Its wealthy clientele from the 1960s aged, and its unswerving conservatism failed to attract new faces. But last year a Frenchman named Andre Jammet became sole owner. He is the son of the man who founded the superb Hôtel Le Bristol in Paris, and Mr. Jammet has infused his restaurant, at 33 West 55th Street (between Fifth and Sixth avenues), with new sophistication and has shored up the kitchen with an eager and capable American-born chef. With a new air, this conventionally luxurious restaurant (at 33 West 55th Street) has gone from seeming old-time to seeming timeless. It remains one of the last bastions of such waiters' artistry as tableside carving, but its lease on the city's high-end social life is now fully renewed. Tel: 586-4252.

Le Cygne broke and ran from the pack. It moved into a new and very attractive Postmodern building (always filled with flowers) at 55 East 54th Street between Madison and Park before there really *were* any Postmodern buildings built. The gamble paid off, for this is the prettiest of the lot, though it isn't roomy. In the last year, the owners brought in a new, young chef, Jean-Michel Bergougnoux, who has truly been cooking up a storm and adding new dishes since his arrival. The veteran serving staff seems a bit dazed by his prodigious energy, but the results are just wonderful. As at most of the other grand restaurants described here, the meals at Le Cygne are at a fixed (high) price. Special goodies generally add a few dollars to the bill, and a useful rule of thumb is to estimate that each person's meal, with drinks, tax, and tips factored in, will come to about twice the fixed price. Tel: 759-5941.

La Côte Basque, at 5 East 55th Street, was in danger of fizzling for many years, bounced back, and is now starting to ossify again, this time from expanding its facilities and letting boredom creep into the menu and the manner of the staff. The shame of it is that the sprightly, luminous murals of waterfront life in Basque country still form a backdrop to what is certainly one of the ritziest rooms in town. Come hell or high water, the frontmost tables at lunch are still occupied by the latter-day equivalents of the ladies who headquartered here in Truman Capote's venomous unfinished novel *Answered Prayers*. They have the Dover sole and skip dessert. Tel: 688-6525.

The creative resurgence in cooking in France that started in the 1970s and shows no sign of slowing down has influenced New York in many ways (right down to goat cheese on salads in bars). But it is most keenly felt at some of the city's French outposts.

Le Cirque, at 58 East 65th Street between Madison and Park, is actually a fairly old restaurant, but it has kept up with the times by hiring highly trained Frenchmen to lead the kitchen. The current bearer of the torch is Daniel Boulud, who was something of a prize pupil of the French titans Michel Guérard and Roger Vergé. He draws influences from traditional French haute cuisine and from French regional styles. A piece of paper pasted into each day's menu gives the latest of his discoveries (which, for example, recently included a "napoleon" of fresh tuna layered between ultra-thin garlic toasts). He cooks fish with unerring accuracy and has brilliant pastry chefs working under him. It is the sort of meal worth setting time and resources aside to enjoy.

Food at Le Cirque is only half the story, however. Under the direction of Sirio Maccioni, a veteran of many decades of restaurant life, the dining room is one of the most frenetic scenes in a frenetic town. Tables are packed together, which the regulars mind not at all. Waiters are constantly on the go, and famous people are making no effort to be unnoticed. Le Cirque is no respite from city living; it *is* city living. Tel: 794-9292.

Le Bernardin, at 155 West 51st Street (between Sixth and Seventh avenues), was at first intended to be the New York branch of a very successful seafood restaurant in Paris owned by a brother and sister, Gilbert and Maguy Le Coze. But given an instant blast of acclaim in New York (and a kitchen that is a professional chef's most glorious dream come true), the Paris operation seemed like old hat and was sold. Now the Le Cozes' unusual cult of fish and shellfish (meat is served grudgingly and only on special request) is centered in Manhattan and has easily as many adherents as it had across the Atlantic. Descended from Breton fishermen, the siblings sell sparkling fresh aquatic fare that has the cold brightness of sashimi and the oceanic goodness of a dockside grill. The food is a study in minimalism, but the dining room is plush and formal, and wonderful genre paintings (heroic fishermen, still lifes of crustaceans) hang on the walls. Desserts are state-of-the-art lovely and yummy. Some people find the seafood regimen more to their liking at midday than in the evening. Very expensive. Tel: 489-1515.

Lafayette, in the Drake Swissôtel, at 65 East 56th Street at Park Avenue, is a showplace for the innovative Alsatian chef Jean-Georges Vongerichten. This smallest of the top-flight French restaurants is quiet and removed, and quite forthright in its fixation with great food: There's a picture window onto the kitchen that keeps the calm, methodical chefs on view throughout the meal. The menu is revamped at least twice a year, and it is a safe bet that many of the dishes will never have appeared anywhere else before. Waiters are unobtrusively helpful, and if the management ever plays favorites with customers, it isn't done to a degree that could catch notice. This would be first choice for a luxurious dinner where privacy was a high priority. Tel: 832-1565.

If you have the time or the resources for but one lavish meal in New York, you might well consider **Le Périgord**, a veteran establishment at 405 East 52nd Street off First Avenue, whose kitchen is in the hands of yet another tireless young genius, in this case Antoine Bouterin. Why here? Well, because the menu reaches in every direction: some very current light food; some conscious throwback dishes; creative *menus gastronomiques;* dessert-lovers' desserts—all served with abundant good humor. It could be the answer to what virtually anyone looks for in a splashy French restaurant. Tel: 755-6244.

AMERICAN

For the purposes of dining out, "American food" has come to mean cooking prepared by chefs with classical training that uses ingredients that most (or at least some) Americans are familar with, but that would force a normally parochial European to do a bit of head scratching.

This outlook has been raised to a highly individual art by American chef Larry Forgione at his eatery **An American Place**, at 2 Park Avenue (32nd Street). He gained attention initially by vowing not to use imported European ingredients (not something New York chefs rely on heavily in the first place), but his talent has been for taking such American vernacular items as corn relish, beef jerky, and apple brown Betty and turning them into dishes that lift the senses as vigorously as French cooking will with its own best ingredients on hand. Naturally the wine list is entirely American, too. The best thing about An American Place is that years after proving his point about American food sources, Mr. Forgione keeps using them with love and gusto. Tel: 684-2122.

Looking approvingly, one imagines, over Mr. Forgione's shoulder is Leon Lianides (both men were championed by the cooking authority James Beard), whose **Coach House**, at 110 Waverly Place (a block south of 8th Street between Sixth Avenue and Washington Square), has been serving gracious American meals (with overtones of the South, although Mr. Lianides is a Greek) for 40 years. Rather than spin out new dishes, Mr. Lianides has spent his career perfecting a set of American basics that includes paradigmatic crab cakes, corn sticks, black bean soup, roast rack of Kentucky lamb, steak au poivre, chef's custard, and, for a few special autumn weeks, quince pie. The staff is all in the near-retirement years, and so a meal is not rapid-fire. Tel: 777-0303.

The fires of youth burn elsewhere, most strongly at Bouley and Aureole, two gracious establishments that are firmly under the control of young American chefs. **Bouley** is the last name of chef David Bouley, and he has fashioned in a southern TriBeCa warehouse zone, at 165 Duane Street between Greenwich and Hudson, a nearly perfect re-creation of the sort of provincial French restaurant where a lovely hedge border protects a parking lot full of large Mercedes-Benzes. Bouley's ceilings are gracefully vaulted, and a dignified calm reigns. The cooking, much of which is very exciting, is French-derived, but with an increasing reliance on local producers of fine ingredients. The chef's geographic center has been moving westward, and the tastes of his customers have been driving him further into seafood. He makes a proud display of his French souvenirs (including an 18th-century walnut front door), but his style is his own. Tel: 608-3852.

Aureole takes up much of a renovated town house at 34 East 61st Street and is home to the generous and nigh-unforgettable cooking of Charles Palmer, a young man raised on an Upstate New York farm whose sheer love of food brings the bountiful image of American agriculture to life and whose training leads him to embellish his meals in ways that other restaurants wish they had time for. If a dish needs some grilled corn-meal spoon bread on the side, it's the best version of corn bread you may ever taste, and the desserts his pastry crew produces are almost too glorious to eat. The after-meal chocolates alone are worthy of a detour, and while prices are high, they are mercifully below the top. Tel: 319-1660.

Other American chefs have worked their way up to splashy addresses after making their initial marks in settings that offered good brunches and other less-formal meals. For years Patrick Clark oversaw the kitchens at both the archetypal downtown hangout **The Odeon** (for discovered and undiscovered artists, loft dwellers, people with defiantly original wardrobes, and people who happened to like a very good, fairly priced meal), at 145 West Broadway in TriBeCa (Tel: 233-0507), and its Upper West Side sequel, **Café Luxembourg**, at 200 West 70th Street west of Broadway (Tel: 873-7411). He left both in very capable hands, and both have stayed very busy (places that are well run do tend to outlive the ones that trade only on flash). Mr. Clark now has his own setup at **Metro**, in the very definitely uptown Volney Residence, at 23 East 74th Street. As he did at his earlier workplaces, Mr. Clark makes his kitchen keep long hours (until 11:30 every night but Sunday), which means that a fine meal can be had long after the other serious places have stacked the chairs. Deceptively simple, lustrous salads are one of his specialties, and so are dishes based around squab and other game birds. Tel: 249-3030.

For nearly a decade **Chanterelle**, at 6 Harrison Street in TriBeCa (at the corner of Hudson Street), kept a nightly vigil on a lonely corner of SoHo that somehow remained untouched by the neighborhood's art and apparel boom. In new, slightly enlarged quarters, David and Karen Waltuck continue to turn out long, exquisite meals. They also have a following among leading artists, many of whom have designed menu covers. These friends of the house include Merce Cunningham, John Cage, and Eric Fischl. (The late Virgil Thomson scored an original number for the Waltucks called "Intensely Two.") David Waltuck's own art has to do with such fine things as seafood sausage in beurre blanc and some surprisingly glamorous approaches to pork and to venison. Chanterelle also offers one of the most extensive cheese boards in the known world—a staggering variety, mostly farm-made, all in peak condition. The evening costs about as much as a minor work of art, but it might hold your affection for longer. Tel: 966-6960.

Chefs are a nomadic lot, and New Yorkers carefully scan the press for the not unexpected news that a cook they admire has just given notice and will soon be appearing at a new stove. Thus when one of these talented drifters finds a place to call true home, the town tends to applaud. Tom Valenti, who opened and left some very good restaurants, has settled down, it would seem, at **Alison on Dominick Street**, a small gem west of SoHo at 38 Dominick Street (between Varick and Hudson streets—an obscure location that baffles even lifelong Manhattanites). It is run by the stylish actress-proprietress Alison Price, and she and Mr. Valenti go for the cooking of Southwest France in a big way, hence lentils, lamb shanks, and ducks are treated with special care, and the wines are robust and affordable. Try going for lunch, when business is slightly less brisk. Tel: 727-1188.

Anne Rosenzweig gained notice at **Vanessa**, which remains a good standby in Greenwich Village, at 289 Bleecker Street just east of Seventh Avenue, especially for Sunday brunch; Tel: 243-4225. Along with a business partner, she opened **Arcadia**, at 21 East 62nd Street, one of the smartest small restaurants in the city (it sports a charming panorama of the seasons by Paul Davis), where she has achieved success with such inventions as a lobster club sandwich (lunch) and "chimney-smoked" lobster (for dinner). She and her partner also took on executive positions at the refurbished "**21**," the hulking Establishment hangout at 21 West 52nd Street that has never quite emerged from the days when executives were fueled by martinis. Her talents have for some reason proven unavailing at turning "21" into a great restaurant. While "21" still needs help, Arcadia hasn't noticeably slipped despite the demands on Ms. Rosenzweig's time. Tel: 223-2900 for Arcadia; 582-7200 for "21."

A far more effective rejuvenation has been wrought by a chef named Andrew D'Amico at the famously beautiful (and formerly scorned) restaurant **Sign of the Dove**, at 1110 Third Avenue on the corner of 65th Street. A few years ago, masses of bric-a-brac went heave-ho, and now simple wrought iron, exposed brick archways, skylights, roomy tables, and a barroom inspired by Josef Hoffmann's designs are part of this long-running establishment's attraction. The house-made sourdough is one of the best loaves in town and it may quite conveniently be used to absorb the last drops of Mr. D'Amico's lovely light sauces. During good weather, the skylights open, but the cuisine is a lure year-round. Tel: 861-8080.

And if these places are insufficiently all-American, then there is now a bona fide **K-Paul's Restaurant** right in little old Manhattan. The hyperbolic Louisiana master chef Paul Prudhomme sent a crew of his New Orleans cooks north and deputized some local talent, and the results are to found at 622 Broadway between Bleecker and Houston streets. The line to get in stretches forever, the service is roadhouse-style, and the prices are steep, but it's the real thing: Cajun martinis, crawfish *étoufée,* flaky-crusted pies, and all. No tablecloths, no food served on Saturdays or Sundays, and no compromises in the kitchen during those thriving weeknights. Tel: 460-9633.

LOCAL PHENOMENA

There are some restaurants that could only happen in New York, because anything more modest than the ambitions of this city could probably not have propelled them into existence.

At the figurative epicenter stands **The Four Seasons**. Philip Johnson designed it 30 years ago under the eye of Ludwig Mies van der Rohe, as a part of Mies's Seagram Building on Park Avenue (the restaurant's entrance is at 99 East 52nd Street). In its looks and manners The Four Seasons may be the purest statement of wealthy, confident Modernism anywhere; it pioneered sans-serif flatware and stemless brandy snifters and elevated basic American foodstuffs to international recognition. Grandly spacious and luxurious in spite of its rigorous geometry, The Four Seasons is something of a law unto itself. Menus and greenery still change on the first day of every season. Hordes of well-attired customers troop past the huge Picasso in the corridor linking the dining rooms or sip drinks beneath Richard Lippold's sculpture comprising thousands of suspended brass rods. Given the size of the place, the kitchen is staggeringly good. The Pool Room, which is named for the square, burbling fountain in its center, offers more elaborate meals than the Grill Room, which is well known for its high-profile clientele at midday (who tend to order the same simple things every time) and its chic and expensive suppers at night. The Pool Room has a long menu (which always includes a superb roast duckling), and its waiters perform the carving and plate arranging at tableside. Luscious desserts are wheeled from table to table on a cart that someone, someday, is going to hijack. As with any New York City restaurant of note, reservations should be made as far in advance as plans allow. Tel: 754-9494.

Recessed into the lower level of Grand Central Terminal is **The Grand Central Oyster Bar & Restaurant**, since 1913 a mecca for seafood lovers, commuters, business folk, and those remaining few travellers who expect a celebratory send-off before a journey by rail. About 2,000 people a day are served under its vast vaulted ceilings, at tables, along counters, and at the granite-topped oyster bar itself, where imperturbable chefs prepare the likes of oyster "pan roasts" or Ipswich clam stews, one portion at a time, wearing what looks like lab gear. Briny fresh oysters (bluepoints, Chincoteagues, Wellfleets, Malpeques, and so on) are pried open all day long to be savored raw, and the kitchen carefully prepares an almost confounding array of the freshest fish, such as yellow perch, Montauk bluefish, smelts, and wolffish, in addition to Atlantic salmon, lemon or gray sole, tuna, and halibut. The Oyster Bar also offers a similarly all-inclusive list of American white wines. Tel: 490-6650; closed on weekends.

Rockefeller Center, between Fifth and Sixth avenues off 50th Street, the visionary office complex in the heart of Midtown, has dramatic eateries at its pinnacle and at its base. At the very top of the RCA Building (now officially known by its new owner as the G. E. Building) is the legendary **Rainbow Room**, a triumph of Style Moderne, recently restored to its 1930s ebullience, with a revolving inlaid dance floor, big-band music, cigarette girls, and fancy, authentically mediocre nightclub food. Many of the dancers on the floor really know their moves; they can fox-trot as gracefully as some of the ice skaters, 65 stories below, can glide. Black tie is never out of step. Tel: 632-5000. (By day the Rainbow Room is a private club.)

Adjacent to Rockefeller Center's sunken rink is the handsomely appointed, spacious **SeaGrill**, another place aiming for aquatic excellence. It lists far fewer fish than the Oyster Bar but prepares them more elaborately. In the months when there is no skating some of the Lower Plaza is given over to umbrellaed outdoor tables (sharing the territory with the less-expensive and less-wonderful American Festival Café). Very properly suited types inhabit it by day, and their very properly dressed families come in at night. Tel: 246-9201.

The magnificent view from **The River Café**, moored in the shadow of the Brooklyn Bridge on the Brooklyn side (at 1 Water Street), takes in Wall Street's towers and the bay and river that almost lap at their edges. The restaurant is a pair of barges in the East River and is also rightly famous for its sophisticated American cooking. The stove's current overseer is a young chef named David Burke, the third in a distinguished line at the River Café. He succeeds Larry Forgione (see An American Place) and Charles Palmer (see Aureole). Given the panorama out the windows, the restaurant would fill if it only sold cheese and crackers, and so the excellence of the cooking just serves to make it a tougher booking. The solution: a weekday lunch. An error: trying to get in on Mother's Day. To reach it by car or cab from Manhattan, take the first exit off the Brooklyn Bridge and follow the road that curves back down to the water. The restaurant will summon a cab or notify a car service, on request, for the return trip. Tel: (718) 522-5200.

The River Café and countless other specks on the cityscape can be pointed to from the restaurant complex **Windows on the World**, which is on the 107th floor of 1 World Trade Center (the north tower). Dinners served in "The Restaurant"—enough table linen here for a tent city—are passably good, but dinners served in the tiny room called **Cellar in the Sky**, which only offers a lengthy, imaginatively orchestrated wine-and-food blowout (it commences nightly at 7:30), are marvelous. The catch is that you are cut off from the view. Windows' bar and self-explanatory **Hors d'Oeuvrerie** permit a look at, on the other hand, the hills of Staten Island and the familiar figure of *Liberty Enlightening the World* without obliging you to stay all evening. Tel: 938-1111.

Tavern on the Green, in Central Park at West 67th Street, does more business than any other restaurant in New York, so "tavern" is somewhat misleading. Tabernacle on the Green might come closer. In any case, it is also the city's leading producer of hoopla (tens of thousands of firefly-size lights in the trees, chandeliers galore, an unashamed leaning toward desserts). Birthdays are to Tavern on the Green as Christmas is to Macy's. People who think hard about their food go elsewhere, but the spectacle is unrivaled. Tel: 873-3200.

Another local spectacle is the fabled **Russian Tea Room**, best known perhaps for its slogan, "Slightly to the Left of Carnegie Hall," which translates into 150 West 57th Street near Seventh Avenue. It is home to the czars and czarinas of show business, who assemble here at lunchtime to do business. This must give the nonindustry people who watch them a delicious thrill—they could not possibly be here for the food, which is quite expensive and is doled out with very un-Slavic stinginess. The decoration is indeed cheery, and the caviar and blini are a delectable splurge after a concert, but if the crummy little pastries that pass for dessert were shown to a real czar he'd call the executioner. Tel: 265-0947.

It has long been pointed out that no all-American city is complete without something called a New York–style deli in which certain facets of traditional Jewish-Romanian party food are sold at varying stages of deep frost. But are there New York–style delis in New York?

"In name only" are the words that might come to the lips of most longtime New Yorkers, for deli food has fallen on hard times, at least as far as eating out is concerned (stunningly fine fare is still available from many sources to carry back to your lair—it's the deli-as-public-accommodation that has suffered lately). The death of Leo Steiner, a voluble, fanatical, corned beef–apotheosizing promoter was a deep blow to the noshing community. Within weeks of Steiner's passing the word was out that his headquarters, **The Carnegie Delicatessen and Restaurant**, at 854 Seventh Avenue between 54th and 55th streets (Tel: 757-2245), had taken advantage of his unavoidable absence and "changed the coleslaw." It was deemed sweeter, more luncheonette-like, and missing its more difficult, sinus-clearing edge. If they could let the slaw slide, might not Steiner's whole legacy be trashed?

The next realization was that aside from the Carnegie, most delis hadn't been very good anyway. They let their meats dry out; the yellow in their chicken broth looked suspiciously industrial; and the chopped chicken liver was clearly made by people who had no idea what it was supposed to taste like. The Carnegie Deli, The Second Avenue Kosher Deli (at 156 Second Avenue at 10th Street), and a bunch of others remain busy and popular, but the boasts about their cooking ring very hollow now. Steiner, who had an awesome temper, must be truly beside himself somewhere.

CHINESE

The golden age of going out for Chinese food lasted from about the time that President Nixon stood on the Great Wall of China until approximately the time of the bicentennial of United States trade with China, a little more than ten years later. These were the years when hot, spicy, colorful, tangy dishes from Szechwan and Hunan provinces appeared in the city, and many dedicated diners had simply never in their lives eaten so well (and for so little money).

The golden age ended as the Grand Openings of Chinese restaurants started to outnumber, by an enormous factor, the number of chefs with even the most modest talent (Chinese restaurants even appeared to outnumber dry cleaners on the avenues of Manhattan). Five thousand years of culinary greatness declined rapidly into the stuff that New Yorkers sat in front of the TV eating on rainy nights.

Visits to the city's Chinatowns (or to the few relatively expensive places outside the Chinatowns that can afford a real chef) are now the only ways to relive the heyday. Nearly any New Yorker who swears that the take-out place on the corner is very good is really talking about how well the place maintains its delivery bikes and not how well it maintains its cuisine.

But out in the city's "second" Chinatown, in the Flushing section of Queens, things are starting to shake again. **Fortune Chao-Chow Seafood Restaurant**, at 135-16 Roosevelt Avenue (from Times Square, Fifth Avenue and 42nd

Street, or Grand Central Station, take the number 7 IRT subway beyond Shea Stadium to the end of the line), is the first restaurant in the city to devote itself to the excellent subcategory of Cantonese cooking called Chao-Chow (pronounced "jow-joe"). The spicing is restrained, sauces are thin and delicate (with a minimum of cornstarch and salt), and the natural flavors of ingredients come singing through (as in a meaty duck stewed nearly to disintegration in an anise-spiked sauce with barely cooked spinach, or warm slices of roast goose breast with lightly pickled vegetables). It is too early to say if Chao-Chow cooking will spark a rejuvenation citywide. Tel: (718) 359-4384.

Not too far away, at 137-40 Northern Boulevard, is **Stony Wok**, a Taiwanese place in a Taiwanese neighborhood that is set up with gas burners at the tables to allow customers to make elaborate meals of more or less their own devising by choosing from a list of ingredients (all priced separately) and using the provided wok to slip them into. Compared with Manhattan's far older and more complex Chinatown, the Taiwanese community in Flushing has an upbeat, spanking-clean atmosphere, and Stony Wok is a cheery sort of place (the teenagers appear to belong to after-school clubs and not to gangs). Tel: (718) 445-8535.

Manhattan's **Chinatown**, however, can still provide some magnificent eating. As the neighborhood has grown—it has essentially swallowed up Little Italy and the old Jewish Lower East Side—it has changed from a tourist attraction into a Chinese city (the eventual transfer of Hong Kong from Britain to the People's Republic has sparked a financial boom here that makes Chinatown seem like wall-to-wall banks). With many, many Chinese people to feed, the newest, biggest restaurants no longer promote such Western concerns as "our Cocktail Lounge" and don't care that their English-language menus hopelessly misrepresent what their kitchens really produce.

The way around this is simply to eat the way Chinese people eat. Gather a group of anywhere from eight to a hundred people, walk into a big, busy Chinatown restaurant at the very busiest time, and order a fixed-price banquet, which might cost $150 but will handily feed ten people. It's still $150 whether you are eight people or twelve people; the quantity of food is not adjusted until your group becomes *two* tables. Even if every dish doesn't meet with universal acceptance, there is still more than enough food to send the gang rolling home.

Grand Palace, at 94 Mott Street, is the sort of place to go for a huge evening banquet (no prior arrangement necessary), and so are **The Silver Palace**, at 50 Bowery, and **The Nice Restaurant** (which has a particularly adept kitchen), at 35 East Broadway. You need the names of at least three of these places because one or more are liable to be booked solid with big parties. The meal generally begins with savory hors d'oeuvres, moves through a velvety soup (often made from winter melon), and usually pushes on through shellfish, duck, chicken, beef, bean curd, and, last but not least, a glorious whole fresh fish. Coke, Sprite, Tsing-Tao beer, and tea are the beverages of choice.

From early morning until about 4:00 P.M. all of these restaurants offer *dim sum,* the small plates of dumplings, fritters, meat morsels, and sweets that are meant to accompany tea, gossip, and newspaper reading (ask for the *better* tea; it's worth the $1.50). Women circulate through the restaurants pushing carts, each laden with several different dishes. The Nice Restaurant has an outstandingly broad and well-prepared selection. **H.S.F.** (for Hee Seung Fung), at 46 Bowery, offers its daytime *dim sum* along with explanations for the inexperienced, and consequently a long line can form at peak times on weekends. You pay in cash based on a tally of your empty plates (the range is from one to four dollars per plate, and four or five small dishes will satisfy most people).

Diners unable to summon legions of companions have their Chinatown options, too. Excellent Cantonese food is offered at **The Phoenix Garden**, a tiny place in an arcade off 46 Bowery, where the specialty is crabs and salt-and-pepper shrimp. **Siu Lam Kung**, at 18 Elizabeth Street, is another seafood haven; the house has a knack for introducing genuine Cantonese dishes to Westerners whose notions of Cantonese cooking were ruined in childhood by bad takeout.

Great Shanghai, at 27 Division Street, has playful Postmodern decor and offers do-it-yourself hot-pot meals with a marvelous sauce you blend to your liking from 12 ingredients. You select the seafood, meats, and vegetables to slip into the bubbling hot pot from a long list—each item is priced individually—and the more you select the more complex and nourishing the cooking liquid becomes when you drink it as the meal's last touch. Whole fish are also prepared particularly well here, and the best dessert in Chinatown, a hot "eight-treasure" rice gâteau (*ba bo fan*), is on hand, too; place the order for it at the beginning of the meal. Tel: 966-7663.

Away from Chinatown are the myriad Hunans (Lake, Park, House, Tower, Cottage, Balcony, and so on) and Szechwans, but few serve food worth stopping for. The hot-and-spicy spirit does live on, however, aboard **Tang's Chariot**, at 236 East 53rd Street between Second and Third avenues, which is run by the family of one of the first Hunan master chefs in New York. It has a moderately formal air and tuxedoed waiters, but the peppers are in the right places. Tel: 355-5096. The heat is also on at **China Gardens**, at 936 Second Avenue between 49th and 50th streets, one of the last of the uptown places that still takes pride in its kitchen (without charging too terribly much). Tel: 308-4777.

Good food, matched with handsome surroundings, is to be found in **Chin Chin**, at 216 East 49th Street between Second and Third avenues, which is run by two brothers named Chin. Elegantly framed studio photos of their Taiwan boyhood line the walls, and the back room is one of the most austerely elegant eating salons in the city. Just the place to gnaw delicately tea-smoked duck. Tel: 888-4555.

Exactingly executed Cantonese cooking is the reason to visit **Fu's**, at 1395 Second Avenue between 72nd and 73rd streets. The decor is hard-edged glitz, and the staff is less than chummy, but there is no argument with the kitchen and its way with glistening fresh seafood. Tel: 517-9670.

JAPANESE

Real Japanese food came to the city not to provide Americans with something new to eat but to supply much-needed tastes of home to the growing numbers of Japanese businessmen dispatched to the New York office. For their sake, Japanese restaurants (down to the actual building materials) were shipped (stamped "Midtown Manhattan," it seemed) across the Pacific. The surprise was that curiosity about a sushi bar or a warren of tatami rooms or buckets of noodles would pull New Yorkers in off the streets as well, and that they would come back for more.

Sushi and sashimi were the Japanese specialties that attracted the most attention, and eating raw fish, like jostling for lox at Zabar's, became a rite of passage for newcomers to the city. The ability to order individual portions of sushi or sashimi in passable Japanese was a badge of worldly sophistication. This fashion for raw fish has waned among the non-Japanese, which must come as a relief to homesick Japanese businessmen who now can peacefully soak up some of the raffish conviviality that characterizes sushi bars in the old country. To this end, the Japanese flock to **Sushiden**, at 19 East 49th Street, an architecturally pleasing spot with two long counters made of traditional Japanese cypress as well as some regular tables. It's best to order "piece by piece" at the counters. Tilefish, ark shell, yellowtail, and *toro* (the richest cut of tuna) all have their seasons, and the chefs behind the counters will gladly point out what is best at the moment. At the tables it is customary to order a large assortment of sushi or sashimi for communal delectation. There are also some hot dishes on the menu. The waitresses are as adept and polite as their counterparts in Japan. Tel: 758-2700.

Of longer standing and in perpetual struggle for the number one spot in the "Best Of" lists are **Hatsuhana** (with branches at 17 East 48th Street just east of Madison and 237 Park Avenue in an arcade between 45th and 46th streets) and **Takesushi** (with only one venue, at 71 Vanderbilt Avenue, which is the street bordering Grand Central Station to the west). Both cater to an interestingly international clientele and have a busy, no-nonsense air that makes you feel you are in the right place. (Tel: 355-3345 and 661-3400 respectively for Hatsuhana; 867-5120 for Takesushi.)

It isn't clear yet what effect New York City's recently enacted ordinance calling for segregation of smokers and nonsmokers will have on sushi bars. Cigarettes (and beer) are as integral to the experience as fish and shellfish, especially at night when the Japanese businessmen come around to blow off some steam.

The latest intrigue is New York's first *okonomiyaki* joint, a type of small restaurant found all over Japan, and especially in Osaka. The term means "as you like it," and that which is made to your liking is a chunky crêpe binding together various combinations of seafood, veggies, pork, and even eggs and noodles. Customers sit at counters lined with big griddles or at tables with a wooden edge and a griddle in the center. At night, *teppanyaki,* the artful carving and quick cooking of sirloin (primarily), takes place on the same surface. The "crêpes" are one of the cheap, sustaining meals (under $10 at lunch) that has made Japan great. **Chibo Okonomiyaki**, at 47 East 44th

Street, is more pleasingly decorated than most of its counterparts in Japan, and service is eager and prompt.

In New York (as opposed to Tokyo), other Japanese specialties such as sukiyaki, tempura, yakitori, and so forth are usually served under one roof. An example of this is **Nakagawa**, a large and fairly formal establishment at 7 West 44th Street, which has a bustling sushi scene on the first floor but also provides as much culinary variety as perhaps ten restaurants in Japan. It has a short menu of savory little bar treats meant to go well with liquor or sake, and tables where people come to eat sukiyaki (the sweet, oniony stew) and *shabu-shabu* (the Mongolian-inspired boiled dinner of beef, many vegetables, and sloppy, slippery noodles). There are also tatami rooms (with wells under the tables to prevent leg cramps in the unpracticed), where long, multicourse banquets can be served in dignified privacy. Tel: 869-8077.

More lavishly lovely is **Seryna**, at 11 East 53rd Street, which, in the spirit of the grandest restaurants in Japan, has very good art, demure, overqualified waitresses, and tiny portions of luxurious food, some of which is cooked at the table on a heated rock. Tel: 980-9393.

Then there are restaurants that have shown what might be considered unseemly Western leanings back in Japan (Kentucky-fried chicken is fine, but not on the same menu with an airy, subtle bean-curd creation). **Nishi NoHo** (380 Lafayette Street near Great Jones Street) is the lofty, gigantic downtown branch of **Nishi**, a very tiny place at 325 Amsterdam Avenue (between 75th and 76th Streets), whose creators realized that a decorous evening of sushi could come to a rousing good finale with an ice-cream sundae (called a Hot Fuji). Some Nishi dishes are dainty, others are in-jokes (a flaming conch shell is a nod to the naïve spectacle of "Polynesian" restaurants), and some, such as various pastas, are in the East-meets-West middle ground that is probably the food of the 1990s. Nishi NoHo is so huge that full-size ceremonial kimonos hang on the wall almost unobtrusively, looking like something some aristocratic ghosts left behind when they fled the Hot Fujis in terror. Tel: 677-8401 for Nishi NoHo; 799-0117 for Nishi on Amsterdam.

Diners looking for the serene, beautiful side of Japanese life (free of commerce, kitsch, and that Japanese specialty, commerce *in* kitsch) tend to find **Omen**, at 113 Thompson Street in SoHo. The cooking is delicious and the pottery is also worthy of contemplation. The crowd is young, poised, and wears its basic black attire in a way that is somehow not glum. Tel: 925-8923.

At various locations in Midtown and elsewhere around town are mid-priced Japanese restaurants called **East— The Town of Taste**, a name doubtlessly selected by one of those writers who also decides what faddish Japanese clothes should have written on them ("Key Staff," "New York Sick—I'll Never Forget You," and so on). An optimistic attempt to make dining sans shoes a part of ordinary Manhattan life, the various Easts have a mission to civilize; they also have good sushi and tasty little beef-and-scallion *negimaki*.

It virtually had to happen: A Japanese corporation had to open the sort of privileged, deeply luxurious restaurant that is so expensive that even rich Japanese think twice about it. **Chinzan-So New York** is actually in New Jersey, perched on the stately Palisades and looking back across the Hudson at a Manhattan Island that is increasingly the property of Japanese interests. The heart of the Chinzan-So experience is a *kaiseki,* or tasting menu of achingly exquisite delicacies served in a serene, art-filled environment. The restaurant is at 595 River Road in Edgewater, New Jersey, about 3 miles south of the George Washington Bridge (take the Lemoine Avenue exit) or 3 miles north of the Lincoln Tunnel (take the Weehawken exit). Tel: (201) 945-9450.

SPANISH AND LATIN AMERICAN

Spanish cooking has a long history in New York, and many denizens of the city fondly remember the Spanish restaurants of their youth, places where brimming pots of paella or *mariscado* fed them amply for very little money on their first big dates. The encouraging thing is that the Spanish restaurants of almost everyone's youth are still in business and still feed all comers heartily.

Most typical of the venerable spots is **Sevilla** in Greenwich Village, at 62 Charles Street near West 4th Street (west of Seventh Avenue). The room is dark and filled with music, the Spanish wine flows freely, and waiters practically buckle under the weight of the pots of food they carry to the tables. The big decisions are whether to have seafood or land food in the paella and whether to try to go it alone or split the main course two ways. Whichever, the prices are an act of mercy. Tel: 929-3189.

Café San Martin, at 1458 First Avenue near 76th Street, is blessedly un-dim. In fact, it has a big skylight, which it hardly needs because its charming host, Ramon San Martin, could easily brighten the place himself. While still an excellent value, dinner here is more elaborate than in the Village places, and the roast meats and splendid desserts are actually to be preferred to filling up on a big rice dish. Some house specialties include *chorizo* sausage braised in red wine, and a genuine delicacy: baby eels from Spain flash-cooked with garlic and hot pepper flakes. Tel: 288-0470.

Just in time to whet appetites for the 1992 Olympics is **Paradis Barcelona**, the impressively authentic New York branch of a chain in Spain, at 145 East 50th Street between Lexington and Third avenues. The look is Iberian-midday-functional, but the Rioja flows and flows, and the meal does justice to anyone's most cherished memories of gazpacho, elaborately stuffed sole, and soothing *crema catalana*. Too bad that being in Midtown sends the prices up a bit. Tel: 754-3333.

Adventuresome diners may want to try **Rio Mar**, a little splinter of Bilbao among the trucks of the meat-purveying district at 7 Ninth Avenue, near Little West 12th Street. The specialty here is phenomenally low-priced juicy steaks with huge fried potatoes, but the bar serves up real *tapas,* the little tidbits meant to foster drink sales, and was doing so long before *tapas* became chic. You are more than welcome to toss your peanut shells on the floor. Tel: 243-9015.

The reason *tapas* became so chic in the first place is that they were offered in glorious profusion by Chef Felipe Rojas-Lombardi at the bar in **The Ballroom**, 253 West 28th Street, near Eighth Avenue. The chef is Peruvian by birth, but he has mastered the Spanish idiom and was a protégé of James Beard. The Ballroom itself is best known for its classy cabaret performers, but Rojas-Lombardi is one of the best cooks in America, and he lends a rich, suave touch to everything on his menu. A dinner can be rather expensive, but the buffet lunch offered here from autumn through spring is a chance to sample some of his best for a ridiculously low price. Tel: 244-3005.

Brazilian cooking can be found in generous supply and close concentration along two blocks west of Fifth Avenue in Midtown. A pleasant introduction can be made at **The Brazilian Coffee Restaurant**, at 45 West 46th Street. Spit-roasted chicken and the Brazilian "national dish," a dark, starchy ham and sausage stew called *feijoada,* are the usual things to order, after hearts of palm and shrimps cooked a variety of ways. To finish: guava jelly with cream cheese and, of course, a cup of Brazilian coffee. The management, which seems far more concerned with soccer than money, asks surprisingly little for such a big meal. Tel: 719-2105.

Not far away, at 123 West 45th Street, is **Cabaña Carioca**, a joint where music reigns instead of soccer and the menu includes a few Portuguese dishes, as well as the Brazilian standbys. The portions of food are gargantuan, which you might not notice after a few shots of *cachaça,* the Brazilian white-lightning sugar-cane liquor (also used in the "Brazilian margarita," the *caipirinha*). People come here to make noise, and the place is built to take it. Tel: 581-8088.

Hearty Cuban cooking is best represented at a long-running establishment called **Victor's Cuban Café**, 240 Columbus Avenue, at the corner of 71st Street, which was thriving long before Columbus Avenue became an elongated shopping mall. This is the place for roast suckling pig, for the stewed beef called *ropas viejas,* and for plenty of rum. Tel: 595-8599.

The IRT number 7 subway train can whisk you from Times Square or Grand Central in Midtown Manhattan out to Jackson Heights in Queens, where at the intersection of Roosevelt Avenue and Junction Boulevard (which is the name of the stop at which you detrain) there is a concentration of Argentine enterprises that includes several good restaurants. One of them is **La Cabaña Argentina**, at 95-91 Roosevelt Avenue. A gigantic wood-stoked grill in the front window should give it away that platters of juicy meats and sausages, the traditional *parillada,* are the house specialty, which is meant to be washed down with robust Argentine wine—all an excellent value to boot. Dinner only. Tel: (718) 429-4388.

STEAKS

You could always get a good steak in New York, from the time when slaughterhouses lined the piers of the East River and the best cattle in the West were sent to New York, where they could command a higher price than anywhere else in the country. The slaughterhouses have been replaced by the United Nations and the leafy tranquillity of Beekman Place, but New Yorkers are still willing to pay exorbitant prices for a good cut of meat.

There are, essentially, two types of restaurants in New York that serve steak. There is the old-fashioned steak house where, if there is anything besides beef on the menu, it will most likely be a lamb chop or, perhaps, a lobster. At the other type of restaurant, steak shares the menu with more ornately prepared dishes, and the beef itself may come topped with a fancy sauce. The old-style steak house tends to have a rough edge, with bare wood or simply draped tables, boisterous crowds, no-nonsense service. All the amenities of a high-priced restaurant are installed in the new steak house: beautiful rooms, fine linen, and service without gruffness, plus wonderful wines. People may quarrel over who serves the best, but it really comes down to how you like to eat your steak. No matter where you go you'll pay dearly, but the steak will be of the very highest quality.

What **Christ Cella** (pronounced Cri-SEL-la), 160 East 46th Street near Third Avenue, lacks in decor, it makes up tenfold in service and the quality of its cooking. Attention is paid to the simple requirements of meat and potatoes as well as to shellfish. There are no menus, so listen carefully to the waiter's catalog of appetizers and entrées—it's not long, but you don't want to miss a single thing. Tel: 697-2479.

Peter Luger is worth a trip to Williamsburg in Brooklyn (where it is located at 178 Broadway). Left behind in what was once a prosperous commercial neighborhood, the restaurant is surrounded by the massive Romanesque hulks of great banks that now serve as social-service centers. But stepping into the restaurant transports you back to a more prosperous time. The waiters, one and all, are good-natured characters, and the steaks—sized for one, two, or three large appetites—are perfect. Reservations are required for dinner; at least a week's notice for weekends. Lunch is less hectic and full of businessmen who have cabbed over from Wall Street. To find Peter Luger look for the big signs at the end of the Williamsburg Bridge. Tel: (718) 387-7400.

Despite Italian origins, **Palm** and **Palm Too** (between 44th and 45th streets at 837 Second Avenue and 840 Second Avenue respectively) are noted for their steaks. There is sawdust on the floor and there are cartoons on the walls, but the loud and at times raucous crowds have been coming here for a good part of this century mostly for the delicious chops and T-bones. But the Italian specials—linguine in clam sauce, for one—are not to be forgotten, either. Tel: 687-2953 (837 Second Avenue); 697-5198 (840 Second Avenue).

Perhaps the best example of the new-style steak house is **Sparks Steakhouse**, 210 East 46th Street just east of Third Avenue. The dining rooms are plush in a manly way, and the brothers Cetta who own and run the place have amassed one of the nation's great restaurant wine cellars—the American offerings are something of an honor roll, and their red Bordeaux collection puts most French places in the shade. This is one-item-per-plate cuisine: The steak comes on one plate, the spinach on another, and so on. Many serious wine types believe that food this simple (and excellent) is what the really complex bottlings need for a foil. In keeping with the times, Sparks has added more fish to the menu—fish that can be served in a steak-y manner, such as swordfish and salmon. Here, as at the two Palms, lobsters huge enough for a horror movie are dug into by ambitious eaters in neck-to-waist bibs. Tel: 687-4855.

The Post House, at 28 East 63rd Street, is a very handsome place with a ritzy clientele that comes for the genteel atmosphere and the excellent wine list. Nothing is a bargain here, but the cooking is carefully done and the restaurant is quiet enough to allow you to actually get some work done or hold a conversation that requires concentration. Tel: 935-2888.

Sammy's Famous Rumanian Restaurant, at 157 Chrystie Street, a few blocks south of Houston Street, is in yet another desolate part of the city, this time the Lower East Side. But the luxury cars are still parked, unmolested, outside, and on winter nights fur coats drape across the backs of chairs and lap into the aisle. It's an experience just to squeeze into this tiny basement room. There are seatings at 7:00 and 9:00 every night, and you are expertly hustled in and out. Cuts of beef stick out over the edges of plates, but no one seems to need a doggy bag. Jars of U-Bet chocolate syrup, seltzer, pickles, and chicken fat threaten you from the center of every table. Tel: 673-0330.

SEAFOOD

Every place serves fish and shellfish these days; it's what New Yorkers like to eat. Thus the old boundary between restaurants that do best by meat and restaurants that do best by fish has blurred. An institution such as Spark's Steakhouse sells virtually as much seafood as it does beef. But there is still a special allure to a place that conjures up sea imagery, and even if the cuisine is no better than it is in less specialized establishments, there is still something joyful in a communal gathering over the bounty of the oceans.

For some of the very best: Refer to the French Restaurants section for Le Bernardin; to Local Phenomena for The Grand Central Oyster Bar & Restaurant and The SeaGrill; to Japanese for a number of sushi bars; and to Chinese for the Chinatown addresses, where the standards of freshness are virtually the highest in the city. Here are other aquatic-oriented places.

Gage & Tollner, at 372 Fulton Street in Brooklyn's reemerging downtown, is a perfectly intact souvenir of the Gaslight Era, and for all of its 111 years it has held a special franchise on shellfish—old menus listed over 50 ways the restaurant served clams (some of these recipes are now lost). The divine fried soft-shelled clam "bellies" are still served nightly, but Gage & Tollner has recently been revitalized by the arrival of chef Edna Lewis, the dean of Tidewater and Carolina cookery. The lure of, for example, her catfish stew, scalloped oysters, and Charleston she-crab soup have brought hundreds of new faces through the ancient door. Yes, the gaslights are still working, and the menu has plenty to offer the landlubber. From Manhattan, take the number 2 or 3 subway trains to Hoyt Street–Fulton Mall or take the number 4 or 5 trains to Borough Hall. By car, cross the Brooklyn Bridge and drive straight ahead, as far as the beautifully restored Borough Hall itself, but look to the left to spot G & T. Tel: (718) 875-5181.

There are two branches of **Dock's Oyster Bar**, one on the Upper West Side at 2427 Broadway near 89th Street, and the other in Midtown on Third Avenue at 40th Street. Both cater to a lively youngish crowd that doesn't mind a fairly long wait for some fairly ordinary seafood. But the prices aren't bad, the white-tiled floors are correct, and the white wine is tossed back merrily. Tel: 724-5588 (Upper West Side) or 986-8080 (Midtown).

Similarly lively, and stronger in the stove department, is **Claire**, at 156 Seventh Avenue, near 20th Street in Chelsea. Claire has a sister restaurant in Key West, and so the mood is subtropical. The Bahamian conch chowder is zesty with pepper, the fish list changes daily, and the Key lime pie wraps it all up nicely. This is also the only place in town where the menu credits the designer of the waiters' shirts. Tel: 255-1955.

For a big, messy crab feast, you may tie on your bib and wield your mallet at **Sidewalkers'**, on the Upper West Side at 12 West 72nd Street, across the way from the Dakota apartment house. The crabs are heaped on your brown-paper-covered table with the Old Bay spices still clinging to them. After a while your fingers may be scratched and weary, but the feeling in your belly is a happy one. An array of other, very decent seafood is available, too. Tel: 799-6070.

Upper East Siders head for the pretty and not inexpensive confines of **Wilkinson's Seafood Café**, at 1590 York Avenue between 83rd and 84th streets. The cooks hit what many feel is just the right midpoint between dressy and plain fish preparations, and not a few indulge in big desserts after the imagined restraint of the earlier courses. Tel: 535-5454.

If only the news were better concerning the seafood available within a short walk of the city's huge, bustling Fulton Fish Market, adjacent to the South Street Seaport in lower Manhattan. **Sweets** and **Sloppy Louie's**, the real old-timers (at 2 Fulton Street and 92 South Street, respectively) serve fish that is only passable, on a good day. Attempts at a large-scale fish place in one of the seaport buildings seem to run aground every year. In this part of town the best bet is probably to order lots of fried *calamari* in one of the bars and wash it down with some interesting suds.

SPICY FOOD

There are a slew of places around town that cater to the craving for spicy food. Some are straightforward, serving the cuisine of countries such as Mexico and Indonesia, where spices are an intrinsic part of cooking. Others are a hodgepodge of styles—Tex-Mex, Southern, Soul Food, Cajun—where the food is often great, but the atmosphere and action are even better.

Cinco de Mayo has two restaurants, the original at 349 West Broadway in SoHo, and another uptown in The Market at Citicorp Center, on the corner of Third Avenue and 54th Street. Both serve respectfully adapted Mexican dishes—robust, lusty fare. These places have perfected the art of providing enough of various treats, such as an improved version of nachos, to turn the pursuit of a few good Mexican beers into a gratifying light meal. Tel: 226-5255 (SoHo); 755-5033 (uptown).

Rosa Mexicana, at 1063 First Avenue on the corner of 58th Street, is a real sit-down-for-a-meal establishment that aims, rather successfully, for true Mexican cooking. The almost mandatory guacamole is made to order, at tableside, in a rough stone *molcajete,* and it really tastes incomparably better this way. Tel: 753-7407.

Nothing beats **Zarela**, a duplex joint at 953 Second Avenue near 51st Street. Zarela Martinez is considered by some to be the best Mexican chef in town, and her exquisite, innovative dishes go a long way to prove it. Her side plates of *arroz con crema* and *torta de arroz* are required eating. Surprisingly inexpensive. Tel: 644-6740.

Nusantara, at 219 East 44th Street between Second and Third avenues, is a startlingly beautiful restaurant, filled with art treasures from Indonesia. The food is intriguing, subtly spiced, and deeply flavorful, and the place is convenient to the United Nations for the Indonesian diplomatic corps who entertain here. Tel: 983-1919.

Tommy Tang's, 323 Greenwich Street between Duane and Reade streets (not far from the river), is both naturally and stylistically hot. Thai food provides the spice and TriBeCa patrons bring the funk. The food is good, though expensive, but portions are shared so a little goes a long way. Tel: 334-9190.

Acme Bar & Grill, 9 Great Jones Street, near Lafayette Street and the big NoHo emporiums, proclaims its theme with hot-sauce bottles—all makes and origins—lined up on shelves around the room. You can even grab one and douse the already spicy Cajun–Gulf Coast food with a little more fire. This is a place to kick back and down a few beers. Tel: 420-1934.

The surprise at **Gulf Coast**, 489 West Street (the corner of West 12th Street and the West Side Highway), is that the restaurant manages to serve some very good Cajun food in the midst of all the drinking going on around the room, the loud music from the jukebox, and its quasi-waterfront seediness. The jambalaya and gumbos are worth the detour around the roistering patrons and their huge margaritas. Tel: 206-8790.

Something of a law unto themselves are the two **Benny's Burritos** (one in the Village at 113 Greenwich

Avenue on the corner of Jane Street, and the other on the Lower East Side at 93 Avenue A near 6th Street). Gently steamed foot-wide flour tortillas with delicious, healthful fillings—some vegetarian—are eagerly consumed under a not unpleasant barrage of rock music, amid 1960s *objets* and some rather more contemporary margarita gulping. Benny's rather blunt slogans are "No Preservatives, No Lard, No Microwave, No MSG," and "Ours are bigger than yours." Very fresh food and very kicky *salsa* at an easy price: Thus, quite a crowd forms at prime hours. Tel: 633-9210 (the Village) or 254-2054 (Avenue A).

Sylvia's Restaurant, at 328 Lenox Avenue between 126th and 127th streets in central Harlem (take the 1, 2, or 3 IRT subway to 125th Street), is unequaled in the city for its Southern cooking. Black-eyed peas, collard greens, and fried chicken are served in great heaps in a casual, homey atmosphere. Pies here are pretty darn good, too, and the breakfasts are life enhancing. Tel: 534-9414.

You can also get some fine soul food at **Jezebel**, 630 Ninth Avenue, at 45th Street. The room is decorated with lace, funky antiques, and lavish flowers. Smothered pork chops and spare ribs are excellent. Tel: 582-1045.

CROWD SCENES

With the exception of a few hushed gastronomic laboratories, all of New York's restaurants are sociable places, but some go a step beyond and are dominated by people who have turned socializing into a craft, or possibly a cause, one that they pursue with more ardor than they do their daytime activities. In some, the clubbishness of Wall Street, the media, or sports devotion transforms the jammed-in conditions of a subway at rush hour into many people's idea of a good time.

Almost every night of the week, a very hip, aggressively dressed crowd packs **Indochine**, at 430 Lafayette Street, just south of Astor Place and 8th Street, across the street from the Public Theater. Eccentric eyeglasses appear to serve as talismans that unleash kooky, insistent behavior among the young things crushed together along the banquettes. Along with the finely prepared Cambodian cooking, you'll get valuable pointers on hair styles, clothing extremes, and conversation stoppers. Tel: 505-5111.

Even more insistently fashionable is **150 Wooster**, at 150 Wooster Street between Prince and Spring streets—

it just happens to belong to the same owner as Indo-chine. Here the oft-photographed come to keep alive their memories of Andy Warhol, Steve Rubell, and the golden age when New York seemed to have more night-life in its old bones. Their solace is some rather good, straightforward food, one another, and paparazzi on stakeout in front. Tel: 995-1010.

After wandering around NoHo (around Broadway north of Houston Street) for a while or flipping through the racks at Tower Records on Broadway and East 4th Street, check out **Bayamo**, at 704 Broadway. The place is huge and often filled to the rafters with New York University students pledging allegiance to their first well-made cocktails and talking up a storm. The rafters themselves are hung with examples of huge, wacky East Village sculpture. The cook-ing is based on the Cuban-Chinese style of the barrios and happens to be delicious. Tel: 475-5151.

Gonzalez y Gonzalez also attracts a big crowd of begin-ning carousers, and no one can deny there's a party going on around here (live music!). The guests of honor are bottles of beer from Mexico. The Mexican food is strictly an impulse-buy but turns out better than you might ex-pect. It takes up a vast block-wide space a few streets south of Bayamo, at 625 Broadway between Houston and Bleecker streets (straight across Broadway from K-Paul's). Tel: 473-8787.

The far smaller **Great Jones Café**, 54 Great Jones Street, just east of Lafayette Street in NoHo, is open very late, and the later it gets the wilder the crowd seems to be. Many of the people pushing through the door haven't seen one another since yesterday, and the sight of these friends being reunited is touching. And if that's not enough, the rib-sticking, down-home food is very good, and the Cajun martinis are narcotic. Tel: 674-9304.

Very serious Cajun-Southern food is dished up at **Memphis**, 329 Columbus Avenue near 76th Street. Remember the address, because the restaurant is unmarked. The activity at the bar, when viewed from a dinner table on the balcony, might recall a big market day in Memphis, Egypt, while the music is a big night in Memphis, Tennes-see. Very high voltage and very high decibels, but the food is even more potent. The mystery is how so many great-looking people can eat this way and still look as though they never have. Tel: 496-1840.

107 West, at 2787 Broadway (near West 107th Street), is an offshoot of Memphis. Columbia students and young people spending the big money they're earning from their first jobs fill the place. From the way they take to the surroundings, you can easily see that many nights in their future will be spent in restaurants. It's more casual and less expensive than Memphis, but just as crowded and hopping. Tel: 864-1555.

A newcomer to the scene is **Delta 88**, 332 Eighth Avenue near 27th Street. Funky, low-life decor meant to seem (somewhat patronizingly) like a Mississippi share-cropper's social seems to heighten the flavors of the Southern cooking. Proximity to the Fashion Institute of Technology means extraordinary clothes on young customers who are very unlikely ever to reel in a catfish on their own hook. Frosted bottles of Dixie beers are the thing to drink. Very reasonably priced. Tel: 924-3499.

The hangar-size hangout of the moment is **Café Iguana**, which tries to dominate the corner of Park Avenue South and 19th Street but has competition from a similarly gigantic bar-restaurant across the way. At nightfall you can see a throng of business-suited Romeos and their Juliets, fresh from work or a workout, hastening down the avenue to take places on the line to get into the Iguana for big drinks and some incidental Mexican food. Places like this don't last long (their formerly devoted customers abandon them without a thought), but their short lives are a blast. Tel: 529-4770.

A crowd scene of foodies—those folks who organize their lives around what exactly will be for lunch or dinner and then love to talk about it—gathers at **Union Square Café**, just west of the Square at 21 East 16th Street. This big, airy, well-run establishment serves its own up-to-date hybrid of Italian, American, French, and grandmotherly cuisine, and it is only modestly expensive. Really, foodies love it, but many other people feel lost here, like the uninitiated watching a game of go. They simply don't see how a plate of perfect mashed turnips could mean so much to anyone. Tel: 243-4020.

B. Smith's is a beacon of civility at the fairly grimy intersection of Eighth Avenue and 47th Street, near the Theater District. It is not only a good place to eat, with a wide-ranging menu, but is also a gathering place for members of New York's soigné black elite, who have coalesced around the gracious and quite beautiful Barbara Smith, a former actress and fashion model, who lends her presence to the place most nights. Many of the impeccably dressed customers have perfected the art of occupying a table with such relaxed, almost Parisian confidence that the act of conversing seems transcended. Tel: 247-2222.

The Upper East Side is dotted with places that have their almost religious adherents among the very-well-to-do who live nearby. **Mortimer's** (at the corner of Lexington Avenue and 75th Street), **J. G. Melon** (at the corner of Third Avenue and 74th Street), **Jim McMullen** (on Third Avenue near 76th Street), **Sam's Café** (on Third Avenue near 80th Street), and many others might strike newcomers as overcrowded, uncomfortable, and charmless, but to many of the locals they are kitchen, pantry, dining room, and clubhouse rolled into one. All serve a reliable hamburger and respectable salads, but their social cachet stems more from what they lack (the obvious trappings of luxury) than what they provide (which is a hearty welcome to the regulars). None is terribly pricey. Tel: Mortimer's, 517-6400; Melon, 744-0585; McMullen, 861-4700; Sam's, 988-5300.

Younger East Siders and young Europeans love to shoehorn themselves into places that specialize in pastas and dressy little pizzas. **Mezzaluna** and nearby **Ciao Bella**, both on Third Avenue near 75th Street, are always hopping, even though tables are so close together you might mistake the neighbors' conversation and food for your own. The style has spread to SoHo, in the form of **Mezzogiorno** at the corner of Spring and Sullivan streets. The meals in all of them are usually simple and delicious, but service is often infuriatingly muddled, and no one speaks with a soft voice. Tel: Mezzaluna, 535-9600; Ciao Bella, 288-2555; Mezzogiorno, 334-2112.

INDIAN

The string of Indian restaurants on East 6th Street, between First and Second avenues, has both contributed to and benefited from the redevelopment of the East Village. The nearby side streets, once dark and grungy, are now well lighted, with fashionable clothing stores and galleries open late into the evening. The restaurants themselves, as befitting the neighborhood's new prosperity, have been spruced up and are very welcoming indeed.

The best restaurant on the strip is **Mitali**, at 334 East 6th Street. Except for very large groups, reservations are not taken—hence the long line outside the door on weekends. Arrive before 7:00 or after 9:00 and the wait won't be as long. Once you are inside the low-ceilinged room, which is hung with tapestries and billowing cloth, such dishes as quail stuffed with almonds and ground meat, or coriander-infused *dansak* curry take precedence. Beer is the drink that helps with the spices. Tel: 533-2508.

The attraction at both **Romna**, at 322 East 6th Street, and **Bombay**, at 330 East 6th Street, is the live music. Sitar and drums heighten the authentic taste of the curries and tandoori specialties. Tel: 475-9394 for Romna and 260-8229 for Bombay. **Passage to India**, at number 308, has the most attractive folkloric decor on the street and is also a contender for the prize for the most irresistible fresh hot Indian breads (*poori, chapati, naan,* etc.). Tel: 529-5770.

Around the corner, on First Avenue, a lavish banquet for a crowd can be had for very little money in **Royal India** at 93 First Avenue. The two long, narrow rooms fill quickly on most nights. The food is a blend of Bengali and Southern styles; the first includes cream-based specialties such as *tikka* chicken *mahani* sweetened with pineapple, and the second means fiery hot ones, as evidenced by the Madras Special's combination of chiles and aromatic spices that have been rubbed deeply into pieces of tender lamb. Tel: 533-2508.

Nizam, at 65 St. Mark's Place (two blocks north of the Indian restaurant row on 6th Street), offers interesting departures from the standard menus, including some fine dishes cooked in a *karahi* (the Pakistani wok). The chef-owner's tandoor oven turns out chickens, lamb, and fish that may be a notch or two better than anyone else's, and his strikingly piquant coriander chutney is without peer in town. Tel: 995-5590.

Another pocket of Indian cooking is on and near Lexington Avenue between East 27th and 29th streets. The sharp, almost sweet scent of heady seasonings fills the air from the many spice shops in the neighborhood.

Annapurna, at 108 Lexington Avenue, is a little fancier than other restaurants nearby. The room is very attractive, and delicious regional specialties are served in a friendly manner. Tel: 679-1284.

Madras Palace, 104 Lexington Avenue, serves only vegetarian dishes from the south of India. Rich sauces and earthy combinations of beans and vegetables, such as cauliflower with ginger and coriander, or potato patties stuffed with lentils and chiles, make up for the lack of meat. The kitchen declares itself "kosher" because it is so rigorously vegetarian. Tel: 532-3314.

Tabaq, at 101 Lexington Avenue at 27th Street, has a tandoor oven in the window. The dining rooms are down a flight of stairs, brightly lighted, and *very* plain. The cooking is rough with spices, so there is a slow, steady burn to the food, but everything is prepared to order and, if you can handle it, decidedly delicious. Tel: 683-1030.

As you head uptown, Indian restaurants become more lavish and seem to compete with one another for grand decor and genteel service. **Darbar**, 44 West 56th Street, has long been considered the most elegant, with its intricately carved screens and luxurious velvet covering the walls. The food is also exquisite. A buffet of wonderful dishes is provided at lunch in the upstairs portion of the restaurant, and that is a real bargain. Tel: 432-7227.

One of the most unusual restaurants in the city is **Bukhara**, at 148 East 48th Street between Lexington and Third. When the restaurant first opened, patrons were provided with eating utensils only on request. The tandoori cooking was so luscious—the meat came smeared with a combination of spices mellowed with yogurt or lemon—that eating with your hands seemed natural. Now forks and spoons are at every place, but the cooking is still wonderful. The restaurant is also a treat for its beautiful display of rugs and copperware. Tel: 838-1811.

Dawat, 210 East 58th Street, is a very spacious and formidably serious addition to the scene. Madhur Jaffrey, star of films by Ismail Merchant and James Ivory and a renowned cooking teacher and cookbook author in her own right, developed the dishes on the menu. Here you'll find *bhel poori,* a plate laden with crisp wafers, puffed wheat, and sweet chutneys that is a re-creation of the legendary street snacks of Delhi; and *rogan josh,* here, goat simmered in a cardamom-infused sauce until it falls deliciously off the bone. These are classic, authentic dishes, beautifully rendered. Tel: 355-7555.

KOREAN

The West 30s off Fifth Avenue is the center of Korean cooking in Manhattan. Surrounded by businesses connected with the Korean community, the restaurants on these streets fill with businessmen on the weekdays and families out on the town on the weekends.

New York Kom Tang House, at 32 West 32nd Street (off Broadway), is noted for its beef barbecue. The diner sits at a table with a metal well in the middle, where a hibachi is placed. The waitress brings a pile of marinated short ribs of beef and spreads it onto the grill. Once the meat is cooked, the diner rolls the meat in a lettuce leaf along with a garlic clove and sliced hot pepper, and dabs it with *miso* sauce. Bowls of *kim chi*—pickled vegetables—and soup precede the meat; fruit and a stick of gum follow, along with the very reasonable check. Be sure to sit upstairs. Tel: 947-8482.

Nearby is **Kang Suh** at 1250 Broadway (32nd Street). Downstairs is a Japanese-style sushi bar; upstairs are the tables with wells. Barbecued pork is the specialty—be sure to let the edges burn to a savory crispness. Tel: 564-6845.

Sae Jip, at 34 West 36th Street, is very popular these days with the Korean community, and they know whereof they eat. The *kim chi* here are silken textured and heady with chile, and *go choo pa jun* (scallion griddle cakes) are just sensational. Braver non-Koreans will try *jeyuk gui*, strips of pork with a menacing red coat of spices. Lots of invigorating food for not much money. Tel: 279-2086.

Woo Lae Oak of Seoul, at 77 West 46th Street, is ideal for pre-theater dining, but make a reservation, especially on the weekends. The large room fills up quickly with families and, later, with big groups of young people, all having a boisterous time as the room fills with smoke from the table grills and the air becomes scented with warm, delicious aromas. Tel: 869-9958.

MEDITERRANEAN AND MIDDLE EASTERN

Many purveyors of Middle Eastern food have come to feel uncomfortable with that designation lately. Somehow the heading "Mediterranean" fits more agreeably, and the justification comes from the interrelatedness of cuisines from Morocco to Turkey to Greece. Fortunately the change hasn't compromised their spice-loving, vibrant style of cooking.

One of the embodiments of it is Andree Abramoff, who, along with her husband, Charlie, runs the charming little **Café Crocodile**, at 354 East 74th Street, near First Avenue. The crocodile motif stems from Andree and Charlie's youth among the cosmopolitan Jews of Egypt (she occasionally offers a selection of appetizers that she calls an "Alexandria Quartet"). Her family was of French nationality, and so she claims Pan-Mediterranean rights as a cook. Her style is earthy but subtle, and Charlie stocks very good, very affordable wines (several bottles can go down for the price of one bottle elsewhere). Tel: 249-6619.

Anatolia is a bright and airy Turkish restaurant at 1422 Third Avenue, near 81st Street. Homesick Turks really do come here for the classic eggplant dish *iman bayaldi* (literally, "the iman swooned") as well as for an ungodly succulent quail grilled in grape leaves. The Turkish desserts are light and delectable (including an authentic pudding made from pounded chicken), and the Turkish coffee is as dark, sludgy, and revivifying as expected. Costs are reasonable. Tel: 517-6262.

Greek food is not the ready-to-hand specialty here that it is in a number of American cities, despite the huge Greek community in Astoria, Queens. But one bright spot is **Periyali** at 35 West 20th Street. It has an uncluttered Aegean atmosphere and lovingly prepared food, some of which is set out on a display table for all to admire. Tangy, garlicky flavors predominate, and dishes such as moussaka are rescued from heaviness by a deft kitchen. Tel: 463-7890.

A strip of little Israeli and Lebanese spots along Mac-Dougal Street in Greenwich Village caters to those in search of vegetarian nourishment and those in search of an inexpensive piquant meal. The street might well be renamed Pita Place someday. Most of the restaurants here are undecorated storefronts where falafel and gyros and salads are ready in a jiffy. You can sit down and spend a little more time in the **Olive Tree Café**, 117 MacDougal Street, a short stroll south from Washington Square, and still enjoy the same restorative, easily affordable cooking. A comedy club beckons from downstairs. Tel: 254-3630.

Couscous, those gentle, nourishing granules rolled from semolina flour, may be chic among the French now, but the real (inexpensive) Moroccan-Tunisian thing is to be found in little places like **Lotfi's Couscous**. One branch is in the Village at 28 Cornelia Street between West 4th and Bleecker streets, and the other is in the Theater District at 135 West 45th Street, between Sixth Avenue and Times Square. Whether laden just with vegetables or with everything in the kitchen, the couscous makes a pleasing and most mercifully priced meal. Tel: 929-3693 (Village) or 768-8738 (Times Square).

BROOKLYN MIDDLE EASTERN

Along Atlantic Avenue, between Court and Henry streets, and a few blocks from Brooklyn's Borough Hall (and easily reached from Manhattan via the 2, 3, 4, 5, N, and R subway lines), there is a high concentration of Middle Eastern shops and restaurants. Jars of spices, nuts, and grains line the shelves of the shops, and from the bakeries comes the smell of honey and ground pistachios and the warm fragrance of baked phyllo dough.

It's impossible to walk down the avenue and not become incredibly hungry. Head for **Dar Lebnan**, at 151 Atlantic Avenue, for some *babaganouj* (smoked eggplant with tahini, garlic, and lemon juice) or hummus (mashed and spiced chick peas) and lamb kebabs. The restaurant is clean and sparsely decorated and, at night, liable to be crowded. It's also very inexpensive. Tel: (718) 596-9215.

Sido Restaurant, 151 Atlantic Avenue, is newer and rather luxurious, with fine wood paneling and beautiful paintings of the major Muslim capitals, but the prices are still low. The "Sido dinner" includes soup, appetizers (hummus, stuffed grape leaves, and *babaganouj*), and kebabs for a main course, all for $14. A good deal by any standard. Tel: (718) 237-4019.

A long and beautiful wooden boat is moored inside the **Tripoli**, at 156 Atlantic Avenue. At night when the lights are low the room seems magically out at sea. The lamb dishes are very good here, and so is the service. Tel: (718) 596-5800.

MIDDLE AND EASTERN EUROPEAN

Like many groups before and after them, the German and Slavic immigrants who came in the great wave that hit American shores in the latter half of the 19th century settled on the **Lower East Side**. What remains today of their early efforts in this new land are a few good restaurants that serve honest home cooking at a very reasonable price.

Chief among these places is the **Ukrainian Restaurant**, at 140 Second Avenue near 9th Street. You enter through a long, drab hallway into a spartan dining room, where the tables are filled with Ukrainian families and the new, more prosperous (or artistically bent) residents of the neighborhood. Bring a healthy appetite. Portions are large, and the food—pickled herring, borscht, variously stuffed pirogi, stuffed cabbage, and *bigoš,* to name a few specialties—is hearty. To wash this all down try one of the rich dark beers. No credit cards are accepted. Tel: 533-6765.

The **Veselka Coffee Shop**, at 144 Second Avenue on the corner of 9th Street, is a neighborhood landmark. The swirling murals inside and outside the restaurant depict shop owners and old residents of the area. The pirogi here are excellent, as are the blintzes—with plenty of sour cream. Veselka is open late and becomes very lively with a good cross section of the East Village population. Tel: 228-9682.

Leshko Coffee Shop, on the corner of Avenue A (number 111), across from Tompkins Square Park, has very good borscht and stews. People tend to linger long in the comfortable booths and watch the street scene through the large windows. Tel: 473-9208.

Jolanta, 119 First Avenue between 7th and 8th streets, is little more than a counter, but it is also one of the finest Polish restaurants in the city. The hunter's stew, a rich, glimmering concoction of meat and cabbage, is delicious, as are the various kinds of pirogi. To feel like one of the locals, just grab a stool and point to whatever you want. Tel: 473-9936.

When the *General Slocum,* an excursion steamer, capsized on June 15, 1904, more than a thousand people from the Lower East Side lost their lives. The victims were mostly of German descent, and the disaster forced the surviving grief-stricken families to move to other parts of the city. One of the areas they settled in was **Yorkville** on the Upper East Side. There they joined Czechs, Slovaks, Hungarians, and a smattering of Irish.

Csarda, at 1477 Second Avenue between 77th and 78th streets, is a reminder of what this neighborhood was like in the old days. A bright and trim room, decorated with colorful Hungarian rugs and glazed earthenware, the restaurant serves big platters of hearty, delicious food. The smell of paprika, sweet onions, and garlic from such dishes as stuffed peppers, roasted chicken, and veal *flecken* fill the air. Tel: 472-2892.

Café Geiger, at 206 East 86th Street near Third Avenue, looks like a pastry café, but it also serves such traditional German fare as *eisbein* (steamed pigs' feet), Wiener schnitzel, and sweet-and-sour red cabbage. The desserts are Old World whipped-cream affairs and all are delicious. Tel: 734-4428.

The Red Tulip, 439 East 75th Street between York and First avenues, is a very lively and pretty Hungarian restaurant. This is no place to go if you're in a quiet mood; the dining room becomes very crowded and gay, with strolling musicians dressed as gypsies. Stuffed cabbage, grilled Hungarian sausage, and crackling duck here are exceptional. Tel: 734-4893.

Brighton Beach has come to be known as "Odessa by the Sea" because of the thousands of Russians who emigrated in the 1970s and settled here. The restaurants in the area not only serve terrific Russian food but offer a crash course in a very lively culture.

The D train stops right in the heart of Brighton Beach, which is also the name of the stop, and the **Odessa** (at 1113 Brighton Beach Avenue between 13th and 14th streets) is close by. Don't come any earlier than 9:30 on a weekend night or you are liable to have the whole garishy decorated room to yourself. And don't order from the menu; have the buffet at about $32 (it goes up, but only slightly, with the quality of the evening's musicians). The price includes a bottle of vodka for a party of four, two trays worth of cold and hot appetizers (anything from homemade ham to smoked fish to ribs with potatoes), main courses (lamb kebab, roast chicken), and dessert. The music is lively, and everyone dances. It makes for a memorable night. Tel: (718) 332-3223.

The action at **The National**, at 273 Brighton Beach Avenue, begins even later but, like the Odessa, it goes on and on. The National holds 200 people and on a good weekend it seems to hold more. Tel: (718) 646-1225.

Gastronom Moscow, on the Brighton Beach boardwalk near 6th Street, is a dimly lit boardwalk café that serves tea and vodka, a bleakly poetic place to linger and watch the ocean, especially when the beach crowds are gone. Tel: (718) 934-7418.

For lunch or supper there is **Café Armenia**, on Brighton 4 Street, just off Brighton Beach Avenue. It's a homey, comfortable little restaurant that serves stews, soups, and spiced meats. Tel: (718) 743-2444.

A PROPER TEA

Not everyone stops for teatime in New York, but those who do don't mind being different. It leaves more room for them. At four o'clock these days it's not just maiden aunts and their visiting relatives who settle down with their cups and plates, but business people, too, who find the calm and elegant surroundings of the best tearooms to be conducive to the closing of a deal. Tea is the relaxed and perfect setting for catching up with friends, cooling your heels after a day's shopping, or simply recharging for the evening ahead.

The Mayfair Regent, at 65th Street and Park Avenue, provides a perfect tea. At four the ivory-colored velvet settees and armchairs slowly fill with an elegant clientele. Potted palms and silk lampshades reflecting soft lights give the room an intimate feeling. There are seven kinds of teas to choose from, such as Lapsang Souchong, Russian, and jasmine. Finger sandwiches are delicious, especially the smoked salmon and chicken, and the scones . . . well, it's hard not to eat a stack of them. Tel: 288-0800.

The problem with **The Rotunda**, where tea is served at the Pierre Hotel, at Fifth Avenue and 61st Street, is that there are only eight tables nestled in this lavishly decorated room. But once you are seated upon a coveted sofa or in the arms of an overstuffed chair, the focus is on the table spread. A three-tiered silver tray is brought to the table, laden with savory sandwiches, Dundee fruitcake, scones, and tarts. The wide choice of teas almost seems to be an afterthought. Reserve a table. Tel: 838-8000.

The Gold Room at the Helmsley Palace, at 455 Madison Avenue at 50th Street, is as beautiful as the Pierre. The room was designed by Stanford White as part of the 19th-century Neo-Renaissance Villard Houses and modeled after the Palazzo della Cancelleria in Rome. The tables are set with gold-trimmed china and, on an overhead balcony, a harpist plays. Eighteen teas are offered with the three-course menu. First there are the properly thin finger sandwiches. Next come warm scones with Devonshire cream and fruit preserves. Last is a tray of fruitcakes, tarts, and pastries. Tel: 888-7000.

For a bit more fun during tea repair to **The Gallery** at the Carlyle Hotel, 35 East 76th Street. Nestled to the side of the lobby, the comfortable arrangement of velvet love seats and upholstered armchairs gives a bird's-eye view of the interesting comings and goings in the lobby. The offerings are not as lavish here as at the three places above, with only a few types of teas available, but everything is quite good. Slipping into the cocktail hour with a sherry is encouraged. Tel: 744-1600.

Downtown at Barney's New York clothing store there is **Le Café**, at 106 Seventh Avenue at 17th Street. On the lower level, in a charming garden setting—complete with a rustic fountain of frogs and hand-painted palm frond mirrors—Le Café offers a buffet of cold seafood, smoked fish, egg salad, and Polish ham. There are also luscious cheeses and many, many cakes and sweets, such as poppy seed, flourless chocolate cake, and profiteroles. And not everyone is sipping tea: A nice wine list is available, too. Tel: 929-9000.

FOR ALL AGES

"In America, there are two classes of travel," Robert Benchley wrote. "First class, and with children." The same could be said for dining out. Given enough money and a few years of vigorous training, it's possible that a parent could walk into the finest restaurant in the city with his or her children in tow and have a pleasant meal. But the evening would do little to promote how much fun eating out should be, and it would do less to improve the quality of family relations.

Better to take the kids to a place where everyone can truly enjoy themselves, like **The Hard Rock Café**, at 221 West 57th Street between Seventh Avenue and Broadway. Everything is here: the constant beat of music, personable, good-looking young help, big hamburgers, and gooey desserts. There is often a long line outside the door to endure before you're allowed in to wait still longer for a table, but once inside you can get a drink at the bar and stare at the memorabilia: Joan Jett's black high-top sneakers, Prince's purple cape, Elvis's guitar, and stacks of Gold Records. Tel: 489-6565.

Across town there is **Serendipity**, at 225 East 60th Street. Young "society" girls who didn't want to go to the Village in the 1960s used to hold court amid the exuberantly funky decor of this toy shop–restaurant. You'll still catch them here, but now they bring their children and discreetly chow down on bowls of chili, hamburgers, and foot-long hot dogs. No one passes on dessert, especially "F-f-f-frozen hot chocolate." Tel: 838-3531.

Outside **Two Boots** at 37 Avenue A on the Lower East Side there's a brightly painted seal balancing a ball on the tip of his nose. A ride on him will cost a quarter. The very good Cajun-Italian food served inside is only slightly more expensive. A hip, East Village crowd fills the place on most nights. Tel: 505-5450.

The second floor of the main market building in the **South Street Seaport** is filled with stalls that offer food of every description. Long curls of french fries, oysters and clams on the half shell, barbecue, deli, pastries—it's a glutton's (or growing child's) delight.

Across the square, at the corner of Fulton and South streets, is the **Northstar Tavern**. Housed in one of the oldest buildings in the city (where slave runners used to congregate), the tavern offers a large selection of domestic and imported beers for adults, and simple, English pub–type food for the young people. Tel: 509-6757.

For dessert, or to hold you over until the next meal, stop in at **Die Fledermaus**, across the square from the main market building at Front Street. There are salads and tiny sandwiches, but they're incidental compared to such Viennese pastry delights as chocolate mousse cake, lemon swirl, and raspberry tarts. Tel: 269-5890.

A few blocks north of the seaport is **The Bridge Café**, a down-to-earth joint that many New Yorkers consider an antidote to the seaport's hype. The oldest restaurant building in the city, it predates City Hall (which went up in 1811). Salads, pastas, fish—good straight stuff—and the help tells the kids some very convincing ghost stories. The Bridge Café may be found by sauntering away from the seaport, toward the Brooklyn Bridge on Water Street. It's at the end, 279 Water Street, on the corner of Dover Street. Tel: 227-3344.

What the **Boathouse Café** on Central Park's Lake, on the East Drive north of 72nd Street, sorely lacks in culinary delights it makes up for in charm. Selections from the Northern Italian menu should be kept simple. Better yet, come for drinks and dessert, then a row across the lake. Tel: 517-2233.

If you've been wandering around the city and you need a respite, give the children a bellyful of good things to eat at **Sarabeth's Kitchen** at 423 Amsterdam Avenue at 80th Street (not far from the Museum of Natural History) and 1295 Madison between 92nd and 93rd. Prices are moderate, and the room is homey and relaxed. Brunch is particularly good and, for munching later, stock up on the brownies and cookies from the case up front. Tel: 496-6280.

Hamburger Harry's has two locations: 145 West 45th Street and 157 Chambers Street south of Canal. A battalion of cooks man charcoal grills on a raised station in the back of the room and flip big, juicy meat patties at an astonishing rate. To go with the burgers there are interesting toppings as well as great french fries. Kids will like to drink the lime Rickies. Tel: 840-2756 (West 45th); 267-4446 (Chambers Street).

On the edge of SoHo, the **Moondance Diner**, at 80 Sixth Avenue (Grand Street), serves standard American road food at a decent price. The diner is open 24 hours; it gets busy at lunch, then again after midnight when the clubs let out. Tel: 226-1191.

A lot of food for a little money is the main attraction at a number of other diners around town. **The Horn & Hardart Dine-O-Mat**, at 942 Third Avenue at 57th Street, is the queen of the pack. Meat loaf and open-faced turkey sandwiches are terrific here, as are the retro decor and old-time rock 'n' roll. Tel: 755-3755.

Ellen's Stardust, at 56th Street and Sixth Avenue, accepts only cash, but the prices seem to be the same as they would have been during the Eisenhower administration. Not to be missed here are Brown Cows and hamburgers. Tel: 307-7575.

Another good buy are pasta restaurants. **Pasta Bella**, at 754 Ninth Avenue at 51st Street, serves big bowls of noodles, generously sauced. For children who clean their plates, the restaurant has been known to add an extra dollop of whipped cream to their desserts. Tel: 307-5484.

BRUNCH

Brunch: gathering to eat at a time when so many needs must be met. Perhaps you crave some breakfast (although it's past noon) while the rest of the crew has already been out and about and needs lunch; or perhaps you need cover for ordering a drink—a Bloody Mary, for instance, to set things back to rights. Some in the group may be famished, others might be a little piqued and would prefer just tea and toast. It was probably all these divergent demands of modern life that put an end to big Sunday dinners (the daylight kind) in New York. Well, it's an interesting subject, the evolution of brunch. Maybe *The New York Times Magazine* will take it up, and we can all read about it over brunch one Sunday. In the meantime, gather up the sections of the paper you like to read and toddle over to any of the following.

The epicenter of brunch has long been recognized as **Café des Artistes**, at 1 West 67th Street. It may have to do with the awakening effect of looking at the sisterly cavorting nudes that Howard Chandler Christy painted all over the walls. Indeed this is one of the best-looking restaurants in town, and brunch dishes and desserts are the kitchen's strong suit. It is also one of the few places in the city that offer truly superior fresh fruit as a final course for those disinclined to eat pastry. This is a dressy and somewhat expensive brunch, but it may be the nicest (and reservations are crucial). Tel: 877-3500.

Another vigorous wake-up call is sounded at **Lola**, at 30 West 22nd Street, a deservedly popular spot for any day of the week that offers a rousing Gospel brunch on Sundays. Just as you might be tucking into your Caribbean-influenced waffles, a dynamic woman in a choir robe steps up beside a piano and, well, hallelujah! The music, the Cayenne onion rings, and the overall cheer of the place should repair any damage wrought by the night before. Tel: 675-6700. A short menu of Southern specialties from Edna Lewis—all are quite heavenly—is offered every Sunday afternoon at **Gage & Tollner** (see Seafood) for an admirably low fixed price. A somewhat fancier brunch with flowers and imaginative food may be enjoyed at **Vanessa**, at 289 Bleecker Street in the Village, just east of Seventh Avenue South. A harpist sets the relaxing tone. Tel: 243-4225.

It might be even more soothing to watch the river flow while you eat a light meal at **The Water's Edge**, a barge restaurant moored at 44th Drive and the East River in the Long Island City section of Queens, just south of the Queensborough Bridge. The view takes in the spires of Midtown and, most spectacularly, the United Nations. Or watch the same river flow past **The Water Club**, docked on the Manhattan side at East 30th Street. A drink outdoors is permitted in good weather, and tables for large groups are easily obtained. The menu will include something pleasing for all tastes. Tel: 683-3333. And, of course, there is also Sunday brunch at **The River Café** (see Local Phenomena).

There are branches of **Elephant & Castle** (named after the London underground stop) in the Village at 68 Greenwich Avenue, near Seventh Avenue, and in SoHo at 183 Prince Street, between Sullivan and Thompson streets. E & C specializes in affordable breakfasts all week long, so no major gears need to be shifted to turn out fluffy omelets and bowls of fruit-laden yogurt frou-frou on Sundays. Both provide simple snug surroundings in which it is permissible to read the paper. Tel: 243-1400 (the Village) or 260-3600 (SoHo).

Many of the major hotels offer big buffet brunches, a fact that most New Yorkers seem unaware of, and so these fine opportunities for grazing are patronized mainly by out-of-towners. Nevertheless, an "all-you-can-eat" for a fixed price is being held weekly in **The Barclay Restaurant** in the Hotel Inter-Continental, 111 East 48th Street, at Lexington Avenue (Tel: 755-5900); and in **The Patio** in the Hotel Parker Meridien, at 118 West 57th Street, between Sixth and Seventh avenues (Tel: 245-5000); and, most elegantly, in the ever-stylish confines of the **Café Carlyle** in the Hotel Carlyle, Madison Avenue and 76th Street (Tel: 744-1600). These generally commence at noon and last until 2:30.

Other ideas for brunch include **Sarabeth's Kitchen**, the baking and preserve specialists (see For All Ages), any of the restaurants in Chinatown that offer *dim sum* (see Chinese), and the delis (see Local Phenomena). For a most intriguing departure, try an Indian brunch. The two branches of **Mitali**—the original on East 6th Street (see Indian) and the offshoot, **Mitali West**, in the Village at 296 Bleecker Street, near Seventh Avenue South—both have Sunday buffets and the kind of hearty spicy food that might be just right before a big afternoon around town. **Bukhara** (see Indian) lays on a special menu for Sundays *and* Saturdays that combines its usual array of *tandoor*-baked meats with a wider selection of Indian delicacies. The kids are allowed to eat with their hands here, and so may the adults.

Should brunch be required on a *Saturday,* **Union Square Café** (see Crowd Scenes) offers an innovative and diverting Greenmarket Brunch, which takes its name from the popular open-air market held every week on that day in Union Square, a few feet from the restaurant's door. The chef always includes dishes that he improvises from the produce that the Greenmarket farm stands have to offer, some of which is quite exotic. But that's just on Saturdays.

OUT LATE

If you're up past midnight there are many places around town where you can still get a good feed. Some are scenes unto themselves, and just getting admitted to them may take until the wee hours of the morning.

Nell's, 246 West 14th Street, **M.K.**, at Fifth Avenue and 25th Street, and **Au Bar**, 48 East 58th Street, are just such places. Nell's began the trend in this category—mock gentlemen's clubs, decorated in English style—but the differences between them can sometimes be detected only by the chosen few who attend regularly. In all you'll find good dance music, a very stylish crowd, a lot of posing, and, surprisingly, some darn good food (especially at Nell's). Reservations for dinner allegedly help, and there is of course a cover charge if you're fortunate enough to be chosen by the nice men at the doors. Tel: 675-1567 for Nell's; 779-1340 for M.K.; 308-9455 for Au Bar.

The Canal Bar, 511 Greenwich Street (corner of Spring Street, west of SoHo), a good-looking, well-run establishment, rathers nicely bridges the gap between club and restaurant. There's less of that wearisome wandering about, and, of course, there's no dancing, but the hipness, the *awareness,* the *attitude* are just so. Having a late dinner here connotes membership in *something,* and much of the food would be quite welcome at an earlier, more gastronomic hour. Tel: 334-5150.

Trixie's, 307 West 47th Street between Eighth and Ninth avenues, is loud and fun, and the dancing in the aisles just goes on and on. Although diners are crowded into small tables, the simply prepared food is pretty good. Entertainment is provided, on occasion, by the illustrious Mr. Spoons and, more often, the audience at large. Tel: 840-9537.

Acme Bar & Grill, 9 Great Jones Street, is a good restaurant that serves fiery Southern cooking (see Spicy Food, above). But past midnight the crowds come more to drink and mingle than to eat. Tel: 420-1934. This is also true at the **Great Jones Café**, 54 Great Jones Street. Cajun martinis and the very good jukebox fuel the frenzy. The cooking is tasty, too. Tel: 674-9304. (See Crowd Scenes above.)

Le Zinc, 139 Duane Street in TriBeCa, is a Paris-style

bistro, a long red room with azure clouds painted on the ceiling. It helps to be dressed beautifully, or just to *be* beautiful, to get a good seat. The food is incidental to the scene after 10:00 P.M. Tel: 732-1226.

For just a good hamburger and beer in a convivial setting there is **The Broome Street Bar**, at 363 West Broadway in SoHo. There's a long bar in front and a pleasant, dimly lighted back room. Tel: 925-2086.

Another good basic joint is the **Moondance Diner**, 80 Sixth Avenue at Grand Street (see For All Ages, above). The menu is pretty standard, but the fare is revitalizing, especially after a night of dancing. Tel: 226-1191.

Breakfast begins at 1:00 A.M. at **The Empire Diner**, 210 Tenth Avenue at 22nd Street. An assorted clientele from all parts of the city congregates for scrambled eggs and hash browns or a very rich and satisfying sundae. Tel: 243-2736.

What's bad about going late to the **Hard Rock Café**, 221 West 57th Street between Seventh Avenue and Broadway, is the line out front. It can get longer and longer as the night progresses. Once inside, and once you're seated (another wait; see For All Ages, above), it's like being at a good loud party, provided you're young and you like your music strong and uninterrupted. Good hefty hamburgers, chicken club sandwiches, and desserts. The food keeps coming until 4:00 A.M. Tel: 489-6565.

RESTAURANTS BY NEIGHBORHOOD

The following is a list of New York restaurants organized by neighborhood; for descriptions, addresses, and telephone numbers, consult the preceding listings, organized by type of food and special interest.

Lower Manhattan
Acme Bar & Grill (Cajun) (see Spicy Food)
Arqua (Italian)
Barocco (Italian)
Bridge Café (seafood and pasta) (see For All Ages)
Bouley (American)
Chanterelle (American)
Die Fledermaus (dessert) (see For All Ages)
Grand Palace (Chinese)
Great Shanghai (Chinese)
H.S.F. (Chinese)
Hamburger Harry's (For All Ages)

The Nice Restaurant (Chinese)
Northstar Tavern (pub food) (see For All Ages)
The Odeon (American)
The Phoenix Garden (Chinese)
Sammy's Famous Rumanian Restaurant (Steaks)
The Silver Palace (Chinese)
Siu Lam Kung (Chinese)
Sloppy Louie's (Seafood)
South Street Seaport (see For All Ages)
Sweets (Seafood)
Windows on the World (Multinational) (see Local Phenomena)
Le Zinc (Out Late)

Downtown above Canal Street
Alison on Dominick Street (American)
Annapurna (Indian)
The Ballroom (Spanish and Latin American)
Bayamo (Cuban-Chinese) (see Crowd Scenes)
Benny's Burritos (Mexican) (See Spicy Food)
Bombay (Indian)
Broome Street Bar (Out Late)
Le Café (Tea)
Café Iguana (Mexican) (see Crowd Scenes)
Café Loup (French)
The Canal Bar (Out Late)
Cent'Anni (Italian)
Chelsea Trattoria (Italian)
Chez Jacqueline (French)
Cinco de Mayo (Mexican) (see Spicy Food)
Claire (Seafood)
Coach House (American)
La Colombe d'Or (French)
Delta 88 (Southern) (see Crowd Scenes)
Elephant & Castle (see Brunch)
Empire Diner (Out Late)
Eze (French)
Florent (French)
La Gauloise (French)
Gonzalez y Gonzalez (Mexican) (see Crowd Scenes)
Grand Ticino (Italian)
Great Jones Café (Cajun) (see Crowd Scenes)
Gulf Coast (Cajun) (see Spicy Food)
Indochine (Cambodian) (see Crowd Scenes)
Jolanta (see Middle and Eastern European)
K-Paul's (Cajun) (see American)

Leshko Coffee Shop (see Middle and Eastern European)
Lotfi's Couscous (see Mediterranean and Middle Eastern)
M.K. (Out Late)
Madras Palace (Indian)
Mezzogiorno (Italian) (see Crowd Scenes)
Minetta Tavern (Italian)
Mitali (Indian)
Moondance Diner (American) (see For All Ages)
Nell's (Out Late)
Nishi NoHo (Japanese)
Nizam (Indian)
Olive Tree Café (Middle Eastern) (see Mediterranean and
    Middle Eastern)
Omen (Japanese)
150 Wooster (American) (see Crowd Scenes)
Onini (Italian)
Passage to India (Indian)
Periyali (Greek) (see Mediterranean and Middle Eastern)
Positano (Italian)
Puglia (Italian)
Quatorze (French)
Rio Mar (Spanish and Latin American)
Romna (Indian)
Rosolio (Italian)
Royal India (Indian)
Second Avenue Kosher Deli (delicatessen) (see Local
    Phenomena)
Sevilla (Spanish)
Da Silvano (Italian)
Siracusa (Italian)
Tabaq (Indian)
Taormina (Italian)
Tommy Tang's (Thai) (see Spicy Food)
Two Boots (Cajun/Italian) (see For All Ages)
Ukrainian Restaurant (see Middle and Eastern European)
Da Umberto (Italian)
Union Square Café (Continental) (see Crowd Scenes)
Vanessa (American)
Veselka Coffee Shop (see Middle and Eastern European)
Villa Pensa (Italian)

Midtown
An American Place (American)
Aureole (American)
Au Bar (Out Late)
B. Smith's (American) (see Crowd Scenes)

The Barclay Restaurant (see Brunch)
Le Bernardin (French)
The Brazilian Coffee Restaurant (see Spanish and Latin
   American)
Bukhara (Indian)
Cabaña Carioca (Brazilian Portuguese) (see Spanish and
   Latin American)
La Caravelle (French)
The Carnegie Delicatessen and Restaurant (delicatessen)
   (see Local Phenomena)
Chez Josephine (French)
Chez Napoleon (French)
Chibo Okonomiyaki (Japanese)
China Gardens (Chinese)
Chin Chin (Chinese)
Christ Cella (Steaks)
Cinco de Mayo (Mexican) (see Spicy Food)
La Côte Basque (French)
Le Cygne (French)
Darbar (Indian)
Dawat (Indian)
Dock's Oyster Bar (Seafood)
East—The Town of Taste (Japanese)
Ellen's Stardust (American) (see For All Ages)
Four Seasons (American) (see Local Phenomena)
The Gold Room (Tea)
Grand Central Oyster Bar and Restaurant (seafood) (see
   Local Phenomena)
Hamburger Harry's (see For All Ages)
Hard Rock Café (burgers) (see For All Ages)
Hatsuhana (Japanese)
The Horn & Hardart Dine-O-Mat (see For All Ages)
Jezebel (Southern) (see Spicy Food)
Kang Suh (Korean)
Lafayette (French)
Lattanzi (Italian)
Lola (Southern) (see Brunch)
Lotfi's Couscous (see Mediterranean and Middle Eastern)
Lutèce (French)
Nakagawa (Japanese)
New York Kom Tang House (Korean)
Nusantara (Indonesian) (see Spicy Food)
Palio (Italian)
Palm and Palm Too (Steaks)
Paradis Barcelona (Spanish and Latin American)
Pasta Bella (Italian) (see For All Ages)

The Patio (see Brunch)
Le Périgord (French)
Rainbow Room (American) (see Local Phenomena)
René Pujol (French)
Rosa Mexicano (Mexican) (see Spicy Food)
The Rotunda (Tea)
Russian Tea Room (Russian) (see Local Phenomena)
Sae Jip (Korean)
San Domenico (Italian)
SeaGrill (seafood) (see Local Phenomena)
Seryna (Japanese)
Sparks Steakhouse (Steaks)
Sushiden (Japanese)
Takesushi (Japanese)
Tang's Chariot (Chinese)
Toscano (Italian)
Trixie's (Out Late)
"21" Club (American)
The Water Club (see Brunch)
Woo Lae Oak of Seoul (Korean)
Zarela (Mexican) (see Spicy Food)

Upper East Side
Anatolia (Turkish) (see Mediterranean and Middle Eastern)
Arcadia (American)
Azzuro (Italian)
Bistro Bamboche (French)
Boathouse Café (Italian) (see For All Ages)
Café Carlyle (see Brunch)
Café Crocodile (Mediterranean) (see Mediterranean and Middle Eastern)
Café Geiger (German) (see Middle and Eastern European)
Café San Martin (Spanish)
Café Trevi (Italian)
Ciao Bella (Italian) (see Crowd Scenes)
Le Cirque (French)
Csarda (Hungarian) (see Middle and Eastern European)
Fu's (Chinese)
The Gallery (Tea)
J. G. Melon (bar food) (see Crowd Scenes)
Jim McMullen (bar food) (see Crowd Scenes)
The Mayfair Regent (Tea)
Metro (American)
Mezzaluna (Italian) (see Crowd Scenes)
Mortimer's (bar food) (see Crowd Scenes)

The Post House (Steaks)
Primavera (Italian)
The Red Tulip (Hungarian) (see Middle and Eastern
    European)
Rosa Mexicana (Mexican) (see Spicy Food)
Sam's Café (bar food) (see Crowd Scenes)
Sarabeth's Kitchen (see For All Ages and Brunch)
Serendipity (burgers and sweets) (see For All Ages)
Sign of the Dove (American)
Sistina (Italian)
Wilkinson's Seafood Café (Seafood)

Upper West Side
Baci (Italian)
Café des Artistes (see Brunch)
Café Luxembourg (American)
Dock's (Seafood)
Memphis (Cajun) (see Crowd Scenes)
Nishi (Japanese)
107 West (Cajun) (see Crowd Scenes)
Sarabeth's Kitchen (see For All Ages and Brunch)
Sidewalkers' (Seafood)
Tavern on the Green (American) (see Local Phenomena)
Victor's Cuban Café (see Spanish and Latin American)

Harlem
Sylvia's (Southern) (see Spicy Food)

OUTSIDE MANHATTAN

The Bronx
Dominick's (Italian)
Mario's (Italian)

Brooklyn
Almontaser (Middle Eastern)
Café Armenia (Armenian) (see Middle and Eastern Euro-
    pean)
Dar Lebnan (Middle Eastern)
Gage & Tollner (Seafood)
Gargiulo's (Italian)
Gastronom Moscow (Russian) (see Middle and Eastern
    European)
The National (Russian) (see Middle and Eastern Euro-
    pean)
Odessa (Russian) (see Middle and Eastern European)

Peter Luger (Steaks)
River Café (American) (see Local Phenomena)
Sido Restaurant (Middle Eastern)
Tripoli (Middle Eastern)

Queens
La Cabaña (Argentine) (see Spanish and Latin American)
Fortune Chao-Chow Seafood Restaurant (Chinese)
Stony Wok (Taiwanese) (see Chinese)
The Water's Edge (see Brunch)

New Jersey
Chinzan-So New York (Japanese)

BARS AND CAFES

By Heidi L. Kriz

Heidi Kriz, a resident of the Upper West Side, is a graduate of Columbia University—as well as its famous bartending course. She has written about the people, places, and bars of New York City for such publications as the Village Voice *and* 7 Days.

Manhattan, an island of countless choices, must be sampled in a discriminating fashion. We have attempted to reduce the hundreds of bars that might interest a visitor to a relatively select few, keeping in mind the broad range required to represent the bar bounty of this city accurately. (There are nice bars in the other boroughs, too, but you'll have your hands full without having to transit a bridge or a tunnel.)

New York City has the good fortune to possess some of the finest restaurants and clubs in the world. They are also some of the loftiest and most exclusive places, seemingly not very accessible to most visitors. But never say die, for the bars of this city are often an entrance into places otherwise unapproachable.

In many ways this survey mirrors the motivations and desires of the people of the city—quirky, quixotic, sleazy, or sophisticated. It also holds, for the careful observer, an insight into the differing characters of the neighborhoods.

THE WALL STREET AREA

The thousands of people who work and live in this area used to have a problem. To have a good meal and drink in a nice place often required a tedious trek uptown. But lo and behold, the real-estate gods heard their prayers, and in what seemed like six days the **South Street Seaport** was born.

If you have made no plans to visit the Seaport, at the east end of Fulton Street, then make them, for it really does have something for everyone. Wander around until you are parched and then choose from the myriad bars and night spots available.

At the end of the pier are two versions of **Flutie's**, a heavy-duty singles scene so vigorous it would make mama blush. Other places to ask after are **Roeblings**, the **Fulton Street Café**, the **Liberty Café**, **Pedro O'Hara's**, and **Caroline's Comedy Club**. Each differs slightly in mood from the others. The **Paris Café** on South Street right in the Fulton Fish Market complex (which is contiguous to the Seaport attractions) and **Jeremy's Ale House** nearby on Front Street are two other busy after-work retreats. **Bridgewaters** stands apart from the others with its spectacular boats, 13 of them, that hang from the rafters on steel cables and look glorious against the midnight sky. On Fridays, a veritable tidal wave of young bankers and stockbrokers washes over the Seaport.

Outside the Seaport area is **Harry's at Hanover Square**, between Pearl and Stone streets, one block from Water Street. Harry's, like every other place in this part of town, has a mostly financial and banking clientele, but it is a bit older here than at the Seaport.

TRIBECA

Even the name of the area known as "TriBeCa" is illustrative of New Yorkers' desire to be distinctive. A chunk of the Lower West Side was annexed, Texas-style, and identified with a name derived from its location: the *Tri*angle *Be*low *Ca*nal Street. The neighborhood's shopkeepers, barkeepers, and restaurateurs have accordingly striven to be unique—resulting in a variety of funky shops and eateries.

Having successfully fended off competitors for the top

spot, **The Canal Bar** (actually just north of Canal, at the corner of Greenwich and Spring streets) remains popular and exciting. The decor is pointedly eclectic, with some details recognizable as requisite Postmodern and other items completely incomprehensible. The bar and restaurant region are perpetually filled, but the people eating are predominantly Armani-garbed businessmen with leggy dates, while those carousing at the bar are younger and firmer—but poorer. There seems to be a tacit, ongoing beauty contest between the staff and the bar folk. *Très cher,* but not *trop cher* to preclude at least one plunge.

The Odeon (145 West Broadway at Thomas Street) began as, and remains, the triumph of TriBeCa. Once a 1950s cafeteria, it kept its clean, streamlined Art Deco feel and spacious, uncluttered interior when it became a restaurant. Having been a pioneer in the now completely transformed TriBeCa, the Odeon has passed, well preserved, into its golden years. Food, drink, and company here are of the highest order, and the Odeon remains one of the few good restaurants in town offering late-night dinner. The crowd has toned down a bit, but there is still a staple of glamorous types: models, celebrities, artists, and the usual associated sycophants. The bar itself is wonderfully large and well stocked, the sign of a quality rare in popular restaurants: encouragement to remain at the bar all night should you so desire. The menu is a little pricey, but worth it. Wear something retro, or black, or better yet, both.

The neighborhood's the same but the **Ear Inn** (326 Spring Street between Greenwich and Washington streets) is a welcome departure from Postmodern everything. Charmingly dingy and rough around the edges, this pub has long been a hardy mainstay for struggling artsy locals of all kinds. All the clients know one another, but they still act as if they want to know you, too.

If you're in the mood for a place like Canal Bar, or the Odeon, but the wait is daunting, **El Teddy's** (West Broadway, between Franklin and White streets) will serve you well. The atmosphere is clean, dry, and Southwestern, with piecemeal mosaics dominating the walls and decor. The crowd is young and casual, and the food is very good.

SOHO

SoHo (*So*uth of *Ho*uston Street) went through the gentrification shakedown a long time ago, and as a result the area has settled into the Middle Ages of its time span. Everything is comfy and prosperous, but there are few vanguard establishments left. SoHo's original character has been obliterated by bourgeois desires.

Speaking of bourgeois, "oenophobia," or an aversion to drinking overpriced wine in pretentious surroundings, has long been the unintended effect of many a wine-tasting place. Put out of mind whatever mediocre glasses of wine in mediocre bars you have already reluctantly swallowed: **I Tre Merli** on West Broadway near Prince Street is authentic and it's good. The menu is heavy with 28 choices of wine, demonstrated by two oversize wine racks, obviously not made just for show. The interior is accented with black and brick and has an exciting cavelike air. The matching black bar downstairs seats about 25; single glasses of wine run about $3.50. The crowd is SoHo, which means wear black again. Anticipate a lively learning experience.

Keep that black outfit on, get a trendy haircut, then enter **Raoul's** (180 Prince Street between West Broadway and Sixth Avenue) with your head held high, nose raised to the ceiling. Actually, for all its hipness, the place manages to be toney without being elite. The decor recalls the look of an early Truffaut film: very French, with brown tin ceilings and warm cream walls. The crowd could be effortlessly transplanted to the Odeon, and vice versa. The bar is always interesting, and sitting next to the likes of Richard Gere is not unusual. Rather expensive, of course.

LOWER EAST SIDE/EAST VILLAGE

For a long time, the Lower East Side of Manhattan had the air of a freshly bombed war zone. At least this was true of the very, very East Side, otherwise known as Alphabet City (Avenue A, Avenue B, etc.). This area was even once the focus of a film by the same name, a B movie about gangs that lived in a desolate neighborhood. Alphabet City and much else of the Lower East Side fit that description—that is, until danger became hip and condemned buildings cool. Like flies to honey, entrepreneurs zoomed in at the first sign of a real-estate gold mine. Overnight, slumlords became landlords and rich kids appalled daddy by insisting on paying an uptown price for a downtown hovel. Consequently, this state-of-the-art scene demanded state-of-the-art clubs, which (along with still relatively low rent) is why most of the city's cutting-edge clubs can be found on the Lower East Side. What is less predominant are solid, made-for-drinking hangouts, places with more gin and less din. Hence, the following selection will be brief and will include bars that actually encourage the art of drinking—along with a few other things.

The Bar (Second Avenue and 4th Street) is completely representative of the East Village gay scene. The tattered awnings and darkened windows make the place look sleazy—and it is. But it's also filled with a very colorful local crowd that makes drinking here (if you're straight and uninformed, that is) a very educational experience. Dress is strictly casual: boots, sweaters, and jeans—the tighter the better. The place is throbbing by 1:00 A.M.

Often a bar's reputation is self-perpetuating, even though yesterday's praises far surpass today's reality. Good for the bar owner, not so good for the potential customer. **McSorley's Old Ale House** (15 East 7th Street) is a prime example. Lines extend outside on the weekends with people willing to cram themselves into the bar for two mugs of beer for $2.00. Its resemblance to a frat party is no accident; the bar did not accept women until 1970. Go on a weeknight, when you'll be able to raise your elbow to drink and the pub itself is rather nice.

It has been around for 50 years and is twice as old as most of its clientele on the weekends, but **Vazac's** (108 Avenue B at 7th Street) will undoubtedly continue to have a long and prosperous life. The scene is simple and mellow most nights, and the massive dark horseshoe bar always offers a place to sit. Proudly calling itself a neighborhood place, it has all the accoutrements, from ceiling fans to pinball and a well-stocked jukebox. The weekends get very collegiate, but Vazac's is commodious and there's nary a class clash to speak of. If the bar looks familiar, it could be because it was the site of Paul Newman's dipsomania early in the movie *The Verdict*.

Part of the charm of Lower East Side bars is their makeshift atmosphere. Falling into this dive-bar category where the emphasis is on alcohol, not ambience, are: **Mona's** (Avenue B between 13th and 14th streets), **Blanche's** (Avenue A between 9th and 10th streets), and **2A** (corner of Avenue A and 2nd Street). The last is more of a dive bar with upward mobility, but they are all places made by the people who go there, who tend to be young, cynical, and creatively unemployed.

GREENWICH VILLAGE

The Village area appeals to the gamut of society—much of it tri-state (New York, New Jersey, and Connecticut) and adolescent on the weekends. Its density of shops and sights reflects this range, and a scrutinizing eye is necessary to catch that gem of a jazz bar, one-of-a-kind clothing store, or art-film house.

Tiny **Arthur's Tavern** (57 Grove Street west of Seventh Avenue across from Sheridan Square), squeezed in between some cheesy "Broadway tune" bars, is worth squinting for. It's dark, steamy, and very sexy, and serves up some of the best jazz in town for the price of a drink—which will run about three dollars but is easily nursed through a set or two. The crowd is mixed: lots of mid-20s one-timers "getting down and dirty," and a few fond regulars who know good jazz when they hear it. This place is a fabulous late-night stop-off, and a good way to impress your companion.

Equally low-key from the outside but very hip indoors is **Automatic Slims** (733 Washington Street at Bank Street). Not only is the crowd eye-pleasing—arty, attractive, interesting—but the conversation here reflects more than the depth of the latest issue of *National Enquirer* or *The Sun*. Generally in their 30s and with friends, the customers make the place lively and fun. The bar is always crowded, but standing won't prove unpleasant; you can always turn and talk to that model on the latest cover of *Vogue*.

Cerebral celebrities whose names are more familiar than their faces can be found at **Bradley's** (70 University Place), a polished restaurant usually populated by very dedicated jazz aficionados. With no cover charge and an accommodating bar, an evening of solid jazz is very affordable here. If you are travelling en masse, get there before 10:00 P.M., grab a table, and pay the pittance of a five-dollar cover charge. Dress is tweedy or upscale post-bohemian.

When the crowd from Bradley's is "slumming it" they might be found at **Chumley's** (86 Bedford Street at Barrow Street—no sign). Homely but cozy, the pub has long served as a wateringhole for neighborhood journalists and the poor but ponderous. A burger and a beer are very reasonable, and the fireplace will help ease a hangover from the night before. (Dylan Thomas used to drink at the nearby **White Horse Tavern**, Hudson at 11th street, and it's still pretty much of a saloon-goer's saloon.)

After you've recovered, you might well venture forth to a Brazilian bar that puts Ricky Ricardo to shame. S.O.B.'s—Sounds of Brazil—(204 Varick Street near West Houston) is a hot, loose club with a knockout mixture of Latin, African, and Caribbean sounds. Brazilians and Haitians mingle comfortably with Wall Street types—all willing to pay the $15 cover charge. The bar is spacious and amply stocked with alcoholic exotica. For bar seating, get there by 11:00 P.M., and expect to dance later.

The Gotham Bar and Grill (12 East 12th Street, off Fifth Avenue near University Place) is a three-star restaurant first, but its bar runs a close second to the kitchen. Columned, marbled, and Postmodern, the place resembles many an upscale restaurant conceived in the past six months, but despite its lack of design inspiration, Gotham stands out for one good reason—people still go there. Gotham, and especially its bar, survived the attack of the "beautiful people," and when the dust cleared and the limousines retreated, a very snazzy, solid group of regulars remained. (No longer young, but no longer living on a shoestring either, many of them travel from the Upper East Side to drink and eat here.) Now the bar itself is less frantic and is a fine place to have an elegant drink in lovely surroundings.

After the workday, professionals are often seen relaxing in a much heralded Village "spot"—the **Union Square Café** (21 East 16th Street off Union Square West, north of the Village proper in the Flatiron District). This restaurant is casual but well bred, and there's a lengthy, gleaming wooden bar holding a variety of bar snacks and relishes. Early evening, women in business suits and Reeboks often sit at the white-linen-covered window tables, looking very relaxed and watching the world go by.

Amidst the carnage of the meat-packing district is a 24-hour metallic bistro called **Florent** (Gansevoort Street between Greenwich and Washington). This sliver of a scene manages to erase the cloud of slaughterhouse smells you passed through to get there.

CHELSEA TO GRAMERCY PARK

The neighborhood known as Chelsea has absolutely blossomed in the past few years with quality shops, sights, and places to eat and drink. A relatively small area, it is thick with attractions for natives and out-of-towners alike. In spite of being flanked by other, trendier neighborhoods in lower Manhattan, Chelsea holds its own with a kind of discount funkiness and continues to grow in popularity and consideration.

The Ballroom (253 West 28th Street) exemplifies the eclecticism of Chelsea. A bar, restaurant, and cabaret all in one, The Ballroom is clean, breezy, and elegant, and the waiters in their stiff black-and-white uniforms convey a formal but unimposing air. The bar area is always bustling, but its popularity rests less on alcohol than a spectacular buffet of *tapas,* Spanish hors d'oeuvres. Two drinks and a plate of hors d'oeuvres will run about $15. Men wear business suits, women wear furs, and both genders tend to be divorced. If appetizers and drinks don't fulfill, there's more to The Ballroom: the cabaret. Amid typical high-tech club decor, performers like Helen Schneider and Jeff Harner sing magnificently, catering to a dressy, enthusiastic crowd. A set costs about $15 with a two-drink minimum. Sunday brunch is also served. Reservations are required; Tel: (212) 244-3005.

New York restaurant regulars are a contingent with almost impossible aesthetic standards, and, in their efforts to please the unpleaseable, restaurant owners often overextend themselves financially or decoratively. The result is often a dark, empty building that a year before was bright and busy. However, the most dour of critics, social and gastronomical, have difficulty finding fault with one relatively recent hot spot near Chelsea, **Lola** (30 West 22nd Street). Even Humbert Humbert, a character of scrupulous taste and European airs, might conceivably have brought his precious charge here in an attempt to find a restaurant that matched her fresh beauty. Highlights include a tiled foyer, fresh flowers, and soft lighting (everywhere the eyes rest they find unique lighting fixtures, lovely artwork, and special details). You encounter the bar in the entranceway to the restaurant. Cocktail tables with upholstered chairs elegantly extend the drinking area. Weekends at Lola are enhanced by jazz combos in the front room. The crowd is youngish but urbane. A two-drink tab runs about nine dollars. Experience this study in New York haute hangouts. You might even catch a glimpse of Lola herself, whose own beauty is unsurpassed by her club.

Those women who frequent **Café Society** (915 Broadway at 21st Street) need to be able to afford not only the prices but also the weekly shopping spree to Saks or Betsey Johnson that will protect them from the humiliation of wearing the same overpriced ensemble more than once. Furniture and attitude are both overstuffed, but if the clientele is sometimes annoying, the grace and beauty of the restaurant itself is soothing. The place is constructed with lofty ceilings and a soaring staircase to the cloakroom, complemented by columns of the currently requisite pink and black Art Deco hues. Imagine Bette Davis descending the staircase, step by step, pausing with a portentous "Fasten your seat belts: it's gonna be a bumpy night," and then slinking down the rest of the way.

Near Café Society, on the south side of 23rd Street between Fifth Avenue and Park Avenue South, is **Live Bait**, a supposedly Cajun restaurant whose cheek-to-jowl crowd starts changing at around 9:00 P.M. from young insurance executives (Metropolitan Life and other insurers are nearby) to probably under-age representatives of the hip demimonde. Crowded and noisy, but the food is pretty good.

Just south of Gramercy Park, on Irving Place at 18th Street, is **Pete's Tavern**, once a drinking place of O. Henry's. The bar itself is most evocative of old New York, with its wood carving, beveled glass, and grime. A slightly younger, more boisterous clientele prefers the likewise ancient **Old Town** on 18th Street between Park Avenue South and Broadway.

The 23rd Street Bar and Grill (just west of Third Avenue on the south side of the street) attracts freshly showered, young middle-management people, hair in place. There's nothing stiff about the well-stocked bar, however, made of gleaming dark wood with plenty of seats. Which it needs, because the cocktail, dinner, and going-out hours Wednesday to Saturday are extremely busy here, and the bar glows then with a warm, chatty atmosphere. Because of its convincing turn-of-the-century decor, this site of casual prosperity has served as a set for some major film releases— including *The Cotton Club* and *Rage of Angels*.

MIDTOWN

Midtown Manhattan is dense with the diversity you find only in New York City. Moving west from the epicenter, you encounter both the glitzy and the grotesque. The glamorous Theater District of Midtown West is only an X-rated movie house or two away from West 42nd Street, rife with street crime, prostitution, and pornography. Midtown East is hushed and refined and far less visually dramatic. A common denominator of the two areas is the presence of some of the finest drinking establishments in New York City.

Midtown East

Bars over here tend to appeal to the rich, famous, and successful. The beauty of barhopping, however, is that you need not be Donald or Ivana Trump to be able to afford to drink in the most elegant of locations.

The Four Seasons, located in the Seagram Building on 52nd Street east of Park Avenue, is a perpetual hangout for political and publishing heavyweights—the names change but the status level remains the same. The bar is located in the Grill Room, which was probably the site of the first power lunch. If you go (which you must, at least once), dress to impress, and try not to stare when a famous politician enters with a leggy blonde on his arm—and she's not his wife.

The glittering grandess of the Helmsley bars at the Helmsley Palace, Madison Avenue and 50th Street, is to be experienced at least once, like Saks Fifth Avenue the week before Christmas. **Harry's New York Bar** is the hotel's one bar that doesn't overtly bear the telltale stamp of Leona's rampant femininity. The room is dark and pubby, with a professional crowd of both locals and out-of-towners. Look in, then move on to the real lookers: first, **The Gold Room**—really an understated name for what must be a replica of one of Leona's living rooms. Men in jackets and women with fresh hairdos drape themselves around the 100-year-old Roman Renaissance–style room. With its gold-leaf walls, garlands of foliage, and stained-glass windows, it is regal and spectacular.

The Hunt Room's name and decor are evocative of those turn-of-the-century English hunt scenes with noblemen and squires relaxing with pipes. Understated and elegant, it's a perfect place to sip fine Scotch and pretend you're landed gentry. Gentlemen, get out your jackets and gray slacks; ladies, look refined and self-possessed.

But wait, the faux gold-leaf paint runneth over, all the way to the **Madison Room**. This is high camp at its finest. With its green marble fireplaces, marble columns capped with bronze mountings, and tinkling pianist, this room could have served as Liberace's mausoleum. Actually the room is fun and splashy, and a drink or two is recommended by the window overlooking Madison Avenue.

Nestled in the block of luxury hotels that line Central Park South, the Ritz Carlton Hotel's **Jockey Club** is why expense accounts exist. Elegant and traditional, the wonderful bar also serves as a place where the upper classes and high-level executives meet and greet, relaxing in the genteel atmosphere. One or two martinis should smooth any nervousness about the horsey atmosphere. Just remember to play dress-up, for this is a place for the "properly attired." Relax in comfort at the bar or at a table in the foyer. Women should check out the w.c.—Laura Ashley would have been green with envy. And bring a wallet fat with cards or cash—such gentility costs.

Finally, in this luxury hotel genre there is the Plaza Hotel's esteemed **Oak Bar**—a venerated New York drinking establishment filled with the very rich and very powerful, or just wealthy women tired from shopping on Fifth Avenue all day. All designer accessories worn here are the real thing, and there are understated signs of money everywhere in this dark, clubby room. While the bar is small, most of the drinking is done at the tables anyway, where you can get a magnificent view of the park.

In the Midtown East area the hotels seem to have a monopoly on good places to drink, but there *are* some standard bars that deserve more than a pass. Reflective of this area's cultural sophistication, there exists a place that is less a bar than a showplace for some of the finest musicians in town. **Michael's Pub** (211 East 55th Street) is a cabaret restaurant where the well-heeled come to catch the best of the genre. Monday nights Woody Allen sometimes leaves his urban angst at home with Mia and plays a damn good clarinet. The trick is to be early to the no-cover, no-minimum bar space and nurse a drink all the way through a show. The menu is solid, however, and the show is always one of the best deals in town.

A horse of a dramatically different color (probably red, white, and blue) is **P. J. Clarke's** (915 Third Avenue at 55th Street), a grown-up frat boy's dream. With an abundant selection of beer, and a big, beautiful carved bar at which to chug it, this drinking haunt accommodates a mass of aging preppies and after-work yuppies. Woody and masculine, P. J. Clarke's exemplifies the best of New York pubbing—and the chili and hamburgers are great. If you go, be prepared to rave about your alma mater.

Midtown West
Over on the west side of town a few new restaurants stand out, either in quality or gimmick. A longtime pio-

neer in establishing regal restaurants in Gotham City, Harry Cipriani bounced back from the closing of the restaurant that bore his name, and did so beautifully. His new place, **Bellini** (777 Seventh Avenue at 51st Street), is the offspring of a stylistic marriage between Harry's first restaurant and the famous Hemingway haunt, Harry's Bar and Grill in Venice. The low ceilings, pale peach fabrics, and Art Deco decor provide a wonderfully elegant atmosphere for sophisticated drinks and drinkers. The patrons, as in the bar that was Bellini's inspiration, often represent the best and the brightest of the local society of the arts and fashion.

Because the "beautiful people" have short attention spans when it comes to night spots, the enduring popularity of **Trixie's** (307 West 47th Street, west of Eighth Avenue, on the western edge of the Theater District) is noteworthy. Trixie is now a regular on M.T.V., but she still finds time to preside over her trendy diners, dance the samba three or four times a night, and generally stir up trouble (which is good for business). The bar is petite and always crowded, but worth the discomfort on a busy Saturday night, offering a prime view of a stream of people rivaled only by the Halloween parade in Greenwich Village. Only beer is served; no matter—the general atmosphere is wacky enough to preclude the need to be gin-soaked in order to be amused.

For relaxing among more cerebral inebriants, saunter over to the **Algonquin Hotel** (44th Street between Fifth and Sixth avenues). Here sat the Round Table, a 1920s ensemble of writers, artists, and celebrated tipplers, caustic wits of the likes of Dorothy Parker, Ring Lardner, and Robert Benchley. (The offices of *The New Yorker* are, not coincidentally, nearby.) The large bar—actually a sitting room—is plush without being prim, and the clientele, literary to international, and always well bred, may remind you of a set of extras for a BBC production. Off the lobby to the right of the entrance is the snug **Blue Bar**.

Another West Side hot spot is **Un Deux Trois** (123 West 44th Street), obviously French and very much the perpetual scene: another "beautiful people" place, only with patrons a bit older than at Trixie's. If you have a contract with Ford's, or at least good bone structure, you'll feel right at home. The bar itself is small but noisy and fun, and you might need the intimacy to decipher everyone's heavy European accent anyway.

THE UPPER WEST SIDE

While no area of New York is truly homogeneous, there are some neighborhoods that seem to be filled with people either from the same year at Princeton or the same jail cell. However, the people and places on the Upper West Side make this neighborhood one of the most varied in all of New York City. In many ways, gentrification has a lot to do with the area's broad range. One day a bodega coexists next to a gleaming new Tex-Mex eatery; a week later, the Tex-Mex eatery is competing with a new sushi place. This kind of rapid commercial turnover helps explain why the neighborhood consists of genteel older men and women who have lived in the same magnificent prewar buildings for 50 years, and the young middle-class men and women who have lived in their brand new condos for six months—and will probably move within a year. Reflective of this dual consumerism are the many bars and restaurants of the Upper West Side.

Lincoln Center

The bars near this epicenter of the arts are of course designed for, and filled with, the pre- and post-theater or concert crowd. But just because they are soliciting the same consumer source doesn't mean the bars look the same. They range from the pedestrian to the posh, and one restaurant that practically defines the latter is **Café Des Artistes** (1 West 67th Street off Central Park West). The fact that this glorious restaurant is praised to the heavens for its food results in its bar being overlooked. This is good, for the bar, though small, is very cozy, and while a meal at Des Artistes would wipe out the wallet, the intimate, romantic bar serves as the perfect alternative. Dress here is stylishly conservative; clothes worn for the theater are probably just fine. Middle-aged men and women discuss the performance they just saw in refined, hushed tones, and the service people glide by so as not to disturb the avid conversation.

Equally stylish, but in a very different manner, is the **Café Luxembourg** (200 West 70th Street, between Amsterdam and West End avenues). It looks like the Odeon (see the TriBeCa section), and its clientele is much the same: attractive and model-like. The decor is very clean lined, done in pink, black, and white Art Deco details, replete with columns and a terrazzo floor. The effect is very 1920s and Parisian; *The Sun Also Rises* comes to mind. The scene, however, is right now, and film and TV stars, young and not-so-young, are often tucked away in the anonymous corners of the restaurant. The bar is relatively small and always crowded, but if you are lucky enough to grab a stool, stay. The atmosphere is lively and good fun, and when you get tired of looking for celebrities, turn to the staff: They all have the bodies of dancers and the cheekbones of Paulina.

A bar that is more representative of the old guard of the Upper West Side is the **Ginger Man** (51 West 64th Street east of Broadway). The bar itself is very tasteful, with dark wood and Tiffany lamps that create the perfect atmosphere for a post-matinee drink, and especially a late nightcap after a concert or performance. The men and women who frequent the bar are older, well heeled, and established. However, there is none of the stuffiness that often goes with such a crowd, and the tone here is usually hale. The bar is, however, compact, thus usually close, so consider the level of intimacy you desire for a setting. The ABC television studios are close by, and the boys from the newsroom often fill the place with smoke and hearty gossip at lunchtime. TV newsman Peter Jennings is also a regular, though he tends to sit at a table in the restaurant late at night, after the taping of his final broadcast. Often there is live entertainment, usually a pianist. The dress is clubby and the prices are right up there, but it's worth it.

So far, every place mentioned in this category has been a little on the staid side. This is perhaps due to the often subdued and reflective audiences that emerge from Lincoln Center. But theater or no theater, that doesn't press upon the wild bunch at **The Saloon** (1920 Broadway at 64th Street). The restaurant's bar is large and commodious, and even offers those displaced from the bar itself an area to stand in. The Saloon obviously caters to a different type of crowd from Café des Artistes, but the diversity exists because of the nature of the Upper West Side, not in spite of it. The drinkers at the Saloon are young, rowdy, and often single; you might leave with a date for your next theater event. When the weather is warm the staff breaks out the sidewalk tables, creating one of the finest people-gazing spots in the city.

During warm weather, out-of-towners and natives alike can be found sipping aperitifs on the brick patio café of **Tavern on the Green** (in Central Park at 67th Street). Ignore the touristy types and the creepy feeling of being in a coffee commercial: The establishment is indeed an

Establishment in the restaurant circles of New York, and Tavern on the Green is a place to have experienced.

Columbus Avenue

A special section has to be allotted for the area known as Columbus Avenue. Once an area filled with bodegas and run-down shops, the upper portion of this broad street has become overrun with designer places peddling designer food, shoes, clothes, cookies, and ice cream. There are even designer pet stores, so your greyhound won't feel gauche. The problem is, the modern definition of "designer" doesn't mean singular or special, it means expensive. And, in the case of Columbus Avenue, redundant. Which is why, despite the plethora of bars and restaurants in this area (and that of the nearby portion of Amsterdam Avenue, which is well on its way to parity with Columbus Avenue), there are only a few bars that distinguish themselves in one way or another.

A respite of sorts from Columbus's usual is the newish **Peter's** (68th Street and Columbus Avenue). The division between bar and restaurant allows you to drink freely without feeling pressured to eat pasta, and its tasteful, muted decor makes it one of the few bars in the neighborhood that looks nothing like a designer shoe store.

The next stop is **Lucy's Restaurant** (503 Columbus Avenue near 84th Street). The girls wear pink, the boys are neophyte investment bankers, and the bar is almost larger than the eating area. With everyone's hormones popping, Lucy's practically oozes sly thoughts. Everybody is having a smashing time, drinking colorful outfit-matching concoctions topped off with a plastic fish. Later in the evening the toy sea creatures often provide conversational access to that hot babe or super stud at the end of the bar. Goofy but fun, this place helps lighten the load of making an entry-level living in New York City.

More contemplative moods are well served by a restaurant a few blocks down the street. **The Museum Café** (366 Columbus Avenue at 77th Street) is sophisticated and serene, with a sidewalk enclosure that allows sitting indoors with an outdoors sensation. The woody interior is dark and polished, and the inside bar is rarely overcrowded. Customers, usually established West Siders, often come alone, read a novel, or just sit and think. The place seems to be very therapeutic and speeds recovery from the night before.

Jazz and the Upper Upper West Side

The one-time countenance of the Upper Upper West Side, rough-hewn but full of character, has developed some unsightly blemishes in the form of pasta pits, sushi bars, and salsa scenes. Even the world-renowned West End Café, site of the sodden scribbling of young Kerouac and Ginsberg and venue for jazz greats like Louis Armstrong, has resoundingly closed its heavy wooden doors. But the owners of the downtown Village Gate (see Popular Music and Nightlife) have opened the West End's doors again— as the **West End Gate** (on Broadway between 113th and 114th streets)—and have pledged to maintain a dedication to pub atmosphere and jazz performance.

For uptown jazz in a more upscale atmosphere, the newish **Birdland** (corner of Broadway and 105th Street) has established itself with a streamlined bar, menu, and jazz. The people and the music are handsome and polished—and so are the bartenders, who are invariably on hiatus from a soap opera.

The final point in the triangular combo is **J's** (on Broadway between 97th and 98th streets), a piano/jazz bar, smallish and cozy, perched a story above Broadway. Red velvet and schmoozy waiters are minor drawbacks; the music and atmosphere are elegant and lively. The well-dressed patrons are either single or in groups, but all look lean and hungry.

THE UPPER EAST SIDE

Maligners of the Upper East Side often claim it is elitist, Waspy, frigid, and unfriendly. Well, it's not exactly untrue. But New York would not be New York without rich people (and would-be rich people) and a place to put them, and the side of town where furs are a familiar sight can also be classy, cultured, and traditional. Rich people like to have fun too, and a nice feature of the Upper East Side is that almost anyone can do as the rich do, by sipping at their wateringholes.

The Beach Café (1326 Second Avenue at 70th Street) does its best to soothe the tender nerves of executives who just couldn't get away to the Hamptons in time. The walls are covered with seascapes that can be purchased for anywhere from $200 to $1,000 (no black velvet, paint-by-number art here). The decor is like a lofty beach house, with pretty tile and brick walls and a lovely mahogany bar that is a delight to drink at. If you close your eyes and sip your Scotch slowly, you can almost imagine being in George Plimpton's country home, chatting about safaris until the Kennedys arrive for dinner. There's even a courtesy Rolls-Royce sponsored by J & B Scotch—ask the maître d' and you can get a lift home.

If it's seclusion you want—and the real thing when it comes to the music—one of the best shows in town still takes place in the **Café Carlyle** (Carlyle Hotel, Madison Avenue and 76th Street). Go on a weekday, sit at the bar in elegant surroundings, and hear brilliant Bobby Short play and sing for only ten dollars—fifteen dollars less than the cost of sitting at a table. Otherwise, the general atmosphere is stuffy, and the place is filled with self-preoccupied businessmen and their much younger dates.

The infamous **Elaine's** (1703 Second Avenue near 88th Street) is a tad tired but still something of a spectacle. Woody is sometimes here eating dinner quietly in a corner with Mia. Powerful publishers and literary giants often dine here too. Elaine's bosom may be generous, but *she* is not, at least to "outsiders." Don't be daunted; the large bar has a very good view of the restaurant, and, late at night, you might catch snatches of conversation and Hollywood shop talk, if you like that sort of thing. Dress here is chic but understated.

An elitism of a different sort permeates the air at **Mortimer's** (1057 Lexington Avenue at 75th Street). Fame (though it never hurts) is not a key to the entrance here, but what might be persuasive is if you and some of Mortimer's regulars had wintered together in Gstaad. Add an Ivy League education (preferably at one of the less "bohemian" schools), no chin if you're a man, and flat chest and bony ankles if you're a woman. Now you not only fit in, you look as if you're related to everyone else in the place. The crowd at the bar is young and boisterous, while those dining tend to be more sedate. The decor is pretty, the waiters are pretty, and Mortimer's itself is a great spot to ogle the rich and feel somehow superior to them.

Specialty bars often lean toward the gauche, especially sports bars, which makes **Rusty's** (1271 Third Avenue at 73rd Street) earthy and genuine, a super exception. Mets paraphernalia abounds, which makes a lot of sense, because Rusty, the owner, is the former Mets right fielder and pinch hitter Rusty Staub, now an announcer and special assistant to the Mets general manager. The bar is always filled with team members—not just of the Mets but of every professional New York sports team, including the Giants, the Knicks, and the Jets. When out-of-town teams come in to play, they can usually be found at Rusty's, and where the pros go, so goes a mob of related professionals—announcers, producers, and reporters—who converge upon the place to interview the players and fans, arranged so nicely under one roof. A great view of the big-screen TV can be had from every cleverly placed table in the main room, but the best seats in the house are at the bar, which actually has indentations for resting your elbow. The walls of Rusty's are packed with photos of sports greats and sure beat yet another curling photo of Brooke Shields in a Chinese restaurant. Rusty's is most busy after work, at dinnertime, and for brunch on weekends during a game. Because Rusty tips his cap to all major athletic events, his bar remains one of the best year-round sports bars anywhere.

Her name, or nickname at least, appropriately up in lights, Mariel "Sam" Hemingway has managed to defy the stuffiness of the bars surrounding her on the Third Avenue strip and create a sincere, light, and airy restaurant dubbed **Sam's Cafe** (1406 Third Avenue at 80th Street). The decor is reminiscent of one of her favorite spots, Ketchum, Idaho, also a haunt of Papa Hemingway. The genuine country feel of the place is a surprise: The tone is low-key and pleasant, and the bar, which runs the length of the place, is filled after work with couples, mostly in their late 20s to late 30s, and usually on dates. Dress is casual.

Down Third Avenue between 78th and 79th streets is **The Ravelled Sleave**, a rather clubby singles bar for workers in the financial industry who were educated, some years ago, at good southern colleges. If you're able to pass for one of them—or *are* one of them—you'll have a good time here.

BARS WITH COUCHES

There is a distinctive style manifested in a number of very popular, very chichi bars about town. One descriptive phrase might be the "parlor phenomenon." It refers to the timely embrace of certain social and political themes by designers of new restaurants: clubs made to look like homes. Not just any homes, but the homes—and specifically the living rooms—of the very rich. The decor of such places usually includes many plush couches, settees, and any type of furniture that indulges. There are often fireplaces and always low, warm lighting. The fixtures tend to be brass. This return to luxury and wealth, combined with the concept of the Great American Home, was practically George Bush's political platform. In any case, the following clubs are something to see, and they *do* serve as relaxing alternatives to the stiffer, stand-up type bars.

A Roman bath may have been one of the first practical temples built in honor of the wealthy (today of course Donald Trump takes care of such things), but the reputation of bathhouses has declined. Nevertheless, **Cave Canem** (24 First Avenue near 2nd Street) attempts to resurrect the Roman Empire and all of its sensual recreations. There are richly upholstered settees that Caesar would have liked, and the marble interior and elaborate fixtures of this former bathhouse are essentially intact. The rooms are dark and smoky and seem ripe for sexual drama—which they might be if the clientele wasn't basically the same tired bunch wearing black that has driven miles (i.e., from the suburbs) to get there. Drinks are, as for all clubs of this order, overpriced, but the setting can be amusing if you come with friends; you could all lurk in the magnificent, empty old marble "Jacuzzi" left untouched in the middle of the floor. If the season is right, not-so-proper bathing attire is encouraged, leaving very little to a prospective date's imagination.

There once was a time when only the very best friends of Jay McInerney could get into this place, but if you haven't had the good fortune to cultivate a relationship with him you're in luck: **Nell's** (246 West 14th Street) has relaxed its entry criteria quite a bit. In other words, it has become a bit passé. The premises are still lovely, though, and very grand, with a number of huge rooms to wander through, all done up in various fin-de-siècle detail. Witty, bubbly conversation is a must, and the owners (the same people who own the Odeon) have thoughtfully provided conversation pits that tend to determine the action of the rooms they are in. Everyone used to be young and gorgeous; now some are a little bit older, but all very gracious and well dressed. The younger set can usually be found on the dance floor (which has an excellent sound system) dancing to the likes of old Madonna. The "madame" of Nell's may look familiar: She is Little Nell from *The Rocky Horror Picture Show.*

M.K. (204 Fifth Avenue at 25th Street) is the inheritor of the Nell's snob crowd, and its previous door policy. Sto-

ries of irate celebrities and power-broker types being
turned away with the same gesture as a carload from New
Jersey has shaken the city's In crowd to the core. But of
course, instead of graciously accepting the rejection, their
ardor to get in is increased exponentially. Since getting in
is damn near impossible, here is a description so that you
can fake having been there. There are three levels to M.K.:
The first is a restaurant with mediocre food served practically all night long. In the basement, where the frenetic
dancing takes place, the people visible are either models
and their dates or someone's bratty teenage son with a
group of bratty friends, the son having coerced someone
with daddy's money or connections. All is flashing, silvery
lights that tend to make people look attractively purple.
People drink at the bar—but don't stand there, or they
would be crushed—and then wander upstairs to the hunting lodge and princess bedroom. Exactly as it sounds, the
denlike trophy room is filled with exotic stuffed animal
heads on the walls, staring down glassy-eyed at the people playing at the pool table. The princess bedroom has
an enormous four-poster bed and various pieces of accommodating furniture. Those in this area tend to be very
young, masterful at draping themselves over select upholstered chairs. Food and drink prices are hefty, but you'll
actually save a lot of money the night you go to M.K.,
because you won't get in.

Sofi (102 Fifth Avenue at 15th Street) takes its name
from the new acronym of the district—*So*uth of *Flati*ron—
but is original in every other way. The breathtaking
textile-showroom space that houses Sofi's is utilized in a
very space-efficient but beautiful manner. The foyer is
dotted with richly upholstered chairs and couches that
invite patrons to sip aperitifs or cocktails before dinner.
The dining room is built on the lower split level, the room
itself long and cavernous, and very impressive looking.
The dark wooden bar is handsome, with green glass
reading lamps that cast a flattering light on each of the 13
places at the bar. The clientele is well dressed and sophisticated, and the atmosphere is perfect for intimacy and
even romance.

Finally, just so you know, there is a new bar gimmick in
certain New York bars: the Jello shot. A shot of schnapps
or vodka replaces most of the water in a fruit-flavored
Jello recipe, and the stuff is sold in paper cups for about
two dollars. This concoction is the nineties' equivalent of
pot brownies. A handful of Jello-shot outlets include:

Ruby's River Road Bar and Café (Second Avenue and 92nd Street); Lucy's (previously mentioned); and the Gulf Coast (12th Avenue and 12th Street). Interestingly, these places also have Tex-Mex/Cajun–type menus in common.

BARS WITH A VIEW

One of the most fantastic sights in New York City is the city itself—seen from on high. A bird's-eye view of the island of Manhattan is a wonder and is fortunately possible to obtain in comfort and style from many restaurants around town that might be called simply "view bars."

The Boathouse Café (Central Park at the Fifth Avenue and 72nd Street entrance) is not on high, but it has a view of skyline and lake that lies somewhere in between the fish and the fowl. With a rear cocktail area that overlooks the lake, the romantic scene is marred only by the plastic cups that hold the cocktails. Bring a sweetie at dusk and hold hands till the sky lights up.

Il Mondo's glass-walled atrium has an incredible frontal view of the Chrysler Building. As if that weren't enough, the position of the restaurant results in a wondrous view of the United Nations building. The atmosphere of the restaurant is tasteful and dignified, and the patrons, 30 and over, are also. The bar itself is small but plush, and there is a prim, elderly lady, a tiara perched on her head, who trills traditional songs and plays the piano beautifully. At the eastern end of 43rd Street off First Avenue.

The Rainbow Room, high atop the RCA Building, is a 1930s dream come true, or, in light of recent renovation, déjà vu. Luckily, the media ballyhoo over the revamping was not for naught: The place is a wonderland; from the staff to the silverware, all looks authentic. There's an air of expectation, as if Fred and Ginger were going to whirl around the corner at any moment. At lunch the two dining rooms are open only to those who are members. The bar itself—called the Grill—is as luxurious and well appointed as the other rooms. Details include a long, gleaming mahogany bar, inviting leather furniture, and deep red carpeting. Then there is the view: Ceiling-to-floor windows reveal a magnificent view of Midtown in all its illuminated glory. This is the spot for a special evening—and special dress. The bar has a light menu; cocktails are $6.50—a pittance for paradise.

When announcing a trip to this next "view bar," ignore the shouting and vehement protests that leaving Manhattan requires a bilingual guide book and a shotgun. This next place is as thrilling as any location in Manhattan, shotgun or no. Taxi, a one-stop subway ride from Wall Street, or a pleasant walk over the Brooklyn Bridge are three easy ways to get to Brooklyn, home of the renowned **River Café** (1 Water Street, Brooklyn); the management will help arrange for you to get back. This gourmet bar-restaurant is built on a barge that sits at the foot of the Brooklyn Bridge. The food is so widely lauded that dinner reservations must be made weeks in advance. Here's where the beauty of the bar comes in. No elaborate plan is needed to drop in for a cocktail, and the extraordinary view of Manhattan costs drinkers a fraction of the cost to diners. This place is so special, Woody Allen would probably film here—*if* it were in Manhattan.

The Terrace (400 West 119th Street near Columbia University) is the place where professors take visiting scholars to dine at their department's expense, and father takes graduate and family to dine at his business's expense. Though the Terrace is known as the gourmet restaurant of the area, its food is actually rather ordinary. The bar is large and has a great view of the downtown skyline, but the decor is hotel-like; after catching the view plan on going elsewhere.

The Top of the Sixes (666 Fifth Avenue between 52nd and 53rd streets) has a memorable address and view, but that's about it. The decor is stale and reminiscent of a family restaurant, and the patrons are not particularly chic or elegant. The view offered is from atop 39 stories, and includes Central Park and Fifth Avenue. This otherwise prime location may one day be given the makeover it deserves.

Imagine Frank Sinatra crooning his trademark about you-know-what city. The camera pans to the Empire State Building, the Citicorp Building, and the 59th Street Bridge—all from the top of the Beekman Tower, 26 floors high. At the **Top of the Tower** (3 Mitchell Place off First Avenue at 49th Street) there's a two-drink minimum from 9:00 P.M. to 1:00 A.M. that will cost close to the price of three elsewhere, but the romance here is well worth it.

Logically, the higher the building, the better the view, right? Well, how does 107 stories sound? The view from the top of the World Trade Center *is* great. The twin buildings are the tallest on the East Coast, and the north tower (number 1) serves as the home of a restaurant with a peerless view of New York City, Windows on the World. Adjacent to the dining room is the bar itself, named the **Hors d'Oeuvrerie**. It should not be missed. There's a $2.95 cover charge for the jazz combo after 7:30 P.M.; drinks for two run $15. Men must wear coat and tie, women, no denim. Windows on the World is an appropriate place to end a visit to New York, and an equally appropriate place to end our bar section.

POPULAR MUSIC AND NIGHTLIFE

By David Frankel

David Frankel, formerly an editor of New York *maga-zine, has written on music for* New York *and for* Rolling Stone *magazine. He is an editor of* Artforum *magazine.*

Generations in New York nightlife come and go, but having gone they don't necessarily disappear—they just move out of the consciousness of the public, or at least of the particular public that decides what clubs and practices are hot and of the moment. For some, New York club life died in 1973 with the closing of the old Copacabana. For others it was 1980, when Steve Rubell and Ian Schrager, the owners of the seminal late-1970s discotheque Studio 54, faced the tax-evasion charges that eventually sent them to jail; or perhaps it was 1982 and the loss, after similar tax charges, of Steve Mass's Mudd Club, a rudimentary below-Canal establishment that began as a kind of artists' and downtowners' bar. Yet not only are people still going out in the evenings, they're going to rooms that are basically similar to those older haunts—or at least to Studio and the Mudd. It's just that they're also going to, and talking about, what came after—or whatever may have come after that by the time you read this book.

The Copacabana is a different story. From the 1940s

through the 1960s, the club defined the image of the New York night spot as many imagined it: big-name entertainers, a floor show, glamour. It had its own chorus line, the Copa Girls (a tall dancer was called a show girl; a short one, unimaginable today, a "pony"), and its ever-so-vaguely Brazilian decor—the palm trees are concrete—was for countless Americans the instantly evocative epitome of show biz. In its billing, the Copa found ways to cope with the times, moving from Brazilian Bombshell Carmen Miranda in designer fruit-salad hats to a twisting Chubby Checker to Tom Jones, creating lines, the story goes, four times around the block. But the club did not survive Las Vegas. The big casino hotels that went up there in the 1960s hired singers like Jones as part of the bait to lure players in to the tables, and could pay extraordinary fees out of their gambling income. Relatively small rooms couldn't compete. The Copa is now a discotheque, and the only regular chorus line left in town is Radio City Music Hall's Rockettes.

For many, of course, chorus-line-type entertainment isn't such a great loss. Still, New Yorkers who remember the Copa kind of club sometimes malign the contemporary scene: It's all geared for teenagers and the rock 'n' roll crowd; there's nowhere left to eat a good supper in a sophisticated surround and see a big star; and so forth. It's certainly true that rock, disco, and their variants are the popular music of the day, that their audiences tend to be young (though aging all the time), and that their settings take rough wear. It's also true that the economics of nightlife have changed; Frank Sinatra doesn't play supper clubs anymore.

As for the rest of us, New York is a very big town with a long and thrilling tradition in every branch of the performing arts. It attracts singers and dancers, pianists and horn players, cabaret acts and comedians, and rock 'n' rollers from all over the country as well as rearing its own, and these people expend a great deal of energy, both competitive and collegial, on figuring out how to put themselves in front of a crowd that will listen while they do what they do. If New Yorkers like to appear jaded to the city's nightlife, that may be because there's more of it here than they can possibly see; and if you have to miss a good cabaret act or club date or jazz gig, why not pretend you did it on purpose.

The different modes of night spots from the different eras cohabit, whether or not they're in the spotlight. Fifty-second Street—Swing Street, the Jazz Capital of the World—once a night owl's delight of side-by-side jazz clubs from speakeasy days in the 1920s on, no longer exists. A row of high-rises has replaced the clubs, but that only means that jazz spots are diffused around town, from a concentration in the Village to a scattering on the residential Upper West Side.

Cabarets and piano rooms are sprinkled throughout Midtown, in the still raffish neighborhoods around Times Square and Broadway, sifting out strollers from the theater crowd; their performers too are sometimes spun out of Broadway, as when singers and musicians from the stage moonlight, or just drop in to some loosely organized bar that welcomes anyone with a voice (and some without). Places like these coexist with well-run cabarets such as Jan Wallman's, a room that's a firm retort to the nowhere-to-go-for-a-civilized-evening-out complaint. The Village still bears traces of its 1960s folk scene, rock 'n' roll is pretty much everywhere, and the discotheques that dominated nightlife in the late 1970s are still laying down their old beat (though maybe lightening it some through the more jittery rhythms of hip-hop and house music). And in addition, of course, there's whatever superseded these spots—whatever's of the moment at the moment.

The most recent real vogue, now seen as distinctly passé though not yet superseded, was what's been christened the Dim Age. This phase was ushered in late in 1986 with the opening of a club called Nell's, far west on 14th Street. Whereas the preceding era of clubs had gone for glitz and light shows and fabulous technology on the one hand, or for hole-in-the-wall funk on the other, Nell's tried to conjure a softly lit sitting-room mood. It may seem paradoxical to line up and pay for something like home, but people do, in a hip, downtown version of 1980s American conservatism. Several clubs that have opened since play variations on Nell's (M.K., and Au Bar on East 58th Street), and preexisting spots have nudged corners of their spaces in Nell's direction. But this doesn't mean that the older disco palaces are empty. Abandoned by the scene setters, they're simply made available for everyone else.

All this activity doesn't mean that New York makes life easy for aspiring club owners. An urgent issue is the city's high rent scale, which to people who live here sometimes appears a threat to all civilized life as we know it. New Yorkers pay for this all around—in their own living expenses of course and (as concerns nightlife) in ever-higher admission fees and cover charges—but also in terms of the community of performing artists here, who need space to rehearse in, experiment in, and, of course, to live in—space that is less and less available. New York State's residential rent-control laws tend to make apartments cheaper in relation to the market the longer a tenant has occupied them (the rent increases less when a lease is renewed than when it changes hands), which is fortunate for the town's longer-standing citizens but unhelpful to its newcomers. And because New York's cultural life depends on its centripetal power to attract to itself the newcomers who will contribute to it and constitute it, some worry is attached to the question of whether those people will find a room of their own here.

The early 1980s saw a revealing confrontation with these issues in the East Village, traditionally a part of Manhattan that was low rent to the extent that large sections of it were derelict (fewer but still numerous blocks remain so). The relative cheapness of life there made the area attractive to artists and other low-budget young people, and some of them opened night spots of a kind, in the lineage of the Mudd Club, with names like 8 BC (on 8th Street between Avenues B and C), Darinka, the Limbo Lounge, and King Tut's Wah-Wah Hut. As these logos may suggest, East Village cabarets catered to a crowd that was youthful at least in heart and usually also in actuality. They were small establishments, storefronts and tenements converted to their new use at minimal expense and often rudely and imperfectly—a 1980s version of the "Hey kids, let's put on a show" movies of the 1930s, and infinitely tackier though just as enthusiastic. The entertainment was of a kind with its location: raw, or at least unafraid to be so. Some East Village performers now have movie careers (Ann Magnuson) or have seen the inner meaning of their work discussed in art magazines and the *Village Voice* (Karen Finley). The unpretentiousness of their environment, which was cultivated, and their own Dada familiarity with the shock tactic as stage business have not obscured their inventiveness.

Today, however, most of these cut-rate nightclubs are gone. As Cornelius Conboy, the former co-owner of 8 BC, told *The New York Times* in 1985 when the club closed, the city government hit them with wall-to-wall paperwork: "license fees, certificate of occupancy, cabaret license, lease or bill of sale, nonflammability of drapes, public assembly permit, fire inspection, electric and gas inspection, health permit, liquor license, consumer affairs. . . ." Few of the Lower East Side cabarets were operating on that bureaucratic level. Though some, such as the Pyramid, have survived, an arrest or two for selling alcohol without a license, or the prospect of having to scrape up lawyers' fees to stay open, was enough to fold the rest.

Now, any visitor to a nightclub has of course a justifiable interest in whether the ceiling will collapse and the sprinkler system will work (or whether there *is* a sprinkler system). Still, given the number of basement social clubs operating illegally in New York—unlicensed rooms offering liquor, some of them staying open for years without police action (a while ago there was a fatal fire in one of these bars)—the city's attention to the East Village scene seemed out of scale. And it played a part in the escalation of rents. The unsafe and empty streets of the Lower East Side had discouraged landlords from repairing the area's derelict buildings. With clubs and art galleries attracting crowds to those streets again, developers began to rebuild the neighborhood, and the shoestring operations that had touched off the cycle were pressured to leave—in some cases, conveniently, by the city—so that more lucrative businesses could replace them. The effect was a contribution to the conservative drift defined by Nell's, a reclaiming of the night by establishments with relatively abundant capital. (And after the East Village, everyone wanted a little comfort.) But clubs like 8 BC did set a vital example, and though the odds against them seem higher with every storefront Lost Our Lease sign, it's worth noting the arrival of Trixie's, a loose and funny restaurant in Midtown with a lot of the old spirit. It and places like it may mark a brightening of the Dim Age.

In one respect the bureaucratic load night spots bear has lightened lately, with the demise, in early 1988, of a cabaret law that had been a consistent source of complaint. Originally passed in 1926 as a tool for crackdowns on speakeasies, the law forbade certain instruments and restricted to three the number of musicians who could perform simultaneously in clubs without a cabaret license. These licenses demanded annual fees and the fulfillment of certain zoning and safety requirements, and many rooms functioned quite well, and quite safely, without one—but they couldn't legally book four or more pieces, or horn players, or even drummers. Bands got around the law by organizing wrestling-type tag teams—

you would see players waiting to step onstage as soon as one of the three already there stepped off. The practice was sometimes diverting but more often distracting. It ended on January 28, 1988, when a New York State Supreme Court judge found the law an unconstitutional violation of performers' freedom of expression. That evening bandstands all over town were packed as musicians asked their friends to step up and jam with them. It was a happy night—and, clearing the way for larger bands, it offered more musicians the chance of employment. Now the city is trying to write a new law, one that will restore its lost control through a form of zoning code. "To some people on the city council," said one cabaret owner a while ago, "all music is noise."

Another legal change in the last few years that directly affected nightlife was the 1985 raising of the state drinking age from 19 to 21—a particularly important development for rock clubs and discos, which have a large teenage clientele. Theoretically, everyone 16 or over can go to a club that serves liquor, though they now have to be 21 to be served a drink. Until recently, it was considered easier to keep under-21s out of a disco than to let them in and then try to identify them at the bar. "Club kids" are important enough to the clubs' image, however, that it is now routine procedure to rubber-stamp adults' wrists or give them a rubber bracelet once they've proved their age; they have to show the stamp to buy a drink. Other places set aside rooms for under-21s where no liquor is served, or open only to teenagers on selected nights of the week. This last wrinkle puts the newly 21-year-old in a novel position: Having spent the last several years trying to persuade a club's bartenders that he's old enough to drink there, he now has to persuade the club's doorman he's young enough to be let in at all.

Doormen have a very up-and-down reputation in New York—doted on by some, loathed by others. The doorman has absolute say as to whether or not you're admitted. And the fashionable clubs use the door as a tool: Creating a crowd outside is the approved way of letting the city know the place is hot. Stories are told of waiting outside the velvet ropes in front of some new venue only to enter at last and find the place half empty. And those who are allowed in, at least when a club is of the moment, are carefully chosen: If the crowd outside is a draw because it creates an impression of the club's exclusivity and of the lengths people will go to to be there, the crowd inside is the main attraction and has to look exciting to be with. Most Manhattan clubs have regulars, a set that goes there all the time and never worries about admission. People outside those cliques tend to show up looking their best, or at least dressed for maximum self-confidence. They arrive early rather than late—late being after midnight, when the clubs fill up, early varying from place to place but probably not after 11:00. They may go on a weekday rather than a weekend. They may try calling in advance to make a reservation, which some establishments accept depending on the positions of the planets. And they try not to take things personally.

The buzz about a nightclub lasts for a while, then moves to somewhere else. The set that once loved the place now complains that it's full of "bridge-and-tunnelers"—off-islanders who, like virtually everyone who wasn't born here, have come to Manhattan by one of those two types of entry. Bridge-and-tunnelers, of course, and every other visitor from outside the club's set, both out-of-towners and New Yorkers as well, are paying guests, and the clubs are in the business of earning money. After making themselves visible by whatever means they can, including invidious door policies, club managements settle down to turnover and emptying the till. Watching outside the Limelight (opened 1984) and the Palladium (opened 1985) recently, we saw no one forced to wait to get in. Watching outside Nell's (opened 1986) we saw a few people waiting; outside M.K. (opened 1988), a small crowd, and outside Red Zone (opened 1989), a large one. If you have trouble (and you may have none), remember it's only a business ploy and go instead to S.O.B.'s, which runs a great live-music program with dancing for a strictly first-come-first-served crowd. Or call the Vanguard, or Bradley's, and see if they can seat you for jazz. It's a big town.

In the descriptions that follow, we haven't tried to provide specific times or prices for the various night spots, since they may change at the drop of a hat. Jazz clubs and cabarets tend to start their programs at 9:00-to-10:00-ish, and run till after midnight. They may open earlier, particularly if they serve food. Dance clubs may not open till 10:00 and close at 3:00 or 4:00 in the morning; or they may move their hours forward on weekdays. Some close in the early part of the week—Sundays through Tuesdays or Mondays through Wednesdays. A lot of jazz clubs close on Mondays, which may also be a cheap night at places that stay open. Many charge a cover plus a drink minimum at your table; it's often worth checking whether the cover is dropped if you sit at the bar. Some discotheques bump up their prices during the course of the night—it's cheaper or even free (try the Copa) early on. (The management's bet is that you'll spend money in the club while you're waiting for everyone else to arrive.) A lot of residents here use *New York* magazine, *The New Yorker,* and the *Village Voice* for listings, ads, and reviews that will tell them what's going on. *Details* and *The Paper* are better for gossip about whatever venues are newest and hottest—those, and plentiful use of the telephone.

We don't talk about a lot of places, just the best or most interesting in a reasonable range of types with various types of clientele. Once you're in one that sounds good to you, you'll have no trouble finding out from fellow revelers about other places to your taste, if you're the restless type.

The telephone area code for Manhattan is 212.

JAZZ AND PIANO

The **Village Vanguard** is the oldest jazz room in the city— it opened in 1935—and a much-beloved local institution. The music that's been played here over the years seems to have seeped into the walls and furniture to give the place its particular jazz-nirvana feel. It's a basement, down a steep flight of stairs from the street; dark walls laden with photographs and posters, red banquettes underneath them (more comfortable than the tables crowded together out on the floor), an informal crowd with high standards in what it expects to hear. 178 Seventh Avenue South, just south of 11th Street; Tel: 255-4037.

A few blocks south of the Vanguard is **Sweet Basil**, a club and restaurant that bills equally classic jazz, if perhaps slightly more eclectically. There's an outer room, a kind of porch, which generally substitutes a view of the street for a view of the stage, though the music is still perfectly clear. Inside, a wood-paneled room under a nice tin ceiling squeezes in a half dozen tight rows of tables full of well-heeled West Villagers on a civilized evening out. 88 Seventh Avenue South, between Bleecker and Grove streets; Tel: 242-1785.

The Blue Note's glass and mirrors, its darkness, and its bluish decor give it an underwater feel. Upstairs there's a gift shop selling Blue Note pens, tee-shirts, spoons, and watches; out in the bar, which you have to pass through to get to the main room, there's a hard stone floor to take the busy milling about that the place seems to attract. Still, the club books good bills, ranging from the R & B side of jazz to (on occasion) Sarah Vaughan, who can fill halls many times this size. 131 West 3rd Street, just east of Sixth Avenue; Tel: 475-8592.

The French *mardi gras* literally means "fat Tuesday," and refers to Shrove Tuesday, the spring day before Ash Wednesday and the beginning of the Christian calendar's 40 days of fasting over Lent. So *mardi gras* was the last chance for a blowout, and in New Orleans and other tropical cultures it became a carnival. In New York, **Fat Tuesday** is a basement jazz club with a pretty good rep for its bookings. 190 Third Avenue, at 17th Street; Tel: 533-7902.

Zinno takes up the ground floor of a nice old brownstone on a tree-lined street in the Village. Inside, it's an elegant but warm contemporary space, and between the bar and the larger main room is an alcove with enough room for a jazz duo or trio to accompany diners through a refined Italian supper. The bar also takes listeners, for the price of two or three drinks, and the music is choice. 126 West 13th Street, west of Sixth Avenue; Tel: 924-5182.

On a good night, **Bradley's** may be as close as a bar comes to a concert hall: Jazz pianists and bass players get a beautiful sound here, and the usual restaurant noises of cutlery, talk, and general coming and going seem voluntarily muted so people can listen. The dark wood paneling and low black-painted tin ceiling somehow help, framing the light in the room the same way a deep double bass frames the clarity of a piano. This is a popular place for serious jazz fans, who stand packed in the bar or who book a table for an unfancy meal. 70 University Place, a block east of Fifth Avenue and just south of 11th Street; Tel: 473-9700.

Greene Street is *on* Greene Street in SoHo, the former light-industry and warehouse neighborhood whose sweeping lofts have mostly been converted into equally sweeping galleries, restaurants, boutiques, and dwellings. This particular place has a 30-foot ceiling so that you dine here in subtle light topped by volumes of dim air. Pianists usually play during the week, trios on weekends. Up the gantrylike stairs by the bar is a cabaret room. 101 Greene Street, south of Prince Street; Tel: 925-2415.

The **Fortune Garden Pavilion** is a Chinese restaurant of

the Upper East Side variety rather than the Chinatown variety—a plush-carpeted, jacket-and-tie kind of place. The olde stone façade on the street is deceptive, as the establishment backs onto a contemporary atrium-type building on Third Avenue, which seems to have determined its interior—a glass ceiling, for example, looking out on the tops of the local architecture and, when visible, the moon. The room also has expensive-looking chinoiserie dotted about and a Steinway for the use of the distinguished jazz pianists who pass through. 209 East 49th Street, just east of Third Avenue; Tel: 753-0101.

Mikell's lives in a one-story postwar building in a neighborhood of modern high-rises on the Upper West Side— a rather aseptic environment, especially in relation to the older tenements it replaced, blocks of which stretch to the north. Inside, however, is a bright, wood-beamed space with ferns scattered about and also crayons, so you can draw pictures on the paper tablecloths. The main room is long and narrow—a bar, a single row of tables, and standing space crammed between; an outer room gives a view through an elongated window. Most often the music is young people's jazz—electric rather than acoustic, and flavored with rock and soul. The juke runs all the way from Dave Brubeck to Michael Jackson. 760 Columbus Avenue at 97th Street; Tel: 864-8832.

The Knitting Factory, a bare-bones but friendly walk-up on the western edge of the East Village, is a pleasant reminder of the city's old jazz-loft days and, at the same time, a workshop for the present Lower East Side artist community. The music here may be rock-based, may be jazz-based, may be the guy drinking beer at the bar (which trembles when you lean on it) getting up to play guitar by himself; generally, it's experimental and personal. On the ground floor there's a small restaurant with speakers hooked into the sound system above, and the prices throughout are low enough that people from the neighborhood can easily drop in. The neighborhood is young and *avant*. 47 East Houston Street, between Mott and Mulberry streets north of Chinatown and Little Italy; Tel: 219-3055.

CABARET AND SUCH

When Jan Wallman closed her cabaret in the Village for a move to Midtown, old friends—Dick Cavett, Joan Rivers, Margaret Whiting, and others—performed in a benefit at Carnegie Hall to help her fund it. The result, **Jan Wall-**

man's, which opened in 1987, is a welcoming room that avoids both the slight pomposity of the hoity-toitier cabarets and the raffishness of its relatives to the west, the Times Square–area piano places. Wallman is a veteran of the business, and a lot of her patrons come to dine and be entertained without knowing the act booked for the evening, relying instead on her knowledge and taste. 49 West 44th Street, west of Fifth Avenue; Tel: 764-8930.

The Carlyle, one of New York's most elegant hotels, runs two music rooms outfitted accordingly. The **Bemelmans Bar** is a tenebrous room, full of dark leather upholstery. (The management has sometimes considered redesigning and brightening up the bar, but neighbors have always written enough letters of protest to forestall them, in the Upper East Side version of social activism.) On the walls are the brownish-toned murals of Ludwig Bemelmans, well known as the illustrator of the "Madeleine" children's books. These paintings, which date from 1947, are whimsical and playful, with balloon sellers and bulldogs and snowy skating scenes and kangaroos. In the middle of the room is a piano; the program changes somewhat with the seasons, but the regular here is Barbara Carroll. Next to the bar is the **Café Carlyle,** with more original murals, these from 1955 by the French artist Vertès—a kind of post-Fauvist idyll of harlequins and horses, musicians and birds. Many of the tables here have cushioned love seats instead of chairs. This rather luxurious space is the supper club in which the supremely accomplished pianist and singer Bobby Short has played, again depending on the season, for over 20 years. Madison Avenue at 76th Street; Tel: 570-7189.

The Algonquin Hotel, where famous *New Yorker* writers used to congregate to cut each other verbally into ribbons (and may still do—the magazine's offices are just down the street), has recently refurbished its cabaret spot the **Oak Room,** which tends to run very polished singers of the evening-dress variety. But the Algonquin has its own idea of progress: At a cost of a quarter million dollars, it has replaced the room's handsome old paneling, in oak veneer, with handsome new paneling, in solid oak, for pretty much the same visual look. (We are reminded of the 1920s Hollywood director Erich von Stroheim, who insisted that the Austrian cavalry officers in his film *Foolish Wives* wear authentic silk underwear.) But those visitors in the know may experience a more tangible sense of luxury. 59 West 44th Street, east of Sixth Avenue; Tel: 840-6800.

On a rather unprepossessing block in north Chelsea is a classy, elaborately Continental restaurant and cabaret called **The Ballroom**. Attended by black-bow-tied-and-waistcoated waiters, patrons snack on *tapas* and martinis at the bar, which is decorated with ornamental foodstuffs—smoked hams, plaits of garlic bulbs, dried peppers—and then take their drinks through a mirrored double door to a dark, simply designed room supplied with a sizable stage and a piano. The tables are on gently descending terraces, so everyone gets a good view of the singers and accompanists and good-taste comedy acts the place books. Some of The Ballroom's performances are in the early evening, right after work, which is unusual for the city. 253 West 28th Street, east of Eighth Avenue; Tel: 244-3005.

The bar of **Michael's Pub** is all dolled up with oak and old mirrors to look like what a visitor from Ireland might—might!—expect to find in some Victorian remnant back home. This is incongruous, given the building's steel-and-glass exterior, but it makes for a pleasant environment in which to hear music. That last comes from an inner room, a supper club, which takes acts ranging from cabaret and stand-up comedy to serious jazz, and regularly bills big names. The Dixieland band that plays here every Monday is known for featuring Woody Allen on clarinet, though he doesn't invariably show up. If you're not in the mood to sit down (the service here, incidentally, is sometimes brusque), all this can be heard, though not seen, relatively inexpensively from the bar. 211 East 55th Street, east of Third Avenue; Tel: 758-2272.

Broadway attracts actors, dancers, and singers to New York, then doesn't hire them all, so the balance have to keep their hand in however they can. **Eighty-Eights**—the name, of course, refers to the number of keys on a piano—is the kind of place where the pianist sings and the waiters sing and people dropping in sing, some of them very well. It's a contemporary room full of blond wood and black glass and dove gray carpeting; there's a cabaret upstairs. The club has a Midtown cousin, **Don't Tell Mama** (same management), which is much closer to Broadway and much more rowdy and casual.

Eighty-Eights, 228 West 10th Street, west of Bleecker Street; Tel: 924-0088. Don't Tell Mama, 343 West 46th Street, west of Eighth Avenue; Tel: 757-0788.

BLEECKER STREET

The string of clubs along Bleecker Street between Sullivan and La Guardia Place is the gradually mutating corpus of the Village's old folk-and-rock scene, now catering to a rowdy mix of tourists, young bridge-and-tunnelers in for the evening, college students from nearby New York University, and neighborhood folk preserving their own corner of the 1960s. With a few exceptions, there's not much to tell between these places. However, the **Village Gate**'s cavernous basement room is large enough to bill significant, mainly jazz, names, with some of the rootsier rock mixed in; every Monday evening it runs a terrific series of salsa concerts that set a jazz soloist in the context of a Latin orchestra and watch what happens.

Along the street is the **Village Corner**, a dark and ancient bar (here in one form or another since 1904) with a grand piano. Since 1975, a regular player here has been Lance Hayward, who is worth travelling to hear.

The Village Gate is at Bleecker and Thompson streets; Tel: 475-5120. The Village Corner, at Bleecker Street and La Guardia Place; Tel: 473-9762.

ROCK AND OTHER LIVE PERFORMANCES

It seems symbolic that Bleecker Street, the main drag of New York's 1960s folk scene, should end abruptly on the Bowery at **CBGB**. In the late 1970s this club was the heart of the city's punk-rock movement, which set out to replace everything sensitive and singer-songwriterly in popular music with the abrasive, the aggressive, the loud. Some of the groups that played here back then (the Talking Heads, for example) have ended up as arty as rock comes, but CBGB hasn't changed: it's the archetypal dive, dark, worn, graffitied, and odorous of beer. Generally speaking, the bands haven't changed either, so the place can be tough on the ears. But CBGB is historic in its way. Old habitués feel affectionate about it, and sometimes musicians now quite elevated in the world come back to play. The letters of the name, incidentally, are not, as is sometimes thought (given the club's aura and skid-row location), a riff on "heebie-jeebies"; they stand for country, bluegrass, and blues, none of which has been booked here in years. 315 Bowery, at Bleecker Street; Tel: 677-0455.

The Bottom Line is a basic rock 'n' roll club, considerably less raunchy than CBGB, where record companies like to see breaking acts showcased for the influential New

York media searchers. It also features long-established people who have sizable followings but may not fill a big hall; recently, for example, Donovan and Laura Nyro passed through. The club is near New York University, so it gets a student audience, and when jazz players like Sun Ra and his Arkestra play here they pull out all the stops to grab the young crowd. 15 West 4th Street, west of Broadway at Mercer Street; Tel: 228-6300.

S.O.B.'s—Sounds of Brazil—grew out of a season owner Larry Gold spent going to Brazilian bars in Paris and wondering why there was no equivalent in New York. Since his club opened, in 1982, the city's enthusiastic dance and music crowd has proven he asked the right question. S.O.B.'s specializes in the rhythms of Brazil, tapping both the country's local expatriate community for acts and bringing them up here from Rio and Bahia and beyond. It also explores the music of Africa and the Caribbean, and the purview is gradually expanding. This is a supper club, and a lot of patrons have dinner here—a Brazilian menu—before settling in to samba. The place is noisy and energetic, the music both ambitious and wildly danceable. 204 Varick Street, near Houston Street; Tel: 243-4940.

Sadly, the Lone Star Café has lost its lease on the lower Fifth Avenue building it decorated with a giant rooftop sculpture of an iguana and a banner proclaiming "Too Much Is Not Enough." That leaves us with the **Lone Star Roadhouse**, a Times Square–area room done up from the outside to look like a Greyhound bus. Inside, the club shows the influence of its location: It's a cabaret-type space, with mirrored walls and pictures dotted around the way rooms in this neighborhood put up pictures of Broadway stars who stop by (though the folks in this little gallery are more Long Tall Sally than Tin Pan Alley). So there's less Texas atmosphere than in the old place, but the acts are still roadhouse rock 'n' roll, R & B, blues, western swing—anything that sounds like a party. 240 West 52nd Street, west of Broadway; Tel: 245-2950.

A little while ago the **Ritz** moved uptown, from the gorgeous East 11th Street Art Deco–style hall that it gave hard wear to a West 54th Street site that is intriguing in a different way—this is the former Studio 54, a crucial discotheque in New York discotheque history. (Somehow these new quarters, once the acme of glamour, now look pretty much like the Ritz always did. It's as if one forgot, in the old days, that this was simply a made-over theater with the ground-floor seats ripped out, but with the vaulted ceiling, balcony, stage, etc., basically intact.) The Ritz bills all kinds of rock 'n' roll, and it's gentler on the feet than it used to be—there's much more sitting space upstairs to complement the big dance floor below. Often, buying your ticket in advance here is a little cheaper than buying it on the night of the show. 254 West 54th Street, east of Eighth Avenue; Tel: 541-8900.

A block of 21st Street between Fifth and Sixth avenues has become a peculiar kind of inner-city entertainment mall: Besides the discotheque **Private Eyes** and the Philippine restaurant and club **Manila** (which seems to book mainly Latin-type jazz, with an occasional touring Filipino pop star), there is a chic, well-lit pool hall called Chelsea Billiards and—an urban rarity, though no great metropolis worthy of the name should be without one—an indoor miniature golf course called Putters Paradise. Understandably enough, the block often fills up with strollers of a late evening, and some of them stop in at **Tramps**, the rock club opposite the golf course. Tramps used to be housed in the Gramercy Park neighborhood, when it was known for awhile as the home away from home of the singer Buster Poindexter. Now the club has moved to a much larger, unpolished but comfortable loft, and though rock bands we've never heard of often appear here, whenever it gets the opportunity Tramps bills blues greats—if they're playing in the city, they're probably here. 45 West 21st Street, east of Sixth Avenue; Tel: 727-7788.

The **Eagle Tavern** is an Irish bar, a basic kind of place, much more like most of the pubs we remember in Ireland than the more deliberately "Gaelic" drinking spots in which the city abounds. There's a back room decorated, inexplicably, with a maritime motif (eagles swim?), and here, on Monday and Friday nights, visiting fiddlers and tin-whistlers and button accordionists spin out jigs and reels. Some of the musicians are Irish-American, some are from the Old Country, and the crowd seems similarly mixed. Saturday nights are for this music's American cousin, bluegrass. 355 West 14th Street, at Ninth Avenue; Tel: 924-0275.

Tommy Makem's **Irish Pavilion** puts a ceramic shamrock over its door to broadcast its national allegiance; inside, a sign reads *Failte* (Welcome), though no Gaelic is needed to read the invitation in the nice old china spirit kegs that decorate the place. Befitting its 57th Street location, the Pavilion is a rather elegant version of an Irish bar, with its brass rails and green walls and gentle light. Downtown is **Glocca Morra**, a darker, homier version of the same institution. (According to the pilfered Irish road sign that is Glocca Morra's principal concession to decor, it is 19 miles from East 23rd Street to Spiddal.) According to both these rooms' billings, the criterion of Celtic music is a tenor voice and an acoustic guitar. Alongside Irish staples like "Black Velvet Band" and "Johnny I Hardly Knew Ye," singers here may throw in Allman Brothers numbers, or "New York, New York"; but then the Irish have historic connections with New York, and songs about the American open road are as popular in Western Eire as in the Western United States. In any case, everyone seems to know all the words. The Pavilion has a musical edge in that owner Tommy Makem, the great Irish singer and multi-instrumentalist, appears here regularly. The Irish Pavilion, 130 East 57th Street, just west of Lexington Avenue; Tel: 759-9040. Glocca Morra, 304 Third Avenue, just north of 23rd Street; Tel: 473-9638.

New York is not the obvious place to go for country music, but it's the city with everything, so **O'Lunney's** bills the stuff seven nights a week. This is basically a simple Irish bar, but it makes a few bows to the West in its decor, has a small dance floor, and if the bands sometimes have accents that seem local, they play pedal steel just like they're supposed to. 915 Second Avenue, south of 49th Street; Tel: 751-5470.

Performance Art

The Pyramid is an unlikely storefront nightclub on the Lower East Side, a home for the unpredictable, no-rules kind of entertainment known as performance art. In the early to mid-1980s the East Village held a sizable nightclub and gallery scene of young entrepreneurs evading the high rents of the established art districts by operating here instead, in pocket-size spaces where they showed the emerging local talent. Today a few remain, but most have either closed or, in the case of many of the galleries, moved to upgraded spaces in and around SoHo. The Pyramid is a reminder of the old days. Outside is an ornately but funkily decorated façade standing out from the grayish tenement fronts around it on Avenue A; inside is a pair of rooms in every shade of phosphorescent, one a bar painted in purple and orange paisley, the second the black-lit performance space. What plays here varies wildly: On quiet evenings it's a loud discotheque (if for a young Loisaida—Lower East Sider—crowd that might be called adventuresome); often it's a rock club for bands unheard of outside a ten-block radius; then there's performance, which is virtually anything the artist in question decides it is, from the humdrum to the hilarious to the cover-your-eyes-and-pretend-you-didn't-see-that. 101 Avenue A, south of 7th Street; Tel: 420-1590.

Performance art also plays in spaces a little more sedate. **P.S. 122**, a former schoolhouse become neighborhood art center, is a few blocks away from The Pyramid, and the auditorium here takes some of the same performers and some of the same crowd, but the mood is more theatrical than clubbish—though with bleacher seating and no air conditioning in summer. Many New Yorkers uncomfortable with the close-packed standing-room-only let's-all-throw-things-at-the-stage exigencies of club life may come here to see a performance artist stretch to engage a larger and calmer audience, or they may go to **The Kitchen**, which also runs an ambitious contemporary-music program. These places, some of whose income comes from public grant money, are less free-for-all than the private performance houses; hey, this stuff is supposed to be art. So a performer may debut with an ambitious project here and then go back to the clubs.

P.S. 122, 150 First Avenue, at 9th Street; Tel: 477-5288. The Kitchen, 512 West 19th Street, west of Tenth Avenue; Tel: 255-5793.

COMEDY CLUBS

In the late 1970s, when the satiric TV show "Saturday Night Live" was at the height of its cult popularity, stand-up comedy took on a whole new glamour in New York. Young comics achieved for themselves the kind of media stardom that had once been linked mainly with rock 'n' roll—which for many culture consumers had begun to seem either overly well established and safe or, in the hands of the punksters who were trying to make the music risky again, a little too confrontational for comfort. Part of rock's role has been to offer an identity, a feeling of group community, to whatever generation is growing up at the time, and as music slackened its hold (not that it isn't still popular) comics were the perfect substitute, especially if their humor was of that nervy kind that kids weren't sure was funny, suspected was shocking, but at least knew that their parents weren't laughing at. That moment has to some extent passed, but its legacy is today's comedy clubs in the city, which are full of young comedians looking for their break. Their models are less Henny Youngman and Rich Little than John Belushi and Steve Martin; some of their jokes you can go to hell just for hearing told. On good nights these places are full of fresh energy.

In comedy clubs, however, good nights are unpredictable. These rooms are where comics learn as well as practice their craft. Sometimes they fly and sometimes they flop, and the best can flop in front of an audience that just isn't amused. A crowd that goes to see Richard Pryor at Radio City Music Hall goes ready to laugh, wanting to laugh, knowing the night will be funny. A comedy-club crowd expects the quality to vary and can be ungenerous. Two clubs on the Upper East Side sometimes demonstrate this clearly. The Comic Strip and Catch a Rising Star are within walking distance of each other, and people who aren't enjoying the one can easily stroll over to the other to see what's going on. If they do, they may find that a comic they saw earlier in the evening has taken the same walk, and though they just watched him bomb, now he's rolling. The act itself is probably identical.

Given the proviso of variable evenings, **Catch a Rising Star** is a good bet for hilarity. It's a popular club (the bigger the crowd, the better the probability of laughter, which is infectious), and it's a comfortable and friendly spot. **The Comic Strip** is a barer and less-polished room, but not necessarily the less funny for that, and it's nice to sit at the bar here and listen to the comics hanging out and telling stories about horrible audiences they have known.

Downtown is **Caroline's** at the South Street Seaport, which is a kind of urban theme park designed for picturesqueness; yet Caroline's is a modern room, and a little antiseptic. It is, however, well sited to attract good crowds. In Midtown East is **Rags to Riches**, an elegant room that offers a "happy hour" comedy special just after the end of the working day, as well as regular evening shows.

A lot of the same performers circulate from one to the other of these clubs—and we've only mentioned a few; check the nightlife ads in the *Village Voice* or the entertainment listings in *New York* magazine for more—which means that the chances for enjoyment are spread around. An evening in any of these places may see a dozen young aspirants chewed up or coming off smiling. And although the clubs may have open evenings when anyone can stand up to take his or her knocks, these are not amateur outfits. Many of the comics who play them are very polished indeed, with a lot of pro experience, and well-known names sometimes pass through.

Catch a Rising Star, 1487 First Avenue, south of 78th Street; Tel: 794-1906. The Comic Strip, 1568 Second Avenue, south of 82nd Street; Tel: 861-9386. Caroline's, South Street Seaport, Pier 17, at Fulton Street and the East River; Tel: 233-4900. Rags to Riches, 226 East 54th Street, east of Third Avenue; Tel. 688-5577.

DANCE HALLS, SOIREES, AND DISCOS

Roseland is New York's classic Broadway ballroom. It has been where it now stands since 1956, but it opened around the corner on 51st Street in 1919. A renovation in the mid-1980s didn't do too much harm. The decor looks pretty much as always, though the red-rose-studded green carpet is actually new; the dance floor, ringed by a sinuous wrought-iron balustrade punctuated by low lampposts, is still half a block long, and there are clubs in the city smaller than its bandstand. The versatility of the lighting system, however, is entirely modern. From Thursday to Sunday people can dance here for up to nine and a half hours a day—disco late nights on Friday and Saturday, ballroom and Latin on Thursday, Saturday, and Sunday, beginning in midafternoon. These events can be fascinating, allowing a glimpse of an older Broadway culture. A "wall of fame" on the way in is a display case of the shoes of famous dancers, from Ruby Keeler to Ann Reinking, from George Raft to Gregory Hines. Pop acts in need of a hall with a floor sometimes stop in, but the air still breathes Stan Kenton and the Dorsey Brothers. 239 West 52nd Street, west of Broadway; Tel: 247-0200.

The Rainbow Room is in Rockefeller Center, and you can reach it from Sixth Avenue and 50th Street, but don't. Take the processional walk in from Fifth Avenue, with your destination, 30 Rockefeller Plaza, brilliantly spotlit in front of you at night above the golden statue of Prometheus. The gentle descent of the pavement pulls you on, and the architecture tells you you're going somewhere big. Inside, the floor continues its easy slope, and you reach the private burl-paneled elevators that will whisk you express to the 65th floor; step out, turn around, and there's a sudden view of the Empire State Building with all of southern Manhattan laid out around it.

The Rainbow Room first opened in 1934, an Art Deco palace in the sky. It reopened at the end of 1987, after a two-year, $20 million renovation, in all its former stylishness, with contemporary design and *objets* artfully complementing the old. The band plays Glenn Miller; the dance floor revolves; the floor-to-ceiling windows frame . . . practically everything. Fred Astaire and Ginger Rogers do not go swinging by, but in the general flurry of evening gowns and tuxedos it's easy to pretend. Dinner and dancing here may run $100 or so a person; from the neighboring bar you can enjoy the same views for the price of a drink, though the music is now remote, and gentlemen still must wear a jacket there. A new addition to the place is the Rainbow & Stars, which combines the same views with sophisticated cabaret acts. 30 Rockefeller Plaza near 50th Street off Fifth Avenue; Tel: 632-5000/5100.

The **Red Blazer Too** is a relaxed dinner and dancing place that specializes in the jazz of the 1920s and 1930s: Dixieland, swing, and the chunkily swinging stuff in between. Some of the bands that run here feature players from those times. There aren't many rooms around anymore in which this music can be heard from a dance floor instead of from a chair, so the people who come to the Red Blazer seem both to know their jazz history and to get up and enjoy it in the best, nonacademic way—in their dancing shoes. 349 West 46th Street, west of Eighth Avenue; Tel: 262-3112.

The **Cat Club** on ordinary days is a standard rock 'n' roll place, but most Sundays since 1985 it has belonged to the New York Swing Dance Society, who use it to do the lindy and other steps of that family to the music of big orchestras (including, one night a while ago, the Basie band). These Sundays are like club nights—a lot of people are regulars, and there's that sociable feeling of a not necessarily fashionable common interest. Some of the dancers remember the Savoy Ballroom (of Chick Webb's "Stompin' at the Savoy," a famous Harlem hall torn down in the 1950s); others barely remember the Beatles. All are welcome. From a framed photograph on the wall, David Bowie looks on, impassive as ever. 76 East 13th Street, west of Fourth Avenue (a southern incarnation of Park Avenue); Tel: 505-0090.

For over 30 years, from its opening in 1940, the **Copacabana**, almost always called the Copa, was a hegemonic presence in New York nightlife. Everybody played there, from Frank Sinatra to Chubby Checker to the Supremes and on. A booking there marked a performer as a star, like a stamp he needed in his passport. There are volumes of Copa lore—how co-owner Jules Podell was an associate of underworld crime boss Frank Costello; how Desi Arnaz and Lucille Ball first met in the club, when she was in its chorus line; how Dean Martin and Jerry Lewis both began and ended their career as a comedy team there. After Podell's death in 1973 the club closed its doors. It reopened in 1976 and is now a regular discotheque, open Tuesdays, Fridays, and Saturdays and booking live, mainly Latin bands. But the downstairs room has been restored rather than renovated and has the same Carmen Miranda–headgear–painted mirrors, the same concrete support columns made over into white-enameled palm trees, the same frond-pattern carpeting that made the rat pack feel at home. 10 East 60th Street, east of Fifth Avenue; Tel: 755-6010.

In a heavily Hispanic Upper West Side neighborhood, above a jeans outlet and beside a McDonald's, is the blue-velvet-interiored **Club Broadway**, an unpretentious but capacious and comfortable ballroom open late weekend nights for dancing to Latin big bands. 2551 Broadway, south of 96th Street; Tel: 864-7600.

The Palladium is housed in a big and battered old theater, from 1926, that used to be called the Academy of Music. This discotheque's designer, the Japanese architect Arata Isozaki (creator of the new Museum of Contemporary Art in Los Angeles, among other buildings), has kept large chunks of the original decor. The parts of the interior that were decaying he preserved or even encouraged in their decay, but he mixed them with decisively modern elements. The dance floor, for example, is encased in a high-tech open-sided cube, with built-in lights and video banks, and paintings and designs by significant current artists are scattered about the walls. This is a spectacular space, full of dramatic lighting effects and vistas, jumbling the antiqued with the contemporary, that makes you feel as if you were living out the transition from one kind of world into another. As architecture it's as worthy of a visit, as indicative of its time as, say, Grace Church or the lobby of the Woolworth Building. As a dance club, it's been on the scene a little too long to be called state of the art—it opened in 1985, a long time ago in some circles—but, at least in its visual style, few of the hot clubs of the present day really advance on it, and many of them are in its debt. Run by Ian Schrager—who, with the late Steve Rubell, created Studio 54, the big daddy of New York's late-1970s disco scene—the Palladium is almost a necessary stop for nightclubbers, if only for the sake of history. 126 East 14th Street, west of Third Avenue; Tel: 473-7171.

The Tunnel is a discotheque built over one of the old railway lines that hauled freight up and down the West Side of Manhattan in the now-vanished days of working docks and warehouses there. As you'd expect, then, it's a narrow, elongated space (well, it's a tunnel), with the old train tracks still visible at one end, though subject to a light show novel in their history. Sitting rooms off the main dance floor are done up in a variety of decors—Aubrey Beardsley, Neoclassical, all-mirrored—and big old-fashioned glass chandeliers above the dance floor sit oddly within the bare-brick walls. This glamour-in-the-ruins effect seems a cop from the Palladium, however. 220 12th Avenue, though the door is actually around the corner on 27th Street; Tel: 244-6444.

Those who see New York as Sin City, a destroyer of all Christian values, might surely support their argument by citing the **Limelight**. For most of the years since the 1840s this building was the Church of the Holy Communion; now it's a discotheque. When the Limelight opened, in 1984, the regional Episcopal bishop pronounced himself "horrified," but the church had already been sold into secular use. Now light towers and catwalks scrape the gothic arches, and dancers pump to disco in the nave. A marble tablet in the vestibule advises them that "this house was created to the honor of God and for the good of His children"; maybe, in their own way, they agree. 47 West 20th Street, at Sixth Avenue; Tel: 807-7850.

When it opened in 1986, **Nell's** was something new under the sun, or at least in the New York club life of the preceding decade. Where discos from Studio 54 on had emphasized a high-tech glamour that reached its peak in the Palladium, Nell's decided to be an Edwardian salon. On the ground floor is a rather beautiful room, all softly lit red-velvet sofas and low coffee tables on faded carpets, with dark wood paneling on the walls and gilt-framed mirrors stretching back under a dim but lustrous chandelier. In the far section of the space you can dine, or you can converse on a couch as if in a more luxurious version of your sitting room, but with a bar. For dancers there's a floor in the basement, so they don't have to go somewhere else. Nell's is one of those clubs that likes to keep people standing outside; but it's not a huge space, and a chunk of its nightly clientele will be the in-crowd "regis-trants," the regulars who get precedence at the door. You can try to assure entry by calling ahead, early, to make a reservation. 246 West 14th Street, east of Eighth Avenue; Tel: 675-1567.

M.K. takes the premises of what used to be a bank, and, like the Palladium, it keeps some of the old interior decor (for example, the marble-paneled walls) and adds some of its own (the balcony restaurant space and the stuffed Dobermans). The art on the walls also recalls the Palla-dium (at this writing a Basquiat, some Schnabels, etc.), the chandeliers recall Nell's and the Tunnel, and the sitting-room mood of the ground-floor bar is definitely out of Nell's. Still, at this writing M.K. is a hot club. In the basement, which used to be the vault, is a late-night discotheque; the coat check is in what was once the safe, with the massive, rather beautiful steel doors standing polished and open. Upstairs there's a nice little balconied window where patrons can stand and watch the bouncer outside turning people away. Those who do get in tend to be young and affluent and very chic. If you must visit here, try calling in advance to make a reservation for dinner. 204 Fifth Avenue, north of 25th Street; Tel: 779-1340.

The World, like the Ritz and the Palladium, is an old auditorium made over to new use, but where the Ritz preserves its original fittings and the Palladium makes decay look dressy, here the dilapidation is a value in itself. Downstairs is a smallish, moderne, relatively soigné space; upstairs is a cavernous hall of peeling plaster and ratty brick, supplied, of course, with high-tech lights and sound. Some evenings this is a regular rock 'n' roll con-cert space, but the time to go is from midnight or one-ish until around 4:00 A.M., say, Tuesday through Sunday, when it turns into a dance club for an eclectic cross section of the city's most knowledgeable nightlife crowd, and a very hot place to be. 254 East 2nd Street, just west of Avenue C; Tel: 477-8677.

Red Zone and Mars are the closest to "new things" to come along during the waning of the Nell's-type club. **Red Zone**, a converted sound studio in the far West 50s, isn't actually that new—a conventional disco with high-tech sounds, lights, and a fancy array of movie screens, in a return to Palladium-style glamour. An upstairs restau-rant with a lounge and its own dance floor is less frenetic, though it may require a second application of talk-your-way-past-the-doorman smarts. **Mars** is more interesting—

a deliberately grungy, five-story interior scattered with odd bits of sculpture and old machine parts, for a German Expressionist, *Metropolis* kind of look. The club's name may come from its remote location, down near the river in the still-seedy meat-packing district; or perhaps the owners liked imagining the cab driver's response when you asked him to take you to Mars. Red Zone, 440 West 54 Street, west of Ninth Avenue; Tel: 582-2222. Mars, 28 Tenth Avenue, south of 13th Street; Tel: 691-6262.

Trixie's is a wonderful anomaly: a hot spot that's actually hot instead of cool. Kids seem to come here to have fun rather than to see and be seen and to demonstrate their hipness. A former Greek diner, Trixie's is actually a restaurant rather than a nightclub—to get in here, you call and make a reservation for dinner—but it's a restaurant that fancies itself a nightclub, though circumstances suggest otherwise. There's no room; lounge-lizard crooners stride up and down the crowded aisles between the tables, singing to backing tapes because there's nowhere to put a band. Or an all-women samba drum outfit in sarongs squeezes itself in next to the bar and ends up snaking through the place in a conga line, followed by half the diners. Between acts, the PA plays loud rock 'n' roll and everyone sings along. 307 West 47th Street, west of Eighth Avenue; Tel: 840-9537.

CHRONOLOGY OF THE HISTORY OF NEW YORK CITY

When Europeans arrived, the land that is now New York City was covered with forest (part of the original, virgin forest still survives in the Bronx), in which roamed black bears, mountain lions, bobcats, minks, foxes, wolves, and wild turkeys. The region was peopled by Algonquin subtribes that belonged to the Wappinger Confederation (Bronx and Manhattan) and the Delaware Confederation (Staten Island and Brooklyn). They subsisted by hunting and fishing and wore deerskin clothing and ornaments made of copper. The Indians greeted the first European arrivals with curiosity and were soon trading furs and wampum (strings of shells) with the newcomers. The harmony didn't last, however. Dutchman Willem Kieft initiated unprovoked attacks on the Indians. They retaliated and soon general mistrust and hostility strained relations between Europeans and Native Americans.

The Dutch Settle New Amsterdam

- **1524**: Giovanni da Verrazano sails into New York Bay and anchors in the Narrows
  Esteban Gomez, exploring for Spain, follows
- **1609**: Henry Hudson stops in Manhattan, then continues up the Hudson River
- **1613**: Dutch captain Adriaen Block winters on Manhattan
- **1624**: The first Dutch West India Company settlers arrive in New Netherland; most go upriver, but eight men stay in Manhattan
- **1625**: Large group of West India Company employees, mostly Walloons, arrives, followed by the first blacks, probably Portuguese slaves
- **1626**: Peter Minuit buys Manhattan from local Indians for $24 worth of goods
- **1628**: Manhattan has 270 inhabitants, 30 houses, 6 farms
  First black women (also slaves) arrive
- **1629**: Dutch West India Company issues land grants (patroonships) to anyone bringing 50 families to settle

- **1631**: Peter Minuit builds an 800-ton ship (then the largest ever built) to demonstrate uses of local timber to authorities in Netherlands
- **1632**: Minuit loses his post; returns to Netherlands
- **1638**: Willem Kieft, new director-general, imposes first known city ordinances (port regulations, drinking laws) and raises tensions with Indians
First school opens (for Dutch and black children)
Ferry begins operation between Manhattan and Brooklyn
- **1639**: First English immigrants arrive in Manhattan
- **1641**: The Wooden Horse, first tavern, opens
New law makes it illegal to drink during church hours
At New Netherland's first hanging the rope breaks; Manuel Gerrit, a slave convicted of murder, is released
- **1643**: Settlers have their first serious clash with Indians
Deborah Moody is the first woman to receive a land grant (in Gravesend, Brooklyn)
- **1644**: Some African slaves are set free and given land
A new law forbids dumping refuse and urinating in the streets
- **1645**: A truce is reached with the Indians; selling liquor to Indians is prohibited
- **1647**: Kieft is replaced as director-general by Petrus Stuyvesant, whose first ordinance is to close taverns at nine o'clock
- **1652**: Manhattan's first speeding law (no galloping allowed in the city) and gun-control law (no shooting in the streets) instituted
- **1653**: New Amsterdam forms a new municipal government, a forerunner of today's city council; its concerns include support of widows and orphans and control of the hogs that run in the streets
City Hall is established in a tavern
New Amsterdam's first lawyer is not allowed to practice because there is no one to act as opposing council
The wall that gave Wall Street its name is built to keep out Indians
- **1654**: The colony's first Jews arrive from northern Brazil

- **1655**: Indians attack New Amsterdam, killing and capturing settlers
  Jews win right to join militia and own homes (against Stuyvesant's protest)
  The first slave ship direct from Africa lands
- **1656**: Population: 1,000; 120 homes
  Sunday laws forbid drinking, tennis, dancing, laboring, bowling, and boating during church hours
- **1657**: The directors of the West India Company uphold freedom of religion after Stuyvesant tries to outlaw all but Dutch Reform
  It becomes illegal to litter in the streets of New Amsterdam
- **1658**: First street is paved (Stone Street, with cobblestones)
- **1660**: Settlers and Indians establish peace
  A hospital is instituted to tend soldiers and blacks

British New York

- **1664**: The English take over New Amsterdam and rename it New York
- **1665**: Thomas Willett is the first mayor of New York City
  Stuyvesant retires to his bouwerie
  New Jersey is colonized
- **1670**: First merchant exchange is established when businessmen begin meeting Fridays at noon on the bridge over Broad Canal (now Bridge Street)
- **1671**: Society of Friends (Quakers) hold their first meeting in New York—in a tavern
- **1673**: The Dutch regain New York; it becomes New Orange
- **1674**: Treaty of Westminster gives New York back to the English; its inhabitants become British subjects
- **1683**: Thomas Dongan, New York's first Roman Catholic governor, calls a representative assembly
- **1685**: Dongan Charter, or Charter of Liberties and Privileges, is New York's first constitution
- **1688**: King James is overthrown and William and Mary ascend the throne; in New York, Jacob Leisler and Jacob Milbourne assume the governing of New York
- **1691**: William and Mary's governor finally arrives in New York; Leisler and Milbourne wait 24 hours to hand over rule, thus angering the Crown, and are hanged for treason

- **1692**: City begins landfill at Water Street, creating Front and South streets
- **1693**: Fearing an attack by the French the city sets up a battery of cannon at the southern tip of the island (the Battery)
  William Bradford opens the city's first printing shop
- **1695**: Parliament pardons Leisler and Milbourne
- **1697**: Streetlight law requires every seventh house to hang a lantern
- **1698**: Census counts 4,937 inhabitants
- **1702**: New York's governor, Edward Hyde, Lord Cornbury, distinguishes himself by promenading in women's clothes
- **1705**: First free grammar school is instituted
- **1712**: Nine whites are killed in slave revolts; 21 blacks are executed
- **1725**: The city's first newspaper, *The New York Gazette,* is published
- **1732**: Bowling Green park is fenced off and used for bowling
- **1733**: *New York Weekly Journal* appears
- **1735**: John Peter Zenger, imprisoned for criticizing the British government in print, wins his case, the first victory for freedom of the press in America
- **1741**: After a number of fires and robberies that come to be called the Negro Conspiracy, 4 whites and 29 blacks are put to death, 71 blacks are transported, and 52 are pardoned
- **1750**: New York's first theater opens on Nassau Street
- **1754**: King's College (Columbia University) founded
  New York Society Library established, first public library
- **1763**: Ferry service to New Jersey begins
  West Indian Samuel Fraunces opens his tavern on Pearl Street

American Revolution and Independence

- **1765**: British pass the Stamp Act; colonists meet in City Hall at Stamp Act Congress and issue Declaration of Rights and Grievances

- **1766**: British repeal the Stamp Act but impose new taxes on tea, paper, glass, paint
- **1767**: Britain passes the Townshend Acts, which impose shipping laws and taxes for a military on the colonists
- **1770**: Skirmish between British soldiers and colonists on Golden Hill (John Street) predates Boston Massacre by a few days
  Parliament rescinds duties on everything but tea
- **1775**: American Revolution begins; Washington makes Richmond Hill house in Greenwich Village his headquarters; British position themselves around the city
- **1776**: The Declaration of Independence is read publicly from City Hall and America's flag is flown on July 18
  August 27: Americans retreat after losing Battle of Long Island; British take Brooklyn Heights
  September: Americans win battle of Harlem Heights and move north; British take possession of New York City (the city remains Loyalist until 1783); American troops and patriots begin to leave the city
  September 21: Nearly a fourth of Manhattan is destroyed by fire; losses include Trinity Church
  September 22: The British hang Nathan Hale, 22, as a spy without giving him a trial
- **1779**: Irish recruited to fight for the British hold New York's first St. Patrick's Day Parade
- **1781**: The martini, the first cocktail, is invented near Tarrytown
- **1782**: Loyalists, almost a third of the city's population, start leaving for Nova Scotia
- **1783**: November 25, Evacuation Day: American troops led by Washington reenter New York, Loyalists and British leave
  December 4: At Fraunces Tavern, George Washington bids his comrades farewell
- **1784**: New York State legislature begins to meet at City Hall
  Bank of New York established (first bank)
  King's College is renamed Columbia University
- **1785**: U.S. Congress meets in New York City
- **1786**: First city directory is issued, listing names, addresses, and occupations

- **1788**: New York ratifies the new U.S. Constitution and becomes the federal capital
- **1789**: George Washington is inaugurated president on the balcony of Federal Hall in Manhattan
  Tammany Society, a benevolent organization, is formed
- **1790**: Federal capital moves to Philadelphia
  First sidewalks are put down on Broadway
- **1792**: Forerunner of the New York Stock Exchange is born when brokers begin meeting under a buttonwood tree on Wall Street
- **1794**: City council changes names of streets and places that have British names
  The city uses Belle Vue farm to isolate yellow-fever patients
- **1797**: The state legislature moves from Manhattan to Albany
  Ordinance against pollution prohibits candle, glue, and soap making inside the city

The 19th Century

- **1800**: African Methodist Episcopal Zion Church, first church for blacks, is organized by a freed slave
- **1801**: Alexander Hamilton founds the *New York Post*
  Botanist David Hosack opens the 20-acre Elgin Garden on the site of Radio City Music Hall
- **1804**: New Yorkers duel: Aaron Burr kills Alexander Hamilton in Weehawken, New Jersey
  New-York Historical Society founded
- **1805**: The New York Free School Society is instituted to educate children who can't afford private schools
- **1807**: Robert Fulton begins steamboat service between New York and Albany with the *Clermont*
- **1809**: Washington Irving publishes *A History of New York from the Beginning of the World to the End of the Dutch Dynasty by Diedrich Knickerbocker*
- **1811**: Randel Plan is drawn up dividing Manhattan into grids with numbered avenues running north–south and streets running east–west
- **1814**: War of 1812 ends

- **1817**: The New York Stock Exchange is chartered
  The Staten Island Ferry begins running
- **1820–1830**: About 4,000 immigrants arrive per year
- **1821**: African Grove Theater, first black theater, opens on Bleecker Street
- **1822**: About two-thirds of the city's population evacuates for Greenwich Village and other country retreats during yellow-fever epidemic
- **1824**: Fifth Avenue is laid down from Waverly Place to 13th Street (it goes to 24th Street in 1830 and to Harlem by 1864)
- **1825**: The Erie Canal opens, connecting the Hudson to Lakes Champlain and Erie
  New York Gas Light Company begins to lay gas pipelines
  Arnold Constable, the city's first department store, opens
- **1826**: All white males over 21 who have lived in the state for one year are given the right to vote
- **1827**: *Freedom's Journal,* the world's first newspaper published by and for blacks, begins publication
  New York State outlaws slavery
- **1828**: New York's first known seller of roasted chestnuts sets up on Broadway at Duane
- **1830**: 14,000 immigrants enter New York
  Parade on Fifth Avenue in honor of the 1830 revolution in Paris starts the tradition
- **1831**: Nonsectarian New York University is instituted as an alternative to Episcopalian Columbia
- **1832**: New York and Harlem Railroad starts running horse-drawn street cars from Prince to 14th Street
- **1833**: The *New York Sun* begins publication
- **1834**: Cornelius Van Wyck Lawrence is the first mayor elected by popular vote
  Steam trains are running on Second, Sixth, and Eighth avenues
- **1835**: 32,715 immigrants enter New York
  Great Fire of 1835 destroys most of old Dutch New York
  Two Democratic party groups, Irish and "native," riot at Five Points
  New York Herald first issued
- **1837**: Financial panic causes a six-year depression

Daily News founded

Tiffany & Company opens

Samuel Morse demonstrates the telegraph at Castle Garden

- **1838**: The *New York Herald* starts using foreign correspondents
- **1839**: Samuel Cunard founds his famous shipping empire
- **1840–1856**: Three million immigrants enter New York, many fleeing potato famine in Ireland
- **1841**: Barnum's American Museum opens, featuring curiosities, freaks, and natural-history oddities

  Horace Greeley founds the *New York Tribune*

  Brooklyn Democrats found the *Brooklyn Eagle*
- **1842**: New York City takes over the public schools and discontinues aid to parochial schools

  Croton Reservoir is built at 42nd Street and Fifth Avenue

  The New York Philharmonic is formed
- **1843**: Brooklyn Institute of Arts & Sciences (Brooklyn Museum) is founded
- **1844**: New York City Police Department is formed (police refuse to wear uniforms until 1853)
- **1845**: The New York Knickerbocker Baseball Club draws up a formal set of rules for the game
- **1846**: Hudson-River Railroad runs along the river from Manhattan to Albany in five hours

  Walt Whitman takes job as editor of the *Brooklyn Eagle*
- **1847**: Abolitionist Henry Ward Beecher begins preaching at Plymouth Church of the Pilgrims in Brooklyn
- **1848**: New York's residential area extends as far north as 23rd Street

  New York News Agency (later renamed Associated Press) established
- **1849**: Supporters of English actor Charles Macready clash with those of American actor Edwin Forrest in the Astor Place Riot, leaving many dead and wounded
- **1850**: Hecker & Brothers millers on Cherry Street install the first freight elevator

  Jenny Lind makes her American debut at Castle Garden under the management of P. T. Barnum
- **1851**: *New York Times* begins publication

- **1852**: William Marcy Tweed is elected to city council
- **1853**: Manhattan hosts the world's fair
  Steinway & Sons piano manufacturers opens
- **1854**: Chester A. Arthur represents Elizabeth Jennings in a suit against Third Avenue Railroad, which had refused to let her ride because she was black; her victory brings an end to official discrimination on public transportation
- **1857**: Financial panic sets off a depression
  Haughwout Building installs Otis passenger elevator, said to be the first in the world
  The Fenians, the Irish Republican Brotherhood, is formed in New York
  Joseph C. Gayetty of West 33rd Street invents toilet paper
- **1858**: The Crystal Palace, a fireproof exhibition hall, is demolished by fire
  Construction of Central Park begins
  New York Symphony Orchestra is formed
  New York City has 16 baseball clubs
- **1859**: Cooper Union, a tuition-free science and arts school, opens
- **1860**: Abraham Lincoln, seeking Republican nomination for the presidency, gives a speech at Cooper Union
  Tweed rises to prominence in Tammany Society
  Four thousand socialites pay their respects to the Prince of Wales (Edward VII) at a spectacular ball at the Academy of Music
- **1861**: American Civil War begins
- **1862**: F.A.O. Schwartz toy store opens
- **1863**: The Draft Riots sweep the city as gangs set fires and attack blacks and abolitionists in protest against military draft; many are killed and injured, many buildings destroyed
  General Tom Thumb, a famous exhibit at Barnum's museum, marries at Grace Church
- **1864**: Songwriter Stephen Foster dies in the Bowery
- **1865**: The city staffs its first paid, trained fire department
  Woodlawn Cemetery opens in the Bronx
- **1866**: New York establishes a board of health
  The Black Crook, progenitor of the American musical comedy, begins a 16-month run

- **1868**: Boss Tweed has virtual control of city and county of New York
  Elevated railway is erected on Greenwich Street
- **1869**: Tweed forms the Tweed Ring, putting control of the city in the hands of four men
  American Museum of Natural History is founded
  Bellevue Hospital starts horse-drawn ambulance service
- **1870**: The Metropolitan Museum of Art is founded
  Alfred Ely Beach builds a wind-powered subway under Broadway, but Boss Tweed prevents him from getting funding
- **1871**: Citizens meet at Cooper Union to protest Tweed's rule; he makes his famous reply: "Well, what are you going to do about it?"
  The New York Times begins printing articles exposing Tammany Hall; with the help of Thomas Nast's political cartoons, it leads to the investigation and downfall of the Tweed Ring
  National Association of Baseball Players is founded in New York; the league includes the New York Mutuals and the Brooklyn Eckfords
- **1872**: Tweed Courthouse completed; massive cost overrun causes scandal
  Bloomingdale's opens
- **1873**: Stock market crashes: Exchange closes for ten days; railroads go bankrupt; six-year depression follows
  Olmsted designs Riverside Park, and he and Vaux finish Prospect Park in Brooklyn
- **1874**: Society for the Prevention of Cruelty to Children is founded in New York
  Henry Ward Beecher is tried for and acquitted of adultery
- **1876**: Central Park opens
  The New York Legal Aid Society is founded; first such institution in the world
- **1878**: Boss Tweed dies in debtors prison
  Elevated trains are operating on Ninth, Sixth, and Third avenues
  Bell Telephone Company of New York issues its first telephone directory
- **1879**: Charles McKim, William Mead, and Stanford White found an architectural firm that will change the face of New York
- **1880**: Electricity lights the streets of New York

- **1882**: Thomas Edison's central electrical plant goes into operation; it supplies electricity to homes and businesses
- **1883**: The Brooklyn Bridge opens the first roadway between Brooklyn and Manhattan
  First Metropolitan Opera House opens
- **1884**: The Dakota apartment house lures New Yorkers to the Upper West Side
  World's first roller coaster is installed at Coney Island
- **1886**: One million people gather for the unveiling of the Statue of Liberty
  "Boodle Board" scandal exposes city officials extorting money from a railroad company
- **1888**: The Great Blizzard dumps 22 inches of snow on the city; falling telegraph and electrical poles and wires prompt the city to move them all underground
  New York's first deli opens on Delancey Street and introduces New Yorkers to pastrami on rye
- **1889**: A wooden arch is raised in Washington Square to commemorate the anniversary of Washington's presidential inauguration (it is recast in marble in 1895)
  Charles Dow and Edward Jones start publishing the daily *Wall Street Journal*
- **1890**: Federal government takes over immigration and moves the operation to Ellis Island (which opens in 1892)
  Thousands attend the opening of McKim, Mead & White's Madison Square Garden
  Movies are first shown in New York
  Jacob Riis's *How the Other Half Lives* exposes the plight of the immigrant poor
- **1891**: Carnegie Hall opens; Tchaikovsky is one of the first conductors to appear
- **1892**: Building of the Cathedral Church of St. John the Divine begins (still not completed today)
  The first of Broadway's monstrous electrical signs is lit
- **1893**: Henry Street Settlement, still active today, opens
  Crane's *Maggie, A Girl of the Streets* portrays life in the Bowery
- **1894**: The city indicts 67 policemen on corruption charges

Theodore Roosevelt becomes city police commissioner

Yiddish-language daily *The Forward* begins publication

Statue of Christopher Columbus is put up in Grand Circle, which is renamed Columbus Circle

Edison opens a Kinetoscope (type of moving picture) theater in Manhattan

- **1895**: First electric streetcars run

  "White Wings," street cleaners in white uniforms, are a visible part of the city's new sanitation system

  Marble Hill, the northern tip of Manhattan, is cut from the island and attached to the Bronx when the Harlem River is shifted and made deeper to accommodate ships

- **1896**: Building of Columbus Park eradicates the city's most notorious slum, Five Points

  Castle Clinton becomes home to the New York Aquarium

  A Clinton Street baker bakes an old German recipe with a Yiddish name, *bagel,* and starts a New York tradition

- **1897**: Dow and Jones begin monitoring the stock market

  Oscar Hammerstein's Olympia Theater is the first in what is now considered the Theater District

  Steeplechase Park, an amusement park, opens at Coney Island

- **1899**: Two million people line Broadway and Fifth Avenue at parade to welcome Admiral George Dewey back from a victorious campaign in the Spanish-American War

  Entire stretch of road from lower Manhattan to the Bronx-Westchester line is given the name Broadway

The 20th Century

- **1900**: Building of subways begins

  Traffic laws, enforced at specific times of day, come into use in New York City

  Madison Square Garden hosts the country's first auto show

  B. A. Mcfadden opens the first of his chain of one-cent restaurants called Mcfadden Physical Culture Restaurants

- **1901**: Macy's opens at 34th and Broadway
- **1902**: The Flatiron Building goes up
- **1903**: C. K. G. Billings gives the famed Horseback Dinner at Sherry's restaurant; the guests, all men, sat on horses—sipping the champagne in their saddlebags through straws—and were served by waiters dressed as grooms

  The Baltimore Orioles become the New York Highlanders (later the Yankees)
- **1904**: The IRT subway opens with trains from City Hall to 145th Street

  The tradition of New Year's Eve in Times Square (up until now known as Longacre Square) starts at the inaugural celebration of the New York Times Tower

  The steamboat *General Slocum* catches fire and sinks in the East River while transporting 1,335 passengers, many of them children, to a picnic; 1,051 die and 124 are injured

  The New York Public Library is built at 42nd and Fifth Avenue on site of Croton Reservoir

  August Belmont builds his own private subway car with a bar, washroom, waiters, and its own conductor

  George M. Cohan's *Little Johnny Jones,* featuring "Give My Regards to Broadway," opens
- **1905**: George Bernard Shaw's *Mrs. Warren's Profession* is closed by censor after opening night
- **1906**: Stanford White is killed by Henry K. Thaw, his former mistress's husband, in Madison Square Garden's roof garden
- **1907**: Stock market panic (Panic of 1907)

  Subway service to Brooklyn begins

  It becomes against the law for women to smoke in public in New York City

  The first Ziegfeld Follies show opens
- **1908**: Eight New York artists (including Maurice Prendergast, John Sloan, and Robert Henri) form group known as the Ashcan School
- **1909**: Hudson-Fulton celebration commemorates Hudson's 1609 excursion and Fulton's 1807 steamboat

  NAACP founded; opens its first chapter in New York City

  Wilbur Wright flies over Manhattan; first plane ever to pass over the island

- **1910**: McKim, Mead & White's Pennsylvania Station opens
- **1911**: After nearly 150 workers (mostly young women) are killed in a fire at the Triangle Shirtwaist Company, changes are made in the city building code and new safety regulations are instituted
  New York City hires its first black police officer
- **1913**: Grand Central Station opens
  Woolworth Building (world's tallest until 1930) opens
  The New York Armory Show, featuring works of European Postimpressionist artists, brings modern art to America
- **1914**: World War I begins
  The Hotel Biltmore opens; "under the clock at the Biltmore" becomes a favorite meeting place
- **1915**: An explosion during subway construction kills and injures many people and leaves a crater in Seventh Avenue
  Provincetown Players founded
- **1916**: New York passes its first zoning law, which requires tall buildings to have setbacks to let more light to the street
- **1917**: New York's last horse car is put out of service
  The Original Dixieland Jazz Band comes to New York
- **1918**: Allies and Germany sign armistice
  More than 12,000 New Yorkers die of influenza
- **1919**: The passage of the 18th Amendment (Prohibition) brings such speakeasies as the Cotton Club, the Stork Club, and the "21" Club into business and contributes to the rise of organized crime
  The Marx Brothers, Gloria Swanson, Rudolph Valentino, and others are making movies at Astoria Studios in Queens, then movie capital of America
  A. D. Juilliard's will bequeaths $20 million to start the Juilliard School of Music
  New School for Social Research opens
- **1920**: American women get the right to vote
  An as-yet-unexplained bombing at the Morgan Guaranty Trust Building kills 33 people
  Paul Robeson makes his professional stage debut with the Provincetown Players
  Coney Island's boardwalk opens

- **1921:** First Quota Law is instituted to help regulate immigration
- **1923:** Yankee Stadium opens; Babe Ruth's three-run homer helps the Yanks beat the Red Sox in the first game
  New York's first birth-control clinic is established
  Saks Fifth Avenue opens
- **1924:** The *Herald* and *Tribune* merge to form the *New York Herald-Tribune*
- **1925:** McKim, Mead & White's Madison Square Garden is torn down
  Eustace Tilley graces the cover of the first *New Yorker*
  Al Hirschfeld's caricatures first appear in the *New York Times*
- **1926:** James "Jimmy" Walker begins serving as mayor
- **1927:** New York honors Charles Lindbergh with a ticker-tape parade after his transatlantic flight
  Holland Tunnel opens
  The Harlem Globetrotters are founded
- **1928:** Arturo Toscanini becomes the conductor of the New York Philharmonic
- **1929:** Stock-market crash sets off the Great Depression
  Museum of Modern Art opens with Postimpressionist show featuring works by Gauguin, van Gogh, Cézanne, and Seurat
- **1930:** Meeting of 10,000 Communists and sympathizers ends in riot in Union Square
  RCA begins a television station in New York
  The Chrysler Building is completed, world's tallest
- **1931:** Empire State Building, complete with a mooring mast for airships, tops the Chrysler
  George Washington Bridge opens
  Ground is broken for Rockefeller Center
- **1932:** Mayor Jimmy Walker, under investigation for corruption, resigns
  Unemployment reaches 25 percent in New York
  Columbia opens its Teachers College
- **1933:** A quarter million New Yorkers watch the mayoral election returns on the Times Tower's moving electric sign, singing "Who's Afraid of the Big Bad Wolf," victor Fiorello La Guardia's theme song
  Prohibition ends

RCA Building is completed

Douglas Leigh, creator of such classics as the Camel cigarette billboard that blew smoke rings (installed just before World War II), puts up his first Broadway advertisement—a giant, steaming cup of coffee for A & P

- **1935**: WPA Federal Art Projects begin

  Alcoholics Anonymous is founded in New York City
- **1936**: Robert Moses becomes parks commissioner (until 1960)

  The bus displaces the electric streetcar
- **1938**: Orson Welles makes "War of the Worlds" radio broadcast

  The Metropolitan Museum of Art opens its branch, The Cloisters
- **1939**: The World of Tomorrow World's Fair is constructed by Robert Moses in Queens on the site of a former dump

  Municipal Airport (later La Guardia) opens

  The Sixth Avenue "El" is torn down
- **1940**: The Eighth Avenue "El" goes the way of the Sixth
- **1941**: U.S. enters World War II

  New Yorkers endure blackout conditions and air raids

  First black is elected to New York City Council, Adam Clayton Powell, Jr.
- **1942**: Gracie Mansion becomes official mayor's residence

  Idlewild Airport (now JFK) opens
- **1943**: Riot erupts in Harlem after a black serviceman is manhandled by a white cop
- **1945**: World War II ends

  Fourteen people are killed when an American bomber crashes into the 78th and 79th floors of the Empire State Building

  Sixth Avenue is renamed Avenue of the Americas
- **1947**: United Nations Plaza construction begins

  Jackie Robinson signs with the Brooklyn Dodgers and helps them win the pennant

  December 17 snowfall drops 28 inches of snow on the city
- **1948**: Bus and subway fares go up to a dime
- **1949**: "Harry Gross Affair" reveals corruption in the police department

Yankees win first of five world series in a row
- **1950**: Port Authority Bus Terminal opens
- **1952**: Edward Steichen curates the Family of Man photography exhibit at the MoMA
- **1953**: Dylan Thomas dies of alcohol poisoning at St. Vincent's Hospital
- **1954**: Ellis Island immigration center closes
- **1955**: Last train runs on the Third Avenue "El"
  The Eagle, Brooklyn's only daily paper, stops publication
- **1956**: Maria Callas debuts at the Metropolitan Opera
- **1957**: New York Giants move to San Francisco and the Brooklyn Dodgers move to Los Angeles
  New York City's last trolley runs (Queensboro Bridge line)
  Leonard Bernstein creates the star-crossed lovers of upper Manhattan in *West Side Story*
- **1958**: Fire damages the Museum of Modern Art
  The Seagram Building goes up
- **1959**: Construction of Lincoln Center for the Performing Arts begins
  City Council considers the feasibility of making New York City the 51st state
  Frank Lloyd Wright's Solomon Guggenheim Museum opens
- **1962**: Nine city newspapers begin four-month strike
  The New York Mets baseball team is formed; New Yorkers fall in love with them for their clumsiness
  The Pan Am building goes up, changing the Park Avenue vista
  Eero Saarinen's TWA Terminal is built at Idlewild Airport
- **1963**: President John F. Kennedy is assassinated
  700 are arrested during demonstrations in favor of minority hiring in construction jobs
  McKim, Mead & White's Pennsylvania Station is demolished; the New York City Landmarks Commission is founded in response
  The New York Review of Books is founded to take up slack during the newspaper strike
  The Guggenheim puts on a Pop Art show featuring the works of Warhol, Rauschenberg, Johns, and others

- **1964**: Harlem and Bedford-Stuyvesant are the scenes of race riots
  Verrazano-Narrows Bridge, the longest suspension bridge in the world, links Staten Island to Brooklyn
  The giant globe known as the Unisphere is the symbol of the second world's fair in Queens
  Shea Stadium is built
- **1965**: Blackout hits the Northeast; 30 million people are without electricity
  Black Muslim leader Malcolm X is assassinated in New York
  Students in Brooklyn demonstrate against segregation
- **1966**: Transit workers go on strike
  Newspapers strike for nearly five months
  New York Herald-Tribune stops publication
  The Brooklyn Navy Yard closes
  The Metropolitan Opera House opens at Lincoln Center
  Truman Capote throws a party at the Plaza Hotel to celebrate the publication of *In Cold Blood*
- **1967**: 700,000 people parade down Fifth Avenue in support of the Vietnam War; Martin Luther King, Jr., then leads march protesting American involvement in Vietnam
  Warhol releases his film *The Chelsea Girls*
- **1968**: Martin Luther King and Robert F. Kennedy are assassinated
  The streets are piled with garbage while city sanitation workers strike for nine days
  A student sit-in closes Columbia University
  Valerie Solanis, an actress, shoots Andy Warhol
  Gerome Ragni and James Rado's *Hair* is staged
- **1969**: The police raid the Stonewall Inn, a private club for homosexuals in Sheridan Square, and a riot erupts when the club patrons fight back; the annual Gay Pride Day Parade is instituted to commemorate the incident
  The Mets amaze everyone when they win the world series
- **1970**: Explosion in a Greenwich Village house kills three members of the radical group the Weathermen
  Construction workers beat up antiwar protesters on Wall Street

The city grants artists legal permission to move into abandoned buildings in SoHo, which they had been doing illegally since the early 1960s

First New York City Marathon is run

- **1971**: *New York Times* prints articles exposing a Pentagon study of American policy in Vietnam—the Pentagon Papers

New York City police go on strike

Off-track betting becomes legal in New York

Bill Graham closes Fillmore East

- **1972**: *All in the Family* introduces Flushing to America

Mafioso Crazy Joey Gallo is shot and killed at his birthday party in Umberto's Clam House in Little Italy

Fiddler on the Roof closes after 3,242 performances

- **1973**: The World Trade Center's twin towers change Manhattan's skyline

Dancers at New York City Ballet strike for job security

- **1974**: Global inflation

Price for a seat on the New York Stock Exchange is lowest in 16 years

- **1975**: New York City nears bankruptcy; secures a federal loan

Last American soldiers leave Vietnam

Bombs at Fraunces Tavern and La Guardia Airport kill 15 and injure 123

Two thousand interns and resident doctors strike at New York City hospitals

Metropolitan Opera names its first woman conductor, Sarah Caldwell

Beverly Sills debuts at the Met

- **1976**: In celebration of America's bicentennial, tall ships from around the world sail up the Hudson while 6 million people watch

Carnegie Hall features Leonard Bernstein, Isaac Stern, Vladimir Horowitz, and others at the "Concert of the Century"

- **1977**: Total blackout in New York City area (affecting 9 million people) leads to 500 reported fires and the arrest of 3,776 people for looting and vandalism

Fatal accident closes the Pan Am Building's heliport

Ed Koch is elected to his first of three terms as mayor

George Willig scales one of the World Trade Center towers and is fined a penny a floor ($1.10 in all)

- **1978**: The *Post, Times,* and *Daily News* are shut down for 88 days by strikes

  David Berkowitz, Son of Sam, gets life in prison for six murders

  Zubin Mehta is the New York Philharmonic's new director

  Sex Pistol Sid Vicious murders his girlfriend, Nancy, in the Chelsea Hotel

- **1979**: New York City passes the Poop Scoop Law, which requires owners to clean up after their dogs in the street

  The Guardian Angels begin patrolling city streets and subways

- **1980**: New Yorkers take to bicycles, roller skates, and sneakers during ten-day transit strike

  John Lennon is shot and killed in front of the Dakota Apartments

  Graffiti becomes the new art form in New York

- **1981**: Gay Men's Health Crisis is founded in response to the recognition of the AIDS virus

  Richard Serra's sculpture *Tilted Arc* is installed at Federal Plaza and sets off eight years of protest (it is finally removed in 1989)

  Simon and Garfunkel reunite for concert in Central Park

- **1982**: Hundreds of thousands attend peace/anti-nukes rally in New York City

- **1984**: Bernard Goetz, the "Subway Vigilante," shoots four youths on a New York subway

  The word "Yuppie" (Young Urban Professional) is coined

- **1985**: Crack cocaine, offering a fast, cheap high, begins to gain popularity

- **1986**: Corruption scandal in city government breaks within the first three months of Mayor Koch's third term, with charges ranging from bribery to extortion

  Donald Manes, Queens borough president, implicated in corruption scandal, commits suicide

  Preppie Murder: Robert Chambers kills Jennifer Levin in Central Park

- **1987**: The stock market crashes

  A young black man is killed and two others are beaten in Howard Beach racial attack

- **1988**: Police are filmed beating demonstrators in Tomkins Square Park by a private filmmaker
Federal government charges investment firm Drexel Burnham Lambert and trader Michael Milken with insider trading
- **1989**: Woman jogging in Central Park is raped and beaten by gang of teenagers
Yusuf Hawkins is killed by a mob of white youths in Brooklyn, fueling racial tensions throughout the city
Hotel queen Leona Helmsley is found guilty of tax fraud
Donald Dinkins beats Ed Koch in the Democratic mayoral primary and goes on to win the election, becoming the first black to hold the position in the city's history

—Amy K. Hughes

INDEX